The
GATE
of FIRE

Tor Books by Thomas Harlan

THE OATH OF EMPIRE
The Shadow of Ararat
The Gate of Fire

The
GATE
of FIRE

Book Two of
The Oath of Empire

Thomas Harlan

TOR®
fantasy

A TOM DOHERTY ASSOCIATES BOOK
NEW YORK

For Suzanne,
without whose love and support,
none of this would be possible

This is a work of fiction. All the characters and events portrayed in this book are either products of the author's imagination or are used fictitiously.

THE GATE OF FIRE

Copyright © 2000 by Thomas Harlan

Edited by Beth Meacham

A Tor Book
Published by Tom Doherty Associates, LLC
175 Fifth Avenue
New York, NY 10010

www.tor.com

Tor® is a registered trademark of Tom Doherty Associates, LLC.

ISBN 0-812-59010-4
Library of Congress Catalog Card Number: 00-023326

First edition: May 2000
First mass market edition: June 2001

Printed in the United States of America

0 9 8 7 6 5 4 3 2 1

DRAMATIS PERSONAE

Thyatis Julia Clodia, Agent of the Western Empire
Dwyrin MacDonald, Thaumaturge of the Eastern Empire
Maxian Atreus, Caesar of the Western Empire
Nicholas of Roskilde, Agent of the Eastern Empire
Shirin, Princess of Khazaria, Empress of Persia
Krista, a Slave
Odenathus, Prince of Palmyra
Zoë, Queen of Palmyra
Dahak, a Persian Sorcerer
Mohammed, a Merchant Prince of Mekkah
Galen Atreus, Augustus and God of the Western Empire
Heraclius, Avtokrator of the Eastern Empire
Anastasia d'Orelio, Duchess of Parma, Spymaster
Khadames, General of the Persian Empire

NOTES ON
NOMENCLATURE

The Roman mile is approximately nine-tenths of an English mile.
A league is approximately three Roman miles in distance.

MAPS

Roma Mater
The Roman Empire
Constantinople

OATH OF EMPIRE
ON THE WORLD WIDE WEB

www.throneworld.com/oathofempire

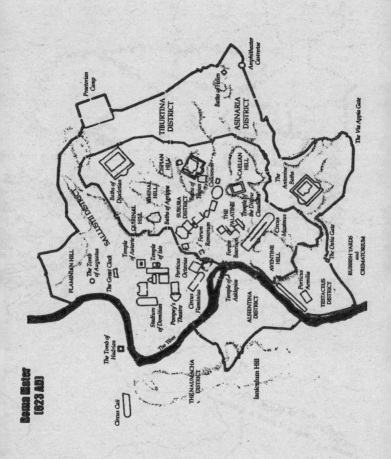

Roma Mater
(623 AD)

Praetorian
Camp

TIBURTINA
DISTRICT

ASINARIA
DISTRICT

Baths of Diana

Amphitheater
Castrense

The Via Appia Gate

SALLUSTIAN DISTRICT

Baths of
Diocletian

VIMINAL
HILL

ESPIAN
HILL

Baths of Trajan

CAELIAN
HILL

Coliseum

QUIRINAL
HILL

Baths of Agrippa

SUBURA
DISTRICT

Temple of
the Divine Claudius

THE
PALATINE

The
Antonine
Baths

Temple of Asiatic

Forum
Romanum

Forum
Boarium

Circus
Maximus

The Ostia Gate

Temple of Isis

AVENTINE
HILL

RUBBISH YARDS
and
CREMATORIUM

FLAMINIAN HILL

The Tomb
of Augustus

The Great Clock

Portico
Octavia

2

TESTACEUS
DISTRICT

Portico
Aemilia

Pompey's
Theatre

Circus
Flaminius

Temple of
Asklepios

Stadium
of Domitian

ALSIENTINA
DISTRICT

The Tomb of Hadrian

The Tiber

THE NAUMACHA
DISTRICT

Ianiculum Hill

Circus Caii

THE WESTERN ROMAN EMPIRE

SA

THE
DANNMARK

DUCHY
OF
POLAND

KHANATE
OF THE
BLUE HUNS

KINGDOM
OF
SAXONY

BURGUNDIA

Krakow

FRANKREICH

PRINCIPATE
OF
BOHEMIA

DRACULIS

SLAVS

GOTHICA

NORICUM

Augusta Vendelicorum

BULGARS

DACIA

WALLACHS

MOE
INFE

HELVETIA

SISCIA

MAGNA
GOTHICA
(Roman Feodorati State)

GEPIDS

AVAR KHANATE

LOMBARDIA

Aquileia

Sirmium

MOESIA
SUPERIOR

SERDICA

Mediolanum

Ravenna

ILLYRIA

MACEDON

THR

Genua

Massilia

Firenza

ITALIA

ROMA

Ostia

Neapolis

Cumer

Tarentum

Thessalonika

Mare Adriaticum

ATTICA

Athens

Mar

SARDINIA

Mare Tyrrhenum

Mare Ionium

SICILIA

Syracuse

Mare Inte

Carthago

Malta

NUMIDIA

Arsinoe

AFRICA

Leptis Magna

**Partial WESTERN and EASTERN
ROMAN EMPIRES
(623 AD)**

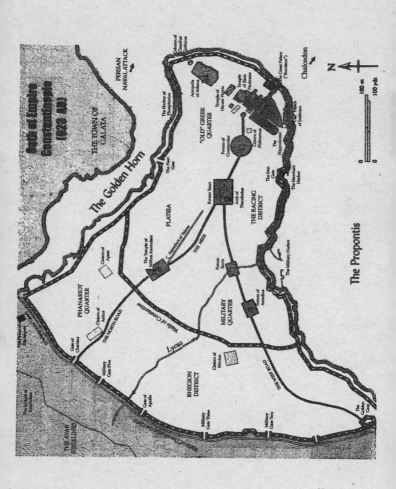

Siege of Imperial Constantinople (626 AD)

THE TOWN OF GALATA

PERSIAN NAVAL ATTACK

The Golden Horn

The Blind at Regium

THE AVAR SIEGELINES

700 Pagan Roman Monuments

Gate of Charisus

Military Gate Five

THE NORTH ROAD

PHANARIOT QUARTER

Cistern of Aetius

WALLS OF CONSTANTINE

Lycus

Gate of Apollo

RHEGION DISTRICT

Cistern of Mocius

Military Gate Three

Military Gate Two

THE WEST ROAD

The Golden Gate

MILITARY QUARTER

Forum of Arcadius

The Military Harbor

Forum Bovis

THE MESE

Aqueduct of Valens

The Temple of Mithra Ascendant

Cistern of Aspar

PLATEIA

Forum Tauri

Arch of Theodosius

THE RACING DISTRICT

The Iron Gate

The Merchant Harbor

Forum of Constantine

"OLD" GREEK QUARTER

Cistern of Philoxenus

The Hippodrome

Palace of Justinian

The First Gate

The Harbor of Prosphorion

The Great Palace ("Theodore's")

Temple of Zeus Pankrator

Temple of Hecate Victrix

Acropolis of Athena

Column of Gaius Claudius Pollheus

Chalcedon

The Propontis

N

0   100 m
0   100 yds

THE SHRINE AT DELPHI, ACHAEA,
710 *AB URBE CONDITA* (31 B.C.)

)H(

The sun beat down, hot, on the narrow courtyard between the house of the Oracle and the columns of the Place of Waiting. The woman stumbled a little on the steps of the house—the stones were deeply grooved from the passage of tens of thousands, and the footing was tricky in her elegant shoes. Guardsmen caught her arms and held her up. She smiled, though her face was bleak, and rewarded them with a light touch on their bronzed shoulders. After the smoky darkness of the Oracle's residence, the brilliant sun and the shining, colorfully painted walls of the temple complex stabbed at her eyes. She drew a veil of dark red silk over her face and walked, slowly, toward the end of the courtyard that faced the south.

There, a line of graceful columns framed a long view of the mountainside plunging down to a gleaming blue limb of the sea. Far below, the water sparkled like a coat of silvered iron. The air seemed tremendously clear to her as she leaned against one of the columns, her hand resting on the dark orchre surface. Paint crumbled away under her touch, leaving a tiny smear of pigment on her fingertip. She felt worn and old; tired—attenuated—by the long struggle. Unseen by her guards, or the servants that had crept out from the House of Waiting to join her, tears seeped from the edges of her kohl-rimmed eyes. She blinked and looked to the west, down the long tongue of water that led to the Middle Sea.

At the edge of vision, smoke rose curling and dark, the breath of wood, tar and canvas.

The release of our dreams, she thought, *Apollo and Ra have called them back to the heavens.*

The tears cut narrow tracks through the artfully applied paints and powders that subtly accented her strong beauty. She stood away from the pillar and turned toward the captain of her guardsmen.

"Rufus, we must . . ." She paused, seeing the servants part. A small figure waddled through the crowd of women, each tiny hand held by a smiling maid. Her heart caught, seeing the wide eyes and beatific, innocent face. The guard captain stepped back, his black eyes flitting over the crowd. One scarred hand rested lightly on the copper pommel of his short sword. The Queen knelt, forgetting to keep the veil across her face.

"Oh, beautiful boy . . ." She held out her arms and her son climbed into them. She stood, swinging him to rest on her hip.

One dream remains on earth, she thought, and the lines on her face smoothed and an iron spark returned to her eyes. *I will have victory yet!*

CONSTANTINOPLE, CAPITAL OF
THE EASTERN ROMAN EMPIRE,
1378 *AB URBE CONDITA* (623 A.D.)

"Make way! Citizens, make way for the Legion!"

The lean, brown-haired man stepped aside, into the shelter of a deep doorway, as a long line of armed men rattled past. The Roman soldiers were clad in patched red cloaks over worn and pitted armor. Their iron helms, snugged taut under their chins with leather straps, were dented and scratched. The rings and scales of their mail were corroded and irregular, patched with rawhide strips. Some had only partial armor, their arms and legs protected by boiled leather bracings over heavy woolen trousers. Their faces matched their gear—worn by months of struggle on the walls of the city. Still, they jogged past with a certain air—something cold and cruel like the winter sky above, certain of victory.

The man settled his shoulder against the doorpost, flicking a dark green woolen cloak around his knees. Droplets of chill water spattered against heavy black boots. The snow that had fallen during the night was melting in the trapped heat of the city, leaving the streets filled with a foul brown slush. A heavy leather baldric was slung over one shoulder, holding a long hand-and-a-half sword in a sheath at his back. Under the cloak the glint of metal scales revealed an iron shirt.

At the end of the double column of men, an *ouragos*—a file-closer in the tongue of the Eastern Empire—passed, his eyes sweeping over the man, seeing the sharp Latin features, a medium height, the trim waist and broad shoulders, and the jutting points of his waxed mustache. The soldier kept an eye on the Westerner as he jogged past, his armor jingling in the cold morning air.

Nicholas kept from smiling and showing his teeth. The cold look in the soldier's eye put him on edge, but there was absolutely no need for a street brawl at this time.

It's the mustache, he thought smugly. *Every man envies what he cannot have.*

Winter had taken its time coming to the Eastern capital. Only after an autumn filled with fits and starts of cold weather, after warm, balmy days and sudden chill winds, had it settled in to stay. Each night, fresh snow settled on the roofs of the temples and *insulae*, covering the grime and filth of too many people packed into a city that had been under siege, off and on, for almost eight years. Nicholas took a long step over cracked marble paving stones.

Steam drifted up from the jagged opening—a sewer ran under the street and the smell was thick. His narrow nose barely twitched at the stench—he had arrived in the city during the summer, when it had been far, far worse. At the end of the street were huge piles of rubble—crumbling clay bricks and broken roofing tiles—blocking the way.

He clambered up over the loose, shifting, snow-covered debris. His hood fell back, revealing a long narrow head with close-set ears. The sun gleamed through heavy clouds, causing him to shade his eyes—an odd dark shade of violet that had gained him the attention of more than one woman—with a gloved hand. Beyond the rubble a boulevard had been forcibly cleared behind the great outer wall of the city. The houses and shops that had grown up under the shadow of the Wall had been smashed down with picks and hammers five years before, when the Emperor Heraclius had first arrived in the city. The space behind the Wall was filled with men, horses, wagons, and all the accoutrements of war.

Nicholas picked his way down the impromptu hill onto the military street. He walked carefully, avoiding the notice of the masons and engineers that were coming and going under the shadow of the massive walls. He looked up, watching the movements of soldiers atop the forty-foot-high edifice. They seemed unconcerned, even nonchalant. This was the inner wall, which had never been breached by an enemy. Great square towers rose along it at regular intervals. The barbarian turned left at the base of the rampart and walked a little way before he came to a gate set into the cliff of stones. More soldiers on horses were filing through the arch, which was deep and narrow, faced with two massive ironbound doors. A grimy statue of a man in an archaic toga and crown of laurels was perched at the apex, a weather-worn hand raised in benediction.

Coming out into the pale sunlight, the man snugged his cloak close around his neck. Between the looming inner wall and the lower, but still formidable, outer works, was an open terrace called the *peribolos*. It was narrow, perhaps fifteen paces across, and filled with more gangs of workers with mauls and picks, engineers in tented hats with wax tablets under their arms, lines of soldiers in red and gray, marching south toward the sea. Rising up above the stream of humanity was a second rampart, the *protichisma*, and that was where the work of battle was focused. This wall was only thirty feet high, but studded with towers and battlements like the inner works.

Nicholas glanced about and then made his way to the base of an open-sided wooden tower that had been built alongside the Wall. As he climbed the stairs housed within, his eyes were restless—counting the numbers of men in the street, gauging the strength of the massive granite blocks that old Emperor Constantine's engineers and the Hippodrome factions had mortised together to make the outer rampart of the greatest city in the world. This was a friendly city to him, at least at the moment, but in this line of work it was hard to let go of old habits. Today, seeing this awesome strength, he was pleased, but he wondered idly what he would think if he stood beyond the walls, looking down from the hills of Thrace at the object of desire.

I would see a damnably huge city, girdled by walls and towers and battlements unmatched in the world. That is what I would see.

The wind out of the north was cold on the top of the Wall, biting at his ears and snapping his cloak around his shoulders. The heavy gray clouds had parted again, letting streaks of wan sunlight through. The air here was fresh, though, and he breathed deeply, smelling the pine resin of distant fires and the sharp tang of the sea. That smell, after the fetid closeness of the city, brought a smile to his face. There were many days when he hated the *urb*. Memories of a pine deck twisting under his feet, sea spray in his face, and the boom of surf from the Caledonian shore tugged at him. Sadly, he put those thoughts away. Fifty paces to his left, the octagonal towers of the Number Two

Military Gate rose up, dark and foreboding, their surfaces scarred by the impact of bolts and stones. He walked that way.

To his right, the crenellations of the battlement jutted up like broken teeth. The embrasures between them were stained with long streaks of dried blood and nicked by the passage of arms that had coursed along the Wall in hurried violence for the past three years. Roman soldiers stood in the lee of the great stones, their cloaks wrapped tight around their shoulders. Some held steaming mugs of hot wine. Each man looked him over as he passed, and he nodded to some. The heavy mail tunic that he wore under his cloak and linen shirt felt close and comfortable on his body. It was backed by a tough garment of felt, and then— in a nod to *vanitas*—a silk tunic. A thin film of ice had formed on the walkway during the night, and his hobnailed boots crunched through it as he walked.

The near tower loomed over his head, rising another twenty feet from the bulk of the Wall. It was squat and massive, brooding over the doubly gated passageway below it. An overhanging platform crowned it, reinforced with a wooden wall covered with hides. It looked out over the half-frozen, blackish waters of a canal that ran at the foot of the rampart. The canal was twenty feet wide and choked with debris; it ran from the southern end of the Wall—at the shore of the Propontis—to the north, where the last half mile descended into a brick-lined tunnel under the old Blachernae palace before it reached the waters of the Golden Horn. All summer the soldiers and slaves of the besieging army had been dumping bundles of brush, wicker, and dirt into it, trying to fill the barrier. The Great Khagan of the Avars intended to break the walls of the city, but his mobs of Slavic spear and axemen had to get at the walls somehow. The Roman defenders had spent just as much time clearing the fill away. Too, the blackened timbers of smashed siege towers and burned-out mantlets jutted from the dark surface of the canal and littered the ground just beyond. Nicholas stopped short of the tower

Wall and leaned out of the nearest embrasure.

An open field lay before the city, sloping down to the distant woods and outlying buildings of the Thracian countryside. The field was scattered with snow-covered mounds and lumps—the detritus of three years of war. Beyond it, a half mile away, the Avars had their siege line—a confused jumble of camps and hastily built fortifications in a long arc facing the walls of the city. The barbarians, horsemen from the steppes beyond Chersonensus in the far north, had overwhelmed the Balkan provinces of the Eastern Empire a generation before, but had only recently tested their strength against the capital. The host that their khagan had raised dwarfed the number of fighting men in the city—Nicholas knew there were at least fifty thousand barbarians out there. More were probably coming. The promise of the sack of the greatest city in the world drew the outlanders like flies to rotting meat.

The Wall had thrown back great armies before, and the men that defended the city were not concerned. Nicholas wondered, as he walked, at the audacity of an emperor who would raise an army and then leave his capital, still under siege, to fight another war far away. It seemed insane—insane and wholly trusting in the work of his predecessors—that this city could stand against anything that the Avar Khanate could bring against it.

He's not been wrong so far, he thought. *But if there is ever a first time . . .*

A sandy-haired centurion was standing at the base of the tower, leaning one thick arm on the top of the fighting wall. His helmet hung at his side, secured by a loop of cloth to his belt. A long sword, thicker and heavier than that usually favored by Imperial troops, was slung at his side. He was staring out over the snowy fields, watching the smoke curl up from the cookfires of the enemy.

"A cold day to be fighting," Nicholas said as he came up to the narrow door.

The centurion turned, watery blue eyes looking the stranger up and down with a patient, steady manner. A little cloud of breath puffed from his chapped lips.

" 'Tis cold," the soldier said. "There will be fighting soon, though. Mayhap not here, but at least down there." The centurion turned a little and pointed off down the line of the massive walls toward the sea. "There, at the Golden Gate. The barbs have ten or twelve engines moving—do you hear the squeak of their wheels? They should use black grease instead of that pig fat—it burns off the axles too quickly."

"I hear it. I'm Nicholas of Roskilde. Things are quiet here?"

"Aye." The centurion gazed at Nicholas steadily. "You've business on the Wall?"

Nicholas looked out over the field, rubbing his chin with his right hand. "Faction business," he said. "I'm owing a favor to a kindly man. I was thinking there might be some work afoot up here, what with your friends yonder."

The centurion raised an eyebrow and made a clucking sound with his teeth. "You come looking for some fighting, go down to the Golden Gate. This section is well quiet. You must owe this fellow more than a little to risk your neck on the Wall."

Nicholas shrugged, looking back at the soldier with a guileless expression. "Three squares a day, plus wine or mead if there is any."

Suspicion flickered across the centurion's face, then it cleared. "You, ah, find yourself without an emperor or two to rub together, then?"

Nicholas nodded, summoning up a shamed look. "I was on a ship—there was a game of chance—I found myself on the docks of this city, wondering at its awesome size and greatness. More than one night I spent sleeping in the alleys of the Racing District."

"And someone took you in?" The disbelief on the centurion's face was almost comical. "This is not a *burg* noted for civility and hospitality to strangers—particularly to *fyrdmen* down on their luck. It seems a poor way of living."

Nicholas shrugged, tilting his left hand a little to the side. "A tavern keeper found me and said his faction would feed me if I'd fight on the Wall in the place of one of their own. So, here I am."

The centurion grimaced. The racing factions of the Hippodrome—the Greens and the Blues—had lost much of their old political power, but their ward bosses remained as canny as ever. They might not be able to make or break an emperor, but they surely knew all the tricks of keeping their clients away from the Imperial levies and drafts.

"Well," said the centurion, turning away to go into the tower, "find a place out of the wind."

Nicholas grimaced and looked out over the Wall again. The land was still and quiet, showing dirty snow, distant leafless trees, and a cold gray sky thick with fat clouds. It would start snowing again soon: he could smell it in the air.

Nicholas swung himself up to sit in the embrasure next to the side of the tower. It made a fine seat, though the wind out of the north slid across his face like *freyasdottir* kiss. He leaned back into the stones, waiting for events to unfold. Though by nature an impatient man, his business had taught him many virtues. Patience was even one of them. Thin fingers pulled the hood of his cloak over his head and he worked himself out of the direct strength of the wind.

He wondered if the men in the camps beyond the Wall were drinking deep of half-frozen mead, crouched in hide tents around their smoky fires. He wondered if slaves, barely clad in tunics of raw wool and graced with thick iron rings welded around their necks, scurried to bring the fighting men more of the heavy drink and thick slabs of meat, dripping with blood and steaming from the fire. His fingers twitched, touching the hilt of the long sword that leaned against the Wall at his side. There had been a rusting iron ring on his neck once. That was the sort of thing that you did not forget.

Once he had carried heavy jugs of mead from the storage house to the feasting hall, his bare feet bloody in the snow. The sky had been gray then, too, for the Storm Lord loved the Dannmark as no other place. Hail had slashed down out of bitter clouds, raising welts on his back. It had been a cruel life for an outland boy with odd-colored eyes, sold into slavery far beyond the frontier of the Empire. The *jarls* of Dannmark were not easy masters.

But without them? Nicholas raised the sword up, still sheathed, and smiled, showing his teeth. His hand moved gently on the sheath. *I would not have met the niebelungen, or gained your love.*

The sun was swallowed by cloud, and the sky darkened. Heavy gray overcast pressed against the earth. Snowflakes drifted down, melting on the stones of the Wall. His breath white in the air, Nicholas made his way down the wooden staircase behind the gate. He had waited on the Wall for three hours, slowly getting colder and colder, watching the distant line of trees. It had been quiet, and then the falling snow had obscured the Avar camps. The noise of the fighting down the Wall, at the great Golden Gate, had slowly risen in intensity as the day progressed. The tower at the Number Two Gate blocked a direct view of the looming redoubt that anchored the southern end of the city wall, but the sound of crashing metal on metal and the high-pitched snap of siege engines firing filtered through the cold air. At the bottom of the stairs a band of knights— no, he reminded himself, an *alae* of *equites*—were gathering in the space behind the gatehouse.

Nicholas jumped down from the next to last landing on the wooden scaffold, landing lightly in a space just off the gate. Horsemen armored in silvery bands of iron were preparing to go out into the snowy fields. Steam rose from the flanks of the horses, and the high arch of the gate rang with voices and the rattle of metal. The knights were checking the straps of their low-cantled saddles, and long straight swords hung to their knees. Many had wooden bow cases strapped behind them, the tops thick with gray goose feathers. Nicholas scratched the back of his head and turned toward the gate. A grinding sound echoing off the barrel vault of the passage drew his attention upward. The long iron bars that secured the gate were being drawn, slowly, up into the ceiling of the passage. The rumble of great hidden wheels echoed through the stout brick walls. Each iron bar was a foot wide, and the width of man's hand thick. Nicholas counted heads: there were thirty or forty men in the entryway—most of them the lead horsemen. He began scanning their faces, comparing them to a half-heard description.

A thin man, half Slav and half Greek, with a pleasant and smiling face. A spy and a traitor to the city.

"A sortie," a voice said from behind him. Nicholas turned, his face casual. It was the blond centurion from the tower. "Going out to burn a tower or two. Teach the barbs not to get sloppy about their flanks."

"You want to teach them to win?" Nicholas regretted opening his mouth as soon as the words had escaped. The centurion glared at him for a moment, then pushed past him through the throng of horses. Nicholas bit his lip in regret and considered going after the man, but there was little time left. The legionnaires by the gate itself were preparing to push it open. The *equites* in the first rank were trying to form a double line with something like proper spacing. The horses jostled in the confined space, and Nicholas was forced back against the Wall. Bricks ground into his back. Without conscious thought, his right hand reached up and tugged the wire loop that secured his sword in its sheath off the hilt. Behind him, out in the military street behind the Wall, a trumpet pealed and there was shouting.

The gate swung open. Nicholas cursed and pushed forward along the Wall toward the edge of the opening hinge. Five men were there, putting their shoulders into the rough planks of the gate. It was heavy, and the hinges squealed in protest at the movement. As Nicholas tried to make his

way though the throng of horses and other men standing
by the Wall, a dim gray light spilled in. Cold air followed,
and the horses whinnied and milled a little before their
riders stilled them. The snowy field was revealed, a foot
at a time, as the soldiers continued to push the gate open.

Nicholas jumped up, trying to see over the bulk of the
horsemen. Legionnaires pushed at his back, trying to move
up to the gate. He turned back and began trying to swim
against their flow. There was a shout, and the horsemen
began to move out of the gate passage. A flash of something catching the light caught Nick's eye and he stared
through a forest of horse legs at the other side of the passage. A bared sword blade flickered in the light from outside.

Nicholas snarled a curse and swung up on a man's
shoulder, planting his boot against the courses of bricks on
the Wall.

The soldier, startled, shouted at him. "Bastard! Get off
me!"

The extra two feet of height was enough. Nicholas
cursed aloud himself. The man he was hunting was across
the passage, only fifteen feet away, screened by the knights
who were filing through the gateway. He dropped down
and absently blocked the legionnaire's halfhearted punch
with a raised hand. The slithering sound of his sword coming into his hand stilled the soldier's protest. Nicholas
glanced right, seeing the gate come fully open, then left,
counting the remaining numbers of horsemen waiting to
ride out. The column was halfway out the gate. He tensed,
preparing to dash through the horses cantering past.

A tremendous, high-pitched, wailing scream suddenly
filled the world. Nicholas ducked down, hearing the hissing passage of hundreds of arrows fill the air. Men started
shouting and screaming. There was a rippling sound of
heavy blows striking meat. Nicholas scrambled away to
the Wall, under the falling body of the soldier. A black-
feathered bow shaft had transfixed the man, spilling bright
blood out of his back and mouth. Nicholas grabbed the

man's arm and hauled the body over his own as a shield.
A horse hoof, driven by pain-maddened rage, smashed into
the soldier's breastplate, cracking the metal, and Nicholas
grimaced, turning his head away as the body jerked in his
hands. More blood spattered on the side of his face. He
wedged himself into the corner of the Wall. Now there
was a wailing war cry from beyond the gate.

Nicholas could hear the company of knights, caught half
in and half out of the gate, being slaughtered by arrow fire.
Shafts continued to whip through the open gate, into the
mass of dying men and horses in the passage. Behind the
gate was loud confusion as men milled about—some trying to get into the passage, others to get away. The bull-
voiced shouts of centurions rallying their men and raising
the alarm rang in the air. Too, there was fighting outside,
in the space before the Wall. The war cries of Avars echoed off the high vault of the gate. A horse, rearing, was
struck down by two black arrows and fell across the body
of the man that partially covered Nick. He twisted away
from the impact, but felt it like a titan's slap against his
back.

Outside, horses galloped away, neighing in fear. The
whistling of arrows faltered and then stopped. There was
a rush of running feet and Nicholas grimaced, pushing the
leaden body away from him with all his strength. The dead
legionnaire, his eyes still round with surprise, fell away,
and Nicholas scrambled up. His right hand, slimy with
sticky red mud, dragged the length of his long sword out
of the gore covering the floor of the passage. Dark figures
filled the gateway, rushing forward with axes and long
spears in hand. Nicholas sprang up onto the unsteady welter of corpses—both man and horse—and bright sparks
rang from his sword as he parried the first stroke of an
Avar axe.

The Avar noble was broad in the shoulder and clad in
heavy capes of ermine and fox. Scale mail glinted under
the fur and rose up to his neck, circled by a thick torc of
gold, and down to his biceps. His eyes were slanted over

high cheekbones, and his nose was broad and flat. The axe whipped around again, driven by dark-skinned arms thick with matted hair, muscle, and a thin sheen of sweat. Nicholas stumbled aside, his foot slipping on the flank of a fallen horse. The iron wedge carved air where his arm had been. Nicholas dropped his shoulder and bulled into the Avar, crashing iron rings against scale. A hand with long dirty nails clawed at his face, cutting his cheek. He grappled, pinning the nomad's free hand between their bodies. Stiff fingers stabbed at the barbarian's eye. The Avar fell backward, clouting Nicholas on the side of the head. Nicholas pushed into the fall and drove his left knee into the inside of the Avar's thigh. The man gasped in pain, feeling his leg go numb. Nicholas lashed down with his right elbow, catching the man on the neck. The torc deformed— soft gold twisting under the blow—but it prevented the barbarian's larynx from being crushed.

More Avars swarmed past through the gateway. As they ran forward they fired short but heavy bows with an odd, long, top stave into the milling crowd of legionnaires who had fallen back into the street. Men staggered and fell as the heavy arrows punched through their leather and chainmail armor. Behind the Avar veterans, a great crowd of Slavs was pushing forward, their red and blond hair standing stiff with grease, their shields bright with geometric patterns in black and red and blue. A forest of spear points danced over their heads. They were running forward, raising their voices in a great shout when they saw the gate standing wide.

The noble squirmed under Nicholas like a Danube eel and threw him to one side. Nicholas slipped and skidded away on the gore-smeared floor. Another Roman corpse stopped him. His sword was gone, lost among the still-dying horses. The Avar sprang up, his right hand already filled with the mirror brightness of a long knife. Nicholas felt a chill, seeing that he was cut off from the rest of the defenders. He rolled backward and then came up, stripping the remains of his shirtsleeve from his left arm. The Avar dodged in, making short, controlled, stabs with the knife. Nicholas skipped back again, over the body of a bay horse, and flexed his left fist outward from his arm, pulling the exposed wire-ring with his thumb.

There was a sharp metallic *twang*, and a six-inch steel bolt punched through the Avar's right eye and rang off the inside of his conical helmet. Blood and white flakes of bone smeared the right side of the nobleman's face as he crumpled soundlessly back into the welter of other bodies.

Nicholas half saw a blurring shape in the air and threw himself forward. One of the long arrows whickered over his head and glanced off the inner gate post with a shrill *tang*. He crawled hurriedly, searching among the bodies for his sword. More arrows flicked past, hunting him. He bellied down behind one of the dead horses and scuttled forward.

Behind him, in the street, was a confused melee. More Avars and Slavs poured through the gateway and piled into the Romans trying to hold the boulevard against them. Legionnaires atop the wall were throwing javelins and stones down into the mass of men struggling on the pavement. The masons and engineers who had been working behind the Wall rushed up, spears and great hammers in their hands. Nicholas heard the bellowing voice of the blond centurion ringing above the din of steel and iron, rallying his men to him.

Nicholas breathed a sigh of relief; *Brunhilde's* engraved hilt was barely visible, jutting from under the carcass of a sandy-colored mare. The grooved leather binding on the hilt met his fingers like a well-loved friend. The four-foot length of rune-carved Scandian steel stuck for a moment, but then slid free with a greasy popping sound. He ducked aside from another arrow, but the Avar archers were now occupied exchanging missile fire with the Romans on the Wall and on the battlements. Nicholas sprinted across the killing ground to the foot of the nearest wooden stair tower.

Taking the plank steps two and three at a time, he leapt

to the second level of the tower, fifteen feet above the battle raging in the street. Two Avars had also climbed up before him and were firing arrow after arrow into the ranks of the Romans fighting below. Nicholas shifted one hand back on *Brunhilde's* long hilt and, taking her two-handed, ended his rush with a hard horizontal chop that bit deep into the neck of the Avar on the right, sending his body sprawling into the other archer. Bright arterial blood gushed out, spraying down on the men below, and the Avar's head lolled at an obscene angle. The other Avar staggered up in time for Nicholas to shatter his outthrust kneecap with a sharp kick. The man was still howling in pain as Nicholas heaved his body over the railing.

Arrows thrummed through the air, spiking into the pillars of the tower. He dodged again, this time up the stairs to the next platform. The tower shook with the weight of more Avars swarming up the steps. Nicholas skidded back on the undressed planks of the third platform, swinging *Brunhilde* into guard position. Four Avars in glistening iron-scale tunics, their furs cast aside, showing long mustaches and lank black hair, stormed up the stairs. Luckily, they blocked the view of the archers behind them for a moment.

The first Avar rushed onto the platform, his axe a blur of short cuts at Nick's midriff. The Roman slid aside, falling back a step, and then feinted overhand with the long sword. The Avar parried up with the head of the axe, and Nicholas reversed his stroke, catching the nomad on the outside of his left arm. *Brunhilde* bit deep, cleaving the muscle and tendon. The Avar cursed and fell back, switching the axe to his off-hand. Nicholas rushed in, keeping the wounded man between himself and the others at the top of the stairs. The axeman tried to block with the haft of his weapon, but Nicholas was inside his guard and jerked his blade upward, punching the triangular tip through the bottom of the Avar's jaw. There was a gelid sound and then a tinny ringing as the point ground on the inside of the man's helmet.

Another Avar stabbed over the first dead man's shoulder with a long spear, catching Nicholas squarely in the left side of his chest. The spear point, a rusty iron wedge with a poorly forged brace running down the middle, ground at the center of one of the links of chain, sending a burst of cold through his chest. Nicholas rotated left, slipping the spear off, though there was a tearing sensation as he whipped *Brunhilde* back out of the dead axeman. The second Avar slid his spear back and jumped up onto the platform from the steps below.

Nicholas ducked low, feeling the point slash across his head, and lunged, extending *Brunhilde* like a spear herself. The Avar tried to dance aside, but more men were pushing up the stairs, and the Nordic long sword punched through the stiff leather armor under his left armpit, blue-black blood gurgling up around the blade. Nicholas rushed again, shoving the dying man back down the stairs onto his fellows.

Cries of rage rose up as the first rank of Avars tumbled backward, arms and legs flailing. For a moment, the stairway was clogged with bodies and Nicholas shook his hair out of his eyes and fell back, sliding his boots across the rough floor, searching for good footing. The sword felt light in his hand and the air danced with tiny points of light. Even the air was warm, almost hot, against his skin. An Avar on the lower platform hurled a small axe overhand at him, but it seemed to hang in the air and Nicholas stepped easily aside, bringing *Brunhilde* up in guard again. The *falx* hissed past, the delicate interlocking carving of dragons and deer spinning head over heels.

Two of the spearmen separated themselves from the mass of bodies on the stairs and scrambled up at him, crouching low and apart, keeping to the railings. The spearheads flickered like snake tongues in the air at him, bright points of iron. Nicholas lunged at the man on the left, near the outer railing, and cut sharply at the head of the spear with *Brunhilde*. A veteran, the man slipped his spear back and slashed at Nick's head. At the same time, the other man rushed in, stabbing low at Nick's thigh. The Roman watched them come, like clockworks advancing in slow motion. Cold burned in his veins, powering his muscles and thought. He leaned back, weaving away from the spear slash and turned right, spinning into the attack coming low. *Brunhilde* brushed the lunging spear point aside, tip arrowing at the floor. Inside the spear's length, Nicholas spun back the other way, the long sword flicking up to intersect with the haft of the spear, shearing it in half, and then into the spearman's shoulder, gouging through light mail and a shirt of leather. The man's mouth opened in a snarl of surprise.

Tiny links of mail ornamented with perfect ruby droplets scattered through the air, whirling like tiny stars.

Nick's hard-muscled shoulder powered the blade through the rest of the arc, plunging into the chest of the first spearman. The man sucked air for a moment, then choked on the blue bubbles filling his throat. Nicholas pushed him off of the blade with his boot, cracking the railing with his weight. The spearman toppled back, hanging for a moment in the air before he slammed into the paving stones below. The other Avar was still gasping at the pain in his shoulder and the ruin of his spear when Nicholas spun back to face him.

The sound of running men rattled the stairs above the third platform, and Nicholas spared a glance upward, catching sight of billowing red cloaks and hobnailed boots pounding on the upper steps. Shouting rose from below, and he turned back in time to see a cloud of arrows hurtling toward him. A cry of rage caught in his throat as he threw himself backward.

Sparks from a burning timber flew up, tracing a slow, whirling dance against the dark sky. Nicholas lay with his back against a stone wall, vision blurry with exhaustion. He could barely lift his left arm but, with a grunt, he stripped the leather bracing of the spring gun off his forearm. Snow was falling again, but the heat from the bonfire kept melting it before it could stick to the paving stones of the street. Legionnaires moved about in the darkness, briefly illuminated by the bonfire or resin torches in the gateway. A cart rumbled past, its high wooden wheels turning slowly over. A thicket of bruised-looking arms and legs jutted from the back of the wagon, and a seep of blood pattered on the street as it passed. They were the bodies of the dead, going to feed the fires that burned in the street the length of the Wall. A sickly sweet odor permeated the air, fueled by sizzling fat.

Clenching his teeth against the pain, Nicholas leaned slowly forward and stripped off the heavy shirt of iron rings. It was fouled with the *thoracomachus* beneath it where the rings had been driven through the thick felt padding by the force of Avar blows. The shirt next to his body had almost disintegrated into a pudding of blood, silk, and sweat. Cold air bit at his exposed flesh, and he hissed in pain as the layers of armor and padding peeled away from his skin.

The left side of his chest and most of his torso was already turning blue-purple. Dozens of cuts where the iron rings had ground into his skin were already clotted. He prodded the longest cut, just under his left shoulder. Clear fluid oozed out of the jagged red gash.

"Huh, you look fine. Another winning mission for you, I see."

Nicholas looked up; in his exhausted state, he couldn't quite place the voice. A stout man stood over him, a deep red cloak rippling on his shoulders. The fellow wore a burnished breastplate over a shirt of fine chain mail links and carried a full helm under one arm. He was clean shaven, though a beard would have improved his pox-scarred face by hiding old wounds. The officer's hair was shaved very close to the scalp, almost bald.

Nicholas squinted against the firelight. A vague knocking in his head reminded him that he knew the man.

"Tribune Sergius . . . *ave*. Hail and well met." Even that much left Nicholas feeling exhausted. "He got away,"

Nicholas muttered almost inaudibly. "Slippery bastard . . ."

The tribune squatted down next to Nicholas and peeled back an eyelid with one thumb. Even that much contact caused Nicholas to turn away in pain. The soldier grunted and put his helmet down, shifting his weight to both feet. The tribune shook his head slowly, surveying the drubbing that Nicholas had endured. One thick finger gently traced over the pattern of melon-shaped contusions scattered across his ribs.

"I came looking for you after I heard that the breach had been thrown back. Some hard work here today, but then you have a very nose for slaughter. . . . I was talking to one of the wall commanders—he says you showed up at almost noon. What the Hades were you thinking? I sent you up here at daybreak!" Sergius paused in his incipient rant, his eyes narrowing. "Can you understand anything I'm saying?"

Nicholas blinked and looked back at the fellow. Why was he talking to him? The thought of sleep seemed tremendously appealing, but at the same time something warned him that it was a bad idea. The image of the man wavered a little, like he was standing in the heart of a fire. "What?"

The tribune sighed and stood up. He gestured into the darkness, and two men in slave tunics and fur-lined boots came up.

"Put him in the litter and take him back to the offices. He's no use to me here. Get some hot food and wine in him and have one of the surgeons check him over. His eyes look like those of a reveler at a Dionysus festival, so—don't let him sleep."

Strong hands grasped Nick's arms and hauled him up. He felt very faint, but the prospect of wine and some fresh bread dripping with oil and garlic roused him a little. The two slaves helped him to a litter and laid him inside. One turned a blanket over him. It smelled of cloves and some kind of perfume. Lying down, he found that he could see. The sky over the city was black as pitch; without the heavy clouds that hung above them, he guessed he could see the stars and the moon. Snowflakes swirled down, passing through bands of gold and red cast by the bonfires. The slaves lifted the litter and he swayed from side to side, then they took a step, and another, and jogged off through the dark streets.

Snow continued to fall.

🔲◖0◗◖0◗◖0◗◖0◗◖0◗◖0◗◖0◗◖0◗◖0◗◖0◗◖0◗◖0◗◖0◗◖0◗◖0◗◖0◗◖0◗◖0◗🔲

THE SKIES OVER LATIUM, ITALIA,
THE WESTERN ROMAN EMPIRE

〤

A young man dressed wholly in black and dark gray climbed stiffly up a ladder made of beech wood handles set in hand-forged iron brackets. At the top of the ladder a metal cover swung away at his touch, flooding the narrow tube he had ascended with sunlight. He squinted for a moment, and then the clear blue of his eyes darkened, deepening to an almost metallic aqua that covered both iris and pupil. Able to see at last, he clambered out of the tube and swung his long legs out into the cavity of the observation deck. A stiff wind rushed past, catching his long brown hair—now beginning to show tendrils of white—and blowing it out in front of him. He slid down into the cavity, lined with wooden seats and stout ropes, with a sigh.

By a trick of the design of the upper surface of the Engine, the roaring of the wind within the cavity was reduced to a dull, basso rumbling. The sound came more from the iron heart of the machine than the air whipping past. The man popped his ears with narrow, long-fingered hands and pulled one of the ropes across him, securing it to a stout bronze clasp set into the metal skin.

"Lord Prince, you don't trust your power so far?"

The young man smiled wryly at the young woman seated opposite him and shook his head. "No, I must be awake and aware to rebuild skin, bone, tissue, the vital humors. A fall from this height would kill me as surely as you or anyone."

The young woman smiled back, a little, but there was a guarded reserve present in her face and the line of her body that pricked at him. He returned her smile with a greater one of his own, genuine and filled with warmth. For a moment the cold cast that governed his features faded, and he seemed the amiable young physician she had first met, neither the Prince of the Realm nor the power that he had become. Despite a deep distrust, she replied in kind, and her own features—a little longer than the classical oval, but marked by striking dark eyes and rich lips, framed by a barely restrained mane of rich dark brown, nearly black, hair—were transformed as well. The man felt a pang in his heart to see her so, beautiful and elegant, sitting sideways on the bench in a thick furred cloak, with neat leather gloves on her hands, and her svelte legs covered by Persian-style silk trousers.

"Don't you get cold, sitting up here all these hours?" he asked.

The young woman's face became guarded again, and she looked away, out over the long, dark pinion of the Engine. It soared between pillars of cloud, bright sun shining on the delicate iron bones of the wings. The metallic fabric that covered them rippled and shimmered in the clear afternoon sunlight. The omnipresent vibration of the Engine filled the world, transmitting itself through the decking to bone and skin. The tail, long and tapering, weaved languidly behind them in the air, its surface gleaming with thousands of tiny carefully fitted metallic scales. The young woman leaned a little to one side as the Engine banked around a vast white tower of cloud, its wings casting a hurrying shadow across the ivory field. The air was crystal clear between her and the brilliant white surface. Deep in the crevices of the thunderhead, lightning muttered and wind howled. The woman looked back at the Prince. "It seems like a different world, here, close to the heavens. Islands of cloud in a sea of air, and we in a ship, voyaging among them. Do you ever think of it, when you look out, what it would be like to stand at the edge of a cliff of cloud, surrounded by billowing white? To see down, a thousand feet, to the land below, tiny and perfect?"

The Prince shook his head. Too many matters weighed upon him to spend time gazing out from the green-tinted windows of the Engine, even those great circular ones mounted at the head.

"No," he said, a faint bitter edge in his voice. "There is too much to prepare—too much to discuss with Gaius and Alexandros. Krista, we return to a dangerous situation! One moment of—"

She raised a hand and looked at him squarely for the first time since he had clambered up out of the hatchway. "Lord Maxian, I feel death at my shoulder as closely as you do. More, as I cannot protect myself. You spend your time plotting and planning with those two dead men and your other servants. That has nothing to do with me—I am your property, a slave, a convenience when you are lonely or in need of comfort. Up here, I can find some space for myself, some peace." She dropped her hand, though her eyes were smoldering with a near-hot anger.

The Prince swallowed, taken aback. He leaned back against the cold iron, thinking furiously. With a sickening feeling, he realized he did not know what to say or do.

Krista watched him, keeping anger in her face, hoping that he would not see the fear and acid terror that threatened her composure. She hated the close, hot confines of the Engine, filled with the woken dead and the servants the Prince had accumulated on his long journey in the East. There was a strange smell about the rooms below, cloying and sweet. Krista did not feel safe, save when she was alone, or surrounded by her Walach boys. The others—particularly the *homunculus* Khiron and that ancient lecher Gaius Julius—watched her constantly with hungry eyes.

Still . . . all within lived or died by the will of the Prince, and she retained some influence over him. She almost smiled to see the struggle of emotions and thought on his face.

Krista unsnapped the restraining rope around her waist and stepped over to the Prince's side. With a deft hand, she caught a band and locked it to the same restraining bolt that the Prince had used. Held close by the rope, she settled into his side, her leg falling over his. He shifted and put his arms around her narrow waist. Krista clasped his hands to her stomach, feeling the tension in them. "My lord," she said, letting her head fall back into his chest and the curve of his neck, "do you know what you are going to do now?"

Maxian stirred, and she felt him mentally veer back onto familiar ground. Something about him had changed, finding confidence and direction. "Yes," he said, and even his voice had changed, becoming almost regal. Inwardly she cringed, hearing echoes of Alexandros' commanding baritone in his. In the time since they had abandoned the crumbling ruins of Dastagird and the ancient secrets of the fire priests, she had watched her master adopt more and more of the mannerisms and patterns of speech of his two advisors.

"We will return, in secret, to the Egyptian House outside of Rome. With the power inherent in Alex and Gaius, I believe—no, I *know*—that I can break the power of the curse. It will be difficult and as dangerous as before, but now I *know* that it can be done."

Krista frowned and turned a little so that she could see his face. "You nearly died in your last attempt, my lord. Does Alexandros represent so much power that you can win through this time?"

Maxian smiled down at her, his teeth bright in his pale face. So much time spent in the dank tombs and catacombs of the ruined Persian city had leached the nut brown tan from his skin. Krista stroked the back of her hand along his cheek, feeling its smoothness. *Much better than some damned bushy beard always tickling my nose*, she thought, distracted for a moment.

"My love," Maxian said, "I have learned a little—no, a great deal—since we went to the East. I nearly died before trying to drive the curse, this corruption, out of that soldier with raw power. That was very foolish. The curse is not a single thing, or a man, that can be overwhelmed by me, or anyone, in single combat." Maxian turned so that he could face her. His face was alight with eagerness. "When I bent my powers upon the old legionnaire, or the stolen child, I tried to drive out the corruption of the curse an organ at a time—from the bones, the heart, the brain. It was fruitless! Even if I expunged every trace of the contagion from a single organ, it would flood back in, tearing at bone and blood. I could not remove it because it was everywhere, all around us, in everything, like trying to hold back the sea with a spade. Impossible." He paused, taking a breath.

Krista almost laughed aloud at seeing him as an excited child, showing off the muddy frog he had found by the bank of some stream.

"But what *is* possible—if we can find the crux, the anchor, the focus of this thing—is to destroy it utterly. Somewhere in the old Imperial archives there must be a record of the first working that made this thing possible. We will find it. The tomes of the old priests contained many secrets, and one of them is perfect for what I intend."

Krista raised a long, rich eyebrow at the confidence in his voice.

Maxian stopped for a moment, nonplussed, then pressed on. "Yes, I see your expression—such a look you give me! No, my love, listen: These things we know—that in the time of the first emperor, Octavian, the words and intent of the legionary oath of allegiance were changed. That new text, imbued with some tiny spark of power, bound each legionnaire to the service of the state—not to flee in battle, not to allow ruin or corruption or disaster. A small thing, in its beginning, a tiny pebble thrown into an empty field.

"But time passes. Thousands and then tens of thousands of legionnaires take this Oath—fighting and dying to expand and protect the Empire of Rome. With each one, another pebble is added to the pile in the field. Some of those who take the Oath have the *power* themselves, and the strength of that original spark gets a little hotter. Too, the Oath and the regulations of service bind the sons of a legionnaire as well, and the Oath passes to them as well, carried in blood and bone from father to son. Generation after generation, it becomes stronger and stronger.

"The pebble becomes a mountain, a very monolith of stones."

Maxian paused. The Engine was beginning to drop through the clouds, and he pulled his woolen cloak—a heavy black fabric that the dead Alais had woven for him—around them both. Freezing rain spattered around them, pilling on the surface of the Engine and flipping away into the slipstream. The sun vanished, swallowed by black clouds, and they rushed through a huge corridor of cloud and smoke. The crack of lightning echoed loud around them as the Engine continued to drop through the storm.

The thunderheads lit up, burning with white-hot light as a trail of lightning hissed past. The Engine continued to speed downward, lashed by rain and lit by staccato bursts of incandescence. Krista turned her head away from a bright flare that danced along the wingtip of the Engine. She felt Maxian's body tremble in response to the enormous boom that followed.

Then there was clear air, and above them a massive ceiling of cloud. Rain continued to fall, but the Engine swerved to the left and suddenly they were flying beside a falling curtain of water. Below them, as the Engine banked again, they could see a gray sea and terraced fields rising up the sides of a huge cone-shaped mountain. White beaches fringed a great bay, and the colored sails of ships could be picked out among the waves. Krista stared in awe, seeing the tiny tracery of roads and towns rush by below. Puffy white clouds fringed the top of the mountain, where a bowl-shaped valley lay nestled at the very summit.

"This is the thing," Maxian continued, his voice fuzzy for a moment, "that we call the curse—the thing that I had thought was a plague, or a contagion. This is the thing that murders in the night, that kills the artist and the innovator. This is the thing that saps the life from every Roman child, leaving them pale and scrawny. It hides in their blood, an invisible guest at every table and in every wedding bed."

Anger, bitter and abiding, began to show in his voice. At her ribs, Krista felt his fist clench.

"It kills our future each day—how many advances might our philosophy have made without the bony hand waiting in the darkness to pluck away our best minds? Those jewelers—what they had made would benefit every man, every woman, every child in the Empire! But they, all unknowing, proposed to *change* the fabric of the Empire— a crime worthy of death for this invisible judge."

"If," Krista said, summoning some strength in the face of the fate that hung over her as well, "it is so pervasive, how can it be driven out? You would have to bend your will upon every person who lives in the Empire—there are millions!"

"Yes—that is what I had thought. But the works of the priests of fire have taught me well—even old Abdmachus had an inkling of what must be done when he offered me a *lever* to move the world."

Krista sneaked a look up at the Prince's face, but saw no feeling was there for the little Persian sorcerer who had joined him when these investigations had first begun. Now the funny old man was one of those in the Engine below who lived only by the will of the Prince. His soft laugh and fondness for plums and pears was dead, like his flesh, though he still moved and spoke—at least when questioned. Unlike Gaius or Alexandros, he did not revel in his "new" life, but rather sat quietly in the darkness, his pale eyes shining in the gloom.

"The mountain cannot be destroyed," Maxian continued, heedless of the sadness on Krista's face, "not one pebble at a time—but it can be moved. I believe that at the root there is a focus or an anchor upon which the entire structure of the Oath depends. Like . . . like the arch of a bridge, with a keystone that locks the edifice into place. This is the thing that we must discover—we must know its nature. Once I have that, then I can shatter it, and the whole Oath will unravel. With Alexandros, the power to my hand is a hundred times what it was before—if we can find the last piece, the puzzle is unlocked."

"And," Krista said slowly and carefully, mindful of being in a flying machine two thousand feet above the earth, "what if Gaius' theory is correct? What will you do then?"

Maxian stiffened and his fists clenched around her hands. Krista breathed slowly out, willing the sharp pain in her wrists to go away. The Prince sat in thought for a moment, and the young woman continued to breathe evenly, though the pain was inching toward agony.

"No . . ." The Prince shifted in his seat and let go of her hands. "I do not think he is right. He has no schooling in these matters—he makes a guess, trying to push me to *his* desired course of action. He has no proof of this, only a *feeling.*"

Krista smiled a little, hearing fear in Maxian's voice. She weighed her options and, seeing the bleak look in his eyes, decided to set the issue aside.

The rain fell away behind them, afflicting the vacationers at Baiae and Neapolis, and the Engine soared over the close-set fields of Latium on a cool spring day. The Prince unwrapped himself from the young woman and returned to the hot, crowded decks below to instruct the Engine as to their landing place. Krista remained above, slowly kneading some feeling back into her hands and wrists. With Maxian gone, her expression settled into a deep frown. She needed to talk to someone about all of this, and soon. The Prince was preparing to embark on some very dubious efforts and could well lose his own life as well as that of countless others.

"But there is just me," she said aloud, to the speeding air. "Just one pretty, dark-haired slave girl with no friends to speak of."

There was a sharp pain in her chest, almost matching that of her wrists. Memories of other times with the Prince threatened to surface, but she held them away with an effort of will. She smoothed her cloak instead, and carefully checked the bronze tube strapped to the inside of her left arm, testing the point of the steel rod that rode inside it. The blood that had come from the eye socket of that fat cow Alais had been carefully scrubbed off after she had retrieved the dart. Touching it now, the slim sharp rod still tingled with the power that the Prince had put into it so long before. Satisfied that the spring was still stiff and the thumb-ring was just a little loose, she checked the rest of her garments—the long, thin knife at her side was secure, the length of wire-cord string nestled at her waist. The familiar routine helped settle her mind.

The Engine slewed to one side and descended toward thickly wooded hills at the edge of a haze-filled river valley. Distantly, marble domes and pillars gleamed in the late afternoon light. Trees rushed up, and the wings of the Engine spread wide, catching at the air like giant sails, slowing the machine. Krista stood a little, one hand on the safety line, looking over the side of the observation cavity at the dead garden and great house sprawling across the hillside below.

"Ah, just as I remember it! A gaudy ruin, filled with the stink of death!"

A thick-shouldered man with a trim waist and a fringe of close-cut gray hair strode down the landing deck of the Engine. He was dressed in the Persian style: soft linen trousers, belted with richly worked kid leather, a close-fitting shirt of silk with an embroidered ox-hide jacket over it. His nose, however, could not be mistaken for anything but a Roman nose, and a patrician one at that. His eyes, cold and gray, were restless, flickering from the roof of the house to the rank weeds that choked the old garden. A short sword of the old classical style hung from his shoulder on a leather strap, and one large-knuckled hand rode easily on it.

"You know it so well, Gaius; your boyhood home, perhaps?"

Another man, this one much shorter, descended the iron ramp that had levered out of the belly of the Engine. Within the looming dark shape was a banging as the other servants began unloading the wooden crates and boxes that held the loot of Dastagird and the libraries of the Persian savants. It was quite cool in the garden, and the smell of freshly disturbed earth thrown up by the claws of the Engine tickled at Gaius' nose.

"No, Alexandros, I grew up by the sea—at the house of my aunt. This place was a fancy of mine when I was a man. Come inside, there is something you should see."

The older man picked his way through the garden and started to mount a series of broad, flat, granite steps that led up to a high-ceilinged arcade of pillars that surrounded the house. Though he was only shod in light military boots, there was a brittle splintering sound as he set foot on the first step. Gaius stopped short, peering down at the slab under his *caligulae*. It had crumbled where he had stepped, cracking in a spiderweb out from under his heel. He frowned and raised a hand in warning to the other man.

Alexandros, his long golden hair tied back behind his head in two bands of copper, also stopped. Like the older man, he was alert, his clear blue eyes scanning the shadows behind the pillars and the brown ranks of trees and bushes on the slopes above the house. He turned slowly, his eyes narrowed over well-formed cheeks and nose. Unlike Gaius, he was wearing only a short white tunic and plain sandals, showing muscular thighs and well-defined biceps. The chilly winter air of central Italia did not seem to bother him. The ramp behind them rang with the tramp of more feet, and Alex turned. "Hold up, lads. Something odd is going on. Don't unload anything yet."

The servants—a collection of dark-haired Valach and Armenians—stopped and laid down their burdens. The tone of command in the young-seeming man's voice did not allow for anything but obedience. Alexandros caught Gaius' eye and nodded to the right, crouching a little. Like the older Roman, the young man carried a blade—a long, straight cavalry sword. The Persian steel rippled out of its sheath, and Alex moved off soundlessly to the left of the house. Gaius watched him for a moment, admiring the play of muscles under the smooth-toned skin and the wolflike quality of the boy.

Gaius shook his head, clearing away unimportant thoughts, and moved off to the right, his ears alert for any sound. Dead grass rustled under his feet.

"Lord Prince?" Krista stepped carefully into the gloom of the Engine. The rumbling had ceased leaving an odd echoing emptiness in the tight little rooms that ran the length of its body. Even small sounds—the *tik-tik* of her sandals on the metal floor—seemed large. She pushed aside the circular door that led into the specially built chamber at the heart of the machine. The well-oiled hinges rolled smoothly, revealing a room of hard-angled iron plates and a slightly raised floor. "Maxian?"

The space echoed with the sound of her voice. The flickering blue-white light of the Engine itself illuminated her face. She moved carefully around the circumference of the room, giving a wide berth to the cage of gold and silver wire that restrained a crystalline orb resting in a cup of rune-carved iron. A high-pitched singing sound followed her as she moved, but it, too, was a sound that she had put aside from her conscious thought. Another circular doorway stood ajar on the opposite side of the room, and beyond it she thought she heard a sound.

That door swung open at her touch, too, still soundless.

The room beyond was quite dark, though the intermittent blue light from the Engine picked out a vague shape. Krista quelled her fear and entered, left hand drawing her cloak behind her back to free her right arm.

Behind her, in its prison of glass and wire and powerful signs, the Engine peered after her with sad, enormous eyes. Its gossamer wings fluttered against the glass, and tiny hands picked fruitlessly at the perfectly smooth surface of its prison.

Krista waited inside the doorway, listening intently. There was the ragged sound of breathing and a sharp smell—sweat and fear—filling the space. "My lord?" She bent forward, one hand out in front of her. It touched a fold of cloth, and then cold flesh. "Ah! Can you speak?"

The flickering light picked out the Prince, huddled on the floor of his room, curled up into a ball. Sweat beaded on his forearms and the side of his forehead. Krista cursed silently and gathered him up in her arms. He was very cold, and trembling slightly. Her long fingers pressed against the side of his neck—there was a pulse, but it hammered like a forge. "What is it?" She rolled back an eyelid and found his pupils wide and black.

The Prince shuddered in her arms, and sudden warmth flushed his skin. "Get me . . . ," he croaked, "get me out. It is too strong here."

Krista nodded sharply and laid the Prince back down gently, feeling a prickling at the back of her neck. With quick hands, she folded a blanket over him and then sprinted out of the chamber.

Her feet rang on the floor, raising the heads of the servants in the cargo space and on the landing ramp. She skidded to a stop and half crouched to see out into the garden. The house of the Egyptian Queen seemed shrunken and badly used by the weather since the previous year. The head had fallen off the sphinx beside the great doorway. The rosebushes and trees that had been growing up among the remains of the ornamental garden were dead and withered.

"Quickly," she snapped at the Valach boys sitting on the metal ramp, "get these things out of the way and into the house. You and you—come with me. The Prince needs our help."

Without looking to see if they obeyed, she spun around and ran lightly back into the bowels of the Engine. Two of the Valach padded after her, as they always did. She ducked back into the room where the Prince lay, finding him half sitting, his face showing enormous strain. She touched the blanket and jerked her hand away in surprise. The heavy wool crumbled to dust under her fingers.

"The house, get me into the house. . . ." The Prince's voice was tight and strained.

Krista knelt and got her shoulder under his. The burlier of the two Valach got his own hairy arm around the Prince's waist. Krista heaved, and the Prince came up off the floor. Crabbing sideways, they slid out the door into the passage. The Prince was a dead weight, his limbs flopping loosely. The slave girl began to hear a sharp buzzing sound in her ears. "Don't stop," she barked at the Valach. "We must reach the house."

The Valach scooped up the Prince's legs and broke into a run in one fluid motion. Krista slid Maxian's arm off her shoulder and ran alongside.

The metal ramp at the mouth of the Engine rang under their feet as they ran out onto the brown dead grass of the garden. The Valach began to labor as he crossed the space between the Engine and the veranda of the house. Krista paced him, watching in horror out of the corner of her eye as the boy's long raven black hair began to dull and turn a pale gray. His steps faltered on the staircase, and more stones cracked and shattered, even under Krista's light sandals. At the line of columns, the buzzing sound soared into a shrieking wail. Krista grabbed for the Prince as the Valach stumbled sideways and crashed headlong into one of the ancient marble pillars.

The other boy, running up behind, threw himself between the girl and the dying Valach. Though lacking the broad shoulders and rippling brawn of his older sibling, the younger man caught the Prince and shoved away from the withered corpse of his brother. Krista cursed and leapt from the top of the steps into the cool darkness between the pillars. There was a moment of suffocating sensation as she passed through the doorway, but she landed lightly and spun around, long hair flying out behind her head. The buzzing sound in her head was gone. The remaining Valach followed close on her heels, the Prince in his arms.

Krista looked out on the garden and saw that the stands of trees and rosebushes that had surrounded the house were all dead. Every living thing within sight of the porch was a drear brown or a rotting black. The Egyptian House stood at the center of quiet devastation.

Gaius picked his way around the corner of the rear of the house, walking carefully on the crumbling bricks that had once made a broad, pleasant patio. The patio had opened out of the dining rooms at the back of the house, overlooking a sloping lawn and more ornamental trees that descended the face of the hill. Once, covered pipes had carried water to fountains and a culvert that watered the lemon and orange trees. Now the trees were dead and overgrown with a thick vine bearing shiny dark leaves. The culverts were dangerous gaping holes in the floor of the patio. Sharp edges of broken ceramic pipe waited for an unwary ankle.

Memories fluttered at the edge of the old Roman's consciousness. He snarled to himself, his face contorting for a moment, and drove them away with an effort of will. Gaius had spent too much time in the pleasant company of enemies to show his emotions or true feelings to anyone else. Only one person had drawn his heart's truth out of him. This house, and much more, had been part of the reward he had intended her.

Now, thinking back upon it, he wondered if this curse that the Prince obsessed about might have had an earlier genesis than they suspected. Would it not explain the circumstances of his own death? It had seemed so petty! Walking into the great Forum of Rome—a man, an acquaintance, a political crony, walking up to him with a raised hand and a strained smile. Sudden burning pain in his side—then falling, and a crowd of faces above him, some familiar, some not. A cold darkness, broken at last by a dreadful awakening in a dank hole filled with bones and mud. The old man shook his head again and stepped up onto the veranda.

Alexandros entered the arcade of pillars at the same time from the opposite direction. Under the shelter of the roof—still mostly intact, and even partially repaired during their previous stay—the floor tiles did not shatter at a step, and the walls seemed strong enough. Gaius raised an eyebrow at the younger man. Alex smiled back, his strong white teeth gleaming in the dim light. The Greek shrugged his shoulders and slipped his sword back into its sheath.

"Nothing—only ruins and dead things. Did you see any animals on your side?"

"No," Gaius said, shaking his head in negation. Alex nodded over his shoulder.

"There are flights and flights of birds heaped on that side, all dead and withered. A strange business—none are rotted to speak of, just sort of shriveled up."

Gaius pursed his lips and slowly turned around, his eyes picking out the faded remains of the marks that the Persian Abdmachus had made the year before on floor and column and wall. He put his own sword away as well. "The curse, then," he said slowly, looking out at the dead trees at the edge of the garden. "It is attacking the house, but the old sorcerer's ward is enough to hold it at bay. We should get back to the Engine and help them unload—I doubt it is safe to be outside here, now."

Alex turned to go back out through the pillars, but Gaius halted him with a touch.

"This way," the old Roman said with a wry smile. "Better not to risk it outside—and there is something that you should see within."

Alex smiled back, but Gaius was slow to remove his hand from the boy's shoulder, and the Macedonian's eyes became wary.

"Who is this?"

Alex stared up at the massive statue that stood in the atrium of the house. Gaius covered a brief smile, though his mind was no longer focused on the younger man. The rooms and chambers they had passed through seemed long abandoned, but small items—a wicker chair in one room— were not where he remembered they had been left. Someone had been through the house, doubtless searching for evidence of what the Prince had been about. The incised and painted marks along the floors and etched into the walls remained, however, and the old Roman was glad. Without the remaining vestige of power that held the invisible enemy at bay, he was sure the entire building would have been reduced to a pitted foundation.

"It is you, my friend," Gaius said at last, turning back to his companion. The old Roman thought it was an excellent likeness.

"Me?" Alex turned, his face a study in comedy. "It looks nothing like me!"

Gaius shrugged. "Those who came after you were fond of embellishing your features, your purpose, your height, your reputation—or blackening it by equal turns. A woman I once knew had this bronze cast in your honor— this was her house, and she revered you as a god."

Alex grinned tightly, a flicker of cold steel in the dimness. "My men always complained about that. It is the way of the people of the East, though, to look upon the lord and master of their time as a living divinity. But not the Greeks!" He laughed. "Not my Greeks . . ."

"Well," Gaius said slowly, his eyes narrowed, "she was a Greek, the last of her house, and she swore by you and the power you represented."

Alex nodded, his eyes seeing something far away. "Women always looked to me as a source of power—for them or for their families. It seems, from what you have

told me of your life, that you forgot that lesson. Your as-
signation with her destroyed your support among the citizens and the Senate."

Gaius frowned and spread his hands. "Who can say?
The accounts of the time are confused, and I did not see
it when I was alive. You are not one to talk, either! Your
drive to build a new civilization cost you your life by poison, and *my* empire still stands while yours is dust."

Alex nodded absently, looking around the dim, old
room. The painted panels that had once covered the ma-
sonry and concrete walls had cracked and splintered, falling away in piles of dust. Still, it was a great chamber,
and he could see that it had—upon a time—been a bright
place, filled with torches and lanterns and the many mar-
velous inventions of the Romans. Still, he thought, it was
little different, this stone and brick and mortar, from his
own palaces, or the cities he had ruled or destroyed. Even
the speech of his countrymen was the same, though centuries had passed by, leaving nations and men in ruin. It
seemed odd, but then, perhaps there was something to this
talk of a curse.

"Yes . . . your empire still stands," Alexandros said,
"though your name stands best as a festival day and a text
for schoolchildren. Do the notables of this time raise statues to you in their entranceways?" The edge of a sneer
had crept into Alex's voice.

Gaius smiled broadly, hooking his thumbs in his belt.
"Why, my lad, you are right. The great houses of the city
do hold statues of me, or my nephew, in honored places.
A great tomb of colored marble stands near the crossroads
of the city, erected in my name. My memory maintains,
as great as yours."

Alex matched stares with the old man for a moment and
was reminded, briefly, of a pugnacious childhood friend
he had not seen in a long time. There was something familiar in the old man's eye and face—but then he laughed
and bowed.

"My pardon, I am your guest and have been inconsiderate. Pray, show me the rest of this place and tell me the story of its building."

Gaius inclined his head, accepting the apology.

Maxian lay still on the floor, wrapped in a blanket. Krista crouched next to his head, lifting it a little to slide another folded blanket underneath. The Prince's breathing had grown stronger since they had entered the house, and he could move his arms and legs. She wiped sweat from his brow with the edge of her sleeve.

"Thank you," whispered the Prince. His voice had not yet recovered.

"No matter, my lord," she said softly. "Without you we are all dead."

"Perhaps . . ." Maxian searched her face, seeing worry and strain there. He realized, again, how much he needed her assistance and support. For a moment, he nearly blurted the words out, but something held him back. A distance had grown up between them since the death of the Valach woman, Alais, at Dastagird. Maxian knew what had happened; old Gaius had taken great relish in relating the story of the struggle in the final chamber of the fire temple. But he had never mentioned it to Krista, or she to him.

"Is everyone else inside?"

Krista nodded and folded back the sleeves on her tunic.

"Yes, the rest of us can still come and go—it just seems to seek you out. The Engine is fine. I've ordered the other servants to move it back into the cover of the trees and set a watch. There will be hot food in a little while, and the plumbing still works." She smiled and knelt at his side, taking his left hand in both of hers.

"What about Gaius and Alexandros?" Maxian squeezed her hand.

Krista shook her head, giving him a despairing look. "They're wandering around, trying to see which is the bigger dog. I took care of everything myself."

Maxian shook his head a little, frowning. Bright white

sparks floated across his vision at this, so he stopped and lay very still. "Go get them and bring them here," he whispered. "We've no time for their bickering."

"You've thought of strangling him while he sleeps, I suppose."

Gaius turned in the darkness, barely able to make out the outline of Alexandros' head. A thin slat of light fell from a broken roof tile, high above, and provided the faintest illumination. The boy's golden hair was white in this light, and his face was hidden in shadow, unreadable and distant.

"Many times." Gaius' voice was very quiet, though they were far from the kitchens, where the Valach and Armenians were setting up shop, or the upper bedrooms, where the Prince Maxian lay with his concubine. A cool, musty dampness surrounded them as they lay on a pallet on the floor of the root cellar of the old house.

"On the road into the East, my thoughts often turned to poison—save that he could doubtless smell it, or feel its effect and cure himself. Sometimes, I thought that the quick stab of a knife into the back of his skull might be enough. But the little witch watches him all the time. This makes it difficult . . ."

Alexandros laughed, a low musical sound that made the skin on Gaius' arms prickle. "Never more in my life," Alex said, "have I hated anything more than another having power over me, controlling my life, pointing my destiny. Such a man was my father, and now this Prince of yours. I had seemed to escape this, only to come home again."

Gaius snorted and sat up, rubbing his face with his hands. "He is not *my* Prince. He is the unwanted friend who rouses you from sleep for some dreadful party or careless escapade that brings the *aediles*. These are fancies, though, that cannot stand the light of bitter truth."

Alexandros sat up as well and pulled on his tunic. He sprang to his feet, limber as the youth that he still was. Gaius watched him out of the corner of his eye, feeling envy creeping in his soul. *He is a pretty boy*, thought the old Roman, *and, now, will always be.*

"Our truth is that he is life." Alexandros, despite the bitter tone, was smiling. "Life is precious to us—to me, at least. Perhaps you are old enough to lay down this burden again?"

"Hah!" Gaius rose as well, though he did not *spring* anywhere. He stood, using one of the broken columns to steady himself. His sandals had gone missing, and he hunted about with his foot, stubbing a toe on a brick. He grimaced at the pain, but it subsided quickly. An unexpected side effect of his condition, he supposed. "I have never sought release from this life. It galls me, as it oppresses you, that I—we—must serve another. Yet, this is the lot we are given. I put to you a thought . . ." Gaius paused, hearing a noise on the narrow stairs that led down from the upper floor. A sound like light footsteps. He raised a hand, and Alex looked up at the stairway as well. The sound did not repeat.

"I put to you," he continued, "that our situation being fixed, we must put all our labors to exalting the position and situation of our master—yes, a cold word, but a true one! As he improves, so do we. Is this not so?"

Alex made a face, but nodded. "You think like a Persian palace servant," the youth said. "But, still, you are right."

"Good," Gaius said briskly, "I will take that as a compliment. Now, our present circumstances are limited, so we must convince the Prince to allow us more freedom of action, both to pursue the goals that he knows he holds and those that he does not."

"What?" Alex raised a hand, glaring at the older man. "You speak like an Athenian jurist—many words with little meaning."

Gaius raised an eyebrow, his lips forming a smirk. "I am—I was—a rather successful one," he said. "This is what I mean, plainspoken boy! Today, our Prince desires one thing: to defeat this curse upon his people. We will bend all our effort to helping him win out. Tomorrow, however, when this affliction is past, then other thoughts will come to him. I say that we help ourselves most by working toward both goals—that of today, and that of tomorrow—now. Let us spare no time while he dithers and struggles with his conscience."

Alex stared back at Gaius for a moment, but then understanding stole up on him a bit at a time. Then the youth smiled back at the old Roman, showing his fine white teeth. "Not just a jurist, but a wise councillor."

This time they both heard the sound of steps, light but unmistakable, on the stairs.

Both men turned to look up at Krista as she appeared in the doorway. "My lords," she said, seemingly oblivious of the dankness of the chamber, "the Lord Prince wishes to speak with you."

Gaius bowed a little, indicating that Alexandros should precede him up the stairs.

The Prince lay in one of the beds in the upper rooms. The wooden frame had nearly rotted away, but enough of the pallet remained for him to lie down on a bed of rugs and quilts that the servants had carried from the Engine. A brace of beeswax candles burned steadily on a table at the head of the bed. Gaius entered the room and drifted to one side to lean against the wall, as was his wont. Alexandros chose to squat on the floor by the foot of the bed, watching the Prince with his deep blue eyes. Krista occupied the lone chair, her legs crossed and a small black cat cradled in her lap. Maxian was still pale and drained looking, but some color had returned to his cheeks.

"My friends, a delicate struggle lies ahead of us. We have returned to the heartland of our enemy stronger by the addition of Alexandros and the secrets of the Persian magi, but now this great power is focused upon me and it bears down heavily.

"Gaius, we cannot wait until I am strong enough to go about in the world on my own feet. There is too much work to be done. You and Alexandros must be my eyes and hands in the city."

The old Roman bowed slightly at this, though his eyes did not leave Maxian's face. The Prince was recovering, but slowly, and Gaius smiled inwardly, seeing opportunities unfold like the leaves of a spring flower.

"How do we avoid destruction by this curse?" Alexandros' voice showed no concern for his possible annihilation. "If we leave this place and its ward, will it not strike us down?"

Maxian shook his head wearily. "Our enemy is neither wise nor cunning," he said. "It is very strong, but it does not look ahead. If you take an indirect approach and do not cause the weave of the fabric of the Empire, as it were, to change by direct action, it cannot tell that you are a threat. Even if you did, it might take some time for it to react and strike at you. It knows me, though! It knows the taste of my will and is always pressing against me. If you and Gaius and Krista go out and undertake activities that are not obviously a threat, then I believe that you can act without fear."

Alexandros shrugged and looked up at Gaius. The Roman nodded slightly and turned back to the Prince. "My lord, what must we do?"

A brief smile flitted across Maxian's face. "First," he said, "we must track down the exact text of this Oath, which means you or Alex must spend a great deal of time within the Imperial Archives and whichever private libraries you can gain entrance to."

Gaius grinned at Krista at this, his eyes sparkling. She answered him with an icy calm and continued to pet the cat. Maxian did not miss the exchange, however.

"Gaius . . . no dallying. Time will be short, and we must move quickly."

"How so?" Alexandros stood, brushing his cotton kilt down over his thighs. "If you surmise correctly, we can take our time with a flanking movement and the enemy will not be able to discern our approach."

"The curse is not our only foe," Maxian said, his voice now very weary. "My brother's agents will also be seeking me out if they learn that I have returned to Latium. After our lamentable conversation in Armenia, I fear my dear brother will think me quite mad. An emperor must, by his nature, look poorly on unstable relatives."

Gaius opened his mouth to speak, but a fierce look from Maxian stilled him.

"No, old man, we will *not* undertake your preferred course of action in this matter. There are other ways to reach my goal. I will *not* take that one. Go into the city and find out the latest news, seek out this text, get supplies . . ."

Krista ushered both men out, and then closed the pale green panel behind them.

THE CITY OF MAKKAH, ARABIA FELIX

><

Uncle Mohammed!" The young woman, her raven hair tied back behind her head with a scarf, looked up in surprise, bright green eyes visible over a light veil of raw silk. She rose from the stone seat just inside the doorway of the house, smoothing the plaits of her dress, and bowed deeply.

Mohammed returned her bow and shrugged his outer robe, dirty with the grime of a thousand-mile journey, off his shoulders. "Rasana, daughter of my wife's sister, greetings."

The courtyard behind Mohammed was filled with noise: men, camels, horses. The sound of swords and lances rattled against the whitewashed walls of the house. Boots rang on the cobblestones. Mohammed stripped the burnoose from his head, unwinding the length of linen. His face was worn and dark from the sun, showing the strain of weeks of hard travel across the wasteland. The girl stared at him, seeing a jagged new scar starting at his left eye and descending sharply into the thicket of his beard.

Mohammed cocked his head a little to one side, dark brown eyes curious. "Niece, kindly summon my wife to me. I would greet her before I enter our home."

The girl's eyes grew wider, as some surprise or shock registered in her. "Uncle . . . you did not hear? I thought you had come—"

Mohammed raised a hand, forestalling her, and turned to the crowd of men in the courtyard. They were a grimy and desperate-looking lot, men of the deep desert with long, curved swords and grim, forbidding faces. Many bore the marks of old wounds and hard fighting. Mailed armor glinted under their patched and mended robes. Mohammed gestured to two of them, hawk-visaged men with the blue cords of the northern tribes wound through their *kaffiyeh*.

"Quiet! Jalal; Shadin—the stables and water are around the side. Take the horses there and see that they are fed and watered. I will send servants with food and drink for the men."

The two men bowed, and Mohammed turned back to the girl in the doorway. She had turned pale, and her soft hands were fluttering at her waist like doves startled from the brush. "Oh, Uncle! I thought you knew! Please, accept my apologies! I am so sorry." The girl bowed again, almost kneeling on the floor.

Mohammed frowned and crossed one leg over the other so that he could take off his boots. "Apologies for what? Where is Khadijah? Where is everyone, for that matter?"

The girl bowed again, placing her head on the floor. "Oh, Uncle, they are in the little house on the side of the hill. The house of white stones! Please, forgive my foolishness, I thought you had come because of the news . . ."

Mohammed's frown deepened, and a shade of fear flickered across his face. "The house of white stones? Who has died?" He stopped, his heart filled with sudden dreadful certainty. The girl remained prostrate; her face against the floor, but now Mohammed could hear the faint sound of tears dripping. He brushed past her and ran through the dim chambers of the house, forgetting to remove his boots as custom and civility demanded.

Mohammed halted, his right fist poised to rap on the frame of the door. His face remained impassive, though anger was close to breaking the surface of his control. Loud voices, muffled by the door, could be heard. He dropped his hand and consciously opened his fist, flexing his fingers.

". . . be mine! They are Bani Hashim caravans, our camels, our goods! By what right do they go to him? He is no blood of ours—a hired hand that did too well! He owes his position to his . . ."

Mohammed grimaced and considered breaking down the door. Behind him, he felt the presence of Jalal close at hand. He raised a hand and gestured for the Tanukh to leave. The Northerner nodded, tucking a knife back into his shirt, and faded away into the dim coolness at the end of the corridor. Mohammed took another moment and mastered himself before knocking.

The door banged open, and a very angry woman of middle age looked out.

Mohammed smiled politely and stepped into the room, ducking his head under the lintel. "Blessings, Taiya, sister of my wife. Blessings, Hala, sister of my wife."

The woman who had answered the door turned her back on him and stalked to a low seat by the window. The other woman, Hala, stood and bowed gravely to Mohammed, then resumed her own seat. The window behind them was tall and narrow, showing a narrow wedge of the innermost garden of the great house. Hala met his gaze with sad eyes. She had been her older sister's favorite and had accompanied her nearly everywhere. Like Khadijah, she was plain featured, with intelligent eyes and a quiet, almost gentle, manner. Mohammed bowed to her and took a chair that had been sitting in the corner of the small room.

It was cool and almost dark, with only a little light coming in from the garden window. Mohammed sat easily, though his heart was still greatly troubled, and waited. The other woman, Taiya, was the youngest surviving daughter of old Khuwaylid and—when he was alive—his favorite. She sat stiffly, looking at the window, fingers picking at the rich brocade of her skirts. Hala glanced at her sister and then turned back to Mohammed, her small hands folded in her lap. Mohammed summoned a smile for her, but he was sure that it seemed false.

"Brother, we feared that something had befallen you when you did not return with the caravan from Damascus."

"Something did," grated Mohammed, suddenly assailed by a stabbing sensation of guilt at the quiet words. "There has been a great war in the North, between Persia and Rome. The Persian armies under the command of their great general, Shahr-Baraz, attempted to capture Damascus. I became involved, and my return was greatly delayed."

"Involved?" Taiya's voice was quiet, but the anger in her voice was as bitter as spike-leaf tea. "With *who*? What was *her* name? Neither Rome nor Persia is any friend of the Quraysh. What is the business of our house to meddle in their affairs?"

Mohammed turned a little in the chair, facing Taiya squarely. "I met a man whom I would call my brother, if he were alive today. A true friend, for all that we met in a *caravanserai* in the foreigners' district of the Red City. He was driven to go north, to Damascus, and then to the City of Silk, Palmyra, and I followed him, for he needed my aid. How could I deny the brother of my heart?"

"You were gone too long," Hala said, her voice rising a little.

Mohammed nodded, still meeting her eyes. Tears threatened them, for Hala had loved her sister very much. Taiya, too, was on the verge of tears, but would fight to the end to keep this *poor cousin* from seeing them. "I know. There was a great battle at Palmyra, and we were besieged for many months. Flight was impossible. I barely escaped with my life."

Taiya suddenly stood up and paced across to the door and threw it open. She looked out into the passageway, saw nothing, and then slammed it closed again. "All the time she lay sick, Khadijah could think only of you," Taiya snapped as she returned to the window. "When she could no longer see, and the fever had settled into her bones, all she asked for was news of you—*you*, the wanderer! The husband who is never in his own house—who spent his brief time at home mewed up in a cave, sharing porridge with beggars and thieves!"

Hala stood and tried to take her sister by the arm. Taiya slapped her hand away, her voice rising still further. "You left her alone and she died! She trusted you when she trusted no one else—and you abandoned her! All she needed to live was your face, or your voice, and you denied her even this! At the end, she thought you had perished in the wasteland and then she died, sure that you would never come."

Mohammed stood, his face tremendously calm. Taiya flinched and shrank back from him, but he did not raise a hand. Instead, he pushed the chair away and knelt on the stone floor and bowed to the two sisters, placing his head on the woven sisal mat that lay across the center of the room. "I am sorry," he said. "Had I known, I would have done anything to be here."

He stood, and Hala stepped to his side, her hand smoothing his tunic, which had turned awry. Taiya just stared, her face a white mask behind the kohl around her eyes and the golden rings hanging from her ears.

"I know," Hala said, tears leaking from the corners of her eyes, making long marks in the powder on her face. "It was an evil circumstance."

Mohammed's left eyelid flickered under the scar, and his face became a degree paler. "No . . . there is true evil in the world, but it is not circumstance. Do not say that this was evil; I have seen its face, and it did not pass this way."

"Evil?" Taiya whispered incredulously. "You know so much of evil that you can see it, touch it, feel it, declare its worth? Neglect is evil; indifference is evil!"

Mohammed's face darkened, and he seemed to grow larger in the room. "I have seen the face of true evil, sister of my wife. It is a dark shape that dims the sun, that shatters towers with its voice, which walks in the world in the form of man. Something that the jinn fear as they cower in the desert. Something that makes the world shake when it walks. It did not lay Khadijah low. I know, for I looked upon it from the rampart of Palmyra and saw my friend die at its hand. If it had come this way, there would be nothing left."

Hala's eyes widened, hearing an echo of fear and battle in his voice.

"Rubbish!" Taiya almost spit at him, but restrained herself at the last moment. "You do not care that my sister," she continued, "whom I loved best, is dead. Well, I do care and my family cares. You came late into our household, al-Quryash, and you will not be master here now that she is gone. I do not care that you were Khadijah's husband—I will take those portions of our father's inheritance that are mine for myself."

Hala turned on her sister, her eyes flashing. "That is not our way! Mohammed and Khadijah wed, and he is her heir. Our clan is rich and prosperous from her wisdom and skill. She chose this man to be at her side, to make us stronger, to be our eyes in the world beyond the desert. Now that she is gone, he will lead us."

Taiya sneered at her older sister, twitching her skirts away. "Foolish little weaver! What did you do all these years but sit at Khadijah's footstool, smiling prettily and knitting? My husband and I made as much as this boy in her service. Our father made us rich! He is the one who raised up this house and made it strong. Without him, there would be nothing here but a hut and scrawny goats!"

Hala stamped her foot, ringing a bracelet of tiny bells around her ankle. "Stupid cow! Father made us a house and the beginnings of wealth—but Khadijah's wisdom delivered us riches! Never was a woman wiser than she, even if she could not bear a living son, or married twice. See him? He is her choice—she who is your master and mine in forethought and care. In life, you took her advice above all others. Now that she lies dead in the house of white stones, you would say she is a liar?"

Taiya did not respond, but stormed out, golden bangles at her wrists tinkling in the sudden quiet. After a moment, there was the sound of another door crashing closed at the end of the hallway. Mohammed stared after her and then sat down, holding his head in his hands.

Hala looked away, then slowly went to her seat on the window ledge. "Will you stay this time?" Her voice was faint. "Tell me what happened in the north."

"No," Mohammed said, raising his head up and looking out the window at the bougainvillea and jasmine in the garden. "This house makes my heart sick."

The sound of crickets chirping echoed off broken gray rock. A boot made of tooled kid leather with small silver studs passed over the stones. A man of almost fifty climbed the side of the mountain under a blazing sun. He wore a long desert robe of tan and white, with a burnoose wrapped around his head. His features were strong—a fierce nose jutted over a thick bushy black beard. His hands, large and scarred with the artifacts of many battles, were a dark brown and grasped at the stones to pull himself up over a ledge. The man's face was bleak, for his heart was greatly troubled.

The peak rose at the side of a deep, broad valley. The summit was bare of trees, though covered with scattered gray shrubs and thorny bushes. Great boulders littered the face of the mountain, all showing deep cracks and crevices where the merciless sun and wind had broken them down. A perfectly clear blue sky rose above the mountain, anchored by the white disk of the sun. There was little wind to break the tremendous heat of the day. Gravel crunched under the man's foot, and the still, hot air was filled with the voices of bees and crickets.

The man passed underneath a cliff of stone, covered with small spiky plants bearing tiny white flowers. In the bare fragment of shade that the cliff endowed, a scrub bush with dark red bark was growing. Triangular waxy leaves covered the branches. The man pushed through the thicket at the base of the cliff and climbed up a narrow passage between the stones. At the top the rocks were hot with the radiance of the sun. Now he could see the summit of the mountain, a tilted pile of barren stone and cracked rock. The air was heavy and hot, like a mourning cloth.

From the mountaintop, the whole world lay below the man in a vast sweep of desert and mountain and hills. The valley below him seemed far away, filled with a faint bluish haze from the cook fires of the villages and the city. No clouds could be seen in all that gigantic expanse of sky. The bowl of heaven shaded from a dusty bone near the horizon to a tremendously deep Chin blue overhead. The sun, standing high in the sky, was a bright flare of white. Beneath his feet, the mountain slept in the heat of the day. Here, exposed on all sides, was a breeze at last, ruffling his cloak and robes. He stood straight, his walking cane at one side, and slowly turned to survey the entire world.

The land was a rumpled quilt of flat plateaus and deep *wadi* cut by summer thunderstorms. Low mountains spiked up out of barren plains of salt pan and rocky fields. No green thing intruded into the sere desolation save below, within the shelter of the valley and the walls of the city. The man turned back, away from the openness of the desert. The valley was long and narrow, with hills marching close on either side and mountains rising behind them. Here, there was green, carefully tended and watched over. At the wells and along the slash of the streambeds, small fields and orchards sprouted from the gray-and-tan soil. He looked southwest, along the length of the valley of Mak-kah, and could, at the edge of vision, make out the green of the oasis of the Zam-Zam. There was a deep well there, surrounded by pools and temples.

The man sat, his legs swinging off the edge of the great slab of sandstone.

The man lay on the mountaintop, his eyes closed, the heat of the sun burning on his skin. The hot wind continued to whisper across him, plucking at his sleeves. His lips were badly chapped, and his skin had become cold, even in the heat of the day. The walking cane lay by his side, thrown down. Even with his eyelids closed, he could see the brilliant blue sky above him. He hid in old memories.

Act!

The man's head twitched a little to one side, though his mind had wandered far from his body and the sound of a voice in the air around him took a long time to register. The sound hung in the air, clear and ringing from the rocks like the chime of a great bell.

Act!

The man's eyes fluttered open, and then he turned his head to one side, away from the merciless sun. His lips moved, but no sound came out. For an instant, he thought that he could see himself as if looking down from above, a battered disheartened man of later middle age, lying on sunbaked stones at the top of a mountain. Then he could feel the hot wind on his arms and legs and taste dust in his mouth.

Act!

The man levered himself up on one elbow and, squinting, looked around. Only sky and boulders were to be seen. The mountaintop was empty. The wind died, leaving a great stillness.

"Who is there?" The man's voice was plaintive and weak, barely a whisper.

I am here. I am in all things. Prostrate yourself, man, and listen.

The man tried to stand, but his legs failed him and he fell down. He bent his head, trying to use his arms to raise himself up. The rock beneath him crumbled, and his hands slipped. A sharp pain sparked on his forehead where the rock face cut it.

"What are you?" His voice was even weaker.

Listen, man, you whom the Lord of the World made from clots of blood, do you know His will?

"Who are you?" the man tried to shout, but there was no breath left in his body.

Do you make obeisance to Him, who made all that is? Do you render Him respect? Come to Him, and listen, and know His will in all things.

The man whimpered, his hands twitching uncontrollably.

Do you see that there is evil in the world? Evil that defies the Lord of the World, that stains His perfect creation?

An image blossomed in the man's mind, horribly real and as fresh as the day he had first seen it. The man's body jerked with spasms.

A dark shape moved on a plain of sandy stones. A great host of men, their spears glittering in the morning light, pressed about the walls of a strong place. The man, clad in bright armor, stood at the summit of a great tower of ashlar stone and fitted granite blocks. The dark shape raised a fist, and the air shook with the roar of unheard words. The man on the tower shouted defiance back into that tremendous sound. A whirl of stones and dust and the bones of the dead skittered across the plain before the army. It grew and grew, until it loomed over the rampart and the man in the tower knew fear. A shape blurred out of the air, enormous and given an impossible outline. The earth shook at its step. The man screamed at his soldiers to flee, to abandon the tower. It was too late. The thing in the air roared and swung down its fist. Stone blocks taller than a man shattered like porcelain under the blow. The tower toppled to one side, and the man threw himself off, out into the air. Wind rushed past, whipping his hair and then there was a stunning blow as he hit the street. The earth shook again, and the man looked up, seeing the whole tower sliding toward him.

The man sobbed, his body aching with pain at the memory that had welled up in his mind.

Act! Submit to the will of your Lord and strive against this, or all your race will be the playthings of hidden powers. Act! You know what must be done.

The man shuddered, his entire body twitching furiously, then he lay still on the broad surface of the great boulder that crowned the mountaintop. After a moment the wind rose again, rattling the leaves of the thornbushes and blowing sand and grit across him.

THE HARBOR OF PHOSPHERION, CONSTANTINOPLE

"T o the left," the centurion's whisper drifted down the line of men. Nicholas leaned out a little, trying to see the head of the line in the pressing darkness. There was the dim glow of a shuttered lantern up ahead and the liquid gleam of its tiny light on water below his feet. White breath puffed from Nick's mouth, and he drew the heavy woolen cloak around his shoulders a little tighter. The man in front of him moved, the boards of the dock creaking under his feet, and Nicholas shuffled ahead as well. He felt awkward and heavy in the thick cork-filled armor. He was used to a shirt of close-linked mail, heavy and snug against his chest and on his shoulders. This thick padding made him feel enormous and stiff.

Another centurion, this one with the Poseidon-blaze of

the Imperial fleet on his shoulder, moved past him, along the line of men. He carried another lantern and moved quietly down the gangway at the end of the dock. Above him the light briefly illuminated the overhanging oar galleries of the three-banked galley—a *dromon* to the Southerners—that they were boarding. Nicholas shivered again, feeling a chill breeze gust up off the waters of the Propontis. All around him the docks of the military harbor, nestled under the walls of the great city, were filled with the muted noise of thousands of men moving quietly.

Nicholas hurried across the gangway when his time came, nervous at the darkness, but once his feet touched the subtly tilting deck of the great oared galley, his heart calmed. Here, on the deck of a fighting ship again for the first time in nearly four years, fear and doubt faded away. He stepped to the side and looked around. The ninety-foot length of the warship was filling up with legionnaires. Great bulwarks of planks faced with hides covered a fighting deck and, below them, three rowing galleries. Nicholas looked down, seeing the white eyes of hundreds of sailors, already seated at their benches, staring back up at him. The ship trembled a little as more and more men clattered over the gangway.

The centurions were herding men aft, toward the rise of the rear cabin, making them file in two lines on either side of the artillery towers that rose from the center of the ship. Nicholas shed his woolen cloak, the sensation of cold having dropped from him like leaves in the Scandian fall, and rolled it up. He swung out along the edge of the bulwark and hooked an arm around a stanchion. Below him the sailors were gossiping and arguing among themselves. Warm air, heated by three hundred bodies in the gallery, billowed up through the opening. Nicholas began working his way forward along the narrow walkway.

The gangplank was hauled back to the dock, and thick hawsers were pulled back aboard and coiled. A soft tapping sound echoed through the rowing gallery, and the sailors fell quiet. There was a rustle of men finding position on the benches and a creak as they tested the oars in the locks. A soft piping note came from the flautist at the head of the rowing gallery. The oarsmen took hold of the oars, making a rattle of great wooden shafts. Nicholas reached the cross walkway of the first artillery tower, where there was a break in the outer wall of the ship.

Creaking, the galley moved, slowly at first, as two long-boats filled with oarsmen began towing it away from the dock, out into the harbor basin. The shore receded, becoming a blur of faint lights at the waterline, and then a vast unseen bulk of darkness that was the seawall of the city; high above, a glittering range of lights on the upper battlements. The massive towers studded along that long line were ablaze with pitch torches and lanterns. A sulfurous glow surrounded the summit of each tower; bonfires wrapped in mist and fog rising from the cold waters of the Golden Horn. Nicholas leaned out, smelling the sea and feeling cold fresh air on his face.

In the darkness he smiled, his heart glad to be afloat, with the quiver of a deck under his feet, preparing to speed to war. The longboats released the towlines and broke away from the prow of the galley. The flute player sounded two sharp notes, and the sailors ran the long ashwood oars out of the locks. The great leaf-shaped blades dipped into the water, then, in one motion, stroked slowly backward. Nicholas felt the ship come fully alive under his feet, and now a feral grin split his features. The flautist called again, marking the beat of the oars, and the three hundred-legged beast slid forward across the dark waters, quiet as some great hunting cat.

Around the *dromon*, in the predawn darkness, the dim, bobbing lights of a hundred other galleys of the Imperial fleet also crept forward. The wind out of the north picked up a little, luffing the sails as the ships turned out of the mouth of the Horn and into the wider body of the Propontis itself. Dawn would come soon, creeping over the rim of the world.

*   *   *

It had been a small, mean room with only a single lantern to push back the shadows. Nicholas entered and sat down; his face half twisted into a grin. He thought it was funny that the men he worked for found it necessary to hide their doings in dolorous places. Most citizens of the Empire wouldn't have noticed if they had discussed their business in the Forum. They never appreciated the humor of it. Sergius certainly did not. The tribune was one of the efficient, vigorous ones. *The Empire Is Our Duty. Our Duty Is the Empire*.

"You're better, then?"

Nicholas nodded. He healed quickly, though he tended to scar. Parts of his back still felt like bubbled glass where lash marks had healed badly. The hold of a Dansk reaver was a poor place to convalesce. Sergius rubbed the end of his nose, considering some parchment sheets on the rickety table between them.

"The offices here are overstaffed," said the tribune, scowling at the roster. "You've been detached from cleanup to fieldwork." He pushed a chit across the table. Nicholas picked it up and turned it over. The fired clay chip had a pair of fish painted on it with black ink.

"The navy has some business coming up in a day or two. Report to them."

Sergius paused, squinting at Nicholas. "You can swim, can't you?"

Nicholas grinned, showing fine white teeth. In the Empire, to career Legion men like Sergius, duty on a fighting galley was akin to a term in prison. Why should Nicholas tell him that the flat, tepid water of the Inner Sea was like some overlarge bath to those who had earned a place at the oars of the Stormlord?

"I'll manage. Is this a punishment detail?"

"For what? For letting that bastard Otholarix get past you?"

Nicholas shrugged, looking away. He had dawdled on his way to the Wall. The smell and filth of the great city might repel him, but that did not mean there were not interesting diversions within the walls. A tinge of guilt touched him, though, thinking of the *equites* who had been cut down in the fight at the gate.

Sergius tapped the tabletop with a wooden stylus. "You've had some good notes, lad, from your other commanders. I've no complaints about your work until this business at the gate. Do well for the navy and we'll put you back on shore."

Nicholas nodded, but he could not pretend he wanted "shore work" any more than a fighting berth on a ship of war. Ten years of his life, before kin-feud and jealousy had driven him from the Dansk court, had been spent on *drakenships*. How was murdering or kidnapping political opponents of the Empire any different from raiding the Caledonian or Hibernian shore? He felt a vague dissatisfaction.

Mists parted, and the iron beak of the ship nosed out of a wall of dim gray. Nicholas hung on the rail of the fighting platform, peering forward through the murk. The fog muffled sound and made the quiet splash of the long oars in the water seem faint and distant. The sun had risen at last, and the mist was beginning to burn away. The Imperial fleet barely moved, creeping forward through the fog bank. The sound of a hobnailed boot on the decking made the Scandian turn.

Another soldier swung up onto the bulwark and pulled himself to the rail. Nicholas nodded politely at him, hiding a frown. The man was stocky and of middling height, with thick black hair hanging heavily around his head and shoulders. Unlike most of the men on the ship, he was not wearing a helmet. Bushy eyebrows crowded over his muddy brown eyes, and though his skin was fair and even pale, he seemed a dark and brooding sort. "Greetings," the fellow said, his dark eyes idly drifting over Nick's clothing, armor, weapons, hands. "I am Vladimir of Carpathos—and you?"

Nicholas frowned openly now, and lifted his head a little, pointing with his chin at the shirt of heavy iron rings that the soldier wore under a tunic of deep green wool. Copper wire bound the rings—each the size of a *solidus*— to a leather backing. He was obviously no sailor.

"You ever go swimming in that?"

Vladimir shook his head, allowing a brief and brilliantly white smile in the shade of his neatly trimmed mustache and beard. "Hate the water, myself, try to stay away from it as much as I can. I've heard it brings disease and sickness."

Nicholas grunted, something close to a laugh, and nodded his head over the rail. "Seems a mighty lot of it about. You volunteer for our little trip this morning?"

"No, I try to avoid getting killed," Vladimir said, shaking his head and leaning easily on the heavy wooden planking that ran along the top of the bulwark. He grinned. "You?"

"Can't say as I did," Nick muttered, turning to the rail himself. "Not beyond saying I'd put my sword to the defense of the city. You plan on walking home if something happens to this tub?"

Vladimir looked down and fingered the weighty armor. His thumbs were thick, too, and gnarled like old roots sunk into a rocky cleft. He smiled again, an almost shy expression. "Oh, I guess it would be hard to swim in this . . . I'd feel naked without it, though."

Nicholas nodded, scratching at an itch at the base of his neck. He felt naked, too, without his good chain mail— but the cork doublet was far better for this kind of work. It had been good enough for generations of Roman marines, and it was good enough for him.

"Know the feeling—just stay in the middle of the ship. They'll be plenty of fight for everyone once the mist burns off."

Vladimir nodded and shuffled his feet on the deck, looking for good purchase. Nicholas got a momentary impression of a stag in the deep forest, pawing at the loamy soil and snorting at the sight of a rival buck. The Scandian cocked his head a little to one side—there was something odd about the Northerner. Nicholas guessed he was Russ, or maybe Sarmatian—though he did not have Hunnic features, so maybe he hailed from the back woods someplace beyond the rule of the Great Khan. Clad in dark colors, in this dim light the man seemed solid and as natural as a stone—but something about his face seemed ephemeral.

Nicholas shook his head in disgust; there was time for idle speculation later. The ship under him quivered suddenly, and a double note from the flute signaled for the banks of oars to lift and hang poised over the oily blue-black waters.

"What is it?" Vladimir's voice dropped, becoming a low whisper.

"The Persians," Nicholas guessed aloud. "I heard that some of the high priest's men learned they would try a crossing today, on the festival."

Vladimir tested the release on his blade. From the corner of his eye, Nicholas caught a glimpse of a red leather hilt with a bone handle and the dull gleam of old worn iron. *Brunhilde* trembled under his own fingers, feather-light on her pommel. Above them, on the fighting tower, was a *clink* as thick glass jugs were carefully moved about. A windlass cranked, its gears muffled by cloths. The *dromon* drifted in the mist, sliding slowly on the strong current that came from the Sea of Darkness. Above, through the murk, the sun was a pale orange disk. Nicholas squinted up—yes, the fog was thinning quickly. In minutes it would be gone. "Soon," he breathed, and crouched a little behind the bulwark. "Get down a bit," he said to Vladimir. "These things always start with sharp objects flying through the air. Our turn will come, though, once we're in the thick of it."

"Oh," Vladimir said agreeably, squatting down behind the wooden planks. "You've done this before, I suppose. I thought you looked like a sailor."

Nicholas glared at him out of the corner of his eye. The fog was almost gone. He bent to untie the leather straps that bound the boots to his feet. Sea work called for bare feet on the decking. He began humming a little tune.

"Ramming speed!"

The shout echoed from the fore fighting tower of the *dromon*. Nicholas leaned out, oblivious to the whistle of Persian arrows filling the air over his head. The sea was bright, the wave tops brilliant with the noon sun, and a crisp wind blew past. Oars flashed into the dark water, and with each stroke the great ship surged forward. Spray from the bow wave blew back over the marines crowded into the foredeck. Nicholas squinted forward, seeing the bulk of another Persian ship swell before them. The nine-foot-long iron beak that jutted from the front of the Roman warship cut above the water, spilling back bright foam. The *dromon* charged down into a swale between the long, slow waves and the beak disappeared again in the blue-black depths.

The Persian, its sail full of the northern wind, began swinging away from the oncoming Roman ship. Nicholas hissed, silently urging the ship on, on toward its victim. The trill of the row master's flute altered, and the oars on the right side of the ship rippled like snakes and rose up for half a beat. The left bank cut to double time, and the *dromon* danced to the right, a hurtling spearhead tipped with hungry iron. The Persians, crowding the rails of their captured merchantman, began screaming. The flurry of arrows from their ship faltered, then stopped. The crewmen, in dirty wool breechcloths, began leaping over the side. Nicholas grinned again, and kicked Vladimir in the leg.

The Northerner rose up, gripping the railing to steady himself.

"Here it comes," shouted Nicholas over the roar of the waters and the thunder of oars in the locks. The Persian soldiers were scrambling away from the side of their ship closest to the great ram. The sea dipped, and the merchantman slid down into a trough. The beak of the *dromon* broke out of the waters, dripping foam, and then arrowed down with the tilting sea, to stab into the foredeck of the sailing ship.

Nicholas flexed his knees in automatic reaction to the shock that shuddered through the length of the ship. The decking under his feet jumped a little, and Vladimir swore as the side of his head cracked against the bulwark. The iron ram punched through the pine planking of the Persian ship with a tremendous *screech*. The booming roar from the dying ship drowned the screams of Persians hurled into the sea by the shock of the collision. The heavy decking shattered, sending yard-long splinters scything across the deck; then the *dromon* plunged through the wreck like an axe head into a rotten log.

Nicholas cursed violently and threw himself down. The sudden wave had thrown the *dromon* into the enemy ship too quickly—the front ranks of oars were still sliding back into the body of the Roman ship. Thirty or more oars on the right-hand side crashed into the Persian ship as it was brushed aside, shattering and snapping like an overbent bow. In an instant the forward gallery was filled with hideous screams. The thirty-foot oars ground through the benches of seated men, smashing bone and crushing flesh. A spray of blood filled the compartment, and bench after bench was torn to splinters. Sixty men died in an instant. The *dromon* staggered, seemingly stunned by the blow.

Nicholas staggered up off the deck, oblivious to the wailing cries of the men trapped below. The Persian ship had fouled on the starboard side of the Roman *dromon*, the remaining oars tangled with the rigging of the merchantman's mast. The enemy ship, its fore torn away, was filling with water at an alarming rate. Those Persian soldiers still alive crawled among the wreckage. Some, weighted down by their heavy scaled armor, had already disappeared under the dark waters.

Nicholas felt Vladimir pick himself up off of the deck and stand at his side. "Watch for boarders," Nicholas snapped and he slid *Brunhilde* back over his back into her sheath with a *click*.

"What?" Vladimir was still dizzy from the blow to his head. "Where are . . ."

Nicholas vaulted the rail and swung down the side of the ship. The *dromon* was beginning to list to starboard as the Persian ship's hold flooded. Behind him, distantly, like the cawing of black ravens in the low hills of the Dannmark, he heard sailors shouting. He stepped out onto a top-bank oar. It was almost a foot across at this point, though it tapered toward the leaf-shaped blade. A grim smile flickered across his face—here, at least, he could miss an oar and escape being beaten.

Behind him, he heard Vladimir shouting in dismay.

He ran forward, springing lightly from oar to oar, his toes gripping the oar-shafts on each step. The oars were jammed up against the Persian ship, offering him a far more stable platform than in the old days. He reached the last intact oar and sidestepped down its length. The deck of the Persian ship, turned almost sideways, was only a dozen feet away. He slid a herring knife out of the sheath strapped to his leg and crouched, his legs balanced on two broken oars. The curving blade—honed to mirror sharpness—cut into the tangled ropes and guylines that bound the two ships together. The ropes, even heavy with seawater, yielded to the knife. The sea rose and fell around him, grinding the broken oars into the decking.

Under the cork armor, Nicholas dripped with sweat. Someone was shouting at him from the *dromon*, but he refused to listen. A wave came up, and for a moment he was up to his shoulders in the cold, dark waters of the Propontis. It slid away, and it took all his strength to cling to the oar. Something heavy slammed into him from the side, and he blinked seawater away to see the crushed face of a man swing past him. He pushed the corpse off with one arm. The ropes were free on this oar.

He dragged himself up, feeling water sluicing out of his armor. The oar trembled and he jumped to the next—a tangled mass of ropes, broken oars, and part of the Persian mast. Behind him the freed oars slid away, pulled back into the Roman ship by the sailors still alive in the forward compartment. The rigging was greasy under his feet, slick with blood and long ribbons of gray intestine. He knelt, one knee pressed into the stomach of a corpse caught in the ropes. The herring knife bit at the hawsers. A groaning sound seemed to come from out of the water itself. Nicholas cut faster, his hand and the knife a blur. He could feel the *dromon* tipping farther, the dark water rising higher and higher toward the open oar ports as the merchantman's hold flooded.

A rope came free, and with it an oar. He kicked it free with his foot, then rolled off the mass of rope and shattered boards into the water as he caught movement out of the corner of his eye. The chill water was a sharp shock against his sweaty skin. A Persian crawled toward him across the wreckage, his chest bare and face spattered with blood. The man had a stabbing spear though, and Nicholas kicked in the water, pushing himself away from the debris. The Persian staggered up on the ropes, his mouth moving with unheard shouts. Nicholas pushed back again, but more broken oars were behind him. The Persian stabbed at him with the spear.

Nicholas ducked under the water, feeling it close with a slap over his head. Dimly, for the waters of the Propontis were thick with the blue-black silt that marked the Sea of Darkness, he saw a bright flash as the spearhead dug into the water and then disappeared again. He tried to dive and swim away from the wreckage. The cork armor was too buoyant, though, and he ground against the broken mast. The spear plunged into the water again, catching him on the shoulder. The armor caught the tip, but now he was driven deeper, spinning to one side, completely submerged. He clawed at the mast, trying to get some purchase. His fingers slipped off the smooth oaken surface.

Vladimir bounced from foot to foot, staring over the rail with mounting concern. The Roman ship was still tangled with the Persian, though enough oars had been cut free to halt the tipping that had threatened to flood the rowing gallery. Roman archers shooting from the fighting towers were cutting down the few Persians left on the foundering merchantman. Still, down in the dark water, amid the flotsam, Nicholas had not reappeared. Too, the Persian that had been stabbing at him with a spear was still there, kneeling amid the broken timbers, slashing at the water.

Vlad looked around; the deck of the *dromon* was swarming with fighting men and sailors. Around them the sea battle was still raging after a brutal day. Hundreds of ships were locked in a slowly swirling melee. Many of the Persian merchantmen were ablaze with the sticky green fire thrown by the Roman ships from arbalests in their fighting towers. Others were trying to flee toward the coast of Chalcedon, but the smaller Roman double-bank galleys were dogging them like wolves. A thick layer of smoke shrouded the sky. No one seemed to have noticed Nick's struggle in the water. Vlad fingered the heavy iron rings of his shirt, then looked around again. No one seemed to be paying him any attention.

For a moment he argued with himself silently, weighing pro and con. Then he shook his head, sending dark locks flying, and swung up and over the rail. His cavalry-style boots slipped on the top-rank oars, and he staggered, nearly falling. He shook his head again and frowned, concentrating. He slid, half falling, half running, down the oar. As he almost reached the bottom, it rose up out of the dark sea, and he jumped sideways to the next. His left boot struck it squarely and he immediately pushed off, springing into the air. The oars began to back against the pull of the sinking merchantman.

Vlad staggered, leaning forward, then windmilling his arms to bend backward. The long oar dipped, sliding under the waves. Water rushed up around his feet, and his footing slipped away. Cursing, he crashed into the water. It flooded cold and numbing into his clothing and armor, pulling him down. An oar rose up, swinging back, and Vlad kicked, surging up out of the sea. His arms wrapped around the heavy ashwood shaft. For a moment he broke free of the water, but then the oar dipped again, and now he was dragged under.

It was dark and cold, but he clung to the oar tenaciously, wrapping his arms around it. It cut free of the water on the upstroke, and—gasping for breath—he flung one arm out. Fingers grazed the next oar as it came up, then dug in, splintering wood away from his nails. Vlad let go and swung out, crashing into the next oar. Breath chuffed out of his chest at the blow, but he held on. The Roman ship edged away from the wreckage. In the gore-drenched forward gallery, the marines were cutting men away from the ruin of the oars with axes and pushing the bodies out of the oarlocks. The tangled oars fell away, too, sliding into the sea. Bodies and wreckage floated on the water, tipped this way and that by the waves.

Vlad let himself slide to the end of an oar as it dug into the water, then—holding his mouth and nose closed against the cold shock as he went under again—let go as it broke free. Water rushed up around him, dragging at his armor and boots. He kicked strongly, and his arms plowed through the water. The wedge of ropes and timber and bodies was very close. He surged forward, even as the weight of the iron on him dragged him down. The Persian with the spear turned at the last moment as Vlad caught a net of webbing on the side of the debris.

The Persian shouted and stabbed down at him. Vlad rolled, his left hand tangled in the netting, and the spear point cut the water beside him. His right hand, free, darted out and seized the haft of the spear. The Persian struggled, hauling back on the oaken shaft. Vlad grimaced, the tendons in his arms bulging, and his face locked in a grim mask. The spear twisted in his hand, then suddenly snapped with a sharp barking sound. The Persian staggered back, then stumbled and fell into the ocean. Spray spurted behind him and he was gone. Vlad crawled up, hand over hand, onto the raft. It shifted queasily under him, but seemed to hold his weight.

"Nicholas!" Vlad's voice seemed thin and hoarse. The sea around him bobbed with debris; broken oars, shattered masts, crates, corpses, the oily shininess of blood on the water. He was exhausted from the tremendous effort. He fell to his knees, digging his hands into the ropes. "Ho, Nicholas!"

The sea tipped as a wave passed under the raft. The *dromon* had pulled away, the rattle of its drums echoing across the water. The Persian fleet seemed smashed, broken into a hundred sinking or captured ships. The Roman fleet, its red sails catching the light, seemed behemoths of war, titanic engines washed in blood. Smoke and haze filled the sky, turning the sun into a monstrous red orb.

"Nicholas!"

The raft tipped suddenly, and Vlad fell heavily into the welter of rope, broken pieces of wood and corpses that formed it. A hand appeared at the edge of the debris, cut and bleeding, gripping a rope. Vlad crawled over to the edge, lying flat to spread his weight on the noisome island. A face appeared out of the water, sodden and bedraggled. Vlad grabbed hold of the man's shoulder, catching an armor strap in his hand, and pulled him up.

Nicholas gasped and sputtered, clawing at Vlad's shoulder to get up out of the chill water. He rolled over, clinging with both hands to the feeble collection of spars and tangled rope. Vlad moved aside a little, grinning furiously through the long trails of black hair plastered to his face by the water. Nicholas coughed up water and sneered at the Northerner. "A brilliant . . . *cough* . . . move, my friend. I could have swum back to the *dromon*, you know, with this armor to hold me up."

Vlad clapped him on the shoulder, still smiling like a loon. "No matter, my friend. I'm sure you sailors know many tricks of the sea to get us home again."

The sun drifted into the west, passing behind a thick band of smoke, its vast red shape shimmering and dancing over the rooftops of the distant city. Nicholas rolled over, seeing the sails of the fleet a mile or more distant. The waves rolled slowly up and down. Fine white ash began falling out of the sky as the upper air cooled. Not too far away was a sudden frenzied splashing in the water, then a short scream. Nicholas shaded his eyes against the glare of the sun. A great white shape rolled over under the water, a massive tailfin swinging from side to side, diving deep after seizing its prey on the surface.

The air filled with the rattle of wings as flocks of gulls and terns rose up at the disturbance. The white birds were streaked with blood on their downy chests and wings. Within moments they had settled again on the water, feasting on the harvest the day had yielded up.

"Brilliant, truly brilliant."

"You're welcome," Vladimir said, wringing seawater out of his hair.

───────────────────────────────

THE HIGHLANDS OF TABARISTAN, NORTHERN PERSIA

A man, dressed in worn robes and grimy armor, looked up out of the shadow of a narrow canyon between towering walls of granite. Far above, a pale strip of sky showed the lateness of the day. He rode a stout-chested warhorse—a Sogdian charger, by the look—and he leaned heavily in the saddle. Weariness was etched in his face and in the line of his shoulders; he had traveled a long road. The clip-clop of his horse's hooves echoed back from the cliffs that hemmed in the narrow trail he followed. Above him all he could see was a jagged strip of blue. He had been riding in deep shade for nearly a day before he came to this place. At his left, below the road, a foaming cataract plunged down the steep canyon, the roar of the waters reverberating among the thick, dark pines and gray-green rocks.

Behind the man, on the road, a dozen black mules strained to drag a wagon up the pitch. Behind them, hundreds of men slowly followed—they were exhausted too, having pressed hard for a month or more to cross eight hundred miles of desert, desolate mountain, and forest. The wheels of the wagon just fit between the looming cliff on the right, a grainy rock with long, deep crevices in its surface, and the crumbling edge of the canyon itself. The lead man gently kneed his horse, and it resumed its slow walk up the winding road. Despite his weariness, he kept a wary eye on the rocks and cliffs above—the land they had entered bore an ominous reputation, long stained with blood and murder.

Hidden away behind the barren peaks and ridges of the land, the sun settled into the west, plunging the dim canyon into darkness well before sunset. The sky itself shaded to pink and then purple, while the mountains assumed a diffuse golden glow that threatened to linger even when the sun was gone and the sky was a black pit. The man on the lead horse reined in and raised his hand.

The wagon rumbled to a halt, and the puffing breath of the mules ghosted through the chill air. On the broad seat of the wagon, a dark shape stirred itself and then stood. Deep black robes of silk rustled away from lean arms and a broad chest. The man on the horse turned in the saddle and nervously smoothed his long mustache.

"Lord? Shall we press on or camp on the road?" Other unspoken questions hung in the air.

"No, faithful Khadames," a voice whispered out of the darkness. "There is but a little to go. Behind this narrows, a valley opens out, and there, amid sweet gardens and lush fields, we shall find rest. Just a little farther and we come to the end of our long journey."

Khadames flinched a little at the sound of that rich, smooth voice. In all the long weeks of grueling passage and intermittent horror, nothing troubled him more than the steady and unmistakable restoration of the man in the wagon. Not long ago, before the looming walls of the City of Silk—Palmyra in the deserts of Syria—that voice had been a hoarse croak coming from a smashed and crippled body. Not much more than a corpse had been dragged from the burning ruin of the Plain of Towers. Khadames had commanded an army then, in the name of his lord Shahr-Baraz, and for a brief moment considered with giddy delight that the black sorcerer was upon the gates of death. But he had bent his knee instead, and pried back a blood-caked eyelid to see if life still flickered in the odd yellow pupils. It had, and they had focused upon him and swelled and rippled like the back of a snake, and he held no will but theirs. The moment had passed, and life had crawled or crept back into the shattered body of the dark prince.

"So . . . so soon? We are there?" Khadames' voice cracked in astonishment.

Laughter echoed out of the dark shape, the sound of an adult amused by a child.

"Yes, Khadames, this is the Valley of the Eagle's Nest. Press on, we are very near."

Khadames spurred his horse forward, and it trotted around the bend of the road, hooves striking on a sudden pavement of fitted stones. The Persian nobleman whistled in surprise as the vast bulk of a fortified gate rose up before him, octagonal towers springing forth from the sinews of the mountain itself. It was hard to gauge their size in the twilight, but the afterglow from the mountaintops picked out a wall of massive granite blocks closing off the canyon. At each side the towers climbed up, a hundred feet or more to the pinnacle of each. Between them a great dam of dark stone arched up, with a crenellated battlement spanning the gorge. A sluice gate roared and foamed at the base, spewing forth the swift stream that they had followed for the past two days. Water plunged another fifty feet to hammer at the rocks below. The road ran into darkness at the base of the near tower.

Khadames let the horse find the way across the metaled road. Behind him the wagon wheels rattled up onto the pavement and picked up speed. A mass of shadow grew before him and, trusting to the words of his master, the Persian rode on. A tunnel enfolded him, narrow—again, no more than the width of the wagon. A chill wind hissed down its length, and he followed as it wound forward. It turned first to the right, then back again to the left. Each time the mules were forced to slow down and make a careful turn. Each time, the wagon barely fit around the corners. All was in complete darkness. Khadames rode slowly, his hand on the left wall, trusting the horse's nose and careful tread.

The wind suddenly stopped, and it took Khadames a moment to realize that he had ridden out of the tunnel mouth and onto a broad road at the foot of a valley. The sky above was pitch black, without even a star to break the ebon firmament. He tasted the air and found it damp— clouds blotted the sky. The moon had yet to rise, too, and Khadames slowly urged his horse to the side of the road. A stone lip ran there, and the Persian stopped.

"This is the valley below the Eagle's Nest," that smooth voice said again as the wagon rumbled out of the tunnel. "You and I will go up the mountain to see what decay the years have wrought. Bid the men make camp by the banks of the stream—they may make a fire, for no enemy of ours will ever find this place."

Khadames watched as the sorcerer rode past with his wagon and the long coffin of gold and lead that had ridden in it, securely fastened with ropes and chains, from the gates of dead Palmyra. The memory of cold yellow eyes remained with him. He even fancied he could still see them hanging in the air when the dark shape had turned away. The Persian reached down to the travel lantern slung on a leather strap by the pommel of his saddle. At least light would be allowed them for this camp.

*   *   *

The moon had risen by the time Khadames made his way out of the camp and onto the road that wound along the side of the stream. For a few moments it had gleamed down over the jagged ridges that ringed the valley, but then the clouds had swallowed it. In that time, Khadames had seen that the valley was broad and fertile, filled with great stands of trees and meadows among the crags. On every side it seemed that impassible cliffs stood as a rampart of stone, closing all entrances save the great gate at the dam. Khadames had ordered guards posted there as soon as the last of his men had entered the valley. The sorcerer had claimed that none could follow them in their long journey through the mountains, but the Persian general was not so sure. Where one man walked, so might another.

Of the 20,000 men who had stormed the walls of Palmyra three months before, he had counted only 516 as they passed through the vaulted gates of the valley. Every man was worn to the bone from his long trek. Still, he wondered why they had come. Some, he thought, followed him as their captain. Others were drawn to the dark Prince and his terrible power—those men Khadames watched closely, for they had come out of the deserts to join them during the flight from Syria. Others, like the Uze mercenaries who had served as the lord's bodyguard since the great battle at Emesa, seemed content to draw their pay and follow. The others? They had fled in the darkness during the march, or deserted in whole regiments whenever the little army passed a city. Some had died during the long journey, and those had been buried in unmarked graves. Khadames raised the travel lantern, letting its wan yellow light spill out on the road before him, and rode up the valley.

In the few moments he had taken to post his sentries at the dam-gate, Khadames had seen that the massive towers and the broad battlement had been abandoned for many years. Small trees grew in cracks among the mighty stones, and a deep drift of leaves and dirt had accumulated on the valley side of the wall. The four heavy gates themselves—

monstrous constructions of oak and iron and steel rivets—
were frozen open in their posts. It would be a great task
to pry them free and set them to close again.

Too, the road, while canted in the Roman style and
marked by stone gutters on either side, was showing signs
of wear. The first bridge over the stream had nearly collapsed, forcing Khadames to dismount and carefully walk
his horse across it. How the dark Prince had gotten the
wagon over was a mystery—but, then, around that creature
were many mysteries. Khadames crossed a second bridge,
and the road began to climb up out of the valley. The night
air was still, hushed, even a little stuffy. It seemed odd,
for a strong breeze blew through the tunnel in the gate.
Now the road cut up the side of a long slope, marked by
great stone pylons on the outer side. In the flickering light
of the lantern, Khadames saw that great chains once had
hung from rings screwed into the stone. Dry streaks of rust
were all that remained of them.

The road turned back upon itself, still climbing, and at
the turn, Khadames passed over a broad circle of fitted
stones and pavement. Whoever had first occupied this hidden valley and raised these mighty works were well-
accomplished stonemasons and builders. Slowly, as he
rode up the long road, as it turned upon itself and turned
again, he began to feel a bitter chill seep through his
clothes. He was warmly dressed, for the mountains of Irak
and Tabaristan are unforgiving and prey to terrible storms.
This seemed to congeal out of the air around him, cold
fingers plucking at his sleeve and creeping around his
neck. A sense, too, grew in him of an oppressive weight
hanging over him, looming above, hidden in the darkness.

The road ended at a narrow platform, perched at the end
of a steep climb. The last length of road was carved from
the side of a great cliff, and ended with an outthrust platform of stone. Great pylons rose out of the darkness below
to support it, and curled around its lip like titanic fingers.
Khadames reined his horse around and peered back, down
in the depths of the valley. Far away and below, like the

sight of fireflies at night, he saw the lights of the campfires of his men. The cold slid along his back and arms, for he guessed at the distance and knew that—should he look down from this precipice by the light of day—he would near swoon from vertigo. He turned away.

A gate rose out of the darkness, hewn from the flank of the mountain. Forty feet or more across and fifty high it rose, a black mouth straddled by carved figures. A portal closed it with two massive valves of stone. Across their face, signs and symbols were graven into the rock face, line after line of them, swirling around a central figure of the Flame Eternal. At each side, the figures of men surged out of the dark rock, their bodies forming the side of the gate, their arms—outstretched to each other—the lintel. Their faces were still in shadow, far above the poor light of his tiny lantern. At the foot of the gate was a puddle of black silk.

Khadames blanched and felt faint. The Flame stared back at him in the yellow cast of the travel lantern. In this place, even graven in stone, it seemed to leap and burn, shedding a fierce light. His right hand twitched to make the sign of the Lord of Light, but stopped, and he forced it back to his saddle horn. The remembered smell of burning flesh and the agonized screams of men echoed in his memory.

If you love the fire so much, said a dreadful voice, *then you shall have it.*

The sorcerer did not countenance that his men, his followers, even his generals, embraced the words of the prophets of Ahura-Mazda, he-who-rules-the-Universe-in-Light. Khadames had not opposed him on this, either, not after the slaughter in the temple at Sura. If you rode at the side of the dark man, you rode far from the light of the Beneficent One. The Persian swung down off of his horse, feeling his legs twinge in response. Now that they had reached their goal, his body—so long driven by his will alone—was beginning to rebel, demanding sleep, food, rest, even a bath. Regardless, he walked warily forward to the body slumped at the base of the mammoth gate. A boot of tooled leather jutted from under the flowing robes.

Khadames knelt, and gingerly turned the man over. The sorcerer's head rolled back, bile-yellow eyes staring into nothingness. The once-handsome features seemed slack and lifeless, but breath still hissed between his fine white teeth. Khadames pulled his hand away, feeling moisture on his fingers. He stared at them in puzzlement: They were damp with tears.

The Uze, their figures bulky in thick furs and glinting with half-hidden armor, stood as one when Khadames rode back into the camp. Their felt tents, low and round, clustered like toadstools around the bulk of the sorcerer's great yurt. Each night on that long march from Syria, they had raised it, then unfolded their own in barrier around it. Tagai, their broken-toothed leader, moved slowly forward and reached up to take the limp body of the sorcerer from Khadames. His thick arms, corded with muscle and ridged with old scars, took the weight easily. The Persian dismounted, his face grim, and gestured for Tagai to take the body into the tent. The other Uze edged toward him, some glancing over their shoulders at their chieftain.

"Go," Khadames growled in the badly accented Sogdian he shared with the Northern barbarians. "Bring each man in the camp, one at a time, to me in the lord's tent. If a man refuses, say that I command him. If he refuses again, say that the lord wills it. If he still will not come, then cut him down."

An odd fever was upon the Persian. He felt odd—light-headed and dizzy—but he knew that despite his fear he must do his honorable duty to the commander he had sworn to obey. Part of his mind, that which still half re-membered the words of the old fire priest in his home village, railed at him to cut the throat of the dark man who now lay on soft cushions in the tent. Those words he pushed away, remembering the bright eyes of another man—one he accounted his true master and friend—the general Shahr-Baraz.

I leave him as your support, Khadames, echoed the booming voice of the greatest general Khadames had ever known. *He is willful, though, so watch him like a spirited horse! If that braggart and fop Shahin contests your command, he will support you. Watch the "great Prince" cower then! He I entrust to you, and you to him, and this army. Do your duty to the King of Kings, old friend.*

Khadames blinked away his own tears. By all accounts, the Royal Boar was dead in the ruin at Kerenos River, laid low with his army by the Roman enemy. Even the King of Kings was dead, his body cut to pieces by the Roman Emperors amid the wreck of his great capital at Ctesiphon on the Euphrates. Khadames wondered if the Empire itself still stood, outside this remote ring of mountains. With the royal seat fallen, and the *shahhanshah* dead and the armies scattered, there was little left and no one to rule. The general sat down heavily in one of the camp chairs within the great tent. The weariness threatened to pull him down into sleep at any moment.

He stood again, forcing his eyes to open, and moved to the side of the cot where Tagai had laid the sorcerer. Khadames looked upon that drawn and pale countenance—*yes*, he thought, *it is as it was before. He has overreached himself, pitting his will against that vault of stone and the emblem of fire.*

The general looked up at Tagai, who squatted on the other side of the cot, a curved blade unsheathed, gleaming, laid over his thighs. Khadames pursed his lips and nodded to the pile of trunks and baggage laid against the felt wall.

"Among his things is a knife of flint. Find it."

The Uze chieftain grunted and moved away. Khadames peeled back the eyelid of the sorcerer with one callused thumb. The yellow orb flickered weakly, turning away from the light of the oil lantern suspended from the center of the tent.

"You still live, then." He sighed and rubbed his face.

His mustache and beard were thick with grime from the long road. "Duty commands, honor obeys." An old saying from his youth.

Tagai returned, gingerly holding a narrow knife of glittering black flint by the hilt. It was an old thing, knapped from a single stone, slightly curved, with a fat haft. Countless strips of pale leather wrapped the hilt, glued together with sweat and old blood. Khadames took the knife firmly, showing no fear to the superstitious clansman. He turned it over in his hand, feeling the weight of it. It was very heavy for its size, and the scalloped facets of the blade gleamed oddly in the light. The Persian looked up and saw fear in the eyes of the Uze.

"Go get the others," grated Khadames, and he adjusted the head of the man lying on the cot, tipping it back a little. He pried the mouth open and pushed a wad of silk into the corner. The sorcerer's breath rasped, uneven and fitful. Tagai slunk away, but Khadames did not notice. He smoothed back the long dark hair, leaving the face exposed, pale and drawn. In another place many might have accounted the sorcerer handsome—he bore a strong nose and high cheekbones, with a noble profile. Khadames did not care; all that mattered to him in this tiny moment in a tent, high in the barren mountains, was the execution of his honor and duty.

The tent door was pushed aside, and men entered. Khadames turned, the corners of his eyes crinkling up as he saw that his detachment commanders had come to see what the trouble was. They were angry already—the Uze were not noted for politeness—and had their hands on sword hilts. Khadames stood up, turning the flint knife into the palm of his hand, its blade lying along his forearm. "Mirza—good. Come here and bare your arm."

The blond Khorasanian, who had served with Khadames and Shahr-Baraz for more than a dozen years in campaigns and battles the length and breadth of the Empire, stepped forward, but his face was closed and suspicious. Khadames stepped aside, showing the man the supine form of the sorcerer.

"Yes," the general said, "he is terribly wounded again— even as after the battle on the Plain of Towers. We must revive him."

"Why?" Mirza's voice was harsh and blunt. He turned to Khadames with cold fury in his eyes. "By the sacrifice of more of our men—by their blood? He has killed us all already."

Khadames nodded, his demeanor calm. "He is a hard taskmaster, and death walks with him like a hunting hound. Do you fear him?"

"Yes," Mirza said, his bristly beard jutting out as he faced his commander. "We would all be well rid of him— enough ruin has come of his work already. We know you are bound to follow him, for you swore to the Boar to stand by him. We follow you—but is there no limit to the demand of your honor?"

"Is there to yours?" Khadames' voice was cold. He straightened his back and his eyes swept over the men, and behind them the Uze, who were crowding at the door of the tent. "We all swore great oaths when we accepted the service of the King of Kings—do you repudiate them now? Do you turn your backs on the honor of your houses?"

"No," Mirza growled, without bothering to look to the outraged faces of his fellows. "And where does that leave us? The great King Chrosoes is dead, and with him his wife and children. *He has no heir!* Baraz is dead, too— damnable Rome casts down the entire world in ruin. We hide in the mountains like beggars, following this storm crow on dark paths. Why not have done with it? Cut his heart out and burn it in the fire of the Lord of Light and we will go forth—back to our homes!"

Khadames shook his head and slowly passed among the men, his steady gaze slowly moving from face to face. The anger in the room dimmed and then quieted. The general turned back to the cot and knelt, turning the face of the sorcerer toward them. He looked up. "Do you remember your oaths? The ones you swore to the House of Sassan before the King of Kings that blustery day in Ctesiphon—victory was ours, the Man of Wood thrown down, and the right, true King raised in his place? They were strong oaths, sworn to the Empire and the man, Chrosoes, who restored it. Do you remember that day? You were there, Mirza, at my side—so were you, Peroz, and you Isfandiar. *I* remember what I swore that day—have you forgotten?"

"No," Mirza said again, "but I say—what of it? All we swore to uphold is in ruins, dead, buried, cast to the winds—there is nothing left of that house. Only memories that will dim with time, leaving cruel Rome in their place."

"Not so," Khadames said, rising to his feet, his voice filling with strength. "The House of Sassan still lives, hidden and in secret, and will rise again—you and I will make it rise, and be strong. Come here."

Mirza stood, rock solid and still, his thick legs apart. Khadames met his gaze and held it. A long moment passed in complete silence in the tent. Then Mirza shook his head and stepped forward. Khadames bent close, whispering in his ear. Mirza stiffened in surprise, but the general's hand was quick, seizing the man's forearm. The black knife whispered, and blood spilled.

Mirza cried out. Outside the tent, the Uze grinned in the darkness.

Khadames sat, again, on the campstool by the narrow bed. Another day had passed, and the sun had fallen behind the fence of the mountains. Darkness filled the valley, and outside the tent the lanterns and evening fires of the little army flickered in the twilight. Tonight the men were roasting goats they had trapped in the higher reaches of the long, narrow canyon that fed the stream. Khadames was beginning to grow concerned that they would have to leave their refuge to search for supplies. At his side the figure of the sorcerer lay still and quiet, as it had done for the past eleven days.

The Persian sighed and scratched a mosquito bite on one ear. The men were beginning to recover some of their strength and would soon grow restless. A tapping sound drew his attention. He looked around, then saw that one of the sorcerer's feet was twitching, banging against the edge of the cot. Khadames leaned over, one hand reaching to check the pulse at the side of the neck.

The sorcerer's eyes opened slowly, blinking in the dim light of the lamps. They seemed unfocused and drifted from side to side. They turned toward Khadames—some flicker of recognition entered them. The yellow pupils blinked again, and awareness crept into the face, drawing intellect with it.

"How long?" the sorcerer croaked. His eyes had focused on Khadames.

"Almost two weeks," said the general, picking up a copper cup from the side of the bed and holding it to the man's papery lips. The sorcerer took a taste of the thin red liquid in the cup and an eyebrow raised, arching like the flight of a raven in the winter sky.

"This has been my milk?" The sorcerer's voice was very weak, lacking all but a memory of its usual subtle power. "You are unexpectedly good to me, faithful Khadames."

Khadames matched the yellow-eyed stare, his face a tight mask. He had done what was needful. "It worked before, so I reasoned that it would work again. How do you feel?"

The sorcerer laughed—a weak human sound.

"Like one on the door of death . . . but worse than my usual state. I owe you a substantial debt, General. It must have been harsh upon you to put men to death."

Khadames shook his head slowly. "No one died for you, Lord. That is *your* way, not mine." He pulled back the sleeve of the green linen shirt with thin red stripes he was wearing, exposing his forearm. Along the inside, slashed across his wrist at right angles, was a puckered white scar. It was ugly and jagged, but seemed to have healed cleanly. He turned his arm so that the sorcerer could see. "I strove to save you to abide by oaths sworn to the King of Kings, Wizard. Nothing of them says that I must gut men and offer up their bleeding hearts to the sky to feed your power. You wax strong on the blood of men, so we gave you enough to live. But each man gave only a part, and none so much that they sickened or died."

The sorcerer blinked slowly at the venom in the general's voice, and with great effort raised his hand to touch Khadames' forearm. One long finger traced the route of the scar, and then the hand fell back onto the coverlet that lay over his body. The yellow eyes closed, and the sorcerer lay still for a long time. Then, just before Khadames was going to rise and leave the tent, they opened again.

"How did you do it?" The voice was little more than a croak.

"With the flint blade from your baggage," Khadames answered. "It seemed proper, from what you had done before."

"How many men gave their blood so?"

Khadames frowned at the sorcerer, but the dark man's eyes were closed again, as if in sleep.

"Not all. A few men were on the watch, or scouting, when I called them to this tent. All told, some five hundred."

"Five hundred . . ." The sorcerer breathed out a long, slow breath. His eyes flickered open again, and his hand gripped Khadames' wrist. "I owe you much, then, General. You are far wiser than I in this matter. I tell you this"— the sorcerer paused and seemed to consider his words, then his voice became stronger—"the day will come, and soon, when this mark—this scar from an ancient knife—will mean more than kingdoms for the men who bear it. I will not forget you or these five hundred who came to my aid when I lay at the verge of dissolution."

The sorcerer sat up, startling Khadames, and swung his legs off of the cot. He seemed suddenly to have limitless energy—the lassitude and weakness dropping from him like a discarded cloak. The general rose, too, though slower, seeing little reason to hurry. The dark man turned, and his eyes burned with something like their old fire. "Bring the sixteen who did not give their blood to me— we go again to the door in the mountain. But no others— you, the sixteen, and myself. It will be enough." With that, the sorcerer strode out of the tent, clad only in a thin tunic and breeches.

Khadames had not come before the massive door and the emblem of fire since the night when he had found the sorcerer lying at its foot. Now he rode up the long series of switchbacks and felt again, even in the dim overcast light of day, the sense of brooding oppression that had come upon him that night. At the end of the valley, where the road of the ancient builders was hewn from the rock itself, rose a peak of black stone. Upthrust from the dull gray rock of the surrounding mountains, it drew every eye to it, but Khadames found that the mountain was featureless and indistinct. The summit was shrouded in the mist that hung constantly over the valley. Tiny black dots circled below the clouds—ravens or crows in flight. Much of the lower reaches were worked by the hands of men; ramparts and parapets jutted from the bulk of the mountain. Long, narrow windows peered down from the recesses, and high up, near the clouds, were indistinct signs of vaulted arches.

Below, in the shadow of the gate, Khadames found the sorcerer crouched before the massive portal. The sixteen men who rode with the general halted and waited for him to dismount. He told four of the men to hobble the horses, and walked to within a dozen feet of the dark man. The sorcerer squatted near the base of the door; he laid his hands on the cold stone, his fingers spread wide on the rain-damp surface. The dark man had found his robes again and was clad entirely in black, save for a gold bangle on one wrist and red lacings on his boots. Khadames settled himself and waited. Behind him, the men did the same.

After a bit, the sorcerer straightened and turned to face

the general. "All are here? Yes? Good. Lord Khadames, take this."

The sorcerer handed Khadames a small clay pot filled with a caked black powder. "Not so long ago," the sorcerer said, standing amid the men, "you were absent from the camp when a ritual was undertaken to save my life. Those men who attended me—who *allowed me to live again*—have won my respect and my debt. Each of you, in pursuit of your duty, was not allowed to partake in that . . . blessed event."

The soldiers, a stolid collection of Lakhmids Arabs, Bactrians, and native Persians, watched the sorcerer warily. They had heard little or nothing of the events of that night, for Khadames had impressed stringent secrecy upon the other men.

"Khadames," the dark man continued, "take the paint and mark each man with this sign." He pulled his shirt open, showing an odd, inverted mark—more like a blunted triangle than anything else—that was painted on his chest.

The general paused a moment, regarding the sorcerer with suspicion. Then he shook his head. If the creature meant ill, there was little need for this ritual. He went to the first man and made the same mark on the Arab's forehead. The man screwed up his nose at the smell—the paint was thick and sour-smelling. Khadames stepped back, checked his work, and proceeded on to the next man. By the time that he had finished, the sorcerer was squatting again, his legs folded under him, at the center of the rough circle of men.

"Lord General," the dark man said over his shoulder, "pray take the horses down to the first turn of the road—there will be some noise and it would not do to affright them."

Khadames nodded, puzzled, but slipped the hobbles from the horses and tied them to a lead line. When he was done, he rubbed the side of their long noses and clucked at his own steed to lead them down the steep road. Behind him, as he descended the slope, he heard the sorcerer begin to chant. By the time he had reached the roundabout and had tied off each string of four horses to the great jutting pylons that marked the edge of the paved space, the air itself was trembling with sound.

He turned, looking back up at the face of the mountain, and felt his knees give way. He fell to the ground, paralyzed and weak.

The sound of the chanting had swollen to fill the world, ringing off the distant peaks and the plunging cliffs that ringed the valley. Blue lightning rippled and cracked along the lines of the black peak, arcing in sheets of brilliant white and orange from stone to stone. A fierce red glow shimmered around the gate itself—the source hidden from Khadames' stunned eyes by the lip of the final platform on the road. Above, the clouds swirled around the peak and a wind rose, whipping at the general as he lay on the half circle of stone. Thunder boomed in the suddenly dark sky, and within the rushing clouds, yellow-orange lightning shuddered, leaping from cloud to cloud.

Then the whirlpool of air spun back with majestic slowness, revealing the peak—a fierce tower of carved stone and battlements. Arch upon arch rose up to the summit, a fortress of native stone and columns and pillars. The sky boiled behind it, sliding into a deep greenish black.

Khadames cried out, his eyes seared by a blinding flare of red light from the gate.

The world shook with a thunderclap like the stroke of the gods. The horses shrieked in fear, tearing at their bridles, then were thrown to the ground by an impossibly fierce blast of wind that howled down from the peak. Khadames was crushed to the stones, his nose grinding into the pavement. He felt blood spurt and a stinging pain. All across the valley the wind bent trees low and lashed the waters of the streams and pools. Auroral fires flickered from men's hands and weapons. In the camp by the lower gate, hundreds of men threw themselves to the ground, overcome by a paralyzing fear.

A booming crack, greater even than what had gone before, smote the air. The horses that had struggled up collapsed and Khadames drooled mindlessly on the octagonal paving tiles. The burning red light flickered and then went out with a sharp popping sound.

Even in the camp of the soldiers, a mile or more distant, the titanic sound of stone grinding over stone could be plainly heard. In the camp, the men who bore the mark of the knife on their right wrist knelt—unbidden—and bowed their heads toward the dark mountain that loomed, revealed at last, at the head of the valley. Some among them exulted, their hearts filled with a great joy. The others, they wept in fear, feeling the last vestige of their old faith wither and die.

Cold stone pressed against Khadames' face when he woke. He felt very cold, and water was dripping nearby. He tried to move his head, but a spike of pain behind his eye ended the effort. Swallowing was no better: The pain transferred to his throat. When he managed to open his eyes he found himself lying on a bed of stone flags set into the wall of a great chamber. Sparkling lights danced in front of his eyes for a moment, but then he was able to focus and see that torches of pitch sparked and guttered on the walls, casting a fitful light. There was a great rattling sound, and the shouting of men. He closed his eyes, trying to gather his strength.

"Here, faithful ones!" The voice was too familiar, and rich with delight.

A banging sound came, and the scrape of metal on stone followed. Khadames opened his eyes again and was rewarded with only mild pain. A door swung clear in one wall of the chamber, and a gang of his men—stripped to the waist and sweating heavily—were manhandling the heavy oblong shape of the coffin of gold and lead into the room. The general rolled over onto his side. The sorcerer strode into the room, his skin flushed with the pale rose of good health, his long, thick hair flowing like a raven's tail behind his head.

"To the stone bier, my friends. Yes—lay it there."

The coffin entered the room by inches, with the groans of struggling men punctuating each movement. At last it was dragged on a sled of wooden rails to the edge of a stone platform set into one wall of the chamber. A vaulted dome of stone rose above it, pierced by triangular windows. Through them, Khadames could see a cloud-filled sky and hear wind and rain. The mutter of thunder growled in the distance, too. With thirty men on a side, the coffin was levered up onto the stone platform and finally pushed to rest.

The sorcerer seemed more than pleased, and spent a long moment caressing the dull metal surface of the funereal casket. "Soon, dear one, you will feel the touch of life again. . . ."

Khadames turned away at the soft voice; he had heard the long litany before, many times, on the road from the ruin of doomed Palmyra. He did not need to hear it now; the pain in his limbs and head was company enough. He tried to find sleep again, but it eluded him.

"You are better, faithful General?"

Khadames started awake—he had not heard the sorcerer creep up to him. He turned his head a little and opened one eye a bare slit. The pale yellow irises of the sorcerer looked back, close over his face. The chill in the room seemed to have flooded around him, and Khadames shivered despite a thick blanket that had been laid over him.

"I did not mean for you to come to harm," said the dark man in a gentle voice. "I sent you away to tend the horses. . . . Such things happen, though."

"Yes," Khadames said, coughing, "they do happen. Where are we?"

"Ah . . . you have missed more than a little, faithful General. We are in a chamber near the summit of the Eagle's Nest—a place once called the *kahar kehediupan*—the Room of Life. Your men have tended you since we entered the mountain. You took a strong blow to the head."

"And you," Khadames chattered through clenched teeth, "what have you done in this place?"

The sorcerer straightened and stood back, putting his hands on his hips. "I have made the mountain wake," he said, his lean face smug and filled with delight. "In ancient days they called this place Damawand and trusted much to the strength of its walls and ramparts. They trusted it to sleep, too, at their command and not wake unless they willed it. An unwise assumption." He smiled down at Khadames and sat on the edge of the stone bench. "This is a place of secrets, faithful General, secrets eager to reveal themselves to me. This is a place of power, power that will come to me, now that I inhabit it. Damawand is mine now, a strong place that will call more strength to it."

Khadames closed his eyes. Thoughts fluttered aimlessly in his mind until one managed to force its way through to his lips. "And the men who stood with you at the gate? What of them?"

"Ahhhh . . ." The sorcerer took a long breath. "You are wise, noble Khadames, far wiser than I. This lesson, above all things, I cherish—that one man, even gifted with the strength of multitudes, is still but one man. He has but one pair of hands, one set of eyes—he can only be in one place at once. Oh, this is the most beneficent lesson!"

The dark man reached out and gently stroked the side of Khadames' face. At the touch, there was a brief sensation of bitter cold and then warmth flooded through the general. The chill that had gripped him vanished, leaving a sense of thick warm blankets piled up to the nose, and a chilly room beyond. Despite himself, Khadames sighed and lay back.

"One man may struggle and fail," mused the sorcerer, "where two may succeed or *five hundred* may triumph. You need not fear, faithful General, the men who stood with me at the door, before the sign of fire; they are precious to me beyond belief—they are my Sixteen now, my hands where I cannot lift, my eyes where I cannot see, my voice where I cannot speak. Oh, they are treasured—they will be well looked after. Just as you will be . . ."

The dark man continued speaking, but Khadames could not make out the words. Sleep stole over him in the delicious warmth, and he yielded gratefully to it.

Drums rolled, making a deep thunder that boomed back from the walls of the great hall. Khadames stood, dressed in full armor and the dark green surcoat of his house. A helm of iron chased with silver and gold was tucked under one arm. His mustache was waxed stiff and jutted from his face like the tusks of a boar. His long gray-brown hair lay on his shoulders in heavy braids. Behind him, in four ranks, stood half of his men, each dressed in their finest attire. The hall itself, a brooding vault of heavy stone bracing and towering pillars, lay at the center of the mountain, just opposite the great gate.

The upper reaches were filled with shadow and the fumes of a multitude of torches that burned in sconces cut into the stone. At the center of the room a dais of blocky steps rose up, and atop it, seated on a chair of plain iron, the sorcerer sat at ease. The five hundred were arrayed in two great wings on either side of the throne, the captains on the steps and the ranks of men sweeping down on either side. The dark man had somehow acquired a rich wine red robe and velvet hood that lay back on his shoulders, exposing the graceful sweep of his neck and head. Beneath it his customary black shirt and long pantaloons gleamed like a film of water over ice. Like his subordinates, he was immaculately groomed. Somehow, during the time that Khadames had lay in his feverish weakness, servants had come into the mountain—groomsmen, washerwomen, maids, even link-boys to light the thousands of lamps and torches that filled the vast warren of the mountain with their fitful dim light.

The drums ceased, leaving the air trembling. The heavy iron and oak doors that closed the main entrance to the great hall groaned and then swung wide, pushed by dozens of slaves in black tunics. Between the opening doors, a small crowd of men advanced slowly. A small drum hidden somewhere in the recesses of the hall began to tap in time with their footsteps. The visitors crossed the expanse of the hall still huddled together. At the foot of the dais they halted, and Khadames observed them carefully.

As the sorcerer had promised, they were the headmen of the surrounding villages, clans, and tribes. The mountains of Irak were riddled with narrow valleys and hidden basins. The tribes that clawed a meager existence from the barren plateaus and rough mountainsides did not welcome lowlanders. Too, they were fractious and given to mutual slaughter and betrayal. These six men, with their escorts behind them nervously fingering their weapons, were the chiefs of the greatest clans in the mountains. Each was richly dressed—by their standard, at least, though they could not begin to match the opulent splendor of the Imperial Court, or even the understated refinement of the sorcerer.

"Greetings, honored guests. Be welcome in my house."

The sorcerer's voice filled the air with warm, good humor. He stood, a lithe figure showing boundless energy and will in each step as he descended to the floor. The tribal chieftains, their eyes either suspicious or filled with fear, backed away from him as he came to stand in front of them.

"Please, you are guests here. There is no need for caution or fear."

The sorcerer motioned to one of the servants standing in the shadows. A young, dark-haired woman, dressed in a plain black linen dress, shawl, and modest veil, came forward with a silver platter. In her white hands was a tray bearing a loaf of bread and two golden cups. She knelt at the sorcerer's side, holding the platter up for him. The dark man produced a knife from his sleeve and cut the loaf. "Here is the bread of my house; it is yours."

He offered a piece of the loaf to the nearest chief—a tall, strapping man with a thick black beard and a turban of red and gold. The hill-chief regarded the bread for a moment, then gingerly took it. It was freshly baked and even on the height of the dais, Khadames could smell the sharp tang of yeast and the rich aroma of the new crust. The sorcerer put the rest of the loaf back on the platter and raised the first golden cup. "Here is the salt of my house; it is yours." He sprinkled coarse-grained salt in the upturned palm of the hill-chieftain. Another young woman with hair the color of fresh rust came out of the shadows behind the throne, bearing another goblet. The sorcerer poured wine from the cup on the platter into the new cup and took it himself. The servant bowed to the dark man and took the first cup from the platter and presented it, bowing again, to the hill-chieftain. Demurely, she did not look up, her face remaining hidden behind the veil.

"This is the blood of my house; it is yours. Drink with me, and know that we are guest-friend and there is peace between us."

The sorcerer raised his cup and drank from it. A thin trickle of wine spilled down the side of his chin and he wiped it away with the back of his hand. The hill-chieftain, his dark eyes intent, watched the dark man carefully. The sorcerer took bread and salt from the platter and tasted first the salt, then took a bite of the bread and chewed. He swallowed and turned to the assembled chieftains. "Welcome, friends, to the house of the mountain of the Eagle. Pray, join me."

The hill-chieftain, the wariness a little gone from his face, tasted salt and bread as well, then sipped the cup of wine. Seeing that he had done so, the others followed suit. After they had done this, they sat on the cold stone floor, crossing their legs under them. The sorcerer sat down as well, flipping the dark red robe behind him. He seemed completely at ease among them.

"You are well spoken," said the first hill-chief, his voice gruff. "You claim much, coming to the hidden mountain and making it your home."

"I only claim what is mine," answered the sorcerer in

an even voice. The hill-chief raised an eyebrow at this. "I have been away a long time," continued the sorcerer, looking around the circle of chieftains. "But now I dwell here again—in ancient days, your forefathers served me well and swore mighty oaths to come to my banner when I called. By my right, I call you to do the same."

The chiefs looked around at the huge hall and the armored men standing by the side of the dais. Some looked up, seeing that above the throne a mighty flag hung down from the hidden ceiling—twenty feet wide and a hundred high, a dark, rippling surface that bore a wheel of twelve interlocking serpents in crimson upon it. One frowned, staring up at the banner, and tugged at his beard. Khadames guessed that the man was searching his memory for some tale of that flag.

"And who are you, to stand in the hall that Faridoon built and claim it for your own?" The black-bearded hill-chieftain's voice was mocking, and he made to stand up.

The sorcerer raised a hand, and his face subtly darkened in anger. He stood in a smooth motion. "That name has no place here now, Khawaj Ali. The brothers of the fire did not carve this hall from the mountain, or raise the fortress that stands about us. No, they came by it by treachery. They stole it." The sorcerer's voice rose, filling with an echo of thunder, and rattled from the roof. "I built this place! I brought it forth from the mountain. At my command ten thousand slaves raised it. At my command ten thousand slaves made these halls and tunnels. This is my place, this mountain called Damawand." His voice softened, standing still among the chiefs, who seemed ready to bolt. "Have you forgotten me so soon? Are the memories of men so short—once my name was known throughout the world, and nowhere better than these hills . . ."

While he spoke, the sorcerer had seemed to grow, standing now a head or more above the men who stood at his back. Too, the drums had begun a low, almost soundless beat, and fires had leapt up behind the throne and in the dark recesses at the sides of the hall. In this new light—

all ruddy orange and flickering—great statues of stone emerged from the darkness, flanking the great pillars and lining the arches of the hall. The first chieftain stood, his feet wide, with a fierce glower on his face. "Name yourself, then, stranger! You summon us but do not give your name. Say who you are, and let us have done with these mysteries!"

The sorcerer turned fully to face the chieftain, and again he seemed to grow. He pulled the wine red hood over his head, and his eyes, now cast in shadow, gleamed and flickered with an odd yellow light. When he spoke, the floor trembled and a wind rose, making the torches flicker. "You do not know me by sign and deed? Then I will tell you, short-lived man. I am Azi Tohak—he who some men name Dahak. I am the lord of this place, this tower of stone, and lord of all the lands that lie under the sky."

The chieftain blanched and staggered a little. The other men gasped and began to crawl away. They could not escape, for at Khadame's signal, the Uze had crept up behind them and now formed a ring of steel around them. The curved blades in the hands of the nomads gleamed red in the light of the fires that now roared up behind the throne. The sorcerer turned and mounted the stairs to his seat of iron. There he sat again, turning his countenance upon the hill-chieftains who now knelt, some whimpering in fear, at the base of the dais.

"Yes, now you remember me, not least from the tales your mothers told you when you were young. Yes, I am a lord of demons, a wizard, and a sorcerer who crosses the night sky on the wings of the great *byakhee*. I have returned to my place of power, and you will bow before me and swear the same oaths that your ten-times grandfather's swore when first I walked on this earth."

Of all the hill-men, only one remained standing—the first, the one named Khawaj Ali. His face was stern and filled with stubborn anger. Of all the chieftains, only he showed no fear. "This is not your place," he barked. "This is the fortress that Faridoon built! The priests of fire will cast you down again, as they did before. You and your dark master have no place here—"

Laughter cut him short, a bitter mocking laugh from the hooded man. Dahak raised a hand, and figures appeared out of the flame-shot darkness. They were dressed in full lamellar armor of steel bands from head to toe, and their helms were contrived to seem as the faces of horned and terrible demons. The red light washed over them, making them seem insubstantial. They carried long poles over their shoulders and from the poles, suspended by blood-matted beards tied around the shaft, were the heads of many elderly men.

"Here are your priests of fire, those who mouth the platitudes of a dead god," crowed the sorcerer, his hand outstretched. "See how they bow to me?"

The armored men knelt, moving in complete silence, and the heads made a wet sound as they struck the floor. Khadames, seeing the sightless, gouged eyes and the cruel wounds that had been cut into the faces, swallowed but did not move from his place.

Dahak stood again and he descended a step from the seat of iron. One hand flexed, and a long, tapering finger traced a sign in the air. "Who am I?" boomed out his voice.

The heads, lying in slowly spreading pools of blood on the floor, began to twitch.

"Speak, O priests of the fire, do you know me?"

There was a bubbling sound, and gore dribbled from the lips of one head. It's jaw muscles twitched and bunched, then the mouth opened.

"You are our master, O Lord of Darkness." The voice was foul—a gruesome parody of the speech of men—but the words were clear. Two of the hill-chieftains fainted, collapsing into the arms of the Uze who lurked behind them. These men were immediately taken away. Dahak turned to the Khawaj chieftain and smiled broadly, showing his fine white teeth. "So will all things bow to me; you not least, brave chieftain."

)¤(

Askiff rode up the side of a long rolling swell. Deep blue water slid past, hissing, under the prow of the boat, curling away from brightly painted eyes that stared out over the broad ocean. High above, gulls and cormorants circled, their plaintive cries faint in the afternoon sun. At the back of the boat a tall, young woman with braided red hair leaned into the oars. They bit the water, and the skiff cut into the side of the next wave and then slid over the top. The woman was deeply tanned by weeks at sea and wore a clingy red cotton shirt half soaked with sea spray. Thin braids wrapped with little blue ribbons fluttered on a stiff following wind at either side of her face, framing high cheekbones and firm lips. She squinted forward, storm gray eyes scanning the waters before her. She backed one oar, and the boat turned a little. "There," she said in a strong voice, "the walls of Thira."

Her companion, seated in the front of the skiff, half turned and stared up at the looming cliffs of dark stone that rose from the sea. A thick cloud of raven hair tied back with silver wire fell over olive shoulders and slim brown arms. The passenger was clad in a fine white linen toga not long from the shops of Alexandria. Silver bracelets encircled her wrists, and necklaces of gold and sapphire glittered at her neck. The passenger turned, enormous dark eyes smiling at the oarswoman. "No beach? No harbor? Must we scale the cliffs themselves?" The olive-skinned woman was laughing, her smile brilliant in a perfect oval face.

"Dear Princess," the red-haired woman said, "I promised

you sanctuary and you will find it here. But have a little patience and some of the secrets of the island will reveal themselves to you."

"So you say, O mysterious one, but I wonder at your daring ... the ship that brought us here is long gone, and my brother and children with it. Mayhap there is no one on this island at all! Do you want me all to yourself?"

The oarswoman lost her paddle stroke for a moment, her expression stilled, and studied the smiling face of her companion through slitted eyelids. She pulled the oars into their locks and braced them with one bare brown foot. Even with the tan that had slowly built up during the long weeks they had sailed in the hot waters of the Persian and Arabian seas, a wash of freckles was clear on her nose and cheeks. She stared away from her companion, out over the bright blue sea and the dark cliffs.

Shirin arched a fine jet eyebrow at the troubled expression on her companion's face. "Thyatis? I meant nothing by it—a jest. I know it must pain you to separate me from my children."

The Roman woman turned back, a little, at the light touch on her arm. Shirin had carefully moved the length of the slowly pitching skiff, picking up her skirts in one hand, showing shapely legs and small bare feet. She sat on the middle seat of the longboat they had purchased from the captain of the *Pride of Ialysus* the day before. The upper part of the dress had fallen away, revealing a smooth shoulder and necklaces that plunged into the cool shadow between her breasts. Thyatis frowned a moment, seeing the pensive look on Shirin's face. "No, Lady Shirin, I separated you from your children for everyone's safety. Once they are in Rome, the Duchess will take them into her care—and no one will know them or be able to match them to you. All *know* that your family perished in the wreck of Ctesiphon—who can threaten the dead? Who would guess that those house monkeys are of the noblest blood?"

Shirin laughed again, flipping her hair over her shoulder.

She took Thyatis' hand in her own. Her own thumbs, smooth and manicured, rubbed unconsciously against the hard ridges of callus and muscle that defined her companion's. "So serious! I know I must be apart from them for some little while . . . The soft life of an empress does not prepare me well for what will come. You do me honor, bringing me to this secret place. I can bear to be apart from those squally brats for a little while—it will be restful, if nothing else!"

Thyatis nodded, quelling the conflict in her own heart for the moment, and released the younger woman's hand. She picked up the oars again and bent to them. There was still a ways to go to reach the island. Shirin turned back and settled herself in the prow again, curling her legs under her and leaning her arm on the gunwale of the skiff. The boat plunged down a steep wave. The sea roughened as they approached the rocky shore.

The walls of Thira towered over them, bleak and almost featureless. The island stabbed out of the bright sea, a non-descript stub of some ancient mountain that had remained above the waves during the Drowning. No sign of green marred the crumbling stone and twisted lava. The skiff slid down deeper and deeper troughs between the waves, and now the roar of their crash against the dark shore drowned out all conversation. Thyatis leaned into the oars, her face lashed with spray and the skiff crabbed to the side. A riptide rose up before the boat, a white boil of crashing water, and in the prow, Shirin pointed urgently off to one side. A dark spine of volcanic rock was momentarily revealed by the surging waves. Thyatis rowed furiously, feeling her muscles stretched to their fullest for the first time in weeks. The boat danced aside, swept around the black tooth by the next swell.

The cliff face before them—a sheer rampart of dark shale and glassy lava—suddenly split, drawing a shout of wonder from Shirin, and Thyatis shipped the oars. With smooth, practiced movements, she lashed one oar with a line from the bottom of the boat and slid the other back into the rear rudder lock. A wave swelled behind them, curling up out of blue-green waters. The skiff was carried up its inner face, and Thyatis held the steering oar free of the water, waiting.

The island and the horizon tipped as the boat rode up, higher and higher. In the front of the skiff, Shirin had wedged herself into the bottom of the boat, her arms hooked around the forward bench. Thyatis half stood at the back of the skiff, her head suddenly outlined against the brilliantly blue sky. She braced her feet on the thwarts, feeling the wave gather strength under her. Before them, a narrow passage appeared in the cliff, filled with the roar of the sea. The wave rushed into the slot and the boat rocketed down its inner face. Thyatis' hand was gentle on the oar, keeping the skiff balanced just before the wave crest.

Towering walls of jagged stone whipped past on either side, and the sea boiled against them. The air was filled with brilliant white spray. From the bottom of the boat, Shirin half saw arches of worked stone blur past above her, then there was a great roaring sound and the skiff spun around like a leaf on a mill-race.

Thyatis dug the steering oar in suddenly, and the boat leapt to the side. Gray-green walls of cut stone rushed past, and they were in a dark passage. Waves slapped against walls shrouded in the gloom, and then the skiff sailed out into the light again.

"You must stand and be seen," Thyatis said from the rear of the boat. Shirin looked back and saw that her friend was drenched from her slicked-back red hair to the bare foot braced against one side of the skiff. The cotton shirt and short linen skirt were plastered to her muscular body like some wall painting from the City of the Great Kings. Shirin swallowed a little whistle and turned away. She stood, one bare foot braced against the prow and the other on the first bench. Nervously, she ran slim fingers through her thick hair. It was not as tangled as she feared. She looked up and around.

A great circle of gloriously blue-green water greeted her. Sunlight danced on the wave tops, barely obscuring the tremendous depth of the water. Shirin looked down and laughed aloud—a merry sound—to see a great school of orange and yellow fish darting through the water below the keel of the boat. Under them golden sand and thousands more fish swam in a lagoon of water clearer than the finest glass. Great towers of coral and sea fern rose from the floor of the hidden bay. Around the lagoon, high cliffs rose up, forming a ring of stone and rock hundreds of feet high. At the far edge was a narrow half circle of pure white sand, and there—where half of the encircling wall stood in shadow and half in sun—a pier of white marble thrust from the strand.

On the pier stood three figures, each dressed in flowing white robes. One held a parasol of pale sea green over the head of the central figure. The others were motionless, waiting. Behind them the pier ran back into the face of a temple carved from the rock and faced with soaring columns. Above it, temple buildings climbed the cliff, seemingly half grown from the dark rock. The gleam of white marble stunned the eye, even as the senses were excited by the beauty of the statues and pediments that were so exposed. Far up, on the rim of the bowl, great colonnaded archways peered down, and in them were small figures, adorned with bright flowers and colorful garments.

"This is Thira, my friend."

Shirin barely heard Thyatis' words. A hidden city lay at the center of the island, a city of beautiful cream-colored buildings and graceful white pillars. The skiff sailed over transparent waters, seemingly aloft in an ocean of blue air. Thyatis guided the boat to the end of the pier with sure strokes of the oar. One of the figures, slighter than the other two and with dusky skin, reached down and caught the prow of the boat with a looped rope. Thyatis bowed deeply to the other two figures and oared the rear of the boat to a gentle contact with the stone of the quay.

"Greetings, Lady of the Island. Two women seek refuge here among the daughters of Artemis."

The middle figure smiled, her long face split with a merry grin. She was almost as tall as Thyatis and lean, but her once-dark hair was streaked with white, and her features showed the graceful onset of great age. She wore a clean-lined gown of simple wool, and her only jewelry was a single sapphire on a pendant around her neck. At her side, holding the parasol, another woman stood, enough like her to be a sister or daughter, but she was of middle age, and her bright eyes measured the two women in the boat.

"Well met, wayward daughter," the Matron said. "We welcome you to the island. Please, step ashore."

Shirin stepped off of the boat and onto the dock, the stone cool under her bare feet. The dusky-skinned woman who had snared the boat held out a hand to help her, and Shirin suppressed a start of surprise when she felt the strength in the thin fingers. This woman was very short, barely four and a half feet tall, olive skinned with a golden tinge to it that Shirin had never seen before. Her oval face seemed made for smiling, but she was calm and self-possessed. Shirin met her coal-dark eyes and felt disoriented for a moment. Then it passed, and she made a graceful bow to the Matron of the Island.

"Greetings, lost daughter," the elderly woman said, a muted smile on her lips.

"Greetings, Daughter of the Archer," Shirin replied, carefully pronouncing the archaic words as Thyatis had taught her. "I seek shelter from storm. I seek shelter from the rage of men. I seek shelter from fate and the gods. Bright lady, hear my prayer and grant me peace and surcease from the world. I pray you let me into sanctuary and I will bind up my hair for you and follow your ways in all the days of my life."

The snow white eyebrows of the Matron rose up, and she darted a fierce look at Thyatis, who had also stepped out of the boat and had stripped off the soaked cotton shirt.

The red-haired woman met her gaze and held it, all innocence while she wrung the seawater out of the garment. The Matron turned back to Shirin, noting for the first time the archaic line of the garment she was wearing and the classical styling of her hair. "I see . . . my lost daughter brings a new student, and a troublesome one at that."

The younger woman with the parasol made a slight coughing sound. The Matron rolled her eyes and batted a hand at her. "Peace, Aurelia, I will abide by the conventions of the island and the Order."

The Matron turned a steely gaze upon Shirin and considered her for a long moment. "O girl, you who come before the goddess as *ephebe*, you give yourself to the Order of the Huntress?"

Shirin knelt, furiously trying to remember the rest of the ritual words. "Artemis watches over us," she recited to the old woman's slippers, "winged guardian of all lost things. I am Shirin of Khazaria. I am lost in this world, I seek shelter. Bring me into your fold, *O Potnia Theron*, and I will repay you with love, duty, and obedience."

The Matron glared at Thyatis again, who had pulled her shirt back on and tied it off under her breasts. Sighing, she raised her long-fingered hand and made a sign in the air over Shirin's head. High above, where hundreds of distant faces watched from the windows and archways of the hidden city, a voice was raised in song. Shirin did not understand the words, but she knew from what Thyatis had told her that it was a song of welcome and an invocation for the blessing of the goddess.

"Welcome, daughter Shirin," the Matron said. "You have found your sanctuary, here on the Island of the Huntress, this blessed and secret place."

Shirin stood up and bowed again. The smaller woman patted her on the arm, and the Matron turned away to lead them down the sunlit pier into the cool darkness of the temple. Behind them, the skiff rocked easily against the pier, born up on bright waves. The song swelled from a single voice to hundreds, haunting and beautiful over the empty waters.

The sun set, turning the sea a deep gold and the sky a wash of pale pink and purple. Thin clouds crowded the horizon, and they burned golden like ingots in a forge. Shirin, sitting in the window of the rooms that had been given to her and Thyatis, sighed in delight. The beauty of the sky and the sea from this height made her heart glad. The window was cut from the rock, sitting in a deep embrasure and looking out over the waters beyond the island. Thyatis looked up from the little table in the plainly appointed room. She had her long sword laid out over her knees on a quilt of wool. A small copper bottle of oil sat nearby, and she had a rag and whetstone in one hand. The warm light of the setting sun, slanting through the window, silhouetted Shirin and painted Thyatis like a statue of gold.

"What is it?" Thyatis' voice was weary—the struggle with the sea had taxed her. Her arms and shoulders were stiff and very sore.

"I have never been in a more peaceful place, my friend. After all our travels, I feel at last that I could be safe to walk about without you at my side."

A glad smile gleamed for a moment on Thyatis' face, and then she sighed herself and looked down at the blade. It shimmered in the failing light, a bar of bright watery silver. Outside the deep-cut window, a flight of terns flew past, cawing, heading home to their rookeries on the cliffs above the temple. "I could think of no better place—no, no other place—to bring you after your old home was destroyed."

Shirin nodded, turning a little on the windowsill. Thyatis did not look up, knowing the look of sadness and loss that would be plain on the younger woman's face. "My home . . . I wonder if Ctesiphon was ever truly my home. I lived there, true, with my husband and my children—but was it a home? Its memory fades, but other places remain bright—the yurts of my uncles; the smell of the horses in the rain; the long, open vista of the steppe. Of those palaces and gardens, I can see only you—my friend—standing in the rain, covered with blood, over my husband's body. That and flames leaping into the night sky."

Shirin paused, staring out the window. The sun at last slid into the blue-black ocean, leaving a trailing green spark on the horizon and then a burning ember swallowed by wine dark waters. The sky shaded to deepest purple, with long fingers of gleaming orange trailing across it, the last vestige of the day. Thyatis remained silent, her long fingers slowly running a cloth along the blade, bringing it to a bright oiled polish. Shirin continued, her voice soft. "It was like . . . I had fallen into a dream or a *soma*-sleep, filled with gorgeous halls and elegant people, fabulous gifts, and a prince of the hidden folk—one who could grant any wish, conjure any amusement. A fair face, hiding a dark heart. I was a doll, perfectly combed and painted, something to hold up to the light and wonder at. Then you came, all unbidden, with that reckless oaf of an uncle of mine—ah, what a risk you took!"

Thyatis grimaced and slid the Indian-steel blade into the long scabbard. "It was his plan," she said wryly, "and I cannot fault it—it worked, and here we are."

Shirin laughed, cocking her head to one side. Her hair spilled slowly over her shoulder, thick and rich. "And here we are . . . you and I, a more unlikely pair than any in a troubadour's tale. I know, dear Thyatis, that you fret that you have done me some disservice—torn me away from hearth and home to journey in some strange land—but you forget that I am not some pampered lady of the court."

Thyatis looked up at the sharp note in Shirin's voice. One pale red eyebrow crept up in amusement at the vehemence in that low voice.

"Do not give me that look!" Shirin stood and strode across the room to stand over the Roman woman, brown arms tensed, fists on her hips. "I rode before I walked, drew bow before I could speak—all my people do, as you well know! I rode at Chrosoes' side in the war against the

Man of Wood with lance and shield . . . braggart Roman!"

Shirin pinched Thyatis' ear sharply and then jumped back, giggling, when the red-haired woman growled at her. Thyatis stood, a blur of motion, and her sword, scab-barded, sailed across the room to land in the pile of bag-gage and clothes they had brought up from the boat. Shirin laughed aloud and stuck out her tongue. Thyatis growled again, though a quick smile was welling in her face like a flower opening to the sun. She slid forward, her bare feet quick on the polished slate tiles of the floor, and snatched at Shirin's bare arm. Shirin spun aside, her hair flashing in a dark wheel, and leapt over the chair by the table.

Thyatis sprang left around the low table, her braids fly-ing behind her. "Insolent Princess," she cried, "slow and fat, like a summer deer!"

"Oh!" Shirin's eyes flashed wide, and she snarled back, "Roman piglet, plump and well fed!"

Shirin danced in, small brown feet light on the floor and her right leg came to her stomach and then snapped out. Thyatis leaned aside, her body twisting to slip the kick, and her right hand snaked out, catching Shirin's heel. The Khazar girl sprang up from the floor, twisting her foot out of Thyatis' grip, and she somersaulted, bouncing off of the floor and up again.

Thyatis shouted aloud in unconscious joy and spun in, body bent parallel to the floor in a whirling leg strike. Shirin dropped in the same motion and rotated on one heel, her long, smooth leg flashing out to catch Thyatis' foot. Thyatis fell hard, but rolled into a ball at the last moment and crashed into the table as she came clear. The table legs broke, scattering splinters and broken wood across the room.

"Oh, now see what you've done!" Thyatis crowed, roll-ing up to the balls of her feet. Without thinking, she tossed the table aside with a great clatter.

Shirin tossed her head, clearing hair out of her eyes, and made a face back at the Roman. "Clumsy ox, anyone could have avoided that! I count a point!"

"Do you?" Thyatis snarled, her eyes filled with wicked joy. She circled to the right, balanced, arms a little out in front of her. "A point of what?"

Shirin kept her distance. The toga was a lost cause, and she undid the remaining knot at her shoulder, letting the thin cotton garment fall to the floor. Thyatis made a short rush, but Shirin dodged behind the bed and quickly tied her hair back with a ribbon. Under the toga she was wearing a short linen skirt and a tight silk blouse with short sleeves. "A point of law," she said, leaping over the corner of the bed as Thyatis made another rush. "The court will find in my favor, uncultured Roman barbarian!"

"Will it, effete Persian?" Thyatis sprang over the bed in a mighty bound. Shirin ducked aside, but Thyatis clipped the Khazar girl with her shoulder. Shirin gasped and rolled back, but Thyatis caught her leg with her own and fell on top of her, pinning one hand. Shirin cursed and squirmed aside, but Thyatis locked her left leg and—after a fierce struggle—managed to pin Shirin's other arm.

Sweat dripped off of Thyatis' nose and made tiny pearls on Shirin's cheek. They slowly slid down the golden skin into the hollow of her throat.

"Just like a Roman," Shirin hissed, glaring up at Thyatis, "all brute force—no subtlety at all."

"Just like a Persian," Thyatis said, smiling, bending her forehead to touch Shirin's, "blame defeat on their enemies failings." She was breathing a little heavier than usual.

"Like schoolchildren, more like," a musical voice said with an odd lilt to it.

Thyatis' eyes widened, and her entire body suddenly surged upward, one arm sweeping Shirin away, behind her, and the other fanning in a block across her head and shoulders.

A thin hand, dusky gold, arrowed past the blocking move and collapsed into a knuckled fist. Thyatis, catching a glimpse of a thin, small woman with a crown of tightly braided black hair, tried to twist aside, her arm continuing to push Shirin behind her. The thin fist tapped her on the inside of her right breast, and Thyatis coughed at the impact. Pain blossomed across her chest like fire in grain dust, and she flew back, crashing into the stone wall by the window. Her mouth was open in an O of surprise, and tears welled in her eyes.

Shirin, thrown aside, attacked in the same instant, her right leg snap-kicking at the stranger's head. She followed with a blurring open-hand strike at the woman's sternum. The stranger barely moved, her head drifting aside from the kick, her black eyes smiling at the rage on Shirin's face. Shirin's fist strike was plucked out of the air by the woman's left hand, moving with unhurried ease. In seemingly the most natural movement in the world, the woman's right hand came up into Shirin's chest as Shirin carried forward with her strike and ran herself onto the open palm.

Shirin gasped in pain, all the breath driven from her body, and stood stock-still, her mouth working to breathe. The woman stepped away, every movement as graceful as a swan's, and smiled again, bowing at the two women. Shirin, unable to breathe, shuddered and collapsed forward onto her knees and then to the floor. Thyatis, with a Herculean effort, pushed away from the wall and crawled to her friend. She rolled Shirin over and, with a trembling hand, traced a line with her two middle fingers from the side of Shirin's nose, down the side of her throat, across her chest, and to the inside of her thigh. The Khazar girl twitched and then gasped for breath, able to breathe at last.

"Well done," the woman said, her voice lilting with amusement. "But you were poorly prepared and . . . distracted."

Thyatis looked up, her face filled with surprise, delight, and fulminating disgust. *"Sifu,"* she croaked, still barely able to speak. "never just a hello?"

The little golden woman shook her head, face sad. "No, not in this world of troubles. Welcome home."

Thyatis stood, lifting Shirin from the tiles with an arm

around her waist. She bowed. "Thank you, *sifu*. This is my friend—"

"Shirin of the House of Asena," the golden woman interrupted, "a new student in the Temple."

"Yes," Thyatis said, her voice edged with suspicion. "I was going to bring her to meet you tomorrow."

"Tonight will do for meetings," the woman said, smiling and showing perfect white teeth. "Tomorrow will do for beginning her training."

Shirin's eyebrows rose up, and she looked sidelong at Thyatis, who was staring at the little woman in concern. "Training? She will not be here long enough—"

"She will be here as long as she is here," the woman said, overriding Thyatis with calm authority. "And while she is here, she will be one of my students. This is the Way."

"Not all students in the Temple are your students, *Sifu*! She does not have to—"

"Wait!" Shirin interjected in a cold voice. Thyatis stopped and looked at her friend in surprise. Shirin met her eyes with an icy glare. "I will decide," Shirin said. She turned to the little woman and bowed, her hands pressed together before her. "*Sifu*," she said, "you are the one known as Mikele? The master of the art of the open hand? The one who taught Thyatis—this great lumbering ox of a Roman—to fight with her whole body?"

Mikele inclined her head, bright dark eyes looking the Khazar girl up and down. "Yes," Mikele said, "I am a teacher of the Way."

Shirin met the dark eyes levelly and returned the slow observation.

Mikele was very thin, even lighter than Shirin, who was not heavy at all. The little woman was a swordblade, balanced and whip-thin, with a core of steel. An enormous amount of pitch-black-hair was curled up on Mikele's head, held in place by silver combs and tiny golden pins. She wore a plain-cotton-shirt, with a round-notched collar, and Persian-style pants with wide bottoms. Her face was serene and elegant, marked by high cheekbones and slightly slanted eyes. Shirin knew, looking upon her, that in her youth the little woman had been surpassingly pretty. But now, age had peeled away everything but a clear beauty that shone from her eyes more than the appearance of her face. Her lips were thin, but creased at the corners by a constant smile. Every thing about her spoke of balance and restraint, nothing hinted at the effortless speed of her movements.

Shirin bowed again, tendrils of raven hair falling around her face. "If the teacher would allow a student to learn, the student is ready."

One of Mikele's eyebrows rose now, and she glanced at Thyatis. "Well spoken, at least. Come, the Matron would have you sit with her at dinner."

Moonlight slanted between round-bellied pillars. Thyatis stood in shadow, leaning against the cool marble surface of a low wall. Shirin stood close to her, a shawl of light knotted wool pulled over her shoulders. They stood in a small circular temple raised on the highest point of the island. A narrow stair of a thousand steps fell away below it, leading down to the hidden temples and rooms below. The night air was cold on the height, and the Temple of Artemis was open on all sides, revealing an enormous vista of barren ocean. Beyond the rocky walls of the island was nothing to the horizon. A full moon rode high in the sky, filling the world with a lush silver light.

A breeze passed over them, and Shirin edged closer to Thyatis. The Roman woman slid her arms around Shirin's waist, and the Khazar girl settled into her chest, pulling the shawl tighter. Somewhere on the barren slope, bats were hunting, their squeaking voices faint in the background.

"Was this the first building here?" Shirin asked in a quiet, dreamy, voice.

Thyatis shook her head and rested her chin on the crown of Shirin's head. "No," she said slowly. "The first temple lies on the floor of the lagoon. Sometimes, when the sun is high in the sky, you can see the roof, deep in the waters. It is nearly covered with sand, though. Once, when I was learning to swim, I dove deep enough to touch it. All the others—the Temple of the Winged Huntress, the dormitories, the kitchens and bakeries, the workshops—were built later. The Sisters came and carved them from the stone of the island by hand."

Shirin clasped her hand over Thyatis' and held it tight to her. Her thumb traced a puckered scar on the back of Thyatis' wrist. "That must have taken centuries," she said in a small voice.

"Yes," Thyatis said. "But the Sisters have been here for a long time."

"There are no men here? Not even slaves?"

"No," Thyatis said, smiling in the darkness, "not even a slave. So it was in old Themiscyra, so it is upon Thira-the-Daughter. The world has enough men in it as it stands. There need be none here."

"How did you come here? Did you run away from your family?"

Thyatis stiffened slightly, but then relaxed again, though she held Shirin tight. "No . . . I did not run away. My *pater*—my father—was a landowner in one of the farming districts south of Roma, but there were hard times, and he fell into debt. I—we—my sisters and I, he . . . we were sold, in the great market."

Shirin turned her head a little, peering up at her friend. Thyatis' face seemed that of a statue in the moonlight, as hard as stone. Thyatis pursed her lips and shook her head a little. Little bells wound through her hair and tinkled softly.

"A woman was in the marketplace, just . . . browsing, I suppose. She saw me, all gangly arms and legs and wild red hair, and took a fancy to me. She was a duchess—the wife of a regional governor in the Empire—and money did not concern her much. I was taken to her house, though I do not believe that I ever saw her at all. I remember little of the day in the market—only a terrible thirst and the great noise, all around me, of thousands of people.

"They sent me to a house on the edge of the city, a temple where women could find refuge. The priestesses fed me and gave me clothes and a bath. I stayed there for a little while, then two women in masks came to fetch me and I was sent far away from Roma.

"I was sent here, to the School, to Mikele."

Even in the darkness, Shirin could feel a wry smile on Thyatis' face.

"I was here five years—oh, and they were dreadful! The School is unforgiving and brooks no disobedience. I must have scrubbed every step and tile in this whole warren. But I did learn—I learned to fight, and to see, and to react without conscious thought. I learned the open-hand Way, and the sword art, and all the other things they teach."

"Was Mikele your teacher the whole time?"

"No, she only teaches the open-hand Way. Another teacher—Atalanta—showed me the way of the sword, and many others taught me to read and to write. There are dozens of teachers in the School—Mikele is only the most memorable."

Shirin felt cold again; the breeze was becoming stronger. She felt a little disgusted—when she had been young, she had run barefoot in snow and barely noticed it. The vast open steppes north of the Mare Caspium were not noted for balmy weather and a comfortable climate. *I have become a soft and spoiled princess,* she grumbled to herself. *But this will change.*

"Do you want to go in?"

Shirin looked up at Thyatis and nodded, smiling.

The moon watched them descend the thousand steps, tiny pale figures in the silver light.

⟨⟩

T his seems impossible. How can such a thing happen?"

The Lady Hala knelt on a padded cotton mat in her sewing room. The room was light and airy, with a high ceiling of cedarwood beams and white stucco. Stone walls closed two sides of the room, painted with pale colors. The other two sides were lined with shutters set in a wooden frame, now open, showing the tops of the orange trees that grew in the garden below. Beyond the green crown of the trees were the roofs of the other buildings in the Bani Hashim compound, then the rest of the city spreading out below. Taiya poured bitter green tea into small white cups. Mohammed sat opposite her on a thick-woven Persian rug. He was staring out the window. Above the red tile roofs of the city, the sky was very blue.

"I wanted only to die," he said in a soft voice, "but this voice commanded me to live. The sound of it filled the air like the voice of a god. I could not refuse."

"Was it?" Hala sat the enameled pot of tea aside and then measured a spoonful of crystallized honey into each cup. The amber kernels swirled into the dark liquid. "Was it a god?"

Mohammed looked back at her from the window. She watched him carefully, for he had been very distant and strange-seeming since waking. A shepherd boy had found him on the mountaintop, very close to death, his body burned by the sun, his lips cracked with thirst. The shepherd had carried him down from the mountain on his back and brought him to this house, to Khadijah's house. Weeks

had passed since then, and only now could he walk and
stand without help. The gray in his beard and hair had
deepened into narrow streaks of silver-white.

"A god? Can it be anything but a god who speaks from
the air, unseen? The voice spoke of powers awake in the
world. It said that I must strive against them. It commanded me to act."

Mohammed slowly picked up one of the cups and
sipped from it. The tea was bitter on his tongue, but then
the warm taste of the honey followed. He put the cup down
and met his sister-in-law's eyes directly. "I must follow
that command. I will go forth into the world, with those
men who will follow me and stand against the powers that
I have seen."

Hala frowned, her eyes glittering over the pale umber
veil that she wore when in the presence of her brother-in-
law. She had spent many hours sitting by the bed where
Mohammed had lain in his convalescence, waiting for him
to recover, listening to his mumbled words. She knew,
perhaps better than he, what had been said to him on the
mountain. "Is this wise?" she asked, picking up her sewing
and smoothing the cloth over her knees. "There are things
that must be done here, in your home, first. The speaking
of a god is not to be ignored, surely, but if you are going
away, then you must settle some matters."

Mohammed scowled. He had fled his wife's house on
the day of his return and gone to the mountain. Since then
he had seen no one save Hala and the house servants, and
that had pleased him. In all the years he had been Khadijah's husband, he had kept clear of the fierce political and
clan struggles that raged among the noble houses of Makkah. Many powerful families lived in the city, or had estates in the valley, and there was constant struggle for
position and eminence. He detested them—he had been a
poor orphan before he had married Khadijah—for their
slights against him. He looked away from Hala, his heart
sinking at the thought of plunging himself into that morass.

"You have not even seen your daughter," Hala continued as she began picking out a poorly sewn seam in the dress. "You should take dinner with Roxane at her house, at least, before you go."

Mohammed sighed, and his fists clenched. He hated this. The demands of family and clan dragged at him like lead weights on a pearl diver.

"She misses you. She came every day while you were unconscious and sat with me at your bedside. That blouse? She brought it for you, sewn by her own hand."

Mohammed sighed, and his fingers picked at the edge of the shirt. "So, what matters must I resolve before you will let me go?"

Hala raised an eyebrow at the bitterness in his voice. She had long wondered if the arrangement between her sister and the wayward husband had suffered from strain. She guessed that this—the matters of the sprawling Bani Hashim clan and the intricate system of alliances and arrangements that had so delighted the subtle Khadijah—put a great fear into the merchant's heart. He was not a man who dealt well with inner fear. Too, being raised an orphan, he had not gained any taste for the business of a great sprawling family.

"No one can keep you anywhere," she replied while she threaded one of her bone needles. "But there is a question among the elders about your status now that Khadijah has left us. Some feel that you should now be chief of the Quryash and the Bani Hashim; one you lead by blood, the other you have gained by marriage. You know, surely, that Taiya and her husband will refuse to acknowledge you as the head of the clan. They argue that since you are not of the blood of the Hashim, you cannot now be chieftain."

"And so? If old al'Uzza had begotten any sons the issue would be moot. Hala, your sister *wanted* to be the ruler of her house, and so it was. I do not. I was content as her husband, but the thought of ruling the rabble of sisters, daughters, and cousins is repellent. Let Taiya and her husband lead if they so choose. I will be gone soon. I will take my sword-brothers north."

Hala sighed and put down the needle. She glared at Mohammed and then smiled a little when he squirmed under her gaze. She had not put all those years sitting at Khadijah's feet to waste. "There is more than the issue of the clan at stake here. You have always had an odd status among us. Your time spent on the mountain has made you something of a holy man to some. Your long absences on the trade road have made you mysterious. Now, you have suffered a vision, and I must say that in your troubled sleep, you spoke of this often. In your sleep, you had no doubts—a God had revealed himself to you. More ears than mine and Roxane's heard your words. Even the servants of this house, loyal as they are, have been known to gossip in the marketplace."

Mohammed looked up, his face filled with dismay. "What do you say? Do all know what happened? Do they account me mad?"

"Yes, some do. Others clamor at the gate of our house each day, begging to see you, to speak to you. They say that the gods have touched you and that you will bring good luck to them, or cure their ills. This has made things worse, in the city, between the other clans and us. Some think you are trying to become the high priest of the Ka'ba."

Mohammed laughed out loud, a sound both bitter and despairing. "At the Well? Do they think I seek the ill luck that befell my father and my grandfather? That warren of temples and altars is even more riven with politics and intrigue than this house! If my mother had just left the valley when old Abd died, then so much trouble would have been avoided."

"If she had done so," Hala said softly, "you would not have met Khadijah, or married her. You would not have been blessed with your daughters, or have been given the time to go about in the world, walking up and down in it and seeing all there is to see. You would still be herding sheep in the wasteland."

Mohammed stood abruptly and went to the window. He

looked out over the broad, beautiful garden and the luxurious furnishings in the patio. The great House of the Bani Hashim was strong and rich, filled with servants and family. Its trade connections reached to Alexandria in distant Egypt, to Sa'na in the far south, and even over the broad ocean, to Sind and India. As its representative and emissary, he had seen lands, cities, and people that no other man of Makkah had ever laid eyes upon. He had looked upon wonders that none here, in this dry and dusty place, could name. All these things his wife had given him as he had tried to still the restlessness in his heart. "You are right," he said at last. "Time and circumstance have given me many gifts. She always carried a heavy load for me. Now the burden lies by the side of the road. I must pick it up."

"Well said," Hala remarked wryly. "Will you really do it?"

Mohammed turned at the sting in her voice and looked at her, cast in silhouette by the light from the window. Something in the relationship between them had changed while he lay in delirium, wracked with fever. Before, she had seemed insignificant and mild beside the burning intellect of her sister, but now he saw—perhaps for the first time in his life—that she was the solid foundation, the steadfast maternal core of the family. Too, though she did not own the sharp tongue and ready wit of her sister, she was neither ignorant nor stupid. Mohammed returned to his seat, feeling a great sense of shame in his heart. "I have done you a disservice, sister of my wife," he said, making a low bow. "I have avoided or ignored many responsibilities for many years. You have not. What must I do to repair this state of affairs?"

Hala sighed and now she looked out the window at the garden. "I do not know—the city is very troubled—but you should see your daughter while you still can. I fear this matter may only be settled with blood. Taiya and some of the other clans are very angry; and others see opportunity where there was none before." She stood, a little stiff from sitting for so long. She was no longer a young girl. "Come with me. I would like to show you something."

A broad splash of faded brown was scattered across a wall. Mohammed bent close, his right hand on the stucco, and rubbed a thumb across the dried blood. It flaked away with a rime of plaster. More stains marked the round cobbles of the narrow street. He stood back, his eyes narrowed to slits, looking up and down the alleyway. "When did this happen?"

Hala, her face covered with a heavier black veil, raised a hand and pointed up the street. Two of her servants stood behind her. One held a broad parasol over her head, cutting the heat and light of the afternoon sun. Behind them, standing easily in the street, were two of Mohammed's Tanukh.

"A day ago. Two of your men, Tihuri and Sayyqi, were returning from the marketplace with some of the serving girls from the house. Men beset them here, as they cut across from the high road. The men were dressed in desert robes, and their faces were covered. Tihuri was killed— that is his blood on the wall—but he wounded several of them. The girls fled, shouting, to the house. Sayyqi killed two of the attackers, but then they ran, taking the bodies of their fallen comrades."

"Has this happened before?" Mohammed turned slowly, surveying the rooftops of the houses that lined the alley. He signed to his men, and they moved away, down the street. "Have the disputes of the families grown so vehement that blood is spilt?"

"Yes," Hala said, turning away to return to the house. "Many hatreds that slumbered while Khadijah was alive are now waking. I have learned a little of this; some say that the Hashim were responsible, others claim that the Ben-Sarid sent these men."

Mohammed lengthened his stride to catch up with the woman. "The Ben-Sarid? What quarrel do they have with us? Old Menachem was one of my father's finest friends—

he even gave me a book of theology once, as a friend-gift, when I first left the city."

Hala laughed and raised a hand to forestall him. "Your father is dead, and so is Menachem. His son, Uri, is the chief of the ben-Sarid now and he aspires to make his house as rich as ours. His factors and ours already quarrel on the docks of ports from Aelana to Zanzibar. Oh, relations between us are proper and polite, but they have cooled of late. He well knows that the alliance of Quryash and Hashim is close to breaking—then perhaps he and his people will become the strongest."

Mohammed shook his head in dismay. In youth he had spent many hours with Uri, running and playing among the statues and altars of the sprawling complex of buildings that made up the district of the Holy Well of the Zamzam. Mohammed's father had once been a benefactor of the Temple of Allah there, while old Menachem had been a teacher and wise man of his own people. To think of him as an enemy roused an ill feeling. Still, he did not quail away from the thought—he had disappointed his family and friends and would not let it happen again. "Then the city is divided roughly into three factions," he said after a moment. "Perhaps only two if this matter with the Hashim—with Taiya and her cousins—can be resolved."

Hala and her servants reached the gate at the back of the great house. A number of Tanukh were loitering around the gateway, sitting or standing in the shade of the great trees that hung over the wall. They were all well armed. One man had a bow leaning against the wall at his side. Mohammed swept his eyes over them with approval—for all their languid air, the desert-riders were alert and wary. Mohammed felt a prickling at the back of his neck and half turned at the gateway. Hala and her servants passed through, but he looked back. Two or three blocks away, a man was standing in the shade of a doorway down the street.

"They watch all the time, Captain."

Mohammed nodded a little, acknowledging the words of the Tanukh at the doorpost. Then he went in. His men remained on their own watch, as they had done since his return from the mountaintop. They, at least, had no concerns for him.

"Here, my lord. This is the house of the Lady Roxane."

Mohammed pressed a coin into the man's hand and nodded in dismissal. The servant bowed, his long robes draping to the street, and then hurried away with his lantern held high on a pole. The merchant paused a moment, tugging at the collar of his shirt. Hala and her maids had fussed over him for an hour or more, combing his long hair and beard, setting the jacket and embroidered shirt properly on his broad shoulders. There had been a short discussion of dyeing the white streaks out of his beard, but he had overruled them. "I am as I am," he had growled, and they had laughed but relented in their plan.

He frowned and looked both ways on the street—here the avenues of the city were broad, and torches or lanterns burned by each doorway. Still, there was a watching feeling in the air, and a quiet stillness that put him on edge.

"Captain?"

Mohammed nodded to his two escorts. One was the previously wounded Sayyqi, who had escaped the ambuscade near the market with only a long gash down one thigh. The other was Da'ud, who had joined them in the deserts south of ruined Palmyra. Mohammed thought him a bit young for the life of a sand bandit, but he showed promise.

"All right," he said, and mounted the short flight of steps that led up from the street to the deeply recessed door to the house of his daughter. He rapped sharply on the heavy wooden panels of the door. Roxane seemed to have done well; the fittings of the door were brass rather than cheaper iron. Within a grain, the door swung open and two servants with very dark faces bowed deeply to him.

"Please inform the lady of the house that her father is here," Mohammed said, stepping into the small boxlike atrium at the door. The servants bowed again, and one scurried away. The two Tanukh came in, hands light on their sword hilts. Mohammed moved away from the door and took a deep breath.

He had not seen Roxane in almost six years. She had been sent away to live with a foster family in the southern city of Abha and when she had returned, he had been in India trading for rubies. When he had returned, she had already been married to a cousin—Sharaf, of the Al'Qusr clan of the Bani Hashim—and gone from her mother's house. He realized with a pang of sorrow that he would not recognize her if he passed her on the street.

Have I been away so much?

The inner doors opened, and other servants beckoned them into the great hall at the center of the house. Fine draperies and tapestries covered the walls, which were hung to make the hall seem like a great desert tent. A walkway had been cleared on the floor, showing polished slate tiles that led between divans and rugs. Mohammed strode quickly forward, passing marble statues and chests of rosewood. At the middle of the hall, steps rose up to a deck. A young woman waited on the platform, her hands demurely folded, dressed in a rich gown of red and burnt orange. A chain of light gold links held a whisper of silk across her nose and chin. Mohammed bowed before her, one hand pressed to his heart.

"Gracious lady, I thank you for your hospitality. I am Mohammed of the Quryash."

The woman laughed, a mellow sound, and took his other hand. "Father! So formal, with your own daughter? Do you even recognize me?"

Mohammed flushed with embarrassment and raised his eyes, his mind trying to find some words to apologize for his miscue. Then he staggered in complete surprise, and no words came.

In Roxane, it seemed that his dead wife lived and breathed again, even as he had first seen her, years before. The same strong nose and plain features, the same brilliant eyes and wild, barely restrained, cloud of hair. Then the vision passed and he could see the subtle differences: Where Khadijah's eyes were pale amber, her daughter's were a rich dark brown like a cup of the Ethiopian "black drink"; where Khadijah had tiny scars from childhood disease, Roxane's skin was fair and smooth.

"Father? Come sit by me, tell me of your travels."

Wordless, he allowed himself to be led through the hall and into a sitting room behind it. Much like in her mother's house, the sitting room looked out over the garden. Now, the garden was filled with night, but tiny candles flickered among the limbs of the trees, casting a *jinn* light over the ornamental pools and pale roses. Mohammed sat on a Roman-style divan covered with plush velvet. Servants moved in the room, carrying wine and cut fruit in small bowls. He shook his head and drank from the proffered cup. His eyebrows rose in appreciation.

"It is rather good, isn't it? I wanted to serve only the best for you."

Roxane settled gracefully into the chair opposite, and Mohammed, looking around him at the luxury of her house, began to realize the depth and breadth of the wealth that Khadijah's family, *his* family, commanded. He put the cup of Falernian—a Latin wine, no less!—down on the mother-of-pearl surface of the sitting table. He was touched by the gesture, and disturbed, too. Hala's warnings about the struggle within the family began to gain weight in his mind. He looked over his daughter and her clothing, her jewels, her servants with a merchant's eye.

The Bani Hashim trade spanned Arabia and, with it, the world. On one hand, to the north and the west lay Rome and its vast luxury-hungry cities. The nobles and potentates of the old gray Empire had an endless hunger for Indian rubies, Javan pepper and cinnamon, Moluccan cardamom, thyme and myrrh. Then, too, there was silk and porcelain and jade out of Serica, and steel from the cities on the Gangetic plain in India. Rubber and poppy paste from the jungles of Sinae, and rare beasts from the wild shores of

Africa. Rome consumed mightily and Rome paid mightily, paid in gold and silver, paid in ceramics and machines that no other nation could contrive. Paid in skilled slaves and weapons. And all this, all this had to move by sea, and the Sinus Arabicus was the pathway from the east to the west. And here, at Makkah, the House of Bani Hashim was perfectly placed to arrange and hold and trade and relay and mark up all the shipments from east and west. Every ship from India had to pass through waters controlled by the fleets of Jeddah and Sa'na; every merchant caravan from Rome had to come to ports where Bani Hashim factors and agents waited, with warehouses and customs levies and the knowledge and contacts to squeeze every last *aureus* out of that trade.

"Daughter . . . Roxane, it has been so long . . . I am sorry that I was not at your wedding. I know that must have hurt you."

Roxane rose out of her chair, brushing the gown aside, and knelt by her father's side, taking his gnarled, scarred hand in her own. Mohammed could smell a delicate perfume in her hair.

"Father, I bear you no ill will. Mama and I spoke of you and your work often—I understand why you were gone so much. I am glad that you are here, now, in my house at last. Unfortunate things have been happening in the city. I know you know of them—there can be peace if you will have it."

Mohammed looked down into his daughter's eyes. She stared back, her face graven with concern. "I bear no one in this city ill will, daughter. But do others desire peace as well?"

"Yes," Roxane said, rising to her feet again. "I have invited two of them here, tonight, to dine with us. You know them both—Uri of the ben-Sarid, and my uncle, Tafiq. You remember him; he married Aunt Taiya."

Mohammed frowned; Tafiq had regarded him as an interloper and enemy from the first day the man had laid eyes on him. There had never been anything but icy politeness between the highborn Hashim nobleman and the baseborn Quryash merchant. Now his ears would be filled with Taiya's vitriol as well.

"Will they come?"

Roxane laughed again, her eyes merry. "They are already here, Father, in the dining hall. Come, let us go to them."

"Jalal?" A whisper came in the darkness. The Tanukh turned, still keeping one eye on the street below him. A figure in dark robes edged forward along the rooftop.

"Shh . . . ," Jalal hissed at the other man, then beckoned him over. The younger man, one of the Palmyrenes who had come with Mohammed out of the ruin of that city, slithered over the tiled roof to join him.

"What is it?" Jalal's voice was barely audible, his mouth close to the boy's ear.

"There are men moving in the other alley," the Palmyrene answered. "Thirty or forty of them."

"Armed?" Jalal turned back to watch the street. It was a narrow alleyway in the older part of town at the base of the hill. Here, in a warren of alleys and overcrowded two- and three-story buildings, were the dwellings of the Quryash. The riches of the Bani Hashim and their estates outside of the city, and their town houses on the upper slopes of the hill, trickled down here, but not enough to keep the stink of tanneries and the smell of too many people from pervading the stones and walls of every building. After the attack on Tihuri and Sayyqi, the captain had sent them down here, among his relatives and blood kin. Jalal felt much better here, where anyone who was not Quryash was viewed with suspicion and even hatred. The Tanukh were outsiders, too, but they followed a well-loved Quryash lord, and that counted for a great deal. A strong watch was kept, too, for the captain was wondering if his enemies would dispense with secrecy.

Now, maybe they had waited long enough. Jalal cocked an ear—yes, he could hear the sound of running feet. He reached behind him and pulled his bow forward. It was a stubby, recurved weapon, like those favored by the Huns on the cold northern steppe. Jalal sat up on the sloping roof and tugged his quiver of arrows over to rest against his leg. The Palmyrene boy sat up, too.

"Lad, go downstairs quickly and wake everyone. Tell Shadin that they are going to attack on this side, too. Then stand ready. This will be some cruel work."

The boy nodded and scrambled away across the roof. Jalal ran a thumb along the curve of the weapon and bent the upper arm down. With a quick motion he strung the bow and slid his left hand into the groove of the armrest. Without looking he found a triangular-headed arrow in the quiver and drew it to the string, pulling back almost to his chin. He sighted down the street. The sound of running feet was growing closer.

Mohammed entered the room, an airy enclosure off of the main hall of the house, surrounded on three sides by light frames holding rice-paper screens printed with subdued images of mountains and clouds. A low table had been set with food and drink. Two men were already seated there, at opposite ends, with cups of wine set in front of them. Neither seemed to have touched the drink. Roxane entered and bowed to each man.

"Dear Uncle," she said to the man on the right, "welcome to my house, and blessings upon you and your family."

Uncle Tafiq, a gaunt man with a long hawk-nose and thinning black hair, made a barely perceptible bow to Roxane and did not even look at Mohammed. He was dressed in long black and gray robes of a traditional cut. He sat again, his back stiff and straight, nervously pulling at a pointed black beard. Mohammed smiled a little, but noted that his brother-in-law's hand was very close to the hilt of a saber that was thrust into his robes.

"Master Uri, of the noble ben-Sarid," continued Roxane,

bowing to the other man. "Welcome to my house, and blessings upon you and your family."

Uri stood, his narrow face wreathed in a big smile. He was thin, too, but it was the whipcord well-muscled fitness of middle age. He had a thin nose and sharp eyebrows and wore his curly hair cut short—it was the custom among his tribe—with a neatly trimmed mustache and beard. He bowed to Roxane and stepped past her to crush Mohammed in a huge hug. "My friend! It has been far too long!"

Mohammed smiled back, his humor improving greatly with the open joy on his old friend's face. He clasped Uri's hand and made a sharp bow.

"Uri the rascal, plague of the markets, now the chief of the ben-Sarid—a chief, by the gods, a chief! Well done, my friend."

"Sit, please!" Roxane said, and shooed them back to their seats. She glided to her own, with her back to the door, as was most polite, and sat, her gown swirling about her. Mohammed sat opposite, facing the doorway, with Tafiq on his left and Uri on his right. He inclined his head to his daughter and smiled. She caught his look and smiled back.

"The first course," she said, "is a light fruit compote— oranges and raspberries, with some lemon to keep it from being too sweet." She clapped her hands, and two comely serving maids entered the room bearing engraved silver trays with small glass bowls. Mohammed accepted the bowl, marveling at the clarity of the glass, and waited for the hostess to take the first bite. Roxane plucked a wedge of orange from the bowl and bit it daintily in half.

Jalal breathed out as he released, the taut bowstring singing at his ear, and snatched up another arrow from the quiver. It, too, was in flight before the first had torn into the upper shoulder of one of the hundred men running down the street. The man screamed as the black-fletched shaft gouged through his shoulder and splintered against bone. Blood welled up around the shaft, and the running man crashed into one of his fellows. The crowd of men raised a great cry, then another suddenly choked as the second arrow pierced his throat above the gorget of his shirt of scale mail. He staggered and fell, blood spurting from his neck. The men behind him stumbled and fell, crashing into his thrashing body.

Jalal fired again, now standing upright, shooting down into the narrow street. The first rank of men had reached the door of the house, axes and mallets already swinging against the oaken planks. His arrow plunged down and sank into the crest of one of the axemen's helmets with a tinny clang. The man swung his axe again, biting a thick chunk of wood away from the door, but then his vision blurred with a red film, and he sagged to one side, dead on his feet. More men pressed at the door, their spears a bright thicket. Jalal switched targets, firing as fast as he could into the crowd. The silence of the middle night was rent with shouts and screams.

More Tanukh ran up the stairs from the house and lined the edge of the roof. Each man bore a bow like Jalal's, and a boy followed him with baskets of arrows. Somewhere behind him, Jalal could hear the clangor of blades on metal, doubtless in the other streets. He fired again, his arrow vanishing into the surging tide of men in the street. Arrows began to flash out of the sky, and more of the attackers fell.

Jalal could smell smoke and the bitter tang of blood in the air.

"This is the second course," Roxane said, handing a silver platter to her uncle. "Please, dear Uncle, take two of the quail—they are very sweet and stuffed with nuts and have a honey glaze." Tafiq frowned, but slid two of the tiny birds onto his plate to rest among the rice and flatbread that was already there. The Bani Hashim passed the platter to Mohammed, who smiled at him politely and took it.

"You see?" Roxane said, when the platter had passed around the table. "We can sit and break our fast; we can share a meal as family and friends without ill coming of it." She inclined her head to Tafiq, and smiled prettily. "Uncle, is not a house at peace a pleasant house?"

Tafiq glowered at her and put down one of the quail. "Niece, a peaceful house is one where everyone knows their place and works to the common good. A house where the servants think themselves the masters is an unhappy house, filled with ill will." He smiled thinly at Uri, across the table. "The ben-Sarid, of course, are happily our equals in blood and breeding."

Mohammed, with a great effort, held his tongue. He would see how Roxane wanted to handle this.

"Uncle, please! No one in our clan seeks to rise above his or her *appointed* station. But you are unhappy—pray tell, why?"

Tafiq opened his mouth, eyes brimming with anger, when another round of servants arrived, this time bearing a great tray with a roasted lamb on a bed of rice and wild herbs.

"Ah," Roxane said, holding up her hand and turning away from her uncle, "the main course! Please, try the mint sauce that I have made—an ancient recipe I learned in the house of my mother. Delicious!"

Flames leapt up at one end of the building, billowing out of the windows that looked over the garden. Jalal shouted at his men fighting among the trees and pointed at the fire. The attackers were pouring over the garden wall—someone had thought to bring ladders. The Tanukh in the yard fell back to the long, shaded porch at the rear of the house. On the roof, Jalal and his archers covered their retreat with a flurry of arrows. A dozen of the attackers fell, pinned back against the wall by the black shafts, but more kept coming.

"There are too many of them," Shadin gasped, who had scrambled up onto the roof. His face had a long smear of blood across his cheek, and he had lost his helmet somewhere. His sword was dripping with gore, and the links of his chainmail shirt were fouled with mud.

"Yes," Jalal said, stringing another arrow to his bow, "we need reinforcements." He sighted and fired, oblivious to the roar of the flames or the cracking sound of roof tiles shattering in the heat. Another of the attackers staggered, the arrow jutting from his thigh. The man stumbled and fell, grasping at the blood flooding from his severed femoral artery. Jalal's eyes moved, seeing the next man as a rushing shape. He plucked an arrow, drew, and fired in one breath. It missed, the man moving at the last moment.

"The Quryash? I doubt they would aid anyone not bound by blood and birth to them."

Jalal lowered the bow. The attackers in the garden had thrown open the gates, and a hundred men or more had rushed in. He gestured for the boy with the basket of arrows to fall back along the ridgeline of the house. The other men were already scuttling back.

"Where is Sayyqi? He has something in his saddlebags we can use."

Shadin shook his head as he jogged along the rooftop. "He went with the captain to dinner. What is it?"

Jalal cursed—he had forgotten about the captain in the rush of battle. Now his liege lord and master was on the hill, somewhere, and might already be dead. Holding this building was a useless task in any case. He turned at an open door set into the roof. Stairs went down into the house. He could hear the shouts and clatter of battle in the building below. It sounded like the Tanukh in the house were still holding the main floor.

"Shadin—fire the back of the house and keep these bandits off of the roof. We're leaving and we'll go out over the front wall. I'll be back with everyone else in a moment."

Jalal slid down the stairs in great haste and began shouting for his men to form up on him. Above him was a cracking sound as Shadin and the others ran back down the roof. Smoke began to creep along the ceiling of the hallway.

Mohammed pushed the plate away from him, feeling very satisfied. His daughter's cooks had not disappointed him—the lamb had been tender and young, the carrots and squash perfectly cooked. Only delicate spices had been used, and just enough to enhance the flavor of the meats and not enough to crush all other taste, as the Romans would have done. Too, it was restful to listen to Uri and Tafiq bicker over precedence and status in the city. It reminded him of his own house.

"This is ridiculous," Tafiq snapped, jabbing at the ben-Sarid lord with a hunk of flatbread. "The Bani Hashim hold place of precedence in the city by right of tradition and—more to the point—because we are the best suited to lead the community. We have the most experience, the most wealth, the most desire to better all."

"Not true," Uri interjected hotly. "The customs laws and tax policies are all weighted in the favor of existing businesses—like yours! Huge fees for new construction or renovation stymie those of us who are attempting to bring new business into the city, or to create new *fabricae*. You are protecting yourself at our detriment—when there is trade and wealth enough for all!"

Tafiq laughed out loud, an ugly braying sound. Mohammed turned his mind back to the matter at hand. Though Roxane had attempted to bring the circumstances of the current dispute between the Quryash and the Bani Hashim to light during the course of the dinner, Tafiq had refused to talk of it. Then Uri had been baited into this argument about taxes and fees. Mohammed caught Roxane's eye and raised an eyebrow.

She shrugged, giving him a despairing look.

Well, he thought to himself, *she's not her mother yet. But perhaps in time . . .* "Lord Tafiq," Mohammed said in a calm voice, but it broke the bickering. "The matter of the leadership of the Bani Hashim must be addressed—as

Khadijah's heir, it is mine by point of law, but I know this is not a popular position. Do you dispute my right to lead our clan?"

Tafiq stopped, his mouth open, and stared in surprise at the merchant. Mohammed could see that he had never expected a bald challenge. Tafiq closed his mouth and his eyes narrowed, considering Mohammed. He tugged at his beard, thinking. "Master Mohammed," he began, but then there was a shout in the great hallway and a clattering sound. Mohammed glanced up to the doorway to the dining area, and barely caught—out of the corner of his eye—the blur of glittering metal that had sprung into Tafiq's hand. Mohammed flung himself to the side, bellowing a great shout of alarm. The knife caught his pant leg and tore through, taking a length of cloth with it. Mohammed rolled up, and his own long sword rasped out of its sheath. At his side, Uri had leapt back from the table and had drawn a short blade of his own.

There was a roar of shouting men outside, in the great expanse of the hallway, and Roxane—who had also leapt up in alarm—cried out, seeing something behind her. Mohammed paid no attention as old Tafiq had kicked the table over, sending a spray of glassware, platters, and lamb bones at him. Mohammed ducked aside, twisting away from the edge of the table as it crashed into the paper wall behind him. He sidestepped and lunged at the nobleman.

Steel flickered and rang, sparking from the edge of his blade. Tafiq bore in, his saber flashing in a blizzard of cuts and thrusts. Mohammed gave ground, shoving the other paper wall over with his shoulder to make fighting room. More shouts rang out, and the sound of men struggling came from the front of the house. Distantly, for Tafiq was a veritable dervish in his attack, Mohammed could hear his guards shouting for him. He parried an overhand cut, and his saber licked out at Tafiq's knee. The man skipped back and Mohammed rushed in, catching the Bani Hashim's sword guard on his own. Tafiq spit at his eye, but Mohammed turned his head in time and muscles bunched and corded in his shoulders. He gave a mighty heave and Tafiq crashed through the light wooden panels of the opposite wall with a ripping sound.

Mohammed leapt over the legs of the table and came down hard on the tiles. A spray of fat drippings slid under his foot, and he fell heavily. Tafiq scrambled up and hacked at him. Mohammed rolled away, hearing the saber ring off the stones. He kicked out with his leg and caught Tafiq on the shin. The Bani Hashim cried out in anger and pain, then cut again, striking for Mohammed's abdomen. The merchant blocked the blow with his pommel and twisted, feeling the angry strength in Tafiq's arm. Mohammed kicked again, catching the Bani Hashim in the diaphragm. Tafiq grunted and fell back, trying to force breath into his lungs.

Scrambling up, Mohammed's sword arm flickered out, and the point of his saber caught Tafiq under the chin and then, with a sickly ripping sound, tore his throat out. Mohammed fell back, wiping his blade unconsciously on his pant leg. The sound of steel ringing on steel filled the air. He turned, kicking the other fallen paper wall out of the way.

The great hall was filled with dead and dying men; and more—Bani Hashim by their headdresses and robes—were pushing into the hall from the doorway. Roxane's servants and house guards seemed to have fallen or disappeared. Sayyqi and Da'ud had fallen back to the front of the dining area and joined Uri, who had retrieved a spear from somewhere. The Hashim spread out, advancing across the floor of the hall toward them.

"Up the stairs," Mohammed barked, pointing behind them to where a broad, flat set of stairs rose up to the second story of the house. "Roxane—run ahead and gather your servants. We need a room with a stout door! Sayyqi, Da'ud—with her! Uri, to me."

Mohammed backed up the stairs, his saber loose in his hand, ready to drink the blood of the first man to cross it. Uri fell back in step with him while the others ran off down the hallway. The Hashim scuttled closer. Mohammed eyed them warily—the clansmen were in heavy robes with light armor underneath. The first rank moved cautiously up the stairs, a thicket of spears and shields tensed and at the ready. Mohammed felt the edge of the carpet in the upper hallway with his boot and jumped backward, onto the landing. There was a pair of lanterns on the walls, cut glass with an oil wick inside. He jerked his head at the one on his left, catching Uri's eye.

The Hashim on the stairs raised a shout and suddenly charged, two men leading the way, springing up the steps. Mohammed took a step down and whirled his sword across their path. The man on the left dodged aside, but the other tried to duck under the blur of steel. Mohammed reversed and cut down, drawing his whole right side back in one abrupt movement. The Indian steel of his saber scissored down and caught the man on the joint of his shoulder and his arm. Metal links sparked and then gave way. The saber bit into the man's shoulder, catching the joint, and Mohammed whipped the blade away, tearing cartilage and bone. The Hashim fighter screamed, and blood spattered from his ruined arm across the other men charging up behind him.

At Mohammed's side, Uri feinted at the man who had leapt aside, then stabbed out with his spear, hooking the oil lantern off the wall and flinging it across the faces of the onrushing men. The glass cracked and then shattered as the lantern flew, spewing burning oil across the Hashim. One man took the brunt of the fire and fell back, his head engulfed in sticky orange flame. He tried to scream, but the oil slid into his mouth and he choked to death on smoke and fire as he fell down the stairs. Uri howled in delight and spun back to the left, catching one of the partially burning Hashim with the spear. The man's sternum caught the tip of the heavy-bladed spear and then cracked nosily. Uri kicked the man off the leaf-shaped blade and threw him into the mass of men on the stairs.

Mohammed fell back again, his saber ringing like a bell

as it fended off three Hashim who were pressing hard. Uri was fighting a step behind and to one side, the gore-streaked blade of the spear darting over the Quryash's shoulder. More Hashim pressed up the stairs and into the corridor. Mohammed backed into a great urn and had to roll away to avoid being pierced by two spears. He leapt back, beating aside the spears, and threw his shoulder into the giant jadeite planter. It creaked and then spilled over with a great boom. The Hashim jumped back.

"Run!" Mohammed yelled at Uri, sprinting away down the corridor. Behind them the Hashim roared in anger, the sound of baying hounds on the hunt.

The roof of the building collapsed with a great roar, flames billowing out of the windows and jetting into the sky. Somewhere within, amphorae of oil or pine resin ignited, sending rich blue flames rushing up amid the orange and yellow of wood and straw. Jalal stood in the street, bodies scattered around him, blood on his face and hands, howling commands at his men. "Form up! Form up!"

The Tanukh spilled out of the darkness, heavily laden with their gear. Shadin ran up, his face a mask in the flickering flame light. He had a staff with him, wrapped in a banner. Jalal laughed with joy to see it—his second great fear had been that it was lost in the burning building.

"Unfurl the banner of our captain," he shouted above the din. Their sudden attack out into the street had driven back the Bani Hashim who had been guarding the front of the house. Their dismembered bodies showed the skill and ferocity of the Tanukh. Shadin grinned in the darkness, his teeth white and his eyes wild in the ruddy light. He swiftly untied the cords that held the banner closed.

Some of the Tanukh turned in the street, once they had reached Jalal and Shadin, and drew their bows. At the end of the street, Bani Hashim warriors were regrouping. Black arrows flicked away, and even in the poor light, two of the Hashim fell. Shadin raised the banner, a long green triangular pennant with a long tail. In the grim light of the burning building, it seemed black with the sigil of a single curved white saber upon it. Jalal's heart soared to see it unfurl and flap in the wind. "For the captain!" he howled, and raised his saber high. "For the Quryash!"

The Tanukh joined him, screaming at the top of their lungs, "For the Quryash!"

Jalal pointed up the hill, where the street wound away between the narrow buildings and mounted up the terraces toward the residences of the Bani Hashim.

"On, lads! On! Our captain needs us!"

The Tanukh moved as one, a thick band of men in arms and armor, bristling with spears over shields blazoned with bright geometric patterns. They jogged up the street, their grim faces lit by the flames of the burning building.

Mohammed threw his shoulder into the door, Uri hard at his side, and the oaken panel slammed shut. A Hashim spear had thrust through the opening at the last instant and had caught at the jamb. Mohammed tried to kick at it with his boot, but it would not dislodge. The door panel shook as the Hashim outside the room slammed against it.

"The spear!" Mohammed shouted, fumbling for his long sword with one hand. Roxane stepped in, swinging a carpenter's axe, and the spear haft snapped under the blow. The broken shaft disappeared back out the door, and the panel finally crashed shut. Uri slammed the locking bar across the door, and the whole frame jumped as the Hashim, their voices filled with rage, hit it again. Mohammed jumped back and seized a nearby divan, dragging it behind the door.

They had fallen back to Roxane's quarters on the top floor of the house. Here, amid perfumed splendor, Mohammed and Uri barricaded the door. Roxane had gathered her servants before her as she ran upstairs, and now they cowered weeping at the back of the room. Sayyqi and Da'ud returned from the other chamber, their faces red and arms straining as they carried a huge clothing trunk. The chest fell heavily against the door. Mohammed stepped back, letting his saber fall to point at the floor. He looked at Roxane. "Daughter, where are your husband and his guardsmen? Surely they must have heard all this noise?"

Roxane stared glumly at her father, her perfect makeup smeared and a trail of soot in her hair. "My husband did not approve of my attempt to bring peace," she said in a bitter voice. "He betook himself to his mother's house for the evening, with most of the guardsmen. I just saw one of his brothers on the staircase . . ."

Mohammed nodded. Open war between the clans had come to Makkah, and it would spare no one. He looked around the room, seeing tall, narrow windows and a stout-beamed roof. He pointed up with his chin. "Is there a way to the roof? Can we escape that way?"

Roxane sat down on a gilded velvet hassock and put her head in her hands. Her long dark hair was a mess, lying tangled around her shoulders. "There is a garden on part of the roof, and racks for laundry, but you cannot get to the stairway without going back out into the hall. My quarters have no exit save this door."

Uri laughed, turning and leaning on his spear. "A fine cage he made you, then, Lady Roxane. We will have to cut a hole in the ceiling."

Mohammed nodded, his face grim and closed. "Yes. Sayyqi, take my daughter and her servants to the rear-most room. Cut a way out through the ceiling with the axe. We will hold this door and these front rooms until you are done."

Sayyqi nodded, picking up the axe. His shoulders were thick with muscle and he lifted the heavy iron-headed weapon with ease. "As you say, Captain."

He herded the servants out of the room. Roxane made to stay, but Mohammed shook his head at her and she left. Uri looked after her, his face a little sad. He wiped some blood off of his chin. "I tried to arrange a marriage between her and my son, Ezekhail, you know. Unfortunately, Khadijah and I did not see eye to eye at that time. Sharaf won that toss of the dice . . ."

Mohammed smiled a little, and nodded. His wife had told him a little of the constant maneuvering and posturing that filled the idle time of the families of the city. When she had done it, he was sure that the match had been in the best interests of their house. A snort of bitter laughter escaped him. He paced up and down along the wall of the room that held the door to the corridor. Faintly he could make out the Hashim running about outside and some shouting. "They will find something for a ram," he mused aloud as he quietly tapped the wall along its length. It seemed to be solid, without stuccoed spaces where the Hashim could break it down with axes of their own. His son-in-law probably had spared no expense to protect his womenfolk. A though occurred to him. "Da'ud, quickly— go through the rooms here and check for hidden doors or passages. Rap on the walls, look for hollow spaces. Go!"

Da'ud nodded sharply and hefted his saber before ducking through the door into the next room. Uri nodded slowly and began carefully moving along the left wall of the room. It was difficult; the walls were covered with woven hangings and, behind them, ornamental woods. Mohammed stayed near the door, listening quietly. Uri was finished with his circuit in a few minutes and returned. "Nothing here," he said quietly. "A wise precaution—I know my own house has such passages. Well, I built them, so I should remember." He laughed and clapped Mohammed on the shoulder. "I have missed you, my friend," he said. "Odd that our paths took such a long journey to come together again."

Mohammed nodded. When they had been little, it had been Uri who had wanted to see the world and travel on the open seas. But he had stayed home, and built his house until it was very strong. Mohammed, the boy who had always been looking for another scroll to read, had been the one who went away. Mohammed frowned. It was very quiet outside. "Get ready," he said, stepping back into the cleared space in the middle of the room. "They are about to try the door."

A moment passed, and all Mohammed could hear was the breathing of his companion and the faint sound of Sayyqi chopping at the roof timbers three rooms away. Then, very faint through the door, was the sound of rushing feet, and a great boom shook the panel. Splinters flew away from the locking bar, but the door held.

"Da'ud!" Mohammed shouted, raising his saber over his head. A few paces away, Uri raised his long spear. "Get in here!"

Boom! The door panel creaked, and the bar split along its length. The Hashim in the outer corridor gave a great shout, sounding like an army. *Boom!* The bar cracked, and the door snapped open, lodging against the heavy chest of drawers. Spears poked through the opening, their flat heads questing like snakes. Mohammed held up a hand, warning Uri off. Da'ud ran into the room and skidded to a halt on Mohammed's right. The chest groaned and screeched as it was ground back across the floor. The black headdresses of dozens of Hashim could be made out through the door. A spear flew into the room and clattered on the floor behind Mohammed. He tensed, preparing for violent action.

The Hashim swung their ram again, and the chest of drawers was knocked aside with a great clatter. Four Hashim, their long robes flying out, leapt into the room. Their faces were obscured with dark gauze, showing only eyes filled with hatred. The first man's saber hacked at Mohammed, and he caught the tip with his own blade and knocked it aside. A cheer went up from the hallway, and more Hashim boiled into the room. Mohammed gave a great shout and attacked, his own blade raining blows on the Hashim. The lead man parried the first two strokes, but then Mohammed caught him on the pommel and knocked the saber away. Other Hashim struggled past, trading sword strokes with Da'ud and trying to close with Uri.

Mohammed punched the man in the face with the pommel of his saber, feeling bones shatter under the blow, then hacked sideways at one of the men stabbing at Uri. The man, caught from behind, cried out as the saber cut into his spine, then fell. Uri rushed into the space in the line of men trying to bring him to bay, whirling the spear over his head, and gutted the man to his right. Mohammed turned, with Uri at his back, and pressed into the door, hewing at the men struggling to pass over the trunks and divans that had been piled behind it. One tried to jump away but fell heavily, and Mohammed's saber sank into the stomach of the Hashim behind him. Blood gurgled as Mohammed pulled his blade free. Uri killed another of the swordsmen with the spear.

There was a cry behind them both, and Mohammed risked a quick glance over his shoulder. Three Hashim had gotten past and had brought down poor Da'ud. They hacked at his body as he struggled on the floor in a spreading pool of blood. Then Roxane appeared in the doorway, straining to heft a heavy Roman-style *arcuballista* of ancient dark wood. A quatrefoil bolt lay in the cradle. Mohammed wrenched his head away, barely blocking the blow of the next Hashim through the doorway. He heard a sharp *twang* as the steel spring released, and a scream of pain, but no more. Two Hashim attacked; their blades a bright blur in the air. He locked one with his own sword and wrenched sideways. The second man's saber could not stop and hacked into his fellow's shoulder. Both men cried out in rage and Mohammed gave a mighty heave, throwing the two men back in a heap.

Uri rushed back and impaled one of the Hashim who had slain Da'ud, running the spear all the way through his body. The noble pushed the fouled weapon aside, and the man slumped to the floor, his hands clawing at the ash shaft that transfixed him. The remaining Hashim in the room had grappled with Roxane, but now he turned, hearing the sound of Uri's rushing feet. The Hashim warrior threw the woman down, and a long knife rasped out of the sheath at his side. The ben-Sarid skidded to a halt, his fine-tooled leather boots sliding a little on the marble floor. His own dagger appeared in his hand; a blade of Syrian steel twelve inches long. The Hashim shouted and lunged, cutting sharply overhand at Uri's head. The ben-Sarid ducked and slammed the Hashim in the chest with his shoulder. The two men grappled, hands locked on their wrists.

Spearmen crowded the door in front of Mohammed and he fell back, staying out of reach of the metal tongues. He tried rushing the man on the right side, but the others covered too quickly. Mohammed snarled at the men. "Uri, finish him and get back to the next room!"

Behind the Quryash merchant, Uri and the Hashim were struggling on the floor, each trying to gain position. Sweat spattered off the Hashim into Uri's eyes. The Hashim's knife hand ground lower, the blade reaching for Uri's face. The ben-Sarid wrenched to the side, escaping the bite of the knife, which scraped on the floor next to his head. Mohammed backpedaled past the two men, jumping over their legs, and—in passing—slashed down with his saber. The curved tip cut into the side of the man's head and blood fountained. The Hashim screamed and tried to roll away. Uri cracked the man's knife hand against the floor, sending the knife skittering away, and drove his own blade sideways into the man's chest.

The Hashim at the door howled in rage and pushed through, filling the room. Uri scrambled past Mohammed, who threw the next door closed. The Hashim were at it in grains, axe blows raining against the decorative ash panel. It began splintering immediately. Mohammed looked around for something with which to reinforce the door.

His daughter's handmaidens had a beautiful sleeping and sewing room, but it was woefully lacking in large heavy objects to block doors with. Uri looked back at him and shrugged his shoulders.

"Back to the next room," Mohammed wheezed. The battle was wearing on him; he was not so young anymore. "Has Sayyqi cut a hole to the roof yet?"

Jalal jogged up the street, twenty or thirty Tanukh and Quryash at his back. Around him Makkah was burning as the pent-up hatreds of thirty years of quiet conflict erupted into open battle. Great mansions on the hill above and below him burned, their windows gaping wide with rushing flame. Clouds mounted to the dark heavens above, lit from below with ruddy light. As the Tanukh had ascended the hill, they passed scattered fighting and many bodies left to lie in the streets. Now they neared the residence of the Lady Roxane, and Jalal slowed. He turned a corner and stopped, raising a hand in warning. Behind him the other Tanukh came to a halt. Some of their number passed the word, even to the clansmen who had joined them in their exodus from the Quryash quarter in the city below.

The banner had done its work, as had their war cry. The clan, apprised of the danger to their favorite son, had risen fiercely against the Hashim, and now the green turbans hunted the black through dark streets and abandoned buildings. Steady streams of people were fleeing the city through the gates left open by the departure of their Hashim guardians. Jalal peered around the corner, his face wrapped in a long green cloth. Distant fires gleamed in his eyes. A street with three great houses on it lay before him. In front of one, where a gate had been broken down, a crowd of Hashim was loitering about, talking. Torches illuminated the scene, showing indistinct lumps in the street.

Jalal signaled behind him for Shadin. The other man hurried up, a great long sword in his hands.

"There are Hashim at the gate," Jalal whispered into Shadin's ear. "Send the archers forward. Everyone else in two columns—we will go far left and far right, running to the attack. The archers will fire down the center. We must take the gate quickly."

Shadin nodded sharply and moved back down the line of men, whispering commands. At the corner, Jalal drew out his bow and strung it, keeping one eye on the Hashim. Very faintly he could hear the sounds of men shouting in the house. Perhaps there was still some resistance. *No matter*, he thought, *if there is no one left alive, then the captain's funeral pyre will be lit by a mound of foreskins.* Jalal grinned unpleasantly at the thought. Shadin returned to his side with a group of men close behind him.

More shouting came from within the great house, and the men at the gate turned to look inside. Jalal chopped his hand down and jerked it forward. The bowmen fanned out past him into the street. Shadin was hard on their heels, and the Tanukh split into two horns, rushing silently forward. Jalal drew his bow in a smooth, violent movement and sent the first arrow hissing away.

The night suddenly filled with the flashing passage of arrows, and the first man at the gate was gasping in pain, clutching at the sharp sensation in his back, then his neck, before anyone had even turned at the sound of the running feeet. The Tanukh flooded past Jalal as he fired and fired again. Half the men at the gate were thrashing on the ground before Shadin leapt through the gateway, his huge long sword whirling around his head. Screams pierced the air from within, and the clash of steel on steel followed.

Jalal swung his bow over his shoulder and drew his saber. "On!" he growled at the other bowmen. "This will be sword work now."

Mohammed spun sideways, his saber catching the down-stroke of a Hashim blade. The shock rang up his arm like a hammer on an anvil. He ignored it. The blood fire was burning in his veins, and the whole world had shrunk down to a gray tunnel filled with the angry faces of his cousins. Blows rang against his guard, and he pushed his muscles to greater and greater speed. A tickling began at the back of his mind, creeping along his spine as three and then four of the Hashim came against him. Their swords flickered and rang harshly, and he parried, spun, and struck again and again. He drove pommel to pommel with one, then threw the man backward with a powerful surge. The other three piled in, raining cuts and thrusts, but his hand was a blur and his old sword slipped two strokes and then blocked the other with the flat. His riposte tore one man's arm open from wrist to elbow, and the Hashim fell away, gasping with pain.

Very faintly, through the enormous sound of blood hammering in his ears, he could hear someone shouting at him from behind. But the Hashim came on again, more men pushing through the doorway to get at him. The floor was slick with blood, and the delicate cushions and silk draperies of his daughter's bedroom were torn and scattered. He had picked up a dagger for his left hand somewhere and when the Hashim came at him again, he blocked one blade into the floor with it, then circle-parried to the right, tangling a man's weapon. The man fell back, freeing his weapon, but Mohammed jumped into the break in the line, taking two blades on his own, and slashed the dagger across the throat of the first Hashim warrior. Blood blinded the other man, and Mohammed gutted him without thinking.

The gray tunnel filled the world, and Mohammed spun and parried and danced at the center of a whirl of steel and blood. More Hashim came at him, screaming curses and oaths, and he chopped them down, or shattered kneecaps with his iron-shod boots, or left their faces a bleeding ruin.

The shouting came again, and this time it registered. His daughter was screaming at him from the hole in the roof, begging him to follow them out. He beat aside the weakening attack of a Hashim spearman, chopped the spear haft in twain, and sank his saber into the man's armpit. Wrenching it out, he leapt backward and swung up onto the great pile of furniture that led to the rudely hewn exit in the roof. Above him he could see Roxane's face and her arm reaching down at him.

A chair toppled away under him, and he grasped at the edge of the opening. Roxane grabbed onto his shoulder, her long nails digging into the torn shirt. Her face contorted as she strained to pull him up. Mohammed's feet scrambled for purchase, and he caught the edge of the other chair, boosting himself up. Roxane managed to catch his belt and heaved, pulling him halfway into the opening.

For a moment he was blinded, his head caught in her gown.

There was a sharp *twang* sound, and the sound, of something heavy slapping into meat.

Mohammed got out both arms out of the hole and levered himself out onto the roof by main force, carrying Roxane on his shoulders. There was a chill on his back and he rolled over, catching her limp body. The night was lit with great clouds of smoke, glowing sullen red and orange. He rolled Roxane over, and her sightless eyes stared up at him. An *arcuballista* bolt had taken her in the side of the neck as she had dragged him out of the opening. Below her pale perfect face was a ruin of white bone and red tattered flesh. Mohammed stood slowly, heedless of the screams and shouts that rose from the ragged gaping hole in the roof. Ashes drifted out of the sky, settling in his silver-streaked hair and on his face. He stared down into the room below, seeing his Tanukh—come at last— hewing their way through the trapped ranks of the Bani Hashim. In his eyes, the fires of the city gleamed.

░▒▓◙◦○◦◙◦○◦◙◦○◦◙◦○◦◙◦○◦◙◦○◦◙◦○◦◙◦○◦◙◦○◦◙◦○◦◙░▒▓

THE ISLAND OF THIRA, SOMEWHERE IN THE KYKLADES

)━(

Thyatis, her long golden red hair tied back behind her neck, slowly descended a flight of sandstone steps. Her gait was stately, her head held high. She was dressed only in a short cotton chiton and a pair of beaten copper bracelets on her left arm. She stepped down onto a floor of marble blocks covered with fine white sand. A great room opened out around her, vaulted above with a huge dome. The walls were lost in shadow, showing only the feet of massive pillars set at regular intervals. Sunlight, dim and diffuse, filtered from a circular opening in the ceiling high above. Within a shaft of light falling from the oculus the slight figure of Mikele stood waiting. As before, she was dressed in long plain white pantaloons of soft cotton, with a tunic of subtle yellow and a round collar. A second, tighter fitting shirt with long dark sleeves that came to her wrists was worn underneath the tunic. Her hair was tied up into a tight bun at the back of her head.

Thyatis stopped at the edge of the circle of light and bowed deeply, her hands pressed together in front of her. Behind her, at the top of the curving set of stairs that ran down the side of the room, Shirin waited in a long loose gown that covered her whole body. Her hair, too, was tied up and bound back behind her head, out of the way. At the edge of the circle, Thyatis looked up and met the little woman's eyes.

"*Sifu*, I bring a candidate who wishes to learn the Way of the Open Hand."

Mikele did not stir, but her voice echoed off the hidden pillars and the dark spaces in the room. "If there is a student, a teacher will appear. Is there a student here?"

"Yes, *sifu*."

Thyatis bowed again and stood aside, stepping to the base of one of the great grooved pillars that ringed the central space of the room. Shirin descended the steps, the light *pit-pat* of her feet audible in the quiet room. At the edge of the circle of light, she stopped and bowed, even as Thyatis had done. "I am a student," she said in a clear high voice. "Is there a teacher here?"

"Yes," Mikele said, still unmoving. "Show yourself in the circle of light."

Thyatis bit back a soft hiss as Shirin shrugged off the loose gown and stepped into the circle. Under the pale light, her skin seemed to gleam with health; a rich dark olive. Her full breasts were bound with a *strophium* of fine Egyptian cotton, and she wore a slight loincloth to cover herself. The months of training on the decks of ships in Arabian and Egyptian waters had trimmed away the baby fat that had accumulated in four years of soft, palatial life in Ctesiphon. She seemed to float in the air, poised and ready. Thyatis swallowed, seeing her exposed in the pale light as if for the first time.

"I am a teacher," Mikele said, and she moved slightly, making a soft bow, no more than an incline of her head. "Do you wish to learn?"

"Yes," Shirin answered, taking a step forward into the center of the circle of light and bowing. "I wish to learn."

Mikele regarded her gravely for a moment, then a flash of a brilliant smile crossed her face. "Then you shall learn."

Thyatis sighed and turned away, quietly making her way up the curving flight of stairs. Behind her, the other students of the Way, who had been sitting quietly in the shadows, came out, their voices and laughter filling the old domed temple that was the center of their school. At the top of the stairs, Thyatis looked down, her face sad, to see Shirin talking earnestly with the other girls. At the edge of their throng, Mikele was looking back at her, her high-boned face calm and serene. The Roman woman turned and left. She felt excluded from the life of her friend, though she had intended this all along. It hurt.

A wooden man stood at the side of a room with a wooden floor. The floor was worn and rubbed smooth by the scuff and passage of many feet. The wooden man, his stiff arms held out before him, was polished, too, though the patterns were uneven. His neck and face, his elbows, his crotch and knees were all grooved with wear. Once there had been features painted on the face—a fierce red beard and bushy eyebrows—but they had vanished long ago.

Thyatis, stripped down to her loincloth and *strophium*, stalked sideways, poised on the balls of her feet. Her arms were up, ready, muscles tensed. She drifted forward, then exploded into motion, sweat flying away from her hair and face. The wooden man shuddered as sidekicks and sharp, fast hand strikes rained against him. Thyatis pushed herself, going through the long series of punches, kicks, and blocks with increasing speed. Her muscles burned with the effort. Suddenly, spinning away, she shouted in fury and lashed out with a flying side-kick that cracked the wooden head. There was a splintering sound, and the round globe of old oak flew away, clattering off the wall of the training room. Thyatis landed on her feet, her breath hissing between bared, clenched teeth. Sweat ran off of her in tiny rivers. The cotton kilt around her waist clung, sopping wet, to her thighs.

She shouted again and her fists blurred, cracking sharply against the elbows of the wooden man. The worn grooves in the wood took her strike like they had taken tens of thousands of blows before. She spun away, her wrists and fists snapping through the blocking patterns at the end of the practice movements. Then she squatted heavily on the floor, holding her head in her hands. Her whole body felt like it had been beaten with a butcher's hammer.

"Ah, dear," a quiet voice came from the doorway, "you mustn't break the appliances. That poor man takes enough abuse as it is."

Thyatis rose, scowling, but then saw the Matron standing in the doorway, her elegant gown falling almost to her feet. The elderly woman's white hair was down, falling around her shoulders, and she held a folding fan in one hand. The Matron stepped into the room, her movements carefully controlled and showing echoes of the grace she had owned in youth. She sat on one of the benches along the wall, her head silhouetted against a deep-set window. Far beyond her, the line of the horizon was an azure slash in a field of white. The fan moved languidly, stirring the air.

Thyatis shook her head and stood up, going to the corner of the room where the broken head had come to rest. She picked it up, making a wry grimace at it, and put it back on its stump. It lolled to one side. "I should make a new one," she said, not looking at the Matron.

"Hmm. That might do your body some good; diving to

one of the wrecks on the Teeth and recovering the wood to make it. But it will not settle your mind, my dear. Exhaustion will only gain you a short respite. Though . . . there are many stones to be quarried and carved for the new Temple of Atargatis . . ."

Thyatis turned to glare at the old woman, but the sight of her calm face and that slight smile that always hovered around her mouth, a dove waiting to unfurl its wings, stopped her. The Roman woman shook her head, sending tiny droplets of sweat sparkling across the room. "I am troubled," she said, gritting her teeth at the words. "I am unhappy. This is what I wanted—and now I feel distraught over it! This is what I wanted and not . . . what I want. Oh, Goddess, I feel directionless now, suddenly. I hate that. There is *nothing* to do!"

The Matron nodded, her eyes sparkling.

Thyatis paced around the room, filled with nervous energy. "Do you think I did the right thing?" Thyatis turned and stared at the Matron with an expression of deep concern on her face. "Bringing Shirin here, I mean. I asked no one's leave . . . it seemed the best course . . ."

"Your instincts have always been superlative," said the Matron slowly, her head cocked to one side like a curious hawk, watching the young woman pace. "Why do you doubt them now?"

"This is . . . this is higher than I have reached before. This is the Duchess's game, not mine. Mine is dark alleyways or deserted roads late at night. The quiet use of steel and wire and murder. But this . . . kidnapping and hiding princesses—oh, that is not a game I've played before. It would be so much easier if I had just followed the Emperor's command!"

The Matron smiled and nodded. She patted the bench beside her with a thin, wrinkled old hand. "Sit, my dear. You have made a serious decision, to contravene the orders of your commander. To go against the will, I suppose, of your mistress, the Duchess. Why do you suppose you did that?"

Thyatis groaned, sitting, and buried her head in her hands again. Through her fingers, her words were muffled, but audible. "I don't know! I thought the Duchess could better use the Princess alive, in Rome, than dead in Ctesiphon. Ayyy . . . but if the Emperor ever finds out! My head and hers will roll for it. . . ."

The Matron laid a gentle hand on the young woman's shoulder. "I think not, dear. The gossip of the markets reaches even here, to our quiet little island. The Emperor of the East—oh, he is beside himself with rage that such a succulent prize escaped him. Yes, that bear of a man wanted your friend as a wedding gift for his brother. But your master? This Emperor Galen? He is quietly pleased, though he would never say so."

"Why?" Thyatis frowned, watching the smiling face of her old teacher intently. "He bade me go into the city of his enemies and be ready and I failed him. I was not there when his soldiers stormed the gates—I was lost in the maze of the Palace of the Swan, trying to find . . ." Her voice faltered.

"Trying to find whom?" The Matron cocked her head again, her fine white hair falling to one side. "You were trying to find your friend, who was in danger of her life. You were trying to devise an escape from the sack and ruin of that great ancient city for not only yourself, but for your men and the family of your friend. Against this, you weigh the guessed-at desire of an emperor?"

The Matron stood and walked slowly to the western wall of the room, leaning a little on the balustrade under the deep-set windows. Beyond the window the sun blazed down on the island, throwing the aquamarine sea into sharp relief against the dark cliffs. She pursed her lips, looking out at the empty horizon. "This business of guessing at the intent and the desire of emperors is dangerous. Their concerns are not yours, or of any man or woman who does not wield such power. Their responsibilities color the world a different shade than do mine or yours. Emperors forget friends and family, or even those who have done them a good turn. They can *never* be trusted, you know."

Thyatis looked up. The Matron's voice had fallen low, and she seemed lost in memory.

"The concern of an emperor," continued the Matron in a very soft voice, "is the cruel business of Empire. I think, my dear student, that in this matter—of following your heart and helping your friend—the scales balance in your favor."

"Then I did the right thing?" Thyatis stood, nervously rubbing her hands on her thighs.

The Matron laughed and turned from the window. "No one can say that," she said, her old face creased by a wide smile. "But tell me this, O impetuous one, if you had left your dear Shirin in the ruin of that palace, and she now was the captive wife of a prince of the Eastern Empire, would you account that you had done the right thing?"

Thyatis stopped cold. An image of the Eastern Prince Theodore flashed in her mind, and Shirin was kneeling at his feet, her face bruised and streaked with tears, her pale yellow silk gown torn. The Prince was laughing, his broad red face flushed. A thin trickle of sweat crept down from his hairline. Without thinking, her lips contorted in a snarl and her fists clenched.

The Matron frowned, her eyes narrowing. "You see?" she said sharply, bringing Thyatis' attention back to her. "You could not bear it. So does your heart weigh the balance."

"Yes," Thyatis said, troubled again, "I suppose it is so."

Shirin leaned back against the cold stone of the wall in the changing room. Wearily, she raised one knee up and began stripping the padding from her shin. Each movement of her fingers as she unwrapped the cloth was filled with pain. Her fingers trembled as she picked at the knots. After a moment she realized she had been fumbling at one knot for an unknown amount of time. It had pulled tight in the exertion of the long endless day of training. Her hand flopped back down into her lap. Slowly, though she tried to fight against it, she slid sideways, unable to muster the energy to stay upright. The bench was carved slate, quarried from the depths of the island. It was cold and hard, but it held her up. Her eyes closed, and her breath ran fast in little short gasps.

She dreamed, and it was a dream of constant motion and pain.

A light touch came at her shoulder, and she sat up, her eyes blinking furiously.

A face appeared at the center of her vision, a delicate oval dominated by enormous dark eyes.

"Sifu . . . ," she wheezed, "I'm sorry! I didn't mean to fall asleep!"

"No matter, little bird," came the calm voice with its lilting undertone. "Let me help you up."

Fine-boned hands slipped under her arms and raised her up, though Shirin thought she would faint from the flush of pain that flooded her brutalized muscles. The months of training on the ships that had carried her and her family out of the Sinus Persicus, into the deep green waters of the Mare Ethyraeum, and finally to Egypt had toned her some, but nothing compared to the first day of her training here. Mikele carried her down a flight of steps into air thick with steam.

Hot water lapped at Shirin's feet and she gasped in relief to feel the warmth flow up her ankles.

"Here," Mikele said, stripping the short cotton *chlamys* off her. "Slide slowly into the water."

Shirin complied, feeling distant from her body as the warm water rose up around her. A glossy marble step ran around the circumference of the great bath, and she settled into it. The water came up to just above her breasts. It felt wonderful. Mikele settled herself above her, on the lip of the bath, her golden-toned legs on either side. Shirin leaned back, a breath hissing out between her teeth.

"Your work today," Mikele said in a conversational voice as she began rubbing the top of Shirin's scalp with her thumbs, her long fingers holding the Khazar woman's head upright, "was reasonable. You are slow, but not without the promise of speed. You are not very strong, but there is a hint of power in your efforts. You are very tight across the middle of your body—you carry too much bad *chi* in your lower back and along your spine."

Shirin lost the thread of the conversation, feeling only the glorious warmth that penetrated her bones and the slow, spreading wave of relaxation that seemed to radiate out from Mikele's thumbs.

"Why did you bring your dear friend here?"

Thyatis put down the wooden mug on the table and wiped her lips with the back of her hand. Across from her, leaning back against an ancient carved wooden chair with a high back, the Matron regarded her. Darkness had come, stealing across the jagged peaks of the island, filling the bowl of the lagoon, covering the hidden windows with the shade of night. Thyatis sat in a small alcove cut into the side of the Matron's quarters, at a table of ancient cedarwood, with her legs tucked up under her. The alcove looked out, hidden by a crumbling out-thrust cliff, over the lagoon. An embrasure had been carefully cut along the natural line of the rock, keeping the little balcony hidden from those who might look up from below. A long afternoon had passed between them, and now dinner was done as well. A few plates stood between them on the table— simple hand-fired bowls and plates such as the Matron loved—and a red-checked amphora of Cretan wine.

"I"—Thyatis smiled, her teeth white in the twilight—"I don't think I even considered taking her anywhere else."

"Hmm . . ." The Matron looked out, over the lagoon, listening to the rhythmic slap of the water on the narrow beach below. "You brought her home, I think. To a place you felt safe. You chose well, my dear. She will be safe among us, while the island stands. But I do not think you made that decision bereft of all thought."

"How so?" Thyatis said, drawing her knees up to her

chin and wrapping her arms around them. "All that time seems a blur to me."

"Oh," the Matron laughed in her quiet way, "your head may not have thought, but your heart surely did. Tell me, why did you bring her to us as an *ephebe*, a student, a novitiate of the Huntress? We would have taken her in without such an ancient ceremony—many women who have found sanctuary here have never taken the oaths. Why bring her to me in clothes of an ancient cut? Why have her recite, so formally, that hoary old greeting?"

Thyatis flushed, and scratched her scalp furiously, looking away. "I don't know . . . it just seemed the proper way to do it. I had forgotten about the Unsworn . . ."

"Pah!" the Matron barked, and she took a shelled nut out of the bowl on the table. She chewed it slowly, her eyes hard on Thyatis, who found that she could not meet them. "There is more than ceremony and tradition afoot in your addled brain. Tell me this, then: If she were gone away tomorrow, would you miss her?"

"Yes." Thyatis sighed, burying her face in her knees. "I miss her now, with her gone each day to train in the Temple of the Way. I should go on to Rome—the Duchess will be angry if I delay much longer—but it is hard to think of not seeing her."

"Ah, I thought as much. Tell me this, my dear, what would you do if she were to die?"

Thyatis looked up, her face grim.

"The man who dared touch her would pay dearly," she said in a tight voice. "Why are you asking me all of these questions?"

"Hmm . . . morbid curiosity, I suppose. Sometimes stray thoughts come to me like kittens seeking a bowl of fresh cream and a warm lap. This is the one that you inspire— you brought the lovely Shirin to us, to the island, so that she might be your *phedaia*."

"My what?" Thyatis squinted at the Matron, who raised an eyebrow at her.

"Old Lycurgus may take offense at my misusing a word

he first coined, but I believe it means something like *shield-sister*. That is what you want, isn't it?"

Thyatis was puzzled, her face filled with confusion. "Shirin? You mean, I brought her here—you think I want to send her into battle? Make her an assassin? No, I don't want that . . ."

The Matron raised a hand, forestalling the confusion that was threatening to spill out of Thyatis' lips. "No, dear, not an image of you—rather an equal, or a partner. Someone who matches you in skill and talent. A sweet thought, if an unconscious one."

"Wait. Do you think—will she stay with me?"

"Stay? No one can tell the future—but that is what you want, is it not? For her to be at your side, as long as you live?"

"Yes." Thyatis' voice was very low. The Matron smiled a little, watching hidden thoughts flicker across the young woman's face like deer racing in the sun and shadow of a forest. "I would like that."

"You *want* that," the Matron corrected her, laying her hand on Thyatis' arm. "You have been her protector, her guide, her rescuer. Is that enough for you, to shield her from the pain of the world and be responsible for her? To see that her children are fed and grow up strong? To have her at your back, at the hearth, waiting for you to return from war?"

"No!" Thyatis looked up, her face filled with disgust. "I do not own her!"

"Indeed," the Matron said in a very dry tone, "you do not. And so you bring her to us—not for sanctuary or to be hidden away from the world while the Duchess and these Emperors decide her fate. No, you are much more trouble than that. . . . This is the thing that you desire: a friend, a partner, this *phedaia* who is your equal—not your master, not your slave—who stands at your side. A like mind and will with which to make delightful compromise. Do you want that?"

"Yes," Thyatis said, almost in tears, "I want that."

"Hmm . . . perhaps you will have it, but I wonder if you will be content."

Waves, curling white and pale green, boomed along the shore. The sun stood high in the sky, a bone white disk. The surf ran up the slope of the beach, tumbling black sand around Thyatis' bare feet. Beyond the breakers the sea was a limpid green mirror. She walked slowly along the edge of the surf, her toes digging into the damp sand. The freckles that hid along the tops of her cheeks and over the bridge of her nose were very strong. Her hair was loose, hanging in a heavy red-gold cloud along the curve of her back. A broad plaited straw hat shaded her eyes, cast a deep sea green by the water that stretched away to the horizon. A jug of wine on a leather thong bumped against a swatch of colored cloth she had wrapped around her hips. The tiny strip of sand turned, running under a great escarpment of towering black stone. Here, on the very northern tip of the island, a shelf of bubbled lava made a catchment for Thira's lone beach that faced the outer sea.

Around the corner the beach widened a little, and there, on a low dune of sand, was a pavilion of wooden poles and plaited rope with a canopy of white linen. Thyatis walked up, her feet splashing in the edge of the surf. In the shade of the canopy, Shirin sat up on her elbows, her sun-darkened face wreathed in a slow brilliant white smile. Her hair was loose, too, save for two braids that fell like gleaming dark ropes down on either side of her neck. Tiny blue ribbons were twisted into the braids. She was wearing a thin cotton top and had kicked aside her sandals. On one slim ankle she had clasped a silver bangle with tiny golden bells. Thyatis knelt under the canopy and turned, brushing the sand off of her feet.

"Ah, you burn so easily." Shirin sat up and ran her fingers over Thyatis' shoulder. Flakes of blistered skin peeled away under Shirin's fingernail. Thyatis hissed and turned. Shirin's face was only inches away. Her dark eyes seemed enormous. Thyatis was suddenly conscious of her friend's breast pressed against her arm. The thin cotton seemed incapable of keeping in the heat of Shirin's body. Thyatis tossed her head a little, clearing rogue curls from her eyes. She felt a little cold. "Yes, I'm not fit for these sunny skies. Some nice gray rain is what I need . . . ow!"

"Shhh." Shirin moved a little behind her, her quick fingers undoing the knot at the back of Thyatis' top. "I've some lotion for this. Auntie gave it to me."

Cool liquid dribbled on Thyatis' naked back, and she hissed in surprise.

"Stay still," Shirin commanded, rubbing her hands together. They made slippery sounds.

"Yes, Your Majesty," Thyatis grumbled, trying to look over her shoulder. Shirin moved directly behind her, sliding her long olive legs on either side of the Roman's thighs. Thyatis blushed at the sensation, skin sliding across skin like silk, and hid her face in her hair. Shirin smoothed the oil over her back, cool and tingling. Thyatis sighed happily and relaxed a little.

"Northern barbarians," whispered Shirin in her ear, her breath a cool touch on Thyatis' shoulder, "should stay out of the sun. Indoors, you know, where it is safe and dark. Otherwise, they become lobsters and blister horribly."

"Indoors?" Thyatis said, though she had trouble talking.

"Yes," Shirin purred, sliding closer, her nipples brushing Thyatis' back, hands slick with oil gliding over her shoulders and inner arms. "Someplace comfortable and warm, like a bed."

"A bed?" Thyatis whispered, then she gasped a little as Shirin's warm, slippery hands cupped her breasts. Shirin moved slowly, her palms covering Thyatis' nipples as she worked the oil in slow circles. Thyatis groaned a little and turned her head to Shirin. The Khazar girl's lips were waiting, soft and moist, and her mouth was hot, and Thyatis felt everything disappear but the sensation of Shirin's hands on her breasts and the kiss. She lay back slowly, and Shirin slipped into the curve of her arm, one leg sliding over her thigh. Thyatis' hand tangled in Shirin's hair.

The wind off of the sea ruffled the canopy of the pavilion, making a slow, rhythmic creaking sound in counterpoint to the muted boom of the surf echoing from the high dark cliffs. The tiny bells on Shirin's ankle bracelet chimed softly as she moved.

〇━〇━〇━〇━〇━〇━〇━〇━〇━〇━〇━〇━〇━〇━〇━〇

ANTIOCH, ROMAN SYRIA MAGNA

〉〈

A young man, his red hair burned almost white by months under desert skies, jogged along a long line of wagons. They were huge, towering over the running youth; their great slab-sided wheels caked with pasty white dust. Striped canvas awnings had been raised over many of them, shielding their contents—crates, barrels, boxes, pretty young men and women in chains, sheaves of arrows and spears, bolts of cloth, statues of marble and bronze and porphyry, wicker baskets filled with plates and bowls wrapped in straw, amphorae of wine and oil in wicker carriers, thousands of wooden crates marked with the sign of the Imperial Persian Mint—all this protected from the rain, wind, and sun that afflicted travelers in northern Mesopotamia. Yoked to each wagon were teams of oxen or mules. The beasts lowed mournfully at the young man as he ran past, his military-issue sandals slapping rhythmically on the hard-packed dirt of the road. In the meager shade of the wagons—for the sun was high and the heat of the day was becoming intense—thousands of soldiers in worn red cloaks and battered armor sat or sprawled, their sunburned faces streaked with road dust.

The young man jogged along, passing the last of the cargo wagons, and found the road crowded with long lines of horses standing in the heat, their heads low. Their riders, Eastern Empire–armored *tagmata*, squatted at the side of the road in clumps. Some had servants holding parasols of dirty orange silk or linen for shade. Most were sleeping by their horses with a blanket for a pillow or talking in low tones. Everyone the young man passed seemed weary and worn from the long march. Beyond the horsemen the road turned and ran down a long slope to the banks of a broad river. The man smiled, seeing the cluster of wagons and pennons that marked his own unit, parked by the side of the road like everyone else. He slowed his pace; the long slope down the hill was marked by cracks in the stone paving and uneven footing. Now he was passing cohort after cohort of infantry—most of them sunburned Goths and Germans muttering in their half-familiar tongues—sprawled in a great mass along the sides of the road. Their officers watched the young man as he passed, but none tried to halt him.

The *caduceus* and lightning-bolt brooch pinned to his cloak lent him gravity, at least, despite his youth. The Emperor gave members of the Imperial Thaumaturgic Corps a great deal of leeway. Even the Germans and other barbarians who filled out the ranks of the Legions acceded to their prerogatives. Angering a wizard was thought to be bad luck—and, well, it was.

The young man swerved off to the side of the road and stopped, leaning forward with his hands on his thighs, breathing hard. A wagon rumbled up the hill, drawn by straining oxen, carrying six great oaken barrels bound with copper staves. The gurgle of the water in the barrels was the sound of sweet relief for the thousands of men lining the road. The boy smiled at the wagon master as he drove past and flashed a cheery salute. This was the third water wagon he had passed since he had left the city gates. He jogged on, closing his nose and mouth against the trail of dust rising behind the wagon. He felt good, running like this, feeling his body exert itself. He ran on down the hill.

*   *   *

A thicket of broad-shouldered men in armor of wired iron rings parted, allowing a grime-covered courier to enter the field tent. The man doffed his leather hat and batted at the thick yellow dust, knocking it to the ground. Two more guards, these hard-bitten–looking Latins with narrow eyes, checked the rider's weapons and cloak. Satisfied, they nodded him in.

Sitting at a folding camp desk, a thin, dark-haired man looked up at the intrusion. The courier knelt on one knee, making the half *proskynesis* that was the rule here in the East.

"Hail, Emperor and God, Galen."

"Greetings, lad." Martius Galen Atreus, Emperor of the Western Empire, put aside his quill pen and rubbed ink from his hands. His was a narrow face, with a cap of lank black hair crowning his head. His eyes were bright and filled with a fierce intellect. "What news do you bring?"

The messenger stood and pulled a scroll case from the carry bag at his waist. He was very young, perhaps not sixteen, with close-cut hair and a determined expression. "A letter, Caesar, from the Empress."

Galen's hand, reaching for the copper tube, paused for just an instant, but then he took it and placed it on the desk. The Emperor summoned a smile and motioned for one of his servants. "Well done, lad. You need a bath and a shave and someaught to drink. Timos, see that this fellow is looked after."

The elderly Greek nodded, smiling at the courier, and escorted him away. The Emperor stared at the message tube on his desk with trepidation. Poking at it with a tentative finger, he rolled it over and saw that it bore the sign and seal of his wife, Helena, Empress of the West. He sighed. He had last seen her in Catania, at their villa on the island of Sicily. There had been words exchanged between them—heated words he had since regretted. She had sent him letters; he kept them in a chest with his personal items, unopened.

In Rome, and even before, when he had been stationed

at Colonia Agrippina in lower Germania with the Legio First Minerva, Helena had gained herself a towering reputation as a poet, writer, and sly-handed wit. Her sharp tongue had laid low many a city. Her volume of correspondence was legendary. In the course of one week at Agrippina, while it rained constantly and steadily, he had watched her write seventy-three letters. He valued her mind above all else. The thought that he had found a mate of equal or greater intelligence still filled him with hidden wonder.

But when it might be turned against him in vitriolic anger? He dreaded her wit, even he, the master of half the known world. Galen took the message tube in his hand and weighed it, feeling the papyrus sheets slide back and forth inside. *What*, he thought, *if it is good news?*

A memory of Helena, her dark eyes sizzling with anger, her voice raised in a particularly cutting rebuke, her thin hands wrapped around the neck of a Minoan jade vase older than the city of Rome, came to mind. He put the message tube down. He had started that argument with a particularly ill-advised remark about her health. She had finished it. *Perhaps later, when I've had a bit to drink.*

"Well?" The young woman's voice was laced with anger.

The young redheaded man shook his head and shrugged. He smiled broadly. He was long used to her anger and abrupt nature. "Nothing to do about it, leader of five. Things in the city are in such a snarl that it will be days before we see the cool porticoes of the agora or even the inside of an inn."

"For this I send you off to scout?" The young woman snapped, smoothing back short raven black hair. Luminous dark eyes and high cheekbones marked her face, which was radiating disgust. Like the redheaded youth, she wore a travel-stained crimson cloak with blue edging and a heavy shirt of leather embossed with bronze studs. The brooch that held her cloak to the shoulder was silver, though, where his was copper. "For this we sit in the heat for hours, waiting for you to finally report in?"

The young redheaded man shrugged again and took a long drink from a leather wine flask that the other man in the back of the wagon had handed him. It was sour *acetum*, but that was to be expected on the third day. It cut a little of the dust in his throat.

"You may bring down the wrath of heaven upon me, O Zoë, leader-of-five, but I cannot change the will of the Emperor! Say, is there anything left to eat?"

"No, Dwyrin," the dark-haired youth growled, leaning back against the wall of the wagon. "We ate everything out of boredom while waiting for you to return."

"Odenathus, you are a pig of a Palmyrene!" Dwyrin punched the other youth in the arm. "Not so much as a fig left, I suppose!"

Odenathus shook his head, his face a study of pitiful sorrow. "No so much as a fig," he said, "or a date, or a roast hen, or a wheel of cheese, or bread or dried meat or wine, or, well, anything . . ."

Zoë made a snorting sound and swung out of the back of the wagon, brown legs showing for a moment under her leather kilt. Out of the wagon she settled her belt and checked to see that her issue short sword, the *gladius*, was snug at her side and that the other gear was in place. Dwyrin and Odenathus crawled to the back of the wagon and sat, their legs swinging over the tailgate.

"Leader-of-five? You, ah, you going somewhere?"

Zoë spared Dwyrin a short, pointed glare and lifted her hat, a battered straw thing with a long woven tail that lay down over her neck, off a hook twisted into the side of the wagon. "I," she said, "am going into the city to find us lodging and food. You two are staying here, with the wagon and our gear. And I do mean *stay* with the wagon. Do not *leave* the wagon by the side of the road—not even for a moment—to be stolen by drunken Sarmatian mercenaries . . . like last time."

"Wait a grain." Dwyrin was frowning. "Won't the army

be pitching camp here? Why do we have to find our own rooms?"

Odenathus laughed, a short barking sound like a dog with a bone caught in its throat. "At Antioch? The luxurious, sybaritic, legendary Antioch? At the end of such a victorious campaign? Oh, my fine Hibernian friend, the Emperor would not retain his red boots with such an act! This is the first fruit of victory for these legionnaires—this city by the languid waters of the Orontes, this city of green bowers and fine wine and beautiful women under the cedar-covered slopes of Mount Silpius."

Dwyrin frowned again, this time at Odenathus. "You wax eloquent, O Buzzard. You've been thinking about it too much, I think. Then it will be a free-for-all in the city—that would drive the centurions insane trying to keep everyone in line! How can the Roman army move without a camp at the end of each day?"

Zoë shook her head and rolled her eyes in despair, hands on her slim hips. "Oh, there is a camp all right, a permanent one, the *campus martius* west of the city on the far bank of the river. And there everyone will—in all regulation—pitch their tents and count heads. But for another week or two, the army will spend all this loot and coin that we've dragged back from Ctesiphon in the brothels and tavernas and gambling dens of the city . . . which, as you can see, has put my dear cousin into a frenzy at the thought that he might not be able to sate his animal lusts." She tossed her head in the direction of the crowded road and the waiting soldiers. "It will take a day or more to sort them all out and get everyone a pass to go into the city. By then all of the good inns and hostels will be filled with officers and the common soldiers will be sleeping in the seats of the circus or back in the *campus*, on cold ground. I want a bath and I know what to do to get one. But the two of you have to stay with the wagon while I take care of it."

Odenathus' bushy black eyebrows narrowed, and he regarded his cousin with a suspicious air. "But you won't be forgetting us while we're dragging this monster wagon around the narrow streets of the city to get to the *campus* and enduring the foul voices of the centurions, will you? You wouldn't mind sneaking off and finding lodgings at the villa of the Palmyrene consul all by yourself? That would offer some fine lounging about in baths and steam rooms, with servants to brush your hair and trim your nails. Even, dare I say it, a handsome young slave or two to oil your back . . ."

Zoë raised one razor-sharp eyebrow at Odenathus, then made a clicking sound with her teeth. "I was *planning* on securing lodging for all three of us, if not in the consul's *domus* then in one of the inns that the city owns here. However, if you would prefer to deal with such matters yourself, feel free."

Odenathus raised his hands in surrender at the icy tone in her voice.

Zoë nodded and brushed a lock of fine black hair out of her eyes. "Get the wagon to the *campus*. I'll find you if you don't get lost and fall in the river and drown."

Dwyrin smiled, watching the young woman as she strode away up the road. She seemed to have grown into herself in the year that he had known her—though she was still impatient, quick to anger, and filled with suspicion, she seemed to have found some kind of balance in the exercise of their common art. Command suited her, too, it seemed, and he was glad the burden had fallen on her. He leaned back against the slats that made up the sides of the wagon, and closed his eyes. His thoughts turned, as they often did in this dry and barren land, to memories of his youth and rich green of Hibernia and the cold dew on the leaves in the morning.

"That is a fine sound," Dwyrin said, motioning with his cup into the firelit darkness. "Those voices were made for singing under an open sky like this."

Odenathus, leaning back on his bedroll, nodded. In the light of the little oil lamp hanging on the back of the wagon, Dwyrin could just make out the motion of the other man's head. Across the camp, now filled with the wagons of the army and thousands of tents and pavilions, clear, strong voices were raised in song. The night seemed hushed around the sound. It rose toward the vault of heaven, where the stars shone brightly in the clear desert night. Dwyrin could not make out any words, but their cant was that of great deeds done in war and the hunt.

"They are called Blemmye," Odenathus said as he refilled his own cup from the amphora of wine that they were sharing. "They come from the black kingdoms at the source of the Nile—Meroë and Axum. Many of them serve the city as caravan guards or mercenaries if there is a war. There are few men fiercer or braver in battle. I think they dislike our cities, though it is said that their homelands have great *metropolei*, as large and prosperous as Alexandria or Constantinople."

"What are they singing about?"

Odenathus shook his head. "I don't know. They sing in battle, too, to give their limbs strength and drive fear into the hearts of their enemies. My grandfather once said that they account themselves in paradise if they die with a song on their lips. He valued their service greatly."

Dwyrin put down his cup and stood, stretching his sore back. It had been a long day, though thankfully the army had not passed through the middle of Antioch. A pontoon bridge had been put across the river just above the first of the islands that marked the urban center. That had allowed the Legions to cross to the western bank and take a road through fields and past little farms to the great *campus martius* that was maintained for the army stationed at Antioch in times of peace. Still, getting the heavy wagon across the bridge—all twisting under their feet as the great planks shifted with the weight of a dozen wagons and hundreds of men—had been some work. His upper arms and the backs of his legs were still burning with the memory. But here they were, in their allotted space, with their tents pitched and a warm dinner digesting.

Around them the camp was oddly quiet, even with the distant singing. Each cohort had pitched their tents in the regular avenues of a traditional Roman camp, but the lively bustle that usually marked the army at rest was missing. Dwyrin could hear snores echoing from the nearest tents, so he guessed that everyone had turned in early. Tomorrow, or so the centurion had said, a quarter of the men would get passes to go into the city, while the others would rest or refit the wagons. Within the week, or so rumor ran, cohorts would begin marching down the military road to the coast and the port of Seleucia, where the fleet waited to take them home.

Dwyrin was not sure what to think of that. He had come into the army in such haste—the fruit of a last-minute levy upon the thaumaturgic schools of Egypt—that he had no sense of a home other than the tiny academy of Pthames. Before that, he had been only a child, barely aware of the world around him, living in contented ignorance in Hibernia. His birth-home seemed impossibly distant now, months of sea travel away at the far end of the Empire, or even beyond, really. The fierce tribes of his home island had never bowed to Rome, nor had Rome cared. Britannia was the edge of the world as far as the senators were concerned. Now he would return with the Wizard's cohort to Constantinople and find himself in a new home—a vast city only briefly glimpsed in his time there before—among hundreds of sorcerers and magicians that served the state and the Emperor.

"Do you miss your home?" Dwyrin tried to keep the sadness he felt from his voice.

"The City?" Odenathus looked up, his long, lean face half in shadow from the lamp. "Her golden walls and bright gardens filled with hyacinth and bougainvillea? Her long arched passages and arcades, her broad, wide streets of paving stones, and the glory of her sunsets? Yes—I do. I miss my family, too, all of them. My sisters and their squalling brats, my gruff old father . . . I miss all of them."

The Palmyrene youth paused, looking off into the darkness. He seemed pensive. He turned his wine cup over and over in his hands.

"Zoë wants to stay, you know, here—in the army. Our term of service was just for this one campaign—a gift of the city to the Empire, but I think she has found something here she lacks at home. A sense of place and purpose. In the city, what could she be? A wife? Do you think that would suit her? Do you feel this is your home now? I know you were thrown into this, too."

Dwyrin squatted, his own face pensive now. "I don't know. The witch finders took me away from my family when I was very young and then sold me to the Empire. The School was my home for a long time, but I cannot go back there, either." He turned his arm and rolled up the sleeve of his tunic. The small, dark mark of the Legion enlistment brand was plain against his naturally pale skin. "Now I have this, and an enlistment to complete. There is really no place else to go. I will miss you two, if you leave. We had some good times, this campaign. We didn't die, for one! We lived and came home rich—if we don't spend it all here in a brothel."

Odenathus half smiled and scratched his head. He stowed his wine cup. "I know what you mean, barbarian. Don't you think she should be back by now?"

"Yes, she should."

Dwyrin stood again and looked out into the darkness. Across the river, the walls of the city were marked with hundreds of lanterns and torches; long lines of jewels hung against the night. "Well, we haven't a pass between us— I suppose we shall have to sneak out of the camp and search all over the city to find her. No telling what kind of low or depraved places we might be forced to endure before we find her."

"Hmmm . . . ," Odenathus said, staggering to his feet. The amount of wine he had swilled was telling a little. "Wouldn't do if we were caught missing. Best to leave a note for the centurion."

"Yes," Dwyrin said, smiling, "we should leave something behind." He pinched out the wick of the little lamp, and it became very dark around their wagon. He found his cloak by feel and could hear Odenathus doing the same. The Palmyrene youth crouched by the entrance to their tent for a moment, and there was a soft, muted flash of light. When he stood, the dissonant rattle of a snore echoed from the canvas. Dwyrin smiled in the darkness, looking up, seeing a vast abyss of velvet night and winking stars. The River of Milk stood out very clearly in this thin desert air.

"Let's go," whispered Odenathus, and they crept away through the neatly lined streets of the camp.

Even with the streets liberally supplied with oil lamps at the corners, it was dark in the district behind the Daphne Gate at the southern end of the city. Dwyrin stumbled on a missing paving stone, then skipped ahead. Odenathus was walking slowly, carefully surveying the porticoes of the town houses. This was an upscale merchant district—the streets were clear of both rubbish and drunken Roman officers—though it was so late that everyone must be sound asleep. The Palmyrene stopped, staring up at an elegant house with four graceful pillars arrayed across its front. He stepped up to the door, which was dark. The common lamp in the recessed doorway had gone out. Odenathus put his hand against the portal and cocked his head, listening.

Dwyrin stood in the street, looking at the other houses. Each showed little traces of light and habitation; plants on the upper balconies, the muted gleam of a candle or lantern in the entrance hallway. They seemed to breathe in the cold night air; even sleeping, they showed some trace of habitation. This house, the one that they had stopped before, seemed empty and cold, abandoned.

"Are you sure this is the place?"

Odenathus frowned in the darkness, his hand brushing against the carved pillars at the sides of the doorway.

"These are the traditional signs of the city; two palms placed at each entrance. I have been here once before, with my grandfather, and thought this was the street. But this house feels empty, which is very odd. I am sure that Zoë would have come here first, to find the consul. If she did, and everyone was out, I don't know where she would have gone. . . ."

Dwyrin decided, pulling his cloak around him a little tighter. It was getting cold in the deep of night.

"Let's go find someone to ask where they went. Perhaps they moved to a bigger place."

"Wait," Odenathus said as the Hibernian turned to walk away. "We've had far too much wine this evening. We're not thinking clearly." He fumbled in the big leather carryall that he wore, like Dwyrin, strapped to his thigh. After a moment he pulled out a triangle of ceramic tile. "Ah," he breathed in satisfaction. "Do you still have yours?"

Dwyrin nodded. His was buried, too, down at the bottom of the carryall. But he found it by touch, just the way their old teacher Colonna had taught them. The piece of tile was notched on one side, chipped a little, but he held it out and Odenathus' piece slid into place like a long-lost mate.

"Do you remember the memory chant?"

Dwyrin bobbed his head, the feel of the smooth tile in his hand had already brought it back to him. He slowed his breathing and let his mind fall quiet. For a moment, as he approached the state of waiting and nothingness that his old teachers had called the Entrance of Hermes, he felt the muzziness of the wine lap around his consciousness, but then it was gone. Once he was centered, he let his sight unfold, focused around the two pieces of tile in their hands. The darkness fell away, replaced by glittering light where the broken pieces of tile met, then deep violet-and-blue patterns that rippled and flowed along the bricks of the street and the fronts of the houses. Odenathus stood out, a burning flame coiling and twisting where he stood. Dwyrin knew that his own hand, his own arm and body, were the same—rivers of fire tracing the beat of his heart and the surge of blood through his veins.

All this, as he must, he pushed away from his consciousness. An old voice, raspy with years of shouting commands over the din of battle, echoed in his memory: *The second enemy of the sorcerer is too much sight, which drowns the mind in confusion and destroys your focus.* The broken tile remained, though now joined by two ghostly cousins, one brighter and one darker. In all, the four made a square; a common flooring tile of fired clay, smooth on one side with a dull blue glaze.

"See," Odenathus whispered, "Eric's is lost, but our leader-of-five still carries hers. Lead us on, O thoughtful hound!"

Dwyrin drew his tile away, slowly, as did Odenathus. The two ghostly fragments hung in the air for a moment, then the fourth—that which had died with poor, Eric in the dark cold of a river before the Persian city of Tauris—vanished, and the third: It spun in the air and then darted away. The Hibernian laughed, for they would have to run to catch it. Behind him, Odenathus cursed vilely. He hated running.

A dim flicker of dawn was showing in the east and it was cold on the docks, but the broad-shouldered man seemed impervious to the chill. A cutting spring wind came out of the mountains behind the port, but even with bare arms and shins the man remained on the pier. His guardsman loitered a dozen paces behind him. Wrapped in their own furs and armor, they doubtless thought the cold spring pre-dawn to be refreshing, but then they were Scandians and Rus to a man and used to far worse than this. Beyond the end of the stone pier the massive shape of an Imperial galley pulled slowly away. Its great sail was still furled, and a dozen longboats crowded around it. Hawsers stretched from the backs of the longboats, and the rattle of their oars and the rhythmic chanting of the rowers carried easily over the open water. The quinquireme *Juno Claudius* would take almost two hours to make it out of the harbor to the open sea. Its decks were awash with light from sea lanterns, too, and the man on the dock could make out a small figure on the rear deck.

The man raised a hand in farewell, his stern face creased for a moment by a smile. He waved, and the small figure on the deck waved back, her pale white face showing for a moment. On the distant ship she moved and held up a warmly wrapped bundle so that he could look upon the face, tiny and indistinct, of his child again. His hand dropped, and he tugged the hood of the cloak over his head and its blond curls. He turned, hearing the rattle of boots on the dock behind him.

"Royal brother! The Empress is safely away?"

Heraclius, Emperor of the Eastern Roman Empire, *avtokrator* and Augustus of the Greeks and Romans, turned to face his younger brother. The open, guileless smile was gone, and now his face was stern, the face of the ruler of half the known world. He raised his hand and clasped his younger brother's fist in his own.

"Greetings, Prince of Persia. Yes, Martina and my son are safely away. They will reach Constantinople and the luxurious refuge of the Imperial Court within the week. While we, dear brother, will still be here sorting out men and cargo and loot and assignment. . . ."

Theodore smiled broadly at the sound of the *loot*, his teeth gleaming white in the thicket of his red beard. Where Heraclius was tall and broad, his younger brother was thick and stout, but each showed an echo of their father's pugnacious nose and blunt personality. The Prince was clad, as was his wont, in cavalryman's leather and half-armor, with a long blade slung over his back and riding boots. While the Emperor's cloak was a thick red woolen with purple thread and ermine edging around the hood, the Prince affected a shorter, Oriental-style cloak with a fur lining and a silk outer layer. Heraclius had considered mentioning to his sib that though Theodore was Prince of Persia in name, he need not ape its fashion—but he had held his tongue.

"Have you eaten yet? My servants are already up and making breakfast . . ."

Heraclius shook his head, no, and began walking along the pier. His brother fell in beside him, as he had done for twenty years, and the guardsmen shook themselves out into a loose cordon around the two. Some of the hulking Northerners went ahead, while others trailed behind. Their cold blue eyes watched everything, even the dark water, and their hands rested easily on the hilts of their swords.

"I have summoned the Legion commanders to join us just after full light," Heraclius said, "and we will begin deciding which cohorts and regiments will return to the capital, or to Egypt, and which will stay. Many of the men will need to return to their farms or cities in the provinces—some will stay, and new recruits will need to be trained and integrated into the existing cohorts. Too, we must decide what to do with the two Western Legions that my brother Emperor left with us."

"Garrison duty!" Theodore scoffed, sneering. "Over-the-hill infantry and engineers! If we were besieging something, we would bless them, but now? We have little use for them at all. He would have done better by us by leaving all those fine Sarmatian knights whom he brought with him."

Heraclius eyed his younger brother carefully; the rash youth who worshiped the horse-god and the romance of the *equites* was showing strongly. For a moment he reconsidered placing his brother in charge of the newly won Persian provinces, but then pushed the thought aside. *I need someone I can trust there*, he thought. *He will have able advisors and cooler heads to counsel him.*

"Emperor Galen left us something we are sorely lacking, dear brother—experienced infantry and specialists. They will be pure gold to train the four new legions of recruits that will be debarking here within the next six months. You will need more than cavalry to—"

Rashly, Theodore interrupted his brother. "I don't need *infantry* to rule Persia! I need horsemen and lots of them!

Persia is vast and lightly populated. I need cataphracts to garrison and rule and patrol. Infantry works here, in Syria and Egypt and Asia, but there?" He pointed east, past where the slopes of Mount Silpius were tinged with pale dawn. "There I need cavalry, and four legions of it will not be enough."

Heraclius caught his eye and raised an eyebrow. Theodore closed his still-open mouth. "I have considered this," Heraclius said after a moment. "I have been considering a massive change in the way the provincial armies work, both within the Empire and in the newly won provinces. In fact, I want to revise the way we raise armed men for war and support them in the field. You know I have made some changes already . . . well, that is only the beginning of this. The current provinces will be reapportioned into themes. . . ."

The Emperor and his brother left the dock, deep in discussion, and the guardsmen drifted with them, a silent wall around the two men. Dawn continued to swell in the east, and light grew on the stone quays and docks of Seleucia. Hundreds of ships rode at anchor there, fat-bellied transports and massive galleys. The streets began to fill with dockworkers and draymen. Too, long lines of Western Imperial troops—notable by their archaic-seeming armor and ready discipline on the march—began to file out of the town, directed by bull-voiced centurions to their ships. They were the last to leave, following their Emperor, who had put to sea the day before.

The ghost of the broken tile faded away, touched by the sun, and Dwyrin came to a halt. The finder had led them on a merry chase through darkened streets and empty plazas, across public gardens and bridges. Finally it came to the eastern gate, the same that Dwyrin had passed through on the great road the day before. The gate was closed for the night, and the torches of the guard post were guttering low. Still, with the dawn coming, there was enough light to see.

"Where now?" wheezed Odenathus from behind him. The Palmyrene was flushed and panting hard.

"I don't . . . wait. There she is."

A huddled figure was curled up at the base of the gate, just by the guardhouse door. Even in the poor light, Dwyrin could pick out the red cloak and dark boots. He ran up, his heart in his mouth, suddenly stricken by unexpected fear. *What if someone had attacked her? Taken her by surprise with a knife?*

"Zoë?" His voice sounded harsh in the still air. He crouched down, Odenathus at his shoulder. There was a sour smell of far too much wine and something else, a bitter aftertaste hanging in the air. "Leader-of-five?" He touched her shoulder.

The figure lay still for a moment, then twitched away from his hand. Dwyrin sighed, smelling the wine, and motioned with his head for Odenathus to take her other arm. Together they dragged her up. The hood fell away, and Zoë's head lolled to one side. Her front was covered with dried vomit and other less recognizable stains. A cheap pottery jug fell out of her hand; she had been wrapped around it. The jug cracked on the pavement, but it was empty. Only a dark trickle, like sap, oozed out of it.

"Oh, that is a fine smell," Odenathus gasped. "What was she drinking?"

"What was she thinking, you mean. So much for finding us soft beds and a hot bath!"

Zoë's eyes twitched open, and she snarled at the light. One weak hand raised, trying to shield her eyes from the dawn. The two lads dragged her away from the gate, into the shade of a nearby shop awning. Soon the street would be thick with peasants coming into the city with wagon-loads of vegetables and goods to barter or sell. Dwyrin lowered the girl to the steps in front of the shop, carefully holding her head so that it did not bang on the wall.

"Zoë?" Odenathus said, crouching down next to her, his lean face worried. "Do you know us?"

The leader-of-five lay back against the door of the shop,

her hair in a tangle around her head. Odenathus held one hand in his own. The other moved feebly to her face and brushed the hair away. Slowly, her eyes came open, but only to a narrow slit. Even the pale dawn was too much light for her head.

"Odenathus?" Her voice was weak and raspy. Dwyrin realized that Zoë had been crying for a long time at some point. He looked around, hoping to spy a well. There was a public fountain at the side of the little square behind the massive construction of the gate. He jogged to it, pulling a wine cup out of his carryall. It only took a moment to fill the cup with water and hurry back to the front of the shop.

He stopped, hard, when he reached the two Palmyrenes. Odenathus was staring up at him with the face of a dead man, bleached almost white, his eyes stunned. The young man sat down heavily, staring sightlessly at Dwyrin. The Hibernian turned, his mouth half open in surprise, and flinched back from the pure brilliant hatred in Zoë's eyes.

The young woman staggered up, one hand against the wall, the other curled into a claw. "Bastard Roman!" Her voice cut the early dawn stillness like a knife digging into flesh. "Your blessed Empire has destroyed us, every single one of us!"

"What?" Dwyrin managed to blurt before Zoë crossed the space between them and slammed her fist into the side of his head with all her strength. Pain blossomed from his ear, and he staggered back.

"Filth-eating Roman pig!" Another punch slammed into his throat and he rolled, gasping for breath. She pounced on him, fists raining down, cracking against his ribs. He scrambled away, breaking free, and sprang up, his face flushed with anger, his own fists raised. Zoë circled, howling insults at him, her entire body electric with rage. She jumped in and Dwyrin blocked her strike frantically, pushing her away. She spun, kicking at his knee and he barely skipped back in time.

"Irrumator! I will kill you and everyone who looks like you, you . . . urk!"

Odenathus, tears streaming down his face, tackled his cousin from behind, and they crashed to the cobblestones together.

"Help me!" Odenathus shouted at Dwyrin as Zoë thrashed and squirmed like a marsh eel under him. Dwyrin piled on, trying to pin the woman's legs. There was a flurry of arms and knees and a searing pain as she bit him. Dwyrin managed to push a wad of cloth between her teeth, and then they had her pinned down. Odenathus was gasping for air, barely able to speak for the tears that were dripping from his face.

"What . . . what is it?" Dwyrin was winded, too, and his head was still ringing like a temple gong.

"Oh, my friend, I cannot believe it . . . our city has been destroyed."

Dwyrin stared at the shock and horror on his friend's face, barely comprehending what he was saying. "Destroyed? How—I mean, who? The Persians? Not the Empire!"

"I don't know, that was all that she said—but I saw it in her face; everyone is dead: my mother, my father, my sisters, everyone I grew up with, or knew . . ." Odenathus began crying then, and Dwyrin could only hold his friend tightly, while all the pain in the world seemed to pour into them from the open sky.

It was night again, as seemed fitting. Dwyrin sat alone in front of the tent. The wagon loomed over him on one side, and the little oil lamp gleamed, shedding a wan circle of light that included him and the edge of one of the big wagon wheels. He had stopped crying with the help of nearly a gallon of wine. The rest of the cohort was in the city, spending their Persian loot and indulging in whatever desire or pleasure they harbored. The night felt very cold and empty. Both of his friends were gone. Zoë had left the same day that they had found her at the gate. Odenathus had tried to convince her to stay, if only for a few days, but she had refused to listen and had stalked out the eastern gate of the city, alone and on foot. After their brief struggle in the plaza, she had refused to look at Dwyrin, and even Odenathus seemed only marginally acceptable to her. Dwyrin had stood in the midday heat of the gate, watching her figure dwindle into the distance. Watching her go, he felt cold, even with the Syrian sun burning down on him.

Dwyrin raised his cup to his lips. The wine didn't even taste like anything anymore. The open hatred that Zoë had shown him had left its mark; he felt stunned and wounded. But there was no blood to stanch or any wound to close up. Some of the grape dribbled down his chin to stain his tunic, but he did not notice.

Odenathus had left only a few minutes ago. He had been crushed by the news, too, but had managed to struggle through and process his paperwork to leave the Imperial Army. Given the confusion in the city, it had not taken that long—only four days of waiting in the stifling heat of the government offices. He had taken his cash-out with a grim face, weighing the heavy gold coins in his hand for a long time before he turned away from the tribune's field desk. He had taken his things and Zoë's from the wagon and loaded them onto a string of heavily laden camels he had purchased in the agora of the city. Dwyrin had watched him dully, already drunk and lying in the shade of their tent. Odenathus had said nothing to him, though Dwyrin hoped that the easy-going Palmyrene did not bear him the same virulent hatred that Zoë had conceived.

Dwyrin put the cup down by the amphora. It was empty; he could tell that by the weight. The little lamp exhausted its oil and flickered out. "Do you want me to come with you?" His voice echoed in the darkness, but there was no one there. He had wanted to say this to Odenathus, but his throat had seized up and he had not. "I will, if you just ask."

The young man lay down, curling his body up against the cold desert night. Stones dug into his back, but for the moment he did not care. "We should stay together," he whispered. "We're a strong team."

High above the camp, on the soft breeze of night, an owl hunted, crossing the moon.

◻◯◻◯◻◯◻◯◻◯◻◯◻◯◻◯◻◯◻◯◻◯◻◯◻◯◻◯◻◯◻◯◻◯◻◯◻

THE CAMPUS MARTIUS, ROME

)(

Gaius Julius squatted in deep shadow, a cloak of dark red wool pulled around his shoulders and falling to the ground around his boots. It was cold among the ornamental trees, but the old Roman grinned to himself in delight. Indeed, he was flexing his fingers and feeling the smooth movement of the muscles and tendons in his hands and arms. Clouds covered the sky, shrouding the sliver of moon that had been peeking over the tops of the cedars.

"What are you laughing about?" Alexandros' voice was edged with tension and excitement.

"I was thinking," Gaius whispered over his shoulder, "that when I was a living man I would be feeling creaky and old and frozen to be out here at this hour. But now? Now I feel fine! I can sense the cold, but it does not dig at my bones."

"Huh." The Macedonian did not seem impressed. The young man continued to fidget, constantly checking the tools and bags that were strapped to his body. "I can still run farther and faster than you. My grip is stronger."

Gaius Julius smiled in the darkness, hearing the utter confidence in that mellow voice. His heart tugged at him, even cold and dead as it was. Something about the golden youth drew him, subtly demanding that he follow the other blindly, even to death. The old Roman was wary and cynical and knew that he had once exerted the same influence upon others. Perhaps he wouldn't be fooled.

"True," the old Roman purred, "but you died so young and with so much left undone. Your restored body is much fitter than mine, which is old and worn out, abused by success . . . but even so, I do not feel the cold, and that pleases me."

Alexandros made a muttering sound and slouched down against the bole of one of the pine trees. They were crouched in hiding within the first tier of the trees. A curving road of gravel and close-fitted stones lay before them, and beyond that the looming circular shape of a great mausoleum. Across the way, a barrier of rosebushes encircled the base of the tomb. High marble walls rose up to a terrace planted with more ornamental trees—lemons and olives intertwined. Two more terraces rose above that, each sloping with green turf and bright flowers. Finally, surmounting the whole edifice, a great brick drum faced with travertine rose up, topped with a stout marble pillar and then a shining golden statue.

Gaius Julius looked up, seeing the thing glittering in the light of torches held in brick recesses at its base. His lips curled into an involuntary sneer. The sight of his so-called nephew, arm raised in benediction over the city of Rome, the crown of laurels upon his head, galled him. "Puppy . . . ," he hissed, feeling envy and jealousy stir in his heart, bitter as wormwood.

"Ware." Alexandros touched his shoulder lightly and pointed.

A dozen yards away was a break in the neatly trimmed rosebushes and a flight of steps that led up to a pair of broad golden doors. The gold panels gleamed in the light of a pair of lanterns that were hung up on hooks at either side of the doorway. A pair of stools and an iron brazier were placed in an alcove just off of the doorway. Two soldiers in the garb and armor of the Praetorian cohort had been sitting there, talking quietly and warming their hands over the coals. Now they had stood up and were belting up their swords.

"The watch is changing?" Alexandros tensed at Gaius' side, ready to sprint out across the road.

Giaus shook his head and laid a calming hand on the young man's shoulder. "No, not yet. They must be going *utmeiant vel in meiantur*, as it were."

The two Praetorians made a careful survey of the dark woods and the sky, then picked up one of the lanterns and sauntered off into the stands of carefully manicured trees. Gaius watched them carefully until the light of the lantern disappeared between the trunks. Then he nodded to the Macedonian. "Let's go."

The long bronze key jiggled in the lock. The doors, up close, were ornamented with incised pictures of the events surrounding the birth of the Empire. Gaius Julius cursed softly and pulled the key out. The hexagonal lock mechanism was sticking. He pulled a second key from a leather bag hanging from his broad military belt. Behind him, Alexandros moved a little, his *lorica* making a soft metallic rattle. Gaius shook his head, trying to get the helmet he was wearing to set properly on his head. It had been a long time since he had worn a full legionnaire's kit, and the heavy armor on his shoulders and chest was slowing him down.

Soft politician, he chaffed at himself. The boy doesn't even notice the weight of this metal.

The second key clicked and engaged a pin somewhere in the lock. Gaius put his shoulder into turning the handle and there was a grating noise as a bar rolled back inside the lock. The complaining screech it made seemed very loud, but Gaius knew that the sound would die quickly.

"Here we go," he said as the door cracked open a little. He put the key away and pushed at the panel. It swung in, creaking on its hinges with the weight of all that gold on the door facing. The dim light of a few candles showed inside, and Gaius slipped in with Alexandros close on his heels.

* * *

"This is all that is left? Just ashes?" Alexandros rolled a carved marble cylinder between his hands, making a tic-tic-tic sound on the top of a malachite coffin. The cylinder was about a foot long and intricately carved on the outside with scenes of men and horses and women and ships and the Forum. "It's so small!"

"Not much left of a man, once he's been rendered down." Gaius was poking around with a dagger in the niche that had held the cylinder. "I guess you Macedonians weren't much for saving the ashes, though."

"No," Alexandros said, his face pensive. "Wind and fire take the dead back to the gods. I sent many of my men home that way." Gaius looked up, hearing an unexpected thread of melancholy in the young man's voice. In the months since the youth's resurrection he had possessed a singularly positive demeanor. The events of his death and return to life did not seem to bother him at all. Gaius had thought that the youth only took it as his due to rise from the dead and walk among the living again.

"I wonder why they did not honor me that way." Alexandros' face, half illuminated by the light of the little candle-lantern that Gaius had brought, seemed drawn and marked with terrible fatigue. "Did they hate me so, after all that we had suffered together, to leave me trapped on earth, imprisoned in gold and lead?"

Gaius slid the dagger back into its copper sheath and stood up carefully and backed out of the brick-lined alcove that held four recessed niches. He untied a silk bag from his belt, where it had been held with purple string, and shook it open.

"Even in death," Gaius said absently while he worked, "you inspired both hate and love, my friend. If the histories are true, terrible arguments followed your funeral. Blows were struck while you lay in state, your body not even cooled. Some of your generals demanded that you be sent to the gods immediately, but others argued that you should be returned to Macedon to be buried in the city of your fathers. Each man strove to better the others in his grief and love of you."

Alexandros made a face at this, and shook his head and shoulders, trying to shake off the image.

"They were dogs," the old Roman continued, his gray eyes in shadow, "that tore themselves apart once the pack leader was dead. It took two years for an army of craftsmen to build your funeral car, your catafalque. The great generals were already murdering each other for control of your Empire before you were even properly buried. It is said, by men who were there, that the procession of your funeral train took five days to pass. No greater tribute has ever been paid to a living man. Entire nations were beggared to build your coffin."

The Macedonian sat down heavily on one of the steps that lined the tomb. It was cold and dark, lit only barely by the little lantern. A domed ceiling receded above them, lined with niches and statues of the dead. The pale circle of light from the candle barely touched the young man's feet.

"Why did they dishonor the traditions of my people so? The sky should be my burial place!"

Gaius looked down upon the boy, weighing his words. "You were no longer a soldier, deserving a soldier's death," he said softly. "Instead you had become the Emperor. The embalmers who laved your body and put the death shroud upon you prayed for a day and night before entering the chamber where you lay, lest they be struck down for touching the body of 'not a man, but a god.' " Gaius knelt, putting one gnarled old hand on the boy's knee.

Alexandros looked up, his eye makeup streaked with tears. "And my son, my wife? My mother?"

"Dead," Gaius said in an even, toneless voice, "within a decade of your own death. Murdered by those in the court at Pella who hated you. No heir of your body survived. It is said that your son by the Empress Roxane, born after your death, was strangled by Cassander. Even your magnificent Empire did not survive your death. By the time the funeral procession left Babylon for the west, five kingdoms stood where you had built one pan-Hellenic-Persian Empire."

Alexandros stared back the Roman, his eyes stricken. "To the strongest—" he whispered, and held a hand to his mouth.

"Ruin," answered Gaius Julius. The old Roman felt for the boy, feeling at last the death of his life's work and great dream. "All in ruin within a generation. In the end, they even fought over your body. You never reached ancient hallowed Aegae; you never lay in the tomb your soldiers had raised there with their own hands. Even in death, you were more than a corpse; You were a veritable icon and a prize for the most ambitious."

Alexandros snarled and stood up, his fists clenched. A vein throbbed in his forehead. "Was there no banner of passage for even my corpse? Did they not even honor that, the journey of the dead? Who stole the coins from my eyes?"

One of Gaius' eyebrows inched upward at the vehemence in the boy's voice. He suppressed a smile with difficulty. The irony of it all was delightful. *Why shouldn't the body of a living god be a tool in the hands of conniving men? Is it not so now?*

"The one who styled himself your brother, of course," Gaius said, gesturing at the cylinder on the floor. "The wily Ptolemy stole your entire funeral away as it passed through Syria. He took you back to Egypt and installed your body in a fabulous tomb—the *Sema*—where it lay in state for six hundred years. I looked upon it, when I was alive, and made homage to you—as tens of thousands had done—in the Temple of Ammon."

"Ptolemy"—Alexandros frowned and smiled at the same time—"that rascal! He would . . . he would dare such a thing. Boyhood friends should never be trusted. They never show proper respect!"

Seeing that the boy was ignoring him, Gaius dragged

the marble cylinder over to him and began unscrewing the top of the urn. It was old and had once been sealed with a band of bronze, but that had corroded away in the intervening centuries. Gaius' hands were quick about their work; even with the door carefully locked behind them, there was no telling if the sentries might notice something and enter the tomb to investigate. The lid was still sticking, though. Gaius rummaged in the leather bag and found a cold chisel and a mallet. The mallet's head was lead with a woolen fleece tied around it to muffle noise. He wedged the cylinder between his boots and carefully lined up the chisel.

"Who won?" Alexandros' voice was businesslike again, and the melancholy tone had vanished. "When dogs fight, a new leader rises. Was it Ptolemy? Antiochus? Pray not that panderer Seleucus!"

Gaius looked up, the mallet in one hand and the other on the top of the cylinder. "None of them, lad. In the end it was brash young Rome that won. By the time of this puppy"—he tapped the top of the cylinder with the mallet—"the Republic had overthrown all of the *Diadochai*—your successors—and conquered the world. Well, save for Parthia . . ."

Alexandros frowned and looked around the tomb as if for the first time. "This was the best you could build, after all that? It's barely bigger than a minor temple in Thebes!"

Gaius raised an eyebrow and bent again to the urn. He carefully positioned the chisel and tapped softly at it with the mallet. After a moment, and despite a seemingly enormous noise, the top budged and then the old Roman could unscrew it.

"Pfaugh! What a must!" Gaius held the urn away from him and nodded at Alexander to hold the silk bag open. Ashes spilled out in a thin gray stream, barely filling half of the bag.

"Must have been a small fellow," Alexandros said, curiously looking into the sack.

Gaius ignored him and tied up the top of the bag with

the purple string. "Take this," he said to Alexandros. "I need to replace the urn so they don't notice."

Gaius wrestled the heavy marble cylinder back into its niche, then pulled yet another bag from his belt. This one was heavy. He pulled the top open and poured the contents into the urn, his face turned away. "Ay! You're complaining about the mustiness of this? What in Hades is that?" Alexandros backed away from the niche, holding his nose closed and breathing through his mouth.

Gaius stepped back and brushed his hands off on his cloak. He was smiling broadly. "Just paying my proper respects," muttered the old Roman. "Make sure everything is picked up."

Alexandros nodded, and they checked the area around the niche carefully, obscuring any footprints in the dust and recovering their tools. There was no reason to leave any clues to their theft. Within minutes they were gone, the tiny bobbing candle vanishing up the stairs that led to the entrance tunnel.

〖◎()-(0)-(0)-(0)-(0)-(0)-(0)-(0)-(0)-(0)-(0)-(0)-(0)-(0)-(0)-(0)-(0)-(0)-(0)-(0)◎〗

OUTSIDE ANTIOCH, ROMAN SYRIA MAGNA

〉H〈

The rattle of wooden practice swords on the heavy plywood surface of a training scutum filled the air over the camp. Among the tents of the Thaumaturgic cohort was an added whine of small rotating fans that stirred the hot, dry air. In one of the larger tents, opened on one side by a raised awning, two men were sitting, discussing a third who sat opposite. The two men were sitting on triangular camp stools, their boots planted firmly on the ground. The young man they were discussing stood at the center of the tent, his hands behind his back, his eyes and body showing great weariness.

"Lad's not good for much now," the first of the two sitting men said, a veteran with a barrel-like chest and sandy, short-cropped hair. "Without the rest of his five, he'll have to be assigned to a new *manus*."

The other, his superior officer, was a redheaded fellow with a stolid, doughy, face. He wore the dress tunic of a tribune, with a gold flash at the shoulders, and an expensive leather belt. There was a streak of grease on his left hand and a smudge by his left ear. Watery blue eyes hid behind twin circles of glass, held in a fragile-seeming metal frame.

"He can't be assigned to an existing *manus*, one lacking a digit? There were losses at Kerenos that have not been replaced."

The tribune looked Dwyrin up and down, measuring him for the market. The Hibernian ignored him, staring dolefully over the heads of his superior officers. Since Odenathus and Zoë had left, he had been at loose ends. There was no one to practice with—all of the other thaumaturges in the cohort were at least a dozen years his senior and far beyond his skills. He had tried to keep up the daily drill, but too much of it depended on having the rest of your five in hand. The Legions taught cooperative tactics in battle thaumaturgy. In the end, all that he had been able to do was practice fire-casting, which came easily to him, anyway, and the most basic wards and signs.

Blanco frowned, considering the tribune's words. He had already thought of moving the boy into one of the empty slots in the other fives. Unfortunately, every five-leader he had approached had angrily rejected the idea. It took too long for a battle-mage group, whether of three men or five, to learn to battlecast together. No one wanted to start over with a boy of little training. Slowly, and with regret, the centurion shook his head no.

"Tribune Quintus, he will have to go to a new-formed *manus* with other fresh recruits."

The tribune sighed, though it was obvious that he was not concerned about the issue. He had rosters to fill out and men to shuffle about. If this boy could fill one of his tally-slots, then so much the better!

"Very well, keep an eye out for him and keep him out of trouble, Centurion. He'll be reassigned once he gets to Constantinople."

Dwyrin felt his heart sink even further. Now he truly had no place here. *It would be pleasant, he thought, to smash in that cowlike face and its bland indifference to my pain.* But he could not. Surely not with Blanco glowering at him, and beyond that? A soldier striking a superior officer got more than the lash, that was a surety. The thought of marching all the way back to the capital, alone and friendless, was a crushing weight.

"Dismissed," the tribune said, turning away to consider his paperwork.

Dwyrin sat alone, in darkness, under a clear night sky. The wagon had been "appropriated" by one of the other units, leaving him with only a blanket and ground cloth for shelter. He could, he supposed, get a bunk in one of the legionary tents that lined the streets of the great camp. There seemed little point in that, not with an endless succession of clear, cloudless, days and nights marking their time in the valley of the Orontes. The moon had not yet risen, letting the vast wash of stars shine in full glory above. The night wind hissed off the desert, too, as he lay on his back, the blanket rolled under his head.

He could hear men on the watch as they passed along the camp-street, complaining about the nip in the wind. That brought half a smile to his lips, even through the deep funk that had gripped him. He was a poor student of the defensive arts that so intrigued the thaumaturges, but he could control fire and heat and warmth. Even enough to summon the latent heat from the rocks that littered the field and wrap it around himself as an invisible blanket. Once, in the high mountains of Albania, he had cursed the other mages for this skill, but it had come easily to him, once he put his thought to it.

Bats wheeled and chittered overhead, hunting in the night. Their voices were indistinct, but they tugged him toward a kind of peace. Bats sounded much the same in his distant home, when they blurred over the fields of wheat and rye. For a moment he wondered why that life seemed so distant. But, in the end, it did not matter. He was sworn to the Legion and owed them twenty years of his young life. *I will be in the Legion until I die.* It was a mournful thought, but it felt true as he thought it.

"MacDonald?" Blanco's voice was unexpected, coming from the darkness. Dwyrin could hear the crunch of boots on the dirt and gravel. "I see you're still awake."

Dwyrin sat up, his forearms on his knees. He was tired, but could not sleep. "*Ave*, Centurion. What brings you out at this late hour?"

Blanco sat, brushing a scorpion out of his way. In Dwyrin's mage sight, it glowed a faint blue as it scuttled away between the rocks. "You," Blanco said in a resigned voice. "I seem to remember tasking someone else with you and your troubles, but she has bunkered off, which means I must deal with these things myself."

"Centurion, you needn't do anything." Dwyrin's voice was resigned, but he had considered this as well as he had sat listlessly in the shade of one of the wagons for the past three days. Like the rest of his unit, he had received three day-pass chits to go into the city. He still had them. The thought of smiling, cheerful people, their faces flushed with wine and dancing, made his stomach roil and brought the taste of bile to his mouth. As long as there was a daily ration of wine and something to eat, he would live. At the moment, beyond that, he had little care. "I'll do my best to stay out of the tribune's sight," he continued, waving a hand. "I'll be no trouble."

Blanco grunted and tapped his fingers on his belt. "That," the centurion said, "is not what I want. You're a soldier in my cohort. You need to learn the skills that the others know, to master your focus and power. You'll ever be behind if you do not. . . . This is my responsibility, to see you trained and equipped and ready for battle."

"Who will train me?" Dwyrin spread his hands wide in disgust. "I hadn't quite caught up with Zoë and Odenathus before they left. Now I'm years behind the next journeyman! I see the regard the other thaumaturges hold for me—not as high as for a trained mouse!"

"This is true," Blanco grated, cutting off Dwyrin's next protest. "No other five will take you. Therefore, you will have to make do with me."

Dwyrin stopped, considering. The centurion was a grizzled veteran, quick with the baton or a mind-whip, never shy about using pain and fear to gain his ends—obedience and instant response. He did not have the technical skill of the other sorcerers, but he had raw power enough and years of experience.

"If you say so, Centurion. . . ."

"I do," Blanco growled, standing up and brushing off his legs. "I'll show you what I can, when I can. It's up to you to make it work."

<hr>

THE CRYPTS OF ALAMUT

))((

Khadames, his face a mask of tension and control, descended a long stair. Thousands of steps, hewn from the living stone of the mountain, receded behind him. Three of the sixteen followed him, their dark masks ill-lit by the fires that roared up from below. The stair turned, reaching a landing jutting out from the rock wall. Fumes rose from the floor of a vast chamber, where great crucibles burned with liquid iron. The air was filled with the

din of forges and hammers falling on ruddy metal. Khadames stepped down, his breath growing short as the air
became thick with noxious vapors. Behind him, the three
of the sixteen marched on, tireless, each carrying twice the
burden of a strong man.

The Persian lord crossed the wide floor, wending his
way between great levered hammers and gangs of men in
dirty loincloths, sweating and cursing the huge machines.
Great chains ran up into the smoke-fogged darkness above,
constantly moving, ratcheting up and up and up. Even
deeper beneath the tunnels and hidden storehouses of Damawand, a river surged in a black abyss. There, great iron
wheels turned, driven by the snowmelt, that power flowing
up through the sinews of the mountain. It drove forging
hammers and bellows, pushing fresh air through the miles
of tunnel, fueling all the constant industry that throbbed in
the heart of the mountain. Khadames reached another stairway, this one cut into the floor of the long hall. Pillars of
brass rose up around the head of the stair, and a crowd of
half-naked Uze squatted around it.

The barbarians, like Khadames, were sweating rivers in
the furnace-hot air, but they still growled at him and
checked his body for forbidden weapons. They had shaved
their heads, and many of them bore new tattoos in black
and red ink. Scars decorated their faces in long stripes.
Each man also bore the mark of his master branded on his
left shoulder—a single black snake, with eyes of blood,
curling into a wheel. The three of the Sixteen they ignored.
Nothing existed in those cold metal shells and clammy
flesh save that which their master desired. Finally, after
examining all of Khadames' accoutrements, they parted,
letting him set foot on the black onyx of the first step.

Khadames had been sitting in his office on the fourth level
above the main gate when the three of the Sixteen had
come to him. The office was notable most for the tall,
narrow shaft that pierced the roof, letting in—for the better
part of the day—a beam of reflected sunlight that illumi-

nated the wooden desk at the center of the room. Khadames had been sitting there, hunched over reams of parchment and papyrus paper, feeling the millstone weight of his responsibilities crush his face into the plank tabletop. Three scribes—two Indian slaves and a Jew—were working in the room, sitting on the thick rugs and working their counting beads. Somehow, as he had struggled to keep the mountain and its inhabitants fed, and deal with the constant flow of strangers who made their way to the great rivergate, he had accumulated a staff.

At night, when he lay in exhaustion on the pallet in the small room behind the office—really no more than a closet with a sleeping platform cut from the wall—he wondered what had happened to him. He had served Chrosoes, King of Kings, for nearly his whole adult life, and most of that time he had been commander of the right wing in the armies led by the great Shahr-Baraz. He thought of himself as a fighting leader, not one of the scroll pushers who always followed the Royal Boar or the King of Kings from palace to palace. Now, in the darkness, he fretted that he was short of men who could use the counting beads and keep track of thousands of items in hundreds of storerooms.

Each day, too, he blessed the five hundred who had followed him and the sorcerer from the wreck of Palmyra across the breadth of the Empire to this forgotten, remote valley. In them he had found the captains and sergeants and drill instructors for a new army. Without them, the slowly accumulating horde of barbarians, hill tribesmen, wayward sons, foreign mercenaries, and feckless wanderers who filled the barracks and dormitories of Damawand would be uncontrollable. But in the five hundred, he had the brutal force and hard-won experience to take the mob and make them an army.

Others had come, too, as individuals and families, making the long, hard trek up the hidden ways that led to the river gate and the scowling faces of the Uze who were stationed there. The sorcerer had never bothered to explain why these peasants and townspeople had come, but when he passed, they bowed low and made an odd sign with their fist before their heart. Many times, Khadames had intended to question them, to ask them what tie or oath or religion bound them to the dark Prince. But time was precious, and the opportunity had never arisen. At first, Khadames had been at a loss to make use of them, but then, while he wandered through the impromptu village that had sprung up at the base of the road that zigzagged up the lower face of Damawand, he had smelled fresh bread baking.

The mountain—a maze of barracks and armories and assembly halls and forge rooms and cisterns and storehouses mighty enough to feed a city—held even more than that. Khadames was used to commanding an army in motion, driving against the enemies of the sons of Sassan. Garrison duty had never been his forte, nor had he ever served as a civil governor. He had never liked the simple truth that armies needed bakeries and seamstresses and carpenters and weavers and laundry operations. For long years in his service to the Boar, he had taken pains to avoid dealing with those matters. But that morning, in the bitterly cold mountain air, smelling the yeasty tang of a loaf pulled fresh from a rock oven, he realized that all of Damawand, with its endless tunnels and vaulted chambers, would soon be filled to overflowing.

That same afternoon, the peasants, artisans, and townspeople who had been drifting into the valley were moved into the mountain. A hundred rooms, long abandoned, suddenly had purpose. At the same time, Khadames had begun to worry about where he was going to get more skilled men and women. Once the full breadth of what was required to support the army that was growing impressed itself upon him, he felt rather ill. That night, Khadames had taken the time to climb the 999 steps to the height of the mountain, to the aerie where the sorcerer sat on a throne of cold stone, looking out upon the world.

"Loyal Khadames, welcome." The full power of that

dreadful voice had long since returned. The human weakness that the general had glimpsed while the sorcerer lay dying was gone. "Is there a problem?"

"No, my lord," Khadames had answered. "I wonder, though, at the patience you showed when I did not understand your purpose in summoning these people. I have only just ordered all your followers moved into the mountain."

The Lord Dahak had smiled, a cold glitter of white teeth in his lean face. For a moment, Khadames felt the full pressure of the intellect and power that lurked behind the odd yellow eyes, and he felt a chill to the marrow of his bones. In that moment, he felt how alone and isolated he was, here at the peak of the mountain, exposed among the clouds. In the short moment, the sky above seemed the mouth of an infinitely deep pit, filled with nothingness. Khadames felt dizzy and struggled to keep from swaying.

"There is still a little time within which to learn, loyal Khadames. I had faith that you would understand and act. If you had not, well, there are others who strive to take your place . . . but I know you. You have not yet been tested to the breaking. Go, see to my people."

One of the three of the Sixteen had spoken when Khadames had looked up from his desk. "You are summoned below," the voice grated. "The master would have you look upon a thing."

Khadames was sure that nothing remained of the men who had climbed the road to the great door and the sign of fire. Some shell of humanity remained; limbs and sinew, hands and arms, but nothing else. Their voices were gone, replaced by a hollow echo. Black pits watched where eyes had once been. The Sixteen did not know fear, or hunger, or weariness. They came and went from the hidden valley and Damawand at the will of their master. The Uze crept aside when they passed, and cursed them silently to their backs. They rarely made a sound. Khadames knew they went about in the world beyond the mountains, carrying messages and undertaking unknown errands for the power that bided its time, here in the mountain.

When they spoke, which was seldom, men hurried to obey. Khadames stood up and carefully put away the most important papers in an iron box. Out of habit, he buckled his old worn saber to his side and shrugged on a light woolen jacket one of the women had given him. It was a faded blue with hunting dogs embroidered along the collar and cuffs in red and green and brown. Then he went out of his office, following the three, and they made their way down into the depths of the mountain. Broad ramps and winding stairs connected the levels, and as Khadames passed, he noted with satisfaction that the buried city hummed with life. Long hallways were filled with bunks and training rooms and men, thousands of men, bent to the tasks of war. Kitchens belched steam and the smell of porridge and roasting mutton. Lines of sweating laborers unloaded wagons and stacked barrels and crates and boxes in storerooms that had lain empty and unused for a thousand years.

Deeper, under the storerooms, they went down into darkness and the forges and armories of the mountain. The valley that lay below Damawand had been stripped of trees weeks ago; just the effort of building furniture for the buried city had consumed the groves of fruit trees and pines on the lower slopes. Now wagon trains of lumber and pig iron and wheat and cloth rumbled up the narrow valley road on a daily basis. Damawand had a huge appetite, but it vomited forth the sinews of war. Above, in his office, Khadames could count the muster of hundreds of thousands of arrows, hundreds of siege engines, thousands of swords, maces, spears, shields, suits of lamellar, and mail armor. Six great workshops, he knew, did nothing but build wagons and a clever Chin mechanism called a wheelbarrow.

Two tanneries worked around the clock, producing a stench that pervaded the second level and turned the valley stream into an odd-colored sewer. Another three were be-

ing built, slowed only by the necessity to bring the great
tanning vats by mule up from the provincial capital of
Rayy. The lack of lumber hampered many efforts. And
below, in the deeper forges, where Dahak was wont to
walk at night, other things were being built of iron and
steel and gold.

The black onyx steps led down three long flights, and then
Khadames felt the air change around him. A layer of mist
shimmered in the stairway, where the fetid hot air of the
forges ended and he passed into a realm of bitter cold. It
was a shock, like plunging into an icy lake. He felt the
sweat on his brow turn cold, and he shivered. The iron
lanterns that marked the upper halls ceased, and he walked
in darkness. But he did not pause, or halt, for one of the
Sixteen walked before him and two behind.

The stairs ended, and a broad passage carried them onward.

Then the passage stopped at a door. It groaned open,
and Khadames felt a breeze on his face. The door was
stone, that much he could hear, and vastly heavy. It ground
slowly across the floor until a thin slat of blue light appeared in the darkness, and then it widened into a doorway.

Beyond, in a room with a ceiling of mortised blocks and
slender pillars, the sorcerer was waiting, leaning over a
long slab of stone. The three of the Sixteen entered the
room and laid, at last, their softly moving burdens down.
Khadames entered, too, though a queasy feeling of terror
threatened to crawl up his gut and strangle him. On the
long table of stone a body lay, one that Khadames had
looked upon before.

Men, women, even children came to the valley by secret
ways. In his office, Khadames interviewed them and
learned a little at a time of the ruin of Persia. Beyond the
rampart of the mountains, beyond their high, snowcapped
peaks, the empire of the sons of Sassan was dying. Rome
had wounded it first; smashing the Imperial Army in the

massive battle at Kerenos River, then driving a steel dagger into its brain by murdering Chrosoes, King of Kings, in his palace at Ctesiphon. But now, with the Emperor and his children dead, the jackals were tearing at the still-living body that remained. The wreck of Ctesiphon had staggered the entire Empire; central control was lost, and the delicate framework of guidance and taxation and aid that had radiated from it was thrown down. The provincial lords and governors, bereft of any guidance from the heart of the realm, had turned inward, trying to deal with their own local problems.

The winter rains had wounded the Empire again. A huge proportion of the able manpower of the Empire had died or been scattered to the four winds in the disaster at Kerenos. Then unseasonably heavy rains in the great flat valley of the Tigris and the Euphrates had overwhelmed the huge collection of dikes and dams and canals that controlled the two great rivers. Massive flooding had ensued, destroying the harvest and isolating large sections of the lowland Empire. The Romans, though they had claimed Persia for their own, even issuing a proclamation that the Prince Theodore of the Eastern Empire was now "Caesar of the East," had not stayed to repair the damage done by their campaign.

Now the fatal wound was brewing. Khadames could hear it in the voice of the latest men to come to the valley. Word had at last traveled the length and breadth of the Empire; from Amida in the west, to Susania in the east— the throne of the King of Kings was empty. Soon, pretenders would arise, and the last vestiges of central control would fail. Civil war would brew up and consume all that remained. Sitting in his office, in the pale shaft of sunlight, Khadames wondered if the sorcerer's ambition reached high enough.

Then he looked out, across the valley, seeing thousands of men drilling with spear and bow and sword, seeing the long lines of wagons inching their way up the road to the great gate, seeing the gangs of slaves digging new tunnels and caverns into the mountains. Smoke and fumes rose above the valley, wreathing the mountaintops in dark clouds.

"Come, loyal Khadames. He is beautiful, is he not?"

The sorcerer gestured, and Khadames forced himself to approach. The body that lay on the slab was withered and turned a little on its side. The face, once handsome, was stretched tight on the skull. The puckered lips of terrible wounds mocked the general, and he could not bring himself to look fully upon it.

"Ah now," the sorcerer said, "he will improve. These men who serve me so well, these Shanzdah"—a pale hand with dark nails gestured lazily to the three of the Sixteen who stood in the shadow—"they will do something about the *parched* nature that he currently exhibits." The hand laid gently on the wrinkled brow of the mummy, then trailed away.

"But there is other work to be done. Look at me, loyal General."

Khadames met the yellow eyes with an even stare. He knew that his freedom had ended the day he had cut his inner arm with the black knife; it was only a matter of how long he could still wake and see the sun above. The sorcerer watched him for a moment, then nodded, slowly, and turned away. "You alone, of all those who serve me, do so without fear in your heart, dear Khadames. I know that you do not put much in flattery." The sorcerer turned, looking back over his shoulder, a merry gleam in his eye.

"But I will pay you a compliment. And in truth, I mean it well. You had no better master or guide than Shahr-Baraz, the Royal Boar, that colossus of a man. And you learned his lessons well. Take heart in his example, for he would be proud of you."

Khadames raised an eyebrow and suppressed a terrible urge to scratch his nose or tug at his whiskers. The obvious good humor of the thing that wore the shape of a man instilled a cold, solid fear in his heart. Part of his mind began to gibber that in this creature's hands there were things worse than death to fear. "Thank you, my lord. I know of no better compliment."

The sorcerer nodded again, seemingly well pleased with the reaction. "Come with me, dear General. I am going to undertake something rather dangerous, and barring that the Boar should suddenly stride among us, I can think of no other I would have at my side."

Beyond the stone table, there was a pit in the floor. It had sloping sides and a ring of low, carved stone around the lip. Cold air breathed from it, making a faint icy mist in the air. The sorcerer went to the edge and stared down into perfect darkness. Khadames, wary of his footing, for the stones were slippery with frost-rime, made his way to the edge as well.

"This, of old, was a door," the sorcerer said, and Khadames quailed inside to hear the murmur of fear in the thing's voice. "I know now some words that may cause it to open. Such a thing must be done—it is my bargain— but I wonder . . . I wonder if it can only be opened a little way."

Khadames turned, staring at the sorcerer, who had turned as well and watched him with troubled eyes. It seemed, in this moment, on the verge of the cold pit, that something of the human had returned to the cruel visage.

"Long ago," the sorcerer whispered, "a boy came to the valley, for there was no place else for him to go. The priests of the fire were still here then, keeping their ancient watch, and they took him in. One day, when he was more than usually reckless, he went into the mountain by a secret way and became lost in the tunnels. He was lost for a very long time. In the darkness his footsteps turned away from the door of fire and led him down into the true darkness.

"After a long time, he thought he heard a voice, just a faint thing, calling to him. There was nothing else to do, no other possibility of escape, so he followed it. It seemed that many days must have passed before he came to a door that he could not open, but the voice was stronger, almost clear enough to understand. Even that muttering offered him hope in the darkness and strength and food and a way out.

"And it wanted so little, just a thought or a gesture. The boy made that bargain."

Khadames watched, almost paralyzed, as a bead of moisture formed at the edge of one yellow eye. The tear, if it was a tear, crept out a little, sliding over the tiny scales that rimmed the eye, and then it froze in the chill air, making a hard little diamond.

"And now, I must make it good." The sorcerer looked away, down into the inky darkness below his feet. "The voice promises much to whoever can open the door, but I can feel the hunger that is waiting on the other side. It is huge—that hunger—and the whole world might not be enough to satisfy it. Do you understand what I am saying?"

Khadames jerked back to full awareness. The sleepy tone in the sorcerer's voice had given away, at last, to an iron tone of command. The general nodded, though there seemed nothing he could do.

Dahak held out his hand. Khadames took the hilt of the black flint knife, feeling the worn leather under his fingers.

"I will speak a word, and the door will open. I pray it will only open a little way. If it does not, if it swings wide, drive this blade into my heart."

The sorcerer shrugged off his robe, revealing a thin torso marked with terrible glassy scars over his chest and upper arms. The cold in the room, which seemed to seep into Khadame's bones, did not seem to bother him. He raised his left arm.

"Here," Dahak said, "between the ribs. It will reach—I have measured it myself. If the moment comes, you must not think, you must strike without thinking."

Khadames hefted the knife in his hand. It seemed to have grown heavier than he remembered, and smoother, too, more like a blade of smooth black glass than the crude flint knife he had used before.

*   *   *

Behind the general, the great stone door began to close. The sound of its grinding passage seemed very loud in the room, though Khadames could not discern a ceiling or walls in the flickering blue light. The three of the Sixteen who had accompanied him had disappeared, though when he turned, he could see their pale fingers on the edge of the door. The stone closed with a heavy thud, and the room was quiet again. Khadames braced his feet against the floor and raised the knife, holding it ready to strike.

The sorcerer ignored him, and turned to face the pit. For a long time he stared down into the darkness, immobile, barely breathing. Khadames felt his arm tire, holding the glassy knife, but he did not waver, holding it poised to slip between the narrow ribs of his patron. Still, the sorcerer waited, watching the pit.

Khadames blinked, feeling his eyelids grow heavy. The faint bluish glow had gone out. For a moment the room seemed utterly dark. Then, below his feet, within the pit, there was a ghost light. It gleamed and danced, seemingly far away, like a shore-bound fire seen from a ship at sea. A great cold flowed up from the pit, and Khadames shuffled his feet, hearing a tinkling sound as ice that had formed on his boots cracked and splintered. He could feel the pit breathing, slow waves of cold spilling up and out over the floor. The light in the darkness danced, seemingly coming closer and closer.

The sorcerer began to hum, deep in his throat, an inchoate sound that reverberated in the floor and the walls. Khadames felt weak again, and managed only though an effort of total will to remain standing. The sound, which had seemed so low and quiet, grew, filling the air and the world.

The light flickered in the pit and then went out.

Khadames blinked again, and squinted. In the complete dark, his eyes began to play tricks on him, summoning up odd white flashes and sparkling lights before his eyes. A slow rain of burning motes passed before him. The air itself seemed closer, and the walls of the room, even unseen, pressed against him.

In the darkness, the sorcerer moved and the hum changed, rising in pitch. High up, almost beyond hearing, Khadames began to hear a whistling sound, or an odd piping. Despite himself, he fell to his knees, kneeling at the edge of the pit, staring down into the utter darkness. The piping and whistling echoed in the room, though in his mind—almost paralyzed by fear—the general realized that though he heard those sounds, they did not come from the air. The knife grew heavy and began to slip from his fingers.

The sorcerer spoke, and that single syllable smote the air, ringing like a massive gong.

Khadames felt the floor rush up and crash against his face. His nose buckled and broke on the lip of the pit, and blood spattered into the air, freezing into tiny spheres and then cracking against the floor. Smoke boiled up from his exposed skin. He tried to cry out, but then all sound ceased and he stared into the pit in horror.

Darkness parted and showed abyssal black. Ten thousand tiny points of light burned in an ebon firmament. The cold that had gone before was swallowed up in icy darkness. Khadames clutched at the lip of stone, screaming in fear that he would be thrown off into that void of night. Great clouds of hanging fire burned and boiled in the titanic realm beyond the door that now yawned wide.

Khadames could feel the stones ripple and contort under his fingers as the door opened, flexing the world around him. There was a massive rushing sensation, and the pit inverted. Khadames clung to the stones, though they writhed like living flesh under him, and the pit became a sky above. At his side, the sorcerer remained standing, though now he did not look down, but out, into the void.

Something was coming, rushing across the abyss of space, there between the dead suns.

Something that blotted out whole constellations with the shadow of leviathan tripartite wings.

It came on, searching, seeking for the door that now stood ajar. Khadames could feel it, though it was still unguessably far away, hunting in the sea of night. Hunting for the scent of living men and a green world under a yellow sun, where blue seas surged against a white shore. Planets cracked into powder in its passage, shattered by the beat of its wings. Suns, bloated and red, withered and were snuffed out, guttering down to coal-black cinders. Khadames scrabbled on the living stone, feeling the heat of blood pulsing under the rock, searching for the glass knife.

The sorcerer swayed, reaching out with a hand for support. Khadames forced himself to stand, though the reptile mind hiding at the base of his skull gibbered and screamed that they would fall up into the sky. Dahak clutched his shoulder, digging sharp talons into the general's jacket.

"The knife," the sorcerer breathed, turning away from the vast impossible shape that rushed closer and closer. The yellow eyes were lit with fire, and Khadames felt the knife pressing into his hand, cutting at the edge of his thumb. Over the sorcerer's shoulder, the sky was blotted out. Something writhed there, in that darkness.

Khadames reversed the knife, the hilt nestling into his palm.

He stabbed, twisting his body into the thrust, feeling the hot breath of the sorcerer on his cheek.

The flint blade met resistance, doughy and stiff, then something parted wetly, and the world inverted. The black sky was below, and the living stone cracked and shattered in the cold. An invisible fist slapped Khadames away like a siege engine's arm, and he felt stone crack against his back. There was rushing air and a shrieking wail. Then Khadames fell forward to sprawl on the stone floor of the room.

The sorcerer staggered back from the lip of the pit, wreathed in cold blue fire. Then he raised an arm, and fire crawled across his chest and upper arms to collect, pooling like mercury, in his open hand. He turned, his lean face lit by the glow. Khadames levered himself up, feeling every muscle and bone groaning in agony. The black knife jutted from the sorcerer's chest, a dark trail of blood seeping down his waist.

Dahak smiled and seemed to swell, filling the room.

"Oh, bravely done," the sorcerer cooed. "Now let us begin."

Nothing human remained in the burning yellow eyes, only an echo of the vast shape that had blotted out the stars.

But the stone door was shut.

The next day, the body that had lain on the slab in the cold room was carried to the height of Damawand, and priests anointed the corpse with oils and spices. Though their eyes had been put out, they labored diligently, laving the withered flesh with scented waters and daubing paint upon it. They worked in great haste, for the desire of their master was like a whip. Jagged stone surrounded the open space where the body lay, and the sky above was filled with troubled clouds. The sun rarely shone down upon the old mountain now, and the valley below was filled with dirty gray mist and smoke.

THE ZAM-ZAM, SOUTHERN ARABIA FELIX

T his is an abomination!"

Scowling, Mohammed pushed through the crowd, the hulking shapes of the Tanukh at his back. Hundreds of men and women crowded into the square, dressed in their holiday finest. Mohammed pressed on, though the crowd was getting thicker and thicker as he approached the gates of the shrine. Around him, turbaned men carried tall poles with offerings and painted cloths hanging from them. Women, dressed in heavy dark dresses, held plates of grain and salt over their heads. A constant noise rose from the crowd like the surf on the distant shore. A tight wedge of Tanukh in black robes, Jalal among them, flowed after their commander. Their swords, still sheathed, held back the crowd like a steel fence.

Within fifteen feet of the temple, all movement ceased, and Mohammed was forced to step back and stretch, looking over the heads of those in the press before him.

Two great doors rose above him, each three times the height of a man, set into a large square brick building. The bricks had been polished smooth and then painted; first black, and then with thousands of tiny white, yellow, and blue stars. Above the doors a great yellow-white disk had been painted—the eternal sun—to signify the center of the vault of heaven. From his youth, when he had spent much time to little end in the precincts of the temples, Mohammed knew that on the opposite side of the building, a moon was painted. At the side of each door, statues loomed, carved from the desert stone in the shape of the gods of distant Greece. Apollo stood on the left, holding a great sun-disk, and Hermes on the right. The likeness was crude and stiff, nothing like the graceful marbles in Caesarea or Damascus, but that had not mattered to the artisans who had labored on them for years.

Jalal shouldered past his master and cracked the man in front of him on the head with the heavy iron pommel of his saber. The man slumped soundlessly to the ground, and Jalal stepped forward over the body. The other Tanukh pushed into the gap, shoving men and women aside. Mohammed opened his mouth to shout a command, but then a way cleared to the foot of the steps before the doors. He shut it with a snap and slid sideways into the gap.

At the top of the stairs, a phalanx of priests blocked passage into the temple itself. They were dour-looking men with long braided beards and heavy caps of black cloth sewn with topazes and garnets. Their long brocaded robes hung to their sandalled feet. Mohammed put his boot on the bottom step, and his eyes narrowed in anger. Some of these men had been acquaintances of his father, in the long-ago days when Abd of the Al'Quryash had served in the temples of the Zam-Zam. Now they held the door to the temple closed against his son, even on a day of worship.

"The Lord who made this world has no shape," he shouted at them as he advanced up the stairs. "You cannot give him a man's face! You are impious to confine him in a form of clay or wood!"

The priests glowered down at him, but did not answer. Mohammed stopped one step below them and put his hand on his saber hilt. Those nearest him flinched, but they did not move.

"You priests, hear me!" Mohammed's voice boomed off the metal doors and echoed across the throng packed into the courtyard. "The murderer of my daughter hides in your house of stone. I will have him, whether you will it or no. Stand aside!"

The priests did not move, and some in the rear ranks linked their arms. In the crowd behind him, Mohammed could hear a muttering rumble begin to rise among the people who had come to lay their offerings on the hundred altars within the sacred precincts. He could hear the Tanukh, too, spreading out on the steps behind him. He raised his arms and turned slowly, watching the crowd with an eagle eye. "Is this your god?" He jabbed a finger out, pointing up at the great weatherworn statue of Apollo. "This is a god of the Greeks, who live far away by the side of the green sea. Is this the god who watches over your flocks? Is this the god who breathes in the deep desert, raising the *kamshin*?"

The faces of the people in the crowd were confused or angry. It was hot in the noonday sun, and little wind made its way into the pillared courtyards of the temples. He caught Jalal's eye, and the burly mercenary shook his head minutely.

"I will show you the voice of the god who made the world!" Mohammed spun, drawing his saber in one quick movement, and it flashed in the midday sun as he clubbed the nearest priest on the side of the head with the pommel. The man's skull made a sharp cracking sound and he fell away, his arms and legs tangling with his fellows. The Tanukh gave a great shout and leapt up the stairs. The priests cried out and cowered away from the glittering blades. Some fell down the steps. Mohammed, sneering, pushed through them to the doors themselves. He put his shoulder to the right panel, feeling the heat of the sun-warmed metal burning through the cloth of his robes.

The door opened, slowly, creaking on ancient hinges. The close smell of incense and smoke and sweat flooded out. Mohammed stepped inside, his saber nosing forward to test the passage.

Around the cobblestoned square a great cluster of temples had grown up over the years. Domes and minarets sprouted from the decaying brick and stone buildings. Narrow passages wound between the temples of great gods and small, opening into unexpected courtyards and upon wilting gardens. Dim passages echoed with the chanting of priests and the stink of incense. All the Zam-Zam lay in a great bowl that had once housed a spring of medicinal repute. Now stone and brick buried the spring and the waters had been driven deep underground. Dozens of wells had tapped it dry, and only a bare trickle could be had. With the flight of the water, the gardens had withered. At the northern end of the maze of whitewashed plaster, facing the city walls of Mekkah some miles away, a great vaulted gate stood.

In the shadow under the gate, a man sat, his lean, dark face creased by a little smile. He smoothed the fine hairs of his beard down and cut an orange in half with his saddle knife. Some of his men, marked by their white-and-blue turban braid, squatted in the shade as well. Some bore wounds from the fighting in Mekkah, but all were alert in the lazy way of hunting cats. Though the gate of the temple precinct stood open, these men held the way closed.

Uri Ben-Sarid looked up, hearing the rattle of hooves on stone, and in the barren upland that lay between the city and the temple he saw men approaching on horseback. Bone-white dust plumed behind them as they came, rising slowly in the still air. Ben-Sarid pushed away from the stone bench and stretched his arms. He yawned and then bit into the orange half. Juice dribbled at the edge of his mouth, and he wiped it clean with the sleeve of his robe. His men, watching with slitted eyes, had seen the dust as well, but they did not get up. Ben-Sarid nodded to one of them, and the tribesman slowly rose and walked off into the twisting passage that led into the city of the priests.

The riders came closer, coming at a good pace. Ben-Sarid stood at the gate, just within the shade cast by the great vault. There were more than a dozen men coming, maybe as many as fifty. He shrugged his tan and white robe off one shoulder, freeing his right arm and the polished horn hilt of his saber. Silver and ruby winked at the cross-guard. Behind him, there was a rustling as his men finally stood, and a light clatter of metal on metal as they drew their weapons. Those men who bore shields shrugged them into place.

Mohammed pushed aside a hanging drape, letting the thousands of tiny onyx beads flow over his arm like a snakeskin. Beyond it, a room opened up. This was the center of the great square building—this room without windows, pierced only by one narrow door—filled to overflowing with thousands of statuettes, idols, graven images, and painted icons. The air was thick, filled with the sweet, waxy smell of hundreds of candles that flickered around the circumference of the chamber. Narrow pathways wound between the looming shapes of great gods and small. On any day but this, a slow procession of penitents and priests would clog the corridor behind and spill into this room, making a slow circuit through it.

But today it was quiet and empty. Mohammed drifted into the room, his saber sliding through the gloom in front of him. Candlelight glittered in its steel depth, and Mohammed moved as quietly as he could. After a moment of listening, he moved to the right, following the twisting path around the tightly packed cluster of statues that stood at the center of the room. As he edged deeper into the room, the beaded curtain shifted a little, tinkling in an invisible breeze.

Behind the statues, the room was darker and Mohammed slowed, letting his eyes adjust to the light. There, at the back of the room, the walls took an unexpected turn. Old stones, still showing the marks of wind and sun, jutted out of the brickwork at an odd angle. A space had been cleared before this ancient remnant, and many small shoe-shaped oil lamps gleamed at its foot. Mohammed felt his heart lighten, seeing that the oldest shrine in this whole dilapidated place still received some small veneration. He bowed his head, feeling memories of his father curling up in his thought.

A candlestick rattled, brushed by the hem of a robe.

Mohammed dodged aside, his boots scattering the little oil lamps. A cold breeze followed the passage of a blade. The assailant, garbed in dark colors with only his eyes showing in the turban wrapped tight around his face, faded back into the gloom. Mohammed grinned, his white teeth catching the candlelight. "Well met, my son!" Mohammed's voice was eager, and thoughts of his father were lost. "Are you mourning, hiding here in shadows with the priests? Do their soft words wash away your blood-guilt?"

Fire sprang up from the spilled oil, lighting the room with dancing shadows. The Bani Hashim Princeling was revealed. Mohammed circled to the right, his saber drifting in the air before him. Sharaf matched him, his saber—clean and shining with oil—almost touching the Quryash chieftain's. There was little space to move, here among the statues, but Mohammed was certain that his bitter anger would carry him through. "Have you wept, boy, knowing that you murdered your wife?"

Sharaf attacked, his blade flickering high and fast. Mohammed parried and parried again, testing his strength against the younger man's arm. The Bani Hashim took a step back, and the echoes of steel on steel faded slowly among the thousands of gods that looked down upon them. Below the ancient wall a pool of oil burned brightly, melting the candles that encrusted the walls. Old colors began to run as the wax melted and the empty eyes of the idols filled with leaping shadow.

"Have you told your sons that their mother is dead by your hand?"

Mohammed leapt forward, his saber lashing out in a blur of cuts. Sharaf barely recovered in time, crashing back into the shape of the god Baal that crouched behind him. The Hashim was quick with youth, though, and Mohammed's blade rang off stone. His riposte cut the air below Mohammed's knees, but the chieftain had sprung up, avoiding the blow. Now there was an exchange at close quarters, blade ringing on blade, in a quick succession of cuts and slashes. Mohammed turned sideways, then chopped down hard, catching the edge of Sharaf's blade, driving the tip into the crumbling brick of the floor. It stuck for a moment, and the older man slammed his shoulder into Sharaf's chest.

The Hashim grunted in pain, and Mohammed jerked his blade back, catching the younger man's chin with his elbow. There was a dull, cracking sound, and Sharaf toppled backward. Mohammed spun, slashing down, and only raw instinct got the hilt of Sharaf's saber up in time to catch the blow. Mohammed's blade ground down, squeaking, against the hilt. The Hashim squirmed on the ground, trying to get leverage to rise.

The fire crept up the wall, filling the air with colored smoke and an odd smell. At the center of the ancient wall, framed by chiseled blocks of fine sandstone, a cube of black rock glittered in the firelight. Its matte black surface yielded neither light nor shadow.

Mohammed snarled, stamping down with all his strength on Sharaf's knee. The Hashim rolled away, but his grip on the saber weakened. Mohammed's blade whiskered, grazing the side of the man's head. Blood spurted, and Sharaf's ear spun away across the floor. The Hashim cried out and clapped one hand over the gaping wound. Sharaf's saber flexed and then sprang out of his hand.

"You will serve her in Hell," snarled Mohammed, slamming his saber down, pinning his son-in-law's neck to the ground. Blood welled up around the tip, thrust squarely through the man's throat. For a moment the youth stared up, eyes wide in horror, feeling his throat filling with blood, and then Mohammed whipped the blade out, sending a spray of ruby droplets across the faces of the gods that loomed over them both. Sharaf jerked, his hands clutching his ruined throat, and then made a bubbling sound as he died.

Mohammed staggered back, anger flowing out of him like the tide rushing away on an Adenite shore. His boots scattered the remains of the burning oil, setting it to lick against the wooden feet of Baal and the other gods. He slumped down against the ancient wall. He felt empty.

Above his head, the black stone was wreathed in smoke.

"Ho! The gate!" The first rider in the column pulled up, his horse snorting and stamping its feet. Uri stood, thumbs hooked into the broad ornamented leather belt at his waist, feet apart, at the center of the gate. He squinted up at the man on the horse. There were more like a hundred riders, as motley a collection of brigands, sell-swords, mercenaries, and landless men as Uri had ever seen. To a man they were filthy from a long haul on desert trails; their beards matted and dark with sweat. Their leader, whose sleek black mare was still eager to run, pirouetted his mount in a circle and then back again. He was tall, with a strong olive face and a neatly trimmed black beard. Uri raised an eyebrow—the chieftain of these rascals was young, barely twenty if a day.

"Greetings," the Ben-Sarid chieftain said, showing an empty hand. "The temples are closed today."

"I heard." The young man laughed, grinning like a cat. "I came looking for Mohammed of the Quryash. I heard he might be here."

"He might be," Uri allowed, "but I think he is seeing to some family business. Perhaps if you come back on another day . . . he might speak with you."

The young man swung lightly down from his horse and tossed the reins to one of his fellows.

"I can wait," the young man said, striding to face Uri. "I have come a long way to see him, to bring him news I know he dearly wants to hear. I had not expected to find the city in such an interesting state, though. I am Khalid, son of Al-Walid, of the House of Makhzum. Well met, Uri of the Ben-Sarid."

Uri raised an eyebrow again and tilted his head to one side. The smirking, confident young man before him did seem familiar—but Uri was certain he knew the faces of every Makhzum clansman in the valley. And this rascal— well, he was none of them! "Well met, then, son of the Makhzum, but I do not know you, and Lord Mohammed is busy."

The young man grinned again, and shrugged in a galling way. "I can wait all day—here in the hot sun, if you like— Grandfather. Will you wait with me?"

The wooden idol of Baal the Devourer burned merrily, the wood spitting and hissing as pockets of ancient rosin caught fire. Jets of smoke billowed from the cracks in the wood and out of the gaping mouth. The other statues, even the stone or ceramic ones, were burning, too, for a thick layer of dust and paint clung to all of them. Flames roared up, licking at the wooden beams that held up the high ceiling. Smoke, flattened into swirling layers, rose up to be trapped against the roof.

Jalal hunched forward on his hands and knees, trying to keep his head out of the poisonous smoke that curled and eddied above him. The heat from the room beat at him like the mouth of a furnace. Behind him, in the doorway, his fellows shouted in fear and cried out for him to return. He did not.

A statue of Baalshamin, cast long ago in some nameless northern city, suddenly shattered in the heat, spraying smoking fragments of pottery across the room. One sliver slashed across Jalal's forehead, making a stinging cut. Despite this and the chokingly hot air, he swarmed forward around the curved path. There, ahead of him, he saw Mohammed slumped under the ancient wall, his head hanging limply to one side. Despairing, Jalal slithered to his side and dug one arm under the chieftain.

Mohammed's eyes opened, and Jalal paused, seeing some flicker of consciousness. Mohammed's mouth moved, but the roar of the flames drowned out all other sound. The Tanukh shrugged and hoisted his commander up on his shoulders. Mohammed struggled, his arm reaching for the wall, but Jalal ignored him and braced for a run through the flames. The smoke had grown so thick, he could no longer see the door.

"Does Mohammed know you?" Uri remained standing in the sun, though the midday heat had grown intense. The rascal in front of him shook his head no, his dark eyes sparkling.

"Ah, but Uncle, I know *him!* Who better than one who watched him for months as he strove against the might of Persia? Who is closer to a man: his cousin, or a man with whom he has crossed swords? No wife studies a husband as I have studied the Lord Mohammed of the Quryash. No man respects him more than I, who have seen him draw a match against the greatest general in the world. Can you say, holding this gate for him, that you know him better than I?"

Uri snarled, and his hand gripped the hilt of his saber

without thinking. The youth shook his head at the movement, raising both hands—empty—to show the Ben-Sarid and the men clustered in the gate. The mercenaries had dismounted and held back a dozen yards or more behind, but they, too, tensed. Uri's eyes flickered over them, but he saw no drawn blade or strung bow. When he looked back at Khalid, the youth bowed to him, as a younger man to his elder.

"I mean no disrespect, Uncle, but I have come a long way to offer my services—mine and my men—to the Lord Mohammed of the Al'Quryash. I knew he would need men skilled in war to follow him, so I gathered those I could and followed him out of the north. My grandmother tells me there has been some blood spilled already—but not all that needs be. I bring him news, too, from the north, from the city of Yathrib, whence we have just come."

Uri nodded slowly and removed his hand from the saber. A hot wind lapped around his ankles. "You were at Palmyra, then? You served the Persian? What did you see?"

Khalid bowed again, pressing his hands together. "I saw a noble city fall, Lord Ben-Sarid," he said. "I saw the Lord Mohammed strive against impossible odds—outnumbered five to one or more—and come within a day's breadth of victory. For months the Persians strove against the walls of golden Palmyra, and each day they dreaded the stroke of his blade. At every turn he was waiting for them, matching wit and skill and cunning not only with the great general Shahr-Baraz, he whom men name the Royal Boar, but with the thing-that-walks-like-a-man as well."

"The what?" Uri scowled at the youth. Many stories had circulated among the followers of Mohammed about the siege of the City of Silk, but Uri had discounted the wilder ones—even when they had come from the mouths of Tanukh well into their cups. Dreadful things had happened in the north, but he could not bring himself to believe all of the stories.

"The dark Prince, my lord." Khalid's face turned grim, and his easy smile faded, leaving him looking old and worn. "The one the Persians name Dahak. The Lord of the Ten Serpents. The destroyer of cities."

Jalal bulled his way through the flames, leaping over a fallen idol that was wrapped in smoke. At the door, the men who had followed him into the warren of the building were gone, and he turned sideways to drag Mohammed through the opening. The chieftain was starting to struggle in his hands, and Jalal was forced to pin the older man's arms to his sides. Grunting, he heaved Mohammed up onto his shoulder.

Even in the hallway outside the burning room, the air was thick with smoke. Jalal staggered under the uneven weight, then righted himself.

"I hear you!" The shout startled Jalal, and he tripped, spilling Mohammed onto the tiles of the hallway. It was dark, only fitfully lit by the flames creeping out of the doorway and drifting along the ceiling. Jalal stared, seeing only Mohammed's eyes, white in the darkness, ahead of him.

"I hear you, Lord of This World!" Mohammed staggered to his feet, ignoring the smoke that curled around him. "I will act! These abominations will be thrown down, and you will be raised into your rightful place!"

Jalal stared around in concern—no one else was in the hallway. The echoes of Mohammed's shouts were swallowed by the darkness and the crackling roar of the flames. Jalal scuttled forward, keeping his head low and out of the slow billowing waves of smoke. Mohammed swayed from side to side. Jalal captured one of his arms again, and yelped as a fat yellow spark snapped between the chieftain and his hand.

"I hear you, O Lord of This World! I will tell men what I have seen and . . ."

Mohammed's voice faltered, and he suddenly slid sideways. Jalal caught him, cradling the older man close to his chest. The smoke was worse, flooding the hallway. Jalal crawled forward, hoping that he remembered the way out.

It was becoming very hard to breathe. Mohammed muttered in his ear, senseless words, rambling and incoherent. Jalal began pushing Mohammed ahead of him, but the air was thinning quickly. Sparks began to dance in front of the Tanukh's eyes and his ears began to ring. He gritted his teeth and crawled onward.

A terrible heat beat against his back, and he heard the sound of stones cracking in the fire.

"For ten nights and ten days, the Persians raged against the city. And when they were done, not one stone remained upon another. Temples were thrown down, and palaces shattered. Those people who had survived the fighting were herded into the wide avenue that ran from the Damascus gate to the great Temple of Bel. Tens of thousands of them packed the street. We were outside the city, in the hills, but we could hear the sound of their voices, raised to the night sky, pleading and begging for mercy."

Khalid paused and uncorked a leather bottle that hung at his side. Uri waited, quiet and patient, while the young man drank from the flask. When he was done, Khalid offered it to the older man, but Uri shook his head. The young man stared out at the desert, and the bleak hills that rose above Mekkah.

"The Persians chained them, all those who still lived, to one another. Later, I saw the iron links themselves, lying scattered in the street. Then the Persians left—every man in that army marched out of the city and over the hills, into their camp. Only he remained; the Lord of the Ten Serpents. It grew quiet in the city, and we strained to hear, but there was no sound. No weeping, no cries for mercy, no voices raised in fear. Then . . . then you could feel it, in the ground, like the rattle of dry bones, and you could taste it, in the air, a sour taste of bile and copper. My men fled, running over the crest of the hill, back to the warm fires and the wine bottles of the Persian camp."

Khalid's eyes narrowed to slits, and Uri could feel tremendous anger welling up in the young man.

"But I? I waited and I watched, though every instinct in my breast screamed at me to run. I waited for *him* to emerge, to come forth from that place where he had fed. I waited for hours. At last, when the dawn was close to breaking, I thought to creep down into the valley and cross the siege-trenches and the fields of broken tombs, to look into the city itself. But then he came forth, a shape of black deeper than the night. I could not see him, no—not in that darkness—but I could feel him, even across the breadth of the valley."

Khalid paused and unsnapped a pouch at his belt, drawing out a sliver of pale white bone. He held it up, and Uri frowned at it—the bone was almost translucent, passing the light of the noon sun through it like a prism. The youth turned it back and forth in the sun.

"Sometimes, when you are watching the flocks, out beyond the lights of town, you can feel the night hunters come. Do you know the feeling? Yes, all of us have felt it—something almost inaudible alerts us as we drowse at our watch to the soft pad of great paws on the sand. Or you are in a city, and a man hunts you, then you can feel it in the air—something is watching you. This was worse— this was being a mouse, hiding beneath a stone while the dragon walks past. I fell down, even before that thing came forth from the gate of the city, and screamed in fear. It felt so gigantic; oozing out of the wreckage of the gateway, like an enormous spider that was fat with blood. I tried to burrow into the earth, but the stones stopped me."

The youth held up his hands, and Uri saw that they were scarred along the fingertips and some of the fingernails were missing. Khalid half smiled at the blanched look on the older man's face.

"I left within a day—as soon as I could ride again. We passed thousands of Persian soldiers on the road, fleeing mindlessly from that same fear. We went southeast, into the deep desert, and I did not look back. One of my men, who caught up with us at the oasis of Sabkhat-Mukh, brought me the bone fragment."

Uri coughed, clearing his throat. He had heard parts of the story before, but he had not believed it. He still wasn't sure he believed it.

"Why did you come here? Why seek the Lord Mohammed?"

Jalal stumbled out of the entranceway of the temple, his lungs burning with smoke. He carried Mohammed on his back, though the older man was beginning to struggle against him. The priests had run away, leaving the Tanukh milling about in front of the building with the hundreds of supplicants who had been trying to enter the temples. Smoke spilled out of the doorway, climbing into the clear blue sky. A great heat radiated out of the portal, making the air shimmer.

"Help me," he gasped at his comrades. The two closest jumped up the steps and took Mohammed from him. The passing of the weight was a great relief to Jalal; the smoke was cutting at his lungs, and he wanted nothing more dearly than to cough furiously. He knelt on the steps, hacking and spitting.

"O impious men!" Mohammed shook off the hands of the two tribesmen who were trying to help him down the steps. "In this place, something holy lives, something that came from heaven on a bolt of fire, a sign and a portent to guide us, to give us focus to our faith! Yet you spit upon it, crowding this house that Abraham built with dross and foul images!"

The Tanukh drew back from Mohammed, who was shouting at the crowd. The people stared back in interest— they had come for the religious festival, but the politics of the city had closed the doors of the temples to them. Now this man was ranting, much like the priests of Baalshamin, or Apollo, or any of the other gods whose images thronged the precincts of the sacred well and the black house. Some of the priests of the smaller temples along the outside of the courtyard shouted back at him. A few people in the crowd were staring at the flames rushing out of the door of the House of the Gods, wondering if it were a sign. Some thought it was part of the festival, and raised their voices in a chant.

Jalal crawled across the steps and tried to capture Mohammed's arm. "You cannot constrain the word of god in stone or wood!" Mohammed slapped Jalal's hand away and turned, staring back into the fire that was roaring in the doorway of the temple. Sheets of heat haze billowed out of the door and up, sending smoke rushing into the higher air. The heart of the doorway burned with a white heat, and the copper facings on the doors were beginning to bubble and melt.

"The dread King Nimrud cast Ibrahim into a furnace, but his faith carried Ibrahim through in safety." Mohammed's voice rolled across the courtyard, amplified by the shape of the doorway, rising above even the hiss of the flames and the groaning sound of stone and brick shifting in the terrible heat of the fire. "This flame will cleanse the heart of the Zam-Zam, this sacred place."

Mohammed began walking forward, his hands held out away from his body. Hot wind rushed out of the furnace, blowing his hair and beard back.

"I hear you, O Lord of This World! I hear your voice calling me! I come to the call! I—"

Jalal tackled Mohammed from behind, crashing to the tiled floor in front of the door. The flames were rushing out only inches away. Jalal swallowed a scream as his hair caught fire and his beard began to smoke. Mohammed turned, his mouth open, but Jalal could not hear anything over the hissing roar. Something gleamed in the older man's eyes, some blue-white flame that sparked and flared like a hammer in the forge. Jalal felt the air around him shift and the heat of the flames was driven back. Mohammed pushed him away, trying to stand, but Jalal—his heart filled with a sudden unexpected fear—lunged forward and smashed his fist into the older man's face. Mohammed went down, his eyes wide in shocked surprise, and blood spattered from his nose. Jalal piled in, smashing his scarred knuckles down, and the chieftain went out like a snuffed candle. The glittering blue-white light faded and then was gone.

There was a huge cracking sound as the roof of the temple suddenly collapsed. Flames billowed out in a rush, sending smoke climbing even higher into the heavens. Jalal rolled away from the door, dragging his master—now safely unconscious—down the steps. The other Tanukh scurried up the steps to haul them away. The crowd stared up at the pillar of fire and smoke in amazement. This festival day would be remembered for a long time!

A rumbling sound drew Uri's attention and he turned, looking back into the temple precincts. He raised an eyebrow, seeing the huge column of black smoke that was rising from the center of the holy grounds. He lifted his chin, pointing at the distant fire, and four of his men jogged off down the narrow street with drawn swords. At his side, Khalid moved restlessly, but the Ben-Sarid chieftain shook his head slightly.

"The Lord Mohammed is about a matter of his own personal business. It may require some stringent measures to flush out the man he seeks. We will wait awhile and let him deal with these matters himself."

Khalid sighed and motioned to his men, who had tensed, to stand down.

"This matter—it would be something to do with the murder of his daughter by the Bani-Hashim? His own relatives, cousins and uncles and aunts?"

Uri turned, his eyes narrowed and his forehead creased in a fierce expression. "Guest-right and hospitality were violated by these men, my young friend. The chief of this clan attempted to knife the Lord Mohammed while they sat at dinner—in his own daughter-in-law's house! These Bani-Hashim dogs are without honor, and they will pay in blood for it!"

Khalid bowed slightly and raised his hands in a plea for peace. "I know this story, Lord of the Ben-Sarid! My grandmother took great and lengthy pains to explain it to me. Still, I wonder if the Lord Mohammed will not bring misfortune to himself and to his house by burning down the temples of all the gods that bless Mekkah and this place with their presence."

"Huh!" Uri snorted dismissively. "There is only one god, and he cares not for graven images."

One of the Ben-Sarid ran back down the street, his cloak askew and his blade bare in his hand. "There's a riot," he shouted to the men at the gate. "Lord Mohammed has fallen!"

Uri cursed and raised his voice, shouting over the babble of the men crowding the gate. "Half of you stand at the gate, the other half with me!"

The Ben-Sarid chieftain threw his sand-cloak aside and took his sheathed sword in one hand. He and a crowd of his men jogged off down the street at a good pace. Khalid, still standing in the gateway, did not follow, but motioned to his men to dismount and join him in the shade of the gatehouse. Within minutes, all of the Ben-Sarid were gone, hurrying off to the sound of people shouting and screaming.

"Well," Khalid said, turning to his men with a feral grin, "it seems we may enter the city to pay our respects to Lord Mohammed after all."

A wall toppled, sending a river of bricks crashing to the ground. A line of statues came with it; the gods of Meroë and Sa'na were shattered by the collapsing wall. White marble limbs bounced across the ground, shorn from their bodies. The crowd in the courtyard, now swollen to hundreds of people, drew back in a flood. The core of the old building now stood revealed, wreathed in rushing orange flame and clouds of billowing smoke. At the edge of the square, the Tanukh had fallen back into the long, pillared arcade, forming a ring of steel around Jalal, who was carrying the unconscious Mohammed. Part of the crowd, urged on by the priests who had fled when Mohammed had broken into the temple, muttered angrily and circled outside the blades and spear points of the tribesmen.

Jalal glanced around warily. The situation was becoming ugly. The novelty of the burning temple was fast wearing off, and the realization that the foreigners had violated their holy of holies was gaining ground. A rock sailed out of the milling crowd and bounced across the walkway. Jalal stepped aside from its path. "There," he rasped to his men, "into the passage."

A narrow corridor opened on one side of the arcade, leading between two buildings. Heaps of refuse lay against the mud-brick walls, but it seemed to offer a way out of the square. Jalal hurried into the passage, turning sideways to keep from cracking Mohammed's head against the walls. More stones clattered behind him, and the mutter of the crowd rose into shouts of anger and a shrill whistling. The other Tanukh filed in quickly behind him, shields raised behind them against the rain of stones and garbage.

Khalid entered the square slowly, his men arrayed in a phalanx around him, weapons bared but held low and out of sight. Thousands of people crowded there now, shouting and screaming. The pyre of the old temple building burned merrily, filling the air with sharp reports as stone and brick shattered in the furnace-like heat. The mob surged first this way and then that. The festival offerings lay scattered on the ground, trampled by many feet. A profusion of spears, rakes, and scythes danced above the heads of the people. Khalid held up a hand, halting his men at the end of the street. He looked around carefully, and cocked his head, listening, but he did not hear any sound of steel on steel. The noise of the crowd was enormous, echoing off of the building fronts and reverberating in the recesses of the arcade that surrounded the square. Many priests seemed to be shouting or chanting at the mob, but none of them had managed to focus the anger that was simmering in the afternoon air.

Khalid motioned with his hand, and some of his men

moved ahead, into the crowd. He looked around again but could not make out the blue-and-white *kaffiyeh* of the Ben-Sarid anywhere. More of his men drifted past, forming a quiet wedge that pushed its way through the people milling around the square.

Another cracking sound echoed from the burning temple and another wall collapsed, spilling bricks and blazing timbers into the square. Only some inner wall still stood, wrapped in fierce yellow flame.

Jalal peered around the corner of the building, his cheek pressed to the rough whitewashed wall. The street beyond was empty, bounded by blank-fronted buildings and a few recessed doorways. The street itself slanted away, winding off through the two- and three-story houses. The dim sound of the mob in the temple square barely penetrated over the rooftops.

"Let's go," Jalal barked in his rough voice. His throat felt like sandpaper and tasted of smoke. "We need to get back to the northern gate."

The Tanukh slipped past, their sabers and long knives at the ready. Four of them now carried Mohammed in a litter. The chieftain was very pale and still. Jalal watched him being carried past, and worry clouded his long, lean face. He wondered if he had struck too hard. The fear had been real, though, and the strange gleam in the man's eye had set him on edge. Jalal turned the corner after the last of his men were past. He was not familiar with the maze of the temple precincts, and he wondered how they were going to find their way back to the gate.

The street ended in a blank wall of crumbling brick and a climbing vine with small red flowers. The lead men were already rattling the doors that led off of the cul-de-sac. Jalal cursed as he came up. Then he froze and motioned his men to the sides of the street. An echo of running feet rippled along the walls behind him. He stepped to the nearest wall and flattened against it. One thick thumb eased his saber from its sheath and he held the leather scabbard across his chest, his left hand wrapped around the hilt. Likewise, his men crouched against the walls, waiting. The four men with Lord Mohammed carried him to the back corner of the cul-de-sac and placed him gently on the ground.

A youth in a long robe and a small striped blue cap trotted around the corner, breathing easily. He had a wooden staff in his hand. The Tanukh crouched at the corner looked down the street behind the lad after he had passed and held up two fingers. Jalal cursed again—silently, this time—and stepped out in front of the running boy. The lad pulled up sharply and opened his mouth to cry out. Jalal's fist cracked him on the side of his head, felling him like a poleaxed ox. The staff clattered to the ground and rolled away to fetch up at one of the doorsteps. The Tanukh tensed, ready to meet the dozen men who could now be heard running closer.

Jalal drew the saber, feeling the metal slither out of the sheath. The air seemed clearer to him, the surfaces of the walls and the edgings of the doorways very distinct.

Khalid stood at the edge of the milling crowd, looking upon the burning ruin of the great temple with wry amusement. Around him his men made a living wall of shoulders and interposed bodies. The fires in the crumbled building were still burning merrily, consuming the shapes of the gods and demons who had filled the temple. The crowd was still angry, but directionless. The priests of the outer temples mocked those who had served within the great building, while those worthies accused the "lesser" priests of black treachery. Khalid turned around, slowly, watching the roofs of the other buildings and feeling the tension in the air. Soon something would spark this tinder, and blood would flow. He smiled again, catching the eye of two of his lieutenants. "It is a sign," he cried out, his clear, young voice rising easily over the bickering of the crowd. "The corruption of the temples will be cleansed with fire! Cast down these foreign idols!"

Around him, people paused, halting in their arguments or gossip. Khalid nodded to his lieutenants, and they took up the cry as well, moving through the mob, their voices raised.

"Throw down the idols! Out with the foreigners! Cleanse the temples!"

Within a grain, one of the priests of Zeus Pankrator shoved a Mekkan merchant who had taken up the cry to "drive out the foreigners." The merchant pushed back, and one of Khalid's men, moving through the crowd behind the two men, threw a wine bottle. The bottle cracked open the head of one of the acolytes of the Pankrator Temple. The acolytes shouted abuse at the crowd and threw paving stones back. The Mekkans, hit by the stones, returned fire.

Within ten grains, the temple square surged with a full-blown riot. Priests were knocked to the ground and trampled by the mob. Massed fists beat acolytes barely out of childhood into bloody ruin. Stones and brickbats and offal filled the air as each temple faction raged against the others. The fire burned on, unnoticed. Khalid and his men regrouped near the entrance to the square, still raising a cry to "tear down the idols." The mob, tearing itself to bits, surged up onto the steps of the arcade.

Khalid laughed merrily and ordered his men back. They hurried along the passage, catching a glimpse of the fighting in the square from time to time through the archways that led out into the center of the temple district. After a few grains they reached the front of an imposing temple to Baalshamin. A cluster of priests huddled in the doorway, under towering statues of the god's winged servants. The scent of incense and myrrh and cardamom drifted out from the half-closed doors. The flickering glow of lanterns and torches highlighted the shaven heads of the priests. Khalid stopped, eyeing the doorway with interest. His men stopped, too, gathering around him.

"I wonder," Khalid said to his lieutenants, "if there might be idols that should be cast down in this place?" His eyes lingered on the rich vestments and heavy gold ornaments on the wrists and necks of the priests. His lieutenants laughed, too, a cruel sound, and nodded their heads.

"Yes, Captain, these idolaters must be *rich* in sin to affront the great gods so!"

"Ay! Lord Uri—you'll come to your death, charging around corners like that!"

Jalal resheathed his saber with a *snap*, trembling a little now that his body no longer expected imminent violent action. The Ben-Sarid fighters and the Tanukh faced off in the little street, half of the men in the shade of the buildings, the others in full sun. The Ben-Sarid were watching their lord for a sign, but the Tanukh made an ostentatious show of putting their sabers and spears away. On the ground between the two parties, the runner woke groggily, holding his head and moaning. Jalal put a friendly smile on his face and offered the lad a hand up. Still disoriented, the boy accepted and fairly flew to his feet as Jalal put some strength to it. "Be careful, lad, you could run into a pointy object." Jalal turned the boy around and sent him back to the Ben-Sarid with a gentle shove.

In the opposite line, Lord Uri frowned, but slowly resheathed his own blade. Jalal watched the older man's expression—reading anger and fear and calculation pass across the aquiline features. Finally, the Ben-Sarid lord nodded and gestured for his men to stand easy. Jalal bowed a little and stepped forward. "Lord Uri, my captain has fallen ill from smoke. Is there a place nearby where he may rest?"

Uri peered over Jalal's shoulder, seeing Mohammed's litter. "Yes," muttered the Ben-Sarid, frowning, "one of my cousins maintains a house here in the temple precincts. We can take him there."

Jalal nodded his thanks, and the Tanukh gathered around him again, preparing to move.

"What is that sound?" Uri asked, staring back down the street. "It sounds like the sea."

"No," Jalal said with a grim smile, for he had heard such a sound before. "It is the mob in full spate, crying out for blood and vengeance upon their enemies."

THE RUINS OF PALMYRA, SYRIA COELE

)ɔÐ(

Z oë walked in a field of skulls. Her legion boots cracked and crushed the pale white fragments that covered the broad avenue. Tiny clouds of white dust drifted up behind her, then settled slowly in the still, hot air. She wore an enveloping white and pale green cloak, a Ghassani *djellaba*. It had a deep hood that fell over her face like a shroud, shading her eyes and the grim line of her mouth. The sun was westering, preparing to fall into hiding behind the barren hills that lined the valley to the southwest. She picked her way slowly with a twisty walking stick of Syrian thorn in one hand. Her other hand was hidden in the folds of her cloak. Ten paces behind her, Odenathus followed her with stricken eyes and a shuffling gait. While she stared straight ahead, her head held high, he looked all around, trying to take in the utter devastation that had been visited upon his home.

The graceful pillars were cracked and tumbled, the broad paving stones shattered by the heavy fall of hammers and siege engines. The fronts of the houses had been pulled down, leaving only hollow brick skeletons. The gardens that had hung down over the street, covering the walls with a lush spray of flowers and green garlands, were burned and dark with soot. And everywhere, in the streets, in the doors of the houses, filling the stairways that led to the upper floors, were bones and skulls and shattered ribs. The wind had worked upon the fallen dead, driving them into drifts along the lines of broken stones in the street. Doorways yawned on empty rooms dark with the mark of fire. White lattices of arm and leg bones cluttered there, making little pyramids.

Zoë marched on, climbing over the broken idols that had marked the tetrapylon. There, in that circular plaza at the center of the city, where the avenues of the decumanus and the cardo met, the bones of the fallen had been ground to dust, and the air itself seemed hushed by the heinous crimes that the buildings had witnessed. Empty eyes stared out from cracked heads bigger than a man. Odenathus climbed over them, too, his heavy boot finding purchase on the shoulder of the great god Baal, his hand in the pit of an eye socket. Beyond the plaza of the tetrapylon a quarter-mile of boulevard inched up to a great raised platform. Like the rest of the city, the opulent houses of the rich that had once lined it were torn down and smashed to ruin. Halfway up the ramp, Zoë stopped and turned, looking out over the wreckage of her city. Odenathus paused at her side, his heart sick with despair.

"Everyone is dead, cousin. Nothing is left alive in our city. We are lost, homeless."

Zoë ignored him, peering out of her cloak, searching the rooftops and tumbled piles of brick and stone for some hint of life. There was nothing but sun-blasted desolation. She turned again to the boulevard, her boots kicking a tiny skull away. It rattled and rolled among the scattering of white sticks that had once been a family of carpenters. The skull bounced away down the boulevard, finally tumbling into the side of an upturned paving stone and cracking to dust.

At the top of the ramp, the walls of the royal enclosure loomed up, a twenty-foot-high rampart of heavy granite and sandstone blocks. At the base of the gateway Zoë paused, and at last a sound escaped her. A ragged hiss of pain seeped out from between parched lips. The entrance, once flanked by two mighty winged lions and a high, strong gate of Lebanese cedar two feet thick, had been ground to ruin. The lions were gone, not even a wing or paw remaining. The sandstone and granite had been gouged out, as if by gargantuan talons, and the door smashed to splinters. Bodies were mixed in with the rubble—some still clad in silver mail. A half-crushed helmet in Scythian style with a tapering crown was pinned underneath a toppled block of stone that weighed at least a ton.

It was hard work to climb the rubble slope where the gate had been. The footing was treacherous, and the sandstone, smashed to powder, was slippery. At last they reached the top and stared into the central compound of the royal palace. Here they had grown up and learned their letters. Their families had worked here, ruling the far-flung trading Empire that had fueled Palmyra's enormous wealth. Here they had sat at the foot of the Silk Throne, listening in awe to the wisdom of the Queen of the city, the noble Zenobia the Fifth, as she held court and dispensed justice. Here they had seen their brothers and sisters born; here they had argued with their parents and fought with each other and played in all the years of their youth.

Now there was nothing.

The graceful white walls of the palace, two and three stories high, accented by red pillars and the long noble frieze of Aurelian's victory over the Three Emperors— they were gone. The frieze had stood twenty feet high, running the full length of the front of the palace; from his acclamation as Emperor of Rome by the Rhine Legions at the northern end, to the tremendous scene of his wedding to the first Zenobia of Palmyra—that which had sealed the Eastern Peace and restored an Imperial dynasty to a Roman empire riven by civil war and barbarian invasion—at the southern end. On the day that Zoë and Odenathus had departed to join the Legions, laden with the voyage-gifts of their family and friends, it had measured 306 feet in length.

It had been one of the greatest works of art in the Eastern Empire.

Nothing remained. The palace had been razed to the ground, and not a brick remained upon brick. The lattices of marble and porphyry were ground to dust. The elevated gardens, watered by an ingenious system of pipes and a hidden reservoir at the height of the palace, lay in ruin, a tumbled heap of glinting copper and burned wood and stone. A thick layer of ash lay across the rubble, drifted into pits and crevices where once stairways had descended into cool storage rooms and crypts under the palace.

Fire had raged across the noble buildings, both before they had fallen and after. The marble slabs were discolored and cracked by heat. Sandstone facings were streaked with soot and distorted by some terrible pressure. In the low places, sheets of bubbled glass shimmered green and gray in the afternoon sun where the cauldron of flame had transformed the sand and dust of the dying palace into a cruel mirror.

Zoë sat heavily on a slanted stone that had once formed part of the wall of the Hall of Oceans. Now it tilted at a dangerous angle. The thorn staff fell from her fingers and rattled dully on the slope of broken stone. Odenathus sat, too, more carefully, and wearily put down the heavy bag of supplies he had carried on a staff over his shoulder since they had left their camels outside of the city. His fingers trembled a little as he worked the cork stopper out of his water bag. For some reason he had trouble making his hands work the way he wanted. There was only a little water left, and he barely wet his mouth before pressing the bag into Zoë's hand. She held it, unseeing and unnoticing. Odenathus roused himself enough to scowl and press the leather mouthpiece into her mouth. She drank, but still seemed vastly distant from this world of bleached sunlight and barren broken stone.

"I'll see if the spring north of the theater is still running," he croaked at last. "We need to find water. Shelter, too. Night will fall soon, and it will be cold."

Zoë ignored him, staring across the ruin of her city with cold, dry eyes.

Odenathus picked his way through fallen pillars and great slabs of cut sandstone that had once formed the façade of the theater of Helios. The street here was very dangerous. There had once been tunnels and rooms dug under it, to hold wild animals and performers for the theater and the amphitheater that backed onto it from the north. Now, whatever had raged through the buildings had torn open the avenue, leaving deep pits and channels gaping wide in the surface of the street. A block beyond the theater there had once been a well that had served the northern half of the city. Odenathus remembered a dry voice lecturing in his youth, speaking of the effort that the city had invested into the aqueduct that had supplemented this water source from catchment basins in the hills to the west.

He stopped at the top of a long, sloping hill of rubble. A great cavity had opened in the street in the street, swallowing two houses and part of the theater market. Its bottom was in shadow, thrown by a lone building wall that stood forlornly to the south of it. Disgusted, he rubbed his nose and sneezed. The city was filled with a fine brown dust that got into everything. It was even worse than the grit that blew in from the desert. Though the collapsed street and the fallen buildings obscured it, he could make out the edges of the underground cistern fed by the spring.

Grumbling to himself, he swung his bag of equipment over his shoulder and bound his long dark hair back with a fillet of twisted green cloth. Two empty water bags slapped against his thighs, tied to his back with leather thongs he had made during the long ride south from Antioch. Prepared, he began to pick his way down the slope, cautious of loose shale.

Zoë sat on the shoulder of a fallen giant—once the image of the god Bel, who had blessed the city for so long. His face was gone, that which had stared down (in grave majesty) upon the supplicants in the court of the Silk Queen. Now, only a white marble shoulder remained. The rich paints that had adorned him and given his cold skin the semblance of life had been burned away. The sun and the wind had done the rest. Here on his shoulder, Zoë sat above the city looking out upon the devastation that had shattered nearly every house and building within the circuit of the walls. Even those granite and sandstone ramparts, rising thirty, forty, or fifty feet high, had fallen to the enemy. Wooden stakes had been driven into the stone and flushed with water until the wood, swelling, had cracked away the ashlar facings, sending the walls crashing down to lie in heaped piles along the outline of the city. The two great gates—that to the west, toward Damascus, and that to the east, toward the distant Euphrates and the trading station of Dura Europos—had fallen. The looming towers had been torn down, leaving only a shell of the once-powerful gatehouses.

She sat, silent and still. The fierce anger that had driven her forth from Antioch and the arms of the Imperial Legions had drained away. A haunted emptiness filled her, looking out at the ruin of all her dreams. She knew deep in bone and blood that not one person she had cared for within the circuit of these walls lived to walk the earth. The windrows of bodies lay too deep to give her false hope. Not a soul had gone forth from this place in chains, the captive of the Persians. No hope of ransom was held out to her, even if she could dig in the ruins and find the treasuries and storehouses of the Queens of Palmyra.

The power that had wrecked the city had spared nothing. She could feel the echoes of it still ringing in the broken paving stones and toppled statues. A great power had walked here in incandescent rage, striving to break the spirit and memory of the city. Little was left of it, all those spirits and lives that had walked in the shaded streets, or sung love songs on the balconies under a starry desert night—they had been consumed. The power that had crushed bone to ash and stolen the lives of the thousands and the ten thousands of citizens had taken the memories, too. Sitting there, cold and alone on the height of the city, she knew its purpose, this power. It intended that no one would remember her city, or the vibrant people who had lived in it. It thought, in its malignant power, that no one remained, that there was no one to sing the tale of her city. It thought it had killed Palmyra and torn out its heart.

Zoë's face darkened, and a little wind sprang up around her, swirling first this way and then that. Her fingers, dark and thin in the desert sun, made a mark in the air, and it hung there shimmering softly for a moment. *I remember*, she thought grimly, *and I will remind the whole of the world that the city still lives.*

Below her, on the long boulevard, a movement caught her eye. Her head turned, canting like a hunting hawk, and she peered down from her perch high on the ruin of the palace hill.

A man was in the city, walking carefully among the bones, leading three camels.

Thin streams of dust fell from the cracked rubble above, filtering down through slanting beams of sunlight. Three stories below the level of the street, Odenathus picked his way carefully across a mountain of paving stones. Below, in the darkness, he could hear water falling into some kind of pool. The sound, magnified by the curving walls, made him terribly thirsty. He negotiated a fallen lead drainage pipe and found himself on a set of steps that emerged from the debris. Heartened by this, he made his way down.

At the bottom, a pool of green water spilled over a section of tessellated floor. Dolphins, mermaids, and high-backed ships cavorted on a pale blue surface. Letters marked out with small black chips of stone spelled the name of a notable merchant house of the city. Odenathus paused at the edge of the floor, looking for a way around to the wall beyond where he could see a bent pipe sticking out, spilling a tiny stream of water. The tumble of stones on either side seemed precarious, though. *No matter*, he grumbled to himself, *you've gotten your boots wet before!* He stepped out onto the mosaic floor, still moving carefully. A stone rattled past from above and splashed into the water. He looked up. Something dark blotted out the light coming from above. He threw up his arm and was smashed down by a heavy weight.

"Roman pig," someone snarled above him in the sudden darkness. "Water-thief!"

Odenathus went down hard, feeling tesserae crack under his back. The weight on his chest squirmed, and he felt a knee drive into his stomach. He gasped and tried to roll to one side. The assailant clipped him on the side of the head with a fist, but got more floor than flesh.

"Ay! Bastard!" the voice squeaked in pain. Odenathus shoved up, catching something that felt like an elbow. He tore at the rough fabric around his head and snagged a finger on a leather strap. The cloth ripped, and he rolled again, suddenly losing the weight. He threw the bristly cloth away. He was soaking wet.

A man in ragged clothing stood over him, wiping water out of his face. Odenathus scrambled up to his feet, though the footing on the wet floor was treacherous. The man scuttled back, fumbling at his belt for some kind of knife. Odenathus slid forward, keeping his boots to the floor, and grabbed the man's shirt. The old stained fabric tore in his fingers. The man twisted away, snarling. "Hands off, Roman pig!"

Odenathus punched the man in the face, then grabbed hold of his hair and kneed him in the stomach. The man's face bulged, and a croaking sound came out of his throat as he fell to his knees. Odenathus reached down and plucked a bone-handled knife out of nerveless fingers. Without looking, he tossed the knife away into the shadows. "Friend," Odenathus said, "you shouldn't attack people trying to get a drink of water."

"You've no friends here, Legionary."

Odenathus turned slowly, hearing now the breathing of dozens of men in the darkness around him. Four stood in the slanting light from the street above, bows in their hands, arrows nocked to the shaft. Behind the four, a stout woman was making her way down the slope of rubble with a long, Persian-style spear for support. The young man raised his hand, raising an eyebrow at the rabble who had inched out of the dim recesses of the cistern. He recognized them well enough; the detritus of a destroyed city, living by scavenging the food, coin, and goods that had been left, or forgotten, by the victors. He had seen the same faces when the Imperial Army had marched out of flood-drowned Ctesiphon. Then he had pitied them and thrown a few coins from the back of the wagon he was riding in.

Anger suddenly bubbled up in his breast—these were *his* people in *his* city, and they would not slink and prowl about in the darkness like rats. He looked around, straightening up, his face grim. "I am not a Roman," he said in a blunt tone. "I am a lord of the great city of Palmyra, Queen of the Desert. Who are you?"

The woman, who had reached the watery floor, laughed bitterly. "The great city? There is no place by that name, stranger. It is in ruins, destroyed. Its people are nameless and faceless—who are *you* to question those who have the advantage of you?"

"I am Odenathus, son of Zabda, cousin of the Queen of the City." While he spoke, he had raised a fist, and fire trickled between his fingers. Tongues of orange flame flickered up, and the room was suddenly filled with light. The scavengers flinched back, and their shadows grew suddenly great against the crumbling walls. The old woman leaned heavily on her spear, her head turned slightly away. Even so, Odenathus could see that her right eye was a milky sightless orb.

"Odenathus?" Her voice echoed hollowly in the domed ceiling of the cistern. "He is dead. All of that house are dead, ground down by pride and the darkness. Dead or fled away into the desert. Not one of the noble House of Nasor still lives."

"Not true," Odenathus said, stepping forward, his boots splashing in the water. "I live and I am here. The Queen is here, and while she lives, the city lives." His words echoed around the chamber. The fire he had called to his fist drifted up and away, forming a slowly spinning circle over his head. The light it cast filled the watery floor with blood, where the dolphins swam in a sea of red. The old woman, both her eyes destroyed, turned to face him fully.

Odenathus' step faltered, and the ring of fire flickered, almost going out. He stopped, stunned. "Mama?"

In a hollow formed by the fallen statue of Bel, Zoë cleared a space among the chipped ceiling tiles and charred beams. Now, with the sun set and full night upon the valley, she huddled in a woolen cloak she had taken from the baggage on the camels. A tiny fire flickered in a ring of stones. Beneath it broad blue-and-white hexagonal tiles could be seen—once they had decorated the floor of the entrance hall to the Little Palace. The ever-present wind still blew in from the desert, making the air chill and cold. Across from her, wrapped in his own blankets and a hood of thick wool, an old man with a bushy white beard was gnawing on a hunk of bread. It had come, like the wine mulling at the edge of the little fire, from the supplies that Odenathus had so carefully carried from distant Antioch.

"Grandfather," Zoë whispered, trying to keep her teeth from chattering, "what did you see?"

The old man ignored her and stuffed the rest of the bread into his mouth. His fingers were cracked and grimy, only partially covered by cloth wrappings. With the bread gone, he rummaged in the bowl she had found for him and found some last morsel.

Zoë frowned. The old man was just going to eat her food and say nothing. She reached out and moved the ceramic bottle of wine away from the fire, closer to her. The old man watched her, his black eyes shining with a tiny reflected flames.

"Tell me, Grandfather, what did you see? You said you had seen something important."

"Wine?" he croaked, edging a little closer to the fire. His eyes followed the bottle.

Zoë frowned again, and the bottle disappeared into the folds of her cloak. "No wine," she snapped. Her fingers curled around the hilt of a Legion *gladius* laid on the ground at her side. "Tell me what you saw, and you will have wine."

The old man drew back again, folding into the cocoon of blankets and sweat-stained cloaks that he carried with him. Only his firelit eyes remained visible in the darkness. He made a snuffling sound. "I saw . . ." He paused and suddenly looked up. The line of his body tensed, and Zoë's eyes widened to see a long, curved knife suddenly catch the edge of the firelight. "Someone is coming."

Zoë stood and waved her hand over the fire. It went out, plunging the hollow among the ruins into complete darkness. The moon had not risen, so only the glittering firmament of stars overhead shed any light. Out on the rubble was the clink of a brick shifting and a low mutter. Zoë squinted, then breathed out slowly, summoning focus. Her vision wavered, and then the tumbled mounds of broken building and snaglike pillars sprang into view. Even in starlight the methods of the Legion thaumaturges could lend her sight. At the edge of the royal platform, where the crumbled gate lay, figures—more than one—were moving in file toward her. Instinctively, she opened her awareness and began drawing the power for a Shield of Athena from the air and wind and sky. Its pale blue tracery began to build, whirling, in the air between her and the strangers. The dim red shape of the old man flickered at her side, the fire of his spirit low and guttering. Across the field of rubble, at least one bright shape moved, burning with its own powerful flame.

"Men are coming," the old man whispered, creeping to her side, his knife at the ready. "Many men."

"I see them, Grandfather, but one of them I know. Do not be afraid."

The shield spun down and dispersed. Zoë sat again, and the fire sparked in the stones and leapt up, making a beacon in the night. The old man flinched from the sudden light and scurried back into his nest of blankets. Zoë pulled the bottle of wine out and waved it at him. "Tell me what you saw."

The old man bowed his head to the broken tiles twice. "Yes, mistress," he muttered. "I was in the hills to the north, when the *dhole* smashed the gates of the city. I was looking for wood in the ravines and gullies. The Persians, my lady, they were paying well for firewood."

Zoë's faced darkened with rage, and the old man paused, then groveled on the stones. "Please, my lady, I am just an old man with no family! I must eat! I only did what I had to do."

The girl looked away and, when she looked back, her face was calm again. She motioned for him to continue.

"My mules ran off when the *dhole* was sent away. That was a great noise! Like the gods raging in the clear sky. I hope never to hear such a thing again. . . . It took me days to find them all and bring them back together. Then I went to the city—but it was gone!" The old man rocked back and forth, wringing his hands. "Everything was destroyed . . . even the stream had dried up and the aqueducts were torn down. I could not find any water. It was very hot, so I went into the city. Oh, it was dreadful: All the bodies withering in the sun . . . I went into a house that still stood, hoping to find a pan of water. There was nothing. But when I was coming out, I heard a noise. I hid, thinking that the Persians had come back . . . but it was not the Persians, oh no." The old man's voice ran down, mumbling and cursing to himself.

Zoë frowned and coughed to get his attention. "Who came to the city? Romans?"

"Oh," the old man said, looking up with a puzzled expression on his wrinkled face. "Not Romans, oh no. Bandits, desert bandits, in their long robes and fierce beards. They had sabers, you know! I saw them at the gate."

"Bandits? What tribe? Why did they come to the city?"

"Oh, they came for . . ." The old man began muttering again.

"For what?" Zoë's patience was wearing very thin. Too, she could hear the clatter of boots coming across the rubble. Odenathus would be here very soon, with these strangers. "What were they looking for?"

"Oh!" The old man looked up, his eyes suddenly bright. "They came for her! Well, for her body, for it was nailed up over the gate then—but they took it down, and very gently, too. Very mannerly, for bandits—"

"Her?" Zoë's voice was as cold as morning frost. "Who was nailed above the gate?"

"Her . . . the most radiant one." The old man mumbled again, then his voice strengthened. "One of them had a scar; he said that she would be put away, safe from ravens and wild dogs. They bore her off on their shoulders. They were singing a dirge, as is right. I saw it all, I heard it from the house inside the gate. I say that it is so!"

"The radiant one . . ." Zoë felt her world spinning out of turn. "It can only be Zenobia."

"Oh yes!" The old man brightened. "That was what they called her, these bandits."

THE HOUSE D'ORELIO, THE QUIRINAL HILL, ROMA

Tiny beads of sweat spilled down Anastasia's brow, pooling in the hollow of her neck. The sweat gleamed in the light of hundreds of beeswax candles placed around the periphery of the room. Anastasia's face was contorted in a grimace of pain, and the thin cotton shawl that had been draped around her shoulder slipped. Her carefully trimmed and polished fingernails bit into the muscular arm of the attendant standing behind her chair. A thin trickle of blood seeped from underneath her nails.

"Aaaaa!" Another contraction ground a low moan out of the Duchess. She panted heavily. "Oh, Goddess," she gasped, "blessed Medea was right . . . aaaahh!"

Between her legs, the midwife looked up, smiling. The woman had short brown hair and a pleasantly plump face. The sleeves of her dark red gown were rolled up and tied back with strings. The *obstetrix* seemed perfectly relaxed and at ease. Anastasia, her body in the grip of excruciating pain, briefly envisioned the woman—still smiling—being torn apart by wild dogs on the hot sand floor of the Flavian. Beyond her, the Duchess was dimly aware of the other two attendants—young women of her house who had borne strong sons—kneeling on the floor, holding long tapers. These four women were her only companions, here in her bedroom.

"Soon now, dear," the midwife chided as she rubbed her hands and forearms with olive oil. "You'll have forgotten the pain in a day or so, mark my words."

"Never!" Anastasia hissed as another wave of contractions rippled across her abdomen. "I didn't forget how it was before . . . oh, Goddess . . . ah!"

"Now, now, you've just been a little time away from children and birthing. It'll all come back to you." The midwife made a clucking sound and slipped a gentle hand into Anastasia. The Duchess tried to concentrate on what the woman was doing, but then another wave of pain washed over her and she could only see the ceiling and hear—distantly—someone crying out. The pain passed, leaving her whole body sore and shaking. She slumped exhausted against the attendant behind her. The midwife stood up, holding something red and wrinkled. The woman was smiling. She held up the red thing, and a glad cry rang out from the two women who had been kneeling on the mats at the base of the birthing chair.

Anastasia's head rolled back, and she stared vacantly at the ceiling. The pain ebbed and began to seep away. One of the girls leaned over her, taking the Duchess's head and laying it back on the padded headrest of the chair. She tipped a *krater* of wine to Anastasia's lips. It was hot and very sweet. The attendant stepped away and took a silver bowl of water from the other girl. From somewhere, the Duchess heard a knife rasp out of a metal sheath.

There was a popping sound, and then a wailing cry. At the edge of vision, Anastasia caught sight of the midwife turning, her forearms covered with blood. The girl with the silver bowl was there, and the midwife rinsed her arms, drying them with a pale white woolen towel. This done, she took a second cloth and poured water from the bowl over it. "This is the water of the river of life," the midwife chanted in a hushed singsong. "This is the purity of the first morning of the world."

Anastasia rolled her head to one side—an enormous effort. The midwife had laid the red thing, all squalling and tiny, on the side of the birthing table in a thick linen quilt. With careful, sure movements, she bathed the baby while continuing to chant in the same low voice.

"O Goddess, bless this child and let it see its father's glad smile in five days. Let it grow strong."

Anastasia blinked tears away, feeling a sudden and unexpected sense of loss. Her husband should have been waiting outside the door, pensive and nervous, dressed in his best formal toga and tunic. He should be knocking at the door right now.

"O mistress of the dawn and the hunt, guide the path of this child through the forest. Let it grow wise."

He would have been so proud, his lined, old face all wreathed in smiles, grinning in that merry way that had melted her heart, even as a young and foolish girl. He should be here, she thought disconsolately. *Why isn't he here?*

"O mistress of the ship that crosses the waters, lead this child from birth to death under your beneficent *aegis*. Let it live with honor."

Anastasia began to cry, entirely silently, her chest heaving. She turned her head away from the child and the midwife and the attendants. This is what she had always wanted for her dear old husband, now dead fifteen years. *How can I miss him so? Will this pain ever grow less?*

"Mistress?" Anastasia turned her head back, smoothing her features with an effort of will. The midwife held up the baby, now swaddled in cotton and silk. The woman was smiling, her round face creased with a broad grin. "This is your son, my lady. Shall I send the girls to put a crown of olive above the door?"

The baby stared back at her with deep blue eyes all round and wide. It looked like a little red monkey. The Duchess's lips trembled for a moment, but then she took her emotions in hand and put them behind her. Slowly, without taking her eyes from the round, wrinkly little face and its button nose, she shook her head.

"Sister, this child will never be known to the world until he comes of age. No crown will grace my door, nor shall he walk around my hearth, little hand in mine."

Anastasia sighed, seeing the pitying look in the midwife's eyes. The woman was of the temple, she thought, and deserved some small explanation. The Duchess tried to straighten in the chair, but she was still too weak. "Sister, this child's father is gone, and his family cannot claim him. I will see that he is well taken care of, and when he comes of age, he will come into the honors that his father would likely bestow. No fear, he will not be sent to the rubbish heaps. But I cannot claim him as mine, either, though he will have the protection of my house always."

The midwife nodded, bowing, and tucked the baby into Anastasia's arms. "You'll wait at least until the tenth day, won't you? He needs a name before he goes out into the world."

Anastasia looked down at the little creature cradled in

her arms. Every muscle was dead sore and tired, but she still managed to lift her hand and caress his soft hair. "He will have a name," the Duchess said, smiling down, "but it will not come from my hand. We cannot wait until the *dekate*."

The midwife shook her head in dismay at flouted convention, but turned away and began to bundle up the cloths and bowls and jars. The two girls had been busy, too, scrubbing up the blood spilled on the floor and lighting scented candles to drive away the *miasma* attendant upon birth. Anastasia turned her head a little and lifted her chin. The attendant who had held her during her labor glided into view. This woman was old and bent, but her arms and shoulders were broad and strong from decades of kneading bread in the kitchens of the House of d'Orelio. The Duchess sighed, looking at her old face and calm, ancient eyes. The *pistrix* had seen so much!

"Maga, bring the Islander to me. There are things that must be done."

The *obstetrix* bowed and went out, her purse heavier by a dozen gold *aureae*. Anastasia stared after her with narrowed eyes, thinking upon the damage that a chance comment might wreak upon her plans for the future. She would have to see that the midwife was carefully watched for some time. She pursed her lips and managed to run a hand through her hair. The lush curls were in complete disarray, and damp with sweat and the sacred water that the girls had laved her with. She felt light-headed. *An apprentice to learn the art of the obstetrix*, the Duchess thought. *Someone who has the patience to watch and listen for ten or twelve years....*

She shook her head and laughed at herself. Even now, half blinded by pain and exhaustion, she was planning and calculating!

Tros entered the room, ducking under the six-foot-high lintel of the door. As always, his massive shoulders and broad chest seemed to make the chamber shrink. She smiled, feeling greatly relieved that he was here. His dark eyes flitted around the room, checking to see if anyone was lurking behind the curtains at the windows or under the raised bed. This done, he bowed his head and knelt at her side. Sighing, she reached out and ran a hand through his unruly black mop. Tonight he was wearing a headband of bronze links, but even this sturdy ornament could not control his hair.

"You see, great ruffian, I live, and so does my son." She turned a little in the chair, showing him the tiny package bundled into the curve of her arms. "I must send this child away, far away, and you are the only one I trust him with."

Tros looked up, his broad, handsome face filled with astonishment. "I?" he rumbled. "You are too cunning by half, my lady. This is a task beyond my simple skill."

Anastasia laughed, saying, "You underestimate yourself, Islander. You will make a fine nursemaid with a nanny goat close to hand. You are not used to sleeping, anyway. You will make the perfect *mater*."

Tros smiled, his black eyes glinting in the candlelight. "Where shall I take him?" he asked, his voice troubled. "Beyond Italy? Beyond Gaul? Where will he be safe?"

The Duchess's face saddened, for she was thinking of the long journey and the dangers that would swirl around her baby boy like the currents of Charybdis. Safety was not counted in leagues, but in a hundred days' travel. Too, Tros would be gone, and it was very likely that she would never see him again. Her face grew longer. "Farther than Gaul, dear Tros. Do you remember where we first met?"

Tros's eyes widened, and for the first time that she could remember, he frowned. His great black eyebrows bunched together and something like anger drifted into his face. "I do not forget those days, my lady. It was a near thing, there in the *tlachtecatl*. . . . I did not expect to live, or see the green hills of Rome again."

"Yes," she said, "but it is far enough away, and entirely outside the power of the Empire. . . . This child will be safe there, I think, among our old friends. You will have to go with him and you will have to stay . . ." Her voice faltered, and she covered her mouth with one hand. The rush of emotion was so hard to control. She had not expected it to be this painful. The thought of spending the rest of her days without the comfortable presence of the Islander always within call was suddenly bleak. She settled back in the chair, letting the riot of her hair fall over her face. "You will have to stay there, dear Tros, until he is fourteen years old. You must teach him all the arts at your command. Then, when he is ready to become a man, you will bring him to me."

Tros' face grew grim, for he knew the daily danger that the Duchess placed herself in. Fourteen years could well eclipse her, leaving the boy without any family at all. "When shall I go?"

Anastasia continued to hide her face in her hair, clutching the baby to her breast. "You must go tonight."

Tros looked away. The Duchess was crying again.

THE CILICIAN GATES, ON THE ROAD TO TYANA

The tramp of thousands of booted feet echoed off high, slate-colored cliffs. Dwyrin walked with his head low, his dull red cloak pulled tight around him. The road climbed slowly up the flank of a mountain, rising by inches above a steep-sided gorge. Below, in the mist that drifted in the canyon, a swift stream thundered over black rocks. Above, the sky was thick with fat, gray clouds heavy with rain. Thin drizzle spiraled down out of the sky, but the mountain peaks were not yet completely obscured. The legions marched west, up the long, slow, twisty road from the Plain of Tauris, through the ancient pass of the gates, and then—in another week—down into the hot plains around Tyana. Dwyrin continued walking, seeing only the tips of his boots and the legs of the man in front of him.

Since the army had decamped from Antioch for the long road by land west to the Eastern Capital, he had lost any interest in the world at large. He marched when told to march, he took his turn at camp duties, and beyond that he coveted the wine jug and the isolation of his tent. Sometimes, when the centurion had a free moment, he would tutor Dwyrin in the arts, but those times were irregular. Blanco had his own business to take care of. Dwyrin, exhausted from marching, no longer looked ahead or at the sky.

The Legions tramped under mossy cliffs and past narrow ravines filled with rushing white water. These mountains were rugged and sheer-sided, with desolate summits white with stone. Narrow valleys cleaved them, arrowing toward the sea, filled with pine and cypress. With little margin the road was narrow, just wider than a wagon, and the long steel snake of the army had unwound to its greatest length. Even now, while the Third Cyrenaica was laboring up the pitch to the first gate, lead elements of the Emperor's army had already passed out of the juniper woodlands on the western side of the mountains. Dwyrin did not care; he only cared to keep dry and to put one muddy boot in front of the other until the centurion told him to stop at the end of the day.

The clouds parted a little, spilling pale sunlight down through drifting mist. The cliffs brightened, showing sprays of gold and red flowers in the nooks and crannies of the mountainside. Above the marching line of men, the road climbed and then turned, passing under an outthrust pinnacle of rock. There, on the dark stones, a square tower rose. This was the first gate. The sloping roof gleamed in the sunlight and the banners of the garrison flapped in the breeze rising from the canyon far below. Cruel battlements leaned out over the road, which passed into a broad gateway and a covered tunnel.

Ravens flew up from the top of the tower, disturbed by a ringing of trumpets as a party of riders in crimson and purple entered the gate. On the road below, Dwyrin heard the noise but he did not look up.

"Arrrh!" Heraclius fell heavily on the wet cobblestones. Intense pain flashed in his right knee as it took the brunt of his weight. For a moment he felt completely weak, unable to move his legs. He tried to raise himself, but the rain on the cobbles made it difficult to find purchase. His feet throbbed terribly. The clouds that had parted overhead closed again, now dropping down to enshroud the tower of the first gate in a cold clinging mist.

"Avtokrator!" One of the Varangians knelt hurriedly at his side. The man's broad, blond face was marked by worry. The Northman slid his arm under the Emperor's and lifted gently. Heraclius felt his face flush with embarrassment. He was a tall, strong man—he should not need any help standing or getting off a horse. Others of the Imperial Guard clustered around him, facing outward with hands on their weapons. Heraclius stood, feeling the weakness in his right leg. He tried to stand on his own, but fierce pain ripped through his feet and lower legs, and he had to take the blond Northman's arm again.

"Let's go inside," he gasped, fighting to keep upright. "I need to take off my boots."

The Varangians began moving, forming a circle around him. The blond man and two others supported the Emperor to the ironbound door of the tower. The soldiers assigned to the tower parted—at first slowly, but then quickly when the purple cloak and golden armor of the Emperor were seen. Heraclius ducked through the door and felt himself lifted up and carried bodily up a wide flight of stairs. At the top, a vaulted hallway ran deeper into the tower. More soldiers, some of them with badges of rank, parted before the Imperials. They turned through a door, the blond

Northman turning sideways to carry the Emperor through
in his arms. The room beyond was small, with a domed
roof and a fire in a grate on the inner wall. There was a
desk and a low chair. A surprised man with short-cropped
white hair looked up from where he had been writing at
the desk.

The two lead guardsmen grasped the man by the shoulders and arms and threw him out into the hallway. The
man shouted in anger and fear, but the other guardsmen
ran him off. The others took up guard positions outside
the door. The quills and ink blocks and paper on the desk
were brushed off, clattering to the floor. The blond man
lowered Heraclius onto the tabletop.

"Ahhhhh!" With the pressure relieved from his feet and
legs, there was a sudden blessed ebbing of pain. Heraclius
lay back on the table in relief. Above him, he saw that the
roof of the chamber was dark with soot.

"What has happened?" A basso shout echoed in the passageway. Heraclius summoned enough energy to grin a
little. His brother had heard something dire had befallen
the Emperor and was quick on the wing to hunt it down.
"Where is my brother?"

Heraclius levered himself up on one elbow. He waved
a hand weakly at the Northman who was still at his side.
"Take off my boots," The Emperor hissed. "They feel too
tight."

The Northman nodded and began tugging at the laces
of the high red boots.

"Brother!" Theodore stormed into the room, his own
equites in full armor at his back. The Varangians bristled
and moved to block the door. Theodore pulled up short,
confronted by the half-drawn swords of four burly men in
heavy mail. The Prince's hand moved reflexively to the
hilt of his own *spatha*, but the growl from the Northmen
brought him up short. For a moment the Prince bristled
and locked gazes with the captain of the Varangians. The
captain, quite sure of his place and the long, bloody history
of the Imperial Guard, gave a wintry smile and stepped

closer to Theodore. The Prince gave ground. Even the brother of the Emperor did not command the Varangians, particularly when their fur was ruffled. Their captain, a squat, thickly muscled black-haired veteran with a pox-scarred face was notorious for his personal loyalty to the Emperor and his rough methods. Theodore had tried to befriend him before and had been coldly rebuffed.

"Brother," Theodore called, "are you well? What happened?"

"Be calm, Theo, I am . . . ayyy!" Heraclius flinched as the blond Northman tugged one of the laces of his boots free. It dragged in the copper grommets, pulling tight for a moment. The Emperor swayed and then lay back down on the table again. The sooty roof seemed very distant compared to the pain that rippled up his legs and into his arms. "Cut them . . . cut them off," he managed to blurt out.

The blond Northman frowned and looked to his captain for guidance. The captain nodded, keeping most of his attention on the Prince, who was still poised in the doorway. The blond man pulled a curved knife from a wooden sheath on his belt and carefully slipped the needlelike tip under the laces. The silk cords parted easily, and in a moment the boots had been reduced to brightly colored strips. Heraclius felt like his legs had been released from iron clamps. He breathed easily, almost normally, and was giddy with release. "Ah—I can think! Centurion Rufio, send my brother in."

Theodore bent at his brother's side, his face a mask of concern. Heraclius took his shoulder and sat up again. Now, with the pinching boots gone, he felt almost normal. His feet were still a little numb, though. He looked down and was shocked to see that his toes and feet were unexpectedly swollen.

"What is this?" Heraclius grimaced in disgust. Each foot was a pale gray color and puffy. No wonder he had nearly fainted trying to walk in boots. He felt queasy seeing that the skin was becoming stretched and almost glassy around the ankles.

"I don't know," Theodore said slowly, his eyes lingering on his brother's feet. "I should send for a physician immediately! There is one I trust among my followers. He studied in Egypt and knows many medicinal arts. Pray, brother, let me send for him."

Before Heraclius could speak, the Varangian captain shook his head curtly. "The Emperor has his own physicians, Prince. One of my men will fetch them from the baggage train." Rufio's voice was a gravelly rumble, long ruined by screaming orders over the din of battle. "No other man will tend to the person of the Emperor save them."

Theodore glared back at the Northman, but Rufio's face was an icy crag, admitting no other counsel to its discussions. Heraclius lay back again and stared at the ceiling, ignoring his brother's questioning look. In comparison to the evil-looking cast to his lower legs, the soot-blackened bricks seemed a welcome sight.

"So be it," Theodore said petulantly. "I will see to getting the army past the gate, then." The Prince stalked out without saying anything to his brother, but Heraclius did not notice; he was too busy trying to calm his breathing. His heart had begun to race as his mind began to catalog the ailments and diseases that might be afflicting him. He felt faint again and chided himself for letting his imagination run out of control. Someone leaned over his legs, and Heraclius peered over his stomach. It was Rufio and one of the other veterans. They were muttering to one another.

"*Avtokrator*," Rufio said presently, turning to face the Emperor. "We will bring you a chair on poles so that we can carry you to a better room. It will only be a moment."

Heraclius nodded and folded his hands on his chest, resigned to waiting.

*　　*　　*

A single candle glowed, marking a small yellow circle in darkness. Heraclius could hear the sound of rushing water somewhere, perhaps through a window. He lay in a soft bed, covered by many quilts. Somewhere nearby, but beyond a door or a hanging, he could hear people arguing. He thought it was his brother and the Emperor Galen—but that was impossible: The Western Emperor had departed their company weeks ago. His legs still felt numb, but he was very tired, and he slept.

Galen had been standing at the base of a loading ramp, shading his eyes from the glare off the water in the harbor at Seleucia Piera. Dozens of great *naves onerariae* were tied to the quays, filling with men and supplies and wagons and mules as the Legions of the Western Empire had been preparing to depart from the East. Heraclius had been on his horse, watching in ill-disguised envy as the Western troops bustled about in practiced efficiency, seeing to the thousands of details attendant on their voyage. The huge, dark ships were filling in a steady, unhurried stream. His own army was still snarled up on the roads leading into Antioch. It would take weeks for them to get straightened out, then more weeks while they exhausted themselves in sport in the city.

"Are the omens good?" Theodore had asked from his own horse, voice edged with spite. "No bad dreams or signs of black goats? Surely you've not dreamed of dark clouds or sharks?"

Galen had smiled back in his faintly superior way. The Western Emperor knew that the Prince hated him, but he did not care. Was he not Emperor? And, unless something dreadful happened, Theodore would never don the Purple. Heraclius had two almost grown sons and a third just born. His dynasty was assured. The younger brother would never see the crown of golden laurels placed on his head.

"No," Galen had said. "The fates smile upon me this day. The sun shines, the wind is right, and soon I will return to Rome and a worthy triumph for my men. A celebration as the great city has not seen in three hundred years!"

Heraclius watched the two men sparring. The Western Emperor was thin, nervous-looking, and phenomenally bright. His lank black hair clung to his scalp like a wet rag, but the mind that dwelled behind the dark brown eyes was unmatched. In comparison, the handsome and broad-chested Theodore seemed a brash red hound, constantly befuddled by the wily fox.

"Why rush so?" Theodore was smirking. "Afraid that your men will lose themselves in the fleshy pleasures of Antioch? Afraid that you might be delayed yourself? In a hurry to get home?"

Galen laughed and ran a thin, tanned hand through his hair, scratching the back of his scalp with his habitual tic. Heraclius knew from these last months' experience with the man that he was considering trying to explain something complicated to Theodore. It rarely worked.

"It is best," Heraclius interjected, giving Theodore a stern glance, "if we are about the business of the day."

The Eastern Emperor swung down lightly from his war-horse and looked around, rubbing his neatly trimmed beard before speaking. As he watched, two cohorts of legionaries were using a ship-borne crane to lift two of the sturdily built wagons used by the Western Empire into the cargo hold of the great ship. Heraclius sighed quietly, mentally comparing the efficient and fluid motions of the Western troopers to the snarl that his own men would have spawned by now.

At least, he thought, *my fleet is by far their master.* The Western army had come in a fleet of bulk corn haulers—nearly half of the yearly Egyptian grain fleet had been rerouted to move the sixty thousand men Galen had brought into the east. That was possible because the Eastern navy controlled the sea. Heraclius, swift triremes and *liburnae* ruled the eastern Mediterranean. Even when they had possessed some port cities along the coast of Bithnia or Lydia during the recent war, the Persians had not tried to wrest control of the sea from him. *And so I live and triumph,* thought Heraclius smugly, *and Chosroes, King of Kings, lies rotting in a common grave.*

"Do you find my proposal an agreeable one, brother?" Heraclius looked around and saw that Galen was speaking to him. "The Western Empire shall undertake the administration, policing, and defense of the coastal provinces of Judaea, Syria, and Egypt so that your own governors and their staffs may move farther east?"

Heraclius nodded, ignoring the petulant look on Theodore's face. "Yes," he said, holding out a hand to the Western Emperor. "The devastation wrought by the Persians and Avars has cost me too many skilled men. It will take decades to restore the administrative corpus of the east, even with my new organizational plan. Those cohorts and scribes and clerks will better serve in the new provinces. My brother has a weighty task ahead of him and he will need all the good men he can get."

"Even so," Galen said, glancing sidelong at Theodore and smiling crookedly, "if I can help in any way, do not hesitate to summon me to the *telecast.*"

Heraclius nodded. He had forgotten the odd device that his wizards had found in the ruined library at Pergamum. Normally an interlocking plate of bronze half circles, the telecast could be brought to life by a skilled thaumaturge, and once it was at speed it could show places and people far away. The Eastern Emperor distrusted the device, but Galen swore by its powers. Heraclius allowed that it was sometimes convenient.

"I will," Heraclius replied. "When can we expect the first of your governors and their staffs?"

"Within three months," Galen said briskly. "Lucius Nerethres should be sailing from Carthago Nova in Hispania even now."

This was a man who was well acquainted with the travel plans, locations, and dispositions of his governors. Another thing that Heraclius envied. While the disasters of the past decade had all but eradicated the ancient professional bureaucracy from the East, it still survived in the West. Where Heraclius grappled on a daily basis with a foment of regional warlords, *thematic* dukes, and unruly priests, Galen presided over a long-established and far-flung network of well-maintained roads, appointed professional officials, regular postal service, and steady tax collection. So it had been for nearly seven centuries.

Heraclius shook his head, dispelling the growing jealousy that threatened to turn his thought. This was why he would return by land to Constantinople. There were towns and even cities in the provinces of Anatolia, Bithnia, and Cilicia that had not seen the standards of the Emperor in decades. The Imperial order must be restored. His passage home would see to that.

Galen had continued speaking, though more to Theodore than to the Eastern Emperor. "Use these engineers well, Lord Prince. They will serve you very well in the plains between the Two Rivers. You saw, I am sure, the extensive damage to the fields due to flooding as we marched back from Ctesiphon? These men can repair the dikes and canals and ensure it does not happen again. You will be well received, I think, if you can rescue Persia from famine!"

"Let them starve," Theodore snarled. "It will leave more land for Roman settlers! A land empty of Persians and Medes is a peaceful land. I would be better pleased, O Caesar, if you left me those regiments of Sarmatian heavy horse. That would be a princely gift, in truth!"

"Really?" Galen's voice was light, but the light in his eyes grew bitter and cold. "You've not had enough of my hospitality and familial affection?"

Theodore stopped, his mouth open, and one hand moved unconsciously to his cheek. The blood that had spattered there from the dying Persian boy, Kavadh-Siroes, was long washed away with scented oils and waters, but the sting to Theodore's pride remained fresh. Galen had wielded that knife with swift assurance, resolving a potentially damaging political issue and sending the last competing heir to the Eastern Roman throne into the outer darkness.

In some ways, Theodore owed Galen a great deal, but the Prince saw only the patronizing smile and pointed wit. Heraclius coughed, drawing both of their attentions.

"We have much to be about, as well, my brother. I know you are anxious to be home. May your voyage be safe and swift."

Galen clasped hands with the Eastern Emperor and nodded in thanks. The great ships would leave soon, first for Egypt on the southerly winds, and then out across the deep blue Mediterranean to Rome.

"Ja, Centurion, I haff seen it before! Mein unkles often suffered from this when they were at sea for a long time. The svelling."

Heraclius roused himself from dream slowly, hearing an odd voice speaking. He tugged at the quilts that lay over him. They seemed very heavy, but then his hand was moving so slowly, too.

"Martina?" Someone was asking for his wife. It took a moment to realize that it must be his own voice. He opened his eyes.

Tall, narrow windows let thin slats of light into a dim room. A charcoal brazier stood at the foot of the bed, vainly trying to banish the chill that hung in the air. There was a scattering of tallow candles smoking in the corners of the room, but on the whole it was dark and dank. *Just like every other frontier outpost*, thought Heraclius wryly. *Cold beds, cold food, cold women.* Rufio was standing at the foot of the bed with another Varangian, a muscular young man of no more than twenty, with long blond hair in braids that hung down on his chest. The guard captain had turned back the bottom quilts from the Emperor's feet.

Heraclius looked away quickly. It did not seem possible that his feet were these shiny distended bags of flesh. He could not even feel them, or really anything below his knees. He closed his eyes again, trying to drive the image away. *They look like fish*, he thought, and then shuddered. *Dead fish.*

"Do you know how to cure this?" That was Rufio's voice, rumbling like a heavy wagon on a rocky road.

"Ja, if I can find the proper ingredients. Mein mama vould make a hot drink of juniper berries and parsley seeds—mein unkles vould drink gallons uf it! This will pass, then, as it did for them . . ."

Heraclius tried to sit up, but the weakness in his legs seemed to have infected his arms as well. He could barely raise his head. It occurred to him that he could not feel his fingers well. He felt nauseous with fear.

"Juniper berries?" Theodore's voice intruded harshly, and the sharp clacking sound of his boots on the stone floor could be heard as he stormed into the room. "A woman's drink, to drive away the bad humors of child-birth!"

"Lord Prince," Rufio growled warningly, "this man is well respected among his people. . . ."

"And our own physicians? The Emperor's priests of Asklepios?" Theodore's voice rose almost to a shout. "You ignore and belittle their skills? They are civilized men—men who have studied in Pergamum and Alexandria! Do you follow their advice? No! You bring in this barbarian to give our Emperor a woman's potion!"

"It iss not a voman's drink!" The young man's voice began to rise in anger. "It vill cure the *altjaarl!*"

Heraclius struggled with his left arm and managed to inch it out from under the quilts. He was terribly tired, even with this little exertion. His mouth was very dry, and he tried to speak, to ask for wine, but he could not make his tongue work. Then he saw his fingers, peeking out from under the quilt. They were swollen, all gray and shiny like fresh sausages. His fingernails were almost hidden by puffy flesh. He gulped.

The Emperor turned his head away from his ruined hand. In his mind, he was gibbering in complete panic. Unable to help himself, he moaned aloud in fear.

"Out!" came a distant shout, then a scuffling sound and more men shouting.

"Get everyone out of here!" Theodore had taken command at last. "Bring my physician!"

This is an ill omen.

Theodore, Prince of the Eastern Empire, commander of the left wing of the host of the Avtokrator of the Romans, ran a hand nervously through his hair. The physicians—his own men, adepts from the temples of Asklepios in glorious Egypt—had gone. A draught of wine, laced with medicinal powders, had been forced down the Emperor's throat, giving him sleep. Theodore fidgeted, tapping his fingers on the badly carved headboard of the canopied bed. His brother, the strong, powerful figure of his youth, was lying under blankets and quilts, a pasty gray color, helpless.

The priests had labored over him throughout the day, bending their hidden powers to defeat this enemy that had come so swiftly upon the Emperor. They had failed. Theodore almost laughed aloud, thinking of the surprise apparent on their features. Rarely did a disease or wound last, if one of the true priests of the Asklepion could be summoned.

Something beyond their skill within the Emperor had gone awry. In the end, all they could say was that he must need rest.

If he dies . . . I could rule the Empire. . . .

The thought was chilling, settling in his bones like ice. Theodore had never consciously considered the matter before. Heraclius was like a mountain, or the sky—indestructible and omnipotent. Heraclius had two sons, but they had not quite come of age yet. There was still a little time before they could don the Purple. In that space, Theodore would have to rule.

No . . . he is strong. He will beat this illness and stand once more, strong and hale, the Empress at his side. . . .

Theodore scowled at the thought of the Lady Martina. Heraclius' breath was ragged and made a bubbling sound from time to time. The smell and the sound drove Theodore to the window. The casement was deep and notched, sealed by a wooden shutter. The Prince undid the latch, feeling the rusting iron bite at his fingers. He pushed the panel open, and a rush of cold, wet air flooded into the room. Gasping in relief, he leaned his arms on the stones to either side, letting the mountain air drive back the miasma.

The frown had not left his face. The thought that Martina should be the Empress-Mother galled him. *She is our close cousin by the Red Bull!* Such a match never should have been made, much less acclaimed by the people or countenanced by the temples. Theodore's face settled into grim lines. There had been heated words between the brothers over that matter. Marrying a second or third cousin—that was acceptable, but your own mother's sister's daughter? That challenged the gods. The Prince never had liked little sly Martina. She had always set him on edge, making him feel small and provincial.

She has eyes like that Western prig, Galen. All filled with secret knowledge and pride.

Theodore turned away from the window, wiping his face with one hand. He felt anger build in him, but he pushed it down, burying it. He considered the days to come. It would be very difficult to carry through with the Emperor's plan to visit the cities and towns of Lycia and Asia on the way back to Constantinople. They would have to send him on by sea, and quickly, too, so that he could find succor among the wise men of the capital.

The Prince banged out of the chamber, his face still set in a grimace. His guardsmen, seeing that one of his moods was upon him, wisely stayed out of his way.

)¦(

"A fine fire," Khalid commented to his lieutenants as they picked their way through the smoking rubble of the old black-walled temple. "It seems to have done a merry job of clearing away the debris in this place."

The Persian officer laughed, though the other man—a Circassian from the north—did not show any expression at all at the jest. Khalid smiled inwardly. His men were simple enough to understand and they understood *him* and what he expected of them very well indeed. Khalid stepped over a charred cedar log that had been, when it had supported the roof of the temple, thicker than a man's waist. Now it was a crumbling log of blackened debris. Smoke rose all around them in thin wisps, marking where pockets of fire still smoldered.

The temple had burned for three days, while the Lord Mohammed had lain in the House of the Ben-Sarid. At last, even as the fires were guttering down, Mohammed had roused himself and been taken off to his household. The Ben-Sarid had gone, too, eager to return to their own business in Mekkah. Some of the Tanukh had stayed behind to take command of the policing of the temples and the precincts of the sacred well. Khalid and his men had stayed, too, though he was sure that no one had really marked their arrival beyond the Ben-Sarid chief, who was now quite busy. One of his men now carried the green war banner of the Quryash, though no one had actually granted Khalid the right to bear such a sigil.

"Round up the priests," he said to the Persian, "and see that all this rubble is cleared away. If they find any trinkets of their old gods, let them carry them away. We have no quarrel with them yet."

Khalid stopped, feeling the dull throb of heat seeping through the soles of his boots. One thing remained at the heart of the burned building. A wall of ancient, weathered stone rose out of the tumbled ash and burned logs and fire-cracked rock. It was no more than twenty feet high, but the upper course showed deep grooves that had once supported the upper reaches of a wall and perhaps a roof pillar. The blocks of stone that comprised the wall were five or six feet high and formed of some close-grained rock. Khalid ran a hand along the middle course, feeling them alive with warmth retained from the fire. His fingers came away black with soot. "All this," he said over his shoulder, "should be washed down and space cleared around it."

At the center of the wall was a recess, a space carved from the massive blocks. Khalid squatted in front of it, peering inside. His brow furrowed in concern, seeing that it appeared to be empty. He drew a pearl-handled knife from his belt and poked around in the hole. Caked ash crumbled away from the tip of the dagger in eggshell-like sheets. Khalid grimaced and put the strength of his arm into it. More ash was dug away and then the dagger tip hit something hard.

"Ah," he breathed, and began breaking away the congealed mass of ash and debris. There was something underneath it, something black and shining. A grin began to creep across his face.

"*Sheykh*, what about those statues?"

Khalid looked up, scowling at the interruption. The Circassian was pointing at the remaining two statues that had survived the inferno of the temple. Each was the rough form of a woman and they stood at either end of the ancient wall. Khalid's eyes narrowed, seeing the rounded, fat stomachs and the crudely carved beadwork that lined their heads. They were not tall statues—each only two or three feet high—but they had been chiseled from some dark green stone that had resisted the heat. Khalid pursed his lips, thinking, and then remembered something he had learned as a small boy. "Those gods have no followers anymore, my lads. Once, they stood at either hand of a statue of the great god Allah, whose sacred place this is. They were his consorts—I forget their names—but he has no need of them anymore. Besides, did not the Lord Mohammed say that a god cannot be captured in stone or wood? Bring some of the mules and drag them away. Perhaps someone will purchase them for garden ornaments! See to it now, in fact."

Laughing, the young man turned back to the little recess. A surface of shining black glass had been revealed, just as he had remembered from long ago. The dagger tip cleared away the last of the ash around the stone embedded in the wall. After a moment, the Circassian shrugged and tromped off through the ruins to find his soldiers. The Persian stayed, waiting quietly.

"There, my pretty. You are still here and none the worse for this housecleaning. . . ."

Khalid reached out a hand and brushed away the rest of the soot. Something tinkled under his fingers and then rattled out to fall on the ground. "Ouch!" Khalid drew back his hand, seeing a thin new cut seeping blood on his forefinger. He stuck his finger in his mouth. On the ground lay three thin wafers of black glassy stone. They caught the sun and gleamed around the edges, but nothing escaped from their murky depths. "Careful, my lad . . ." breathed Khalid to himself, bending over the fragments lying in the dust. Delicately, he picked up one wafer with his thumb and forefinger. It seemed fragile, but the edge was razor-sharp. His thumb was still seeping blood from the cut he had received.

"Now this," Khalid mused aloud, "will make a fine gift."

"Those paltry things? A gift?" The Persian *dihqan* sounded almost insulted.

Khalid grinned and pulled a scarf of dark blue Chin silk out of his belt. He wrapped each wafer individually in the scarf and then wrapped it around them, making a thickly padded package. This he put into a leather pouch that he wore around his neck.

"Long ago, Patik, my father, demanded that I learn from the holy priests of these temple grounds. Such was a fate visited upon all the youth of my tribe—our schooling as it were. So I came here often." He waved a hand airily around, indicating the tumbled ruins of the temple. "I sat in these stifling rooms, listening to old men ramble about the history of the world and the doings of the fathers of fathers of men. Do you know what that was like, my Persian friend?"

Patik shook his head, his thickly bearded face revealing little emotion. He was a stolid one, was Patik, steady and sure. Khalid did not think he had an ounce of imagination. Still, he was a useful fellow to have about. He was quick and ruthless with the men and he could ride and fight like a demon. Khalid had welcomed him when the Persian walked out of the wasteland and into the light of the Arab's campfire. Patik knew many of the tongues of the eastern lands—and by the chance of war, Khalid accounted more than one Easterner in his little band. These were uneasy times, and many a lion lay down with a wolf for safety.

"It was dreadful," Khalid continued, looking away at the clear blue sky, seeing something out of memory before him. "Boring and dull and useless . . . all save one old man who actually tried to teach us something interesting. Do you know who that old man was, Patik?"

Patik made a face and shook his head again. All of this made no difference to him.

Khalid spread his hands in resignation. "No matter. Of all the boring old men who have tried to shape my life, only he made some small dent in my thick head! But these little trinkets, they are going to become something larger than themselves—even as we are now larger than just men, Patik. Did you know, O reliable one, that you are walking at the edge of legend?"

"What? Here?" Patik said, looking around at the barren square and the piled rubble and the crews of men working in the sweltering heat of day to move stone and wood. Tanukh guards loitered in the shade of the pillared arcade and the entrances to the other temples. It seemed a quiet enough scene.

Khalid laughed again. "Never mind, my friend. Come, let us find a sword-smith—that should cheer you up."

THE EGYPTIAN HOUSE, OUTSIDE OF ROMA

)(

T hunder muttered over the hills to the east, showing brief flashes of yellow lightning in a wall of dark gray clouds that had been gathering since morning. To the west, in contrast, the sky was still clear and blue, though the permanent haze rising over the city of Rome turned the setting sun into a huge orange ball of fire. Krista sniffed, smelling the odd lightning odor that always seemed to taint the air around the villa. She was warmly dressed for late spring, in a long gown of heavy charcoal gray wool. Her hair, usually unbound, was carefully pinned up in a bundle behind her head, and a shawl rode on her shoulders. She stood quietly beside one of the pillars on the western side of the house, watching the golden afternoon light creep down the walls of the portico. In that magical light the fading paint on the walls seemed to restore itself, showing again the brilliant frescoes of dancers and acrobats, of bulls and Minotaurs, which had once graced the long western face of the house. In earlier times this had been one of her favorite parts of the day—the sun almost setting, its slanting light burnishing everything with a warm golden aura, the air quiet, waiting for darkness to fall.

Now it was an *important* part of the day, a time where

she needed to be alone, if only for a moment. Within an hour the sun would go down and the Prince's ceremonies would begin in the deep, cold cellars under the house. Thinking of the chill, she drew the shawl tighter around her. Up here, in the open air, it was still warm with heat from the day. There, in the depths below, it would be bone chillingly cold. During their previous stay the cellars had held a pleasant, even temperature. Now the Prince's exercises had leached the heat from the rooms and chambers until frost accumulated in the corners. Thick woolen hose graced her legs, too, and she wore stout leather boots.

Krista smiled, fingering the shawl and thinking of the nimble fingers of her Walach boys. They were clever with any kind of needle, thread, or fabric. The thought made her frown. Emotional attachments were proving dangerous enough as it was. She stood away from the pillar and turned slowly, looking first to the right and then to the left. The vaulted portico was empty, though she could hear noise from the kitchens. Satisfied that she was not observed, Krista raised a small silver mirror—a gift from the Duchess on her fourteenth birthday—and held it up to the sun. She felt the warmth of that distant orb glowing in her hand for a moment and then turned the mirror slowly until it faced the wooded hillside at an angle.

Her hand dipped the mirror once, then twice. *Today*, flew the signal.

"So," Maxian said, "we come to the crux of the matter."

The Prince stood and rotated a sheet of plain brown parchment on the table. A series of diagrams and symbols had been inked on the double-wide page. The table was crowded with scrolls of papyrus and burnished red-and-black bowls holding half-eaten pheasant, peeled fruit, and shelled nuts. The Prince traced a set of interlocking symbols with one long, thin finger.

"We still have not acquired the text of the original oath, but the tireless efforts of Abdmachus here"—the little Persian was sitting at one side of the table, his dull, flat eyes staring into empty air above the center of the oaken table-top—"have yielded this much to us. The structure of the Oath—or curse, if you prefer—is built upon a similarity lattice. Well, I should say that it is built upon an inter-locking series of lattices."

Krista was also sitting at the edge of the table, though she had commandeered a wing-backed chair with sweeping padded arms and thick cushions. She had a bowl of grapes, cut pears, peeled tangerine sections, and sliced apples in her lap. The little black cat had wormed itself into the crook of her arm and was lying across her stomach, purring like a little mill wheel. Krista's white teeth bit into a slice of pear while she listened with half an ear to the Prince. The little cat yawned, showing a pink mouth in the supple black felt of its face. It nosed at her hand as she reached into the bowl for more fruit. It wanted its tribute.

"Bad kitten," she whispered to it. "You'll be round as a gourd if you keep eating all that bird."

The kitten's yellow eyes blinked up at her, and it squirmed around onto its back. She smiled secretly at it and rubbed its warm tummy with her free hand. The bad little kitten wrapped itself around her palm and bit her fingers lightly. Krista smiled again.

"The lattices anchor the image of the Empire that the curse operates from." The Prince had continued on without noticing the little cat's antics. "Each lattice contains, as best we can tell, one or more *forms* of some aspect of the Empire. The matter in which bread is baked, for example, may exist in one of these lattices. Even the kind of ovens that are *allowed* are held in these patterns of forms. These forms, however, do not exist in the reality that we can feel or touch or see."

The Prince rapped his knuckles on the smooth surface of the table to show his point. Gaius and Alexandros, sprawled on separate couches set beside the dining table, watched him carefully. Krista watched them in turn, which was a task she had taken upon herself once she had marked how much time they spent with one another. The old Roman leaned on one arm of his couch with the ease of long practice and equal patience. The young Macedonian, however, fidgeted constantly. He would recline for a time, then suddenly sit up and plant his elbows on the tabletop. He could not sit still. Krista hid a smile, thinking that he looked like a small boy who desperately needed to go to the privy.

"But these forms of the 'ideal' Empire do have an existence," the Prince remarked. "They must, for otherwise the Oath could not constrain the rest of the Empire to them."

"Lord Prince," Alexandros interjected abruptly. "If they do not exist in a material form, how can they affect anything else?"

Maxian smiled, his handsome face marked by a long-held weariness.

"Not all things," he said, "that exist can be touched or felt or seen. There are things that affect each of us every day that are not . . . um, material, I suppose."

"Like what?" Alexandros was sitting up again, seemingly poised to leap to his feet. "How can something affect me if it does not have a means to effect me? Something cannot touch *me* unless it itself can be touched."

Maxian sighed and seemed on the verge of glaring openly at the young man. Then he took a deep breath and rubbed his chin in a nervous gesture.

"Ideas," the Prince said slowly, "affect the world. They affect you. You are constrained by honor, are you not?"

"Yes," the Macedonian said equally slowly. The young man's eyes narrowed, and Krista was put in mind of a cagey horse suspecting that the man with an apple might have a lasso behind his back. "I must act as honor and the gods demand. To be otherwise is to court the fates and disaster."

"Exactly," Maxian said sharply, "but you cannot touch *honor*. You cannot see it, or feel it. But it affects you, it affects me, and through us it affects all around us. So it is with the curse—this idea of an Empire of Rome—all fixed in its expression at the time of the Divine Augustus."

Gaius snorted and made to sit up, his eyes dancing with indignation. "Puppy!"

Maxian smiled crookedly and waved for the older man to sit back down.

"The traditions of the Senate promulgate this idea, too, and its expression is written down and passed from father to son throughout the generations." The Prince paused, looking thoughtful. "This is the core of the power of the Oath—the Empire that *should* exist lives in the minds of men, in their memories of the past and belief of how things should be. So are these lattices of form maintained, but then the Oath has the ability to seek out and destroy those who would change that fabric of memory. Too, it can exalt those who would reinforce or maintain these beliefs. So do our armies still fight in the way that they have for two thousand years. Our language maintains, unchanged, such that a man of Alexandros' day can still understand our speech today. The Oath freezes the Empire in amber, a trapped fly with a beating heart. A bee constantly building and reinforcing its own prison."

The Prince's voice ran down, and a cloud seemed to pass over his face. Krista leaned a little forward, her liquid brown eyes watching him carefully. After a moment, Maxian shook his head and looked up again.

"All these lattices, my friend, give the Oath its shape, its purpose, and a form. They interlock in a manifestation of dazzling proportions, reaching from one end of the Empire to the other. They penetrate into the very blood and bone of the people. It is mindless, but subtle. It has no forethought, but it has great purpose. As we have seen, it is surpassingly powerful."

"And you, my Lord Prince, will overturn all this?" Gaius' words seemed mocking, but his face and voice were utterly sincere. "In previous discussions, you and the Persian felt there had to be a keystone that tied all of this together. I know what I believe that key is. Have you found the thing itself?"

Maxian's eyes glinted in anger, but it did not reach his face.

"Yes, Gaius Julius, we have found this key and anchor. It is—I grant you—as you suspected."

"The Emperor," Alexandros said, grinning. "Your very brother."

Cold air lapped at Krista's ankles, seeping through her woolen hose like the icy water of some black Germanian river. She shuddered as she descended the stairs, feeling the clammy air lapping up around her waist. Even here, at the top of the steps, she could hear the droning chant rising from the hidden rooms. The sound set the hairs on the back of her neck up. The Walachs—her Walachs—could be heard as a basso counterpoint to the higher pitch raised by the Persian and Nabatean servants that Abdmachus had gathered. The sound echoed and rolled around the ceiling of the long hallway. For all the volume of the humming drone, it did not pass the top of the steps. There on the crumbling slate a line of pale green glyphs shimmered in the near-darkness, forming a barrier to stop the cold murk and the odd sounds that emanated from the basement.

Icy air closed over her head, and she shuddered, but then smoothed her features and straightened her shoulders. Lanterns gleamed in corroded green sconces, lighting the hallway with pools of pale blue light. Inside each sphere of glass something buzzed and flicked against the glass, casting vague shadows. At the end of the hallway was a turn, and a flight of narrow steps led down into the central room that lay at the base of the house. Here, standing in the doorway of the room, the hum and drone and buzz was loud, like the roar of the crowd in the circus at midday. Even the half-hidden smell of old dried blood that hung in the air was reminiscent of the Games.

At the center of the floor, a circle seven feet wide had been incised in the paving stones and marked with salt and green powder. Outside that circle lay six more layers of ever-expanding rings, each cut an inch or more into the floor of the room. Signs and symbols had been precisely marked into the spaces between each circle until they filled the room from wall to wall. Beneath these new markings, the remains of older signs and symbols could still be seen. This was not the first time the Prince had attempted such a working in these dank chambers. The servants sat along the outside of the outermost ring, each in their own carefully marked space. Candles burned at the cardinal points of each servant's tetrahedron and at the corners of the room.

In the center, at the heart of the innermost ring, lay a marble table the length and breadth of a man. Within the central ring, three triangles formed of silver and gold lines converged upon the table, making a hexagon out of their intersection. Above, the ceiling shimmered and gleamed with a layer of oddly colored green mist that cast a sallow pall across the faces of those gathered in the room.

The Prince Maxian stood at one side of the innermost ring. He wore long dark blue silk pantaloons and a belt of lead links. His chest was bare and smooth, anointed with marks and signs painted in white and purple. His long dark brown hair was tied back behind his head and fell in a tight braid to the small of his back. While the Prince stood, Gaius Julius, Abdmachus, and Alexandros knelt in the triangles, their bodies naked to the waist, free of the kabalistic symbols that marked the Prince. On each forehead, an inverted triangle had been marked in purple dye.

Krista entered the room quietly and stepped off the lowest stair into a pentacle of miniature lead cones that stood nearby. This was her place in the ceremony, where she could watch both the door and the room, and stand apart— or so the Prince had promised—from the power that he sought to unleash here.

Within a grain of entering the room, her hair began to rustle and lift away from her shoulders, charged by unseen forces building in the air and stone around her.

*   *   *

"Yes, the Emperor is the focus and anchor of the curse." Maxian's voice was cold and hard, admitting no interruption. "Through him, as in the state, all things flow. But I warn you, Gaius Julius, that attempting to murder him will not only fail to break the power of the curse, but is the surest road to annihilation that you can possibly devise."

"Surely," Gaius responded with an easy air, "any direct attack upon the person of the Emperor would only draw the full power of the thing upon us. But, I say in all deference to your familial love, there is *no way* the curse can be broken without the Emperor—he who is the very keystone of this thing!—being removed from that position. An arched bridge can carry an enormous burden—a hundred wagons or more—when fully intact. But remove the one stone at its heart? Then it is torn apart by its own weight!"

Maxian was silent for a moment, his eyes locked with the older man's.

Finally, Gaius looked away and raised his hands in surrender. "So be it, my Lord Prince. We will undertake whatever plan you have devised to circumvent this problem. Please, enlighten us!"

"Wait," Krista said quietly, drawing all eyes to her. She had sat through countless sessions among these men, but rarely spoke herself. That she did so now gained her their undivided attention. A knot of tension began to grow in her stomach. "I have a question."

"What is it?" Maxian seemed relieved that the nascent argument had been interrupted. But there was irritation and wariness in his expression, too.

Krista suppressed a raised eyebrow at the look on his face. *So the pretty girl might have a mind and you're surprised? Even disappointed?*

"If, my lord, there is an . . . an image of how the Empire is supposed to be, something like the time of the Principate, then why are there two Empires today?" She smiled slyly sideways at Gaius Julius. "Surely the Divine Augustus would have been displeased with such a division . . ."

Gaius ignored her barb and stared up at the ceiling. Beyond him, however, Alexandros chuckled in delight to see the discomfiture evident in the set of the old Roman's shoulders. Maxian turned a little to Abdmachus and indicated the old Persian with one hand. "I had the same thought when first Abdmachus and I discussed this. Abd'?"

The Persian roused himself, his head rotating slowly first to look to the Prince and then back again to view the others. Krista crushed an instinct to flinch away from the cold, dead eyes and expressionless face and remained seated, smiling pleasantly at the old man.

"The Empire has sustained terrible shocks over the past four hundred years. Barbarian invasions have threatened to overwhelm the frontiers. Intrigue and jealousy have threatened to tear it apart from within. The economy was driven into collapse by unwise fiscal policies and its own failure to evolve." The Persian's voice was toneless and even as a measuring bob.

"Yet through all this, through plague and war, the Empire has been sustained by the power of the Oath. Legions that might have mutinied over back pay soldiered on. Men who aspired to murder capable emperors died themselves. The army, even overmatched by a hundred times, fought on grimly. Men who could have taken their *honesta misso* after six years of service stayed in the Legions for ten or twenty years. Their sons and grandsons willingly followed them into that same service."

At that, Gaius Julius and Alexandros both perked up, though Krista did not know why.

"There is strength in a wholeness—the Oath proves this as no other test or example could. Why then two Empires, side by side?" Abdmachus' flat eyes slid from face to face, his old, lined face immobile save for the movement of his lips.

"There are two Empires because the Divine Diocletian had no choice but to take firm action while he was master of the world. In the year 1037 *ab urbe condita* the man once named Diocles made himself ruler of an empire threatened on all sides by turmoil and invasion. He was a wise man, he who named himself Diocletian upon his assumption of the Purple. He knew that a single man could no longer rule the whole vast sweep of the Empire. All men know this, that the wise Diocletian divided the Empire into East and West."

The old Persian stopped, seemingly lost in thought. Maxian, after waiting a moment, spoke: "But remember, my friends, that Diocletian was Emperor of the whole of the Empire. He appointed a *junior* Caesar and Augustus to rule by his side and entrusted the loyal Maximian with the eastern half of the Empire. The core of the Empire, upon which the Oath lies most heavy, remained under Diocletian's direct control. So was the Oath satisfied—it is not a wise thing, this curse—and as long as Rome remains and the Empire remains, it can countenance in its blind way the passage of provinces into and out of the Empire. And then, with the loyal Maximian ruling the East, the division of the Empire was in name only."

"Then what happened?" Gaius Julius was at last paying full attention. "It is clear there are two entirely separate Empires now, each naming itself Rome."

"The mighty rebel Constantine happened," Maxian said in a wry voice. "After the death of Diocletian the Empire remained divided for administrative purposes. Two separate Augustii could more effectively govern the vast state that had arisen and deal with the constant troubles that assailed it. For a time, this worked well, but in the East, where the General Constantius had succeeded loyal Maximian, trouble was brewing. While the West remained under the firm hand of Galerius, the adopted son of Diocletian, in the Asian provinces the son of Constantius was plotting to outdo his father." The Prince paused and drank from a brass wine cup set on the table.

"The elder Constantius lived only a year as Augustus. His son—a man of enormous energy, conviction, and military ability—was acclaimed as Emperor in the East by the Legions in Thrace and Macedonia. Galerius, the Western

Emperor, protested this appointment, but Constantine was already moving against him."

"There was war," Abdmachus said, suddenly speaking. "Roman strove openly against Roman for the first time in four hundred years. How could this be? Because the Eastern Empire had already passed from under the aegis of the Oath. Though to a thing with mind and forethought the loss of half of the Empire—the richer and more populous half by far!—would seem a thing of dreadful aspect, to the Oath it knew only that Rome still maintained and that the Emperor on the throne still upheld the acts and usages of his father."

"Galerius sent his armies against Constantine," Maxian continued, "and attempted to overthrow the usurper, but the Eastern Legions threw back the West, soundly defeating them in a great battle at Thessalonika. The next year Galerius died of a terrible wasting disease. To my mind, looking back over the centuries, I think the curse removed him from the field of play. It may have been that Galerius was considering peace with the Eastern rebels. The ever-crafty Constantine offered peace and proclaimed himself 'senior' Augustus. In Rome, Galerius' old friend and subordinate Licinus was proclaimed Emperor, but he was of no mood to be subordinate to a younger man.

"The war continued, but it was Constantine who felt the sting of defeat next. Despite outnumbering Licinus' army by three to one, his invasion of Italy was a disaster, and his fleet was scattered by a great storm off Tarentum. Thereafter there was an uneasy peace . . . other troubles and threats rose up to command the attention of the Emperors, and in time the two Empires came to live side by side."

"But," Alexandros said with a lilt in his voice, "the Eastern Empire was no longer under the sway of the Oath. True?"

"In part," Maxian replied, "vestiges of it remain—they still call themselves Romans and try to maintain the ancient traditions and honors. But you can see the change that centuries have wrought—their language is Greek now, and they no longer rule themselves as Rome did."

"But," Alexandros said again, his eyes bright, "they have placed themselves beyond the Oath by this?"

"Yes," Maxian said wearily, missing the look that passed between Gaius and Alexandros. "But the West is still its slave."

Maxian grunted a little, lifting a cylinder of carved marble from the floor up onto the tabletop. The Persian slaves had found an old burial urn for the stolen ashes. It seemed almost new, save for its archaic design and corrosion still clinging stubbornly to the bronze fittings.

"Here is what will be our keystone," Maxian said, turning the cylinder about. "These are the mortal remains of the first Emperor—Gaius Octavian—now better known as Augustus. It was he who first commanded the changes to the soldiers' Oath that gave rise to this curse. It is he, now, who will help us break it. Gaius Julius has been adamant in his belief that we cannot break the Oath without involving the current Emperor, my brother."

Gaius Julius leaned back on his couch, a half smile lurking on his thin lips.

Maxian nodded to him and raised up the cylinder. "Our dear Gaius believes," Maxian continued, "that only the death of my brother will free the Empire. He has a cruel and bloody mind, our Gaius, but he is not a sorcerer. I have, I believe, found another way to take the key from the lock, to bring down the Oath, without this murder. . . ."

Krista pulled back the ears of the little black cat, making its yellow eyes into narrow slits and showing its fangs. The little cat shook its head, freeing its ears from her light touch. It yawned up at her, showing sharp white teeth. Despite this byplay with the little scamp, she was listening intently to Maxian's voice. There was hope in it, and certainty, and her heart veered toward believing in him again. Duty warred with the remnant of affection in her heart— once, she had believed in Maxian, perhaps even loved him as much as a common woman may love a prince. She knew he believed that he loved her, though that was such a fickle thing, she had put no credence in it. Many men had said they loved her—some had even said they would buy her from her mistress, the Duchess, and free her. They had lied.

Would they have made the offer, she wondered, *if they had known she was in truth no slave?*

Only this man, this Prince, had made her a real offer of freedom, though it had been in extremis at the edge of the world, preparing for battle against the Persian magi in their old, dead city. Then, that had counted heavily for her, that he would make the gesture when he desperately needed her at his back. But now? With Gaius Julius and the golden youth filling his ears with their thoughts, their desire, their plans, and schemes? She saw him less and less, His mind and mood had turned away from her and down darker paths. The inevitability of some action against the Emperor seemed to grow stronger and stronger.

And now duty wars against my heart, and the heart loses.

"My brother, friend Gaius," Maxian said, "is currently the keystone we seek. But he need not remain so. Here is an ancient law of the sorcerer's realm—that thing that owns the seeming of another thing may become that thing. A hair, taken from the head of a man, can be used—by this law of similarity—to affect the man himself. At this instant, the Augustus Galen is the crux of the Oath, but with this"—he rubbed his hands over the top of the cylinder—"we can bring forth an older precedent. We can bring forth Augustus himself, and through him, strike at the Oath without touching my brother."

Alexandros made a sound, more than a snort of disbelief and less than outright laughter. Maxian turned his head, glaring at the youth, but Alexandros shook his head and showed his palms.

"Mummery! If you say it will work, perhaps it will, but what will you do if this *substitution* does not work? What will you do if, in the throes of battle, you find your knife at your brother's throat?"

Maxian's face darkened, and Krista tensed, seeing the imminent dissolution of the golden youth at hand. Her right hand clenched into a fist, and the smooth, cold tube of the spring-gun filled her palm. She rummaged the little cat with her left hand, making it squeak. Gaius Julius turned a little at the noise, and she caught his eye. She shook her head minutely, pinning his gaze, and the spring-gun eased out of her sleeve, focusing on him under the cover of the table. The old Roman raised his eyebrows and put a blank look on his face.

"Noble Macedonian," Maxian hissed, "I will not murder my brother. I know it was the common sport of your youth, but here, in my Rome, we will sustain the family that I love. Do you understand me?"

"Oh yes." Alexandros smirked, standing away from the table, his blue eyes hard with old knowledge, dearly bought in a bitter childhood. "You will send tens of thousands to their deaths to salve your conscience, where the death of one—even a dearly beloved one—would suffice. It is good you are not Emperor, for you have not the stomach for it."

"I will never be Emperor," Maxian grated, his left eyelid twitching in barely repressed fury. "My brother and his sons will found that line. What we do is for the Senate and the people, not for personal gain."

Alexandros shook his head, disbelief plain upon his noble face. His thought was clear to Krista, who had relaxed a little. The youth knew in his heart of hearts that the only prize, the only goal, was to rule and to command the world. The Macedonian bowed insolently and then stalked out of the room. The Prince stared after him, then turned to Gaius Julius. "Ensure that he is ready for the ceremony tonight. We are prepared. We will make the throw."

The storm crawled down over the hills, sending rain and wind in front of it. On the hillside above the old, decaying villa, the trees shook and bent under the force of the wind, creaking and groaning. Icy rain spilled down between the trunks, spattering on the thick loam under the limbs. In the near darkness, now that the storm had covered the sun, two men crouched in the lee of a snag. Even here, where they were out of the wind, they could feel the temperature dropping rapidly. Thick woolen cloaks and padded hauberks kept them warm for the moment, but one of them was pulling on thick gloves to keep some feeling in his fingers.

"This is a storm like on the grasslands north of the Azov," the taller man shouted over the whistling roar of the wind. "Comes up out of nowhere and leaves frozen men and horses behind."

The other, shorter man nodded and peered between the thick trunks of the trees down at the villa in the clearing below. He had a weathered tan face, with a short stubble of beard, a bald pate, and a stubby nose. He was stocky and thick-wristed, with a wrestler's arms. Under the cloak he wore a shirt of thick iron rings over a heavy woolen undershirt. A legionary's short sword was strapped to his belt along with knives and pouches of well-worn leather. The taller man at his side had long, curly hair tied behind his head, an aquiline nose, and liquid brown eyes. Unlike his companion, he was well armed with a long cavalry sword—the *spatha* of the Eastern Empire—and a bow, enclosed in a *gorytos* or bow case of stiff leather, was strapped to his back along with a wooden case for black-fletched arrows. Their horses were hidden behind them, deeper in the hazel and witchberry bush that covered the hill.

"Can you see anything?" The taller man was still shouting, trying to make himself heard over the din of the trees being lashed by the storm. The rain began to fall heavily, and sight of the villa disappeared into a dark mist of falling water and blowing leaves. "Nikos?"

The shorter man shook his head, and his fingers made signs in the air. The taller man frowned, trying to follow the quick succession of signs. After a moment, and after Nikos repeated them, he made out:

The lights have gone out. And then, *If the others do not arrive quickly, we will go in ourselves.*

The tall man frowned at that, but made no answer. They had been expecting their backup for three hours, but the other Khazars and the maniple of legionaries that the Duchess had borrowed from the military camp north of the capital had yet to appear. Some deviltry was at work down in the ancient ruin. Their spy inside had only said that something was in the offing, something against the Emperor. Something that would happen tonight.

Jusuf, Prince of the Khazar people, settled himself back down in the shelter of the tree. The Illyrian, Nikos, continued to watch and wait. The storm howled, and small branches, broken from the crown of the trees, began to rattle through the canopy. Lightning flared in the heavens, sending a brief brilliant flash through the forest. Below, roof tiles shattered under the blow, sizzling and crackling with the heat of the stroke. The storm was getting worse.

At the center of the chamber, within the boundary of gold and silver, the Prince stood at the head of the marble table, a silk bag held reverently in his hands. He raised the bag, still tied closed with purple string, toward the northern corner of the room. As he did so the chanting of the Nabateans died, dwindling away to a low, almost inaudible mutter. The Prince turned and raised the bag toward the east and as he did so, the droning sound from the Persians faded away. He turned to the south, and the Walachs fell silent, and last to the west, where even the last low mutter of the Nabateans ceased.

"This is the body of our Emperor," Maxian declared to the still air. Even the odd mist along the ceiling had stilled, ceasing its constantly roiling movement. "This is the body of the state, of the Senate, of the people, and of the city of Rome. Praise him, our Emperor, from whom all order and justice flow."

Maxian bent over the marble table and took the bag in his left hand. With a quick movement he unknotted the string with his right hand and took the cord in his teeth. Carefully, he opened the top of the bag and shook it lightly to break up any clumps that might have formed inside. On the tabletop, the outline of a man with arms at his sides had been marked in purple chalk. The Prince's forehead creased in concentration, and he bowed his head, holding the open bag in front of him cupped in both hands. His eyes closed.

Krista started nervously and cocked her head. Some sound trembled in the air, just past hearing. A thin hum filtered out of the stones under her feet, and the shimmering echo of a distant gong. The sound rose, pulsing like a beating heart, making the air quiver in anticipation. The sound of horns rang, and the wail of the *bucina*—all faint, like the memory of some ancient battle renewed by the light of a dying sun—then a vague tremor of men's voices raised in a thunderous shout. Krista's head snapped around, her eyes wide in alarm, and a flickering glow of ultraviolet and static blue washed over her face.

Power crackled in the air around the Prince, a slow dance of standing lightning flaring between the Prince and his three companions. The air shifted, wind rising up and blowing past Krista, rushing out the door of the chamber. The Nabateans and Persians and Walachs bowed their foreheads to the paving stones of the floor and—almost unheard over the building roar of lightning and thunder that growled at the center of the room—they began to chant again.

The Prince forced his hands apart, crackling and burning with crawling rivers of red and electric blue. His eyes were black pits, thrown in sharp relief by the flare of light that streamed out of his hands. The bag disintegrated, but the pale ashy dust inside did not. Wind caught at it and swirled it up, whipping the dust this way and that. The Prince's mouth moved, speaking a single word.

The air boomed, and Krista found herself on her knees,

gasping for breath, one hand skinned on the stone floor, reaching for some support. At her fingertip a lead cone rattled, almost unbalanced. A smear of blood marked the paving stone. The green mist rushed away, spilling through the doorway in flight, and the ceiling, now revealed, seemed to recede into an infinite distance.

The dust whirled in a broad circle over the marble surface, still just contained by the boundary of gold and lead that circumscribed the table and the Prince. Maxian, his face marked with concentration, pushed his hands against the air, drawing them farther and farther apart.

Krista, crouched within the pentacle by the door, could hear his voice at a great distance, speaking like a god in the mountains, a vast and enormous sound.

"We honor and obey our Lord, the Emperor of all Rome, the master of the world."

The dust whirled even faster, but now grains of it, sparkling in the shuddering light, flashed out of the stream and snapped to the tabletop. One by one, the grains flew to lie within the outline of the man marked on the marble. One by one, they rushed together, piling higher and higher.

Krista squinted. It was hard to see with the shimmering heat haze in the air and the rippling lightning that still danced between the three men. Gaius Julius and Alexandros seemed to be screaming, or crying out, but she could not hear their voices, only that of the Prince. Abdmachus had only slumped to one side, dull eyes staring straight ahead.

A body formed with dizzying speed on the table; that of a man of middle height, stooped by age, his face lined with wrinkles and long-held care. One foot was a little twisted, some ancient injury leaving a long scar along his leg. The Prince raised his hands up, into the air, and the last of the dust settled. The corpse was whole, knitted together by sorcery and trapped lightning.

"We honor him, the Emperor, and make sacrifice to him, blessing him and his regal name, Imperator Caesar Divi Filius Augustus."

*   *   *

Thunder rattled the wooden window shutters that lined the upper floor of the house. A blue-white crack sizzled in the air, sending echoes rolling over the hills. Rain continued to pour down, filling the dead garden with slowly spreading pools of mud. Along the main hall of the villa, now empty and dark, was a flicker of red light along the floor. Tiny signs and symbols of protection marked there months before by the Persian sorcerer Abdmachus flared up brilliantly and then died. A tide of black mist began to creep in from the garden doors. Where the mist touched, the tesserae of the floor crumbled to dust, and the stones and wooden supports of the roof and the walls began to flake away, eroding at a fantastic pace.

At the center of the house, in the barren inner courtyard, where once ten thousand flowers had bloomed in spring to bring a smile to the face of a young queen, a figure stood, alone, exposed to the fury of the storm that rippled and cracked in the heavens above. Dark clouds swirled in the sky, glowing with the constant flash of lightning. Ice and rain fell, lashing the tiled roof. The garden was filling with water from the torrential rain.

The figure stood, inviolate and uncaring, in the storm. A dull yellow gleam marked the slits of its eyes. Water sluiced off a bony skull, ridged with long, twisting lines of tiny stitches. The *homunculus*, Khiron, waited patiently, watching and listening to the roar of the storm. Hail drummed on its ancient flesh, but the thing did not feel the blows.

The mist drifted into the rooms on the main floor, filling them slowly with dark poison.

"Here is our Lord, the Emperor of all men, we praise him!"

Maxian struggled in the grip of lightning, his voice rasping with the effort of forcing words from his throat. The vertices of power—ultraviolet and pale green—that whirled around him, linking him, the old man, the Persian, and the youth in a blizzard of hurtling sparks, were enormously strong. The power inherent in the youth and his legend, coupled with the ever-growing strength of the Prince and the bedrock solidity of the old man, cascaded into a dizzying pattern. At the center, now whole and fleshed, the corpse of the first Emperor twitched and shuddered in time with the beat of Maxian's heart. The circles of ward and protection were ablaze with light, straining to contain the maelstrom that the Prince had unleashed.

"Here is the ruler of the world, Imperator Caesar Divi Filius Augustus! Emperor of Rome!"

Maxian opened his hands, spreading them out and away from him. As he did so, his sight expanded, swelling beyond the immediate confines of the buried chamber and the rings and circles of power. He descended into the universe of forms, and there he beheld the full power of his enemy.

The curse had come against him with all power, a black tide that overtopped the house and filled the whole land around and about him. Maxian shuddered, seeing the enormous malignant strength that arrayed itself against the villa. He felt the bones of the house corrode as the black mist attacked them. He felt the dying of every living thing that did not hew to the Oath for miles around. Inverted lightning rippled along the face of the storm front, black tendrils of corruption lashing at the shields that protected the chamber and those within it. Abdmachus' painstaking work was dying, ground down by the massed will of tens of millions of people, all bound to the Oath and the destruction of this threat.

Maxian's hands blurred into motion, the vortex that roared and raged around him would smash down the barriers in a little time, so he worked quickly. The form and substance of the first Emperor shifted and shuddered on the table before him. He must now find the keystone and invoke it, passing the anchor of the Oath from his brother to this ancient thing. His thought leapt out, burning bluewhite through the storm and chaos around the villa.

At a great distance, he could feel the thought and shape of his brother.

"Go!" Nikos chopped his hand down, pointing off through the blinding rain in the direction of the villa. The boom and crack of the storm had risen to a pitch that constantly lit the air with a blaze of lightning. Hail and rain were smashing the canopy of the trees to nothing. Men moved in the murk, all around him, running forward down the hill. Nikos held his round shield over his head, trying to keep from being struck down by the fist-sized ice that was falling out of the sky. The temperature had continued to drop, and it was well below freezing.

The Illyrian loped down the face of the hill, feeling the ground sliding and gelatinous under his feet. So much rain had fallen that the ground was beginning to liquefy. Jusuf was hard at his heels, running flat out. Twenty or thirty other men ran at their side—the praetorians had finally managed to reach the hill. Their commander had tried explaining why they were late, but Nikos had been unable to hear him over the thunder. Regardless, the praetorians, bulky in their heavy armor and thick red cloaks, rushed forward with them. The band of men hit the edge of the gardens and scrambled over the brick wall at the bottom of the hill. The wall crumbled under their boots, the bricks shattering and breaking apart at the touch of a hobnail. Two men went down, struggling in the mud. Nikos ignored them and pressed on, bent nearly double in the face of the howling wind.

Maxian's thought arrowed out over the broad ocean, his spirit seeing waves and islands and the coastline of southern Italia flash past under him. The sun had set, dropping behind the curve of the world, and the night was dark and moonless. Miniscule lights of cities and towns fell away behind him, and then, sparkling on the surface of the waters, his spirit eye saw the gleam of lanterns. A fleet plunged through the dark sea, great ships cutting through the waves, driven by an eastern wind.

There, in the cabin of the flagship, his brother lay in sleep, dreamless and content in his thoughts of victory. Maxian's will penetrated the walls of the ship, passing guardsmen and sailors on watch, passing unhindered through planks and stays. His brother slept. His thin, narrow face, usually so marked with worry and grim with the concerns of Empire and the state, was peaceful in the light of a single candle. One hand was clasped on his chest, covering an unopened letter.

Maxian hovered over him, looking down on the face of Galen, seeing in him an echo of their gruff father and warm mother. For an instant, memories of old times—in childhood and youth—flooded over him: Galen laughing, holding up a brace of tigery kittens that the barn cat had birthed one summer in Narbo. Galen and Aurelian rolling on the lawn of the summerhouse at Cumae, brambles and twigs in their hair. Maxian reached down, his spirit hand ghostly and indistinct, wavering in the dim light, and brushed back the lock of lank, dark hair that always fell over Galen's forehead.

Pain flashed at the touch, and Maxian froze, feeling the black corruption welling up around him, seeping out of the timbers of the ship, from the close weave of the linen sheets, even from blood and bone of his brother. The Prince felt threat hanging around him, but he steeled his will and made a sign in the air.

The glyph sputtered and flashed, hanging afire in the world of forms. Maxian summoned up a long invocation— carefully memorized and drilled over and over—and let it form in his mind. Despite the lurid descriptions of the popular ballads, the words he summoned did not shape the world. Instead, they served as a mnemonic that described patterns of force that he put into play with his will. Into the shape of his brother as Emperor—a thing that hung like a shroud around the bright golden flame of Galen himself in the world of forms—he sank deep hooks of intent and desire and thought. The curse boiled up around him, black as the pit, and attacked, lashing at him with fangs of deep blue night.

Maxian howled in anguish, feeling the teeth bite into him. But his will did not waver. The shroud of Empire was torn away from the sleeping Emperor, and Maxian fled, all thought focused upon returning to the Egyptian House and the shuddering half-alive corpse of Augustus.

A burly praetorian with shoulders like Atlas crashed through the wooden door. It shattered as soon as he put his full body against it, sending the soldier sprawling on the ground amid a cloud of sawdust and broken hinges. Nikos leapt over the man without even pausing and darted down a long hallway. Black mist boiled around his feet, but the dreadful corruption did not touch him. It was a tremendous relief to be out of the storm and under shelter. The hallway was dark, but Nikos had come prepared. He skidded to a halt and unclipped a storm lantern from his belt. Behind him, more praetorians clambered through the doorway, their swords out. Every third man fell aside as they entered and shifted lanterns from their backs. Leather hoods were removed, and flints sparked in the darkness. A flame leapt up, casting a pale yellow glow on the walls and the faces of the men.

Thunder rumbled in the sky, and the crack of fresh lightning sent white bursts of light through the windows. Nikos looked around, finding his squad leaders by the plumes on their helmets. "Break out in groups of five," he rasped in his command voice, "two lanterns with each. Check each room, each hallway, each cupboard. Prisoners are to be taken alive if possible. There is one friendly, a young woman with dark red-brown hair. Go!"

The praetorians clattered off down the hallway, their swords and spears bright in the lantern light. Nikos looked over at Jusuf, who had unslung his bow and had a long dark arrow fitted to the notch. Here, in the darkness, with unknown enemies about, with some undefined conspiracy against the Emperor afoot, the Illyrian wished devoutly for the presence of his old commander, the Amazon Thyatis. She never had a queasy stomach on an operation like this. *Enough moping*, he snarled to himself. He moved forward through the dark house, Jusuf ready at his back with a strung arrow.

Here, in the dim confines of the house, the storm was muted. Trickles of water spilled down out of the ceiling.

Maxian fell through clouds boiling with fire. Black flames licked at his spirit form, sending agonizing jolts of pain through his mind. He fell through night sky, curled around the cloak of the Emperor, and was in the buried chamber again. The standing ring of power continued to howl and buzz, rushing around the triangle formed by the three men. Maxian settled again within his body, all concentration focused upon the shifting pattern of forms that he had stolen from his brother. He launched into the next phase of the incantation, all effort at last collapsing upon this one single thing.

At the side of the room, Krista covered her head, flinching aside as rock flakes spalled down out of the ceiling. The house above shuddered like a dying thing, shaking with each new peal of thunder. A fine rain of dirt and rock fell from the roof of the buried chamber. She had already pulled her cloak over her hair, and crouched at the join between the wall and the floor. The chanting of the Persians and the Nabateans had begun to waver as stone chips pattered down around them. An ominous groaning sound had begun to make itself heard as well, and Krista felt the wall at her back tremble.

Fire rippled in the unseen world, brilliant shapes invoked by the mind of the Prince hovering around the shape of the first Emperor. He felt a gradient growing as he rushed through the invocation; each moment cost him more and more as he bound the shape of the Imperial duty to the corpse. Greedily, the action drew more and more from the old man, the Persian, and the golden youth. Still,

Maxian rushed on, heedless, his thought and will stitching the garment of sparkling form to the body of Augustus. In a moment, he knew, he would reach a critical point. He could feel the fury of the Oath raging around him, only bare feet away beyond the shining barrier.

Krista flinched again, feeling wetness along her cheek. One of the Persians cried out as a rock sliver, curved like a scythe, slashed across his eye. The man gobbled in pain, his chanting cut off, and clutched at his eye. As he did so, his hand strayed out of the circle inscribed on the stones of the floor, and he screamed in horrible pain. His hand smoked with dull fire, and as Krista watched, her eyes wide in fear, the man's arm withered and crumbled away. Insane with pain and fear, the Persian leapt up and bolted for the door. His feet went first, corroding to dust in an instant, and then his whole body was consumed. She turned away, keeping her hands and feet inside the circle, curling ever tighter into a tiny ball.

Maxian put forth the totality of his will, grasping the raiment of the Emperor, now bound to the corpse of Augustus, bending his power against the last single silver thread that bound it to the distant, sleeping shape of his brother.

Nikos skidded into the dining chamber, his blade up and the lantern flaring in his other hand. Men struggled, crying out, with a fast blur of darkness. A praetorian lunged, his whole weight behind the stroke of his *spatha*, and missed, cleaving air where a shape had stood only an instant before. A gray-green hand, tendons standing from it like iron bars, snaked out of the darkness and crushed the man's throat. Blood spattered away, soaking fingers that punched into the flesh and tore away the soldier's trachea. Two more praetorians lay dead, scattered on the floor, their arms and legs at odd angles.

Jusuf loosed in the same moment, his bowstring thrumming sharply against his wrist guard. The arrow flickered across the space and sank to the fletching in the chest of the creature.

Nikos stumbled, seeing the thing in the light of the lantern for the first time.

It wore the shape of a man, but its skin was gelid and cold, like the intestine of a snake. It had a man's head, but the yellow eyes that burned in the narrow skull had never been human. It was naked, but its slick, wet body was a confusion of tattoos and scars and long, thin ridges that clung to the curve of muscle and sinew and bone. It blurred into motion, faster than the eye could follow. A lantern was smashed aside, spattering burning oil and broken glass against the far wall. Another praetorian was flung down, bones snapping at the force of the impact, his iron helmet caved in by the blow of a fist.

Nikos cast aside thought and leapt forward, his *gladius* whispering in the air. He had faced men and beast for twenty years and he could not conceive of an enemy that would not bleed and die at the touch of his sword. The thing whirled to meet him, its claws snapping toward his head and face. The Illyrian twisted, taking the first blow on his shield at an angle. The thick buckler—an oaken roundel covered with a layer of cured hide and then a metal facing bound through with wire—shattered like a cheap amphora. Nikos felt his arm break in two places, and the jolt of pain slashed up into his chest. The claw faded back into darkness and Nikos leapt up, curling his legs under him. A long leg, tipped with clawlike nails, flashed past underneath him. The point of the *gladius* arrowed at the thing's eyes, smoky yellow in the lamplight. It bobbed away from the blow with effortless ease. It rapped the blade away with a forearm, and Nikos howled in disgust as the blade was torn from his hand. He ducked, feeling the rush of air where his head had been.

Another arrow sprouted from the thing's chest, then another. Jusuf and other men crowded into the room, their bows singing. The thing looked down, seeing the cluster of black fletching dancing in its torso. It looked up, and smiled, its dead mouth stretched into a dreadful grin.

Nikos rolled away, his useless arm blazing with pain. He dragged a long knife from his boot and reversed the point, crouching and circling away. The thing followed him with its eyes. Nikos wheezed in pain, hoping the blood-fire would kick in and elevate him past the crippling damage to his arm. More praetorians, drawn by the sound of battle, rushed in from the other doors.

The *homunculus* laughed—a long, cruel sound—seeing a feast laid out before it.

The entirety of the world collapsed to a single point of glittering white, immensely heavy, and Maxian struggled to contain the power he had summoned. The old man had failed, collapsing into a heap within his triangle of invocation. The golden youth staggered, falling to his knees, his face a rictus of pain as Maxian leached his bones for more power. The raiment of Empire distorted and flexed, slipping away from his will like quicksilver as he tried to fix it to the ancient corpse. Dust spurted up, and the body threatened to dissolve at any moment. Sweat ran in rivers down the Prince's face and soaked his chest. On his forehead the trapezoid of focus burned like a single eye, nearly overcome by the power he had invoked.

Still, the silver thread would not break. Maxian hammered at it with all the strength at his command, trying to sunder the gleaming cord. The Oath raged outside the wards, shattering stone and brick, flooding the upper floors of the house with water and mud, smashing the roof with its fury. The raiment shifted again, sliding away from the face of the old Emperor. Maxian turned his will aside for an instant, fixing the similarity again. The silver cord vibrated like a gong struck by a mallet.

Maxian looked up. At the far, distant end of the silver cord, he saw, for a split second, the face of his brother.

Galen's eyes were open, staring back at him out of a waxy, ashen face.

You murder me, came the thought, speeding across the leagues.

Maxian looked down and saw that the silver cord that ran from the heart of the raiment was the soul of his brother. He flinched away, his will lost for a brief instant.

The *homunculus* howled in joy, its torso slick with the blood of the dead, its claws raising high another praetorian. Entrails spilled from the man's stomach, torn open by a single raking blow. Soldiers surged around it, raining blows from axes, spears, and swords. The thing's dead flesh was hacked and torn, with bright white bones peeking out and half its face carved away. But still it whirled, spilling blood and crushing the faces of its enemies. Manic energy filled it, and shattered flesh reknit itself, bone crawled back to bone. The skin of the creature drank the blood that filled the air.

At the back of the room, Nikos scrambled away, seeing death itself walking in the enclosed space. Jusuf dragged him through the doorway into the hall. The house groaned around him, and tiles and broken timbers clattered from the ceiling.

Khiron closed on the last of the soldiers, a burly youth with a long, iron-headed spear. The man, blinded with fear, charged, screaming in defiance. Khiron turned his body into the blow, catching the point of the spear with his chest. The iron head, tapered and sharp, ground through bone and muscle, scraping across his rib cage. Khiron laughed, his voice ringing from the domed roof, and clawed forward along the shaft. The soldier barely had time to gasp in pain as an iron-tipped thumb punched through his eye socket. Khiron shook its long, lean head in delight and twisted. The man's head tore free from his spine and neck with a sickening pop, and the body fell, twitching spasmodically, to the floor. Khiron bit into the base of the jaw, feeling the flesh part under its white teeth, and tore away the top of the skull with its other hand.

Nikos and Jusuf stumbled away from the dining chamber, hearing only a little of the gelatinous slurping sound that filled the room. Stone and tile jumped under their feet, shaken by some cataclysm in the earth. The Khazar scooped up his friend and ran, his legs pumping furiously. Nikos tried to protest, but Jusuf just kept running. The door to the garden suddenly appeared out of the murk.

The matrices of forms that Maxian had raised shattered in his moment of inattention. The black tide of the Oath stormed in, smashing through the outer wards that ringed the buried room. The Persians and Nabateans wailed in torment and died within a grain, their flesh burned from their bones, souls consumed by the torrent of corruption that flooded into the chamber. Maxian staggered up, whirling around to see the wave of power lash against the innermost shields.

The tide broke, surging up around the final barrier like a sea of acid, but Maxian cried out in horror.

The ward around Krista shattered, crumpling like an eggshell under the foot of an elephant, and she cried out in terrible pain as she was crushed into the wall at her back. Pain burned at her, etching her bones, and she blacked out, falling into a heap on the floor.

The Prince's eyes darkened, and he raised his hand. Words came to his mind, unbidden, and the earth shook. The Shield of Athena that had held to the last suddenly flared bright and expanded, driving back the sea of corruption that surged around him. The shield slid over Krista's body and the Prince knelt, scooping her up in his arms. At his back, Alexandros crawled forward, dragging the still form of the old Roman. The body of the Persian lay behind, unconscious within its triangular ward.

Maxian looked down at the girl in his arms, seeing the deep bruises on the side of her face, feeling the shattered ribs and punctured lung in her chest. Her breathing was thready and bubbled with the sound of liquid spilling into her throat.

"I am a fool," the Prince whispered, seeing his love dying in his arms. He raised his head.

Nikos' skull rapped hard against the side of a log, drawing a weak curse from him, and then Jusuf pushed him over the lip of the fallen tree. He fell on his broken arm, and the whole world suddenly burst into pain and an agonizing throbbing light. The Khazar rolled over the log right behind him, landing on the Illyrian's legs.

"Mars! Get off me!" Nikos barely had the strength to curse, but Jusuf managed to crawl away.

Nikos could only see the log in front of him, but suddenly the whole sky lit up with a blue-white light. Instants later a vast booming sound flattened the two men into the mud, and then a rush of flame and ruddy red light filled the world. The villa in the swale below them shattered, granite pillars weakened by the curse shattering like reeds, long tile roofs flying up in the air on a billowing pillar of flame. Walls tumbled down, crushed by the blast of fire, and the dead trees in the garden and on the surrounding hillsides burst alight.

Jusuf and Nikos burrowed deeper, trying to get away from the stunning noise.

Something rose from the fire, a long dark shape with wings of iron. It twisted, its scales shimmering in the heat haze, and bunched its mighty limbs under it. There was a shriek like a dying city and it sprang away into the black clouds. Thunder cracked in its passage, and a great hiss of steam rose as rain continued to pour down on the burning ruins of the villa.

On the hillside, Jusuf raised his head, blinking mud and water from his eyes. Something rushed away overhead, high in the air, but he could not make out what it was. He spit mud and a broken tooth from his mouth. He rolled over, his mouth open in a cry of pain. Something had slashed his back open. Rain sluiced down over him, washing the mud from his face.

Nikos, still stunned by the blast, and shocky with the

pain of his shattered arm, tried to roll over. He was too weak. Mud slopped around his face, and he felt the hillside quiver.

"Jusuf?" His voice was so weak, he could barely recognize it.

The Khazar turned, his dark eyes slitted against the rain. Nikos gestured weakly at the hill above them. Jusuf looked up, seeing nothing but fire, dark trees, and an ebon sky. Then he squinted again; the trees were swaying, toppling over even as they burned fiercely. A haze of smoke and steam billowed up into the sky, joining with the clouds.

As he watched, a tree, its crown burning merrily, slid sideways and crashed into one of its fellows. Then Jusuf felt the quiver under his feet and heard the rumbling of boulders grinding under the earth. The entire slope above them, loosened by rain and the eroding influence of the Oath, had separated. The Khazar looked around wildly, seeing the burning villa suddenly rush toward them. He cursed, a dreadful oath of his people.

THIRA

)⚬(

This is *Herakles*," Thyatis said with a grin. "He is the only man allowed on Thira, for he serves the Matron of the Island, and the Goddess."

Shirin smiled back and ran a slim hand along the curving prow of the ship. It was a single banked galley, no more than forty feet long, with sleek flanks and a wickedly sinuous line. Two deep steering oars were slung at the back, and it was built low to the water. The flanks were Miletian oak, carefully carved and bent to form the hull. A black varnish covered the ship, both the planking and the seating on the low rowing benches. Thyatis swung up onto the railing and dropped inside. The ship trembled, even at her weight. Shirin followed, her sandals—calfskin with long, thin lacings that ran up to just under her knee—squeaking on the deck. The whole vessel breathed speed and power.

"There are no other men on the island?" Shirin considered this and found it pleasing.

"No—nor have there ever been." Thyatis walked aft and stepped up onto a bench set behind the two steering oars. She sat, folding her legs under her. The Roman woman was clad in the dark green tunic, bronze greaves and arm-brace of one of the *parthenos* of the Order. A round straw hat hung at her back from a thong looped around her neck. Shirin came up to stand by her, but she leaned on the stern rail and looked out into the lagoon that lay behind the ship. The Khazar woman was wearing only a short cotton shift, bound at the waist with a belt of pale-brown leather, and her hair was braided back in a single thick ponytail. She had spent the day in the training circle, sparring with the other students. Her first examinations were coming up soon.

Herakles was nestled in a deep-mouthed sea cave that opened out onto the central lagoon of the island. Once, ages before, a cyst had formed in the flank of the ancient volcano. Over eons of time, the shell-like walls of the cavity had worn away until, at last, the sea spilled into the lagoon. In time, the Sisters had come and found the island and made it their home. Then the opening had been carefully widened and improved. Two quays of black basalt had been built out into the cave, providing mooring for the ships that plied the waters of the Mare Aegeum on the business of the sisterhood. This late in the day, the sun had already fallen behind the towering cliffs that ringed the lagoon, plunging the center of the island into a twilit gloom.

Still, from the back of the galley, Shirin could see the sky—fading to purple and deepest blue—reflecting in the quiet waters of the lagoon. Even here, in the cave, the sweet smell of the sea and the flower gardens of the hidden city reached her. The Princess marked the quiet that had settled upon them, rocking gently in this ship of war. *So like Thira*, she mused, *filled with unexpected moments of solitude*.

She turned, looking down upon her friend. Thyatis was sitting quietly, her legs crossed in the manner favored by the teacher Mikele, watching Shirin with troubled eyes.

"Oh, such a look you give me! Are you sad?" Shirin sat and took Thyatis' hand in her own.

"I will miss you," Thyatis said, her lips quirking down on one side. "I wonder if we will see each other again after I go."

One of Shirin's eyebrows crept up toward her rich dark hair. She frowned. "You had better return," she growled, squeezing Thyatis' hand. "I'm not going to spend the rest of my life cooped up on this island—as restful as it may be. Too, you and that mean uncle of mine have spirited my children away. I miss them terribly."

Thyatis smiled wryly and raised Shirin's hand—slim and dark—to her lips. "I know you miss the little ones," she said, "and all of us will be back together as soon as it is safe. As soon as I reach the Duchess I will find out if the Eastern Emperor is still hunting for you. If he has abandoned that stratagem, we will all go to Rome together."

Shirin cocked her head to one side and pointed with her chin. "They cannot come here? Wouldn't it be safer on the island? Rome must be a very hive of intrigue, even in times of peace. I know you hold this Duchess in great trust, but these are my children."

Thyatis laughed and brushed a tangle of curls over her shoulder. Shirin was half standing again, her eyes flashing in almost anger. "Pax! Pax! Your daughters could come, but Avrahan and little Sahul could not. We will meet Jusuf and Nikos and the others in Rome, then find someplace safe for you to raise them up."

"Perhaps," Shirin said, sitting down, her face serious. "Have you thought upon what we will do—being together, raising this family—beyond just these moments? Our time on this island? Escaping these troubles that now circle us around like dire wolves in winter?"

Thyatis' face blanked for a moment, her thought turned inward, but then her eyes cleared and she nodded slowly. "Yes, my love, I have thought on it." Thyatis took a small cedar box out of her blouse. It was a deep red and delicately carved with winding flowers and tree trunks. A copper clasp held it closed. She held it for a moment, looking at it, and then offered it to Shirin. "I once spoke with your cousin Dahvos about the customs of your fathers, while we were mewed up in an attic in Tauris. He said that among your people it is customary to give a parting gift to those you love, something to indicate you will return and that they are close to your heart while you are away."

Shirin took the little box and turned it over in her hand. Her deep brown eyes looked up, and Thyatis felt a little shock at her gaze. The Princess was smiling, the hidden smile that meant the most to Thyatis.

"Among my people," Thyatis continued, clasping her hands together nervously, "we have no matching tradition, or any way for a woman to express to another woman what she might feel. But here, on the island, there is the hand-fasting that one Sister may make to another. Such things are sealed with a token. This . . . this I brought for you out of the house of dreams, out of Ctesiphon. I saw it, and knew that it was meant for you."

Shirin opened the box and her eyes lit up and the cupid's bow of her mouth curved into a smile. She reached inside and drew out a fine golden chain. At the end of the chain, set into a simple curve of white gold, was a single perfect bloodred jewel the size of Thyatis' thumb.

"The Eye of Ormazd," Shirin breathed in delight. She held it up, and the jewel caught the light of the torches at the end of the quay, shining like a fallen star. Golden red light played on her face, highlighting her high cheekbones and the curve of her neck. "The rarest of jewels—the fire opal of the uttermost East. The wedding price of Shapur the Victorious to his lover, the Queen Yehana of Balkh. Carried out of fallen Amida by the warrior king in his greatest triumph. Worth a kingdom—"

"Worthy of an empress," Thyatis said, her hand tracing the line of Shirin's cheek. "Worthy of you, my love. This is my pledge: I will return to you, I will bring you to your children. I will stay by your side until the end of our days. Will you take it?"

Shirin's eyes glistened, and she settled the gold chain around her neck. The Eye nestled between her breasts, still glowing with captured firelight. It was warm to the touch. Under her fingers the surface of the jewel was as fine as silk. "I accept your gift and your promise, dear barbarian." Shirin's voice was thick with emotion. "I will wait for you to return, but heed me! If you do not come soon, I will come looking for you. Do not think that a pretty bauble like this will keep me locked away and content!"

Thyatis laughed, her face wry. "I would not dream that it would. If the winds are fair, I should be to Rome and back within six months. Can you wait that long?"

"Perhaps," Shirin said, looking away with an imperious mien. "I may become bored here on this island with nothing to do but train and think and meditate. . . . I may go mad, too, if nothing exciting happens."

"Pray, beloved!" Thyatis raised a hand in a sign of warding against disaster. "Take the peace that comes with this blessed isle—do not seek out trouble or excitement! The Matron is getting along in years, and her heart may not bear up. . . ."

Shirin laughed, her eyes shining, and tweaked Thyatis' nose. "You are a silly and beloved barbarian. I am a guest here and I will not dishonor the guest-right."

Smiling, Thyatis leaned close and Shirin met her lips.

After a time, they parted and sat in silence, listening to the waves lap against the quayside and echo from the high ceiling of the darkening sea cave.

* * *

"Back oars!" The steerswoman of *Herakles* had a voice like a bullhorn, echoing loudly in the sea cave. At the prow, Thyatis let go of Shirin's fingers and pressed fingertips to her lips. On the quay, Shirin stood up and returned the blown kiss. The galley, trim and riding even lower to the sea now that forty of the strongest *parthenae* on the island had taken their places on its rowing benches, slid backward as the leaf-shaped oars bit the water. Behind the Princess, the Matron and her attendants were gathered in a silent cluster. *Herakles* scudded out into the brightness of day, onto the glassy green surface of the lagoon. Thyatis stared into the dark entrance of the sea cave, momentarily blinded, and Shirin was gone.

Herakles spun around its long axis as it slipped across the lagoon, one bank of rowers digging in while the others held their oars, shining with seawater, high in salute. Thyatis sat down, taking her place at the first rank of oars. The galley completed its evolution, and the gleaming walls of the city, bright with summer flowers and the muted splendor of the statues and temples, rose up before her. Facing the stern, Thyatis watched the sea cave as it receded. It hurt more to leave than she had expected.

Herakles moved swiftly across the water of the lagoon, leaving a fine curling wake in the crystalline water. Behind her, Thyatis could hear the booming roar and thunder of waves in the passage. At the base of the stern, an elderly woman raised a hand, her head cocked to one side. The rowers halted their stroke and shipped oars a half-length. The ship slid forward, carried by momentum into the passage. Vast, dark volcanic walls rose up, closing off the sky. The temperature dropped, and a wind picked up, driven out of the bowl of the lagoon. The steerswoman leaned on the oars, guiding them down the narrows. A dozen yards were all that stood between the walls of the passage and the sides of the ship.

All this Thyatis ignored, watching the distant black cavity of the sea cave until at last, as the passage turned a little, it disappeared from view. At that last moment, as the jagged cliffs closed off the view of the lagoon, there was a momentary bright red flash, an eye winking in darkness, and then the hidden city and all that it contained were gone.

The tumultuous sound of the waves in the entrance to the passage rose higher and higher, drowning out even the loudest shout. The current picked up, rushing through the passage, a swirling boil of violent waters. Only twice a day did the passage run out, pulled by the sun- and moontide in conjunction. At these times, carefully charted by the *astrologos* of the Temple, it was possible for a ship to escape the island. Otherwise, only ruin waited for any ship foolish enough to dare the sharp volcanic teeth of the passage or the reefs beyond. Now they ran with the current, the ship bucking and twisting as the sweep of the waters swerved first against this cliff face and then against the other.

Suddenly, darkness closed in around them—they were in the heart of the passage—and then sunlight fell upon them again; they were in the Crucible, where the passage turned a little, making a bowl that in all other times was a howling whirlpool. The Titans flashed past, their massive graven arms and legs standing out from the cliffs. Even now, when she had seen them before, Thyatis felt a chill at the grim faces that loomed out of the rock, half entombed, a hundred yards high. Then they were gone, and the steerswoman leaned hard into the current. The old woman at the base of the stern made a sign, and the rowers prepared to unship oars at her signal.

Herakles burst forth from the wall of Thira, a wooden bolt shot from the engine of the passage's wave surge. For a sickening instant the ship rode up the side of a massive breaker that was gathering itself up to smash into oblivion on the crags of the island. The old woman's hand slashed down, and the rowers struck the water as one, their oars biting into the curling green wall that loomed over them. The ship shuddered as the oars caught the water and dug deep. *Herakles* surged up the rising wall, already raised twenty feet or more by the growing mountain of water. The prow suddenly cut free of the top of the wave, spearing into the air, and a fierce shout from behind warned Thyatis to ship her oar as fast as humanly possible. *Herakles'* limbs scuttled back inside the body of the galley as the ship tipped and then rushed down the back slope of the wave like a thrown javelin. It splashed deep, the nose of the ship digging into the valley of water between the wave and the open sea, then surged up again, spilling bright water over the foredeck.

Thyatis laughed in joy at being alive, drenched as she was, and she and the thirty-nine *parthenos* slid oars out. As one, they pulled and the ship leapt forward, on the open sea at last. *Herakles* surged forward, foam boiling at her prow, the wine dark sea open before her. The steerswoman began to sing, her strong voice rising above the creak of the oars and the murmur of the sea.

Behind them the crag of Thira rose, barren and bleak, a sullen black thumb thrust from a turbulent ocean.

The sun settled on the horizon, a great orb of red and gold, turning the wave tops and the sea into an ocean of fire. The sky, clear and cloudless, shaded from pale gold to pink and then to the deep of night. Stars began to gleam in the firmament above, slowly crowding the eastern sky. Shirin walked alone on the northern shore of the island, her bare feet leaving a long line of tracks in the fine black sand of the narrow beach. The moon was rising, huge and yellow, over the eastern rim of the world. Soon the sea would disappear into a black void, marked only by the phosphorescence of the breakers: The Princess was troubled and had been sent away from the day's training by Mikele.

Your mind and body are far apart, the Chin woman had said. *Go find them.*

Shirin stopped, feeling the edge of the surf curl up over her toes. The water was warm and it spilled around her ankles, sighing. She looked out over the waters. Somewhere to the north and west, her friend sped away from her, driven by wind and oar toward distant Rome. Rome and her children and her uncle. Her family was far away, and she was alone. "Is this what I want?" she spoke aloud, though there was no one to hear her. Shirin bent her head in thought, casting her mind ahead, over years and decades that might come. Some things made her smile, others frown. So she walked, under the moon, alone on a deserted beach by an empty sea.

⊡()-{O}-{O}-{O}-{O}-{O}-{O}-{O}-{O}-{O}-{O}-{O}-{O}-{O}-{O}-{O}-{O}-{O}-{O}-{O}⊡

THE FORUM, ROMA MATER

)(

T he sun stood high in the sky, shedding its beneficent rays upon glorious Rome.

Galen Atreus, Caesar, and Augustus, wiped sweat from his brow as he came to the last and highest step of the great staircase that vaulted up from the floor of the Forum to the gatehouse of the Temple of Jupiter Optimus Maximus. Behind him, filling the plaza of the Forum to capacity and beyond, sixty thousand Roman citizens raised their voices in a chant of victory. Here, from the height of the Capitoline hill, looking back upon them, Galen saw a shimmering sea of color and upturned faces. The beat of their voices in the air washed over him like the surf of some fantastic sea. He raised his arm, saluting them, proclaiming victory. Their voices raised up again, and the sound was a storm on the height.

"*Ave! Ave, Imperator!*"

At his side, Galen felt his brother raise his arm as well, and then the ranks of legionaries both in the plaza below and arrayed along the sides of the steps. Each man saluted the city and the people, and there—across the plaza—on the steps of the Curia Julia—the senate of Rome. The senators, as one, raised their arms in reply and great horns sounded, winding a long, solemn note. At this, the lictors and attendants who had preceded Galen up the long staircase turned and entered the platform that housed the Temple of Jupiter.

"Has our brother returned?" Galen whispered out of the side of his mouth as his Imperial party entered the temple. Ranks of praetorians lined the portico, their armor gleaming and bright. The clang of their salute, mailed gloves on cuirasses, was sharp as he passed between them.

"No," Aurelian whispered back. "He came to see me a month or so after you left, saying he had struck upon some secret business he had to deal with. Then he vanished."

Galen bent, kneeling, and bowed his head before the statue of the King of the Gods. At his side, staunch Aurelian on his left and the white-haired Gregorius Auricus on his right, his companions knelt as well. Outside, in the bright sun, the voices of the crowd were raised in song.

It was the first time Galen had ever felt that Rome was a city filled with people. For seven years it had seemed a half-empty tomb, inhabited only by the shades of its residents and the echoes of memory. Today, riding in the white chariot through the avenues, seeing the endless lines of people thronging the streets and alleyways, their voices cheering him as he passed, at last he saw the city that had raised an Empire. At last, after years of struggle, it was alive.

"Has there been sign of him of late?" Galen worried at the question of his missing brother like a dog with an old bone.

"Sign—no, but rumor? Yes. The Duchess sent word to me no more than a week ago that one of her agents had reported that our little piglet had returned to Italy and was hiding out in the hills above the city. I sent men to investigate, but I have not heard what transpired. The Duchess and I are meeting in a few days."

The praises of the priests ceased and the Pontifex Maximus came forth, holding aloft the signs and symbols of his office. Incense drifted around him, making white trails that tracked into the dim recesses of the vault that towered above the great statue of the god. Around the fringe of the temple, a thousand acolytes and priests bowed their heads. Galen, seeing the movement, composed his face and did the same.

"The omens are good!" the voice of the Pontifex rang throughout the temple. "The gods are pleased. Let the Imperator enter his city."

Galen stood, his knees sore from so much kneeling and the long, slow ascent of the steps of the temple. He turned, clasping his brother's wrist with his right hand.

"Well met, brother." Aurelian smiled back, his broad grin shining in his face. "This is a doubly joyous day!"

"Come," Galen said to the assembled host of priests and his Legion commanders, "let us proclaim the celebrations."

"They will drink and carouse and dance and sing until the day comes again," Aurelian said, still smiling, as they stood on the balcony of the Severan Palace at the south end of the Palatine hill. A hundred feet below, in the long rectangle of the Circus Maximus, great bonfires were burning. The sky above was clear and dark, scattered with stars and Venus, bright on the horizon. But below, amid the smoke and fume of hundreds of roasting cattle and swine, the populace of the city celebrated the return of their Emperor and of the Legions, victorious against an ancient enemy.

Galen answered with a nod, leaning against the marble balustrade of the balcony. Here, safe at the heart of his domain, he had released his men from the long discipline that had held them in check from the sack of Ctesiphon. Finally they could celebrate their great victory, spend some of their loot, drink and tell tales of their valor and bravery to wives, barmaids, and maidens. Across the whole city, in every public place, the Emperor's purse was open, filling the bellies of the citizen and the slave and the visitor with wine and bread and hot pies and roasted flesh from every kind of creature. Below, in the circus, with its great doors flung open, the men of the Legions held forth—seeing their families again, meeting old friends and new. For this whole day and night, the city reveled in triumph.

"Maxian came to me in Albania," Galen said, turning to his brother with a pensive face. "All unbidden, he appeared—a ghost in black and gray—as I sat in my tent late at night, working. He was so thin and worn looking! Have you ever seen him in such a state?"

Aurelian shook his head in negation. He was disturbed more, now, by the pain in his brother's voice.

"He told me a tale," Galen said, "an impossible fancy. But *he* believed and asked me for my help. I could not believe it . . . it seemed so fantastical!" The Emperor's voice faded to a whisper.

"What happened?" Aurelian was staring at his brother with unaccustomed concern. Though the brothers had bickered and quarreled over the years—even fought on occasion, when they were in their cups—none had ever refused another's plea for help. The bonds of family ran that close. What would *pater et mater* think if they fell out among themselves? "What did you say to him?"

"There were harsh words," Galen said in a small voice, refusing to meet his brother's eyes. "My guardsmen took him away to sleep—he was so tired! I was sure it was fatigue that made us quarrel. But then morning came and he was gone. Not even one trace of him remained. Aurelian, he was a ghost . . ."

Aurelian shook his head and took his brother by the shoulders, shaking him lightly. "The Piglet will come back," he said softly. "He always does, beard half grown in, stinking of wine. Put those thoughts aside for now; today is the day of your victory, of your triumph. Listen to the night, to the cheerful songs of men who you led to victory on a foreign field. Hear the city rejoicing."

Galen looked up and sighed, then ran a thin hand over his face. "It was very fine to ride in that chariot and hear the adulation of the crowds. It was a good show today."

"But, brother—no races? No gladiatorial games or elaborate staged battles in the Coliseum? No *munera* to please the gods?" Aurelian was grinning, but puzzlement marked his bluff, open face.

Galen shook his head, pursing his lips in a quiet smile.

"My gift to the city is the safe return of these men. Besides, any eager senator can put on a giant octopus and shipwrecked Numidian fishermen show in the Flavian. This does not obscure the joy a mother feels to see her son come home again, alive and whole."

The Emperor turned, putting his back to the railing. Above him, he could see the courses of the Capitoline ablaze with light. Every window held a lamp, and the lines of the rooftops were shining with torches and lanterns. The whole of the city, sprawling away behind him, was glowing. Rome could be seen, he was sure, from a hundred miles away. A breeze off the mountains ruffled his lank dark hair, and the Emperor signaled to one of the slave girls loitering just out of earshot. "Vidia, bring us hot wine, please."

The girl bobbed her long blond hair and hurried off, her short skirt showing fine pale legs.

"I am not an emperor given to excesses, my brother, you know that!"

"True," Aurelian said, shaking his shaggy head, "but it strikes everyone as odd that you do not lavish such gifts and exhibitions upon the city as others have done in the past." Aurelian avoided mentioning the other words he had heard: *miserly* or *cheap* or *penurious*.

"Let them think it odd," Galen growled, finally rising to his brother's bait. "In another time the Emperor would have unleashed each and every man in the army—their shoulders bent with the weight of their looted coin and jewels—all willy-nilly upon the city in a storm of debauchery. Half the army would be drunk and useless for a month from it. And all that silver and gold would be gone from each soldier's purse in half the time. Prices would rise, driven by such an influx of coin, and the poor man in the street would be pinched worse than ever."

Aurelian frowned and scratched his nose. "That has been the tradition," he allowed, and took a goblet from the tray that Vidia had brought. "Why meddle with tradition? It pleases the men, and the innkeepers, too!"

"That is so," Galen said, taking the other goblet. The surface of the wine, a deep red Falernian, was steaming in the cool air, and he drank thirstily. It had been hot work, riding in the chariot through all the winding ways of the city, passing through each square and market, so that all could look upon him and his men and see that Victoria had graced Rome with her favor again. "But it would not please me, nor you if you thought beyond the next horse race or bottle of wine. I have held back each legionnaire's share of the booty from Ctesiphon to place in the Treasury. A third of that sum due each man will be paid out to them when they leave Legion service as an addition to their *honesta misso*. For many, that will double the coin they would receive on their discharge day. Another third will be paid out over time as a supplement to their pay. The last third, they have today, to spend in the fleshpots and tavernae and baths."

Aurelian shook his head. He did not see the point.

"You have ruled the Empire in my name for nine months now," Galen said, an acerbic edge coming into his voice. "Surely you have noted the volume of coin that passes through the Treasury just to sustain day-to-day operations? Yes? Good. I tell you this: The loot our army has brought home is enough to pay for a hundred and sixteen days of Imperial operations, a staggering sum. And that is the Imperial share! The share due the men in the Legions accounts for another hundred days' worth. Now, think of the price of bread or wine today in the marketplace. If I allow all that gold to flood into the Forum Boarium and the brothels and the shops on the Porticus Aemilia in one huge wave, prices will rise like the chariot of Apollo. That, my brother, will make the cost of daily operations for the fisc rise as well. A hundred and sixteen days will become eighty, or sixty."

"Oh," Aurelian said, at last comprehending something of what his brother was saying.

"So," Galen continued downing the last of the wine, "we do not spend all this bounty at once. Instead, we stockpile it in the Treasury and we spend it a bit at a time. The third share that each legionnaire will receive in his pay will take two years to pay out. A sufficient span of time, I think, to dilute the effect on the price of bread. I have other plans for the Imperial share, but it will not be used frivolously or extravagantly."

"Of course not." Aurelian sighed. "Never extravagant . . . you'll not raise a triumphal arch for this, but repair a mile of road or a bridge instead."

"My very thought." Galen snickered, putting the wine goblet aside. "Though I had my heart set on dredging the big harbor at Portus, and perhaps—if your heart can stand the excitement—restoring the old military highway through the Alpes from Mediolanum to the Lacus Brigantinus."

Aurelian made a sour face at this, and looked away in a feigned pout.

Galen clapped Aurelian on the shoulder in great good humor and turned again to look out upon the city, bright with celebration.

Dawn was near when Galen made his way, at last, to his rooms in the Severan wing of the palace. He was bone tired and feeling the effects of too many goblets of wine and too many garlic prawns in pepper aspic. Guardsmen in red cloaks and burnished steel breastplates opened the doors to his chambers and saluted as he passed in. The rooms were dark, barely lit by a single oil lamp that burned on the mantelpiece of a fire grate. One window was open a little, letting in a cool breath of night air. The breeze stirred the gauzy curtains that hung around his bed. It was a huge old thing, with heavy carved wooden pillars at each corner holding up thick beams of aromatic Mauretanian cedar. Once it had stood in his father's bedroom in their family home in Narbo. The door to these chambers, first built by the Emperor Alexander Severus, had been specially widened to get it in.

Galen, feeling much like an overworked shopkeeper at the end of a particularly grueling day during the holiday season, kicked off his boots and pulled his tunic over his head. His entire body ached, and the beginnings of a blinding headache were lurking behind his eyes. He slumped, his head in his hands, and considered calling for one of his servants to rub him down before he went to bed.

"Husband?" A faint whisper from the vastness of the bedclothes caught his attention.

"Helena?" Galen turned, surprised. He had not received a letter from the Empress in weeks, the last coming from her villa at Catania. No one had said anything about her being in the city. Yet here she was, turned on her side, staring at him with sleepy dark brown eyes. "What are you doing here?"

"Waiting for you . . . I fell asleep, though."

Galen slid under the heavy covers, feeling the glorious sensation of a freshly made bed with clean sheets at the end of a taxing day. Unexpectedly, Helena moved to press herself against him, curling around his arm and side. Her sleek dark hair tickled his nose. Nonplussed, for their last parting had been particularly bitter, he slid his arm around her and held her close. She sighed, holding him tight, and the intimacy of their embrace tickled at his heart. He had a sudden, dreadful, premonition. "Helena, are you well?" The Empress had never been a healthy woman, suffering from the cough in her youth, and prone to colds and summer flu. Galen's mind, still wound up from the long, busy day, spun in a thousand directions, finding nothing but disaster in any path it followed. "Are you sick again?"

"No, husband." There was an odd tone in her voice. With another woman, one less given to the furious single-minded pursuit of her interests, he might have thought she was laughing at him. But Helena had never mocked him. "Did you miss me while you were in the East?"

Galen made a rueful face, though she could not see it in the darkness. "Yes, I did. I regretted the words exchanged at our last parting."

She snuggled closer, running a hand across his chest. Galen caught it and brought it to his lips.

"Did you get my letters?" She was still almost asleep.

"Yes . . . but I thought you might take me to task again, so I did not read them. I wanted to see you myself, to apologize."

"Do you mean," she said, rousing herself from near sleep, "that you take back calling me the 'failed broodmare of a dynasty'?"

Galen flinched, feeling the echo of terrible anger in her voice. "I do," he said, kissing the crown of her head.

"Good," she said, putting her head back down on his chest. "Because it's not true anymore. I am a successful broodmare."

A bright light seemed to fill the room, blinding Galen for a moment as his normally quick mind processed the incongruous comment. It did not seem to match up with any previous conversation.

"What?" Somehow it was all that he could manage.

"I became pregnant the last time that we lay together," Helena said, raising her head again and enunciating carefully. "I bore you a son, a healthy son, three weeks ago."

"You did?"

"I did. He is here now, in the palace, in the care of *domina* Anna from your house at Cumae."

"I have a son?" Galen was puzzled; why did he keep repeating himself?

"Huh. As brilliant as ever. Go back to sleep."

Galen lay in the darkness, wondering if there could be a more perfect day in all the history of the world. Eventually, without noticing it, he fell asleep.

THE HILL ABOVE PALMYRA

)-(

There!" Zoë gasped in exhaustion as she hauled herself up over the last pitch of rock. Negotiating the glassy lip of the waterfall had been a tricky piece of business. Two great sandstone boulders towered over her, jutting from the side of the dry canyon like the pillars of a temple. Under them was a little shade, and she collapsed into it, ignoring the pain of the long scratches on her arms and legs, and the parched feeling in her mouth. Sitting, she untangled the cord of her broad-brimmed straw hat from her neck. The canyon fell away below her, lit by the unceasing sun and shimmering with heat. Acres of tumbled stone and cracked tumulus lay below her perch, bare and dry. The canyon bottom itself wound down out of the barren hills that crouched above the city, a narrow thing carved by intermittent rains. Thornbush and gnarled little trees clogged the stream bottom, making passage up it almost impossible. But she had come, following the faint trail of many men over sand and rock.

It had led her up here, to these sentinels on the mountainside. A hundred feet below, she had found a lost buckle, still relatively new, and it had pointed her into this draw that plunged down the side of the mountain. On the gray-green trees that clung to the rocks she had found the marks of cord and the knives of men. Something heavy had been dragged upward, carried in a sling of ropes. It had come here.

There was a scrabbling sound on the rocks below her, and she leaned out, seeing that the old man had finally made his way up to the base of this little cliff.

"Wait," she called down, beginning to uncoil a rope from around her slim waist. "I'll make an anchor."

"Good!" floated back the reply. The old man sat down on a stone at the base of the waterfall, wiping his brow with an ancient and foully stained cloth. His desert robes had suffered, too, in the climb up out of the canyon bottom. He had preferred to wear the full *kaffiyeh* and robes and camel-boots that were the garb of the desert tribes. He and Zoë had argued, in the early morning shadows, under the ruin of the Damascus gate. She had chosen to wear a light cotton kilt and tunic, her legion boots, and her gear slung on leather belts around her waist and over her shoulder. He felt it was unseemly to go into the hills in such a state. She had overruled him.

Now he panted in the heat, below, while she felt fried like a griddle cake in a pan, above.

"What do you see?" the old man shouted.

"The two stones," she called back, "and a hidden place between them."

She thumbed the waxed plug out of one of her waterskins and took a long drink from it. The water had been cold when she had filled them from the cistern under the city, but now it was lukewarm and smelled faintly of sheep. Odenathus had urged her to take one of the copper Legion canteens with her, but it was heavier than this with all that weight of metal. Her cousin had barely marked her going—he and his mother were locked in one of their endless arguments about how to rebuild the city.

Zoë did not care. The city was dead to her. They could clear the debris from the cisterns and open the streets again, even restore the Temple of the Four Gods, or the plinth of Bel, but it would not bring back the bright, glorious city of her youth. That was dead. This dark man, this Lord of the Ten Serpents, had smashed it down in the wake of Rome's betrayal.

The young woman snarled unconsciously, her narrow, elegant face transformed by pure unadulterated hatred. Rome will pay, she vowed in her heart, *Pay for each mur-*

der they committed. Pay for each child's skull that lines the city streets. Then I will find this dark man, and he, too, will pay. . . .

Weeks of unceasing labor had not even recovered all of the bodies from the ruin of the city. Even burying them in a series of mass graves would be fruitless. The sand would cover the city soon enough, and bury everything.

Zoë stood, brushing dust and grit from her bare legs. She bent down and picked up the waterskin, tying it back to her leather harness. There was something barely visible in the deep shadow under the two monoliths; some edge of worked stone. It bore investigation.

"All together, now, heave!" Odenathus, stripped to the waist, his muscular frame glistening with sweat, put his shoulder into the pulley rope. Around him, a dozen men did the same, pulling with all their might. Others crowded around the sides of the obelisk, hands on guide ropes. Once it had stood in the square that backed onto the theater and the edge of the spring. Now it had fallen, its base cracked open by the Persians with chisels and wooden splitting stakes, and lay across the old stairway that led down into the cisterns. "Heave!"

The ropes pulled tight, and Odenathus and his men dug in, pulling with all their might. Slowly the obelisk began to turn, and the men beside it were quick to slide rollers hewn from the few unburned logs found in the city underneath the massive sandstone cylinder. The obelisk groaned and threatened to roll back, but others had jammed stakes in behind it.

"Heave!"

The cylinder turned over, slow and ponderous, but it caught on the rollers and suddenly jumped ahead. Men scattered in all directions, and Odenathus felt the rope over his shoulder go slack. He turned, eyes wide. The pillar was rolling toward him, a massive, suddenly mobile block of stone weighing a dozen tons. Scattered bricks and broken statuary shattered to pale dust under it. Odenathus leapt aside, his blood afire with shock, and threw himself into a side street. The cylinder bounced past and slammed into the side of a half-burned storefront. The facing of the building collapsed with a loud *boom* and showered the street with dust and fragments of travertine facing and ground brick.

Odenathus rolled up, coughing in the thick haze of rock dust, and looked around. "Anyone hurt? Hello?"

The others called back, their voices harsh with grit. Everyone seemed to have survived.

"Well," a querulous voice came from behind him, "you seem to have cleared the stairwell."

Odenathus made a half smile–half grimace and stood up, brushing debris from his pantaloons. He had added a fine new scrape and a thin cut along his arm to the pale scars that already ornamented his chest. "That we did, *mater*. How go things in the kitchens?"

"Poorly," his mother said, taking him by the arm. She led him a little bit away, where the workers marveling at the destruction caused by the runaway obelisk could not hear her. Her old face, tired and framed by white curls, was solemn. He looked away from her blind eyes, unable to bear the sight.

"We're fast running out of food, my son. There just isn't enough left in the stores we've excavated to feed everyone for more than a few weeks. The gardens outside the city were all stripped bare by the Persians, and no caravans will come soon. Every merchant from Edessa to Aelana knows that the city has been destroyed."

Odenathus frowned, considering the options. They did not seem good. He wanted, in his heart, to start anew here—to raise up a whole new city from the ashes of the old—but so many things stood against them. The matter of water was almost resolved. During the siege Persian engineers had cut the aqueducts that ran into the city from the hills in the west, but those catchments had been added to support a city of fifty thousand people. Now there were perhaps six hundred in the city. A few more arrived each week, travelers who had been away during the siege, or expatriates who had forced themselves to return one last time to their homes. In the beginning, he knew, the city had risen from less—no more than a wandering band of desert tribesmen had laid the first stone—but they had flocks of sheep and goats and camels and were used to living on very little.

He looked around; seeing the scarred faces of the men at his command, the thin, pinched look on the few children who were watching the business of the day from the shoulders of a nearby colossus, now fallen into the street with every other statue or idol in the city. These people were born and bred to live in a modern Roman city, with running water and a market and specialized crafts that allowed one man to purchase bread from another. All of those things were gone. If they were to remain, they would have to become nomads again, if only to gather the food they needed to live.

"Do we have any money?"

Ara laughed, putting a wizened hand to her mouth. "Oh, my son, we have plenty of good red gold. The Persians were in haste when they left, and more than one hoard of coin was left unmolested. Our own fortune, that won by your father with his caravans and ships and kegs of spices, is untouched. If there was anyone to buy from, we could buy aplenty. But no one comes here anymore—all that is dead and gone now."

"We could," he said in his stubborn way, "send a party to Damascus to buy food, livestock, tools. All the things we need here. It will be very difficult, but we can remain. The city will rise again, bit by bit."

Ara took her son's face in her hands, her fingers light, feeling the noble nose and the high cheekbones. She felt the close-cropped shape of his hair and the firm muscle along his jaw.

"In this darkness," she said, her voice sad, "you sound so much like your father. If you will it, all these people of the city will remain, but it will be very hard for them. It will be harder for the children; so many of them cannot sleep even now, thinking that the dark one will return. This place is haunted, my son, but perhaps you can make it live again."

Odenathus took his mother's hands and clasped them to his chest. "*Mater,* the city is our life, our home, the reason we are here. If we go away—if we took the gold and jewels that are hidden and passed on to some other town, some other city, we would be strangers. Outsiders, never feeling at ease. If we are to survive as a people, if our tribe will sustain, we must remain here."

"Perhaps," Ara said, freeing her hands from her son's strong grip. "But what thinks the Queen of this?"

Zoë ran her hand over a smooth surface; granite hewn from the mountains of Syria and carried sixty or seventy leagues to this hidden canyon, polished smooth and graven with long lines of the old script of the city. A door stood in the hidden space under the twin boulders, sheltered by their vast red sandstone bulk. Statues emerged from the rock face, flanking the door, statues of the first kings of the city. Their empty eyes stared out at the desert, watching the wasteland. Zoë was a tiny figure between them, crouching at the door of stone. Her fingers traced the worn lines of script, racking her brain in an attempt to decipher the words.

Crows circled high above, cawing listlessly in the hot, still air.

Zoë stood; at the bottom of the stone door the thirty-fifth line was freshly carved, and not in the old tongue. Instead, in the common Latin, it said ZENOBIA V SEPTIMA, QUEEN OF PALMYRA. Zoë's face blanched, becoming almost white. Until this moment, seeing her aunt's grave marker, she had not truly believed that the fiery, dark-haired woman of her memory was dead. But even here, in the hot air, feeling the ruin of her city at her back, Zoë did not cry. Indeed, no tear escaped her eyes, though they looked upon an abyss of pain. She staggered, and fell against the door. The stone, cool to the touch, pressed against her cheek, and her own voice cried out in her mind: *While the Queen stands, so stands the city*.

Face grim, she pushed herself away from the slab and stood back. She folded her hands, closed her eyes, and sought a calming meditation. The craftsmen who had laid the door of stone had wrought it cunningly. It sat in a groove cut from the living rock, a slot a foot or more deep that held the weight of the stone and fixed it closed. Around the edges were splintered markings where grave robbers had tried to penetrate the slab, but they had failed.

It weighed a ton or more. It was impossible for one young woman, no matter the depth of her pain, to lever it out. Twenty men, working under the eye of a master half insane with grief, had taken five days to move it before. Two had died in the effort, but the scarred chieftain had counted that good luck, that servants would join the dead queen in her journey into the afterlife. Their bodies, wrapped in grave cloths, had gone into the tomb with her.

The craftsmen and tomb architects had commissioned spells, too, to be laid upon the door, to keep away the unwary and ensure the long, peaceful sleep of the inhabitants of the royal tomb. Those wizards who had laid them had done passable work, but they had not put their heart in it.

Zoë raised her left hand, and thunder muttered in the clear blue sky. She raised her right hand, and fire spilled from her eyes and swirled around her feet. The slab creaked and moved, rattling with a delicate sound in its frame of polished sandstone. Sweat seeped from her brow, and Zoë lifted, raising up her hands, gripping an image of the door of stone. A ton and a half of granite rose, inch by inch, grinding out of its frame, and then, as Zoë cried out in anger and rage, flew over her head.

In the canyon below, the old man, sitting on the stone at the base of the cliff, leapt up at the dreadful shout, and then stared in awe as the granite door sailed across the width of the canyon to smash in unrestrained fury against the opposite cliff. Dust vomited out, making a great cloud that drifted across the canyon, and then the cracking *boom* of the impact reverberated from the walls. Out of the dust cloud, the door, broken into three great pieces, plummeted to the canyon floor, bouncing once and then shattering into a million fragments. The stricken cliff, cracked by the blow, suddenly shaled away from the ridge at its back, and—with a thunderous roar—plunged down into the streambed. Dust billowed up, and tiny fragments of stone ricocheted off the cliff behind the old man. He ducked down and cowered at the base of the waterfall, hiding his head under his robe.

On the lip of the cliff, Zoë turned, a glad, light feeling growing in her chest, and entered the tomb of her ancestors.

Odenathus sat, dressed in a coat of scale mail the scavengers had dragged from the wreck of one of the great houses, a spear across his legs, at the gate of the city. The twin towers, once faced with slabs of granite, lay scattered behind him. Only the arch of the gate remained, though the doors themselves had not been found. Two of the men who had been working with him to reopen the cistern sat nearby. They stood their watch at sunset, watching the sun fall beyond the hills, turning the sky a brilliant orange gold. All three were exhausted from a long day of hauling stone and clearing the stairs. They would do the same the next day as well, and the one after that. Even repairing the cistern and the pipes to the underground baths near the old library would take weeks of unremitting effort.

The young man sat with his back to a remaining fragment of the old wall of the city, feeling the chill of evening grow, even while the stone still yielded up the warmth it had trapped throughout the day. When first he and Zoë had come to the city, a tablet of black stone had stood above the gate, driven into the remaining wall with iron pins. Old writing, predating even that which had been used by the founders of the city, had covered it. Odenathus did not know that tongue—it was lost to all but a few—but the evil chill that radiated from that tablet had told him all he needed to know.

He had cast it down, wrenching it from the wall with his power, and smashing it into dust.

Now he sat, his eyes closed against the slanting last rays of the sun, and thought upon the ruin of his city.

Something moved, out on the western plain. Two tiny figures trudging along the Damascus road, passing now between two of the ancient tower tombs that dotted the rocky valley. One was bent under a great weight. Odenathus stood up and ground the butt of the spear against the rock of the gateway.

"The Queen approaches," he said quietly, for he discerned the flicker-bright aura of Zoë even at this distance. "You men go into the city and inform my mother. I will bring the Queen to her house as soon as she arrives."

The two men, a stonemason and a carpenter by trade, stood, yawning, and went through the gate, their spears over their shoulders. Odenathus sat again, his legs were too tired to waste time standing around if he could sit instead.

The figures drew closer, step by step, even as night fell.

"My son? Who is here?" Ara struggled to rise from the chair that had been set for her in the tent. This place had once been the garden at the rear of her noble house; a place of refined parties and long afternoon conversations with close friends. Now, with the house itself in ruin, a jagged forest of pillars and cracked walls, it was the only safe place to set a *bedu* tent. The old matriarch, now wearing a strip of salvaged cotton across her eyes, groped by the side of the chair for the javelin that served as her cane and finding-stick.

"I am here," Odenathus answered in a hollow voice, ducking under the flap of the tent. "Zoë is with me."

The young woman, now Queen of the dead city, followed, grunting, as she turned sideways to enter the tent.

Reverently she settled to the ground and shrugged the burden off her back. Ara settled back in her chair, turning her face to one side. Odenathus sat heavily in one of the other chairs and held his head in his hands.

"My lady," Ara ventured after a moment of silence had stretched in the tent, "what have you brought with you, such a heavy thing to make your breath so harsh?"

"Auntie," Zoë said gravely, standing and making a formal bow, "I have returned the Queen to the city, as is right."

"The Queen?" Ara was puzzled, and she settled her grip on the spear. "You are the Queen, my dear."

"No," Zoë said in a grave voice. "I have brought the true Queen home. I carried her on my back from where she lay. Now that she is here, we may ride against our enemies. She will lead us."

"Who is here?" Ara stood now, her face filled with fear. Her knuckles were white on the spear. "What have you done?"

"Zenobia is here, Auntie." Zoë's voice was very calm. She leaned down and, grunting a little at the weight of the corpse, dragged it up into a chair. "Your cousin sits before you. Listen, you can hear her, if it is quiet and you empty your mind. Do you hear her? I do."

Zenobia's corpse, horribly mutilated, her head stitched back to her withered body with crude leather straps, lay askew in the chair. The rags of a funeral sheet were still wound around her, but the cracked skin that still clung to her body had not yet yielded to corruption. Her long dark hair, once the glory of the city, was thin and patchy. Much of it had been gnawed away by something that crept with cold eyes in the tunnels under the mountain. The beautiful face was shrunken and creased with dreadful scars. The eyesockets were chipped where crows and ravens had pecked.

Zoë stood over the body, her face seemingly lit by an inner light. Her voice was sure and clear. "She says—and I hear her oh so clearly—that we must ride against the betrayer, Rome. That old gray empire must be torn down in fire and storm, even as our dear city fell to its treachery. The Queen calls for her horse—where is Bucephalus? Odenathus!"

Odenathus looked up, his face streaked with tears. His cousin stared back at him, her eyes hard as steel.

"Odenathus, where is the Queen's horse? She must ride in the morning. We march upon Damascus as soon as light touches the hills."

⊡0⊢0⊣0⊢0⊣0⊢0⊣0⊢0⊣0⊢0⊣0⊢0⊣0⊢0⊣0⊢0⊣0⊢0⊣0⊢0⊣0⊢0⊣0⊡

CHALCEDON, ON THE ASIAN SHORE OF THE PROPONTIS

)〓(

Wind gusted out of the north, bringing the briny smell of the sea and ruffling Dwyrin's hair. He stopped at the side of the road, stepping off of the broad metaled surface, out of the way of the wagons and marching blocks of men who clogged it. He adjusted his right hand on the walking stick he had fashioned from an oak branch. That had been in Galatia, as the army had crossed the vast interior plain at the heart of the Empire. Now it was carved with interlocking dogs, their long tongues hanging out. It hadn't taken much, just a little time by the fire each night, before he fell asleep, exhausted from the day's exertions.

He did not mark it, but even the long days, marching thirty miles at a crack, no longer exhausted him. Like the twenty-year veterans, he had become used to the rhythm of the army. They rose, broke down the camp, digging up the palisade of stakes that had been erected the night before, filling in the latrine pits, and covering the cook's fires. Wagons were loaded, and the auxiliary infantry and the mercenaries rousted out of their unkempt sprawl. Then, with the full sun risen, they marched through the day. Luckily, from the Cilician gates to the Propontis, it was all on good, hard-surfaced road. Towns and mountains and vast lakes passed by, making a slow-flowing montage of temples; barren, sheep-ravaged hillsides; and endless miles of orchard.

It had gone faster than Dwyrin had expected, and the funk that had clung to him in Antioch had been burned away by the Anatolian sun and the relentlessness of the daily routine. Even the frigid reserve of the older thaumaturges had failed to hold back his spirits. The weather had been good, too, and those rains that had gusted out of the north and east had not turned the land to mud. Dwyrin missed the gray mist and rain of his homeland, but he did not miss mud! No, not after months of slogging through it in Mesopotamia!

Crossing the old heartland of the Empire had been sobering, too, to see the marks of war that had come with the depredations of the Persian armies. Burned-out temples and ruined fortresses dotted the land, along with empty houses and abandoned villas. More than once the Legion outriders had flushed out bands of escaped slaves or other brigands in the hills as they had passed.

Dwyrin had heard that the Emperor had planned to make a great procession out of the journey, but there were odd rumors in the camp that Heraclius had become ill. In any case, he had not been seen riding one of his matching bay stallions in a long time. Still, the standard of the Imperial House rode at the front of the army, glittering and gold in a special wagon.

But now, after three weeks of marching beside a river, through rich farmland beneath snow-capped mountains thick with pine and spruce forest, they had come, at last, to the sea. Dwyrin walked a bit away from the road, up the side of the hill that the highway descended. From the height he could see out across the flat, rolling plain of Chalcedon to the blue line of the sea and a distant glittering white city.

"There she is, the heart of the world." Blanco's voice was gruff in the wind, and Dwyrin started a little when a heavy hand settled on his shoulder. "Behind white walls and beside the Golden Horn, the richest, most powerful city known to man."

Dwyrin nodded. Even at this distance he could catch the glint of golden temples and colorful marble balustrades. He turned, leaning on his staff. "What happens to me?" he asked, raising his voice above the wind. "Will I stay with this cohort? Will there be new recruits to join me in a five?"

Blanco shrugged, his face impassive. Despite this, Dwyrin could tell that the centurion was unhappy.

"Everyone says the Emperor has a new organization in mind for the field army. Until that is revealed to us—mere mortals that we are—no one is willing to commit to anything. You're to go into the 'pool of available recruits' that are handled by the office of the *magister militatum*. What that means, my lad, is that you will sit around in the barracks in the old palace for weeks, waiting for some pasty-faced clerk to get their thumb out and assign you to a new unit."

A long-held aggravation crept into the centurion's voice. Dwyrin frowned.

"It's purely possible you'll be assigned back to this cohort," Blanco said, looking away at the sea, his eyes squinting into the wind. "But more likely you'll go someplace else entirely. You'll have to carry on your training on your own, which will be difficult."

Dwyrin shaded his eyes, looking up at the slightly taller man. "Is that safe?"

Blanco shook his head. "No, but it's the best you can do, for the time being. I received travel orders this morning. I'm being sent back to Antioch to take command of a new thaumaturgic cohort forming there." His face split for a second with a rueful grin.

Dwyrin stared at him in amazement. "We just came from there! Now you have to go back?"

The centurion nodded, hooking his thumbs into his belt. "By sea, at least," he said, pursing his lips. "I've had enough of marching for the moment."

Dwyrin shook his head. *The army surpasses all understanding!*

<hr>

ON THE HEIGHT OF DAMAWAND

ᚺ

Khadames stood in the lee of a tall, dark pillar. It was one of the jagged teeth that rose from the very peak of the mountain, circling around the narrow little space where a bed of stone lay. A cold wind whistled between the monoliths; a northern wind that carried down the chill icy smell of the mountains that ringed the valley. When looking up from the valley floor, Damawand seemed massive; in comparison, its brothers to the north and east stood head and shoulders above it. The general tugged his heavy woolen cloak tight, hoping to keep the ice from his skin. The sun had risen, but it only rarely peered through the thin clouds that shrouded the peaks. It gave no warmth. Khadames rubbed gingerly at his right eye. Endless long hours sitting at his work table, laboring to keep the mountain and the army and the craftsmen fed, were beginning to tell upon him. If he closed his right eye, his vision was still sharp, but with it open? Half the world seemed lost in a dim haze.

The sound of heavy boots on stone drew his attention. Four of the Sixteen appeared, their black helmeted heads rising up from the stairway like puppets in a storyteller's wagon. On their shoulders they bore the body of a man— the captive the lord had taken from the wreck of Palmyra. His face hidden by a knotted scarf, the general grimaced in pain. The man had fought with honor, striving to save his city. There was no call to do these things to his body, or to defame his memory. *It is not*, thought Khadames wearily, *what the Boar would do*.

The four dark figures brought the body to the bed of stone and carefully laid it down. This thing done, they turned as one and returned to the stairway. The narrow space, carved up through the rock of the peak itself, echoed with the tramp of their passing. In time, the noise died and the sound of the wind filled the space atop the peak. Khadames rubbed his hands together. They were cold, even with three layers of gloves on them. It seemed, even if the calendar of days said that summer was upon them, that winter had not lifted its grip from the valley.

The body lay, naked, exposed to the air and the sky. It did not feel the cold.

The wind stopped, and the Lord Dahak was there, standing at the end of the bed of stone. Khadames froze, putting his thoughts away into a place at the back of his mind where they were, perhaps, safe. The dark man leaned over the body, gazing down into the withered face.

"Three men have caused me pain, faithful Khadames. One lies dead, his body rotting in a common grave. One is beyond my reach, but this one is here. He was strong, for a moment, there on the Plain of Towers. He scarred my face again."

Dahak looked up, catching Khadames' eye. It seemed that a smile, or the ghost of one, was hiding in his face. The sorcerer smoothed back his hair. The wind caught at it, making it a dark cloud behind his head.

"You should know, faithful Khadames, that your best ally is a strong enemy."

The sorcerer produced a small package wrapped in pale yellow paper from somewhere in his night black robes. Deft fingers unwrapped it, revealing a metal nail, a small envelope, and a tiny crystal vial of liquid. Dahak picked up the nail gingerly with his thumb and forefinger. It was old iron and rusted, twisted a little, a finger's length or more, with a broad, flat head. This he put to one side.

"O kalaturu and kurgarru, hear me as you heard pure Ereshkigal in the old time."

The wind died as the sorcerer began speaking. His voice was soft, intimate, and he leaned close over the corpse's head, speaking down into the dry hole of the mouth. The parched lips, cracked and dry, had been forced open with silver tongs. Khadames became aware that the wind outside the circle of pillars had risen, that it must be shrieking like the damned in the pits of Ahriman's realm. But here, inside the dark teeth, the air was still and placid. The general looked about, expecting fires to creep from the stones, for darkness to gather, pooling at the feet of the lord. It did not.

"O Anunnaki, who keep the dead in their place beneath the earth, hear me as you heard pure Ereshkigal in the old time."

A tremulous sound entered the air, the tonalities of it twisted and disturbed. A whining screech rose, vibrating from the flat stones of the floor. The pillars echoed it, and Khadames cowered down, hearing each stone suddenly stir to voice.

"I offer you the water of the river," Dahak said, raising up the vial. Something in it sparkled and shimmered like a living jewel. The keening of the stones rose up, rising and rising in pitch. The sorcerer tipped the vial, and quicksilver fell from it in tiny perfect spheres into the mouth of the corpse.

Šu nummagidde.

Khadames shuddered, hearing voices rise from the black stones and the wailing pillars.

"I offer you the grain of the field," Dahak said, raising up the small envelope. He opened it with one hand, deftly, and spilled a trickle of tiny particles into the mouth of the corpse. As he did so, the vibration of the stones changed in pitch and tone, dropping into a vastly lower scale. The rumbling hiss made Khadames shake to his boots. Eyes wide, he watched pebbles and sand dance across the stones, stirred to life by the vibration.

Šu nummagidde.

The stones muttered, and Khadames could feel their hatred of those who lived and walked like the heat from one of the forges in the deepest pits of the mountain. The sorcerer swayed for a moment, but caught himself on the edge of the bed of stone. Dahak closed his eyes, gathering his strength.

The vibration in the earth ceased. Something entered the circle of the pillars—Khadames could feel it come, tentacular limbs caressing his face with a thousand fronds as it passed. On the platform, sheets of shale, carved and fitted to make the floor, cracked under the weight of some unseen thing.

Gagta la šummeb innanneš.

The voice of the thing hummed and buzzed, replicating itself a thousand times in the space of a single word. Khadames steeled himself for worse, for the promise of that voice was madness and the incalculable horrors that hid in the darkness behind the stars. Dahak raised his head and stared into the air, unafraid. "The corpse, it is your king's."

Nig lugalme ea šummeb innanneš.

The unseen thing shifted, and a cold feathery touch passed over Khadames' chest and the thick woolen cloak froze and shattered, falling to the ground in a rain of silver fragments. Dahak raised up the nail, still holding it between thumb and forefinger, though now the old rusted iron was gone and it shone, new and clean, as if fresh from the forge.

"I give you the corpse hung from the nail."

Dahak drove the nail into the forehead of the corpse in a single violent motion. The metal ground against the bone of the skull for a moment and then there was a cracking sound and it sank in, flush to the withered dead skin. Dust puffed up around it, then settled. Dahak stepped back, his hands raised in a gesture of power. A line of glyphs blazed a fulminating green in the air before him.

The unseen thing shifted and coiled in the space between the pillars. The air filled with a gelatinous sound as if millions of beetles were squirming in a vat of gelid blood. The air above the corpse shifted and deformed, creasing for a moment. Khadames stared in awe as the space between him and the sorcerer twisted like a poorly cast mirror, showing multiple images of the sky, the pillars, the sorcerer, even the corpse on the bed of stone.

I'am'u nam-til-la i'-am'a.

Pale dust, like ground bone, fell from the air, settling on the face of the dead man. Khadames blinked, unsure of his sight, but the sparkling motes were gone. He felt uneasy—there had been the impossible notion of squirming motion in the falling dust and some afterimage lingered, that the dust, so silvery and fine, had burrowed into the wrinkled flesh.

Nam-til-la ugu-a bi-in-šub-bu-uš.

Something dripped out of that impossible space above the dead thing, a thin stream of virulent black, gleaming with shades of purple and nacreous green. No more than a single dram fell, spattering on the forehead of the corpse, staining the clean iron of the nail. At the touch, the corpse jerked sharply. Dust drifted up from its skin, disturbed by the motion. The black liquid was gone, swallowed by the thirsty flesh.

"He rises," Dahak said in that same quiet intimate voice.

Khadames covered his eyes and turned away. The feet of the corpse had begun to twitch, and then suddenly thrashed into violent motion, drumming on the edge of the bed of stone. The bones made a dreadful clatter. He put his hands over his ears, but even so, he could not help but feel the air twist again as the unseen thing departed.

A cry rang out, there in the cold place on the mountaintop, a wail of horror at birth.

Inana ba'gub.

Even more warmly dressed, with a brazier of glowing coals close to hand, Khadames stood on the rampart of the

Iron Gate, looking down upon the narrow road below. Fifty of his best bowmen were crouched under the lip of the battlement, in hiding, with heavy arrows nocked in their longbows. Three of his captains, clad from head to toe in the scaled overlapping mail of the *clibanari*—the heavy armor of the Persian *dihqan*—stood at his side. The general himself wore only the heavy black robes and brocaded red vest that were his appointed uniform. Behind him, on the pinnacle of the gate tower, the charcoal black banner of the lord flapped in the strong breeze.

Khadames' lip curled unconsciously in a sneer—the embassy before the gate raised the hackles on his back and set his hand to the hilts of his saber. Had he dared the anger of the sorcerer, he would have them slain and all like them. Too many of the friends of his youth had died, choking blood, on their lances or under a storm of their arrows.

A thick cluster of Hephthalite Huns—those called the T'u-chüeh by the Chin merchants who sometimes came to the court of the King of Kings—stood waiting on the road. At their head, a chief rode, marked by the ermine fur cloak he wore and the glitter of iron mail at his chest. He rode a barrel-chested roan stallion with a fey look in its eye. Even Khadames, who felt nothing but hatred for the Hun, noticed the noble breeding of the horse. The man was swarthy and strong-featured, with the slanted eyes and sallow skin of the eastern Turk, and he wore his mustache very long and waxed with grease. His coal black hair hung over his shoulder in many small braids, each twisted with the knucklebones of dead enemies. The men that followed him were equally fearsome in appearance, but Khadames let a small chuckle escape his cold lips.

The Hun would not come before the Iron Gate in embassy, bearing the serpent token of his lord, if they did not come to beg for life.

"Who comes before the Gate of Iron?" he called down, his voice imperious.

The tail man on the stallion stirred, and the horse raised its head, evil black eyes looking up.

"I am C'hu-lo, *yabghu* of the White Huns. Let me into your house of stone. I would have words with your master, this Lord D'ay'hay'ak."

Khadames grinned to hear the barbarian mispronounce the name of the lord of the valley.

"You are a civil barbarian," he shouted down over the rumble of the stream plunging from the water-gate into the narrow canyon, "Who comes politely to the door. You have fallen far, C'hu-lo. Should you not come with armies numberless as the stems of grass on the steppe? Should not the forest of your lances blind the sun with their brilliance? Are these few men, these boys, all you have left?"

A stormcloud of anger gathered on the face of the Hun chieftain, but he mastered himself and did not draw his bow as he might have. Instead, the chieftain, gritting his teeth, answered in a civil voice:

"A messenger came to me, bringing this token." He held high a black knife of the kind that the Sixteen carried as they passed through the land. Along the blade, etched in the steel, was the rippling shape of a serpent. Even in this dim light, under the shadow of the mountain, the red scales glittered. "I am interested to hear the words of this lord of yours. Let me enter as a guest, and we will not dishonor that right."

Khadames nodded to one of his captains and leaned out on the wall. "You may enter, C'hu-lo, but know that no man who does not please the Lord Dahak leaves this place alive." The general took great pleasure in stressing the proper pronunciation of the sorcerer's name.

The wall trembled a little as the gate opened, chains rattling through their sockets as a hundred men turned the hidden wheels that raised the three gates of iron. The Huns entered, their eyes slits, glancing this way and that. Khadames paced along the inner battlement and descended the broad stair at the back of the gatehouse. He knew they were measuring the depth of the walls, the strength of the gates. *Let them*, he thought to himself with a smile. *This fortress will never fall to the race of men.*

Khadames vaulted onto his horse, feeling a twinge of envy at the speed and power of the roan that the Hun chieftain rode. He gestured with his chin, up the valley. "Come, poor C'hu-lo, let us go into Damawand and you will speak with the lord and learn, I imagine, more than you expected."

There was singing—soft voices raised in melody. The man woke, feeling a deep ache in his bones. For a moment he lay still, feeling the smooth, cool fabric under his finger-tips. A delicate perfume filled the air, bringing memories of lemon trees and running water to his mind. His eyelids flickered and opened and beheld soft drapes of silk and saffron linen hanging above him. He moved his arm, test-ing the flex of his fingers—they moved unexpectedly. He had thought, no—he was sure—that they had been crip-pled, broken, unable to move. He held his hand before his face—a brown palm and long, thin fingers greeted him.

"My lord?" a soft husky voice penetrated. Something, no—someone—warm moved at his side. "Are you awake?"

The man turned his head and found a young woman by his side. Her skin was soft and pale, highlighting her long dark hair. It spilled over her white shoulder like a river, gleaming in the light of lanterns with faces of cut crystal. Her lips were pale rose, soft and full. She moved closer, and he smelled cinnamon perfume in her hair. She kissed him—a long, slow kiss—sliding on top of him. Her firm breasts rubbed against his chest. The man lost himself in sensation for a long time.

Later, his stomach growled, and the girl laughed and rose up, drawing a thin drape of golden silk around her body. "We will bring you food," she said, and went away.

The man lay on the cushions, fully awake for the first time. He sat up, feeling a delicious lassitude in the muscles of his arms and back and legs. A tent of silk surrounded him, lit by small lanterns. The air was sweet and he could hear, a little ways away, the chuckle of a stream running over rocks. He stood, finding his legs strong under him. He rubbed his face—there was a memory of a beard—but found it clean-shaven and smooth. The drapes of the tent door parted and two young girls entered, their long red-brown hair tied back behind their heads with scarves of gold. They carried trays of silver, laden with fresh fruit, sliced meat, and fine cheeses. The black-haired girl entered after them bearing a chalice of chased gold, heavy with wine.

"My lord." The black-haired girl bowed. "Please sit and break your fast."

The man sat, looking up in admiration at the supple forms of his attendants.

"Pray, good ladies," he said as they laid out the feast before him. "What are your names?"

The two girls with hair of red-brown giggled and hid their faces, but they sat close to him at either side, their thighs touching his. The black-haired girl knelt before him and poured wine into a cup of gold.

"My lord," she said, blushing, "we have any name you care to give us. Your will is ours in all things."

"Oh," the man said, and then had to stop as one of the younger girls had deftly slipped a choice bit of roasted meat between his lips. He chewed and his eyebrows raised at the rich, taste. The girls smiled back at him, pressing close.

After another time, spent in delightful repast, he stood again and brushed his long hair back. He took the ends in his hands—his hair was dark, too, like the raven's tail, and glossy with good health. The two maidens with red-brown hair slipped away, carrying the dishes and plates of the feast. Memory tickled at his thought, but then fled when he turned to seize it. "What is my name?"

The black-haired girl had remained. He looked down upon her, cocking his head in puzzlement. Memory stirred again, far back in his thought. Her dark hair should not be straight, but rather a mane of curls, each catching the light like a black pearl. The girl bowed again, pressing her lips to his foot. "Your name is Arad, my lord, or so I have been told."

"Told by whom?" Arad reached down and touched the girl's shoulder. She rose up, slim as a reed, and nestled against the hard muscle of his body. "Who rules this place?"

The girl looked up, her eyes bright in adoration. Her breath tickled his chest. "The lord of all the world, master. This is his *an-na-ki*, his heaven upon the earth. You are the most blessed of his servants, dwelling among us in this garden."

Arad looked around, seeing only the pleasant walls of the tent. "What is outside?" His voice trembled, feeling strange fear at the thought that something unknown might lurk beyond the saffron and ultramarine walls. "I must see."

"No, my lord . . . is it not better to lie here with me, to have every pleasure to your hand?"

Arad turned and stepped out of the tent, though the delicate fingers of the black-haired girl trailed along his arm. Outside, he found himself on the top of a hill of green grass that swept down to a lake of cerulean blue. Orchards heavy with fruit rose from rich soil all around. Below, at the verge of the lake, maidens sported in the water, their tan bodies silhouetted against the warm waters. Above, a sky of pale blue-white covered the world, spotted with fleecy clouds and a warm, forgiving sun.

Arad felt the heat of that sun on his face and turned away, looking behind him. Twin mountains rose up in the distance, capped with snow. Storm clouds swirled over one, while the other stood in sunlight. A fragrant breeze caressed his face. He frowned, for a strong memory rose out of the depths of his thought, breaching like leviathan in the sea of his consciousness.

"I do not belong here," he said aloud, his hand going to

his face again. "These are not the Offering Fields! Where are the guides and the judges?"

The sun flickered and grew dim. The maidens sporting in the waters looked up and then fled, crying out in dismay. Arad looked around in apprehension, seeing the rich orchards and fields of wheat shimmer and fade away. Darkness flooded into the world, and a dim, flickering glow emerged where the bright sun had once stood.

"There are no judges here," came a voice, strong and powerful and filled with great amusement. "There is only I, the Lord of the World."

Arad turned, and a dreadful chill touched his heart. Out of the darkness a figure came, tall and lean, with a narrow head and a sweeping mane of ebon hair. Robes of night fell from the figure's shoulders, and a shirt of blood red silk glittered like scales on his chest. Pale yellow eyes gleamed in the dim light.

"I know you," Arad said, forcing sound from a throat constricted by the memory of horrible and endless pain. "We struggled on the Plain of Towers—I cast out your creature, the *dhole* you had summoned from the black abyss."

"Yes," the Lord Dahak said, canting his head like a hunting wolf, a sly smile on his face. "But you failed, and the city was thrown down in ruin."

Arad staggered, remembering horrors and the wailing of tens of thousands.

"I broke the memory of the city," whispered the figure in the pooling darkness, "but I did not forget you, O my beloved pet. You I brought forth in state, though your body was torn and cold."

Arad remembered, and shuddered at the defilement of his body. He looked down, seeing smooth flesh and strong muscle where only corruption and worms and the bitter taste of embalming salts had been.

"Now you are strong again, your body restored by the breath of the keeper-of-the-dead. Your mind is almost whole; soon the healing will be complete and you will know all that you knew before, comprehend all that has transpired. Your skills will return."

"This pleases you?" Arad's voice was thick with contempt. "I will only raise power against you. I will strike you down and drive you from the world of men."

"Will you?" Dahak laughed, and stepped out of the shadow. Arad felt cold air eddy around him and realized that the beautiful garden had wholly vanished, leaving only a cold stone room with a bed of rushes and rough woolen blankets behind. "Serve me, O risen man. Show me the proper respect—the respect due your lord . . . No. Your King."

Arad opened his mouth, a furious retort on his lips, but found himself instead kneeling before the dark figure. Unbidden, though his mind raged against it, his forehead pressed against the rough stone of the floor in the "little" proskynesis. His mouth, though his will strove to silence it, issued words.

"Yes, dread lord. As you command, so I obey."

"Good," Dahak said, laughing, a chill sound reminiscent of children drowning under thick ice. "Rise up, noble Arad"—and in his singsong voice was a great laughter at some joke known only to the sorcerer—"rise up and come with me. There are things to be done."

In his mind, Arad struggled to command his arms and legs, but they followed the sorcerer eagerly.

C'hu-lo leaned against a wall of worked stone, idly looking out a tall, thin window. The window was tall—over five feet—set high on the peak of the mountain, and looked out over ramparts of black stone and walls of obsidian. From what he could see, a pitch of almost three hundred feet yawned under the sill, and there was neither a bar nor shutters to close it off. Far below, he could make out—for his eyesight was better than that of most men—the smokes and fumes that rose from the floor of the valley. The sight of that valley had troubled him as they had ridden up the long stone road from the Iron Gate. It was thick with buildings—storehouses, barns, foundries, tanning sheds, work-shops—and all the appurtenances of a great city. The valley had been filled with people; men with spades and picks; soldiers marching in file, carrying long spears; women with heavy bundles—all coming and going.

He hooked a thumb into his belt, checking to see that the knife secreted within was still there. He and his men had submitted to a great indignity when they had yielded up their curved swords and bows upon entering the mountain. But no T'u-chüeh would go anywhere—even under guest-oath—without some kind of blade. Another, a flat-headed stabbing knife, was still in his boot. This hidden place intrigued him as little had done in years. There was a power here, a strong power. He smoothed his long mustache and turned away from the window. A fire burned in the wall grate, and there was wine and freshly killed meat on the table. He did not touch them. Instead, he smiled and carefully examined the walls and furniture.

His time in the court of the Celestial Emperor had not been wasted. He had learned a great deal there, under the unsuspecting tutelage of the ministers of the Jade Court. His fingertips found a crack in the wall counterclockwise from the door, and he rubbed them together. A little grit came away.

A door in use, he thought to himself. He turned, alert, brushing the grit away on the side of the table.

The door swung open, and a naked man entered. C'hu-lo raised an eyebrow and smiled at the sight. It was not warm in the room. The man was dark brown, with long straight black hair and a noble profile. The man turned and stood against the wall. Another figured entered, and C'hu-lo snarled involuntarily, seeing something out of legend enter the waking world. An old prayer to the god of storms flashed through his mind, preparing his soul for immediate death.

"Ah," the figure of a man said, this thing with the eyes of a serpent and the cold aura of the corpse-feeders. "The Lord C'hu-lo, once the *yabghu* of the western T'u-chüeh—

those called the Hephthalite Huns by the Persian scribes at the court of the King of Kings. Welcome."

C'hu-lo inclined his head, as was proper when greeting the king of another nation. The cold thing waved a hand to the chair set before the grate.

"Please, sit with me that we may talk. I am Dahak, the master of this valley."

Curiosity and great fear warred in C'hu-lo's heart, but the thing—for he knew without any doubt that this was no man, though it wore a man's shape—seemed polite and to understand the business of guest-hearth and hospitality. The steppe-lord moved carefully to the leftmost chair and sat, turning it so that he might see both doors. The Lord Dahak sat as well, folding one leg under the other with easy grace. The naked man remained standing against the wall.

"I am still *yabghu* of the People Beyond the Rampart of Heaven," said C'hu-lo in a flat voice. "The pawn, the *toy* of the Chin, he who is named Shih-kuei is a false Khagan. Men follow him because they are sheep—worse, they are children who cannot tell a ewe from a wolf."

Lord Dahak inclined his head, showing his acceptance of this statement.

"Yet," the sorcerer said, "he commands thirty *umen* of strong warriors and you barely one. His hands drip with Chin gold, and you must murder and rob in poor villages for your supper. Is this not so?"

C'hu-lo had always accounted himself a sane person, and a sane person did not attack an enemy who could destroy him in an instant, so he held his tongue. The blaze of fury at his heart he held, and contained with his will, and turned it to stoke the old anger that he had kept for the architects of his defeat.

"This . . . this is so." C'hu-lo accounted himself a strong man, but admitting this thing before the slitted yellow eyes of the corpse-feeder made him feel weak and small. "I did not understand the power that was arrayed against me. It was deftly done, and I cannot admit otherwise."

"You were tricked," the Lord Dahak said in a companionable voice. "The agents of the one called P'ei Kiu bribed your chieftains and whispered sweet words in the ears of the clan elders. Chin gold flowed in rivers to those who would acclaim the boy, Shih'kuei, as Khagan of the People. It seemed so reasonable to everyone—all but you, and those true men who rode with you."

C'hu-lo's heart burned with shame, hearing his downfall spoken of so easily. He had ridden with his own men for so long—men who knew never to mention the disaster that had thrown down their war chief from the pinnacle of power and made him a vagabond in the wilderness. Memories flooded into him, so strong that he failed to note the sorcerer had begun speaking to him in the tongue of his own people.

"But they were tired of war, those of the people who live on this side of the rampart." Now Dahak seemed to be musing, thinking over deeds and agonies long gone. "No matter that the people had assailed the very walls of the Chin capital within living memory. No matter that when the people were united they were unstoppable. Even Persia bowed down and paid tribute; even the mighty Rhomanoi sent embassies, begging for help. All of those things, they were forgotten, were they not?"

C'hu-lo looked up and froze, meeting the burning eyes of the sorcerer. Hot words failed on his lips.

"Did it please you, noble C'hu-lo, to take food from the hand of the very man—this one named P'ei Kiu—when he had arranged your shame and downfall? Did the wine taste sweet, when you raised a cup to the honor of the Chin Emperor in his very court?"

The Hun's face blanched, blood draining from his cheeks. He tried to stand, but he could not. The shame of his service in the Chin court, the depth to which he had fallen before he could take no more, burned in his throat and tore at his vitals. C'hu-lo gasped for air, hearing a tremendous rushing of blood in his ears.

"Calm, my friend," the sorcerer said in a lazy voice.

"All of these things are past you now. Your long wandering in the wilderness—all these years of mercenary service, drifting from one court to another, always seeking some grain of the honor that you had lost—they are at an end."

C'hu-lo felt the cold touch on his wrist and looked down. Dahak had laid a blade—a curved silver dagger—across the Hun's wrist. It was finely tooled, with the markings of the smiths of the Issyk-Kul upon it and a hilt of dark red stone. C'hu-lo knew the blade. He had placed it himself—a remembrance of childhood friendship and lifelong loyalty—in the great tomb of the last true Khagan of his people, Tardu, the noble grandfather of the pustule Shih'kuei. Tears, unbidden, sprang from his eyes and leaked slowly down his cheeks.

"How"—C'hu-lo picked up the dagger and held it in both hands—"the tomb is sealed . . . I rolled the closing stone myself. . . ."

Dahak smiled and stood. "The tastes of the boy Shih'kuei are lavish, I am told. This came to me from a Rhomanoi merchant, who had it in turn from an Armenian. The tomb was robbed long ago, while you were exiled in Chin lands, and the contents sold or traded for slaves."

C'hu-lo could not move. The enormity of the crime threatened to shatter the world.

"You must gather strength to you, my friend." Dahak paced to the window and looked out, finding the view pleasing. He turned back, looking over his shoulder. "I offer you friendship and men and gold and arms. I, too, have been denied my patrimony. I intend to get it back, and you are a mighty captain. You can help me retrieve what is rightfully mine. We can aid each other."

C'hu-lo looked up, tearing his eyes from the dagger that lay so heavy in his hand. The fury he had struggled for so long to contain was close, close to the surface. It threatened to break free, but he held it back and struggled to force it back into the dark places in the back of his mind.

"What have you lost, thing-in-the-shape-of-a-man? What do you know of dishonor?"

"I know this," Dahak said as he paced back to the table. "I am a man, though I have made a dreadful bargain. My throne has been stolen from me, even as yours has. My brother murdered, my family scattered. All that is mine by right of birth, denied me. But I will not slink away into the darkness, I will fight and I will win. Even as you will. We will both win, and laugh to see our enemies dragged before us in chains."

"What throne . . ." C'hu-lo stopped, coughing, and cleared his throat. "What throne was yours?"

"My true name," Dahak said, and his face changed subtly, his eyes becoming brown and his skin lightening ever so faintly, the ridges along his skull shrinking, "is Rustam Aparvez. My father was the King of Kings, Hormizd the Fourth. I am the younger brother, now the heir, of the great King Chrosoes, called the Second. Now that he and his son lie dead, I am the last of that line. But I will ascend the Peacock Throne again, and I will rule Persia, even as did my fathers. Even as you will once again rule the T'u-chüeh."

C'hu-lo felt a shock run through him, and he knew—suddenly and completely—that this was the truth. The corpse-eater, the *lich*, the grave-walker that stood before him with those damnable yellow eyes was in truth a king. The Hun stood, his legs still shaky from the shock of seeing the grave-gift of his old friend, and he inclined his head to the dark man.

"I will stand by your side, Persian King, if you will stand by mine. We shall be restored, and our kingdoms whole again."

"Yes," Dahak said, his face serene in victory. "And doom to all our enemies."

Against the wall, the man Arad remained, quiet and still, unable to move. His eyes, though, were filled with pain, though he could not cry out.

)=(

Kurad, captain of the eastern gate, stood, shading his eyes with his hand. Shouts and the sound of horns had risen from the ranks of the Mekkan besiegers. On the barren plain before the wall, he could see spearmen running from their tents, out on the siege line. He squinted, wishing for younger eyes.

A band of horsemen stormed down out of the dun-colored hills behind the line of the *wadi*. Fifty or more, riding hard. The Mekkan camps were stirring as the sound of the alarm spread. Men ran to horses, or jogged out from the shade of their tents, spears or bows in their hands, angling to intercept the hard-riding horsemen.

"Captain, what is it?"

Kurad looked aside, seeing the clan-lord Al'Jayan come up at his side.

"I do not know, my lord. A troop of horsemen are trying to ride through the Mekkan lines."

Al'Jayan shaded his brow as well, peering out with his dark eyes over the tumbled rocks and scattered fields that lay between the gray-green walls of the city and the palms and scrubby trees that lined the *wadi*.

"Who can it be? All our clansmen are within the walls."

Kurad pursed his lips, thinking over the roster of the Bani-Hashim exiles and their cousins who ruled this city—the second-largest metropolis of Arabia Felix. He could think of no one who was not accounted for.

"I know not, Lord—" He stopped. Al'Jayan had suddenly leapt up onto the battlement, waving his hands, shouting.

"Al'Aws! Al'Aws—here, here is sanctuary!"

Kurad cursed, taking the name of Hubal in vain, and leaned out from the battlement himself. The band of riders, still coming on hard, had burst through the scattered lines of the Mekkans. Now they thundered closer, and he could—at last—make out what the younger eyes of Al'Jayan had already discerned: The lead man, a young man by his bearing and the speed with which he drove his horse recklessly across the stone-littered fields, held the banner of the clan of Aws at his side. Kurad squinted, making out the streaming red and green *Kaffiyeh* and he cursed again and leapt down the steps to the gatehouse in haste, taking them three and four at a time.

The arrival of the Al'Aws was unexpected and unlooked for, but Kurad had crossed blades with the young bandit more than once in the internecine strife that had plagued the city. Only in the last year had the Khazarj clans driven out the Aws and their adherents, in great part with the assistance of the Bani-Hashim from the south. Still, the Aws held no love for Mekkah, and the heart of the fiery young chief was true to this city of his birth. Kurad hustled into the dim recess of the gatehouse.

"Up lads! Up! A band of horse are coming—friends of the city—prepare to let them in!"

The Yathribi militia boiled out of the cool shade like ants from a broken hill and swarmed about the great wooden doors that held the eastern gate closed. Kurad shouted above the din, and used his boot and fists to get them in order. A great bar of oak, shipped down years before from Phoenicia, held the gate, and now fifteen men struggled to lift it from its iron hooks.

On the wall above, the young Lord Al'Jayan continued to howl encouragement at the riders, who must be coming close now.

Fifteen men removed the bar and staggered aside, faces pinched with pain at the weight of it. Others, their spears and swords a bright thicket, dragged at the gate. It stuck, grinding across the stones and gravel of the gateway. Kurad, his saber out and ready, pushed through them, his eyes on the slowly widening slot between the gates.

Dust billowed up behind the Aws as they thundered ahead, horses running flat out for the safety of the gate. Behind them, the Mekkans surged forward, their arrows arcing high into the air. As Kurad watched, men fell, stricken from their saddles by the Mekkan archers. Bands of spearmen ran in pursuit, howling their southern war cries. Too, the horsemen from the Mekkan camps south of the city had to hove into view, though they were far away and too late to catch the Aws and their brash young lord before he reached the gate.

The gate swung wide, and Kurad put his shoulder to it, shouting commands at his men.

"When they are through, fill the gate with steel," he shouted, "and close it quickly! The Mekkans are hard on their heels."

He looked up, seeing the Aws horsemen loom large, their mounts streaked with sweat, their heads low, close to the reins, speeding like the wind. Behind them it seemed that the whole army of the Mekkans was in pursuit, covering the fields with lines of running men. Their distant war cry rose and rose, echoing back from the towering walls of the city.

Ah-la-la-la-la-la! The Aws rode on; the hooves of their horses striking sparks from the scattered stone and gravel of the road that led to the eastern gate.

Kurad leapt aside, his face creased by a wild grin as the first of the Aws—the brave young man in chieftains robes, still carrying the bright banner of his house—thundered into the gate and spun his horse, its head turning and rearing, to get out of the way of his fellows. Sweat spattered from its flanks.

The Aws streamed in through the gate, a river of men and horse, green and red, with bright steel in their hands. Kurad leapt to seize the bridle of the rearing horse, his voice raised in welcome.

"Well come, Lord of the Aws! Well met indeed!"

The Lord of the Aws looked down, his eyes bright over the tan drape of his desert scarf. "So it is, man of the city. We are well met."

Kurad paused, his hand tight on the bridle. The man looking down at him had dark eyes the color of well-steeped tea, that and the edge of a scar along his right eye. The Lord Al'Aws—his eyes were light, almost the color of the stones of the mountains. . . . Kurad shuddered, feeling the steel-bright saber of the stranger punch through his larynx. Blood flooded his mouth, and he tried to shout, to raise the alarm. He made a gobbling sound and slumped forward, dragging the head of the horse down.

Khalid al'Walid cut again with his saber, severing the hand tangled in his reins at the wrist. Around him the screams of dying men rose up, filling the air with a cacophony of angry shouts and the ring of steel on steel. His men swarmed through the gate, hewing down the Yathribi milita, driving the defenders back into the streets of the city.

"Wedge the gate," he shouted at Patik as the Persian, his armor soaked with blood, emerged from the door of the gatehouse. The stolid Persian was the very devil at close quarters' work in his heavy interlocking suit of mail. He bore a dripping mace in one hand, and a short sword in the other. The soldier raised his head and nodded his understanding. Khalid turned, his quick eyes scanning the rampart and the rooftops. Yathribi soldiers were running toward the gatehouse along the top of the wall.

"With me," he called to a band of his men just come through the gate. "We must secure the wall." With that he swung down off his horse and bounded up the steps to the rampart, his saber gleaming with blood in his hand. At the top he ducked under the spear thrust of the first militiaman and hacked at the man's arm. Blood gelled around his blade, and the man screamed. Khalid tore the blade away and shoved the Yathribi back, into the next spearman. That fellow ducked aside and thrust hard at Khalid. The sheykh weaved aside and then slipped on the wear-polished stones, sliding in the blood and bile spilling from the first man. He went down hard, the man dying on the rampart clubbed him with a bloody fist.

Khalid tried to squirm aside, seeing the spearman raise his leaf-bladed weapon in both hands to plunge into the Arab's belly. The dying militiaman hit him again, making sparks fly across his vision. Khalid twisted hard, snatching at the fallen man's arm. The spear flashed down and plunged deep into the shoulder of the man as Khalid dragged him across his body. Something cold touched Khalid's chest, and then his own men surged along the battlement, their bows snapping in the hot air. The spearman turned to run and took two arrows in the back, toppling with a wail from the rampart into the street below.

Khalid shoved the body of the fallen man off his chest. The spear had dug into his mailed armor, the thin tip wedging into the center of one of the round links. Khalid let out a shuddering breath and stood, retrieving his saber. Fighting continued on the rampart, and in the city the sounds of battle were growing. The first column of Mekkan infantry—spears and shields raised high—jogged through the gate below him. He smiled, suddenly feeling the blood-fire wash over him. He jumped up and down, crying out in joy.

"What is this atrocity?" Mohammed's voice rumbled through the square as he swung down from his horse. At his back, Jalal and Shadin remained a-horse, their dark eyes surveying the men milling in the plaza. Each of the Tanukh carried a bow at their saddle horn, an arrow ready at the string. While their chieftain stormed through the knot of men clustered at the entrance to the Temple of Hubal, they kept a weather eye on the rooftops and archways. More than one victorious general had found his prize a poisoned well. A wedge of Tanukh followed Mohammed, though, keeping close to his back.

In the foyer of the temple, Mohammed strode up the steps and came to a halt, his eyes filled with tremendous

anger. Two of his allied clan-lords—Mekkan Quryash, by
their Kaffiyeh and the cording on their armor—were shouting at a cluster of kneeling captives. Long knives were in
their hands, one already dripping with blood. Between the
Mekkans and their intended victims, the youth Al'Walid
was half crouched with his saber raised in guard. The temple was lit by many torches of pitch, and their guttering
light shimmered in the surface of his blade like a setting
sun.

"What goes here?" Three heads snapped around at the
sound of Mohammed's voice, and he stepped into their
midst. "Who gave the order to kill these prisoners?"

The Mekkan with the gore-stained blade—a fellow Mohammed dimly recognized as being one of his cousins—
stepped forward, his black beard bristling and his eyes
filled with hatred. At his back, Mohammed felt the whisper
of air as the Tanukh spread out, covering the doorways of
the temple and the great apse of the sanctuary of Hubal
itself.

"I did, Lord Mohammed. These are the kin-slayers who
fled from Mekkah—we caught them hiding in the cellar
of this temple. They owe us—and you, Lord—blood in
plenty. This man"—he kicked the corpse on the floor—
"he burned the house of my father and killed a dozen of
my servants. I am owed blood-debt!"

Mohammed surveyed the scene, seeing the bloody and
battered faces of the captives, their fear, the wounds they
had already suffered. The brash youth, Al'Walid, caught
his eye and made a show of resheathing his blade, though
he took a moment to wipe old dried blood from the edge.
Mohammed nodded at him absently before turning back to
the Hashim captains.

"In the eyes of Allah, the great and merciful, we are all
children and brothers. I gave orders that all captives were
to be spared. There will be an amnesty, and many will be
paroled if they accept my rule and follow my law."

Mohammed stepped in close, looming over the slightly

shorter man. The Quryash lord matched Mohammed's gaze with a steely glare of his own.

"We are owed blood recompense for our loss," the man snarled, his sword still bare in his hand.

Mohammed nodded gravely, never taking his eyes from the Quryash.

"Murderers will be punished, but they will be judged by the law, and the great and good god will look to their punishment. Are you the Lord of the World, that you will take his justice into your hands?"

More Tanukh, and others, crowded into the temple. There was an angry muttering when the men saw that the kin-slayers had been brought to bay. The Quryash captain, seeing something terrible growing in Mohammed's eyes, suddenly backed away and bowed his head.

"Those who follow the law," Mohammed said, turning, his voice rising to fill the great hall, "will be rewarded by the blessings both of man and God. No captive will be slain out of hand, no man put to death without a trial before a judge. This is the *shari'a*—the law—and all will follow it."

Mohammed turned to the captives, who were still kneeling on the floor, though now some of the Tanukh had moved behind them and were loosening the chains that held them.

"Without the law, that which has been spoken to man by the angels of the Lord of the World, we are beasts. In this place and time, I have heard the God speaking in the clear air, and I *know* that if His law is not obeyed, then eternal suffering and torment are our reward. I do not presume to set the terms of His justice, but no man who has not been given the chance to submit himself—as I have done—to the mercy of the God who dwells in the wasteland will die by my hand. Let these men be taken from this place, this house of idols and sacrifice, and let them be judged by the laws of our city."

Mohammed jerked his head at the Tanukh who had surrounded the prisoners.

"Take them away." The Tanukh and other Quryash in the crowd of soldiers opened a path, and the whole collection of men began to file out into the plaza. Mohammed sighed and ran his fingers through his beard. The white streaks that had begun to mark it at Palmyra were growing, twisting through it like snakes in the high grass. *Soon*, he through ruefully, *I will look much like a patriarch or an elder! And I only forty-three years old, too. . . .* He sighed, feeling the terrible weariness that came in the wake of hard fighting. He gestured at the youth, Al'Walid. "Lad," he said, "what brought you here? I would have expected you to be still at work in the city. Is all secure?"

"No, Lord Mohammed," Khalid said easily, coming to stand next to the chieftain. "Some houses are still in the hands of the Yathrib—but the city has fallen. In truth, I came here seeking you, expecting that you would take this place"—he motioned to the vast bulk of the temple that rose around them—"as your command post. I found it almost empty, save for those captives who have just been dragged out of the cellar."

Mohammed's eyes narrowed, and his eyebrows beetled together. "Why not let them die?" he said in an even voice, watching the young man closely.

"The captives?" Khalid seemed nonplussed by the question. "I had heard you speak of the mercy of your faceless God, so I assumed that—*at least*—you would want to question them first. Was I wrong?"

"No," Mohammed said, something in him satisfied by the answer. "You did well today, very well. Your gamble at the eastern gate paid handsomely."

In the early dawn, when Mohammed had gathered with his lieutenants and chieftains to plan the day's assault, the young mercenary had made quite a stir with his proposal to take the eastern gate by a ruse. The Mekkan clan chiefs, who supplied the vast bulk of the army that Mohammed had raised to besiege the hiding place of his daughter's murderers, had thought it mad. But Mohammed had spent too much time in siegework already—the memories of the

long, grueling battle for the City of Silk weighed upon
him. He had no desire to tie down this army, so fractious
and riven with internal dissention, in a lengthy operation
against the gray-green walls of Yathrib. *Besides*, he
thought smugly, *it is such a plan as I would have hatched,
if I had but a moment to think of it.*

"It did, didn't it?" Khalid smiled, the wild assurance of
youth plain in his face. "I was not so sure, for a moment,
as we hurtled toward that gate. I thought it might fail . . .
and I would still be feeling the pain of it! What now, Lord
Mohammed? Now that the city is ours . . . do we return to
Mekkah?"

Mohammed looked around, seeing the vaulting hall and
the towering graven image of Hubal that rose over it. He
saw, too, the rich draperies and carved wooden panels that
hung in that place. His heart felt sick, seeing the long years
of effort that the men of Yathrib had invested in it—knowing as he did that it would not gain them entrance into the
paradise of the afterlife.

"All of this," he whispered to himself, "is a trap . . .
Shaitan speaking to men in their dreams of glory and pride.
All their faith turned aside from the True God, their love
and honor swallowed by nothingness. . . ." For a moment
he felt tears welling, but he calmed his mind, and the emotion passed.

"My lord?" Khalid was still waiting.

"Burn it," Mohammed said, raising his head, his eyes
dry. "Tear it down and leave nothing."

)I(

"G uuhhh!" Blood oozed around the edge of the wound. Maxian, his face ashen, held a trembling hand over the deep gash. He swallowed convulsively, trying to keep from passing out while he worked. Pale green fire flickered in his palm. Yellow serum bubbled out of the wound, then a spoke of green fire stabbed up. Maxian gasped, his breathing harsh, and closed his fist. A fragment of stone, almost five inches long, emerged from the wound, wrinkling its way free in fits and starts. A halo of viridian fire burned around it. Once free of Krista's stomach, it spun away to clatter off the wall. Maxian slumped over the girl's body, bending the last vestige of his will to knitting the ruined skin closed.

The taut skin of the girls' stomach crawled back together, covering the wound. The blood, soaked into the flesh, making it smooth again, and he collapsed at last, utterly exhausted.

Gaius Julius stirred himself, getting up from the moth-eaten couch that he had appropriated. With gentle hands he lifted the Prince's arms and took him on his shoulders. Turning sideways to get around the wobbly table where Krista lay half covered with a dirty woolen sheet, he ducked under the low door to enter the other room. There was something that passed for a bed, though the previous owner seemed to have spent little time in it. The apartment itself was on the sixth floor of a ramshackle insula high on the Aventine hill. Its only redeeming value was the view from the balcony, if one could risk negotiating the termite-eaten wood and the fraying ropes that held it together. Too, it was high enough above the noxious reek that emanated from the laundry on the first floor for a man to breathe comfortably.

Gaius turned the sheet over his nominal master and laid the back of his hand on the boy's forehead. The Prince was sick with fever, almost burning hot. The old Roman frowned—this was a puzzle indeed. If the boy could rouse himself, he could bring his own power to bear, repairing the burn damage and restoring his own health. But now? Unconscious and wracked by fever-dreams? This required a delicate touch.

"Will he live?" Alexandros stood at the door, a jug of wine in his hand and a loop of smoked sausages slung over his shoulder. The golden youth was smiling, and Gaius Julius hated him for a moment. The climb up all those flights of stairs taxed him, even with this body that felt so little pain.

"I pray so, for our sake. No cheese? No olives? No dormouse, fat with figs and candied nuts? Not so much as a sweet onion?"

Alexandros grinned and shook his head. He put the wine on the floor by the door and hung the sausage from a hook twisted into a very precarious-looking timber that held up part of the roof.

"I did not go far—there is a butcher's on the corner, but I did not see another place to get food."

The Macedonian looked around, a wry smile on his face.

"This is your bolt-hole?" Alexandros was grinning, waving a hand at the holes in the roof and the warble of pigeons under the eaves.

"I sublet it," snapped Gaius Julius, "at a low rate. The man is an imperial clerk, so I doubt we will draw any official attention while we are here." The Roman produced a knife and cut a hunk of sausage from the loop. "In any case, we will not be here long. The girl will soon be well; she sleeps now, I think. As soon as our *master* is awake, we will move him as well."

Alexandros sat, shrugging his muscular shoulders. He

leaned back, watching the old Roman while he ate. After a time he rubbed his nose and looked at Gaius. "Why do you do that?"

"Do what?" Gaius washed down the last of the sausage with a draft of wine. It was a poor vintage; he could tell by the taste that it was not from a Latin vineyard. Sicilian, perhaps. It had a rustic and disreputable edge to it.

"Eat. Drink. Sleep. All these things that I see you do, see you waste your time upon."

Gaius Julius frowned at the Macedonian youth. Sometimes the mind that lurked behind those pretty blue eyes baffled him. "They are necessary," Gaius said in a gruff voice. "You eat, you drink, you even sleep, upon occasion."

Alexandros smiled, showing his perfect even white teeth. "Not for some days," he said, the corners of his eyes crinkling up. "I found that sleep is not required by those of us in our current condition months ago. All that sausage gained you was the necessity to expel it later."

Gaius Julius made a face, saying, "I do not believe you. The shock of our recent reversal has unhinged your already addled mind."

Alexandros leaned forward, his hands upon his knees. "Try. Tonight, when the Walach bed down, or the slave girl falls into slumber, do not yield to Morpheus. Simply stay awake—it is so simple! You will find, as I have, that you need never sleep again. It is only the memory of hunger, or thirst, or exhaustion that afflicts you. None of these things are real anymore. Not for us."

On the table, Krista made a small moaning sound, and Gaius Julius stood and stepped to her side. The girl's eyes fluttered open, and she stared up in confusion. "There was fire . . . ," she said in a faint voice. "Something struck me."

"Yes," the old Roman said, gently holding her head up, his arm behind her back to help her rise. "The old villa was destroyed—we only escaped by a hair. Fortuna smiled on us, my dear. The Prince carried you out."

"Where are we?" Krista looked around, rubbing her

eyes. She made a face at the smell in the little apartment. "Another fine hiding place, I see."

Gaius Julius shrugged and tossed her a vile orange tunic he had found in the bedroom.

She raised an eyebrow, but pulled it on regardless. "Thank you," she said, and swung her tan legs off of the table. "We are in the city?"

"Yes," Alexandros said with an edge in his voice. "Despite our flight in the Engine, our dear Roman friend decided that we should walk right back into the den of the enemy instead of resting at ease someplace far away—like Novo Carthago on the sunny coast of Hispania, or perhaps Tyre in Phoenicia."

Krista turned her head, wincing at the pain that came with the movement. "Why?"

Gaius Julius rolled his eyes. No one seemed to see the logic in it. "Praetorians attacked the house during the ceremony," growled the old Roman. "I saw their bodies as we escaped. By the grace of the gods, Khiron was a match for them. That means the Imperial Offices are hunting for us—doubtless our descriptions have been circulated far and wide."

He raised an eyebrow at the girl. "In particular," he continued, "by your former mistress, the Duchess of Parma. So, there is only one place—if we are to continue with this harebrained plan of the Prince's—to operate from. Here, inside the city, hidden amid a population of a million people. This rat's nest gives us more cover, and opportunities, than we would ever have in the countryside."

Krista nodded, feeling queasy and sick. Her stomach hurt dreadfully, but when she felt it, it seemed whole and unscratched. She shook her head, but then realized that she knew the feeling. *The aftereffects of his power*, she thought to herself. *I must have been near death.* "Where is the Prince?" she said aloud, glaring first at Alexandros, and then at the old Roman.

"Here!" Gaius said quickly, brushing aside the curtain

that closed off the bedroom. "He sleeps, but there is a fever on him."

Krista got down off of the table, feeling a jellylike shudder in her legs. She stopped, breathing hard, and then managed to make it to the doorway. Her face turned grim, seeing the pale, feverish face in the bed.

"We need help," she said, casting about in the room for some sandals. "I will go to the Temple of Asclepius on the Isla Tiberis and get a priest. You two, find us better food and drink than this slop you've been living on. Go to the market by the circus and get meat broth and oranges or lemons and fresh garlic if you can."

Gaius Julius and Alexandros exchanged a look, but then shrugged. They had plans of their own. Being out and about would not displease them.

"Well," the Lady Anastasia de'Orelio said, entering the room. "You live, at least."

Jusuf stood and bowed deeply, motioning for the Duchess to take his seat. She smiled, her violet eyes meeting his for a moment, then sat, arranging her dark green gown so that it did not bunch or wrinkle. Her little blond shadow moved to stand discreetly behind the high curved back of the wooden chair. Jusuf leaned against one of the walls of the room, choosing a wooden stanchion that separated two sections of fresco work. He had already learned the hard way that the paintings, old as they were, crumbled if too much pressure was applied.

Ensconced in the bed, fairly buried under heavy quilts and thick fluffy woolen blankets, Nikos tried to nod his head in greeting. Half his skull was wrapped in bandages that covered the cuts he had sustained during the mudslide. His one unobscured eye glittered in anger, however. He hated being bedridden. His grandmother had taught him at an early age that people tend to die of sickness in bed, so he avoided them whenever possible—unless of course the bed wasn't being used for sleeping or convalescing.

"I live," he growled, "and thanks to the barbarian, too.

What gall he has, dragging me from the fire!"

Anastasia turned, dimpling her cheeks, and smiled at Jusuf again. Today, with her hair piled up on her head like a storm cloud, bound back by thin strings of pearls; narrow, diamond-tipped pins; and a particularly well-contrived corset, she looked both at ease and stunning at the same time. The expanse of carefully presented bosom and the long, smooth neck that it ornamented had not gone unnoticed by the Khazar prince, who smiled back. His long, usually dour face fairly lit up in comparison with his usual expression. Silently, in his mind, Nikos groaned. He had worked for the Duchess for six years on her "special" teams. He had started as a doorman, using an iron crowbar or a ram. Before being tagged to follow Thyatis and see that she learned the business, he had been a team leader for a little time. He thought the Duchess was beautiful, too, but it never ever paid for the peasants, as his father was fond of saying, to stomp grapes with the nobles. His father, Mithra bless him, had been a wise man.

"My lady?" Nikos coughed politely.

The Duchess turned, making a pout that only Nikos could see, and her eyes hardened. Nikos felt a great sense of relief seeing her slide her business face on, crushed amethyst eyeliner and all. "So—I have the tally of the dead," she said, pursing rich red lips. "Sixteen men, all veterans, lost, as well as a building destroyed by the emergence"—the Duchess held the sheet of parchment up to the light from the window and raised a thin, elegant eyebrow—"of something that you can only describe as an *ignis dracorus*."

"Yes, milady," Nikos said, struggling, he managed to free himself from the sheets and blankets. Sighing in relief, he squirmed up until he could sit with his back to the wall. The pain in his arm and leg and side, or the throbbing sensation in the shattered half of his face, he put aside. There was business to be done. "A winged creature, nearly a hundred feet long, with a long tail and a flat, triangular head. It burst free from the burning house—it *flew* away.

Our horse handlers on the hillside saw it. It had wings like an enormous bat—dear lady, do not laugh at me!"

The Duchess put a carefully manicured hand over her mouth. Rings of lapis and rubies and emeralds set in bands of white gold and silver glittered on her fingers. Her nails were painted a forest green to match her gown. She smiled, but then took command of her features again.

"I *saw* it, mi'lady—it was real. Someone, a powerful someone, a wizard or sorcerer, was at work in that house. Whoever it was, they fled on that fire-drake. We got there just a little too late—"

"No," Jusuf interjected, ignoring the Duchess, who had opened her mouth to speak. For a moment, cold anger flickered across her features, but then it was gone, like it had never existed. "We did arrive in time," the Khazar continued, his voice filling with anger, "but we could not pass their guardian. That thing gave them the time they needed to flee."

"Ah," the Duchess said, a grim shadow around her eyes. "The monster."

"More than a monster," Nikos said in a heavy voice. "A killing machine; something out of the African jungles, perhaps, or the uttermost East. A creature that lives—*loves*—to kill and hunt. It was waiting for us—for someone to come—and it took joy in that slaughter."

The Duchess nodded. The loss of the praetorians was a heavy blow. She had only gained influence over a portion of their number, and now most of those were dead in this disaster of an arrest. She pinched the bridge of her nose, thinking. "If . . . if you were to meet this thing again, now that you have gauged its speed and power, could you best it?"

Nikos looked to Jusuf, who shook his head sadly. The Illyrian's face settled into grim lines. "My lady, this thing was the match for twenty experienced men. It was faster than anyone—anything—that I have ever crossed blades with. Even if Thyatis were here . . . this thing is wicked."

Anastasia raised an eyebrow again. "You would not set

Thyatis against it?" She cocked her head to the side, regarding Nikos as a Nile crane might a tasty frog. "She who is the best of us, to hear you tell it?"

Nikos flushed and wiped sweat from his brow. He nodded his head slowly. "One on one, we have no one to match it. Our only hope—if we were to hunt this thing—would be a trap, or a cage, or some stratagem . . . catch it while it sleeps, perhaps. . . ."

"A thought for another time," the Duchess said, twisting slightly on the couch so that she could see both men. "You saw no one else—no other people in the house, no sign of our informant?"

Jusuf shook his head.

"No," he said, "only fire and the storm and dead men. Whoever else was there got away, as clean as the snow fox in a hencoop."

"I'm sorry," Maxian whispered, squeezing Krista's hand as she sat on the side of the bed. "I brought you near death again."

Krista, smiling, shook her head. She smoothed his hair back, then turned her hand over to test the temperature of his forehead. He seemed better. Not well, perhaps, but past the fever and mending.

"Since you were here to bring me back, I'll forgive you this time."

She smiled again and put her hand on his cheek, though fear seeped like ice in her heart. This bed was better, at least, than that hovel on the Aventine where Gaius had taken them. At her urging, one of the physician-priests in the Temple of Asclepius had taken her coin and come to look at this patient. The man—a stout fellow with a short, thick beard—had not seemed surprised to find a feverish patrician with scattered burns holed up in a slum. He had taken the thick gold *aureus* that she had pressed into his hands, too. The Duchess had always told her that heavy red gold worked wonders, even among the principled and devout. Maxian's fever had broken, and once he woke he had completed the restoration himself.

"Did anything happen," the Prince asked, his voice still a little weak, "while I was in the fever? Are Gaius and Alexandros well?"

Krista cocked her head to one side, frowning in incomprehension. "What do you mean?" she asked, pursing her lips. "They seemed fine, just tired after a time. For a little while they could barely walk, but it passed."

The Prince nodded and tried to sit up. He failed, and she pressed a hand on his chest and gently pushed him back down on the bed. They had found sanctuary in one of the many houses that the Duchess maintained throughout the city. To the best of her memory, Krista did not believe that this one had been used in more than a year. It sat, perched over a narrow, brick-paved street, on the side of the Ianiculum hill, outside the walls of the city to the west of the Tiber, in a "good" neighborhood.

Well, good for brothels and outlawed temples and lotus-eater houses, she thought, grinning to herself. It had a pleasant garden in the back, with a fabulous view of the city across the river. At night, it looked out upon a galaxy of jewels. You could even see the temples of the Capitoline and the Forum Romanum from here if it wasn't too hazy. There was enough room, too, for the Walach to come in from their hiding places in the rubbish yards south of the city. *And a fine private bath*, she sighed to herself. *With blessedly hot water . . .*

"I feared," the Prince said after he had recovered his breath, "that they would suffer when I was unable to maintain the shield around us. What of the others?"

Krista shook her head, feeling both relief at their escape and disgust that certain other things had managed to claw their way free of the rubble of the burning building and live—in their own fashion—as well.

"Abdmachus did not make it out," she said softly. "He must have died when the roof of the cellar collapsed. All of the servants he had gathered—the Persian singers and those funny-smelling Nabatean monks—are dead as well. We four came away in the Engine, with those Walach who were hiding in it from the storm."

"And the *homunculus*?" the Prince whispered, his eyes sliding away from hers. "Did Khiron escape?"

Krista shrugged in resignation. "I was unconscious, too, my Lord Prince. I do not know if he reached the Engine or not. But he is here now, in the basement of this house. Sleeping, perhaps, or whatever he does when he closes his eyes."

"Where is the Engine?" Maxian's face was filled with worry. "Was it damaged?"

"No," Krista said with an edge of irritation in her voice. Did men think of nothing but their toys? Did it not matter at all that the old Persian—*his friend*—was dead? "By Gaius' account, the Engine carried us to safety—far out to sea, where no one would see. But we needed a refuge with food and news, so he ordered it back to the coast. Now it lies hidden in the marshes south of Ostia, well away from the coastal road."

"Good," the Prince said, turning his face away. His mind was beginning to wake again, and his thought turned once more to the struggle before him. "Bring Gaius to me, and the Macedonian. We must take steps to ensure that we may work apart from one another in safety."

Krista sighed, seeing that even this brush with dissolution had not turned him away from this impossible task. Anger warred with sullen resignation in her heart, but she damped both, though fear stirred in her. She listened quietly, and made the notes he requested on one of her waxed tablets, but he seemed already distant from her, a stranger.

She went downstairs, looking for the two dead men, resolve hardening in her heart and, with it—as she made her decision—a curious lightness as her worries eased.

Galen, Emperor of the West, made a face like a small boy confronted with steamed asparagus. "This is disgusting," he said, pushing a silver platter away from him. "What have you done to the cooks, my brother, killed them all and replaced them with trained monkeys?" The platter was swimming with thin fillets of fish in a creamy orange sauce.

Aurelian looked up from his platter, which had once held the same kind of fish. A trace of the orange sauce streaked his beard. His eyebrows, bushy and red, rose in puzzlement. "You don' like it?" Aurelian was still chewing. "It's good and peppery!"

"That," Galen said with a freezing glare, "is the problem. This fish—if it ever had a pleasing taste—is so drowned in pepper and thyme and basil that I cannot discern a flavor . . . other than pepper and thyme and basil. Please tell me, brother, that you have only *instructed* the cooks of the palace, not *replaced* them?"

Aurelian shook his head in negation and waved to one of the servants lurking about at the edges of the dining chamber. The man, a coal black Nubian in a plain white tunic, padded forward and took the plates from the table. The Emperor and his brother were sitting in a half-circle room that had been added to the original Severan wing of the Palatine complex by one of the "short" Emperors— perhaps Decius or Phillip the Arab. It looked out from the height of the palace down upon the eastern end of the Forum and the line of temples that led up that shallow valley to the great edifice of the Coliseum. Tonight Galen had chosen to sup here, enjoying the breeze that fluttered the long drapes hanging by the windows and it's relative isolation. It was far from the kitchens and the hurly-burly of the lower palace.

"Do you want that?" Aurelian looked hopefully at the plate of fish.

The Emperor shuddered slightly, handing over his dinner. Galen sighed, watching in sick fascination as Aurelian emptied his plate and looked about for more. With weary resignation, he pushed a shallow glazed bowl of honeyed rolls in his brother's direction. It was odd, returning to this place, this palace that he viewed more as an extended office than a home. Home was the old villa at Narbo, or even the Summer House at Cumae. When he had left for the campaign in Persia he had not given any thought to the arrangement of it, or to the practices of its inhabitants. Now that he had returned, he found that the busy nature of his brother had rearranged everything to suit himself. The servants, used to the parade of emperors and caesars, had complied, and now Galen would have to restore everything to a state suiting him.

Worse, glaring at Aurelian was useless because the big horse was too busy stuffing his face with honeyed nut rolls to notice.

One of the guardsmen who were sitting just out of sight, around the bend of the hall by the doors, stood and gave a low whistle. Galen looked up, checking the slow passage of sand in the hourglass set by the table. As expected, the Duchess was almost exactly on time. *Neither a grain too slow, nor too fast.* Galen had tried to push his native distrust of the woman aside, but it was hard. Very hard.

The door opened, and Anastasia entered. Tonight, attending upon the Emperor and his brother, she wore simple white—a traditional Hellenic *chiton* of matte silk, dyed with powdered abalone shell. Her sandals were small and gold, with tiny straps that only left a trace of glittering color around her ankles. A dozen paces from the Emperor's table, she paused and knelt, bowing to them. "Augustus Galen. Caesar Aurelian. I bid thee well."

Her hair, carefully coifed and arranged to fall behind her, seemingly loose, struck Galen as familiar. She rose and smiled and glided in her catlike way to a chair set at the end of the table. She sat, folding her legs under her, and put down a pair of wax tablets.

The Emperor's eyes narrowed, seeing the gleam of blue and aqua at her throat and wrists. "Ah," he said, smiling. He remembered where he had seen the arrangement of her hair and jewels before. "Apelle's *Aphrodite Anadyomene.* Subtle, my Lady de'Orelio, and very well executed."

The Duchess smiled brilliantly back at him, her eyes

meeting his for just a moment, and then, demure, she dropped them. She clapped her hands together, pale and white, like a schoolgirl showing her appreciation. "You have a discerning eye, Augustus. You honor me with your praise."

Galen looked over at Aurelian and was well pleased, seeing that his brother had missed the reference and was trying not to show it. For a moment he thought of tweaking the lummox with it, but then put the small pleasure aside. There was much business to be done, and it was already late. "What troubles do you bring us tonight, my lady? Is there new word out of the East?"

Anastasia moved the tablets onto her lap, opening them. She took a stylus from her girdle and flipped open the first book. "Augustus, shall I begin with the figures from the corn harvest, or with the intrigues of the Eastern court?"

Galen sighed, settling back himself. This was the meat of the day, here in the late hour, by lantern and candlelight.

"And finally," Anastasia said in a tired voice, "the Princess Shirin, late of the House of Chrosoes Aparvez, grand-daughter of the lately departed Khazar Khagan Ziebil, remains at large with—one presumes—her children in tow. I have heard nothing to indicate, my lord, that she has returned to her native home, in the grasslands above the Mare Caspium, or that she has fallen afoul of the agents of the Eastern Office of Barbarians."

The Duchess closed her books and arranged them carefully on the tabletop. She met Galen's eye with equanimity, for they were both quite tired and thinking more of their beds than protocol or matters of state.

Galen rubbed his eyes and signaled to the servant by the door for more coals for the brazier. It was becoming chilly. The African added more, and then closed the tall windows and pulled the drapes tight. When he was done, Galen poked Aurelian—who had nodded off—with one of the eating prongs left behind from dinner. "Wake up, horse. We're not done yet. A matter remains, my lady—

something very troubling to me. It is the matter of our brother . . ."

The praetorian at the outer door sprang up, his hand going to the *gladius* at his side. At the sudden movement, Galen stood and shrugged his cloak back, freeing his right arm. Aurelian, without thinking, rolled off of his couch and drew—with a cold rasp—a cavalry *spatha* from its sheath. The sword had lain hidden beneath his seat the whole evening. Galen, of course, knew that it was there, but in this—of all things—he trusted his brother with his life. Anastasia closed her mouth and sat very still, though she reversed the writing stylus in her hand.

A knock came at the door, a firm rapping sound.

The praetorian half turned, his *gladius* now in his hand, to see what the Emperor desired.

Galen stepped aside from the table and nodded. *Most assassins*, he thought, *do not bother to knock.*

The door opened and a thin, tired-looking man entered. He wore a hooded cloak and scuffed mud brown boots. The man threw back his hood, running a thin hand through his long brown hair, and pulled up short, staring at the tableau before him.

"Pardon," Maxian said, looking about in surprise. "I did not know you were in a meeting."

Galen let out his breath in a whistle, and Aurelian slammed the *spatha* back into its sheath.

"Piglet," the middle brother said in an aggrieved voice, "you've missed dinner again!"

Galen, who had sharp words on his tongue, stopped, speechless, and stared at Aurelian in disgust. "He missed nothing," he snapped. "Now he can have dessert at least— without so much pepper!"

Maxian looked from one brother to the other and felt an iron grip loosen from his heart. He had not even realized that it had been there, and he laughed out loud in relief. Aurelian, grinning shyly, came around the couch and picked him up, wrapping him in a bear hug.

"Ay," Maxian cried, feeling his ribs grind in that embrace, "have a care! I'm fragile—only human, not one of your giant horses!"

"That," Aurelian said, turning around and setting his little brother on the end of the couch beside Anastasia's chair, "is because you are always late to dinner."

Maxian looked up, smiling at his great redheaded bear of a brother, and then turned, making a sketchy bow to the lady. Anastasia contrived a faint smile and returned the bow, though her heart was hammering like a mill-wheel at the sight of the young man. Maxian turned to his eldest brother and bowed, too, but Galen reached out and mussed his hair instead.

"You," Galen said in a gruff voice reminiscent of their father's, "are a dreadful child! We were worried," he said in his normal voice. "I regretted those words we exchanged in Albania in the Legion camp."

Maxian met his eyes and nodded, rubbing his temple. "I am sorry, too, Gales, I was very tired and too wrapped up in my own thoughts."

"No matter," Galen said, making a dismissive motion with his hand. The Emperor sat and signed to the servants who had peeked out from behind the drapes. They scurried off to get more food. "Are you well?"

Maxian looked haunted again, the brief moment of respite from his cares washing away. He glanced at Aurelian and the Duchess—he had truly hoped to find his older brother by himself—but plunged ahead, anyway. "I live," he said after a pause. Troubled thoughts churned in his mind. He had intended to bring Galen up to date on what had transpired and what he now intended. But he could not do that now, with Anastasia and Aurelian in the room. That would seal their fates like the stroke of an axe in the slaughterhouse. "The business I spoke of before . . . have you mentioned it to anyone?" Maxian made a slight motion toward the Duchess and Aurelian.

Galen shook his head minutely, eyes narrowing in calculation.

Maxian bit his lip, making a silent appeal to his brother.

"Pray, Gales, do not." The youngest Prince turned to Anastasia and Aurelian, his face clouded with worry. "Do not take offense, my friends, I do not mean you harm or insult. This is a very delicate matter. If I can contrive a way to tell you in safety, I will, but at this moment only Galen and I may know of this."

The Duchess, ever polite, inclined her head in understanding, though she held very still and hoped beyond hope that the naked fear gibbering in her heart did not show in her face. Krista's enigmatic messages from the villa in the hills had moved her first to the raid, and then—in its aftermath—to extensive excavations in the cellars. The bodies her men had recovered, even crushed by falling stone and burned by fire, told a grim tale of what could only be dark sorcery. This young man, for whom she had such great hopes, now trafficked, not only with the ancient enemies of the state, but with inhuman powers. If the reports were true, he himself was possessed of tremendous strength. "Secrets are fragile things," she said in an even voice, though her hands were sweating. "Lives oft depend on their wholeness. Augustus Galen, I will leave you and your brother in peace. It is late, and there is still much to be done. Lord Caesar Aurelian, will you walk me to my litter?"

Aurelian, making a face, stood and bowed. "Of course, noble lady."

The Duchess rose, bowed again to the two brothers, who remained seated, and glided out, the train of her *chiton* leaving a faint glittering trail of sparkling dust behind. Aurelian stomped along behind her, thumbs hooked in his tooled leather belt. When they were gone, Maxian slumped back on the couch, exhausted.

"Did you find the weapon you needed?" Galen leaned forward, his lank dark hair spilling in front of his eyes. "What happened after you escaped from the encampment?"

Maxian summoned up a chuckle at the characteristic bluntness of his brother. He smoothed back his hair with his hands, feeling a dull throb behind his eyes. "I thought I did . . . I came back here with it. I put it to the test, but . . . it failed. Did you see me in your dreams, when I strove against the Oath?"

Galen's head came up, and he thought back. *On the ship*, he thought, vaguely remembering something . . . *yes, his face, at the end of a long tunnel of gray.* "I think so," he said slowly, trying to remember. "No matter—the situation is unchanged then."

"The same," Maxian said with a mournful tone. "I have put myself and others at risk for nothing. It is just so strong!"

Galen raised a hand, for the servants had returned. When they were gone, the table between the two men fairly groaned with food and drink. The Emperor, pledging himself anew to a life of stoic moderation, took only a bowl of fresh cherries in heavy cream and honey. Maxian, after staring blankly at the food, dug in with a will. Galen, watching him, smiled, seeing an echo of the legendary appetite of Aurelian in the youngest brother. Finally, after nearly an hour, the young man fell back on the couch, groaning. "I had almost forgotten what food tastes like," he said, staring at the ceiling. "I do not know what to do, my brother."

Galen put down the empty bowl. "Can you abandon this course? Walk away and leave it be?"

Maxian shook his head and sat up again. "No," he said. "We are enemies now. To live, unless I go far away, beyond the boundaries of the Empire, I must triumph." He ground a fist into his knee. "There is so much to gain by victory!"

Galen wiped his mouth with a cloth and leaned forward, his hands palm up. "You are still young; there is plenty of time left to you. Can you defend yourself enough to take the time to consider, to think, to plan? A few months, perhaps—you are on the ragged edge now, exhausted and hurt. Gather your strength and try a different approach."

Maxian nodded, smiling wryly. "Surely . . . ," he said,

ducking his head. "I am so tired. There must be a way. . . ."

Galen stood, surreptitiously loosening the clasp on his belt dagger, just in case. He walked around the table and mussed Maxian's hair again. The youngest Prince stood, and they embraced, Maxian leaning his head, weary, on his brother's shoulder for just a moment. Then he stood away, his eyes clear. "Go to the Summer House," Galen said with a contemplative look on his face. "At Cumae. No one is staying there now. It is out of the way, and quiet. Go there and take your ease for a little while. Take a good cook with you! Rest, far from the city. Then come speak to me again, and we will contrive a plan together."

Maxian smiled and gathered up his cloak. "Thank you, brother. I will. Rest and time to think are like gold to me . . . a princely gift."

Galen smiled back, though when Maxian turned to the door, his eyes were hard and cold. He, at least, had seen the naked fear in the face of the Duchess, even if no one else had. His brother, curse the Fates, was dangerous. Very dangerous. Though his heart broke to think of it, sometimes an emperor could not bear the weight of an errant brother. Galen walked with Maxian through the halls of the palace, then bade him good night in the lighted courtyard on the northern side of the hill.

The young man vanished into the darkness of the city, and the Emperor watched him go in silence.

"This tempts fate and the gods," Alexandros muttered as— once more—he and Gaius Julius loitered in darkness. This time they were garbed in dark clothing; tunics, long capes with hoods. Gaius Julius had smeared lampblack on their faces and hands, taking great amusement in smearing the black ash in Alexandros' golden curls. "It is bad luck to disturb the spirits of a *bibliotheca*."

In the darkness, Gaius Julius' teeth appeared in a grin, pale and white against the black of his face.

"That is the joy of this, my young friend. By tradition, the contents of this place are yours, so console yourself with the thought that you are retrieving stolen property. Rome stole it from you, looting your legacy, so now you steal it back from them!"

Another shadow moved in the gloom that surrounded the door. The *homunculus* had been feeling around the locks, searching with cold, patient fingers for a point of leverage. The thing's head turned, and Alexandros felt an atavistic thrill of dread, seeing the gleam of the pale reptilian eyes in the darkness.

"Here," the thing said in its grave voice. Gaius Julius moved to the entrance of the vestibule, looking out on the dark, deserted alley. The buildings of the Forum towered around them, rising up in the thin sliver of moonlight, white and pale. The vestibule itself backed onto the huge wall that divided the graceful colonnades and temples of the Forum from the close-packed noisome slums of the Subura just to the north. The fire wall was a hundred feet high and nearly a mile long, a great heap of brick plated with cheap travertine facing on the Forum side. Here, hidden down at its base behind the massive square edifice of the Temple of Pax, was a stolid rectangular building. Gaius, Alexandros, and Khiron were at its rear door, which was a heavy construction of oak and iron bands.

"Quietly, quietly," Gaius Julius whispered, and there was a rattling sound. A tiny point of light appeared, the yellow glow of a tallow lamp in a hood. The old Roman played it over the locks and stout facing of the door. Khiron's arm, mottled and gray, showing a vague, disturbing impression of translucency and muscles and tendons just under the surface, was poised above the larger lock. "Time we have; sound we cannot afford. The *aediles* do, occasionally, patrol these streets."

Alexandros felt a cold chill of apprehension wash over him, and almost laughed. This was but a door, a stout one, nothing like facing a man in armor and a fine oval shield in battle. Still, his hand brushed the hilt of his sword—a straight-bladed thrusting weapon he had purchased in one of the stalls in the market along the river. The old Roman with pale eyes had laughed at such a thing—*The blade is too long*, he had scoffed. Alexandros ignored him, remembering a fierce battle in driving rain, his body steaming with humidity, and his own life nearly ending on the point of such a weapon as he struggled to rise from thick red mud. The youth shook his head and banished the memory. That was far in the past.

"Now," Gaius Julius hissed, satisfied that the street was clear.

Khiron tensed its arm, and an iron-tipped forefinger dug into the ancient black oak over the lock. There was a squeal as wood twisted aside, but Khiron grimaced, muscles bunching in its arm, and gripped the mechanism of the lock with its other hand. The squeal rose sharply in volume, causing Alexandros to wince and cover his ears. The old Roman hopped from foot to foot in dismay. The *homunculus* ignored him, and there was a grinding screech as the lock mechanism was torn from the door. It groaned and there was a sharp snapping sound as Khiron wrenched the last of it out of the oaken panel. "Here," it said in a gravelly voice, handing the ruin of the lock to Gaius, "the door is open." The *homunculus* reached into the gaping hole gouged out of the door, ignoring the spikes of twisted nails and bolts, and there was a grinding sound as the locking bar was pushed back.

"That was the very soul of quiet," Gaius muttered as he pushed the door open, raising the lantern. The room within was dark, and a dusty smell of age flooded out. Alexandros wrinkled up his nose, but peered in nonetheless. In the pale light of the hooded lantern, he saw the dim outlines of row after row of tall shelves, each pierced with thousands of pigeonholes. In each, the dusty outlines of scrolls and books could be seen.

"Ahhh . . . ," Gaius breathed, stepping into the room. "A true bounty—and this only the extras at the back of the building. Come quickly, we have to cross over the main floor and go up a flight of stairs to reach our goal. Khiron, with me. Alexandros, get the wagon."

Alexandros grimaced, and pride warred in him for a moment with a relief at not violating the sacred precincts of the library. *Stop this*, he commanded himself, *Gaius knows where the books are, and Khiron can carry a vast burden*. The slight still rankled, though, but he had resigned himself to waiting, to being patient, at least for a little while. It had been a long time since he had stood a watch. In the darkness, under the domed roof of the vestibule, he smiled to himself, knowing that by the power of this Prince of the Romans, he had cheated his old bargain with the gods.

Old age I traded for fame, he mused, standing the darkness, alert and wary. *Yet here I am again, young, and— now, perhaps—eternal*. He almost laughed, but then remembered his duty and remained silent, watching the night.

Anastasia rubbed her eyes, which were burning with fatigue. Sighing, she laid aside the reports from her man in Aquileia. The return of the Emperor to the capital had not eased her burden, for now he had to be brought up to speed on the thousand and one details of what had happened in the Western Empire in his absence. The Duchess looked out the window, seeing dawn rising over the mountains in the east. The city was still sleeping, but she had yet to taste the comfort of her bed. Betia, at least, was curled up under a blanket on the couch by the window, sound asleep. Anastasia smiled and rose stiffly, feeling the night chill in her bones. She pulled a woven linen stole from the back of her chair and draped it around her shoulders. Around her, the house was quiet and still, without even the rattle of the cooks in the kitchen.

Soon, she thought, *all will rise and the house will come alive with music and noise and the chatter of my servants*. She closed the door to the study quietly, letting Betia sleep. The floor of the hallway was cold on her bare feet, but she did not have the energy to put on her sandals. She went downstairs, moving like a pale ghost through the dark house, passing the rooms where Jusuf and the other Khazars were sleeping—the rattle of their snoring bringing a smile to her face. At the door of the children's room she paused, opening the door and looking in. They were all piled together on one bed, a softly snoring heap of arms and legs and tousled dark hair.

What beauties, she thought, a warm, unaffected smile growing in her face. *Their mother must be stunning.*

The kitchen was almost dark, but a dim glow came from the roasting oven and she bent to it, igniting a punk from the embers.

She lit one lantern by the carving table and yawned. These long nights were wearing her down, but she had become lax during Aurelian's time as ruler of the West. He did not push her like Galen did; he accepted what she gave him without dispute or comment. *It was too much for him*, she thought as she poured wine into a copper cup. *He was not ready for the weight of the burden.* Still, the middle brother had not done badly in his time, though if it came to his ascending the Purple for true, she would have such a struggle on her hands.

She rooted around in the bins and wicker baskets hung from hooks along the preparation tables and found a brace of pears and some bread that had not gone moldy yet. *Hah, what would my cooks think*, she thought to herself in weary amusement, *to see me making a muss of their kitchen at such an hour?* There was still butter in a chilled urn by the rear door. With her breakfast bundled in a napkin, she climbed the stairs again. They seemed much steeper this morning than last night when she had come home—her nerves fired with the echo of the terror she had felt when Maxian had appeared in the Emperor's dining chamber. "To think," she said aloud, "that I thought him such a nice young man only last year. . . ."

At the top of the stairs she turned, hearing a soft knocking sound echo from the front hallway. She paused, hand on the banister, looking back down into the sweep of the front hallway. She could hear, magnified by the smooth

marble floor, the sound of her watchmen rousing themselves and the rattle of a bolt being withdrawn from the
spy hole set in the door. She bent her head, listening.

The mutter of voices came, and then the sound of the
door opening. Anastasia turned and descended the steps.
When she reached the entryway, she found that three of
her guardsmen, still blinking sleep from their eyes, had
admitted a swarthy and nervous young man. The Duchess
frowned, but saw that two of the guardsmen had their
weapons drawn and that the other had locked the heavy
door behind the visitor.

"Who are you, lad? What brings you to my house at
this hour?"

The barbarian boy looked up, and she felt a strange
crawling sensation in her back and shoulders. His eyes
seemed huge and luminous; when he blinked, the feeling
passed. He had long, unruly hair, black as squid ink and
possessed of a shine that caught the light of the lamps set
beside the door. He wore an embroidered vest and a thick
white cotton shirt under it. His feet were bare, though he
did not seem to mind the cold and his legs were clad in
the rough woolen pantaloons favored by the Goths or Germans.

"I am Anatol," he said in a thick accent. "I bring a
message from our mistress, the Lady Krista. She bade me
hurry—please, I must make my way swiftly before anyone
notices that I am gone."

Hearing him speak, Anastasia knew that he was very
young, perhaps only thirteen or so. Her mind considered
and discarded a dozen replies before settling for the simplest one. She would investigate this matter of the *Lady
Krista* at a later date. "We will not keep you," she said,
touching the boy's hand. "What is the message?"

Anatol ducked his head nervously and drew a scrap of
parchment from a pocket of his vest. He pressed it into her
hand, and she felt his long nails, tapered and sharp, press
into her wrist. She met his eyes again, smiling, and inclined her head. "Tell the Lady Krista that I think of her

often, and miss her company." She nodded to the guardsmen. "Open the door and let the boy go. He must hurry."

"Thank you, noble lady." Then he was gone, slithering out the door like a black streak, and she could hear him running, his feet soft on the stones of the street. Anastasia turned from the door, unrolling the scrap of paper. A vague foreboding threatened, inchoate fears and worry clouding around her.

My lady, said the paper in the brisk angular letters that Krista favored. *I am with the Prince, who has returned to the city. We will be leaving soon for the South. He says Cumae, but I do not believe it. He is dangerous, but you must tread carefully, for he has powerful servants. He will not abandon his purpose.*

Anastasia hissed, feeling a deadly weight settle around her heart. The stairs to her study seemed even steeper now, and she felt terribly alone. Krista, Tros, Thyatis—all were gone, and she felt the weight of their absence keenly.

THE MILE MARKER, CONSTANTINOPLE

Nicholas pushed through the crowd, a garland of flowers twisted around his head. The thunder of the mob of people in the Forum of Constantine rolled over him like the sea. He had never seen so many people in one place before in his life. The energy of the crowd—its delirious good humor and relief—was infectious, filling him like the finest wine. Vladimir, his dark face grinning fit to burst, pushed along behind him. The Northerner had a blonde on his shoulders; her pale, plump legs tucked in his armpits. She was laughing, wine spilling down her chin and soaking her blouse. Nicholas had a girl too, but she was pressed close to his back, her slim hands in his belt. The crowd surged around them like a riptide, pushing them away from the line of columns that ringed the Forum.

Nicholas looked over his shoulder, catching Vladimir's eye. The Northerner's hands were curled around the blonde's smooth white thighs. Nicholas jerked his head, shouting, and Vladimir grinned back, mouthing, *I can't hear you!* Waves of sound battered them, drowning all else. Somewhere, across the vast circle of the Forum, lines of victorious soldiers were marching, their armor bright and shining, their heads held high, their spears and lances sparkling in the sun.

Of all days, the gods had blessed this one. The dreary clouds of winter and the haze of the campfires of the Avars had been blown away by a southern wind. The sun rode high, shining down upon a jubilant city, summoning the populace to the greatest revel that anyone had ever seen. The Emperor, crowned in majesty and favored by victory, would enter the city this day to be greeted by his people in unrestrained joy. The army, hardened by war and laden with loot, had been unloading from the fleet for three days. The civil authorities, however, had begged the Emperor to delay his entrance until they could prepare.

Now he entered, and the city met him with open arms.

Nicholas squeezed around the side of a heavy cart filled with jugs of wine. The merchant was selling them out of the back of the wagon in job lots, passing them over the heads of the crowd that thronged about him. Coins sparkled in the air, cast by thirsty citizens. The merchant was laughing, his face red and flushed, while his assistants—two scrawny boys—scrambled to catch the *denarii*. Nicholas reached a wall, marked with the painted sign of a tailor's shop, and turned, taking the redhead in his arms. She smiled up at him, her full lips moving, saying something. Nicholas smiled back and shrugged. Over the din of a hundred thousand people shouting, singing, releasing all the pent-up joy and jubilation at their delivery from their enemies, he couldn't make out a word anyone said. He kissed her, instead, feeling her press tight against his body, her breasts firm and round against his chest. She dug her hands into his hair, dragging him down to lose himself in her sweet lips.

Vladimir banged into him, pressing his mouth close to Nicholas' ear. "This one says she does not live so far away!" the Northerner was shouting at the top of his voice.

Nicholas nodded, his hands under the redhead's tunic, warm on her bare skin.

Vladimir turned away, the blonde pointing down the street and waving the wineskin like a banner.

Reluctantly, Nicholas followed, pushing the redhead in front of him, though he kept his hands on her stomach. Leg in leg, they squeezed forward through the crowd.

Flowers and a blizzard of cut colored paper rained down from the balconies above, along with the ringing of bells and gongs and the stentorian wail of trumpets and *bucinas*. Constantinople would not sleep tonight.

"Please, my lord, you must come out and greet the crowds—you must make the sacrifice of the bull. The gods are watching!"

Heraclius flinched, seeing the round face of the priest Bonus peering in at him. The Emperor slid back to the other side of the litter, even that simple movement bringing tears of pain to his eyes. Outside the wicker-and-gold conveyance, he could hear the rolling shouts of a mighty assembly. He knew, even though he had passed into the city closed in the darkness of the litter, borne by twenty of his guardsmen on a great platform, that a vast throng crowded the Forum. The thought of stepping out, of feeling the terrible pain in his legs, of feeling the dreadful weakness shoot through his body, unmanned him. The Emperor of the East bit at his hand, trying to keep from crying out in rage and fear at his helplessness. The knuckles were scarred already.

"Avtokrator." Rufio's blunt, scarred face replaced the worried visage of the priest. The centurion was well used to this by now, having carried the Emperor by force of will from Cilicia and the high pass of the gates. "I will be at your side, as will the faithful guard. We will see that you do not fall."

The centurion's black eyes were fierce. Heraclius grimaced, seeing the challenge there. He almost wept, feeling the fear of pain clawing at his will. This should have been the greatest of days, his redemption for the long years of struggle and disaster that had followed his overthrow of the madman Phocas. Instead, he cowered in a litter, afraid to step out into the sunlight. Afraid, though he did not admit it, to be seen by Bonus or any other man. His lower body was distended, swollen with this malignant edema. He could barely walk and could no longer suffer anything but the softest fabric upon his skin. His legs were a gruesome parody of the firm, muscular shape of his youth. Gray and stretched, ballooned out like overstuffed sausages.

But this was the day of days, he railed at his mind, at the fear. *This is my triumph, as no emperor of Rome has ever held! Persia is thrown down, after centuries of struggle! This is my day, my blessed day!*

Rufio, snarling under his breath, half climbed into the litter and wedged a thick muscled arm behind the Emperor. Heraclius cried out, whimpering, and the centurion, his face a mask, bodily lifted him out of the litter. The sun was westering, and the slanting light fell on the face of the Emperor as he emerged, here in the great open space of the temple atrium. Marble pillars faced with gold towered around them, a forest of majesty. They stood on the steps of the Temple of Sol Invictus, that which had once been—in the youth of the city—the abode of Zeus Pankrator. It stretched before them, arcades of marble a hundred feet on a side. Within, in the rectangular apse of the temple, the brilliant disc of the god shone in the late afternoon sun. Thousands of noblemen, their wives, the priests, embassies from the tribes beyond the Empire stood waiting, crowded behind ranks of iron-chested guardsmen. All were silent.

Heraclius put down his feet, swallowing a gasp of pain. From the litter at the entrance to the temple to the gleaming marble altar below the sun disc was a distance of 120 feet. A thick purple carpet, edged with golden thread, lay before him. He took a step, the guardsmen close behind him, Rufio's left hand under his arm, unobtrusive and strong as a bar of steel. He leaned into it, trying to take the weight off of his legs. Even so, the pain was blinding. He took another step, unable to even feel the rich luxurious pile of the carpet. His eyes watered, and a thin trail of tears seeped down his cheek. *This is my day!* he shouted in his mind, trying to override the pain. *My day.*

He took another step.

Her face shrouded in a dark veil of silk, a woman stood at the peak of the little Temple of Hecate Victrix, looking down upon the murmuring crowd below. Though the rays of the sun fell upon her, gilding the dark rich fabrics that she wore, painting golden stripes on the black and gray and charcoal of her raiment, she felt wry amusement. The *a'ha-tri'tsu* children thronged the precincts of the old Acropolis and the grounds of the temples of the young gods, but none marked her, high above them. They were often a blind people. Statues of the goddess lined the roof of the Temple of Hecate, affording the woman cover as she stood quietly, watching their ceremonies.

The roar of noise from the crowds that had surged out into the city streets had woken her, called her forth to this place, the one remnant of her youth that still stood within the confines of the city. She looked down, seeing the pain and agony of this king of the day-people as he staggered to the altar. She smiled, smelling the poison and disease that was upon him. She wondered, shading her eyes from the burning rays of the sun, which of his servants had turned against him. Who had put the golden droplets in his wine or the shining white crystals in his meat? His fear was rank in her fine white nostrils, even at this distance.

A doomed man, she thought, finding a small pleasure in

his agony. *Another soon to pass from this way station on the Wheel.*

The dark lady turned, fading into the shadows behind the lithe statues of the goddesses. Her pale blue-white eyes blinked, and she smiled. With so many out of their homes thronging the streets, there would be good hunting once darkness fell. She smiled, and the tip of a pink tongue appeared between her sharp white teeth. The pain curdled in her blood, but soon she would have surcease from it, respite in the panting fear of a dying day-man. Like a ghost, she passed among the statues and descended a stair that led down into the nave of Hecate's Temple and thence to the cellars below.

Nicholas staggered down the hallway of the apartment, his head spinning with excess. Behind him, in the room with the balcony, the redhead was sprawled amid the tangled sheets and blankets of her too-comfortable bed. She was snoring, overcome by exhaustion. For a moment, as he groped in the darkness, trying to find the edge of the door, he remembered. Then his fingers found it, rough and poorly planed, and he made his way into the stairwell. The insula was a three-story building of cheap brick and half-cured wood quite close to the western end of the Hippodrome. It was not an elegant district—where else could two attractive young seamstresses find lodgings for themselves without undue comment?

Weaving down the stairs, Nicholas felt pleasantly exhausted, the memory of the woman, her skin gleaming with a sheen of sweat, her mouth hot on his, playing back in his memory. He smelled the common privy on the ground floor and managed to keep—by blind luck—from braining himself on the low doorway. He pushed aside a heavy curtain, hung on copper rings from a crossbar, and stepped into the common area between the washroom on his left and the toilets on his right.

There was a sound, an odd moan, and he turned, one hand fumbling for the hilt of his sword.

He had no sword; *Brunhilde* was upstairs, hanging in her leather and cloth sheath on the head of the big carved bed. *Not good*, his mind started to say, and then he stopped, eyes widening.

Vladimir was in the washroom, his lean, muscled form naked but for a loincloth, bent over the still body of the blonde. In the flickering light of a night lantern in the hallway between the two rooms, her flesh had turned a pasty white. Nicholas hissed in surprise and backed up. Vladimir turned, his dark eyes enormous and gleaming like the moon with the reflection of the lantern. There was blood streaking his chest and his hands. Behind him, the girl lay half in and half out of the big stone washtub, her hair drifting in the water, the side of her throat a bloody mass of skin.

Vladimir blinked, his eyes focusing, the snarl fading from his face. Nicholas watched in sick fascination as he wiped the clotted blood from his mouth and his bright white teeth. In the dim light, the long narrow head and wiry body seemed streaked with fur. Even the man's hands were twisted and strange.

"Vlad?" Nicholas felt behind him for the edge of the door, his mind, dulled by wine and exhaustion, groping for words. "What happened?"

Vladimir shook his head and then looked around, awareness entering his eyes. He frowned, confused, and put out a hand on the doorjamb of the washroom. "Where am I?" The Northerner's voice was thick, his accent coming back. "There was a woman with hair like pale gold. . . ."

Nicholas cursed, a vile string of words he had once heard a Roman sea captain use, seeing the sleek gray ships of the Scandians closing on his fat merchantman in the waters off the Batavian shore. He stepped forward and grabbed his friend by the arm. "Come on," he snapped, "we have to get out of here."

Vladimir nodded, still confused, but he followed along readily, taking the steps up to the second floor two and three at a time, like Nicholas. The mercenary's mind was spinning, desperately trying to figure a way out of this fix. *All we can do*, he realized as he skidded to a halt in front of the redhead's bedroom, *is slip away in the night and hope that this one is too drunk to remember what we look like.*

He snatched up Vladimir's breeches from the other bed and threw them at the Northerner. "Get dressed, we've little time."

Vladimir nodded dumbly and began putting on his pants. Blessedly, the redhead was still snoring, sound asleep. Blood, dripping from Vlad's chest, spattered on the floor in tiny red dots.

"Get out!" Heraclius' voice rose in a scream, and his arm, still strong, hurled a heavy porphyry vase at the priest. The holy father fled, and the vase shattered on the facing of the wall by the door. The Emperor cast about for another missile. The other priests who had made to enter his chamber also fled, seeing his intent. It was dark in his chambers. He had knocked down or put out all of the lights save one guttering candle. In the darkness he could not see his legs, or the bulbous protrusion of his lower body. In the dark, if he lay still, he could still believe that he was a whole man again. Weeping, he crawled back onto the bed, dragging his useless feet. Even those movements, jarring as he rolled onto the silk sheets, sent jagged spears of pain through his abdomen. His breath was hoarse, but he managed to turn over.

The canopy of the bed was a dim shape above him. If the room were lit, he knew that it would be rich velvet, a cerulean blue, like the sky. Now he could distinguish nothing. He could hear voices raised in fear and anger outside, in the hallway. His councillors were arguing among themselves. The Emperor made to rise up, for he could hear the dissention and distrust in their voices. Only his will had bound them together before, and now the bonds that tied the state together would begin to fray.

His leg twinged, and he lost his breath. The pain washed

over him, and he shuddered. He lay back down in the quiet darkness.

After a time, the voices quieted and went away. The Emperor dozed, feeling some surcease from his fear in dreams and fantasies.

"My lord?" Heraclius raised his head. It was Rufio—the only one who did not fear him, save his brother Theodore. The scarred face of the centurion was a jarring sight, his dark eyes in shadow. The man was carrying a lantern, half shuttered. In the light of the oil flame, he seemed ominous. "My lord, Empress Martina is outside. She wishes to see you. Shall I let her in?"

"No!" Heraclius blurted before he could think. But the fear was there, and a terrible shame washed around him. "No, good Rufio, send her away. Tell her I will come to her when this . . . this affliction has passed. Let me sleep, just for a little while. I will see her in the morning, I am sure of it."

Rufio's face was stolid, but Heraclius thought he saw a flicker of distaste in the man's eyes. The Emperor knew that his voice held the edge of a whine in it, and he loathed himself even more. But the centurion turned, and went away, taking the lantern with him. The darkness returned, cool and soothing, and Heraclius surrendered himself to his dreams again.

Nicholas sat on the edge of his bed, *Brunhilde* bare on a towel on his knees. He held a whetstone in one hand, and oil in the other. While he worked, keeping just the right edge to the sword, he listened.

"It comes upon us all—the people of my tribe—when the hunger grows too great. The pain, you see, the pain can become too much." Vladimir's voice was low and filled with shame. The Northerner was sitting opposite, on his own bunk. Nicholas, not trusting the night, had lit all of the candles he could find, and they clustered on the tiny wooden table like a forest of stars. Their smoke, sweet with the smell of honey, curled toward the ceiling. On any other night he would have thrown the wooden shutters of the window wide, but now—with the image of the dead girl in the washtub floating behind his eyes—he did not. They were latched and locked.

"I did not think it would happen here . . . but I drank too much wine. I am sorry, my friend."

Nicholas looked up, his eyes cold and guarded. Vladimir had cleaned up in a public fountain, washing the crimson stains from his chest and face. The crowds that danced in the streets had not marked him, no more than any other man nursing an incipient hangover in this city of its millions. "When this hunger comes," he said, his words bitten out, "can you choose who to take? Can you sate this thirst before you lose control? Can you drink just a little?"

Vladimir hung his head again, burying it in his hands. "Yes," the Northerner said. "I could . . . I should have, but I have been trying to master myself, to better it by my will. Some few of us, the *rashkashutra*, can do so. They are our wise men, our war chiefs. They can command it. I thought that I could . . . it is . . ." The Northerner paused, groping for the words he wanted. Nicholas felt a change in the air in the room and half turned.

"It is dangerous to hunt here," whispered a rich voice, redolent of dead flowers and the curling vapor that rises from newly turned earth, "without my leave."

Nicholas froze, hearing the scrape of the door closing. There was a presence behind him, something cold and old and very angry. Under his hand, *Brunhilde* quivered, sending up a faint almost imperceptible keening sound. By sheer will, he mastered the gibbering fear that the voice engendered and he turned, rising, the blade in his hand.

There was a woman at the threshold of the room, with a face like the moon in clear water. He met her eyes—a blue so clear, it was almost white—and felt the blow of her will. He stepped back, between the woman and Vladimir, and *Brunhilde* was singing in his hand. Pale light gleamed along the spine of the dwarf-steel blade. The woman stepped forward from the door, her thin white hand on a staff of bone as tall as a Varangian. Her bracelets made a soft clinking sound. Nicholas did not move, though he felt Vladimir's fear at his back like the heat from a fire.

"What a sight," she said, low voice purring, "the *a'ha-tri'tsu* child defends the murderer, the one who has taken a day-walker woman without my leave. Stand aside, O man, and let my justice take him."

"No," Nicholas grated between clenched teeth. Fear ran riot in him, the sight of those white eyes triggering a heedless desire to run. Only the shudder of *Brunhilde* in his fist made him stand his ground. "He is my friend, and I owe him my life. You cannot have him."

"I cannot?" The woman circled to the right, her dark red hair spilling over her shoulder like a wave of drying blood. Her cloak shifted as she moved, showing deep green glints in the fabric that he had first thought black as night. Her hair was bound back by thin silver wires, and the gleam of ruby shone at her neck. "You should welcome me and my justice. The *k'shapácara* are not well known for their mercy toward the children of the day."

"He did not hunt in your domain," Nicholas said, thinking furiously, "save in extremity."

"Cannot he speak for himself?" The woman edged closer, and Nicholas felt the wash of fear at his ankles, rising like a cold chill tide. "Why does he hide behind you, O man?"

"I can speak for myself," a quavering voice came over Nicholas' shoulder. "I beg your indulgence, *bidalak'sha-virazh'oi*—the pain was upon me! Please, I did not mean to trespass."

The woman stopped and smiled, her fine white teeth gleaming in the candlelight. Then she laughed, a sweet sound like the chime of silver bells. Nicholas felt a pain in his bones at the sound and memory stirred in his heart. An odd longing came upon him, but he pushed it away.

"You are a polite creature," she said. "It has been a long time since one of the *dushkula* spoke so to me. Indeed, I am flattered. But you know the law. You may not feed, even among the least of the *a'ha-tri'tsu*, without my leave. Death is the price of your weakness."

"No," Nicholas quietly said, his jaw clenched. "Not without passing me. This man was driven to break your law by hunger, but he is still my friend, and I will not let you take him."

The woman drew back, seemingly growing in stature, her presence filling the room. "You put great trust in that sliver of iron, day-walker. Do you not believe that I can put forth strength enough to overcome you? Do you not believe that I may summon my pack to me, and they will rend you with tooth and claw?"

"There is no need of that, noble lady. I will vouch for his parole—let me take him away from this place, from your city. He will trouble you no more."

Nicholas felt Vlad tense, gathering his legs under him. The woman's eyes met his, and Nicholas felt the world spin around him, the room growing faint and distant. Pools of blue-white opened before him, and he felt the feather touch of a power on his soul. *Brunhilde* keened sharply, but her warning and anger seemed very far away.

"Ah . . ." The woman sighed in surprise, and her staff made a tapping sound on the brick floor as she turned. "You have your parole, day-walker child. But do not waste it, for even in age, my patience is short." Then she was gone, a dark blur, and the door swung slowly closed.

Nicholas shuddered, feeling his muscles relax and tension flood from him. He stepped to the door and pushed it tight. The bar had moved aside, and he replaced it, sliding it firmly home, with a bleak face. When he turned around, he found Vladimir curled into a ball on the narrow cot. "Are you all right?" he asked, though his voice seemed very distant.

Vladimir whimpered, though at the sound of Nicholas' voice, he slowly uncurled, looking this way and that, sniffing the air. "The Surāpa Queen is gone?" Vladimir's voice was shaky.

"Yes," Nicholas said, sitting heavily on his bed. "For now."

)-(

T'u-chüeh banners snapped sharply in the cold wind, whipping out from standards thrust into the ashy ground. The man, Arad, stood on the edge of a terraced hill, staring across the shallow valley. It was night, and the moon was riding low on the horizon, barely above the mountains. The man now possessed clothes, given from the hand of his master; a tunic of black wool with a short cloak and a hood. His feet remained bare, though the night was quite cold. Some fraction of his power clung to him, keeping him warm.

In the chill darkness, he could hear the mutter of men and the rattle of horse tackle, and the clink of metal on metal. The Lord Dahak had come to look upon the stronghold of his enemies, but he did so cautiously. A dozen paces behind Arad, the sorcerer stood on the summit of the hill, in quiet conversation with the barbarian chieftain, C'hu-lo, and the Persian officers. Arad ignored them, treasuring this small moment of peace and solitude, feeling the wind brush over his skin. It was a little place of privacy, and he clung to it with all his will.

In the valley below, men were sleeping, exhausted from a hard day of labor. On the opposite slope, under the eaves of a high ridge and beetle-browed granite cliffs, the ruins of a huge building climbed up from the bottomland. Once it had boasted long pitched roofs and hundreds of columns of painted marble. In the fading light of the day, when Arad had first come to the hill, the remains of a massive staircase could be made out. Now everything was covered by the mantle of night. Still, Arad could see in the dark—

another remnant of self-willed power—and the extent of the burned-out, shattered building was impressive. The men who slept in the valley below, men who labored in daytime under the aegis of a double-peacock banner—the *senmuru*—were striving to clear the rubble and restore some portions of the building to use.

Arad let his sight settle into the second opening and reveal the clusters of firefly lights and swirling patterns that marked the encampment below—the subdued red glow of men sleeping, the friendly brassy fire of horses and mules dozing in their corrals, the flickering yellow of waking men on patrol and watch. Even the lambent purple fire of wizards or priests in the big tents. A corner of his mind felt the numbers of points resolve into a discrete symbol in his mind—there were just over four thousand workers in the camp below, and some three thousand soldiers, priests, and engineers. Or so the corner of his mind, busy in its purposeless way, had concluded. Arad blinked, letting the gossamer veil of invisible fire fall away from his sight.

Cool darkness flooded in, for now even the moon had slunk away behind the hills in the west.

"Beloved servant," a cruel voice came on the wind, "attend me."

Helpless once his master's thought had touched his mind, Arad turned and climbed over the tumbled stones and low-growing gorse bushes to the summit of the hill. In the darkness, he could feel the lord standing, leaning against a slab of granite, a burning black point of infinite cold. The Persian captains and the barbarians seemed half shadows already, their essential spirit already dimmed and clouded by the presence of the Lord Dahak.

"Good Arad," Dahak purred, his eyes glittering yellow in the darkness, "you have looked upon the valley, seen the men who toil in the service of my enemies, seen the great house they seek to put aright?"

"I have, lord." Arad's voice was a little slurred. He was still remembering how to speak this tongue of the Eastern

men. "There are many in their encampment—many soldiers—many strong priests."

"Yes," Dahak said, his long head nodding in the darkness. "For all their faults, the peacocks that nest on the
throne of my father have some small sense of the importance of such a place. Thus, we must take steps to see they
do not have their way with us."

"What is this place?" Arad's voice was calm and without inflection. Though rage and hatred and shame might
etch his soul like acid, expression was denied him. "What
happened here?"

"Good friends," the Lord Dahak laughed, "came here
and smashed it down. They doused the fire that had once
burned here, lighting all the world. Though they knew it
not, they gave me the most precious gift. There is no limit
to the love I feel for them. But now, as these peacocks
strut and preen, defying me, I must complete the work."

Dahak paused, soft laughter echoing. Arad felt that
black joy beat against him like a wave. The lord was filled
with secret amusement and ached to tell of it. Discipline
held in the creature, and his thought again turned to the
matter at hand.

"Loyal Khadames—you and your captains I have
brought here to observe and watch. No finger will you lift
against the *nindingir* in the valley below. This is work for
our good friends from the east. Noble C'hu-lo, have you
looked upon the land? Have you seen the position of your
enemies?"

The T'u-chüeh stirred in the darkness. Unlike the Persians, who fidgeted and spoke softly among themselves,
thinking that the mantle of darkness made them invisible,
he had sat quietly in the shadow of the slab of granite,
keeping—even now, after nightfall—his head and body
below the crest of the hill. Now he stood and leaned
against the rock, the shape of the Lord Dahak between him
and the priests in the valley.

"I have seen them, Lord Dahak. They have taken some
precautions, though not many. They think themselves in a

safe land, free of enemies. What would you have us do?"

Dahak shifted, and Arad felt the lord turn his attention to the camp.

"Ah, we must fall upon them, these *mobehedan* and their servants. We must scatter the workers, tear down their equipment, murder the priests in their beds, kill the soldiers. This work will stop tonight. By morning, only crows must remain, feasting on the flesh of the dead."

There was a hiss of indrawn breath and the metallic rustle of one of the Persians making some movement. Arad felt Dahak turn, and the sorcerer's voice was soft in the dark.

"I did not bring your men, noble Khadames, because they are not ready for what must be done tonight. But these T'u-chüeh—they are hardened fellows, used to the smell of innocent blood. I brought you and your captains so that you would know what will be required of you and your army in the future. That place"—Arad knew that the sorcerer pointed across the valley—"is the last vestige of a dead faith. An empty shell that Rome cracked open, revealing its bankrupt heart. Rome quenched the fire that burned in that place, but it was down to the last dregs of its fuel. Tonight, we will complete what Rome began. Tonight a new faith will be born, one that will make Persia strong again. You will see and you will believe."

After a moment, C'hu-lo broke the difficult silence that had descended upon the hilltop. "In darkness it will be difficult to make sure that none of them escape."

"That is not necessary," Dahak allowed, gathering up a long staff of iron. "The peasants may flee into the hills. It is the priests I want—the *mobads* and their temple guardsmen. Come, the night is waning. Take your men, C'hu-lo, and come up the stream, against the wind. I will be close by. You need not worry about their priests."

The staff made a faint ringing sound on the rocks as the sorcerer moved away down the slope. Arad followed, feeling the thought and desire of his master. C'hu-lo had already disappeared down the hill in the other direction.

On the hilltop, the Persian *dihqans* huddled in the shelter of the stone, feeling the night grow colder.

"Stop," Dahak whispered, his hand on Arad's shoulder. The man had followed the sorcerer down the hill and into a dense thicket of bramble and lilac. The Lord Dahak had passed through like a ghost, Arad at his side. Now they had reached the jumbled boulders at the edge of the stream that ran along the base of the hills. The fires of the encampment were very close, just beyond the water.

"You are strong," the sorcerer hissed as he climbed onto Arad's broad shoulders. The man staggered a little, but then the hard muscle of his legs took over and he regained his balance. The flesh of the sorcerer was like ice against Arad's neck and arms. "Cross, beloved servant." Dahak's voice was filled with cruel laughter again. The man eased out into the water, feeling the gravel and stones of the streambed shift under his feet. The rocks were slippery and the water rushed past, chilling his legs.

Despite this, Arad reached the far shore without incident, though his muscles were burning with exertion when he clambered up the bank on the far side.

When Arad's feet were on dry ground again, Dahak alighted, twitching the hem of his long dark cloak to dry it. The sorcerer raised his head, sniffing the air. Arad could smell pine smoke and the hearty aroma of lamb stew and brewing tea.

"Attend me," the sorcerer said in a low voice. "Soon the Huns will attack, sprinting up out of the darkness to the south. When they do, the *mobehedan*, who lie not far away, will rise up, filled with furious anger. Then, my beloved Arad, you will go among them, wielding the lightning. I will watch over you, for I prize you above all other possessions."

The man did not move, waiting for his master's will to send him forth. Dahak waited, a shadow wrapped in shadow. The night passed over them, and Arad heard an owl as it ghosted past on the wind.

*　　*　　*

Arad measured the passing of an hour by the beats of his own heart and then another.

When the fire came, blossoming in the center of the camp, he moved. Grass and small stones blurred under his feet as he ran. A rough fence marked the border of the encampment—no more than wooden poles staked in the ground, supporting a barrier of twisted brush. Without thinking, he sprang up and flew over the fence, landing lightly on the ground within. Behind him, in the thicket of scrawny trees, he could feel the cold shadow of the Lord Dahak watching. Shouting and screams rose up, then a confused babble as the Persians scrambled out of their tents. The fire climbed into the sky, lighting the trees with a ruddy orange glow.

Arad felt the chains and coils that bound his mind slip and he paused, standing in the shadow of a large tent, and settled his breathing. The first and second entrances unfolded before him, yielding up visions of infinite spaces hiding within the crushed stems of grass inside the compound. Men ran past, ignoring him in the confusion. Despite the fire and the screams, it seemed that the Huns had not yet attacked the camp. Soldiers jogged by, holding torches aloft and shouting at the workers to return to their beds. The peasants, staring forth from their ragged shanties of canvas and brush, watched with wide eyes.

Boom! A jarring sound rippled through the air. Arad's head rose, pointing like a hunting dog toward the west. Blue-white light flickered among the tents, then there was a ripping sound like a sail shredding in a high wind. The man could feel the power unleashed there like a rush of hot wind in the invisible air. More soldiers ran past, heading toward the flare of light. Arad, unnoticed, slipped in among them, running alongside.

At the center of the camp was a cleared space, now thronged with hundreds of workers milling about. The soldiers were struggling with them, trying to restore order. Two great bonfires had been lit, casting a shifting orange light upon the mobs of men who pushed this way and that. At the edge of the crude plaza, Arad turned aside and slipped along the line of tents that faced the bonfires. He could feel something in the air, an obscure tension. As he moved from shadow to shadow, the man realized that the cold presence of the sorcerer had not left him. Suddenly aware, he knew that the Lord Dahak was riding behind his eyes, seeing all that he saw, hearing all that he heard.

Horns suddenly sounded, away across the tents to the south, and a shrill keening sound cut the air. Arad crouched down in the lee of a wagon he was passing, pressing himself close to the rough wood of the wheel. The air hummed, and suddenly a long black arrow was shuddering in the earth within inches of his hand.

C'hu-lo's *umen*—nearly seven thousand archers on horseback and on foot—had finally attacked.

The arrow storm whispered down out of the night sky, plunging at a steep angle into the crowded center of the camp. Among the triple-edged shafts, whistling arrows fell as well. Their cunningly worked heads, carved during the long steppe winter, raised a shrieking sound as they flew. Arad felt panic bubble up in the minds and hearts of the men in the camp like water rushing up a dry well. Fire-arrows fell as well, and the cloth tents burst into ready flame. Men fell, transfixed by the arrows that crowded out of the sky. The Persian soldiers lost control of the mob, and it stampeded away to the north, trying to flee the invisible death.

Arad crawled under the sheltering bed of the wagon and lay down under the axle. Even with a good six inches of stout lumber above him, he did not feel safe. An armor-piercing shaft tore through the wood a foot from his head, making a high screech. The arrowhead ground to a halt inches from the ground. Men stampeded past, and one staggered, crying out, at the end of the wagon.

The body fell, twitching to the ground. An arrow had punched into the top of the man's clavicle and torn through his spine and out his lower back. Already dead, the corpse shuddered on the ground, and Arad's nostrils flattened as the stench of death flooded the air.

Lightning crackled from the west, the same blue-white refulgence shimmering on the sides of the tents. Men screamed anew, but now, almost unheard over the shrieks of dying men and the lamenting wail of the mob, Arad could hear the ring of steel on steel from the south. A wind blew past the wagon, tumbling men before it. Arrows, still raining from the sky, clattered aside, falling in drifts around the edge of the miniature cyclone. The wagon rocked back, almost tipping over, and Arad clung to the earth, feeling the thick, muddy loam well up around his fingertips.

Power walked close by, ringed by a whirling belt of lightning and howling wind.

Now, my pretty, breathed the soft voice of the sorcerer.

Arad stood, and the wagon toppled away behind him. The *mobehedan* priest was only yards away, his hand raised in a motion of power, directed toward the south. A half sphere of sizzling blue-white fire ringed him, setting all that it touched alight. A path of burning tents and scorched grass wound away behind the priest. Arad could feel the flow of power from the sky and the earth rush past, fueling the priest's defense.

The third entrance was waiting, and beyond it, the power to shake the earth.

Arad raised a hand, scribing a swift pattern in the air. His fists clenched at nothing and he drew them in, toward his center. Hissing power flooded into him, shattering the wagon and shriveling grass. He stabbed out his right hand, palm out, fingers stiff.

For an instant, all that Arad could see was a jagged ultraviolet flash and a burning arc of darkness between his palm and the *mobehedan* priest, half turned. All else seemed to stop, even the wind, even the arrows that continued to rain down out of the sky. Fifteen feet away, Arad could see an arrow paused in flight, hanging frozen in the air.

Then, with a clap of thunder that blew down the remaining tents, time resumed. The bolt of darkness shattered the whirling shield of lightning, and the priest was slammed to the ground, crashing through a line of tents and into the side of a watchtower. The tower was already burning fiercely, set alight by the arrows of the Huns, and now it toppled, thick timbers shattering and the roof of planks cracking apart as it fell. Arad felt the earth jump under his feet as it slammed into the ground with a roar.

But he did not wait to see if the priest would rise again from the shattered logs. He leapt forward, his hands sketching a pattern of glyphs that spun out and rotated around him in the air. Lightning licked out from him, stabbing into the collapsed tower. Fierce explosions rocked the camp, and a rain of debris was thrown up. Something buzzed and flashed in the ruined tower. Arad ducked aside. A sickly white sheet of flame rushed past him, thrown in desperation by the priest who crawled from the wreckage, his face covered with blood. Arad spun, slashing his hand down. The earth rippled, tearing in a line between him and the Persian. The priest rolled aside, mouthing an incantation of ward. The stroke cracked across a half-raised shield of power, and the air shuddered. His mouth in a grim line, Arad sprang across the smoking logs, his braids blowing out behind him in the rush of air from the fires that raged around him.

Blood caked his fingers as he pulled the priest's head back. The Persian was barely alive—the side of his face crushed in by the Fist of Geb. Arad surveyed him with dispassionate eyes and then, without his command, his hands jerked, cracking the priest's neck. Dim light died in the dark brown eyes.

Arad shuddered, his body quivering as the Lord Dahak boiled into the shell of his body. Yellow fire gleamed in his eyes. Thin fingers crawled over the dead man's face, and Arad, free of the compulsion that had driven him into the camp, raged in his mind at the cold thing that possessed his hands and feet and eyes.

He was still screaming, all alone and unheard in the prison of his own skull when the Lord Dahak consumed the dying spirit of the priest. For a brief moment, Arad felt the *ka* of the other man rush past him, shrieking in fear and agony, before the dreadful cold that controlled him destroyed it.

Arad fell terrible anger fill his heart, but he could do nothing.

Come, beloved servant. The Lord Dahak's thought was filled with hunger. *We hunt.*

The night was filled with the sound of battle. The Huns were in the camp.

C'hu-lo sat on a fallen pillar, his legs crossed. A haunch of venison, taken from the burned camp down by the stream, was in his hand. He carved slices off it with the curved knife. It had been well seasoned, but he liked the salty taste. The valley between the frowning cliffs and the ruin of the great temple was filled with the sound of mallets driving posts into the ground. C'hu-lo was watching his men supervise the few hundred remaining peasants. His men were taking great joy in putting the lash to the poor wights, or cutting their throats if the dazed men fell.

The poles rose in a thick forest around the base of the ruined temple. A long slope ran up to the base of the stone walls. Once, it had been covered with trimmed grass and a garden of ornamental trees. Once, a stream had chuckled merrily down the slope, held between retaining walls of fitted stone. Now the trees were lumber for the poles, or for the fires that smoked and burned at the base of the hill. The stream was dry and filled with stones. A dim haze lay over the valley, cutting the light of the sun. Smoke rose in long, trailing columns from the fires. The air was thick with the sweet, cloying smell of roasted human flesh.

C'hu-lo took another bite of venison. He had taken wine, too, from the tents of the priests. The holy men had come well equipped to this place—they had not lacked for luxuries: soft cushions, exotic garments, iron braziers to hold coals in the cold night. Books filled with their blocky writing. C'hu-lo had thrown those things into the inferno of the bonfires himself. The silk of the double-peacock banners had burned merrily as well. The wine, however, was a strong tart vintage, from Shiraz in the south. C'hu-lo did not believe in wasting wine.

The sound of mallets rang across the valley, each dull thud driving a sharpened pole deeper into the ground. The Persian slaves wept in fear as they tilted up each pole, for those that they had emplaced before were now festooned with the bodies of their fellows.

C'hu-lo thought it was a good touch to put the bodies of your enemy's strongest men on display. Each priest of the twelve who had fought and struggled and died in the camp during the night battle had merited his own post. Some of them could no longer be recognized as the bodies of men.

The T'u-chüeh Prince took a long swallow of wine. This was thirsty work.

"You see? The fire is dead. Even the ashes are cold."

Arad felt nothing, staring down into the rubble-choked pit. Some fragment of his consciousness railed at him, urging him to lash out at the serpent who walked beside him. But his limbs did not obey his will, and the anger had dulled, becoming a dim flicker in the back of his mind. The horrors of the night—the heady rush of a dying soul flooding his body, the taste of blood and cracked bones, even the sickening delight that seeped from the cold mind of the sorcerer as his thumbs punched into the gelid wetness of a man's eye sockets—they were muted. The sun, riding high above the haze, seemed cold and distant.

This place, this acre of shattered walls and gravel and splintered marble strewn across the hillside, felt empty. The sorcerer crawled among the rocks and poked down into dark recesses in the tumulus with a long iron staff. Dahak seemed filled with a bubbling joy, constantly talking to himself as he bent to pick up a broken bit of pottery.

"They thought that this fire would burn forever," Dahak said, smiling as he rummaged among the stones. "See? They were wrong. This fire will never be lit again."

Arad looked away at the sky. It was a pale blue. Mountains rose up in the west, high and dark with only a glimmer of ice crowning them. He ignored the sorcerer, who continued to talk to himself while he dug about in the ruins. Memories stirred in the man, something bright and shining with the sun, somewhere in the west. *Was it beyond these mountains?* he wondered. *Something beyond this cold world?*

"Their light has failed!" the Lord Dahak screamed at the sky. The sound died quickly, swallowed by the empty air.

<hr />

THE KA'BA, NEAR MEKKAH, ARABIA FELIX

T he old house stood alone at the center of the plaza. After the fire had gutted the temple, workers had cleared away everything but the original, open-roofed building. Hundreds had labored for weeks under the guidance of the Ben-Sarid, carrying away the broken stone and brick. The ash had been swept up and carried out to fertilize the fields that lined the *wadi*. The old statues had been broken up with mallets and iron bars and used to repair the walls of the city. Only the oldest temple remained, as Ibrahim had raised it at the founding of the shrine. It was small and dark, its walls of fieldstone blackened by centuries of ceremonial fires. At one corner of the square building, a section of the old wall was still smooth. In some unimaginable past, men had carved a block of fine-grained sandstone and—by great labor—had carried it to the precincts of the well of the Zam-Zam and placed it here.

Within that smooth facing, in a cavity worn by the hands of countless pilgrims, a stone gleamed. It was a stolid black, uncut, unmarked. Altogether unremarkable to the eye.

Mohammed stood before the stone and heard it singing.

Though he knew that no other person in all the great throng that filled the plaza to capacity and beyond could hear it, he knew it was the voice of his god, the great and compassionate one who had made the world. "And men," he whispered to himself, "from clots of blood."

Clad in enveloping robes of white and brown, a tall, thin young man edged his way through the throng of people standing in the square of the Ka'ba. His face, half shrouded by a gauze scarf, was grim. He limped slightly, for he had taken a bad fall from a horse. Despite this, he wore heavy armor of iron lamellae bound with loops of wire to a tunic of cured leather under the robes. It was blasphemy to bear arms within the precincts of the Zam-Zam, but the young man was well past caring.

Before the fall of Yathrib, he had been an acolyte in the Temple of Hubal. He had been a quiet, rather reserved young man. Like his father before him, he was named Maslama. Thoughts of his family brought fresh pain. They were all dead, murdered or killed in the fires that had raged through the city in the wake of the Mekkan capture of the eastern gate.

Under his robes, his fingers were firm on the hilts of a sword. He had found it—along with the armor—on a dead Mekkan soldier outside the city. It had taken a long time to crawl through the desert night and steal the body. But it was worth it. Ancient tradition drove him—his family had been killed—and he was due recompense in blood. His height let him see over the heads of the men and women pressed together. The old temple-house loomed up. The chieftains of the Mekkans would be nearby.

*   *   *

It was midday. The sun rode the meridian, a pale white disk of fire. The air was still.

Even among the tens of thousands of men and women and children that filled the square, there was silence. It was not complete—robes brushed against robes, children coughed, there was the quiet susurration of a multitude breathing—for there is always sound. Mohammed bowed and stepped back from the stone. He felt a great peace fall over him, even as it had upon the mountaintop once he had heard the voice speaking from the clear air.

The Tanukh that hovered nearby, their dark faces taut with worry, moved away and the crowd pressed back. The Ka'ba was ringed by a thick crowd of those who had followed Mohammed to fight at Yathrib. Beyond them were the multitudes of the city and the surrounding districts. The word of the war among the Mekkans and its fierce end in the fall of Yathrib had traveled far and wide. Men and women alike had come on camel or horse or shank's mare to look upon the man who had ended a generation of strife.

Mohammed heard the stone singing, and he paced along the outside of the old building.

The Tanukh moved with him, hands on spears and bows. As the Tanukh moved, so did the crowd of veterans of the fighting against the Hashim and their allies. Mohammed circled the building, listening to the song, letting his heart fill with the word of the Lord who spoke from the air.

This place was raised by the first of men, he thought to himself. His eye sought out the careful placement of the stones in the foundations. He knew that the first man had raised up the black stone and had placed it in the wall. He knew that six hundred years later, the sons of that first man had carefully removed the stone from its crude mortar and placed it within the sandstone facing. He knew that those men, who could still hear the Lord of the World speaking in the dawn and in the dusk, did not bow down and worship the black rock.

How could they? The stone was not the merciful and compassionate one.

Mohammed completed his circuit of the house of the black stone. He looked up and saw the crowd standing in the hot sun. He was surprised to see the number of people who had gathered.

"Jalal?"

The burly mercenary came up, his eyes squinting and nervous. The soldier was watching the crowd, one hand close to his saber. Mohammed frowned, but then saw that all of his other men—the companions who stood with him in his struggle, these Sahaba—were equally wary.

"There are enemies?" Mohammed looked around in surprise.

Jalal almost laughed aloud in relief, seeing that his chieftain had roused himself from the waking dream. It had been weeks since the Lord Mohammed had been alert. The Tanukh grinned and scratched his beard. "There are always enemies of the righteous, my lord."

Mohammed smiled back, feeling suddenly awake. There was an odd feeling in the air, like the bitter taste that comes when you ride into a steep-walled *wadi*, expecting an ambush. "Men who follow the straight path," Mohammed said, checking his own blade, "need not fear unrighteous men. The great and good Lord will provide."

Jalal nodded agreeably. "My father always said that a righteous man should not fear to look after his own business. He gave me my first bow and sheaf of arrows. My lord, there are many people here, and it crosses my mind that more than one of them might mean you ill. We should go, if you are finished with your devotions."

Mohammed's brow creased in puzzlement. "My devotions?"

Jalal indicated the old house and the stone. "It seemed that you prayed before the stone. I thought that you made obeisance to it."

Brief anger glittered in Mohammed's eyes, but then he remembered that Jalal had not heard the voice coming from the stone. *How can these men understand me?* he wondered, *if they cannot hear.* . . . "Jalal—send a man to bring my horse."

Maslama turned sideways and pushed through the mob. Everyone was standing so quietly that it unnerved him. He gripped the hilt of the sword tighter, feeling the wires that wrapped it dig into his palm. It was unnatural for the air to be so still, for everyone to be so quiet, in a crowd this size. He reached the edge of the Tanukh line and stopped. He was scrupulous to avoid meeting the gaze of any of the northern mercenaries. Up close they seemed very grim and terrible. Their faces were scarred and pitted, showing the echoes of a lifetime of battles.

The young man made to touch his face with his free hand. There was a scar there, too, gained from a falling timber in the Temple of Hubal as it burned. He stopped, wondering if the same bleak expression marked his face. He looked upon the Tanukh, seeing their well-worn weapons and sturdy armor. He felt the weight of his own shirt of mail and the heavy sword at his side.

Thoughts of his father, lying dead in the apse of the temple, roused themselves in his mind.

Mohammed looked around, seeing the lines of temples that surrounded the square, his dark eyes noting the presence of young men and children sitting on the rooftops. Matrons hung from the windows of the houses, their faces pale ovals in the shade. He felt, now that he looked out upon the sea of faces in the crowd, the pressure of their expectation. Here was nearly the whole population of the city, all waiting.

Jalal returned to his side, though some of the Tanukh were bulling their way through the crowd in search of Mohammed's flea-bitten mare. Mohammed jerked his head toward the mob of people beyond the grim line of the Tanukh and the other Sahaba.

"Are they waiting for me?"

Jalal nodded, shading his eyes with a thick-callused hand. "They have been coming for days. Many have heard that you listen to the voice of God on the mountaintop. Many have heard that you have torn down the temples of the sacred precincts and have driven out the priests. They are curious."

Frowning again, Mohammed began pacing, walking along the line of the Tanukh, looking over their armored shoulders into the eyes of the men and women waiting in the crowd. He saw men both rich and poor. Craftsmen, shepherds, potters, merchants, priests, scholars—and women and children. In this manner, he passed again around the old house and the stone. When he returned to the place just opposite the stone, he saw that the rangy, raw-boned mare was waiting. He swung up into the saddle with the ease of long practice.

In his heart, he heard the voice speaking, and he opened his mouth to let the words go forth.

"It was told to me that a band of jinn listened to the revelation of the god who speaks from the clear air." Mohammed pitched his voice to carry, sitting astride the mare. It was so quiet in the square that he was sure that many, perhaps all, could hear him. "They listened and then they said, 'We have been given guidance to the right path. We believed in this and henceforth we serve none but the merciful and compassionate one. That power that has taken no consort, begotten no children. We sought this god in the high heavens, and found our way barred by mighty wardens and fiery comets. We sat eavesdropping, but eavesdroppers find comets lying in wait for them. We cannot tell if this bodes evil to those of us who dwell upon the earth or if the great and compassionate Lord intends to guide us.' "

Mohammed paused, thinking that his throat was dry and parched. But it was not. "These jinn said, 'Some of us are righteous, while others are not, each of us follows different ways. We know that we cannot escape from the Lord of the Heavens while on earth, nor can we elude His grasp by flight. When we heard His guidance, we believed in Him and we knew this—he who believes in the merciful God shall fear neither dishonesty nor injustice.' "

While he spoke, his clear, strong voice ringing out over the great crowd, Mohammed slowly circled the old house and the black stone. The mare was content to slowly clop in a wide circle between the old house and the ring of the Tanukh. The great silence remained, so much so that Mohammed could hear the faint echo of his voice coming from the marble facings of the old temples at the edge of the square.

"Some of us who stand here are righteous men and some are not. Those who submit themselves to the way that has been revealed pursue the right path. Those who do wrong—they shall become the fuel of Hell itself."

As he said this, Mohammed shuddered, the brutal vision of Palmyra dying coming before his eyes. Now his throat was dry, and he swallowed hard, gathering his strength to continue. "If men pursue the straight path the Lord of the Wasteland will vouchsafe them abundant rain, and show them the proof of these words. He who pays no heed to the warning of the Compassionate One shall be sternly punished."

Mohammed paused and turned the horse. He stood once more before the black stone. He half turned in the saddle, looking back upon the old house with its smoke-blackened stones. "Temples," he shouted, raising his voice to be sure that all could hear. "Temples are built for God's worship; invoke in them no other god besides Him. When God's servants rise to pray to Him, a multitude will press around them. No one can protect you from God, nor can you find any refuge besides Him."

The mare turned at the nudge of Mohammed's knee, and he rode back to the edge of the crowd. He leaned on the saddle horn and searched the faces of those who pressed close. Some were weeping. Again, he thought of the dead city and the thing that had feasted within its walls. "A scourge is coming. I cannot tell whether the scourge the compassionate and merciful God has promised is imminent, or whether the Lord has set it for a far-off day. He alone has knowledge of what is hidden: His secrets He reveals to no one, save to the prophets He has chosen. He sends down guardians to walk before them and behind them, that He may ascertain if they have, indeed, delivered the messages of the Lord of the Wasteland."

Mohammed paused, meaning to speak, but his throat closed up. He tried to cough, but could not. A whispering buzz rose in his ears, and he suddenly felt his skin crawl with the invisible touch of thousands of insects. The mare reared, and Mohammed, clawing at his arms, fell heavily to the ground. The buzzing in his ears roared louder, drowning out the cries of his men and the shouting of the crowd. The sky darkened, and he tried to stand. A wind whipped across the square, blowing a wall of dust before it. Grit stung his face and eyes.

Jalal was shouting, trying to reach his chieftain's side. The wind held him back.

Mohammed staggered to his feet, standing at the center of the whirlwind. Beyond the rushing wall of air he could see the crowd surging back and forth. Many people had been knocked down and were being trampled. He felt faint, and the roaring sound in his ears was a sharp spike of pain. Enraged at the threat to the people in the plaza, his hand groped at his waist for his sword. It had fallen to the ground, torn from his belt.

He turned toward the blade, his shoulder against the rush of the wind.

A blow smashed into his back and threw him to the ground. Something flowed over him, and there was a scent of ancient dust and withered crops in his nostrils. He rolled, feeling the thick, muscular power that pressed against him. The skin of the thing, all unseen, was scaled and cold like a great serpent. A snarl of rage split his face, and Mohammed struggled, trying to pry the coils from his neck. Scales slid across his face, trying to crush his skull. His fingers clawed at it.

Hot breath washed across his face, stinking like the Pit. Mohammed cried out, feeling the air being crushed from his ribs. The sky cartwheeled above him, spinning, and a gray tunnel closed down his vision. The wind continued to roar, though he could feel his bones crack under the incredible pressure.

"O Lord of the World," he wept, feeling death close at hand. "Deliver your servant . . ."

Mocking laughter hissed in his ears, and then the pressure around his heart became too great.

Maslama was thrown down by the surge of panic. Men crashed into him, trying to flee the blast of wind that howled forth from the whirlwind. Rocks and small stones lashed the crowd, and they surged back. Maslama rolled under the feet of the stampeding people. Someone kicked him in the side of the head and then fell down, pinning him to the rough cobblestones. A roaring sound filled the air. People were screaming and shouting in fear all around. The young man, gritting his teeth against the pain that stabbed in his temple, surged up, trying to stand.

More men pushed against him, and he fell heavily on one knee. He threw up a mailed arm, fending off the elbows and arms of those running past.

Suddenly they were all gone. The wind buffeted him, and he bent his head against it. The desert robes shielded him from the worst, though his hands—bare and scraped bloody on the ground—were suddenly touched by a chill.

He looked up, one hand down to help him raise up, and saw the old stone house limned by crawling blue flame. A darkness covered the sky, and something titanic and foul was struggling at the center of the plaza. The Tanukh had scattered, leaving behind a drift of bodies. The crowd was pressed back against the walls of the temples, trying to force their way to safety. Beneath the coiling, rugose, tentacular limbs was a figure in a dirty white robe and battered armor, struggling on the ground.

Maslama crawled forward, his heart hammering in his chest.

Red shuddered at the heart of the thing and sparked across the stones of the plaza. A foul stench rolled off it like the odor from a freshly ruptured corpse. Maslama gagged, retching. Something squirmed across the stones toward him. He struggled to pull the sword from its sheath.

There were words—Maslama knew that he had heard them—but though he felt their shape and color and *knew* what they meant as they sounded, ringing clear and true and perfect in the air, he could put no name to them. With them, blooming like the sun suddenly breaking through the clouds on a day of heavy rain, came light. A pure white radiance flooded forth, and Maslama, squinting in the glare, could see that at their center was the figure of the man in the dirty robe.

The thing, the crawling leprous inchoate form that had loomed over the ancient ruin, shuddered and then turned sideways and folded itself up into nothingness. Maslama gaped, his mind shrieking at the impossibility of what it had—dimly—perceived, but then the light touched his face, feather-light, and all horror and pain and suffering was gone. The sword slipped from his fingers and clattered on the ground.

All across the square the people—almost driven mad with fear and terror at the power that had protruded into their world—stopped. They turned, like flowers tracking the sun, and the light fell across them. Many cried out in joy, or fell to their knees, or fainted.

Only two men stood unmoved by the power that—briefly—flared into existence before the old house. One turned immediately and walked away into one of the streets of the city. The other raised himself up from the ground and brushed off his cloak. A brace of wainwrights had trampled him in their haste to flee. Outweighing him by five to one, they had won the argument.

The light faded, curling back into the shape of the man lying on the ground.

Khalid al'Walid looked about him, seeing the throng standing stunned in the wake of the efflorescence, and he rubbed his smooth-shaven chin.

"Well," he mused to himself, walking toward the old house and the supine form of the chieftain Mohammed. "This is the truth of the Lord. Let him who will, believe in it, and him who will, deny it."

High above, the sun moved in its courses in a bright blue sky.

THE HOUSE D'ORELIO, ROMA

The little blond maid, Betia, moved around the room lighting oil lamps. The lamps were set into brass holders shaped like conch shells and painted a light pinkish white. As each lamp flared to life and then settled into a warm glow, the room shrugged off the night. At the end of the room, a pair of double doors opened onto a balcony. Below the balcony the secluded garden at the center of the house lay sleeping. On other nights, the ornamental paper lanterns in the trees would have been lit, but not tonight. Betia returned to the head of the long porphyry table that stood at the center of the room and replaced the candle she had used to light the lamps in its archaic-style Greek candelabrum.

Nikos watched the little Gaul out of the corner of his eye. He was sitting by the window on a chair of painted wicker. The Khazars, despite the presence of couches and chairs, were sitting on the floor in the corner, throwing knucklebones and talking in low voices. Something about the slave had bothered him for some time, but he was just beginning to understand her place and purpose. The girl, who must have been no more than sixteen years old, was in constant attendance upon the Duchess. For all that—for all that he knew that she was an ever-present fixture—the Illyrian had begun to realize it was very difficult to mark her presence. It was more than the casual indifference of a citizen to a slave; that was a habit Nikos had never developed. In his profession it never paid to be unwary or to discount the inoffensive.

Smiling, Nikos realized the girl was very good. She was quiet and graceful. She did not drop things or bump into the edges of tables. She went barefoot nearly all the time and walked quietly.

That which does not draw attention is unseen. Thyatis' voice drifted in his memory.

Betia placed green enameled bowls of shelled nuts and cut fruit on the tabletop and then departed. Nikos watched her go in interest, suddenly seized by the desire to follow her in his own quiet way and see where she went. But there was no time for that, and he put the thought away for a later time.

She must be, he thought, *from the island.*

Rubbing the back of his head, feeling the bumps and knots in his skull and remembering each one and how he had gained it in the service of the Empire and then the Duchess, Nikos wondered if he ever dared broach the matter of the island with his employer. No one had ever talked of it directly, or spoken of it aloud in his presence, but Thyatis had been comfortable enough to mention that she had once been on the island. Nikos was sure, from watching the Duchess and her servants, and the masked women who came and went from the secret entrances of the house, that the island must be the fixture of a mystery cult. Nikos had considered poking about, just to see what he could see. He had not. Some things, he thought, were better left undisturbed.

The mysteries of women and their ceremonies were one

of them. His father had said that. Nikos put great store by his father's wisdom and daily vowed to follow it as soon as he had time.

The sound of low voices came from the door and Nikos rose, walking to his place by the head of the table. The Duchess entered, her hair bound up in a short waterfall of ringlets. Her arm was entwined with that of the Khazar Prince, Jusuf. Nikos suppressed a grimace at that, for the content expression on his friend's face was hard to dismiss. Anastasia laughed, a low throaty sound, at something the tall, rawboned man was saying.

With a flourish of her dark blue skirts and the gold-colored gauze drape laid around her smooth white shoulders, the Duchess sat in a wide-armed round-backed chair the girl Betia had pulled out for her. Nikos blinked in surprise as he seated himself and had to bite his tongue to keep from speaking. He had not even noticed the girl, though she must have come into the room in the company of the Duchess.

Nikos glared at Betia, his brow furrowed. She gazed back, meeting his eyes for the first time.

They were a liquid blue like the light on northern sea under a cold summer sky. For a moment, he was transfixed, seeing unguessable depths reflecting there. Then she smiled and the corners of her eyes crinkled up as she winked at him. Nikos banged his knee on the table, then winced.

"Come, my friends," the Duchess said, ignoring the look of pain on Nikos' face. "We have much to discuss." The Khazars got up from the floor, gathering their coins and scooping the bones up into a bag of soft velvet. The mute, Anagathios, joined them, sitting cross-legged at the end of the table, where he could see the lips and faces of his companions. Nikos caught the eye of the Syrian-born actor and smiled. The mute bowed back to him, making a courtly flourish, even when seated.

"Do not take this amiss, but I fear that we face quite a difficult situation." The tension in the Duchess' voice focused all of Nikos' attention. Even in this muted light he could see that she was drawn and tired. Her gorgeous violet eyes, usually lighted by the fire of her personality, were hooded and distant. The Illyrian sat up straighter in his chair. Anastasia looked around the table, meeting the eyes of her men, nodding to some, smiling at others. "A problem has arisen that involves the Imperial family."

Anastasia stopped and seemed lost in thought. None of the men spoke. Any matter that involved the Emperor could only be a dangerous and difficult one. After a moment, though, she visibly gathered her strength and resumed. "The youngest Atrean prince, Maxian, has returned from the East. Of itself, this would not be notable, save that he has returned in the company of Persians and others. Some of you know that just over two weeks ago, Jusuf and Nikos led a raid against an abandoned estate in the hills to the East of the city. They were accompanied by almost twenty of the Praetorian Guard."

The Khazars and others around the table perked up at this. There had been some ferocious rumor attendant upon the failed raid. The men who had come with Nikos from Egypt and the East had been disgusted that they had not received the tap to join in. Now, however, they congratulated themselves on avoiding disaster. Nikos knew that the Duchess—not having served with the Khazars and Armenians in the Persian campaign—did not trust these men. Nikos she trusted as she had trusted Thyatis, and Jusuf had found his own favor in her heart, but the others? She was not sure of them.

"I had received word that the Prince was attempting some kind of conjuration in that house. It was said that this effort—this sorcery—was directed against his brother, the Emperor Galen. Such things are not to be allowed. The raid, for all the blood spilt in the process, was a failure. The Prince escaped, and with him some unknown number of his servants and allies. The house was destroyed, and the praetorians massacred."

A chuckle ran around the table, though it stilled quickly at the fierce look on the Duchess' face.

"Nikos, relate what transpired there."

The Illyrian stood and bowed and hooked his thumbs into his belt. He turned to the assembled men, his face grim. It was not a pleasant tale.

The *carnica* rattled through the Ostia gate, its high wooden sides swaying as it rolled over the cobblestones of the street. The sun had set, bringing darkness to the city and allowing, at last, the entrance of draymen and wagons into the Imperial capital. Bolts of cloth were carefully piled in the back, bound for a dressmaker's shop on the northern side of the Aventine hill.

Sprawled on the top of a leather sheet spread over the cloth, a straw hat pulled low on her face, snoring, rode a tall woman with tan legs and tangle of red-gold hair. Her travel cloak, once a dark green, was now a muddy gray. She had pulled her travel bag and the worn leather sheath of her sword onto her chest and had wrapped her arms around them.

It had rained much of the afternoon as the wagon had lumbered up the long road from Ostia and the port. Despite the clatter of the big wooden wheels on the stone street, Thyatis slept, exhausted from her journey.

The Duchess coughed, covering her mouth with a fine-boned white hand. Nikos had finished telling what they had seen and fought. The Khazars were openly interested—none of them had ever matched wits or sword with a demon before. Anagathios' striking features were filled with worry. He did not like battles. His particular skills were of little use once things had come to blows.

"My other servants," Anastasia said in an even, controlled voice, "have excavated the house and pulled many bodies from the cellars. The effects of these dead men have been examined. It is all too clear that the Prince—once accounted a friend and welcome guest of this house—has taken to trafficking with the abominable Persian magi and other foul spirits. It is clear he has summoned, or gained control of, an inhuman thing of unsurpassed ferocity and power. Many of the bodies recovered from the house in the hills show signs of torture and necrothia."

The Duchess paused, seeing that those seated at the table did not know the term.

"*Necrothia*, I have recently learned, is the technical term for the markings apparent upon a body that has been revivified from death by the application of certain powers and rituals."

She surveyed the men seated at the table and saw that a chill had fallen over the gathering.

"Yes, the Prince or someone among his party dabbles in the arts of necromancy. He is served by the living dead."

Nikos was hard pressed to suppress a shudder at this. Even among his usually hardheaded and stoic people the corpse-walkers were a night terror.

"We do not know if the Prince himself has the strength to undertake these acts, or if he is accompanied by others who do. We know, from two exceptionally reliable sources, that he has lately been in the plain of the Euphrates valley—even as were you—and that he undertook excavations in one or more of the dead cities there. What he may have recovered is unknown, but it may be that the thing that Jusuf and Nikos crossed swords with in the ruined house was the fruit of his labors. We know, too, that he is possessed of a flying creature out of legend—something that can carry him great distances at great speed—this thing that resolute Nikos terms an *ignis dracorus* or *fire-drake*."

Jusuf turned to the Duchess, making a slight bow with his head. "What then, noble lady, will we do?"

Nikos repressed a bitter laugh. It was clear that the Duchess had scripted parts of the meeting.

"We must undertake," the Duchess said slowly, "to secure the person of the Prince and return him to Imperial custody. We must attempt to destroy this thing that accompanies him and to capture or kill his servants. We must do so quietly, without arousing undue suspicion on any part."

"Including the Emperor's?" Nikos flushed, for he had spoken without thinking.

The Duchess turned, her grave eyes meeting his. She nodded, though she said nothing. Nikos understood all too well. The Emperor would not be told, informed, or involved until all was done. If the wayward Prince could be brought down and returned to his family, the matter would be closed. If the Prince escaped, or was killed, it would be an unfortunate accident. No taint of this cruel business would touch the Emperor's cloak.

"I have been informed," the Duchess said, "that the Prince is in the city, though hidden. He plans, however, to move his entourage to the South, perhaps to the coastal town of Cumae on the Bay of Neapolis. I have considered, and rejected, a plan to apprehend the Prince within the confines of the capital. The powers he has shown are too dangerous to risk within the walls. We will wait until he moves away and goes to ground. Then we will strike."

Nikos raised a hand. His mind was filled with questions of tactics and the matter of execution.

Thyatis bit a hunk off the end of a loaf. She was very tired and coated with dust and grime from the road. The bread was a little stale—no fresh loaves had been available at this late hour. Her boots needed mending, too, and the climb up the street that wound up the side of the Quirinal was hurting her feet. She had two bags slung over her shoulder—one of her personal things and the other of presents she had spent long hours scouring the markets of Athens and Syracuse to find. Shirin's babies would not look kindly upon her if she arrived without the appropriate tribute!

She resumed walking, though the final pitch of the hill seemed much steeper than she remembered. Around her, in the night, the city spread out like a mirror of the sky, filled with sparkling orange and red jewels. The familiar stink of the air was like incense to her. She usually thought of Thira as her home, but tonight, as she climbed the side of the hill, this felt like a homecoming.

"What will we do about the hell-caster?" Kahrmi, the eldest of the two Khazar brothers who had escaped with them out of burning Ctesiphon, leaned on the table. His brown beard, as thick and curly as a bramble thicket, barely disguised the concerned look on his face. At his side, his brother Efraim nodded in agreement. "If this boy-prince can summon the powers of air and darkness, we stand little chance against him. None of us."—Kahrmi gestured around at the men at the table—"are skilled in those arts. We need assistance; our own witches or warlocks to match power with this boy."

Nikos turned to the Duchess, raising an eyebrow. He had the same questions, though he had not broached them yet.

"I have sought this assistance," the Duchess said in a tired voice. "We cannot use the thaumaturges from the Legion or the Imperial Academy without the permission of the Emperor. This counts them out. I have approached, by messenger, many of the independent wizards who make their home in the city. None have responded. I fear we will have to handle this ourselves."

"What?" Nikos stood, his face the very picture of alarm. "My lady, this is a bootless task! We are strong men, skilled and well versed in the arts of war and murder. But the whole lot of us, even together, even with a plan or a trap, will be very hard pressed to match this thing of theirs, this monster. If we must go up against the lad and his own powers . . . well, that will be the end of us."

"It will *not* be the end of you." Anger at last sparked in Anastasia's eyes. "You are thinking men. Crafty hunters. You can track down this boy and his creatures and kill or capture them. He is a living man, so he bleeds and he can die. You said that to me once, if I remember right."

Nikos flinched at the cutting tone in her voice. "That," he said in a hollow voice, "was before we matched blades with this thing. Jusuf—you were there, you saw how it moved! It is *so* fast . . . more, I do not think that it bleeds, my lady."

Anastasia turned to Jusuf, her kohl-rimmed eyes searching his face.

The Khazar looked back, his long face drawn and grim. "It is true," he said softly. "Petronius speared it through with a clean blow and it laughed. It wanted him to pin it, to show that it could not be killed by our weapons. Then it crushed his skull in its fingers. If you say that the bodies recovered from the villa in the hills show signs of being the risen dead, I wager that the thing is of that same ilk."

Anastasia seemed to shrink in upon herself, her face closing up. Nikos fidgeted, his hands shifting on the tabletop. He could see no way to accomplish what she desired and wondered if she would back away from the task. But that would not be like her.

"My lady," he said when she did not speak. "If we are careful, we may be able to take down the boy if we move while he is still in the city. If there is conscience left in him he may not wield his full powers when there are citizens about. If we let him get away, out into the countryside, then we are at his mercy. By the gods, the *fire-drake* can fly! We have nothing to chase him with if he decides to flee. We are outmatched by this if we cannot bring in help—Imperial help."

"No." The Duchess roused herself at last, sitting up again. Jusuf tried to touch her hand, but she stopped him with a cold glare. She looked around the table, and Nikos felt every man sitting there stiffen. "This is the task that I lay upon you," she said in a brittle voice. "Devise a means to bring down the monster, capture the boy, and return him here, to me. I would advise that you keep him unconscious while he is in our custody. Find a way to win. You are the best that I have to hand, you will *have* to do. All this without drawing the attention of the Emperor or the State. Do you understand me?"

Nikos felt the venom in her voice like a back-handed slap on his face. He nodded jerkily.

"Good." Anastasia relented a little, allowing the ice in her voice to thaw a fraction. "Now, how will you deal with this monster?"

Nervously, Betia bit at her nails. She knew she wasn't supposed to, but she was beside herself in disgust. Distracted, she sneaked a look around the back of the big chair that the Duchess was sitting in. It was hard to make out the muscular, blocky form of the man who had been staring at her, but she could see his hands on the tabletop. They were big and callused and strong. She looked at her own hands, pale and small in the light of the lamps. She had heard that the Illyrian had been a wrestler in his youth. It seemed very possible, particularly since his wrists were like tree roots and almost as big around as her upper arms. His arms, she thought morosely, were worse—ridged with hard muscle and as big as her thighs.

I'm too small, she whimpered to herself. *Too small and weak and careless.*

Worse, he was covered with fine white scars and jagged puckered welts. He was bald and grim-looking, with a mean look in his brown eyes. *I shouldn't have looked right at him*, she thought, berating herself for the lapse. It only compounded her error in letting him notice her being unnoticeable. Behind the shelter of the chair she hung her head in shame and almost sniffled. A student of the art was supposed to avoid notice by simply being a part of the background of the scene or room or crowd. It was against the rules to be invisible all the time.

Betia steeled herself and pinched the bridge of her nose with thumb and forefinger. Crying was forbidden, too. She knew where she had fouled up, but it had been a joy to pass through the house or the market or the temples without anyone noticing her. It had given her a delicious sense of freedom, knowing that she could pass into any place, all unseen, without having to explain her presence or ask for admittance.

I was too confident, she lectured herself. *The Lord Nikos is a professional, not a student. Of course, he would notice me! Perhaps I will not get too bad a beating.* . . . Her face fell at the thought. Her mistress was quite strict about these things. Drawing attention to oneself, particularly in such an odd way, was sure to disgust her. She considered throwing herself on the Duchess' mercy, but then remembered that the lady was rather lacking in patience these days.

She sneaked a look around the corner of the chair again. The Lord Nikos was standing, his eyes flashing as he argued with the Lord Jusuf about some plan or trap or mechanism. Betia noticed that the Lord Nikos had a very muscular chest, all smooth and brown and well defined, which you could kind of see through his tunic.

"And these servants, what of them? Are they men or monsters?" Nikos put his fists on the table, leaning forward. Maps had been brought out, showing the land between the capital and the great bay a hundred miles to the South. A dozen possible strategies had been raised and discarded. Servants had brought wine and cooked meats and more shelled nuts. The Illyrian turned to the Duchess, raising an eyebrow.

Anastasia sighed and put down a goblet of watered wine. She was tired, though this kind of thing had once fired her blood like a drug. Now it seemed much the same as another hundred sessions late at night in just another room half filled with a smoky haze. "I am not sure of it," she said, "but it may be that some of the Prince's servants are not human. They walk like men, wear the clothing of men, but . . ." She paused, groping for the word.

Jusuf looked up from where he had been puzzling over the notes written by the foreman of the excavation crew. He turned one of the sheets of thin-scraped parchment around and pushed it across the table to Nikos. "Some of the bodies that were found in the rubble," he said, "seemed to be those of men. But look at the drawing here—see the foot?"

Nikos turned the parchment around and squinted at it. The light was poor, for the candles had begun to burn down. Then it brightened, and he saw out of the corner of his eye that the little blond slave had slipped up beside him and was replacing the candles. He frowned, but pretended not to notice her. The drawing on the parchment was well executed by a man the Duchess employed to paint not only her wall frescoes but also various buildings, people, machines, and other items of interest to her. Things like dead bodies dragged from the ashen slurry of a ruined house.

The drawing showed a foot with a cut made along the line of the body and the skin pulled back. It seemed to be the foot of a man, but there were extra muscles and tendons, and above each toe—big to small—was a sheath of some kind. Nikos squinted again, unable to make out the fine details. The drawing was beautiful, etched on the parchment in a dark brown ink with a tiny quill.

"It is a claw," Jusuf said in a tight voice. "Some of the Prince's servants are animals that wear the shape of men. Among my people, we call them the *ursakurt*—your term, I believe, is *lycanthrope*. I have heard tales from my grandfathers of such—but they left our lands long ago, before even the Gok Turks came from the East."

Nikos cursed again and rubbed the back of his bald head. This just got worse and worse.

Betia almost laughed out loud, seeing the face that the Lord Nikos made. After sitting here worrying for almost an hour while her elders argued and cursed and exclaimed to one another, she had realized that his bald head and its smooth tan surface reminded her very much of a brown hen's egg. With that she had become much more relaxed and had even stolen some of the food from the trays that were brought in. The Duchess, of a mercy, had seemingly forgotten that she was there.

But Betia had learned the hard way not to forget that the Duchess could command her at any time.

A breath of air touched the little blond girl's neck, and she sprang to her feet in perfect silence, turning toward the door, sliding her body between the door and the back of the Duchess' chair. She had heard neither the pad of a servant's step outside nor the *tink-tink* of one of the Khazar boots on the tile.

A figure was there in a dirty dark robe and a funny smell, like dust and mud and the marketplace. One hand was on the door, and the other was already over Betia's mouth. It was a strong, slim hand, with short-clipped nails and the ridges of callus that marked the swordsman.

"Hello friends," a familiar voice said. Nikos turned in puzzlement and saw the Duchess's eyes open in surprise as well. "Why the long faces?"

Nikos' heart skipped a beat, and the figure at the door shook the hood off her head, letting a river of red-gold curls spill down over her shoulders and the tattered tunic and robe. There was a hiss of air as every man in the room took a breath to speak.

"Nikos!" Thyatis swung around the side of the table and wrapped the stocky Illyrian in a bear hug. She was laughing, her grimy face split with a huge grin. "You didn't get lost on your way home!"

Nikos laughed, feeling a huge weight—it might be the whole world—lift from his shoulders. He hugged her back, unable to speak.

Thyatis turned, her grin lighting the room, and made a half bow to the Duchess. Anastasia's eyes were shining, too, and she raised an elegant hand for Thyatis to kiss in greeting.

"My lady," Thyatis said, pressing her forehead against the back of Anastasia's hand. "You see, I did come home. Late and much delayed, but I am here."

"Welcome," Anastasia said, her old beauty suddenly returning to her face. To Nikos, it seemed she was young again in her smile. Her weariness fled. "You've come at the best time."

"It seems so," Thyatis growled, still holding the Duchess's hand as she turned to look upon the rest of the men in the room. The Khazars crowded around her, pounding her on the back and exclaiming at the wear on her boots and cloak. Jusuf smiled across the table, though he did not move to embrace her. Thyatis raised an eyebrow, noting the hand that the Khazar had laid on the back of the Duchess' chair.

"You've all been about some tomfoolery, I see." Thyatis gestured at the maps and papers on the table. "There is a hunt in the wind—I could hear it in your voices as I came up the stair. Tell me all."

Steam boiled up from the surface of the big cedar tub, and Thyatis lowered herself into it with a groan of pure relief. The water was hot and fresh, and there was plenty of it. The young Roman woman had bound her hair up in a bun at the back of her head. Every muscle in her body had decided it was time to wake up, start aching and demand immediate attention. It felt so good, after weeks of dogging around the Aegean ports on a succession of lugs and coasters before finally reaching Rome.

"The children are fine." Anastasia was sitting by the side of the tub on a marble bench. The Duchess was tired, too, but the haunted look in her face had passed, replaced by something approximating her old confidence and demeanor. "They made a horrible ruckus in the house—running about like wild monkeys—and drove the maids and the cooks to distraction."

"Ah-huh?" Thyatis had settled into the water until only her firm, rose-colored lips were above the water. She leaned back into the side of the tub, letting herself float in the steaming water. "Did they break anything?"

"Oh yes," Anastasia said with a faint smile. "It took a great deal to keep track of them."

"I brought them presents," Thyatis said dreamily as the

heat seeped into her sore muscles. "Are they here?"

"No." The Duchess reached over to the wall and took a stiff brush from its hook on the wall. She handed it to Thyatis, though the young woman let it go in the water and watched it float. "I sent them with Betia to the circus— there was a wild animal show—and then they wanted to see an octopus and a sea serpent and all sorts of things. So I packed them off to my beach house at Baiae for a couple of weeks in the sun. We'll go see them soon."

"How much did they grow?" Thyatis was sad, thinking of Shirin all mewed up on Thira while her children frolicked in the surf on the bay. The Princess would doubtless have a few words to say about the soft life that her children had been living in her absence. "Are they completely spoiled?"

"Yes," the Duchess said, smiling. "I fear so. They are precious. I understand that their mother is quite beautiful."

Thyatis raised her head out of the water, steam curling from her forehead. Water sluiced down her neck, and her hair clung to the shape of her head like a pelt of fur. She raised herself a little out of the water, putting her arm on the lip of the tub.

"Who told you that? Surely not Jusuf—he blushes when anyone talks about her having children. It must be that wretch Nikos."

"It was, but I could see her face in them, too," Anastasia said, laughing. She smiled down at Thyatis, her hands folded on her lap. "He told me a great deal about it— you've set his Roman standards on edge, I think."

Tension stole across Thyatis' face, and she met the calm, quiet eyes of the Duchess evenly. "Do you think I did the wrong thing?"

Anastasia considered her for a moment, gauging the depths in the younger woman's eyes. She marked the planes of the face and the hard muscle that girded her shoulders and arms. The Duchess nodded, seeing that she had sent away a brash youth, still incompletely formed, and had received back—safe by the gods!—the full measure of an adult woman. The Duchess picked at the hem of her gown, thinking. "Thyatis . . ." She stopped, suddenly unsure of what to say. *That is a wonder*, she scolded herself. "My dear, once we discussed the day that I purchased you and brought you into my family. I told you then that I bought you because there was something unbroken in your eyes, standing there in the slave coffle in that hot dusty market. That was true, but once you had left for the East, I found that I missed you. I have realized that I purchased you because you reminded me of . . . me."

Thyatis canted her head and turned, putting her arms on the edge of the tub and her chin on her interleaved fingers. "How so? I was a dirty peasant girl in a torn tunic, barefoot, and only moments from a brand."

"True," the Duchess said in a sad voice. "And so was I, on just such a day, many years ago. I was an orphan— my parents murdered by pirates off of the coast of Sicilia. They were Vandal raiders, I believe, who still held some strongholds on the coast of Africa in those days. I was very lucky to leave their hands—but among them, odd-colored eyes are considered a mark of bad luck. I was sold in the great market on Delos." The Duchess' face seemed shadowed by the old memory. Then she smiled and it passed. "Agents of the Matron purchased me in a job lot with six other girls. It was the eyes again. I was to be had"—her voice held an edge of bitterness—"at a discount. But I do not regret it."

"They took you to the island?"

Anastasia shook her head. "No, things were in too much confusion then. No one was admitted onto or off of the island until Imperial order had been restored. I do not know if it still exists, but at that time there was another sanctuary in the mountains of Epirus. We were taken there and trained in secret. Oh, those were a cruel six years!"

"Six?" Thyatis touched Anastasia's foot, gently squeezing the older woman's big toe. "How you must look down upon the younger generations who must only suffer for five . . ."

Anastasia touched Thyatis' hair and bent down, kissing the crown of the younger woman's head. "Ah, but we did not have the benefit of the Lady Mikele's ministrations then. . . ."

"Oh!" Thyatis stood up and made a face. "That was a soft life, then!"

Anastasia laughed and held up a robe of soft cotton. Thyatis bowed and slipped the garment over her broad shoulders.

"Perhaps it was, but I think that you followed your heart and I could not—will not—gainsay that. You matter too much to me."

Thyatis smiled and embraced the older woman and knew that she *was* home.

▣()-▣

DAMASCUS

)=(

A spinning wheel of fire drifted over the arches of a stone bridge. The span had three courses, rising almost sixty feet above the bed of the Baradas River, and it was wide enough to allow a cohort of men to march abreast. The wheel blazed in the air, spinning faster, and slammed into a barrier of overturned wagons at the northern end of the bridge. There was a hissing sound like a hot blade plunged into a quenching bucket and the line of wagons exploded in smoke and flame. One wagon was catapulted into the air, wheels flying off as it disintegrated. The Syrian militiamen behind the barricade scattered, running pell-mell for the safety of the walls of the city. The remaining wagons burned fiercely, sending up a billowing column of pitchy black smoke.

Odenathus and his cavalry galloped across the bridge.

Some of the Palmyrenes were armed with bows and sent a ragged flight of arrows after the fleeing Syrians. Odenathus pulled up as he reached the smashed barricade. While his men trotted past, he concentrated and reached deep into the earth, touching the flickering fluid glow of the river. Power came to his hand, and the remaining wagons, still burning, toppled away from the road, clearing it.

A hundred yards away, across a leveled field that usually served as a farmer's market for the city, the other Palmyrene horsemen had turned as well and were exchanging arrows with the city. Two huge brick towers rose at either side of the Jerash gate. Covered walkways crowned them and were filled with militia. An arrow, its flight almost spent, wobbled through the air past Odenathus and clattered on the roadway. He turned his horse and urged it up the road. Behind him, the rest of Zoë's little army was trotting across the bridge.

The gates of the city, set well back within an overhanging archway, were already closed. From previous visits to the metropolis, Odenathus knew that a long tunnel led through the walls, guarded by three heavy gates of iron and wood. All three would be closed now, though the young Palmyrene almost laughed aloud at the thought of the city cowering before his pitiful band. More arrows whickered past him and he raised a hand, sketching a glowing sign. A flutter grew in the air between him and the city ramparts. Arrows staggered in flight and dropped from the sky, sticking up in the dirt like a bed of new saplings.

"How strong is the gate?" Zoë rode up, her long hair tucked up into a braid and coiled behind her head. Like Odenathus, she wore an open-faced Legion helmet and a shirt of linked mail under a tan robe. A horse-bow jutted from her forward saddle holder, and a sheaf of arrows matched it on the other side of the four-cornered saddle. Her face was flushed, and her eyes were dark with anger.

Odenathus sighed and gestured toward the huge square towers. "Look," he said, keeping an eye out on the flanks of the three hundred-odd riders who were now re-grouping at the head of the bridge. "Look and see the labor of a thousand years of the art."

Zoë glared at him, her eyes flashing. They had gone over this matter for days while they had sat in the hills above the city, watching the comings and goings of the citizens. She tossed her head and turned away, guiding her glossy black stallion with her knees. Bending her head for a moment, she leaned toward the massive gate, seemingly listening.

"Tiris, Gadama!" he shouted, his voice well used to the carrying volume that being the war leader of this band of ruffians required. "Take ten men each and circle the walls. Stay alert—they may sortie from another gate. If they do, don't forget to come back and tell me!"

Damascus was a city of a dozen gates; some small, some large. Odenathus knew that their effort here was fruitless. Zoë cried out in rage, drawing his attention. He turned in time to see her stab an angry fist at the looming gate.

The air twisted and buckled between the young woman and the gate and Odenathus flinched back, feeling the rage and hatred that howled around her. Stones in the field at her feet shattered, crumbling to dust, and the sky darkened. A wind rose up, whipping grit against the horses.

The main gate, a thirty-foot-wide expanse of iron and wood, shuddered, booming like a bass drum. For an instant, Odenathus could see the gate and the surrounding towers flare up with a tracery of dark red light. Ancient spells and wards, bound into the rock and wood and iron of the gate from the days of the first men, flickered and refracted. Zoë's stroke spattered on the ancient interlocking vertices. Odenathus blinked, calling up the sight he had set aside, and saw the fading echo of the bolt draining away in a hundred traps and guides, flowing across the front of the gate like water spilling on a stone. "It is too strong, my Queen." His voice was quiet and soft, so that no one else could hear.

Zoë spun, her face a mask of rage. Smoky power burned

behind her eyes, only barely restrained. "We will break this city." Her voice was still soft, too, but he could hear a scream building in it.

"We will not." He urged his horse up to hers, wither to wither. He leaned close, his gray eyes matching her dark brown ones. "This is a city of almost five hundred thousand souls—we have but three hundred men, and there are only two of us with the power. Listen, you can hear the citizens jeering us."

Zoë looked over her shoulder, and it was true. On the ramparts, thousands of Syrians—men and women alike—were shouting and screaming. Stones and refuse and offal rained from the wall, though none of the Palmyrenes were close enough to strike. The young woman shuddered, leaning against the high cantle of her saddle. "Rome has betrayed them, too." Zoë's voice was thick with emotion. "Will they not rise up? Will they not stand with us against the Empire that uses us and then discards us?"

Odenathus caught her shoulder and turned her around, gently. "My Queen, it is not *their* city that Rome offered up as a sacrifice. They do not care what happens to us. Come, let us go."

Zoë shook her head, a track of tears on one cheek. "I will not slink away like a whipped cur," she snarled. "She is watching. She would find a way to bring down those gates in ruin and fire."

Odenathus' face closed up, and he forced himself to keep from turning to look back across the bridge. There, on the far side of the river, another cluster of riders guarded a wagon. In the back of the wagon, carefully tied to a chair of gold and ivory that had once graced the Garden Room in the palace, was the body of Zenobia, once Queen of Palmyra. The body was ancient and withered, horribly scarred and disfigured, but it rode in the wagon in state, clothed in gold and samite and silk. Zoë had insisted, once she had returned from her long days in the hills above the city, that the dead Queen still ruled the city. Hidden wires and rods of copper held the body together and kept it upright. Odenathus felt a chill whenever he looked upon it.

"She," Odenathus said, his mind working furiously, "would have come with a great army and a plan to get through that gate and friends within the city, waiting for her word to rise up."

Zoë looked up, her eyes bleak. She opened her mouth, a hot retort on her lips, but a cry came from the west. Odenathus turned, raising his head. Tiris and the horsemen he had sent that way were riding back in a great hurry. The last men in the column were turned in their saddles, firing their bows at something behind the curve of the city wall. Odenathus wheeled his horse and raised his voice in a shout.

"Fall back, over the bridge! Lycius, send a rider to get Gadama and his men. Move!"

Without regard for the black look that Zoë gave him, Odenathus turned again and galloped over the bridge. The crowd of Palmyrene horses followed, flowing across the span in a brown, red, and black stream. Tiris and his scouts thundered after them. Zoë was last, walking her horse back, as she watched the walls in fury. No sooner had she reached the far side of the bridge than a strong troop of cavalry in Imperial red came trotting around the corner of the wall. She ground her fist into the saddle in disgust. Her quick eye counted at least a cohort of Imperial armored knights in scale and lamellar armor. If they were here, then a Legion or a goodly part of it must be hard on their heels.

The first rank of *clibanari* reined up at the other end of the bridge and drew long shafted arrows to their curved horse-bows. Zoë turned her horse and slashed her hand down before she kicked the stallion and it bolted away to the east in a cloud of dust.

Behind her the Imperials swerved aside from the end of the bridge. The span suddenly trembled, sending dust spurting from the sides, and the roadbed jumped as the entire structure gave voice in a tremulous groan. At the top of the slope, from the river, Zoë turned, watching with angry eyes. The structure settled again, sending down a rain of rock chips and dust into the river that rolled slowly between the piers. Her face contorted in anger, and she chopped her hand down again, her will sending a shockwave of power lashing out at the stone and brick. It shook again, quivering along its full hundred-foot length, and part of the facing on the stone pier nearest the city suddenly peeled away and toppled into the river. A white spray of water roared up as the marble and travertine crashed into the stream.

But the bridge held. More Imperials were arriving every second at the far end. Some of them lifted their bows, and Zoë could see the flicker of arrows reaching high into the air. Their thaumaturges had to be close by. She goosed the stallion again, and it blew its nostrils and then sprinted away, its mane streaming in the wind.

"I will not allow it." Zoë and Odenathus were crouched near the back of the wagon that carried the throne of gold and ivory. Their faces were in shadow. Sunset was only minutes away. The rear axle had cracked, spilling the wagon into a ditch as they had attempted to cross one of the *wadi* that crisscrossed the Syrian highlands south of Damascus. It was rocky country and hard going away from the metaled Imperial roads. At first, it had seemed that the Legion would not pursue them, but Odenathus was not willing to risk it. They had pressed hard for two days, seeing no pursuit, but then, at a crossroads sixty miles from the city, they had nearly blundered into an ambush. Only the fierce and sudden application of their combined power had extricated them alive from the trap.

Odenathus stood, brushing sand from his leggings. The wagon was a lost cause. "We cannot repair the axle. Those Hunnic light horse are closing hard on us. Even now they are making up ground while we argue. My Queen, we will have to leave it."

"And her?" Zoë stood, too, her thin frame trembling with anger. "Shall we cast the Queen aside, leaving her to lie in a ditch while we slink away into the night? She is our honor!"

Odenathus controlled himself, chanting a calming meditation in his mind. He had argued long and hard with his cousin. It was insane to take those few souls left to the city and launch a raid into the Imperial provinces. Better, he had argued, to rebuild the city and allow the scattered children of Palmyra to come home again. The city, he knew, was still rich with ships and warehouses and trading contacts throughout the whole of the world. If the center could be rebuilt, even enough to allow the lost to find their way home, they could—in time—restore the city. Zoë would not hear of it.

"Then," he said simply, "we will have to put her on a horse, wrapped in blankets and tied to the saddle."

Zoë had been sure that if they struck against Damascus, the Syrian populace would rise in their favor and throw out the Romans. Odenathus had simply not believed it, but Zoë's madness had infected the others, and nearly all of those who remained had pledged to follow her. His heart breaking, in the end he had agreed to follow her. They would have little chance without him and his power to back up Zoë's. Now, standing in the twilight, looking into the grief-stricken face of his cousin, he wondered if she had not bent her will and power to influence all of them. This was a mad thing.

"I will carry her," Zoë said, climbing into the wagon. "She is my burden."

Odenathus looked away, his heart sick, as the lithe figure of his cousin bent to undo the wires that held the corpse of the dead Queen to the chair. He climbed up out of the bottom of the *wadi* to his horse and swung into the saddle. The western sky was a riot of red and orange and purple. Night was coming, and the track they were following was climbing up the side of a long, rocky ridge. Somewhere beyond it, beyond this last vestige of cultivation and fertile land, rose the vast highland plain of the Hauran. A bleak land, shattered by ancient agonies deep in the earth. Nothing grew there save endless fields of sharp-edged black rock. The Hauran was a haunted place, a hundred-mile-wide wedge of devastation that thrust into the Syrian heartland like a spear flung from the wastelands of Arabia. It would be hard going, with little water and searing heat by day, chilling cold by night.

"But," Odenathus said to himself, motioning to the others to ride on into the night, "it has been the refuge of bandits and friendless men for centuries." He looked down into the *wadi*, his mage-sight showing his cousin struggling to pull a harness onto her back. The dead Queen had been strapped to it, the empty pits of her eyes staring up at the evening stars. Zoë shrugged the corpse onto her back and, with the help of her two guardsmen, managed to climb into her saddle.

"And we are friendless," he finished, gently nudging his mare to move. The horse flicked its ears and ambled back onto the road. Odenathus rubbed his chin, feeling the stubble growing in. He had not had a chance to shave in days. The Imperial pursuit was pressing them too hard for a proper camp. Tired men rode past him, squinting into the dark. After a moment, Zoë followed, avoiding his glance. The dead Queen bobbed at her back, withered hands crossed over her breasts, legs pulled up to her chest and bound in place with wire.

When the last man had passed, Odenathus turned in behind the column and muttered something under his breath. A tiny mote of light, no more than the gleam of a firefly, drifted away from him and skipped forward along the line of men and horses. When it reached the front of the column, it brightened and cast a pale glow over the desert before them.

Following the witch-light, the band of men pressed on into the night. Somewhere ahead the badlands of the Hauran were waiting, and beyond them the jagged spirit-haunted peaks of the Trachontis.

W hoa!" Maxian stood from the seat of the big wagon and waved behind him at the others, signaling a stop. Sitting beside him on the high driver's seat of the *carruca*, Krista leaned forward and looked out from under the canopy she had rigged over the seats. The little caravan—three wagons filled with boxes and crates made of pine boards, their bedding, food in wicker hampers, bags of fruit, amphorae of wine in wooden carriers—had spent the afternoon in a long, slow climb up the side of the mountain. Now they had reached some kind of crossroads, and Krista shaded her eyes against the sun, making out a plinth of weatherworn gray stone. There were markings and arrows chiseled into its surface, showing the distances in miles to the nearest towns, to Roma, and to the provincial seat at Neapolis.

The Prince sat back down and flipped the reins. The four mules hitched to the front of the wagon flicked their ears irritably but then began clopping forward. With their grudging assistance, Maxian pulled the *carruca* off to the side of the road. Krista fanned herself with a cotton spring-fan dyed with small scenes of men and women picking grapes. She had purchased it for a copper from a vendor in the last town.

"Where now?" Her voice was languid, though she had been observing the Prince closely since they had slipped out of Rome three days before. Cold conscience disputed the feeling of her heart. She had to make a decision about this man, and soon. "A nap, perhaps, under a shady tree?"

Maxian grinned and shook his head. He reached under

the seat and pulled out a flagon of wine. After taking a long swallow, he offered it to Krista. She shook her head slightly. A headache was already tickling around the edge of her consciousness; she didn't need to help it along.

"I think this is the turnoff to an old estate that came from my mother's family." Maxian pointed between the trees that lined the road, up the long slope of the mountain. Acres of vineyards and orchards sprawled away from them, reaching up into the fluffy white clouds that were clinging to the summit. It was a hot day, and the air was sticky with humidity. Flies and bees hummed in the air, and the thick green smell of the countryside was overpowering. Krista wrinkled her nose. She preferred the clean breezes of the seaside to this soupy atmosphere.

"The last that I heard, it was deserted save for a caretaker and some tenants. We should find plenty of quiet."

Gaius Julius came up on the side of the wagon, his leathery old face fairly beaming with the genteel beneficence of a patrician on summer holiday. He was wearing a short-sleeved white tunic that showed off the muscles of his upper arms and an impossibly broad straw hat with a pointed top. A pair of *legionaries caligulae* that showed off his splayed toes and hairy feet completed his outfit. Krista looked away, stifling a laugh. The old Roman had conceived an abiding love for this image of the patrician farmer on holiday. "Ah, my lad, this is a fine day! We should have taken a holiday earlier—have you ever tried the wine from these parts? Oh, it has a particularly stiff taste—metallic almost. . . ."

Krista rolled her eyes and tried to ignore the old Roman, whose tendency to maunder on about vintages and vineyards and casks and aromas for hours induced an overwhelming urge to sleep. Maxian's eyes were glazing over as well.

"My lord," Krista interjected in a sharp tone. "Are we stopping for lunch, or taking a nap, or getting wherever it is we're going?"

Maxian's head jerked as he woke up and he nodded, his

eyes bleary. Gaius Julius had continued to propound on the waters of the district and their undoubted effect on the vintages derived therefrom.

"Yes," the Prince said, "we turn right here. It is only a mile or so to the house."

"Good," Krista said, giving Gaius Julius a slit-eyed glare. "Let's go."

Krista watched the old Roman swing down off of the wagon step with relief. Gaius Julius had begun wearing a strong lemon pomade of late, and it turned her stomach. At her side, the Prince flipped the reins and the mules shuffled their feet and leaned into the traces. The wagon rolled slowly forward.

A thick overhang of twisted dark brown vines and prickly bushes made a wall on either side of the road that led off the main highway into the old estate. The stoutly built *carruca* barely fit into the dim green passage. Krista leaned back in the wagon seat, watching the leaves pass by overhead as the wagon rocked back and forth, rumbling up the long, shady road. Her fingers toyed with the amulet around her neck, feeling the smooth bronze links of its chain and the incised symbols on its surface. Maxian was oblivious, staring up at the mountain that slowly grew before them.

The Prince had given her the medallion—a circle of brass with a plain surface, marked with rings of small letters that radiated out from a central point. That center was a hole cut through the brass and notched with tiny marks. For a brief moment, since it was so obviously something that he had made with his own hands, she had been very happy. No one had ever given her something they had made expressly for her before. The visitors that had come and gone from the Duchess' house had often given her flowers or gewgaws or presents refused by the Duchess, but they were second-hand things.

Then, of course, the Prince had explained what it was for, and her heart had turned cold.

In this amulet, he had explained in a brisk, professional

tone, *is trapped a fragment of my power. It holds a similarity of the Shield of Athena that I maintain around all of us at all times. While I live, the device will echo my power and my shield—though around you rather than me. It is less powerful, but it should serve to protect you if you are away from my immediate presence. I have made others for Gaius and Alexandros, of course.*

Though she feigned sleep as they rattled and rolled and creaked up the mountainside with Gaius Julius and the others in tow, her mind was turned to thoughts far away from the Prince. She thought more of her home and a hot bath and even the hectoring voice of the Duchess.

The Prince *tsked* at the mules, and the wagon passed under an old arch of hand-carved stone. They had entered the domain of his patrimony. The clouds seemed very close, and the sun waned. Krista sat up, disturbed from her doze by the chill in the air. It was not cold, exactly, but cooler than it had been down on the plain. Orchards surrounded them, grown wild from lack of care. High grass heavy with seed pods and flowering weeds clogged the ground under the apple trees. The hedgerow that marked the road fell back, becoming a low wall that ran along the verge of the track.

"Just a minute more." Maxian smiled at her, his face open and cheerful. Krista smiled back, though there was the hint of a shadow in her eyes. "Fret not, love. We should be quite safe here."

Clouds parted again as they came out of the apple trees and a house lay before them. Krista smiled involuntarily, seeing the simple, clean lines of the brick walls and the slightly canted roofs of the buildings. This was the kind of place that she knew well—a classic Roman rural villa, all square buildings and tiled roofs, pillared colonnades, and atriums open to the sky. A brick wall, overgrown with roses and creeping yellow vines, surrounded the house. The front gate stood open, the old iron latticework green with rust.

"Ah." The Prince looked abashed. "It's smaller than I remember."

Krista laughed and put her hand on his arm. He flicked the reins, urging the mules to hurry up, and then they rolled through the gate, the stretched cloth top of the *carruca* barely passing under the archway. Within, an open square of hard-packed earth sat between the out buildings and the main house. The edge of the yard was piled with reefs of blown leaves and twigs. Krista stepped down from the wagon and looked around with wary interest. The place was empty and abandoned, with closed doors and shutters on all sides, but she did not feel like a stranger. It had the feel of a place where the hostess had stepped out and she would be back in just a minute. The walls of the buildings were still plastered and trim, without any fallen-in roofs or broken doors. The other wagons rolled up and parked in a line along the side of the yard toward the mountain. There were Barns clustered there, and the faint smell of old manure.

The Walach boys ran past, freed at last from the boring confines of the wagons. They sketched a bow as they ran past Krista, their bare feet thudding on the ground, and loped off between the buildings. Krista took a straw hat—much smaller and more demure than Gaius Julius'—out of the wooden box under the wagon seat and tied it on her head. After undoing a lock, the Prince and Alexandros were opening the doors to the main house. Gaius Julius had already disappeared; doubtless off to find the cellars and winepresses.

A pitiful mew drew her attention, and Krista smiled, her teeth flashing white in the shade under her hat. Two little yellow eyes peered at her out of a red wicker basket stowed behind the seat. Reaching in, she dragged the basket out and held it up. The little black cat was sitting in a nest of old sheets, staring out with wide eyes at the yard and the sky. It mewed again, imperious in its desire to be let out.

"I think not, little squeak." Krista pulled her bag of

clothes and sundries out, too, and walked toward the front door of the house, now standing wide, with the faint gleam of sunlight on tiles shining from within. "We have to get settled first, but then I'll get you some cream."

Old wooden shutters creaked open, and Krista coughed as dust hazed the air in the kitchen. Unlike the dark, enclosed rooms of the kitchens in the Duchess' house in Rome, here, a long rectangular chamber set at the far end of the house held the iron stove and marble countertops. Next to the stove was an open, bricked, fire-pit with a griddle built over it. There was a big basin-shaped sink fed by round ceramic pipes, too, which sat under a long series of windows that looked out on the north side of the big house. With the shutters opened, the room was flooded with a cool, northern light and treated to a fine view of the mountain sloping away above the villa. It would be cool in the summer, with its high ceilings and a row of grillwork-covered windows under the eaves.

Krista clapped her hands together, trying to get the dust and grime off. It was no use; the whole house needed a thorough cleaning, and she grimaced, realizing she was likely the only one to care. All of the Persian and Nabatean servants Abdmachus had gathered were dead or missing, which left her only the Walach boys for helpers. They were not very good at cleaning, having a tendency to get into fights with one another or loll about grooming themselves or sleeping. If there was hunting to be had, or some dark business in the nighttime, they were the very soul of attention. But sweeping or scrubbing down countertops? Never.

Footsteps clattered on the smooth tiles of the kitchen floor, and she turned.

"Would you like to go for a walk with me?"

Maxian had changed into a short kilt, leather sandals, and a Greek-style tunic that bared one arm and shoulder. Krista blinked, not having seen him look so, well, rustic before. She stifled a laugh, imagining him with a crown of laurel leaves and an amphora of wine under one arm. He looked relaxed, and the thin creases of strain and worry around his eyes had faded. "What is so funny?" He leaned on the counter, his head at a slight angle, looking down at her.

"Oh, my Lord Bacchus," she said, turning away and smiling over her shoulder, eyes twinkling. "have you come for a revel?"

Maxian was perplexed for an instant, and then looked down at his costume. "Brat! We're on holiday in the country!" He grabbed her waist, and she skipped back, laughing. "Come here!"

"No!" she caroled, and darted out the door to the back garden. Behind the house and lying under the kitchen windows had been a large vegetable garden fronting on a brick porch with a stout roof. Now it was as overgrown as the orchards or the cattle pens, but a walkway of round stones had been laid from the back door to a gate in a fence of wooden slats. Krista sprinted across the garden, laughing, and the Prince was hard on her heels. "You're too slow, my lord! But catch me if you can!"

Inside the house, Gaius Julius leaned out of one of the windows on the second floor of the sleeping quarters. His old face creased with a smile, the corners of his eyes crinkling up. Like the kitchen in the lower floor, the sleeping rooms were graced with big, tall windows and latticework shutters of thin-cut pine. He had found a chamber to his liking and opened them, letting the late afternoon sun stream through. Even the dust was not so bad. He leaned on the windowsill, watching the figure of the Prince disappear into a stand of olive trees.

"That seems a delightful pursuit."

Gaius turned a little and saw that Alexandros had entered the room. The youth had stripped off his shirt, and the sunlight played over supple muscle and smooth flesh. Even the welts of two deep scars, one along his side and the other just below his shoulder, did not mar his beauty. He had tied his hair partially back, which left it hanging in a thick mane of blond curls behind his head. Gaius Julius grinned wryly, reflecting on the true age of the "young" man. "Would you care to test your strength?"

The old Roman raised an eyebrow and turned around. The Macedonian's eyes met his, and Gaius Julius felt the shock of the man's power to attract and command. "Ah, lad, you know how old I feel . . ."

"Illusion," Alexandros said, grinning like a god, and took his hand. "Let me show you."

Maxian and Krista climbed through stands of cypress trees, sunlight and wind in their hair. The trail, twisted and strewn with rocks, turned and they stopped, looking back. Far below they could make out the red tile roofs of the villa and the outline of the wagons, still sitting in the foreyard. The clouds had blown away to the northwest, out over the Bay of Neapolis. From this height they could see out over the long curve of the shore and toward the headland that held Puteoli and the great military harbor at Misenum. Somewhere below the blue-and-white haze, beyond the sparkling bay, was Cumae and the summer villas of the rich.

"This was my mother's own house," the Prince mused as they walked, clambering up over black rocks with rough pockets cut out of them. "She had it from her father—she was his only heir—and she kept it as she liked. Father built her a whole new house at Cumae when he was made governor and tribune, but this place was the dearest to her heart."

"What happened to your mother?" Krista scrambled along behind him, feeling the twinge of exertion in her thighs. It had been some time since she had had a chance to work up a real sweat. The cool mountain air was refreshing and clean, far better than the humid lowland vapors. She noticed that the Prince had gotten back a little color on his legs and thighs. He seemed fitter, too, though that might just have been the skimpy outfit. She grinned again. This was a thousand times better than spending the whole of the day and the night in some noisome cellar, watching him mutter and chant, bent over some ancient tome.

"*Mater* died in the first plague—the one that made you cough until blood came out of your mouth. She and *Pater* were in Narbo at the other house. I only found out by letter. I was away in Africa, visiting cousin Antonius in Leptis Magna. I came home as fast as I could, but she was already gone. Father kept the household on here for a time, but then the War of the Pretenders began, and they must have fled."

Krista skipped ahead and came alongside the Prince. His face was sad and touched by old pain. She caught his hand and squeezed it. He grinned, and his mood passed away when she smiled back.

"What is your best memory of this place?"

Maxian took her hand and turned it, bringing her wrist to his lips as they walked. Dark-needled trees were intermixed with the cypress now, and the air had a faint piney scent. The ground changed, too, becoming rockier, the lower slopes and their thick rich black soil left behind.

"You are good to try to distract me," he said, kissing her hand. "That is an old pain, my love. She had a long, full life, and saw her sons grow to manhood. Galen missed her most, I'm sure. I remember, when we had come to Rome in victory and the Senate had proclaimed him Emperor and God, that he looked over his shoulder, standing there in the Curia Julia on the speaker's platform, looking to see if she was there, in the wings, watching him."

Krista squeezed his hand and slipped her arm around his waist. They walked under the trees, talking, until the trail ended in a forest of great boulders and a thick tangle of brush. Stones towered up around them, rough and jagged, and she saw that they stood at the edge of a round bowl at the very top of the mountain. It was a mile or more across and jumbled with pillars and boulders and thickets of boscage. Hawks circled in the air above the summit, coasting on the wind.

"Ah . . ." The Prince scratched his chin. "This is a good memory. See this wilderness? It is very famous—long ago there was a great rebellion among the slaves. They fought hard against the Republic but were defeated in the end. This was their stronghold, here in the high air on the mountain. Three Legions besieged them for two years before the end. When I was little my brothers and I would come here to play, sneaking among the rocks, climbing down into all the hidden places, pretending to be soldiers. . . ."

Krista looked around, feeling a chill. She knew this place from whispers in the slave quarters late at night. Even in the house of the Duchess there were some stories that were forbidden. This was one, a tale of gladiators and rebellion. The bravery of the Thracian and the greed of Crassus, the cruelty of the Legions and the dreadful cost in lives that brief freedom cost. It grew cold on the mountaintop. The bright sunlight seemed thin now, and she thought she could see the spirits of the dead slaves in the shadows under the boulders.

"Come on," Maxian said, his voice filled with rediscovered joy. "There is a hidden place at the center, a grotto of soft green grass and flowers. I am sure I can find it again!" Ignoring the bleak look on her face, the Prince dragged her into a passage between the boulders.

Anatol peered around the corner of the big house, his hands on the white plastered wall. Three of the other Walach boys crowded behind him, snickering and tugging at his shirt. The yard in front of the house was empty, save for the wagons that they had ridden up from Rome. The corpse-man was in the yard standing still and quiet as a gravestone. Anatol rubbed his nose furiously and nerved himself up. He looked all around, cautious and wary. He was pretty sure that the young master and his woman would not be back for a few hours—Anatol could smell the heavy scent in the air as well as anyone. The late spring was blooming on the mountainside; flowers were opening,

filling the air with delicious smells and the thick taste of
their pollen. Foxes yowled in the hedgerows, and birds
made a graceful dance in the air. Even the two dead men
were upstairs, locked in sweaty contest. It was spring.

"Go on," whispered Vitaly. "It's just standing there."

Anatol smoothed back his unruly shock of thick black
hair and squared his shoulders. His brothers gave him a
good push, and he skipped out into the yard. Glaring back
over his shoulder, he scuttled up to within ten or twelve
feet of the thing standing in the yard. It remained quies-
cent, staring off into the sky.

"Khiron?"

The head of the thing turned, swiveling like a clock-
work, and Anatol felt a chill from the top of his head to
the bottoms of his bare, furry feet. The corpse-man's eyes
were black and bottomless, filled with pain and a hint of
the lash. The mottled yellow-gray skin of the creature
barely flexed as it bent its head to look upon him. Anatol
gulped and backed up a foot or two. All the Walach boys
had seen the speed of the corpse-man; it was like one of
the *surāpa*, striking like the wind. It was strong, too, strong
enough to bend iron in its fist, strong enough to crack
stones to powder. The young master had ordered it to wear
a long gray tunic with a hood, but in this bright afternoon
it had thrown back the woolen head covering and stood,
watching the birds circling in the sky.

"Khiron," Anatol said, his voice growing stronger as the
thing remained standing quietly. "The master Maxian di-
rects that you should unload all of the wagons and put the
crates inside the big house, in the atrium."

The thing stood quietly, staring down at the Walach boy.
Anatol gulped again and began to slide slowly backward,
angling for the edge of the house and his confederates.
Muscles and veins moved under the skin of the thing,
squirming like worms crawling under a gelid surface of
translucent wax. Anatol blinked, preparing to bolt if the
thing moved toward him.

Khiron smiled, face sliding into a ghastly rictus. Long

yellow teeth, sharp and pointed like needles, were exposed. A tongue darted, a black point that vanished, leaving only a memory of its presence on the mind of the viewer. The thing turned toward the house, the break between stillness and motion undetectable.

"I will place the crates and boxes in the atrium." The thing's voice was hollow, a dry well lined with fragments of bone and dust. "I will empty the wagons."

Anatol and the other Walach boys were long gone, a cloud of white dust drifting in the air of the villa yard. Khiron's face collapsed back into its usual blank state as it unhitched the back of the first wagon. Four wooden crates—each the length of a man—lay within, filled with books and scrolls. Khiron grasped the first with its fists. Wood squeaked in protest as the long black nails ground into the pine planks. Khiron lifted the crate out of the back of the wagon and carried it inside, resting on one shoulder.

On the second floor of the big house, the little black cat peered down between the crossbars of the railing that lined the balcony. Its yellow eyes followed the passage of the corpse-man as it passed below and into the house. When it was gone, the cat turned, tail in the air, and padded away into the dim hallway that ran the length of the upper floor.

"Do you feel it?" Maxian lay on the ground, his face pressed against the earth, his eyes closed. Krista stood over him, her arms crossed over her chest. Her face was pinched in worry, and she could feel a cold, uncomfortable eddy in the air. "Can you hear it breathing?"

They stood in a grotto, as the Prince had promised. It was lined by mossy boulders and floored with thick soft grass and dusted with tiny blue flowers. Water trickled over rocks somewhere nearby, but Krista could not make out where the stream was. Dim green gloom crouched under the overhanging trees and puddled underneath the walls of stone. The way into it had wound down through hidden passages in the brush and brambles, over smooth rocks and past sharp-edged cliffs. It lay, she guessed, at the center of the bowl on the mountaintop, the uttermost secret within the wilderness of rock and thorn. Pollen drifted in the air, catching the last light of afternoon, sparkling in slowly falling clouds. The blue sky seemed far above, distant beyond the tops of the boulders.

The Prince had seemed giddy, almost drunk, since they had climbed that last little way down the rocks into the grassy sward. He had run out into the center and whirled around, his arms spread wide. Krista had crouched, nervous, at the edge of the open space. Her arms were covered with goose bumps. This place made her uneasy. Maxian had been laughing and talking to himself the whole time. It set her nerves on edge, hearing him chatter like a little boy.

"Listen!" Maxian looked up, his eyes crinkled up in a grin. "Put your hand on the ground."

Krista, swallowing nervously, knelt on the grass and placed her palms on the thick loam. Sweat beaded on her forehead. Grass twisted under her hands, and she felt the crumbly soil. She closed her eyes.

First there was nothing, only the cool feel of the ground. Then there was something, a hum or a trembling sensation. Then she felt it, deep and distant, muted by unimaginable distance. A slow, heavy surge, a throbbing, the beat of a vast drum. Breath hissed between her clenched teeth, and she jerked her hand away as if burned by a hot skillet.

The mountain had a heartbeat, as slow and regular as a sleeping child. She looked up. The Prince was standing, his face filled from within with joy. It seemed that years of care had dropped away from him.

"Can't you feel it? The power in the earth? It burns like a star, like the sun."

Krista shook her head. She felt nothing but growing fear and a trickle of cold along her back.

"Don't you feel the air?" Maxian was grinning fit to burst. "This place is free of the curse, held in balance by this power in the mountain. I can rest here. I can *work* here." He rubbed his hands together in delight. "This is what I was missing all along—a sanctuary!"

Krista summoned a smile and accepted his embrace, though she felt cold even in the warmth of his arms. When he spun her around, picking her up off of the ground, her eyes were bleak.

Song rose from the dining hall, echoing off firelit walls and round columns in the garden. Alexandros was singing, standing by the fire with his hand on the back of a couch covered with a blue-and-red quilt. He had a strong voice, and it carried well, filled with longing and a hint of glory won. Gaius and Maxian were reclining on couches under the sloped roof that ran around the inner garden of the house. The remains of a hearty dinner were strewn about, and the Walach boys were curled up under the table, snoring softly, their bellies full of roasted pork and grape leaves stuffed with raisins and nutmeats. A round yellow moon had risen and it peered over the peak of the house. It was bright enough to send the stars hurrying before it.

White-armed Hera smiled, and smiling, took the cup.

Alexandros' rough voice rose, ringing through the empty halls and rooms of the house.

Dripping nectar sweet, from the mixing bowl she poured it round.

Krista moved quietly in the room the Prince had chosen for them, slim white hands gathering up clothes and a comb from the side table.

Laughter broke from the happy gods, watching the god of fire breathing hard.

She twisted the bundle into a carrying roll and bound it round with a long length of cloth.

From that hour and all day long they feasted, and no god hungered or lacked a share.

The straw hat hung down her back, held by the twisted leather plait. She turned at the door, frowning, a wicker basket tucked under one arm.

Gorgeous Apollo struck his lyre, calling the Muses sing-

ing, their voice and voice in choir, their vibrant music ringing.

Alexandros' voice faded as she slipped down the hallway, calling softly into each room. She was beginning to sweat, fearing that the Prince or one of the men would come upstairs at any moment.

Sun's fiery light set, each immortal going to rest in his own house, those splendid high halls Hephaestus built in craft and cunning.

There was a clattering sound, and Krista froze, sliding to the nearest wall, her heart hammering. Her hand was tight on a thin knife of iron. Something darted past her feet, small and black as night, skittering on the smooth tile with tiny claws.

So went Olympian Zeus, lord of lightnings, to his bed. There, welcome sleep lay for him.

Krista sprinted down the hallway, her soft-bottomed shoes flashing on the tile, and scooped up the little black cat with a swift jerk. The cat squeaked plaintively as Krista stuffed it headfirst into the wicker basket. She came to a halt—barely daring to breathe—at the top of the stairs down to the garden. She could see Alexandros still standing in the garden, his voice raised to the open sky. Maxian was draining a cup of good red wine. She turned away, her face composed and still.

There he lay, and there he slept and at his side, Hera the Queen, goddess on a golden throne.

Clapping echoed and faint voices rose as Krista slipped out the door into the side yard. Looking up at the moon, she pulled the hood of her cloak over her head. The carrying roll was slung over one shoulder, and the basket was tight in her hand. The side yard was empty and desolate in the pearly light of the moon. Without a sound she slipped away along the line of outbuildings, her face in shadow.

The rattle of pans in the kitchen woke Maxian. Groaning in pain, he screwed his eyes tight. Bright bars of sunlight were slanting in from the high windows of the sleeping room and falling like hammers on his face. He rolled over, pulling a blanket over his head. Drums rattled and rolled in his head, and he could hear the rush of blood in his ears like a waterfall. A hint of jasmine lay on the pillows.

O brilliant physician, he thought, dreading the hurt of further noise. *Heal thyself.*

"My lord?" Someone knocked lightly on the wooden frame of the doorway. Maxian flinched at the noise, but threw back the blanket. Gaius Julius was standing in the doorway, his leathery old face hiding a grin. "Did you sleep well?"

Maxian snarled and rolled out of bed. He was wearing a wrinkled tunic and a variety of wine stains. He ran his fingers through his hair, feeling it lie lank and greasy on his scalp. He scratched an itch behind his ear. His eyes felt like they had been used by mollusks for a mating bed.

"Yes, Gaius, what is it?"

"We've unloaded the books and put them in one of the rooms downstairs as a library, but where do you want the thaumaturgic apparatus? Also, will you summon the Engine to us today? There are more things we will need that are stored in its hold."

Maxian put his head in his hands and concentrated. Blue fire seeped from between his fingers and washed over his face for a moment. When he stood up, his stubble was gone and the hangover was a memory. He smiled at the old Roman, his great, good humor of the day before restored. There was a great deal of work to be done, and he was eager to be about it.

"I have an excellent place to put the Engine, my friend."

Deep in discussion with Gaius Julius, the Prince bustled out of the room and clattered down the stairs. A scrap of scraped parchment that had been laid on the pillow by his head was lost in the tangle of blankets.

* * *

A *carruca* with white-painted sides and a cover of faded blue cloth rolled slowly north along the Imperial road that followed the line of the coast. Four oxen plodded along in front of it, their driver nodding in the midday heat on the high seat at the front of the vehicle. He was a grizzled fellow, a slave with a white beard and a balding pate. A conical hat of straw was perched on his head, but his shoulders were bare and burned red by the sun. Beside him, exhausted from the long hike down the western slope of the mountain, dozed a young woman with a red wicker basket in her lap. With the steady, even pace of the oxen, they would reach the coastal town of Herculaneum by lunchtime. The slave was in no hurry. His cargo of wine tuns wasn't going to spoil if he was a little late, and bouncing it over the graveled road might even ruin the vintage. The patricians who thronged the streets of the port during the summer liked their wine, and it meant a pretty sesterces to his master for the grape to be delivered in full flavor.

Krista clutched the basket to her chest, her eyes slitted against the sun off the ocean. It was bright and muggy. The headache that had nearly driven her to the ground during her nighttime journey down the mountain had begun to ease, receding slowly like the tide on a shallow shore. The amulet burned against her chest, a hot point on her skin. She dared not take it off yet. *I will kill the Prince and his servants,* she chanted to herself in the safety of her mind. *I will ruin his plan.*

With each recitation, the headache eased and the flickering black glow that came and went at the edge of her vision faded a little more. She shivered, feeling cold creeping along her bones. Even the hot sun did not drive it out. Only one thing would.

I will kill the Prince. He will fail. He will be destroyed.

The wagon rolled north, great wooden wheels rattling on the road.

I will kill him.

THE PORT OF LEUKE KOME ON THE COAST OF THE
HEDJAZ

)(

Black smoke crawled into the upper air, a curling pillar rising slowly over the town. Mohammed strode down a narrow street, the gravel and stones crunching under his boots. The sun was high, and he was feeling the weariness of the day. The port lay ahead, near the burning buildings that fueled the smoke cloud. The Quryash chieftain turned as the street ended in a dusty plaza. One- and two-story buildings built of pale tan lime-and-sandstone blocks surrounded the square. White plaster covered most of the walls. No one was in evidence, though by this hour the streets should have seen some traffic. A squad of the Sahaba trotted along after him, the iron rings of their armor jingling as they moved. Like all the men in his army, they had put aside the colored braid of their tribes, choosing instead the green and white of the Tanukh. About half of the men carried round shields of wood with iron bosses, adorned with a cheap russet paint. The others bore bows and quivers fashioned of boiled leather, packed with black-fletched arrows, on their backs.

A sloping street led off of the plaza, leading down to the harbor. Mohammed walked stiffly—he had spent too much time on a horse in the past week—and the descent made his thighs and ankles complain. From the vantage of the little hill, he could make out the ships tied up to the stone quays in the harbor and the bulk of the warehouses that lined the bay. Leuke Kome stood on a barren shore, a dozen leagues from anything that bore green leaves or a hint of water. The town existed only because it owned the sole harborage along this long stretch of desolate coastline. Despite that, there were still a dozen ships in the harbor. A hundred and eighty miles to the north, along a long, narrow valley, stood the Nabatean capital of Petra and the road to the great cities along the Strata Triana.

Leuke Kome had served as an entrepot for the Petran trade in silk, cotton, perfume, rare spices, steel ingots, poppy paste, and gems for eight hundred years. Its wealth, its whole reason for being, lay in the safe harbor and the stone warehouses that rose two and three stories tall behind the road that ran along the piers. Most of the black smoke was billowing from the windows of one of those warehouses.

Mohammed's face was storm-cloud dark with anger. A faint breeze was blowing up from the sea, carrying a sharp smell and bending the pillars of smoke inland. Ten years spent in the trade, traveling the length and breadth of Arabia and beyond, even to India and the glorious, decadent cities of the Empire, had not been lost on him. He knew many spices, fabrics, and woods by taste and smell.

The Quryash chieftain and his bodyguards reached the bayside road and turned. Other bands of Sahaba soldiers were beginning to gather as they finished their sweep through the town. When the sun had risen, hours ago, the port had still been in Imperial hands. Now it was Mohammed's possession, and he was furious that a quarter or more of its worth to him was being consumed as he watched. One of the Sahaba guardsmen coughed, catching a whiff of the sting in the air. Mohammed raised his riding scarf over his mouth and nose. Burning pepper let off a dangerous humor.

Mohammed had thought to leave Mekkah in secret, accompanied by only a few of his companions. The Tanukh, he knew, had sworn themselves to his service. Those bonds, forged in the battle furnace of Palmyra, would endure until his death or theirs. The men of the city, even his kinsmen, he had not expected to follow. Even after the capture of Yathrib and the extirpation of the Bani-Hashim and their allies, it had not occurred to the Quryash chieftain that he had become the ruler of a people.

The Mekkan clans had fought and feuded and spilt each other's blood for centuries, and Mohammed had not thought to change them. He had sought to take the blood-price from the murderers who had left his child dead in his arms. He had hoped to crush the resistance to his adopted house and secure the patrimony of his children. In that, the promulgation of a common law for the people of both cities had been his aim. The friendship of the Ben-Sarid and the obedience of the Quryash had been a welcome surprise. He had not told Jalal or Shadin about his dreams or the full truth of what the voice had said on the mountaintop, but they had followed him forth from the city nonetheless.

They had ridden out before dawn, in full darkness, finding the road only by the faint light of a crescent moon. Even then Mohammed had been wrapped in thought, listening to the echoes of the voice from the air. He had not noticed that the ranks of the Tanukh had swollen as they had ridden north. The appearance of Uri and his Ben-Sarid horsemen had seemed natural, for the Sarid had fought at their side at Yathrib.

Then dawn was almost upon them, and Mohammed had stopped. He knew that the Lord of the Seven Heavens had chosen him to undertake a dreadful task in the world. That thought filled his heart with a sense of rightness that had always eluded him. That emptiness in his soul, that yearning to find something to set his shoulder to, some task worthy of his full devotion, had driven him out from his house and across the face of the world. Now it was filled, and he knew that thanks were owed.

So, with the sun preparing to crawl over the jagged peaks and desolate mountains to the east of Mekkah, he had reined in his horse and dismounted. Without looking up, he had unrolled a blanket from the saddle of his mare and knelt on the gritty sand. Even though the white fire that had filled him that day before the Ka'ba was gone, there was never a moment when he did not feel the distant voice of the stone. He knelt on the blanket and bowed toward the southeast, toward the sacred precincts.

Make your place of worship free of ornament and distraction, the voice had said from the clear air. *How can you come to know the mind of the merciful and compassionate god if your eye is assailed by graven images and your ear by the importuning of priests?*

Mohammed did not bow down before the Black Stone or the ancient house; he knelt before the Lord of the Wasteland that was in everything he could see or touch. The priests of the temples that his men had torn down had not understood that. In time they would.

When he stood he brushed the sand from the blanket and rolled it up. As he did so there was a susurration in the cool morning air, a rustling and a muted, clinking sound. He looked about, puzzled, and stopped in surprise, the blanket half folded.

Ten thousand men were rising as well all around him. The road behind the clot of Tanukh was clogged with horses and camels and pack mules. Tribal banners and flags fluttered in the air, lending the army a festive air. Men of every tribe in the city, and some he had never seen before, were rolling up their own blankets or swinging back into the saddle. Mohammed raised an eyebrow and turned to find Jalal standing at his side, fists resting on the top of his curved bow. Shadin and Khalid were already seated on their horses, long *kaffiyeh* trailing in the dawn breeze.

"Who are these?" Mohammed gestured toward the columns of men and the thickets of lances, sparkling in the light of the rising sun. Jalal smiled, his grim, scarred features cracking like a stone splitting under the stroke of a chisel.

"Men who would follow you wherever you may lead them, my lord."

And so they had ridden forth from Mekkah with an

army, and made their way into the wastelands of the North, into the barren desolation of the Hedjaz.

A timber, burned through by the inferno raging inside the pepper warehouse, cracked like a sling-bullet against a shield. Part of the roof of the building fell in with a roar, sending sparks and a plume of thick black smoke roiling up. Waves of heat beat against Mohammed's face, and he took a dozen steps back. That left him at the edge of the stone pier, his hand on a stumpy round piling. The inside of the warehouse was a raging red heart as the close-packed barrels of pepper and marjoram burned. Mohammed felt the heat like a blow to his heart—the contents of such a warehouse were worth a thousand times their weight in gold on the trading tables of Constantinople or Rome or Saguntum. Any kind of spice—pepper was most highly prized—was easy to ship and carry and in vast demand. The Roman fondness for hot spices was legendary across the length and breadth of the world. The craving had made Palmyra and Petra rich. It had made Khadijah and the House of Khuwaylid wealthy, too.

"How did this happen?" Mohammed's voice rasped with repressed anger. To him the contents of these warehouses meant even more than they had to his dead wife or the Palmyrenes. Every ounce of spice that whirled away into the sky or fell as a fine ash over the town meant fewer sheaves of arrows, fewer suits of armored mail, fewer swords and lances and spears for his army.

Jalal squared his shoulders and stepped forward from the company of Sahaba, who had deployed themselves as a cordon around the burning building. His face was carefully blank. The Tanukh captain knew what lost supplies and arms meant to an army on the move. It might be his life that the fire cost, a month from now or more. "We were a fraction late, lord. I tried to take the merchant down with a bow shot, but he managed to get an oil lamp cast inside before he went down."

Mohammed met the man's eyes, and they were steel

hard for a moment. "Where is the merchant?"

"There, lord." Jalal pointed with his chin to a huddled form lying at the edge of the dock. A dark stain of dried blood pooled under the corpse.

"Are there others still alive?"

Jalal nodded and motioned to two of his men. The Sahaba spearmen disappeared into the ground level of one of the two-story brick buildings that lined the waterfront. This one had a balcony on the second floor with ornamental railings of crisscrossed wooden slats. Mohammed had seen the style before, in the Roman cities that ringed the Inner Sea. When he had been among the Imperials for a long time, it had seemed natural. Now it seemed wasteful to use wood carted down from the mountains of Syria when brick or stone would do. The guardsmen returned, escorting a thin, worried-looking man with close-cropped hair and a smooth-shaven face.

"What is your name and business?" Mohammed felt his Latin come with difficulty. It had been some time since he had needed it. The Palmyrenes and his friend Ahmet had spoken Aramaic, even as he had done since he was a child. The Roman merchant seemed relieved to hear his mother tongue, and shook his arms free of the Sahaba guardsmen.

"I am Marcus Licinus, factor for the House of Flavius. I trade in slaves, fine woods, timber, ivory, and salt."

Mohammed nodded to himself, gauging the truth of the man's words by the style of his tunic, the well-worn leather belt around the Roman's waist, and his scuffed boots. The fellow had callused hands, worn from pulling a sail-rope or handling a horse or camel. This was a working merchant, not someone who grew fat and slothful off of the work of others. The deep tan that marked the Roman was a good sign, too: He had been in Arabia for some time.

"I am Mohammed," the Quryash chieftain said simply. "The warehouses are full here, and ships ride empty in the harbor. Why is that?"

Marcus Licinus' eyes narrowed, taking in the simple white robe that Mohammed had chosen to go over his scaled iron armor and the pearl-handled saber at his side. The Roman spared a glance for the Sahaba standing nearby, too, and Mohammed could see that he was puzzled by the absence of tribal markings. Too, the green banner of the Sahaba, marked only with a curved white sword and a simple crescent moon, was unfamiliar to him.

"Lord Mohammed," the Roman said carefully in precisely enunciated Aramaic, "is there a quarrel between your people and mine?"

Mohammed raised a hand, stopping the merchant from continuing, and shook his head. "There is no quarrel between our *people*, noble Licinus. But I have a dispute with the Emperor of the East, this one called Heraclius. He has done great evil, and I will call him to account for it before the great and merciful God. I see the question in your eyes. I have taken this town into my hand because it furthers the will of the Merciful and Compassionate One. No one will be taken slave or murdered while I command."

The merchant's face was a carefully controlled mask, but Mohammed had stood across the bargaining table from too many men like this one. Each word was being weighed and considered while an agile mind tried to piece together a fabric that bore a recognizable pattern. "You have not answered my question, noble Licinus. Has trade from the north ceased?"

The Roman nodded sharply, having come to some conclusion in his own mind. "Yes, Lord Mohammed. The last two caravans that we expected from Petra have failed to arrive, while ships have continued to come in from the south. The town sent a party out to the north a week ago, attempting to find out what had transpired. Do you know?"

Mohammed shook his head and turned away, lost in thought. The Sahaba took the Roman by the upper arms and marched him back into the taverna. Jalal stood waiting, now joined by the blocky shape of Shadin and the leaner more elegant figure of Ben-Sarid. Mohammed nodded to them, his mind turning over the meanings of the merchant's report. "Jalal, send scouts out to the north and east," he said. "Find out if the way to Aelana and Petra is clear or not. We must know, and quickly, if we are to make our way past the Wadi Rum before full summer is upon us. Find the missing caravans, if you can. Shadin—quarter the town and bring me every merchant you can find. I will want to speak with each in turn. Round up all of the horses, mules, donkeys, and camels that you can find as well. This is our last opportunity to outfit our men before we enter the Empire. Do not waste it. The Lord of the Wasteland loves a well-prepared man."

The two Tanukh nodded and moved away through the loitering crowd of Sahaba, gathering up their lieutenants and subcaptains in their wake. The Ben-Sarid raised a thin, elegant eyebrow and leaned forward on his spear. Mohammed clapped him on the shoulder, inclining his head.

"And you, my friend, I need you to find me guides— both men who know the way from here to Nabatea and those who have been into the Empire before . . . we will need to move quickly. Apportion these men among the *qatiba* so that each squadron has a guide of their own. Go among the townspeople as well and find those who can work metal or stone. We will need engineers where we are going. Sailors, too."

Uri nodded sharply, his dark eyes sharp with appreciation. The army of the Sahaba would not be a motley horde of desert bandits once it reached the Roman border.

Five days on the road from Mekkah, after his evening devotions, Mohammed had been walking among the campfires of his army when he had heard the ring of steel on steel and harsh shouts of rage. Even his Tanukh guards had been surprised by the speed he showed, sprinting among the tents and into the middle of a knot of struggling men.

"This is not the righteous path," Mohammed had shouted, clouting one of the two men locked in a death embrace on the side of the head with his pommel. The man went down hard, sprawling on the sandy ground. "We are brothers here, and brothers do not raise a hand in anger against one another!"

The other man, shouting in rage, tried to shove Mohammed aside. He was an al'Taif tribesman, his face marked by ritual scarring and lines of ink driven into his flesh with needles. The Quryash chieftain shrugged aside the man's hand and cracked him in the face with his fist. The al'Taif warrior staggered, turning and seeing Mohammed for the first time. The man's eyes widened, making out the simple robe and the bristly black beard. Then the Tanukh were there, forcing themselves into the crowd.

"All those who ride under my banner are brothers." Mohammed raised his voice, letting it carry over the heads of the men at the campfire and beyond. The noise and commotion had drawn many from the other tents. "Why did these men fight?"

There was a moment of silence, and Mohammed saw that there were two groups: more al'Taif and some of the Ben-Sarid. *So*, he thought, a *clan feud*. He considering unleashing his anger upon them, but then a thought occurred, and he put the blazing rage away. "The al'Taif was insulted by the Ben-Sarid?" He motioned to the Tanukh to clear a space around the fire, which was still burning merrily. "There was old blood between them? A matter of a cousin's uncle, killed in a night raid a generation ago?" He stopped in front of the al'Taif that he had struck. The man's nose was bleeding, matting his beard. "Had you seen this Ben-Sarid before today?"

The man refused to meet his eyes. Mohammed nodded, his face marked by disgust. "Alone of all men in the world, you are Sahaba, you are my companions. You put behind you the race or a clan or a tribe of your birth when you joined me. Each day you bow down before the Great and Merciful God, submitting yourselves to His will, as is right. In the eyes of the Lord of the Heavens, you are all equals. There will be no matter of grudges or revenge in this brotherhood. Our enemy is terrible and strong, grown fat with hate and sin and fear. If we are to throw him down, we must be as one—a single hand striking a furious blow."

Mohammed turned, leaving the harsh words hanging in the air, and stalked off into the night.

The next day, each man in his army was assigned to a squadron or *qatiba* by lot, without regard for clan or nation. Henceforth, each man would eat, drink, ride, and sleep only with his *qatiba*-brothers. The Tanukh, Quryash, and Ben-Sarid troopers—by necessity—were parceled out as officers and commanders. Jalal was placed in command of the left wing of the army, what Mohammed termed the *maisarah* and Shadin the right or *maimanah*. Had the brash youth Khalid been with them, Mohammed would have set him to command the scouts, foragers, and outriders. Instead, he placed Ben-Sarid in command of the *muqaddama*. For himself he retained command of the core of heavy armored cavalry, the *qalb*. So ordered, the army continued riding north through the harsh land.

The house of the governor of the port was a simple two-story affair, set back from the shore a hundred feet or so. Mohammed stood on the roof of plaster and mud over interleaved timbers. At some time in the past the governor's wife had erected a sunshade of striped linen held up on wooden poles. Today it was welcome, for the heat of summer was beginning to make itself felt. The sun was a brassy disk in a pale white sky, and even the waves of the sea seemed flattened and subdued. Sahaba messengers squatted in the shade, waiting for Mohammed's word. His bodyguards were downstairs, sleeping in the cool recesses of the house's common room and *triniculum*.

Mohammed shaded his eyes, peering out to sea. Bright-colored triangles in red, blue, and green could be made out on the horizon. A fleet was coming up from the south, making slow headway with the mild wind. Within the day the ships would make landfall in the port, carrying unknown cargoes and news from Yemen or San'a or India. Ben-Sarid's outriders had seen them first, down the coast, and had hurried back with the news. Mohammed was unsure as to whether he considered this a good omen or not. The loot of the port was in hand, most of it already packed onto mules and camels. He had little drayage for more, though he could be supremely lucky and find that a shipload of Indian water-steel blades was about to fall into his hand.

He doubted it, though. Most likely it would be more pepper and cotton and bolts of raw silk. He scratched his beard in thought, wondering if there was anything else that it could be.

Bah! Shadin's men are in place. They know the plan. We shall just see what we shall see.

The new war banner, a triangular pennant of green cloth with a crescent moon and a white saber marked on it, flapped slowly in a desultory breeze. Mohammed looked at it as he turned to go downstairs, shaking his head in amusement. Jalal had been quite proud of it when a contingent of the men presented it to Mohammed the day before they had attacked the port.

"A crescent moon?" Mohammed had not liked the symbol. It reminded him of the statue-crowded temples that infested the cities of northern Syria. "What does that mean?"

Jalal had grinned and stroked his curly salt-and-pepper beard. "It is the moon that watched us go forth from Mekkah, my lord. You say that the merciful and compassionate one watches us always; well—he watched us from the moon that night."

A sixty-foot coaster, lateen-rigged and showing a high prow and stern, drifted close to the stone quay. The ship was painted with cracking light blue paint and ornamented with yellow and black eyes facing forward. Sailors in turbans and loincloths leaned on the railing, long poles in their hands. A pair of long sweeps, driven by the hollow beat of a drum, had edged the ship into the harbor. A dozen more merchantmen just like it were also crowding into the bay. Two of Shadin's men were on the pier, reaching for the first rope to be thrown from the ship.

Mohammed stood in shadow, just inside the open double doors of the warehouse at the end of the pier. The building had been emptied out and was now filled with his men. The small Imperial garrison had been overwhelmed in the initial attack—many of them had still been in bed, sleeping off a night of drinking—when the Sahaba had swarmed over the walls and through the southern gate of the town. The legionaries were now living on bread and water in the basement of the governor's house and their *lorica segmentata* were providing a brace of Mohammed's men with badly needed armor. The Quryash did not think he would need men armored from head to toe in *spangenhelm*-style helmets and full armor for today's work, but it never paid to underestimate one's enemy, even unsuspecting sailors and merchants at the end of a long haul up from the ports of Aden and Abyssinia. Most, like the crews of the *dhows* that were coming into the harbor, would be more interested in drink and food and women than girding their loins for war.

The coaster bumped against the quay and settled. Shadin's men tied the ship off to the stone buttresses that served as mooring poles. On the ship, the sailors clustered on the central deck, and a long plank walkway appeared. It dipped in the air and then fell, rattling, to the stone pier. A man dressed in a flamboyant orange hat shaped like an inflated octopus with tassels coming off it strode down the springy walkway. When he reached the shore, he fell onto his knees and kissed the earth. Behind him a crowd of men were piling off the ship, their legs wobbling. Some of them had spears.

Mohammed hissed, and the Sahaba in the warehouse tensed. There was a faint rattle of metal on metal as men drew their swords or put arrow to string on their bows. At Mohammed's side, Shadin was whispering quick orders to his runners. Two boys slipped through the press of men in the dark warehouse.

"Bowmen, front." Shadin's growl seemed loud in the enclosed space, but Mohammed knew that no one outside could hear. "Make ready to charge."

On the quay, men continued to pour off the boat. Another coaster had tied up at the next pier to the south, and more men were debarking. They had swords, spears, and bows as well. Mohammed felt a sick queasiness in his stomach. An army was debarking on the docks, and he had only Shadin's *maimanah* to face them. Jalal, the heavy cavalry, and the scouts were all up in the hills behind the town, learning to fight in formation. The Quryash clapped Shadin on the shoulder and moved up to the edge of the door. The armed men on the dock were moving forward carefully, their spears a thicket in front of them. The captain in his ebullient hat was at their head, looking about carefully. The town remained sleepily quiet, dozing in the sun.

Mohammed squinted at the bright light. The fellow in the hat seemed to be peering back at him.

"Hello? Is anyone around?" The voice sounded familiar, but it was out of context here.

Mohammed grunted in surprise as the sea captain took off the orange bladder and wiped sweat from a high and noble brow. The Quryash stepped out of the warehouse and slid his saber back into its sheath with a *ting* of metal on metal. The sea captain and his men started with surprise to see the figure appear before them.

"Are you lost?" Mohammed's voice rang off the storefronts and stone walls of the harbor. "This is not Yemen and San'a! You will have to turn around and go the other way." He raised his hand and pointed south.

The sea captain laughed in surprise, showing bright white teeth and a neatly trimmed black beard. He swept the fantastical hat into a flourish and bowed, going down on one knee. Some of his men knelt as well, though others were looking around in suspicion, their faces clouded with uncertainty. Mohammed strode forward, and the warehouse at his back suddenly vomited armed men. The men on the quay backed up hurriedly, taken aback by the appearance of grim-looking Sahaba.

"I am not lost," declared Khalid Al'Walid in a loud voice as he tossed the hat into the water. "I am returned from the south, from San'a and Yemen! Just a little early, is all."

Mohammed looked the youth up and down, his beard lighted by a grin. When the army of the companions had left Mekkah, the Quryash had sent the young rascal and his band of mercenaries to the south, toward the coastal highlands of Yemen. That land had been under the sway of the Sassanids for almost thirty years and there was supposed to be a Persian garrison at the city of San'a. Mohammed had wanted to know if this was still true and if it was, to make sure that the Persians did not meddle in the affairs of the Arabs while he was in the north. After he had scouted the Imperial frontier and divined the lay of the land, then he would deal with them.

"The Persians ran you off, did they? Where did you steal these boats? They're not mine, are they?" Mohammed's eye glinted dangerously. It would be just like the pup to commandeer Bani-Hashim or Quryash ships from one of the coastal ports to catch up with the army.

"No!" Khalid looked hurt at the implication. "These are spoils of war—and fairly gained, too. We captured them in port at Muza. They were just sitting there, and everyone was so eager to meet you . . . I decided that you needed a fleet. Here it is!"

Mohammed turned the youth around and gestured at the ships that had come into the harbor. All of them had found a place to tie up, and more men were debarking from each one. The ships seemed to be packed to the railings with men, hobbled camels, bundles of goods, and barrels. "I sent you south with two thousand men—both yours and mine—to scout a position of the enemy. You seem to have come back with rather more than that . . ."

Khalid clapped the older man on the shoulder, still grin-

ning widely. "Come, let's get in out of the sun and I'll tell
you all about it."

Mohammed shook his head—more troubles were sure
to come of this. He signaled to Shadin, and the mercenary
moved to join them.

"Shadin, incorporate these men immediately. Separate
them out, one or two to each *qaitaba*. All save Khalid's
own men—put them with the other *muqaddama* scouts."

Shadin nodded sharply. They had already gone through
all of this before, during the ride north.

". . . and so I told them that you had foretold a great war,
one that would drive the demons from the earth and cast
down Rome and Persia both. I told them of your visions
and the Light that touched us all at the Ka'ba. I tell you,
Lord Mohammed, it was like a spark in grain dust—there
were four thousand men pledging themselves to the
Straight Path before I could blink."

Khalid leaned back on the couch, scratching at his
closely cropped beard and smiling at the memory. He, Mohammed, Shadin, Jalal, and Uri were sitting in the upper
room of the governor's house. Platters that had held bulgur
wheat in paprika sauce and roast lamb and hummus were
scattered on a low table between them. The Quryash was
seated at the head of the little gathering, his back to the
window, facing the door. Outside, warm night lay on the
port and the town, broken only by the lights of watchfires
on the crumbling walls and the murmur of men going
about their business after dark. Mohammed looked around,
gauging the mood of the other men.

Jalal and Shadin were as solid as ever, their weather-
worn, scarred faces at rest. The brothers had seen armies
come and go, fighting in a hundred wars around the rim
of the world. He supposed they had been born in some
dusty frontier town—Rome's frontier? Persia's?—it did
not matter. They had sworn themselves to him in the ruin
of Palmyra and had not left his side since. Jalal looked
back, the corners of his eyes crinkling with a hidden smile.

The bowman had never been a general before and found that it suited him. Shadin nodded, too. The hulking swordsman would do whatever the situation demanded.

Uri was another matter. The Ben-Sarid had always found Mekkah a hostile place because they lived apart with their own traditions, laws, and God. It must grate upon the proud chief to see his tribesmen subsumed into the Army of the Companions. The lean, dark man had the bearing of a prince. Was Mohammed his king, then? Mohammed lifted his chin in question, catching his boyhood friend's eyes. Uri shrugged and then nodded. Mohammed made a mental note to talk to Uri later, alone, to see what troubled his mind.

The Quryash turned back to Khalid and nodded slightly himself. The addition of five thousand fresh troops was welcome, even though most of the men who had followed the youth from the south were sailors. Then there was the matter of horses or camels for them—they had brought only a few hundred in their ships. The rest would have to walk. The Lord of the Wasteland had blessed them, though, for the capture of the Persian armory in San'a had netted them a full hundred suits of the lamellar mail favored by the Sassanid knights. The Sahaba now counted nearly eight hundred fully armored horsemen among their number.

"Well met, then, young Al'Walid. We had been waiting for the next merchant convoy to come into the trap, but now that you are here, we will move north."

Mohammed unrolled a map inked on a scroll of parchment. It had been part of the spoils of the governor's house. Spidery lines and crabbed little writing in the Imperial script showed the land between Leuke Kome at the southern end of the map all the way to the highlands of Nabatea and beyond, up into the Decapolis on the east and Judaea on the west. Mohammed traced a line overland from the port along the narrow arm of the sea that ran up to Aelana. "Our first march must be to follow the garrison road to the Roman port of Aelana, here at the southern end of the Wadi Arabah. My intent is this, to make a strong raid into the Nabatean heartland, here beyond their capital at Petra, and see what forces have returned to the area."

He looked up, his face grim. The singing voice that had first come to him on the mountaintop urged him to all speed, but he knew that he had to temper that with caution. He did not have an army of *jinn* at his disposal.

"All of the Imperial Legions were stripped out of the entire Judean coast last year and sent into the far north to fight the Persians. The armies of Nabatea, Palmyra, and the cities of the Decapolis were smashed at Emesa and then ground to bits in the siege of Palmyra. If luck holds, there will be little to prevent us from ranging far and wide, unhindered."

Jalal raised an eyebrow, his own eyes straying over the map.

"And our destination, Lord Mohammed? We can strike as we please with this force, but the changes you have made and the training we undertake at your direction— these things indicate that you have more in mind than a simple raid."

Mohammed smiled grimly. If the singing voice in his mind did not fill him with surety, he would have turned aside from his course as a sure road to death and bleached bones beside some desert road.

"Our first destination is here." His forefinger marked the distance from the symbol that represented Petra to the north and east, to a square marked in red squatting at the center of the Decapolis. "The great Legion encampment at Lejjun. If memory serves, there is a great armory there and, more to my liking, a store of heavy siege equipment: rams, disassembled towers, ballistae, all kinds of artillery. Enough for two full Legions."

The Arab generals raised their heads at this. The use of such equipment was known to all of them, but it was not the way of the tribes to spend effort against the walls of cities and fortresses. That was Rome's game, and its great strength. The desert peoples came and went like the wind, taking what they would and then retiring in the face of the plodding Legion. A siege? That was not in their blood.

"What city?" Khalid leaned forward, his face filled with eagerness.

"You will see," Mohammed muttered, looking down at the map. It was a long way to go to reach the great Legion camp, and anything could happen between here and there. "But there is little time . . ."

"My lord, if that is so, then let me take our fleet and some reliable men." Khalid's eyes were ablaze with his eagerness. His thin, well-manicured finger stabbed at the map. "While you advance along the coastal road, let me land at Aelana—even as I planned to land here today. By the time the Sahaba reach the port, it will be in our hands."

Mohammed grimaced and opened his mouth to refute the boy's plan, but Jalal was leaning over the map, too, and there was a gleam in his eye.

"My lord," the thick-shouldered Tanukh said, "we can send the infantry by sea with all of the heavy supplies in the ships. Then we won't have to drag them across a hundred miles of desert and badlands. Wagons, too, if there is space in these fat-bellied coasters . . ."

Then Mohammed did smile.

THE ISLAND OF THIRA

Groaning in pain, her limbs loose with exhaustion and trembling, Shirin flopped down on the bare cot that served as her bed. A thin cotton blanket lay across the pallet, and it possessed a prickly straw mattress that never failed to stab her in the back when she was trying to sleep. The dormitories for the *ephebe* of the Temple of the Huntress were neither gracious nor comfortable. One of the older sisters had mentioned in passing that the dormitory was one of the original caverns hewn from the rock of the island by the first Sisters. To Shirin's eye, they had not been improved since that time. She knew from experience that the higher chambers, cut into the cliffs above the lagoon, were both inviting and well furnished. The student dormitories, however, were not. She lay on her back, a little twisted to the side to avoid the worst of the prickles, and stared at the rough, gray ceiling in a daze.

It was the end of another day of the backbreaking torture that comprised their physical conditioning. Unfortunately for her bruised and tortured muscles it was not the classical Persian gymnasium, filled with a lot of baths, massages, light sparring with a blunted spear or sword, recitations of epic lays by notable poets, or even ignoble lays conducted by sweaty would-be playwrights in the back of the towel room. It was hard work, harder than the late fall hunt or the exercises that Thyatis had put her through on the long trip by sea around Arabia. Shirin lay still, trying to keep the muscles on the insides of her thighs from seizing up due to sheer fatigue. Worse, the Princess had thought that she had been in good shape when she had arrived on the island.

Someone touched the bottom of her foot, and she blinked awake. She had not realized that she had fallen asleep. The dim radiance from the high circular windows in the roof of the hall had gone, leaving only the pale guttering flame of a torch by the door. Her cot flexed as someone sat down next to her.

Shirin's nostrils flared, and she knew that it was the Gothic girl, Claudia. Even in the spare confines of the dormitory, the willowy blonde managed to find some kind of sweet scent for her hair. It might be jasmine or juniper rosin. There was a touch on her arm.

"Shi? Are you awake?"

"Yes," hissed the Princess, suddenly feeling the throb of her upper arms and the insides of her wrists. A four-hour stint with the wooden man left the muscles of her arms like jelly. "What time is it?"

"After dinner," Claudia answered with a smile in her voice. "I brought you some. Cook was not pleased, but I told her you were studying extra hard in the *bibliotheca,* and she relented."

Shirin levered herself up and wedged her back against the smooth stone wall of the cavern. Claudia put a wooden bowl in her hands—it was still warm and smelled faintly of fish. Shirin wrinkled up her nose. The diet of everyone on the island was, not surprisingly, mostly fish. The dark blue seas around Thira yielded an enormous variety of shapes, sizes, colors, and tastes of fish—but it was all still fish. Shirin had never really liked fish. She took the cover off the bowl and put it aside. The warm, tart smell of fish stew assailed her nostrils and she sighed, picking up the spoon. At least there was a pickle.

After she was done, Claudia took the bowl and spoon away. The Gothic girl had sat quietly on the end of Shirin's bed the whole time, which Shirin thought was a little odd, but it seemed perfectly reasonable to the barbarian woman. Shirin flexed her fingers, feeling the tremor in her muscles. It was a bad day, she thought sourly, when even your fingertips were sore.

"Shi? Is it true what they say about you?"

Shirin folded her legs under her as she had seen the Lady Mikele do. It was more comfortable for sitting than squatting was. "What is true? And who are *they?*" Inwardly Shirin shook her head in dismay. The gossip in the Palace of Birds in Ctesiphon had flown faster than a shrike; why should the temple be any different?

"The older girls—the ones who are about to go out into the world—they say that you are a princess, that you were married to an emperor. Is that true?" The Gothic girl's voice was tinged with a little awe and a little envy.

Unseen in the dark, Shirin rolled her dark brown eyes. *Oh dear,* she thought, *some things never change* . . . "I will answer your question," she said with asperity, "if you will answer some of mine."

"Oh, of course!" Claudia clapped her hands together in delight. Shirin gritted her teeth.

"Very well," the Khazar woman said, "I was a princess and I was married to an emperor and I did live in a great palace in a rich and lovely city far away. It was like a dream, but eventually I woke up."

"Oh, no . . . did something bad happen?"

Shirin nodded in the darkness, though she wasn't sure that the Gothic girl could see her. "Ah, now, it's my turn to ask a question. You've been here longer than I—when can we leave this place?"

Shirin took two paces, her back stiff with repressed rage, turned, and then took two more back. The cell was not large, only big enough for a woven reed mat on the floor, a bed no larger than Shirin's own cot, and a folding screen made of pale white paper painted with delicate images of birds and a mountain shrouded in clouds. An oil lamp made from a ceramic bowl and a wick provided a wan yellow light.

"This is insane. I will not stay *here* on this fish-stinking island for another four *years* before I am allowed to see my children." The Khazar woman's voice slid unerringly upward in scale, trembling toward a scream of rage.

"That is the rule and the law that binds the *ephebe* once they have sworn themselves to the service of the Goddess." Mikele's voice was quiet and calm, with only a hint of the lilting accent that normally colored her speech. "You have sworn yourself to her service—before the Matron, no less."

Shirin spun savagely on her heel. She wanted very much to smash her fist into the calm, round face of her teacher, but raw animal instinct held her back. Her training had progressed well, but there was no way that she could face the supple skill of the master with her mind clouded with rage. The result would be painful and quick. "I will not abandon my children," she bit out between clenched teeth. "I will not come back to them after four years denned on this island to find them fully grown and looking upon me with strangers' eyes."

Mikele nodded her head, letting the long wave of her unbound black hair fall over her shoulder. She had been combing her hair when Shirin had barged into her room. The Chin woman was sitting on the bed, her legs crossed under her, with a mother-of-pearl comb in one hand. Her hair was very long, reaching well past her waist. During the day, on the training floor of the gymnasium, she kept it bound up and held in place by long silver pins.

"If you go out now," Mikele said in an infuriatingly calm voice, "you will place yourself and your children in greater danger. This is why Thyatis brought you to this place."

"She brought me here to keep me safe!" Shirin's fists clenched hard, the knuckles whitening. "I am mewed up here for my safety? For my children's safety? Everything is for safety's sake!"

Shirin bit her knuckle, her fine white teeth digging into the flesh.

"I traded one prison for another, one with harder beds and worse food. . . ." Her voice was a harsh whisper.

Mikele stood, unfolding gracefully from sitting to standing like a crane dipping toward the water. "You are not here to be safe," she said. Her hands gathered her hair and pulled it behind her head. "There is no safety in this place, or any other. Remember that, Shirin. Thyatis brought you here to be trained, so that you could go about in the world with open eyes."

"That is not what she said," Shirin muttered in a petulant tone. "She said that I would be safe here."

Mikele nodded again, her quick hands braiding her hair and arranging it. "Thyatis loves you and wishes to keep you from harm. She is a sweet girl, but she is still naïve in the ways of the world. Hiding you here will only delay the attentions of these Kings. This is a time for you—and it will prove little enough, even if you stay here the full term of years—to find some focus."

Shirin hung her head. She had not thought about the agents of the Eastern Emperor that were still, doubtless, watching and listening in the eastern ports and cities, waiting for news of her to come to their ears. Her body and blood were the prize for these Emperors, and if she were found, her children would be forfeit.

"While you and your children are apart," Mikele said, seeing Shirin's thought like a cloud in a clear sky, "each of you are anonymous. They could be any four youngsters, you any woman. But if you are found together, there will be greater danger. If you stay here, you will learn how to deal with that danger."

The Khazar woman looked up, meeting the older woman's eyes. Fury burned in them. "I am not a prize," she said in a flat voice. "I refuse to be a bauble passed from hand to hand. I will find my children and take them out of the Empire, beyond the reach of Theodore's agents."

"And Thyatis?" Mikele cocked her head to one side, her calm brown eyes fixed on Shirin. "What of her?"

Shirin shook her head and stood, her full lips compressed into a tight line. "Thyatis can take care of herself. If she wants to come with me, we will be together. Otherwise, I will find someone else—someone who treats me as an equal rather than as a pretty necklace to be put away in a lock-box until festival day."

Mikele turned up the sleeves of the long, roomy shirt that she wore. Her wrists were graceful and slim, though her grip was strong enough to match any man. A lacework of tiny white scars marked the insides of her wrists and arms.

"If you leave without the permission of the Matron," Mikele said softly, "the Sisters will turn their backs on you. You will not have their help or guidance. If you leave now, before you have completed the training, you will not be fully awake or aware. You will continue to move in a world of shadows."

Shirin shook her head. The loneliness in her heart and the longing to see her children again, to feel their arms wrapped around her neck in a hug, to see them laughing, was far stronger than the teacher's warning.

"My children are more important than this training. They are more important than your sisterhood."

Mikele arched an eyebrow at the spite in the words, but she said nothing as Shirin stalked out. When the Khazar woman was gone, Mikele leaned over and snuffed the lamp wick with her thumb and forefinger. She sat in the darkness, her breathing steady and even, eyes closed while she waited for the dawn.

Surf boomed against the cliff, sending foam rocketing into the air. It fell in a sparkling mist on the black rocks, making them shine and glisten. Shirin, her hair bundled up under a straw hat, clung to the cliff face, feeling it tremble with each blow of the waves. Her tunic was soaked with spray, clinging to her like a skin. In the stiff wind it was cold on her flesh. A hundred feet above her, the top of the cliff leaned out over the precipice, held together by a verge of fat-leafed shrubs and a scrawny tree. Below her, the sea thudded against the walls of Thira, surging with enormous power in its blue-green depths. Shirin grimaced, feeling her toehold slowly slipping as seawater flung up from the wave tops pooled around the toe of her boot.

She reached out and snared the lip of a jutting piece of stone. The cliffs were old lava, fused by the terrible heat in the core of the ancient mountain. They were pocked with air bubbles and cavities. Some of them were big enough for a man to stand up in. Shirin got a good grip, though the edge of the lip was sharp and it bit into her palm. Putting her weight on the handhold, she swung forward, letting her foot slip from the toehold. Her boot found another. Slowly, she inched down the face of the cliff.

Waves hammered at the shore, billowing white with foam. Ahead of her, though, there was a slick glassy section of water that lapped at the foot of the black cliffs.

Pillars of twisted black flint rose up in the sea before it, breaking the force of the waves. A boat could go out from the shore and make it to the open sea without being smashed into kindling on the reefs. Shirin was sure of it; she had seen it with her own eyes.

Following her midnight dispute with Mikele, Shirin had begun to pay attention to the other students and teachers. After two weeks of watching, she had determined there were four hundred and thirty-seven women living in the confines of the island. The kitchens made fish stew every day, too, and only rarely lamb or venison. Despite that, there did not seem to be any fishing boats or dorys in the harbor caves around the lagoon. There were two more of the light galleys and a sturdy hulled merchantman with a sail and mast that could be taken down, but nothing that passed for a ketch.

Someone had to catch all those fish. Shirin started looking for the fisherwomen and their harborage.

Shirin reached a long, narrow slot in the rock. It thinned to nothingness a dozen feet above her head, but below her it widened out. Down at the base, where the cleft plunged into the water, it caught the spume of the waves and shot them upward like a millrace. Shirin snarled in effort and reached around the edge of the crevice, her fingers stretching for the far side. It was just narrow enough. Her fingertips brushed across the smooth black stone. Nodding to herself, she pulled her hand back and got a good grip on the edge of the cleft. Grunting, she hooked her right leg around the edge and felt about for a ledge or crevice. A foot down, she found one. Hoping against hope that it would hold her weight, she swung around the edge and into the crevice itself.

The little ledge held, and she braced her back against the wall of the slot, breathing heavily. Her arms burned from the effort of carrying herself and the bag of tools and rope down the face of the cliff. But now, supported by the leverage of her own weight, she could rest for a moment.

She pulled the bag into her lap and let the top fall open. After flexing her fingers to get some sensation back in them, she dug around in the bag and pulled out a mallet and a flat-headed iron spike. There were dozens of spidery cracks in the black rock already; all she had to do was find one that would take the anchor and not come loose when she put her weight on it.

A trail ran along the height of the cliffs that girded the island. It was rocky and ill-defined, but the *ephebes* sometimes ran along it at midday. Mikele was fond of strenuous physical exercise. The trail made a course three miles in length as it wound around the crown of the island, rising and falling, climbing cliffs and plunging down into narrow ravines. When Shirin had taken to running the trail at dawn and at sunset, the teacher had seemed pleased.

Shirin knew little of a fisherwoman's life, but she had heard they went out at dawn, and returned before nightfall. The mindless exertion of the trail and the effort it put on her muscular legs was good, too, for it took her mind off the aching in her heart. Each day she woke possessed of a nagging fear that she would forget what the faces of her children looked like.

Two weeks had passed before she caught sight of a fishing ketch slipping through the waves below the clifftops. She had skidded to a halt and crawled to the edge of the cliff, peering down. The longboat had a triangular keel and sharply pointed bows. It was painted a sea green on the sides and blue from above. Against the surface of the Mare Aegeum, it was almost invisible. On this day, a sparkle like the sun catching on an Immortal's shield caught her eye. The boat was heavily laden with the catch of the day; some large fish with skin like shining mail. Two of the Sisters drove it through the water with leaf-bladed oars, cutting deftly between towering pillars of black stone that jutted from the sea.

They had disappeared into the cliff below her, and Shirin knew there must be a sea cave. Pressing her cheek and ear to the ground, she could feel a hollow booming sound echoing in the rocks.

Shirin worked her way down the cleft, her feet against one wall, her back pressed against the other. As she descended, the rope in the bag spooled out. One end was tied under her armpits in a crude harness; the other was looped around a series of iron spikes driven into the rock fifty feet above her head. The roar of the sea hammered at her. Though the water just before the sea cave only showed a slight chop, the cleft magnified the sound reverberating through the rock. She stopped. The crevice had grown large enough that she was about to lose the friction that kept her up. Shirin leaned out, craning her head around the edge of the cleft, looking to see how far she was from the sea cave.

A black mouth yawned up from the waterline only a dozen feet away. The rock face between her and the cave was thick with barnacles and encrusted salt. She reached out and grabbed at the nearest handhold. The white stone crumbled under her fingers. The sea was wearing away at the island, a finger's width at a time. The Khazar woman cursed luridly. The sea heaved underneath her, its shining green surface only feet away. She licked her lips. This was not going well. It seemed to have risen during her slow, agonizing crawl down the cliff. Perhaps the tide was rising?

Oh, curse me for a steppe girl! What do I know of the tide? Panic trickled in her mind, threatening to overcome her. An image of children intruded, and her face became still and grim. *They need me*, she snarled at herself. Bracing with her legs, she twisted around and leaned around the corner of the cleft, the mallet in her hand. The corroded rock gave under her first blow, the sound of the hammer ringing on the rock lost in the rush and roar of the surf. A foothold formed with gratifying speed.

Minutes later, she clambered out of the cleft and onto the open face. There were still a few iron spikes left to her, and they sank into the crumbling rock with ease. She crabbed sideways to the edge of the sea cave. Heedless of the possibility of a watch, she swung around the corner, feeling the cold bite of the water as it rose up around her ankles. It was dark inside the cavern, and she pressed herself against the wall, waiting for her eyes to adjust.

When they did, she found herself at the mouth of a half circle. A long ramp of worked stone rose out of the water and ran to the back of the cave. A wall of fitted stones blocked off the back of the cavern. There were no boats in evidence, but the ramp had two long grooves cut in it, grooves that were spilling water down them as the waves lapped in and out of the cave. With a gulp, Shirin untied the rope under her arms with one hand. She had reached the end of the tether.

It fell away and the water caught the line, spinning it out of the cave mouth. She moved along the wall, finding it slow going until she reached the edge of the ramp. The stones were slippery under her feet and she felt utterly exhausted. Despite a ferocious desire to lay down on the damp stone, she made herself climb the ramp and look over the wall. The thick smell of fish greeted her.

Two sturdy-looking fishing boats stood on heels of stone, but beside them, gleaming in the wavering light that reflected on the roof of the cavern from the bright sea outside, was a skiff with a folding mast and a sail of sea-green canvas. Shirin's eyes widened, and she scuttled to the side of the little craft.

Spiky Greek letters gave it a name, *Hector,* and carefully painted eyes of red and gold gave it spirit. It was light enough for her to push off of the mooring block, too, after she had thrown the bag with her supplies of food and clothing into it.

The sea waited, surging at the mouth of the cave, as she struggled to climb into the boat. It danced on the water like a skittish horse, slipping and sliding this way and that. Shirin grinned—part of the training of the *ephebes* was to handle small craft in the lagoon of the island. She shipped an oar of polished oak with a leaf-shaped blade and a painted handle. *Hector* darted forward. Shirin's hair lifted behind her in a dark wave.

The sky was bright as a mirror as the little ship cut through the water.

THE PALACE OF JUSTINIAN, CONSTANTINOPLE

T he sharp rap of knuckles on the doorframe of his room woke Dwyrin. His eyes opened slowly, not because he was deeply asleep, but because his whole body seemed weary, even his eyelids. The Hibernian rolled out of his cot and stood, letting his hair—still tangled and mussed by the thin pillow—hang lankly around his shoulders. A man of medium height and thin, with a narrow waist and broad shoulders, was standing in the doorway. Dwyrin blinked and made out a serviceable dark blue tunic, leather cavalryman's leggings, a pair of dark-colored belts at his waist, and the scabbard of a long, straight sword slung over his back on a baldric of black leather.

"You'd be Dwyrin MacDonald, late of the Ars Magica of the Third Cyrenaica?"

Dwyrin blinked in surprised. The man's voice carried the burr of the northern seas, and he'd even managed to pronounce his name correctly. The youth straightened and ran a hand though his hair. "Aye, sir." He tried to stand, but a fierce headache intervened and he had to lean against the wooden frame of the bunk.

The man stepped into the room and turned a little to the side so that he could stand comfortably. It was not a large room. Dwyrin could make out his features for the first time. He was thin faced, with a narrow nose and dark brown hair. A pair of mustaches jutted from his lip, the ends waxed to sharp points. It was hard to make out his eyes in the poor light, but they seemed a strange violet color.

"Nicholas of Roskilde, centurion on detached duty," the man said, and extended a hand in greeting. Dwyrin took it, gripping the other man's wrist. The fellow was strong—his forearms were thick and muscled like a wrestler—but he felt no need to try to crush Dwyrin's grip in his. "You've been assigned to my cohort."

"I have?" Dwyrin was surprised. The last time that he had trudged across the complex of government buildings to the offices, there had been nothing for him. Of course, when he tried to remember what he had done the day before or the day before that, it was all a sort of pine-rosin tinted haze. These Greeks brewed some fierce wine. Dwyrin rubbed his face and grimaced to find it spiky with stubble. He had only begun to grow a beard and now it felt like a rat's nest stuck to his face. "Where are we going?"

The man nodded to himself and looked around the little room. It was part of a warren of cubicles in the basement of the "old" palace that housed soldiers in transit through the Eastern capital. The room was small and mean and almost filled by four bunks of splintery pine boards and musty straw pallets. "Come on," the man said briskly. "Get your gear and let's get on the road. We've got a boat to catch."

Dwyrin blinked again and rummaged under his bunk, pulling out two leather bags of gear that held his mess tin, his short Spanish-style sword, a saw, some wheat cakes, salted bacon, and other accoutrements. He slung them on a stout wooden pole that doubled as a tent post and hoisted that onto his shoulder. The man was already striding down the hallway, his head bent to one side to avoid striking his forehead on the low arches.

Dwyrin hurried after him. *Well,* he thought, *at least I'm going somewhere!*

* * *

"Lord Prince?"

Theodore turned, his face still damp with sweat from his morning ride. The arches of the Imperial stables rose over his head, framing small square windows that let down bars of dusty yellow light. He rubbed his chin, feeling the stiffness of his beard. He would need a bath soon. His guardsmen loitered close, checking their horses' hooves and rattling about with their saddles and tack. "What ails you, Colos? You look like you've eaten a raw quince."

The man, short and balding, with thin arms and a long, narrow nose, shook his head. Theodore had met him before, many times. Colos was the scroll-pusher in charge of works within the city. Heraclius had always accorded him considerable respect, listening attentively to the man and his endless descriptions of wall repairs, sewer cleanings, aqueduct extensions, and so on. Theodore squared his shoulders and worked up a pleasant expression. Colos looked about and frowned at the number of groomsmen, guards, and other layabouts in evidence.

"Lord Prince, may I speak with you a moment, outside?"

"Surely." Theodore motioned to the stable boys to take his horse. It was bright outside, with the sun shining down out of a sky empty of clouds. The air had been nippy when Theodore had left the city in the predawn darkness, but now it promised to be an exceptional day. The bureaucrat turned left as they left the stables, and they passed through an arched passage. Beyond lay a small garden, filled with vines and spindly looking trees with white flowers.

"What goes?" Theodore turned, leaning against a wall.

Colos squinted in the sunlight, fidgeting. Now that they had some privacy, he seemed even more loathe to speak. The Prince cocked his head, eyeing the man. *Something must be afoot*, he thought with interest. *This fellow is about to wet his pants. . . .*

"Ah . . . there is a delicate matter, Lord Prince. It . . . ah . . . it involves your immediate family."

Theodore frowned, his eyebrows crawling together. A dangerous light entered his eyes. "Which members of my family?"

Colos flinched, but he continued. Now that he had managed to force out the first words, the rest came much easier. "Lord Prince, some matters concerning the Emperor had sought his attention. Of course, since he is ill, he has little time for the business of state! Yet these things must needs be done. . . . I took the matters in my own hands and went to see the Emperor's secretary."

Theodore nodded. Heraclius was barely cognizant of his surroundings for more than an hour or two a day. It made the simple business of government very difficult. Still, the matter had not caught Theodore's particular attention before.

"Again, I was told that the Emperor would see me later." Colos' voice rose a little as he spoke. "I pleaded with the clerks to, at least, let me leave the edicts, petitions, and proposals for his consideration at a later date. At first they refused me, but then she came out."

Theodore looked up from where he had been picking at some dirt under one of his nails. "She?"

"Yes." Colos nodded, his mouth twisted a little on one side. "The Empress and her maids came out of the inner audience chamber. She asked what I desired, and I told her. She said . . . she took the papers from me, saying she would see that the Emperor saw to them. I did not know what else to do, so I acceded to her demand."

The Prince pushed away from the wall, his face stiff. He stared at Colos, and the man stared back. "What happened, then?" Theodore's voice was soft. He realized with a sudden cold certainty that the enjoyable time he had spent riding with his friends in the hills of Thrace, or hunting in the forests of his estates in Bithnia, had been sorely wasted. "Were these items seen to?"

"They were, Lord Prince." Colos' expression changed, becoming, if possible, even more sour looking. "Documents were signed with the Emperor's seal and edicts approved, military dispositions were made and taxes levied. All very neat and tidy and properly done."

Theodore regarded the man, seeing him in a new light. Such words would not come out of Colos' mouth unless the man were sure of himself. Sure that he was supported by the other ministers and bureaucrats within the palace. Sure that the Prince would understand what he was implying. "So . . . despite this proper procedure, you do not feel that the papers and edicts and writs were, in fact, properly issued? You think, you *suspect*, that perhaps the Emperor did not pay overmuch attention to them? That, perhaps, some other person, familiar with the doings of these offices, might have taken it upon themselves to act in the Emperor's stead?"

Despite the menace inherent in the Prince's words, Colos nodded simply. "Lord Prince," he said, "the best-governed household is one where the father is honored. If the father is away, then the eldest son must bear the burden of providing proper guidance and direction to all."

Theodore nodded, though he felt a faint pang for the riding and hunting that would be lost to him. "I understand," he said, smiling. "I will see that proper direction is provided to the Emperor's household while he is ill." The Prince's face was cut by a feral grin. *This could be better than hawking!*

Summer had finally come to Constantinople, and the chill of winter had passed. Today, as Nicholas and Dwyrin tramped through the streets of the city, there was a clear blue sky overhead. The morning haze that had clung to the docks and low-lying brick buildings had burned away in the bright sun. Even the bitter wood smoke of the Avar encampments beyond the walls was gone. The great Prince Theodore had sortied with the Imperial Army a month ago, after the soldiers had recovered from the week-long revel that had accompanied their return to the capital, and the Avars had scattered. The great Khan's morale had been broken by his failure to carry the walls and by the destruction of the Persian fleet. The latest word that Nicholas had heard in the senior centurion's mess was that the Avars were already abandoning Thrace and falling back behind the mountains of Moesia. Within the year he expected that Macedonia and Moesia Inferior would be recovered as well.

Nicholas whistled a lilting tune as he walked, long legs eating up the distance between the old palace and the military harbor. He would be glad to leave the narrow, twisting streets of the city and the unrelenting noise and crowds. The youth dogged along at his side, his shorter legs scrambling to keep up. Nicholas looked down, measuring the unshaven face with its fuzz of red whiskers and the nonregulation hair that was a tangle behind the boy's head. Nicholas had been rather surprised when he had looked over the roster of his command and found that it contained a thaumaturge detached from a frontier unit. His experience in working for the Office of Barbarians had always been marked by a penurious atmosphere.

Now, seeing the boy and the bleary eyes and the shuffle that marked a particularly tremendous hangover, he wondered whether he hadn't gotten shorted again. Of course, the locals were fond of very strong wine, spiked with pine rosin to "give it flavor," as he had once been told.

"So, lad, where have you been? What experience have you?"

Dwyrin looked up blearily and opened his mouth, then closed it again. They walked a distance before the Hibernian could muster enough brainpower to put one word after another. In his current fog, it took a lot of effort to put one foot in front of the other.

"I was with the army in Persia, Centurion. I was at Tauris and Kerenos and Ctesiphon."

Nicholas whistled in appreciation. The boy had seen some action then. Perhaps he had gotten a good draw after all. Not that this job needed it really. "How long have you been in the thaumaturges, MacDonald? Which circle have you attained?"

Dwyrin smiled grimly. He got that question a lot, more so since Zoë and Odenathus had abandoned him at Antioch. "Just about a year, sir. I'm still first circle."

Nicholas raised an eyebrow and shrugged. Back to getting the short stick. Still, an inexperienced hell-caster was better than none, right?

"Sir?"

Nicholas nodded for the boy to go on.

"Where are we going?"

"In a minute, lad. Once we're on the boat and have met the rest of our little crew I'll fill you in."

Ravens flew past overhead, cawing in delight at the warm air. A procession of priests passed them on the raised sidewalk, the voices raised in a chant to the eternal sun. Golden disks were stitched to their long robes, and the lead man carried a solar emblem on a tall pole. Nicholas stepped aside to let them pass, even though it meant that he had to squish through the offal in the middle of the street. Dwyrin hopped after him. The street canted sharply downward, plunging off the hill that held the Hippodrome. A boulevard led down to the harbors on the southwestern side of the city.

Dwyrin was winded by the time they crossed the Racing District and reached the huge brooding gate that opened through the sea walls. A broad road disgorged from the Bovine gate and led down into the controlled chaos of the military harbor. His pack seemed to have become much heavier since he had arrived in the city. His head was still throbbing, too. *No more wine for me*, he pledged, raising an image of the shrine of Macha in his village before him. *Particularly this nasty resinated stuff they serve here.* The free-flowing wine, meat, and bread of the Imperial Triumph had left their mark on him. The excellent muscle tone that he had gained under Blanco and Zoë's tutelage and on a thousand miles of Asian road was suffering.

They passed out of the shadow of the towering brick seawalls and walked down a wooden pier broader than the main street of Dwyrin's home village. A forest of ship's masts rose around them, and the air rang with the cry of quartermasters and sailors and the cawing of seagulls. Flocks of the dirty white birds filled the air, casting endlessly moving shadows on the men laboring in the harbor. Nicholas counted piers, finally turning at the sixth one. The wooden quay was choked with piles of crates under nets and rows of barrels. Dwyrin stuck close to the taller man as they wove through the press. Lines of soldiers squatted or sat on the dock, their kit bundled at their feet. Most of them seemed to be Imperials with short-cropped dark hair and proud noses. They watched the two barbarians pass without comment.

Nicholas continued on, past the hulking shapes of troop transports, and finally reached the end of the dock. A low-sided ship with peeling paint, a dingy cabin, and faded markings was moored there. Nicholas bounded up the ramp, the springy wood flexing under his boots. "Ho, the boat!" His voice rolled out over the craft and roused a sailor who was napping under a striped sunshade hung over the stern deck. The man, a dark-skinned fellow with a beard of tightly curled ringlets, opened one eye and waved, his hand languid in the air. Dwyrin took the gangway at a more sedate pace and put down his bags with a hearty sigh. The smell of the sea, sharp with the smell of rotting fish on the shore and cast-up garbage thrown from passing ships, was beginning to cut through the haze in his head.

Nicholas waved to the sailor as he went forward and banged on the door to the fore cabin. There was no answer, so he gave it a kick and it bounced open, making a tremendous rattle. He turned, looking back up the deck. The Hibernian boy was picking up his bags again. "We can leave when you please, Master Tirus!"

Nicholas flashed the sailor a broad smile. Even the feel of a ship at rest, barely shifting in its mooring, made him feel at home. So much better than the grim, tight streets of the city! "Come on, lad, we've much to discuss."

Dwyrin sighed deeply and slung the tent pole on his shoulder again. The centurion's obvious good humor and nervous energy were giving him a new headache.

The fore cabin was little bigger than the cubicle that Dwyrin had been sleeping in, but it had two windows on either side with wooden shutters and four beds. A table folded out from the far wall. Dwyrin ducked under the door lintel and blinked as his eyes adjusted to the dim light. Nicholas had unstrapped the long sword from his back and pushed it into a pile of gear on one of the bunks. The other bunk was occupied, though the man sleeping in it was turned away with a blanket pulled over his head.

"Vlad, time to get up. The reinforcements are here." Nicholas poked the sleeping man with the tip of his boot. There was a grunting sound. Dwyrin dumped his gear on the lower bunk on the side opposite. His head felt better now that they were in out of the sun. The forge hammer that had started to beat in the back of his skull receded somewhat. It was still there, but now it was muted.

The sleeping man grunted again, but threw back the blanket and shifted himself out of the bunk. His shirt was off, and Dwyrin's eyes widened at the thick pelt of hair that covered his chest and back. It was low and napped like the fur of a shorthaired cat, though it covered only part of his arms. The man had a mane of blue-black hair, too. The fellow looked up, and Dwyrin stiffened, seeing the line of his skull and the cast of his eyes.

Nicholas turned, his lips twisted in a wry grin. "Dwyrin, this is . . . what in Hel's name is that?"

Dwyrin had stood, though his legs were shaking, and his hand—seemingly so slow—traced a mark in the air. It hung, flickering and green, in the still air of the cabin. The boy's face was taut with fear and his lips moved, though no sound came out. Nicholas felt a humming in his head, a whine that was rapidly rising in tone. In the pile of his baggage, *Brunhilde* was quivering, her blade echoing the sound with its own vibration. Nicholas felt Vladimir stiffen and stand up. The glyph was beginning to spin on its long axis, tumbling faster and faster in the air.

"Centurion, get behind me." Dwyrin's voice was harsh with worry. "Quickly!"

Nicholas raised his hands and moved forward between the boy and Vladimir. His heart was thudding with the rush of blood-fire. He hoped he could manage to coax a soothing tone out of his throat. "Lad, it's fine—Vladimir is with me; he's in the cohort . . . He's no danger to us."

Dwyrin flicked his eyes from Vladimir, who was half crouched on the floor, his hands on the decking, for an instant. Nicholas caught them and nodded, trying to put all the meaning he could in the glance.

"Centurion. . . . this *creature* is not any human soul. It feeds on blood of your kind and mine. Are you sure you want to call it friend?"

Nicholas nodded sharply and dropped his hands. "Yes, lad. I owe Vladimir my life. We are bound to one another by our own debts. Put the . . . whatever that is . . . away before it does someone a harm."

Dwyrin shuddered, remembering a time of slow, cruel terror in the hands of just such a creature, but he saw the calm appeal in the centurion's eyes and he broke his concentration. The glyph shimmered, sending a fall of sparks like flower petals to the floor, and then faded away. The humming and the metallic keening in the room faded away as well, though Dwyrin now realized that there were four beings in the room, rather than just three. When the green fire had died, the beast-man named Vladimir breathed a sigh of relief and stood.

"Thank you," said the Walach to Dwyrin, sketching a half bow. "It is not easy for me, either, living among the children of day. But I pledge you that I mean neither you nor Nicholas any harm."

Dwyrin's eyes narrowed to slits, hidden anger threatening to boil forth in fire, but he repressed the urge to call forth the embers hiding in the creature's blood. He wiped his forehead, which had beaded with sweat during the exertion of summoning the ward. It seemed more difficult now—he had grown used to feeling Zoë's touch, and Odenathu's, through their battle-pattern. He kept waiting for them to slide into the matrix, adding their own strength to his.

"Come," Nicholas said, clearing some dirty plates off of the little folding table. "We will be underway soon, and I need to tell you what we are about."

". . . and that is about it." Nicholas tapped his teeth idly with a stylus. Night had fallen on the nameless ship and it rolled easily, cutting across the swells coming up from the south. Vladimir had lighted a small lantern with a body of brass and thin windows of close-cut mica. The stone had been poorly shaved, so the light was muted and dim, but it was better than an open flame in the cabin. Round shutters had been pulled back from the windows, too, and the fresh breeze off of the sea made the little room pleasant. Dwyrin sat on the edge of his bunk, his eyes never far from the hunched shape of Vladimir. The "man" had put on a loose shirt of white cotton with large sleeves to go with his dark leggings.

Dinner had been a thick fish stew, spiced with an inordinate amount of garlic. Dwyrin had almost gagged at the taste, but Nicholas and the Walach had dug in with such relish that he felt he had to go along. His throat was still burning, and he knew that he would be tasting the bulb for a long time. Some loaves of bread, purchased fresh from a bakery in the city that morning, and watered wine completed their meal. The Hibernian toyed with a crust, thinking that it was one of the better meals—not counting the garlic, of course—that he had enjoyed in the past year. Legion food was not much to speak of. Nicholas had made the stew, which explained the garlic and the robust flavor.

"Have you been to this place before? This Aelia Capitolina?" Vladimir's mouth was full, but he managed to get the words out, anyway. The way his long white teeth worried at the bread set Dwyrin on edge, but despite his first impression, the man was not one of the dead-that-walked. The set of his eyes, though, reminded the Hibernian far too much of the Bygar Dracul. That one was dead, but the memory remained like a lesion on his spirit.

"No," Nicholas said, picking his teeth with a sliver of wood. "Constantinople is the farthest east I'd been before this. Lad, have you been there?"

Dwyrin shook his head. Aelia Capitolina was one of the hill-cities in Judea, across the wasteland of the Sinai from Egypt. He had heard a little about it—a rough land with rocky valleys and hilltop orchards—but had never set foot there. "Sorry, Centurion, I've been in Egypt at the School and up in Armenia. We kind of skipped the whole middle part . . ."

Nicholas sighed, then flicked the splinter out the window. "No matter. We're supposed to meet up with the rest of the century in Caesarea, and they—by this roster—are all veterans. They'll know the lay of the land, I'm sure. That will bring our strength up to just over a hundred men. Hopefully it will be enough to deal with these bandits. Hmm . . . I hope they can all ride, otherwise they'll be in for some rough instruction!"

Dwyrin nodded, though his thoughts were far away from the little cabin on the ship. Aelia Capitolina was not so far from Palmyra; perhaps he could work a finding pattern on his friends—if they could bring themselves to speak to him again. The raw pain throbbed in his gut again, and he reached for his beaker of wine. The sweet grape brought relief from the memories of Zoë's face and her terrible anger.

Nicholas looked over and grinned at Vladimir. The lad had fallen asleep, curled up in the bunk, his gear-bag under his head as a pillow. The Walach shrugged, but he seemed to have relaxed a little. "You're too nervous, my friend. He's a good soldier—he'll follow orders if nothing else. He won't singe your tail . . ." Vladimir grimaced at the jibe and put his head in his hands. Nicholas watched him carefully. The nervous energy that had marked the Walach the day that they had met the two girls during the Triumph was absent, but something was preying on the dark-haired man's mind. Nicholas' fingers drifted to *Brunhilde*'s hilt, which was close to hand. The touch calmed him, and her whispering voice settled his nerves. Despite what he had told the boy, he kept a very close eye on the Walach. They could not afford another incident, not while on a mission.

"Vlad, something is troubling you. What is it?"

The Walach looked up, his liquid dark eyes filled with lingering fear.

"We left just in time . . . ," Vladimir whispered. "The dark Queen came to me in my dreams last night. If we had not left today, she and hers would hunt me tonight. I care not where we go, as long as it is away from that cursed city."

Nicholas nodded sagely, feeling the weight of his coin purse. It was a good day to leave—before a certain moneylender realized that the Gothic merchant he had lent so much coin to was not a merchant at all. Vladimir got up and crawled into his bunk, his face turned from the dim light of the lantern. Nicholas sat up, and went over the maps and scrawled notes he had received from the office. He was puzzled by the mission. The rapacity of desert bandits was trouble, to be sure, but not usually the kind of thing that he undertook. His masters back in Rome usually set him to hunt a man. This business of a whole province was new.

Rummaging in the dispatch bag, he took out a copy of the original report. It was penned in a straight, strong hand and had come from this hill-town in Judea, this Aelia Capitolina.

To the Magister Militatum, Eastern Empire,
Constantinople.
   Greetings,
   Noble sir, I wish to draw your attention to the
depredations of fierce bandits that have taken to

infesting the hills around our town. As you know, this
place has long been a hotbed of rebellion, religious
fanatics, necromancers, and thieves. It pains me to
admit that the local garrison, though loyal, is not able
to deal with the troubles that beset us. To understand
this, I must relate some of the history of this old city,
once called Hierosolyma in the time of the Divine
Emperor Trajan, or—in the native tongue—
Jerusalem . . .

Nicholas read on, seeing a litany of feuds and wars and
petty death. At last, his eyes grimy with exhaustion, he put
the documents away and climbed into his own bunk. The
roll and slap of the waves lulled him to sleep in moments.
Soon they would reach the coast of Judea and get all these
troubles straightened out.

THE JABAL AL'JILF, OUTSIDE PETRA,
CAPITAL OF ROMAN NABATEA

Mohammed crouched down, his black beard and
face thrown in sharp relief by the light of the
hooded lantern he held in his hand. The lantern was a
bronze box with an iron loop and a wooden handle. The
candle inside was of the best beeswax that his foragers
could find and it burned cleaner than he had hoped. His
hand moved over the planed surface of the tunnel wall,
feeling a rough patch. At some time in the past there had
been an earth tremor, and the underground passage had
been damaged. Part of the mountain that the tunnel bored
through had slipped a foot or more. Artisans whose skill
did not match the craft of the men who had first cut the
tunnel had repaired it, leaving a jumble of bricks and plas-

ter at the slippage point. Mohammed held the lantern out, peering into the tunnel beyond.

The passage continued, though it would be a bit of a squeeze to make it through the break. The Quryash turned and nodded to the men behind him. Then he ducked down and crawled through on one hand, the other holding the lantern just above the dusty floor. Like the long flight of steps that he and his army had ascended to reach the passage, it was cut from the raw sandstone of the mountains.

A hundred of the Sahaba followed him through the heart of the ridge, their swords sheathed or their spears muffled with wool. Despite this, the sound of their movement seemed very loud, magnified by the close space of the tunnel. They had crossed a highland plateau just after dark, after spending the heat of late afternoon toiling up into the hills that held the hanging gardens and water cisterns serviced by this passage. The main entrance to the city, the Siq, lay barely two hundred yards to their north. That passage was a narrow road that wound through a tight canyon. It was dark and twisty, with a man at midday unable to see the sun above his head. A dozen soldiers could hold it against an army, where it reached the first sight of the city. An elaborate tomb was there, where the passage suddenly opened out into daylight, and a garrison post. Mohammed had no intention of trying to force his way through that dogleg trap.

His army moved through the fringes of the rugged terrain that bounded the hidden city, following a goat path and tracks worn by farmers who cultivated tiny crops of wheat and rye and squash in meager patches of soil in the high canyons.

Steep cliffs and round-browed mountains ringed Petra in a fierce barricade. There were no gentle slopes of pine or juniper, but sheer wind-carved red stone instead. To the undiscerning eye, the heights of Kubtha and Al'Madras seemed impassable, the city impregnable behind the great gate and dam that closed the entrance to the Siq. Mohammed had often come to the Red City in his travels and he knew that there were other ways into the fastness. This was one, shown to him by a shepherd with a taste for foreign wine.

Mohammed smiled grimly, thinking that an Arab tribe—not grown soft in this easy northern land—would have put a guard on the dams and springs that provided water to the city. But these were troubled times, and the city garrison might have other concerns. The Quryash laughed inside at that. For his people, water was always the first concern. That, and secret ways into their city that might allow enemies to surprise them while they slept in their beds.

The tunnel ended, opening out onto a wilderness of great round boulders and canted slabs of sandstone. The moon had risen and the rocks were bathed in a cool light. Mohammed cast about with the lantern and then found a stairway leading down to the left. Beyond it, a path wound between the huge monoliths, cutting across the head of a narrow streamed that had worn its way into the rock of the mountain.

The entrance of the army of the Sahaba into Aelana had been a surprise to Mohammed. He knew that the ships of his small fleet could make better time on the wave-road than his cavalry could in the rocky uplands and desert that they crossed to get from Leuke Kome to the northern port. He had not expected, however, to find the green-and-white banner of the Sahaba flying over the white-painted gate tower of the town, or to be met by a smiling and relaxed Khalid in the shadow of that same gateway.

"There was no garrison?" Khalid had nodded in assent as they had climbed the steps to the dingy tan building that had held the customs office.

Mohammed shook his head in amazement. "They were withdrawn to the north a month ago, according to Feyd here." Khalid had indicated a stooped man with a sun-browned face who had joined them once Mohammed's command staff had reached the center of the town. The man, obviously a local, had a green-and-white flash on his tunic loop. "There is some trouble brewing up in Judea and the governor has summoned all available troops to a muster."

Mohammed had turned, his hand on the hilt of his saber, and surveyed the big room with its arched roof. Once, it had held the men who worked in the customs house; now it would hold his messengers and staff. Windows with triangular tops pierced the southern wall, showing bits and pieces of the blue gulf beyond and the broad golden beach that marked the seaside. Aelana was not a big town, but it had long piers of fitted stone over compacted rubble that provided a fine anchorage for his ships.

"What kind of trouble?" Mohammed leaned close to the youth, his hand on Khalid's shoulder.

Khalid smiled. He loved to tell a tale no one had heard before. The three weeks that he had been in the port had allowed him to gather up every scrap of gossip and rumor he could find.

"The cities of the Decapolis are in an uproar," he said with a grin. "Word has gotten around that the Empire left Zenobia and the Petrans out to dry during the invasion. Apparently some new detachments of Imperial troops have come down from the north to take up the old camps, and people have noticed that their sons and husbands have not returned at all."

Mohammed had nodded, a shadow falling across his face. Obodas of Petra and Zenobia had led the whole might of the Decapolis and Nabatea and Palmyra into a butcher's holiday first at Emesa and then in the siege of Palmyra. Some thousands had escaped from the Persian victory on the field of Emesa, scattering off to the south, but the rest had followed Zenobia to Palmyra.

"Then," Khalid continued, "someone started a rumor that there was to be a census."

The remaining manpower of this whole region had died there, trying to hold on until the Imperial Legions could reach them, paying in blood for each day, trying to buy

Heraclius the time he needed to break the Persian armies in the north. Mohammed turned away, his throat bitter with the taste of bile. He leaned on one of the windowsills, his bushy eyebrows beetling over closed eyes. It had been a trap, but not for Persia. Heraclius had never intended to turn south and succor the loyal cities of the Decapolis and Judea. He had struck east, instead, and seized the Persian capital at Ctesiphon and won his war.

"And that, of course, means new taxes." The youth smiled grimly, his eyes never leaving Mohammed's face. "No one was pleased about the news."

But every man who had followed Zenobia into the gilded cage of Palmyra had died; all save Mohammed and his handful of Tanukh, who had only escaped by a hair. Jalal had seen to that, dragging Mohammed's body from the ruin of the Damascus gate and fleeing before the Persians could recover from the mage-battle that had flattened half the city. The Tanukh knew secret ways into and out of the city, ones they had used to harry the Persians during the long siege. They had served, too, to let them flee. Zenobia had bought them that time, at least, holding out in the palace until the end, drawing the full attention of the dark power that strove against her.

"How goes the provisioning? What supplies did you find here?"

Mohammed pushed himself away from the windowsill and turned back to Khalid. The youth was ready, a marked tablet in his hands. The Quryash smiled, seeing the eagerness of the young man to excel.

He will be an even greater general than I, mused Mohammed, bending over the table to see how many barrels of water, sheaves of arrows, tuns of figs, and casks of dried meat were to hand.

The moon continued to rise as the Arabs climbed up out of the *wadi*. A wide plateau of stone tilted up from the streambed, and cairns of rocks marked a path across it. Now, Mohammed knew, they were nearing the head of the

Siq, where that narrow slot canyon opened out into the valley that held Petra. He looked back, seeing his men toiling steadily up the slope, a dark line of figures with long shadows reaching before them. The moon was very clear in this high place and they moved swiftly.

A little time passed as they crossed the open plateau, passing before the gaping mouths of abandoned tombs cut from the rock, and then they came to another slot canyon athwart their path. A cairn marked a place where the path plunged down into the shadowed ravine. Mohammed could smell water and green growing things in the darkness below. Crouching at the lip of the slot, he listened, his eyes closed, his mind quiet.

No sound of man or beast came from below, only the ripple of water on stone and the drip-drip-drip of some seeping spring. If he remembered aright, this canyon led down past two or three catchment dams to a bowl in the mountain where the passage of the Siq ended and the city itself began. There would be guards there in plenty.

He shuttered his lantern and motioned for the men behind him, squatting on the ground, to do the same. Here they could descend behind the guards at that gate, taking them by surprise, but sound carried easily in these canyons and they would have to go slowly and carefully.

He stood, squinting back at the shadowed lumps of his men, and motioned for Shadin. Jalal and Khalid, along with the bulk of the army, were waiting in the swale of the Wadi Musa, beyond sight of the first gate into the Siq. They were waiting for a signal that the raiding party had seized the entrance to the city from behind.

A dark figure detached itself from the shadow under one of the great boulders and scuttled toward him.

Listen! Do you hear it? Do you hear the doom of men?

Mohammed started, surprised. But the voice had already faded. There was a sound, a whisper, carried on the night wind.

Mohammed stopped, listening. Then, faintly, he heard it: massed voices on the air. He looked up and saw, on the mountaintop that rose to the south of the city, the glare of a bonfire and the outline of hundreds of people standing in the High Place. The people of the city raised their voices in homage to some god that lived behind the sky. When Mohammed had passed through the red city before the furtive nature of the locals, their odd, secretive customs and the bitter aftertaste of the water had just set his nerves on edge. Now the sound of that chanting and the half-heard words ignited a cold anger in his breast. He stopped, feeling his arm trembling.

"My lord?" The Quryash turned, his face grim. The bulky Tanukh was at his side, his helmet and armor wrapped in dark cloth to muffle the sound and prevent any betraying gleam of light. The man's eyes glinted in the darkness, catching a reflection from the lights of the city and the fire on the mountaintop. More Sahaba moved past, as quietly as they could, filtering down the stair with their weapons out.

"There is a ceremony underway, there on the High Place." Mohammed pointed up, indicating the red glare that lit the mountaintop. "I must stop it. I will take half of the men and go up the Long Stair. You take the rest and seize the guardpost at the end of the Siq. With luck, Jalal will be waiting for you. Then follow the plan."

Shadin nodded his understanding and turned, catching the shoulder of one of his lieutenants. Mohammed hurried down the long flight of steps that wound down to the streambed, taking them two and three at a time. The memory of a voice echoed in his mind, urging him to hurry. The faces of the Sahaba flashed past as they turned in surprise. If Shadin could open the gates at the Siq, then the army could pour into the city unopposed. The next good place to mount a defense would be on the steps of the palace. Taking away half of the men that were to accomplish that task would not make it easier, but Mohammed was sure that he had to get to the top of the High Place as fast as possible.

Fly, O man, fly! The voice was urgent, thundering in his mind.

Tradition said there were nine hundred and ninety-nine steps from the red sand of the streambed at the base of the mountain to the twin obelisks that stood on the verge of the High Place. Mohammed had not bothered to count them tonight, but his thighs and the backs of his calves had marked each one and were ready to tell him all about it if he stopped for a moment. The fifty Sahaba at his back were winded, too, and they held their mouths open, gasping for air as silently as they could manage.

Beyond the great obelisks, each towering twenty feet into a dark and cloudless sky, a saddle opened out on the summit. To Mohammed's left, a jumble of slabs marked the head of another set of stairs that led down the far side of the mountain. To his right, where the peak of the High Place rose up, jutting out over the central valley of Petra, a redoubt of squared stones had been raised to bar passage into the sacred precincts.

A gate stood at the base of the tower, though it stood ajar, lit by two large iron sconces holding torches of pitch that guttered in the night wind. In their light, stairs could be made out, marching up the last ramp into the temple itself. The chanting was louder now, though broken by the wind, and the blaze of fires and torches could be seen in the darkness above the stone wall. Bats and nightjars swooped through the illumination, feasting on clouds of insects that had been drawn from the wasteland.

The High Place was a pinnacle of bare rock rising at the southeastern corner of the valley of Petra like a helmet. Here, near the summit, Mohammed could see a vast sweep of desert and mountain and valley lying about him under the moon. A cold wind ruffled his robes and plucked at his hair. It was odd to look out over the tumbled massif of the Ad'Deir hills, here in the heart of night, and see them illuminated by the moon as if by day. He tore his attention away from the vista and the knowledge of the three-hundred–foot drop just beyond his right hand.

There did not seem to be any guards at the gate, but nothing prevented them from standing just within the entrance, hidden in shadows. Mohammed crept forward, his saber out, and held parallel to the ground. The first five men behind him were archers with long black arrows already fitted to the bow. Wind whipped the sound of the chanting away, but now Mohammed could feel it in the stones under his feet.

The tip of the saber passed through the gateway, and Mohammed felt it tremble, meeting some unseen resistance in the cold night air. He stopped, his hand raised in warning to the men behind. A sudden sense *she* was with him made the hairs on his arms prickle up. The blade trembled, for it seemed *her* cool touch was on the back of his hand. He remembered her, standing in the darkness of her chambers in the palace, her hand touching his wrist as he prepared to go out to die on the walls of the city. Her city. He remembered that she had given him this blade after his own had been chipped and nicked beyond use. He looked through the pillars of the gate.

The stairs were empty. There were no guards. Beckoning to his men, Mohammed sprinted up them, pushing the pain in his legs away. There would be time for groaning and lying about while dark-eyed servant girls rubbed his thighs with cool minty cream later. Unlike the plain stone steps in the canyon below, these were faced with marble and fitted into a brick support. He leapt up them, two and three at a time.

At the top of the stairs was a second gate in a wall of brick, marked by twin slim columns of marble. The summit of the High Place made a rough trapezoid, bounded by cliffs on three sides. On the western side, facing the setting sun, perched high above the center of the city, was a rectangular raised dais. Before it a deep pool had been cut into the rock of the mountain. On the dais, an altar of uncarved stone flowed up from the rock like a man's fist rising from the earth. As Mohammed came up to the top of the stairs, there was blood on the altar and the body of a young woman squirming under a stone knife.

Priests in long red robes crowded around the altar, their hands gripping her white flesh, holding her down. The girl was trying to scream, but only a bubbling red froth almost the color of the priests' raiment came out of her mouth. At the head of the altar, a figure had his hands raised to the sky and saffron-colored heat lightning flickered and flashed around him. Between the gate and the pool, hundreds of supplicants knelt, their voices raised in the long rolling chant that Mohammed had heard on the wind. The parishioners wore hoods of red laid over their workaday clothes, but even those were rich and finely detailed.

You will make no sacrifice of blood at my altar, boomed the voice in his mind, making him stagger. *You will submit yourself to the straight path and you will live a righteous life!*

The line of Mohammed's chin tensed, and his eyes narrowed, taking in the scene. There were no graven idols here, no statues crowded together like a forest, but he knew as surely as the voice had spoken to him on the mountaintop that darkness was oozing into the world here, called by blood and iron. He pressed hard with the saber and felt the resistance in the air seize up, testing his strength.

O my Merciful and Compassionate Lord, give me the strength to meet this test!

A bright white flash cut the night, throwing the carvings and pillars of the temple in the cliff face into sharp relief. Shadin's head jerked around involuntarily, his saber rising to ward off whatever made the light. The snapping crash of thunder rolled right behind the glare and the men in the little oval valley cried out, clapping hands to their eardrums. In the residue of the brilliant light, Shadin was left with an image of hundreds of the Sahaba pouring out of the narrow Siq into the broader stream bottom before a great tomb. The rattle and boom of thunder echoed again, and the summit of the High Place lit up like a thunderhead.

"That's done it," he howled over the rolling echo. There would be no surprising the city now. "Forward!"

Jalal ran up, his boots splashing water from the streambed. Centuries of current had worn it smooth save for a thin layer of sand. He had his bow in hand and an open-faced helmet tied under his chin. Men in half armor and shields ran past, their banner leaders and lieutenants urging them on. Around the inner gate, the scattered bodies of the Petrans who had been on watch lay in pools of blood. The attack from the hidden stair had taken them completely by surprise.

"What is that?" Jalal shouted over the thunder, pointing up at the mountaintop.

"The Lord Mohammed," Shadin cursed as he turned to join his men running into the city. "He left us up there in the pass. He's about his own business."

The slim gateway had shattered, cracking lengthwise, when Mohammed had thrust the cold iron of the Palmyran blade through the invisible membrane. The shock of the blast had thrown him down the marble stairway, crashing into the Sahaba behind him. The crowd of men and women on the mountaintop began shrieking in fear. Some had been felled as well by flying debris. The Quryash, his ears ringing, clawed his way out of the tangle of bodies. A blue light flickered beyond the gate, illuminating the shattered pillars.

Act! Time is fleeting!

The voice that spoke in the empty places roared in his mind. Mohammed hurled himself forward through the gateway, even as the Sahaba behind him were shaking themselves out of their daze. The blue flare surrounded him, and he skidded sideways, avoiding a figure that staggered toward him. One of the worshipers stumbled past, a man with a ruined face covered with blood. Mohammed raised his blade, holding it up against the light.

The pool of water was gone, and in its place was a dreadful radiance. Something had risen from the womb of the mountain, a whirling amorphous thing that crackled and shuddered with lightning. Ultramarine fire washed off of it, spinning out in the night and falling in sheets of flame toward the rocks and buildings far below. All of the worshipers on the mountaintop lay dead or dying, their bodies scattered in windrows. Only one remained, the figure who had raised the stone knife to the sky. That one stood behind the altar, his face raised to the pulsating blue cloud that drifted and buzzed and hummed above the dry pool.

Mohammed scuttled forward, crouching low to the ground, leading with the tip of the saber. Arrows snapped overhead as the Sahaba reached the gate and saw what lay before them. Mohammed's face was grim and set—he had seen such things before, like the monstrosity that had stood above him at the Damascus gate. Wind howled around the mountaintop, and lightning jagged through clear air, dancing on the cliffs. Thunder rolled in an unceasing wave, shaking the stones on the ground, making the world shudder and dance.

The priest behind the altar slashed down his hand, pointing with the stone knife, and the whirling chaotic sphere drifted toward Mohammed. The arrows of the bowmen at the gate flashed into the blue haze and then drifted to a stop before they burst into flames and were consumed. The Quryash suddenly leapt to his feet and dashed to the right, heading for the precipice over the canyon. Flickering light followed him, reaching out with spiky fingers. Blue radiance strengthened and washed over him. He skidded to a halt at the edge of the cliff, stones flying away from his boots to rattle down into the dark abyss.

Sahaba spearmen dodged in behind the whirling ultramarine blue refulgence. They sprinted toward the priest, their spearpoints glowing with echoes of the thing that had Mohammed distracted. The Quryash leapt into the air, slashing out with his saber, and the steel tip sliced into one of the glowing tendrils that had suddenly sprouted from the amorphous center of the blue light.

In his mind, Mohammed could see the white arm of the

Queen and her chain mail glove lunging, the saber gleaming in the sun, as it touched the crawling lightning.

Beyond that vision, the priest in red turned too late, and his eyes widened in horror. Three Sahaba spears of cold iron, driven by all the might the soldiers could muster, pierced his torso. Blood suddenly welled in his mouth, and the priest convulsed as one spearpoint tore through his spinal cord. The others punctured a lung and cut into his heart. The stone knife slipped from nerveless fingers, sliding to the ground and cracking in half with a hollow sound.

Mohammed's sword blazed like the eyes of the angels he saw floating in the air around the mountaintop, trapping the white-hot fire that boiled and howled at the center of the blue light. A vast, colorless radiance flooded the world, and Mohammed felt his *kaffiyeh* and riding scarf burst into flames. Across the narrow space at the top of the mountain, the Sahaba cried out as the intense burst blinded them or threw them to the ground.

A third enormous flash lit the valley of the city, and Jalal turned away from the mountain, his eyes screwed shut, his shield raised to block out the infernal light. But this time there was no mind-shattering crash of thunder or rolling boom that cracked temple doorways and tumbled the stone seats of the theater into a ruined pile. Instead, there was complete silence, without even the sound of running feet. All across the valley of Petra, there was utter quiet. The Sahaba, driven to the ground, lay where they had fallen. None dared raise their eyes up to the sky for fear of what they might see there.

Jalal crouched on the ground, tears streaming from his eyes. Sound slowly filtered into his consciousness, and it was the crackle and snap of burning wood. He raised himself up, blinking furiously, and saw that the nearest building—a stall in the colonnaded street that led into the city—was on fire. The dry canvas and light wood had ignited in the titanic flare of light. Jalal brushed soot from his eyes, and his hand came away covered with curled, burned hair.

He held his hand up, seeing it double and triple in his sight.

Cursing, he touched his face and found it raw and sore. His beard came away in his hand, all shriveled and falling to ash. Tears streamed down his face, cutting tracks in the white dust that covered him and every other thing within the valley.

The sky was dark again, free of the strange blue light.

Cries rose from the city as men stirred themselves. Jalal shook his head and tore the ruined *kaffiyeh* from his helmet. The cloth was burned, too.

"To me," he croaked, finding his throat constricted and dry. "To me, Sahaba!"

The kings of Nabatea had raised a fine temple at the center of their city. It held echoes of the Greeks, with long lines of columns carrying understated capitals and a pitched roof. Unlike the other buildings that crowded the valley floor, however, each course of fine-cut stone was separated from the others by a layer of wooden spacers. Where earthquakes had damaged the other buildings over the centuries, or even cast down the Temple of the Winged Lions in ruin, the great temple stood, serene and intact. It stood at the heart of the city, where three streams joined at the western end of the valley. A hill rose behind it, covered with villas and houses with flat roofs. The buildings that flanked it were raised up in the same red sandstone as the rest of the valley, but inset panels lined the walls, covered with painted carvings. Kings and heroes stared out of the stone, frozen in their moment of triumph. A grand Roman theater also graced the city, but it could not compare with the elegant beauty of the massive temple.

Mohammed had taken it as his residence while he remained at Petra. The statues had been covered, for the moment, with burlap and the fires of sacrifice put out. An iron chair with a padded cushion served him as a throne, though in no way did he think of himself as a king. All those notables of the city who had survived the slaughter in the High Place knelt before him on the smooth marble floor of the temple.

The Quryash scratched his bare chin idly. It itched terribly sometimes, though he was always surprised when he touched his face and found it smooth. The ruin of his beard would take some time to grow back, and he had thought it better—though he was sure that the elders of Mekkah would not approve!—to start afresh than have it grow in unevenly. He looked around, smiling at the discomfiture of many of his men who had suffered the same fate.

Those forty men who had followed him up the Long Stair and survived were beardless, too, and the other Sahaba had taken in grave jest to refer to them now as "the children." Mohammed knew, despite the gibe, that those who had survived the test on the mountaintop had earned an honored place, both in the hearts of their companions and in the eye of the great and merciful God. Any man who placed himself against the dark powers that infested the earth, sullying the Lord's perfect creation, would find a place in Paradise.

"This is the law," he said, turning his attention back to the city fathers, still kneeling on the temple floor before his chair. "The Compassionate One does not seek the sacrifice of goods or gold or children. He offers you a choice—to submit to His will and choose the Straight Path and find the joy of Paradise at the end of your days, or to err into sin and find fire and torment. Each man among you, each man in this world, must make this choice for himself. I have placed this city and all your domains under my protection, and while that stands, you will abide by the law. The law will guide you to the Righteous Way, but you must choose to submit to His will or not, as your heart dictates."

Mohammed gestured to the covered statues and the temple around him.

"This place, and all others like it, will either be turned to the contemplation of the Great and Merciful God, or it will serve the State. These works of art will be taken away.

They do not have a place here, nor does any depiction of a form or shape of God. No sacrifice will be made at the coming of the sun, or at the turning points of the year. Five times in each day, you will bow down before the Merciful and Compassionate One and you will pray, submitting yourself to His will. Beyond these things, you will live and work as you did before."

The city fathers remained kneeling, their eyes downcast. Mohammed knew that they were filled with confusion. They may have railed against the rule of the Empire when in their cups, but they looked upon him with naked fear. *The master that is known must be better than that unknown?* It did not matter; he did not intend to tarry here.

"Sit with me, good men of the city." Mohammed gestured for the guards to bring chairs from the nave of the temple. "There is much to discuss, for I will not be here long. First, there is the matter of the taxation of trade that comes through these lands. . . ."

Each hour weighed heavy on his heart, for the voice from the clear air remained with him and urged him to all speed.

ECBATANA, CENTRAL PERSIA

A n oak leaf fell, its shiny green upper surface flashing as it twisted and drifted in the air. Clear evening light, a cool pale blue, fell upon it. The man Arad watched it flutter past his outstretched fingertips. He tried to catch the leaf, bending his will upon his hand to force it to movement. His hand was a dead thing, frozen, stopped in mid-motion, half raised in the air. He stood under a crown of old trees, looking over the crest of a ridge. The slope before him was rocky and strewn with small boulders. The ground was almost bare. Goats and sheep from the village had been grazing along the rise. Tonight, the sky would be clear and cold. Even the sunset was muted, finding nothing to catch its golden glow.

Men's voices came from behind Arad, and he could hear gravel scattering down the slope as they trudged up to where he stood. They came from the Lord Dahak's encampment, which sprawled in a confusion of tents and wagons around the village. The sorcerer had finally moved in strength from his mountain fastness, coming down into the highland plains of old Media with nearly twenty thousand men. This time the army was composed mostly of Persians. C'hu-lo had been sent off to the northwest on another errand with his Huns. Had the sorcerer given Arad leave to speak, he would have advised against such a thing. It was not wise to let a T'u-chüeh army wander about unescorted. His desire did not matter; Arad stood frozen, trapped by the will of his master.

Two Persians in felt caps and long black tabards came into his field of view. Each man bore a long sword in an ornamented leather scabbard at his side and a small, round shield slung over his shoulder by a strap. Their beards were cut square in a style made popular by the late King of Kings, Chrosoes, and were thick with ringlets.

"Come along," the first of the two men said. Arad felt sensation and movement suffuse his body with those words. His master's will withdrew for a moment, leaving an invisible trail of smoky black power in the air. The guardsmen motioned down the slope. Arad complied, turning and picking his way over the stones and raw red gravel. In the poor light, a diffuse gray that made everything seem equally indistinct, whether it was near or far, he took his time. The guardsmen, silent and wary, followed him, each a step behind and aside. At the base of the ridge the trees ended, and a pitiful-looking field of wheat stubble began. As he crossed the field, Arad made a cautious effort with his will.

Grudgingly, the mage-sight that came with the first opening unfolded. Now he could see the individual stalks of wheat, the crumbled dry clods of earth, the line of tents ahead, the faces of the men standing watch. In recent days, as he had spent a great deal of time in thought walking beside the wagon that carried his master, some disquieting aspects of his condition had impressed themselves upon him.

Despite the shock of sensation and delight that had accompanied his birth into the service of the sorcerer, he had slowly realized that his native eyesight, taste, and touch were poor in comparison to that enjoyed by living men. Too, there was a grainy feeling that never left him, even with sleep and rest. It seemed that a dirty gray film lay between his mind and all that was around him. He knew, for memory was still etched bright, that the hue of a rose on a marble wall carved with horsemen should be brighter. The taste of fresh water sprung from a mountain stream should be sharper. The touch of a beloved hand should bring a tingling shock. Of all the bindings laid upon him by the sorcerer, he wondered if this was not the cruelest. The pain that came of that, particularly when he allowed himself to think upon the memories of his life before, pierced him. Arad tried to keep the best of those memories bright in his mind, as a bulwark against the constant horror that surrounded him, but it cost so much.

Bright blue eyes in a pale oval face haunted him.

The army of the Lord Dahak had found a camp among the foothills of Mount Alvand. Snowcapped peaks rose up just to the west, and the village was sheltered in a rich valley that spilled down toward the plain of Ecbatana in the east. They were close enough to the city to reach it in a day of marching, but not so near as to draw unwanted attention. The village was a trim collection of whitewashed brick buildings with canted roofs. Some of the scouts had reported that a ruined palace lay just west of the town, choked with brambles and willow saplings. Some of the Huns who had followed C'hu-lo now ghosted through the pine forests and ravines of the valley, keeping a watch for the sorcerer's enemies.

Arad entered the camp. Men clustered in front of their tents, eating and talking, hands busy cleaning weapons and armor. They looked up at him as he passed. Nearly all wore the black tabard of their master—a long plain garment of dyed wool with a hole for their head and open on the sides. It was worn belted, with a leather girdle closed by an iron buckle in the shape of a curled serpent that bit at its own tail. The front of the tabard was plain and dark, but upon the back the busy needles of the women of the mountain had stitched a single half-curled red serpent. The camp had an uneasy air, for the Lord Dahak had ordered his army into the south without explanation. They had marched down out of the grim mountains without complaint. Even the lack of horses that made most of the men march afoot had not roused a grumbling word.

A single tall standard, a long trailing flag of black with a wheel emblem upon it, stood at the entrance to the sorcerer's tent. A palisade of iron staves surrounded the pavilion, making a clear space on all sides. There was one gate through the paling, though there was space enough between each stave for a man to pass. Arad knew that no man in the camp had tried, nor would any dare. The iron strakes were carved with thousands of tiny incised glyphs in the spiky cruciform lettering that the sorcerer favored. Arad felt the air tremble as he passed through the gate. It grew chill, but his step did not falter.

"Ah . . . our most beloved servant attends us."

Arad stopped, standing still and quiet, his hands clasped behind his back. This was the will of the figure that lounged in a seat of bone at the center of the tent. Upon leaving the fortress of Damawand, the sorcerer had adopted a regal costume—long black silk pantaloons thrust into the tops of tooled kid-leather boots of dark curdled red. He habitually wore a shirt of fitted iron mail, composed of interlocking metal lozenges, though Arad knew that no blade of steel could kill this thing in the shape of a man. Each link of the mail had been enameled with indigo, and it shimmered in the light of the lanterns like the skin of a snake. Over this armor he wore a voluminous cloak with a peaked hood. The cloth was thick and heavy and it made a dry rustling sound as he walked. It, too, was indigo as pure as the night sky. Despite all this, and the thin circlet of gold that he wore on his high brow, he still remained clean shaven. His pale skin gleamed like a candle against the firmament of his clothing.

"You see, Khadames, he comes most readily when we summon him. He is the most loyal of all those who follow us."

Arad remained silent, for no word had been addressed to him. From the corner of his eye he could see that the stocky general remained impassive in the face of the Lord Dahak's banter. The general had adopted a stance with his feet apart and his face schooled to a calm impassivity. He had a helm of painted steel, conical and pointed, under one arm. Arad could feel the tension in the older man, radiating like the warmth of a charcoal brazier. Streaks of gray had begun creeping into the general's thick black beard even during the short time that Arad had been awake and aware of him. Khadames' face seemed graven in stone, and he stood like a mountain.

"Arad, my beloved, come sit with me." Dahak indicated an empty chair close by his side. It was plain and wooden, without cushions or ornamental carvings. Arad did not blink, but stepped to the chair and sat, folding his hands in his lap.

Dahak turned again to the general, his long thin face suffused with a wicked delight.

"You see? He is the most dutiful of men."

Dahak stood, gliding to his feet, letting the long robe fall behind him. He motioned to a man who had been squatting in the shadows by the door of the tent. The sorcerer brooked few servants, but those he maintained were well schooled in remaining invisible until desired. The man who came forth was bald, short, and gnarled, with a twist in his shoulders. His face and arms were marked with many thin scars, each making an odd, shiny ridge on his dark skin. He carried a ceramic bowl covered with a gauze cloth that steamed in the cool air. The man also had a bag slung over his shoulder. Dahak turned his chair of bone so that he could face Arad.

"Begin!" The sorcerer leaned forward, all attention on the small, twisted man.

The man placed his bowl on the ground and opened the leather bag, taking out shining, well-honed knives and curved lengths of metal. He removed glass bottles filled with odd-colored liquids and two cloths. A wooden box burnished dark with wear and about nine inches long on a side followed. Arad remained motionless in the chair, staring straight ahead. The will of his master held him tighter than any vise. The twisted man uncorked one of the glass bottles and moistened a cloth with the fluid inside. This done, he rubbed the cloth over the whole of Arad's head, coating it liberally with a clear, gel-like substance. When the man reached Arad's eyes, still open, he raised a razor-thin eyebrow and carefully closed them with his thumb.

In sudden darkness, Arad could feel the man at his shoulder working. After a moment, there was a rasp of metal, and then the man began carefully shaving the fine down of hair from Arad's neck and face. Arad, by custom long engrained, went clean shaven both on face and head by nature, but this man seemed intent on making sure that not a single hair remained on his pate. The curved shape of a razor wielded with exquisite skill glided over Arad's skin. When this was done, the man moved away and then returned with a warm cloth. With swift, sure movements, the man scrubbed all of the remaining gel from Arad's face, head, and neck. A pause followed, marked by a faint *tink* and the rattle of razors and knives being carefully put away in the wooden box and the leather bag. Water or some other fluid made a splashing sound.

The man bent again at Arad's shoulder, and there was a pungent smell in the air. Another cloth moved slowly over Arad's newly shaven scalp and face. This time the man was very careful to work a layer of oil into and across each ridge, bump, hollow, and opening of Arad's visage. The oil lay heavy on his skin, feeling like a close-fitting mask. The man worked his way around to the back, covering the neck and the back of the skull as well. He ended by swabbing the inside of Arad's nostrils with a small, round-ended wooden dowel. The man was clearly immersed in his work, for he had begun to hum a tune under his breath.

Arad remained patient and still, though in the cell of his mind, he was becoming restless.

The ceramic bowl rattled a little as the twisted man stooped to pick it up. A cloth was laid on Arad's lap, and his hands moved reflexively to take hold of the bowl as it was placed on his thighs. The twisted man paused—Arad could feel him looking across at the sorcerer—and then continued about his business. Warm steam drifted up around Arad's face, and in the cool air the touch was a blessing. The twisted man moved around to the back of Arad's head, and there was a light touch as a sheet of silk was laid over Arad's skull. The fabric fell down just past his mouth, tickling his chin. The leather bag rustled again, and something larger was taken from it. Heavy wood touched Arad's neck and settled there. Something like a yoke rested on his shoulders, coming up almost to his ears. Metal buckles clinked as they were closed on either side, holding it firm.

Arad could hear the General Khadames shift his feet, and there was a hiss of indrawn breath.

The bowl moved as the twisted man reached into it. In the cell of his mind, Arad suddenly felt a chill as an old memory began to work its way out of the back of his mind. Very long ago, when he had been a small child living with his uncle in the sprawling metropolis of Alexandria, he had seen such a wooden collar. Something hot and tacky touched the back of his head. The twisted man's hands moved strongly, pressing a thick, waxy substance across the back of Arad's head. The man scooped more material out of the bowl, building it up quickly across the nape of the neck and the line of the skull. The substance was very hot and almost liquid. Some of it seeped down, pooling against the wooden yoke before it stiffened and set. Arad's nostrils twitched, and he knew by the smell that it was fine beeswax. The twisted man quickly covered the back half of Arad's head, then pulled the silk drape back away from his face, laying it back over the wax. Then he shifted around to the front, even as the wax was beginning to congeal and shrink against Arad's flesh.

Wax touched Arad's throat like a hot compress, and his body trembled. In the cell of his mind, Arad remembered what he had seen that long-ago day, and he began to whimper. The man worked swiftly, building up a thick layer of beeswax, pressed close into the flesh, up over Arad's chin, then mouth, then nostrils.

Arad's eyes flew open, defying the implied will of his master. The twisted man was bent close, his fingers covered with wax, his eyes squinting in concentration. Wax covered Arad's nostrils, being carefully moulded into the cavities and around the nose. Then the cheeks were covered. The wax seemed tremendously hot, and Arad's skin felt like it was being burned away. His whole head was almost encased in hot wax, and the heat was incredible inside the mask.

Arad gathered his strength, trying to ignore the sensation of suffocation that clouded his mind. His lungs labored to breathe, his nostrils to inhale, but there was nothing, only a choking sensation. Within the cell that held his mind inviolate from his body, Arad marshaled all the will left to him. A single burning point of concentration gathered, shining like the tip of a hot poker fresh from the forge. He settled his ragged mind, trying to center himself, trying to find some foundation from which to work.

There is no wall that does not have a weakness. He chanted an old litany from his master. One blow of his will, directed with infinite precision, might rupture the iron bands of thought that held him long enough for him to tear away the wax and take a breath.

The twisted man covered his forehead, leaving cylindrical pits clear where Arad's eyes stared out. His body suddenly ceased breathing, having discovered that there was no air to draw into the lungs. A trembling shuddered through him, making his hands twitch and rattle the bowl. Arad was distracted, feeling the blood suddenly stop moving in his veins. His heart thudded to a stop, leaving blood to lie stagnant in its cavities. The rush of life, sustained by ingrained memory and all the autonomic systems of the body, failed. Arad's thought careened wildly in its cell, filled with a crushing fear of dissolution. The blazing spark of will fluttered and scattered.

The twisted man leaned close, peering into the pits left for Arad's eyes. His quick fingers scooped wax from the bowl and made a matching cylinder. He looked again, his bright black eyes gauging the depth he would need. Arad stared wildly back out. His eyes were still working, though a thin veil had fallen across the world he could see.

The little old man pushed a cylinder into each eye with his thumb, closing off even that sight. The wax burned against Arad's eyelids.

Arad whimpered, his mind folding up into itself over and over and over . . .

A good road wound down the northern slope of Mount Alvand, broad enough for two carts to pass, with a drainage ditch cut on the uphill side. Afternoon haze lay over the valley below, and the chattering of birds in the trees was muted by the late spring heat. Arad strode briskly, a walking staff of blond wood in his hand and a felt hat with a dimpled crown on his head. His face and skin were still pink and raw from where the wax had been peeled carefully away in two halves by the twisted man and his apprentices. They had seemed very pleased with the casting. Arad's feet were bare, for he had become used to the lack of pain that his current state allowed. Though he would not feel more than the memory of a sunburn, his master judged that he should not peel overmuch, as it might attract flies. A carry bag was thrown over one shoulder with a bowl and some oddments.

He wore the off-shoulder tunic and robe of a traveling priest. That familiar touch soothed him, though the brittle laughter of the sorcerer riding in his mind reminded him that he had wandered far from that path. Arad passed under an arch of oaks, descending down out of the pinewoods into the thick lowland forest covering the feet of the mountain. Alvand towered behind him, rising up in the air to find peaks capped in snow the year round. Robins flashed past on the wing. It was a peaceful afternoon. There was a touch of thought in his mind, and at this command he began to whistle a merry tune.

In his mind, Dahak laughed like winter coming in summer, restless and watching.

Flame curled from broken rock, hissing and spitting yellow in the air. Arad paused, looking down in interest at the cracked shale tumbled below the level of the road. A ridge of toppled stone ran down from the slopes of Alvand, intersecting the High Road as it came from the mountain passes of the west to the gate of the city. The High Road ran toward the sunset like an arrow, heading over the Zagros massif and then down through narrow passes to the great plain of the Tigris and the Euphrates. This passage was the single fastest way from east to west in the realm of Persia. Armies, kings, priests, merchants, and pilgrims thronged it by day. Here, where the road came up over the crest of the ridge on a long ramp of filled stone and rubble, a cliff had slid down, breaking open the earth.

A thick, cloying smell rose from the shale, and the air was filled with odd humors. Fires flickered among the rocks, and one flame burned continuously. In the early evening, now that the stars had come out, it cast an eerie glow over the crushed gravel of the roadbed. Arad resumed walking, his staff making a *tik-tik* sound. At this hour, well

after any responsible fellow would be within four walls
and under a roof with his feet up before a fire, the High
Road was deserted. Soon he would come to the city.

There, whispered Dahak, crowding forward in Arad's
mind until the man experienced a disorienting double vision as the loathsome touch of the sorcerer crawled in his
own perception.

*A city of circular walls, the Greek called it. Strong bat-
tlements, one within another, seven in all and within the
innermost, the palace of the King of the Medes. The first,
closest to the King, was gold, then silver for the great
lords, then orange for the priests of the fire, then blue for
the men who trade in goods, then red for the soldiers that
raised such strong walls, then black. Black for those who
till the fields and drive the lowing kine to the market. And
finally, ringing all about, white and the abode of the foreigners that came to pay homage and obeisance to the
King who is not to be seen.*

Arad shook his head, trying to drive out the singsong
chanting of the sorcerer. Arad was faintly aware that the
tongue that Dahak used when in this incorporeal state was
none that he had ever heard upon the lips of a living man.

The western door of royal Ecbatana rose up, strong and
proud, out of the night. Torches blazed on the battlements,
and fires had been set before the gate. The portal was
flanked by two enormous stone lions done in an archaic
style. Sturdy sandstone wings swept back from their shoulders, making their length from the proud nose to the curled
tip of their tails twenty feet or more. They stood, trapped
in stone, their grave faces staring west along the High
Road. Countless years had weathered them, taking an ear
from one and the tip of the wing from another, but nothing
dulled their majesty. The firelight gleamed on them, making their old faces come alive.

Behind the lions, square brick towers loomed up, sixty
feet high, their faces pierced by arrow slits and—high up—
a fighting platform of wood covered with hides and iron
plates. The gates stood open, the huge cypress doors

swung wide. In the gate passage a hundred soldiers stood talking in low tones. Arad approached openly, staying to the center of the road. The soldiers were clad in mail of iron rings on long hauberks that reached below their knees. Surcoats of yellow and red lay over the armor, and each man bore a plume of peacock feathers at the crest of their conical helms.

Brash children! Dahak's thought was filled with anger, and Arad staggered, nearly struck down by the ferocity of the emotion that flooded his mind. The sight of the peacock blazon lingered in Arad's mind. *Left too long without their elders to teach them manners and humility! Do they think that they play in the Garden of Kings, safe and sound, without a care in the world?*

"Ho, the gate." Arad found it difficult to force words from his mouth, and he struggled to maintain enough control of his hand to cling to the staff. "May a pilgrim enter the City of the Kings of Old?"

A tall man with a long beard of tiny curls stepped out from the cluster of men loitering just within the gate. He had a noble visage and piercing eyes set around a strong nose. The gildwork on his armor and the jewel on the hilt of his saber said *noble* and *dihqan* to Arad.

"A pilgrim may enter the city," the man said, his voice strong and even, ready to carry loud and clear over the din of battle. "You are late on the road, Holy Father. Do you need a meal and a bed for the night?"

Arad inclined his head, leaning on his staff. The walk down the mountainside would have been tiring for another—but it was best not to advertise his lack of exhaustion. "Yes," Arad said, surveying the wariness of the gate guards and the weapons they kept close to hand. "A roof and four walls would be a blessed change. Tell me, noble lord, you stand garbed for war, yet the gate is open after the fall of night . . . what transpires?"

The noble smiled, his teeth flashing white in the dark splendor of his beard and mustaches. "There is still trouble in the land, Holy One. Yet the hospitality of the Empresses

knows no bounds. We wait for late arrivals. Come within
and sup. If you make your way across the city, you will
find that the magi are welcome in the court of the Queens
of Persia."

Arad affected surprise. "The Birds of Paradise are in
residence here? I had not known . . . surely every bed and
nook in the city is filled."

The nobleman laughed and smoothed down his mustache with a habitual gesture. "Ahura-Madza bless them,
yes, the Empresses Azarmidukht and Purandokht grace the
old citadel with their presence. That hoary old stone monster wakes with new life as the *spabahadan* of all Persia
come to do them homage."

The *diquan*, for there was no mistaking the casual ar-
rogance and accent of one of the hereditary landowners
who made up the backbone of the Persian state and society,
turned and pointed down the avenue that led from the gate.
"Follow the main road," he said. "You will cross a pillared
bridge and see to your left the hill of seven gates. Ascend
and present yourself at the palace—you will find a warm
welcome—for the Empresses love holy men above all others."

That is fitting, laughed Dahak in the silence of Arad's
mind. *You have some experience of that!*

Arad felt numb, for the jibe awakened memories so
painful, he thought he would faint. The sorcerer did not
allow it, making his body bow to the diquan and pass
through the tunnel. Within the walls, fine two- and three-
story buildings clustered close to the road, and the streets
were filled with people and lights.

Agamátanu has changed of late, mused the sorcerer. *Yet,
it is still the same city I walked in my youth. Move, beautiful Arad, make haste to this palace of the seven gates.*

Whatever the nameless diquan at the gate thought of the
palace, Arad was impressed. Driven by the desire of the
sorcerer, he had hurried across the city, passing over the swift
current of the Alusjerd and through the districts that lay

below the hill of the palace. As the Lord Dahak had said, seven battlements each overtopped by the one behind it rose up on a hill set square in the northeastern quarter of the city. Deep gates pierced each wall, and a road paved with broad stones switch-backed up the hill between the ramparts. It seemed a strong fortress to Arad as he walked up the road, looking up at the merlons frowning over him.

The sorcerer hiding behind his eyes was not impressed. In truth, in comparison to the stupendous fortifications of Damawand, it did seem paltry. At each gate and each turning of the road, a company of guardsmen stood, their armor burnished bright and their helms carrying the same peacock token. At each gate Arad bowed to the commander and begged entrance and at each gate he was allowed to pass. These men were watchful, but a single priest without so much as a wooden spoon to his name did not strike them as a danger. Arad at last came to the summit of the hill and the plaza before the palace itself. Temples crowded the edges of the square, and lanterns burned before their doors. Indeed, the whole of the palace hill was lit up with all imaginable kinds of lights, sconces, torches, and open fires.

How pious, Dahak snickered, and Arad marked that as he passed, flames flickered and sometimes went out. *They feel the touch of night at the hem of their jeweled robes and they are rightly frightened.*

The plaza itself was filled with people. Arad moved through them, marveling at the appearance of those who had come to this place. Merchants from a dozen lands, from India and Serica and Egypt, haggled among themselves. Tribesmen in colorful turbans and beaded headdresses squatted or stood. Many men in armor with peace-bonded weapons chatted among themselves beside the bonfires that lit the square. Slaves in light blue tunics moved through the throng, carrying wine and honey-mead and plates of roasted lamb. Arad realized that these were the followers or servants of the *spabahadan* who had come to pledge themselves to the Empresses. Those, or embassies from surrounding lands, or those seeking favors from the new power that was trying to rise from the ashes of the old.

They have not wasted the trip! Dahak laughed again, a cruel, chill sound. Arad mounted the steps that led up into the palace itself. Here, too, the doors stood open, though now a band of massive men in surcoats of red with a yellow sign marked on their chests blocked the way. The guardsmen, mercenaries, and followers in the square seemed small beside these men. Too, they seemed alert and aware and their captain, when he stepped out to block Arad's advance, did not dismiss the priest before him. Here was a man who knew all too well that treachery and deceit came in every shape and size.

"What is your business here?" The man's voice was the growl of a dire wolf. Rings of gold were on his fingers and twisted into his beard. Scars marked his forearms in the small space between heavy leather gauntlets and armor of overlapping metal plates sewn to a linen backing. The other men were not distracted from their watch, either, though two of them observed Arad carefully with their hands on the hilts of bone-handled swords. These men wore long face masks of close-set iron links that exposed only their eyes. The masks gave them an ominous look.

Pushtigbhan, muttered Dahak and Arad could feel the sorcerer recede, slipping away from the man's consciousness. *The Imperial bodyguards.*

Arad bowed deeply to the man and said, "The captain at the gate of lions said that I could find shelter here in the hospitality of the noble Empresses Azarmidukht and Purandokht. If I have come in error, I will take myself away."

The Pushtigbhan captain grunted noncommittally and looked the priest up and down like a merchant in the marketplace viewing a fine ram. Arad could feel the man's almost perfect balance and the readiness with which violence could erupt.

"Do you have a patron?" It impressed Arad that such a

deep sound could come from a man, even a man with a chest as broad as this one's. "Other than the word of that popinjay at the western gate."

"No, noble lord. I have just come to the city from the west and I know no one within these walls."

The captain nodded, and a stubby finger scratched the side of his nose. He made to speak, but there was a sudden shout from within the palace.

Arad leapt back, down the steps, and barely missed having his throat cut by the lightning-quick draw of the Pushtigbhan captain's long sword. His men spun, blades half-drawn, a shout on their lips.

A man staggered through the doorway and fell heavily on the steps. Two more of the Pushtigbhan came through the portal, dusting their hands of him. Unlike those who stood without, these men's faces were bare, showing their curled beards.

"The gracious and merciful Empress Purandokht bids you a good night, my lord Faridoon. Pray, take her mercy and have done—no one here is interested in the ravings of a madman."

Arad rose and straightened his tunic, hearing the sarcasm dripping from the soldiers' words. The man on the ground rose stiffly, brushing back long, wild hair from his face. He was quite old, past fifty, and his face was deeply lined by starvation and the cruel hand of long days spent unsheltered among the elements. His clothes had once been fine and well made, but a seeming eternity upon the open road had worn them down, leaving them patched and mended and ill-used. For all this, there was a fire in his eye as he stood, picking up his cap. His beard was ragged and shot with white, but there was the remnant of a noble bearing.

"Shout all you will at the night," he boomed, for Faridoon's voice was deep, deeper even than the guard-captain's. "Those things that walk in it are not afraid of the cries of children. Rather, my lords, they sup at fear, growing fat in the darkness. I have been to the great temple at Ganzak, not a score of days ago, and there is nothing in that place but dust. Heed me! Do you know what this means for the children of man?"

The Pushtigbhan guard strode down the steps and struck Faridoon on the face. The old man buckled at the blow and fell to his knees. Blood streamed down from a cut on his forehead. The guard stood over him, glowering, his hand raised for another blow.

"The fire that lit the dawn of the world has gone out." Faridoon remained on one knee, his eyes hard as he looked up at the guard. "Beside that one, all other lights are dim. Hope, noble lords, flickers and goes out. Strike me, if you will, but listen. There is little time left to us."

"Bah!" The guard turned on his heel and walked up the steps. The captain of the guard watched the other Pushtigbhan go back inside the palace. He raised an eyebrow and crossed his arms across his chest. The man Faridoon picked himself up again, wincing at the pain in his head. With a last look at the soaring walls of the palace and the lamps of crystal and silver that lighted the doorway, he turned away.

This one, we follow. Dahak inched forward into Arad's consciousness. *But carefully . . .*

Arad shrugged and turned away from the palace door. Where his master willed, so he would go.

Can this be the one who plagued me so? Arad felt the sorcerer seize control of his limbs, pushing him to break into a trot. They had followed the man Faridoon down into the warren of the lower city, through alleys and dark passages between crumbling brick buildings. Now they paused in shadow, watching their quarry lean against the wall of a doss-house with a weary air. The street was foul with slops and refuse, but a reed taper guttered before the door of the boardinghouse, giving a wan light. *If it is he, he has fallen far in the world.*

Despite the apparent satisfaction in those words, the sorcerer was loath to approach the tired old man. Arad waited patiently in the darkness, his tireless body willing to remain until the snows came again. Finally, the old man pushed himself away from the wall and dug in the coin purse at his belt. Even in the poor light, Arad could see that only one or two copper coins were yielded up.

"Master Faridoon?" Arad stepped out into the little circle of light. The old man started and raised a hand to ward his face, but then lowered it slowly as he took in the poor robes and sandals of the priest. "Fear not! I am a fellow traveler and I saw the poor way they treated you at the palace. I am Arad."

Faridoon raised a tired eyebrow at the priest's name but made a shallow bow.

"Well met, then, Master Arad. I remember, you were getting out of the way of the guardsmen. What drives you to follow me on this black night?"

Arad leaned on his staff and motioned with his head toward the doss-house. "I am equally poorly provided with coin. It seemed that you might know the way to lodgings that might provide for me as well."

Faridoon laughed and relaxed a little. Arad moved closer and dug in his own purse, pulling forth four copper coins. "You see, here are the sum of my riches. Will this suffice?"

Faridoon nodded, his weather-beaten old face settling into a long familiar grimace. "For tonight, at least, friend Arad. Come, let us dine on the watery gruel they call soup here."

"Master Faridoon? That name is well known to me from the readings of our temple—are you descended from the great hero's line, or is it a name of honor?"

Faridoon turned on the step, his hand on the latch. Great sorrow seemed to pool behind his eyes. "I am the five hundred and fifteenth to bear this glorious name," he said in a sad voice. "But I cannot spring from mountaintop to mountaintop or break a dragon's back with my bare hands. Time has attenuated that blood in my veins. Now I am only the vessel of strange dreams and portents, without the strength to raise the spear of fire against the darkness."

Faridoon stopped the rush of long-pent words with his hand, bowing his head in embarrassment.

Good, Dahak purred, and black strength flowed into Arad's limbs. He stepped forward and placed a hand on the old man's shoulder. "You must rest," Arad said, feeling his voice and the sorcerer's overlay in a gruff echo. "Sleep and put these troubling dreams aside."

Faridoon frowned at the odd tone in the priest's voice and looked up. He was too late, for Arad's grip closed on the old man's throat and his fingers, burning with the hidden venom of the sorcerer's ancient hatred, crushed his larynx. Faridoon struggled, thrashing, his hands clawing at the priest's face. The pain was nothing, only a distant memory. Arad raised the old man from the ground, letting his feet kick fruitlessly. There was a cracking sound, and old Faridoon, the last of his noble and blessed line, went limp.

Ah, this is a day of joy. The sorcerer's voice bubbled with glee and an all-encompassing relief. *I never dreamed that it would be so easy!*

Arad carried the body of the old man into one of the alleyways and laid it gently on the ground. With a short prayer, he folded the man's arms on his chest and closed his eyes. Then he walked away, trying to ignore the voice of the sorcerer chattering in his mind. Arad settled his mind, trying to keep the buzz of questions and conjectures from his conscious thought. He did not mark that the reed taper by the door of the doss-house had gone out.

Arad came once more to the door of the palace, though this time the sorcerer had crept forward enough in his consciousness to peer out through the windows of his eyes and mark the formidable barrier of the Pushtigbhan. The same scarred captain was still on watch, though now that a deeper night had fallen, most of the hangers-on in the courtyard had left. Only the two bonfires continued to crackle and blaze, holding back the night a little. Down in the city Arad had acquired a parchment and—at the direction of the sorcerer—had made some marks upon it. Though Arad knew six languages well, he could not ken the meaning of the spiky letters.

The Pushtigbhan captain raised his wooly eyebrows to see the mendicant come before him again, but accepted the proffered sheet of paper with equanimity.

"When I was here before, noble sir, you said that I needed a patron's token. I pray this suffices."

The captain squinted at the paper in the poor light, but on the sheet he saw what he expected to see.

"Enter, then, good priest, and may you find the hospitality of the twin Empresses to your liking."

Arad nodded and entered the great vault of the first entrance chamber.

The Lord Piruz sat before the western gate of the city on a stool with three legs. His personal guard stood at the watch, nearly 120 men in lamellar half-armor with parade helms, long swords in tooled leather scabbards, and their bow cases strapped to their backs. Piruz accounted his duty both honorable—was this not the main gate into the city and the very artery of the Empire?—and easy tonight. Only one ragged priest had come through the gate since the sun had set behind the rampart of the Zagros Mountains. A folding table with copper legs and a porphyry top rested beside him, holding a silver kettle covered in parallel designs of men hunting and small porcelain cups of tea. Piruz smoothed his mustache, considering what to wear in the morrow, when he appeared before the twin Empresses to swear his pledge of loyalty.

He had come well equipped to the court, not only with hardy fighting men from his province, but with silks and jewels and finery of all kinds. None of these things would suffice for a *gift* to the Empresses—they had any luxury they might desire—but *he* needed them, for one could not make a mark in the court of the Birds of Paradise without a sufficient wardrobe. Piruz smirked to himself, for he knew himself a handsome man and well endowed with vast estates. Balkh may be at the uttermost east of the

Empire—by the accounts of the courtiers at Ctesiphon, a
howling wasteland filled only with savages and the Hun—
but Piruz could count as well as any. With the Imperial
capital in ruins and the land between the two rivers
shocked by massive flooding, plague, and famine, remote
Balkh had suddenly become not only the most populous
city in the Empire but the richest as well.

He smiled again and fingered the supple silk doublet he
wore under his armor. It was a pure gold color like nothing
seen in the western half of the Empire. The Chin merchants
who had sold it to him called it *"dew of the sunset,"* and
it had cost him thirty talents of silver to gain enough for
a shirt. Of course, here in the west, or even farther, in the
cities of the Romans, it would sell for a hundred talents or
more . . . such was the wealth that flowed through *his*
hands.

"Lord Piruz!" One of his guardsmen had stiffened and
pointed out onto the dark plain that lay west of the city.
"Someone is coming."

Piruz rose, his hand already on his saber hilt. One could
not fault the Prince of Balkh for going unarmed or unready
for battle. For all their wealth the lands along the
Amu'Darya were not peaceful. The collapse of the Gok
Turk khaghanate that had ruled from Ferghana in the east
to the Russ forests in the west had not engendered stability.
The men of Balkh knew battle and raid and alarms in the
night from birth. Around the Prince, his men shifted to
block the gate and two squads moved inside, ready to
swing the massive oaken portals closed at a moment's notice. Piruz squinted out at the darkness.

There was a light on the plain, flickering and bouncing.
A rider, thought Piruz.

The light grew closer, and Piruz could see that it was
following the road. Then another light appeared behind the
first, then another. Within a minute, Piruz whistled in
alarm as the plain lit up with lines of flickering lights. One
great column was advancing down the road at a walk,
while two others followed on either side.

"Close the gate," he rasped, waving his lieutenants back through the passage. He stepped forward, onto the brick paving before the towers. His bodyguards closed in behind him. There was a booming sound as the portals closed and a rattle of chains as the locking bar was dropped. Piruz grounded his saber and rested his hands on it. No man would say that the Prince of Balkh fled in the face of an unexpected visitor. Many of the great *spabahadan* of the realm were expected here: it would not do for them to find the gate closed against them, and met with spears and arrows.

The tramp of marching feet came out of the darkness, and the bouncing lights resolved into a troop of armored cavalry riding on the road. Two figures led them on coal-black stallions. Piruz squinted again, trying to make out the crest on their banners, but failed. Every man seemed to be garbed in black, and it reduced them to faint outlines in the darkness. The horsemen were clad in mail from head to toe, in the style of the *clibanari*, with barely a slit for their eyes to peer forth from conical helms. Lances, bows, and heavy maces hung at their saddles. Out on the plain, the other two columns came to a halt a hundred yards from the gate, and fell out into ranks.

Piruz guessed that they must be infantry with long spears and rectangular shields of laminated wood and round iron bosses. There were many of them.

The two horsemen in the lead of the column cantered up to the edge of the light cast from the gate towers. They turned their horses, looking down upon Piruz. The Prince was impressed; their horses were as fine as any Sogdian charger, glossy and black as a raven's wing, spirited and tall in the shoulder. Like the men who stood on the plain, the tack of the two horses were black as night, fading almost to invisibility against the glossy hide.

"Greetings, noble lords." Piruz' voice hung in the air, calm and even a little cheerful despite the possible danger.

"Greetings, Captain of the Gate." The voice filled the air with power and strength. The speaker was obviously the lord of this host: a tall, thin man with a clean-shaven face and dark eyes. His skin was pale, but Piruz could see a lean, wiry strength in the set of his shoulders. Too, the charger knew his master was astride, and was calm and poised. Supple armor like a snakeskin gleamed at the man's chest, though he did not seem to bear a sword or a bow. "I have come to pay my respects and pledge to the Empresses, those known as Azarmidukht and Purandokht. Pray, noble Captain, may I enter the city?"

Piruz' left eyelid twitched at the slight implied in the man's speech. Still, the stranger was polite and possessed of strength.

"It is late, my lord. The Empresses will have retired. Too, I see that there is no room in the city for your men. I will send a messenger to the court, saying that you have come . . . what was your name?"

The man on the horse smiled, inclining his head a little at the rebuke. "I have been remiss," he said. "Say to them that their uncle comes to bend his knee before them. Tell them that Rustam Aparvez has returned unlooked for to aid them in this difficult time."

Piruz hissed in surprise despite himself. He had not known that the dead Chrosoes Aparvez, once King of Kings, had a living brother. This was news indeed. He made a half bow to the man on the horse and turned to the gate. The portal ground open a crack, and he stepped to the opening. "Send a runner to the palace in all haste," he said, his voice low. "A man claiming to be the uncle of the Empresses has come to the gate of the lions with an army." Within, Piruz' captain nodded sharply.

The Prince turned back to the men on the horses. "A delay may ensue, noble lords. Would you care to sit and take tea with me?"

Dahak smiled politely and swung down from his horse. His eyes were distant and unfocused. Khadames followed, rubbing the side of his nose as he looked around in interest. It had been some time since he had passed through Ecbatana. Little had changed. The general grinned up at the guardsmen watching from the rampart. Their faces were stony in response. Khadames did not think they would wait long at the gate; perhaps they would not even wait for the messenger to return.

Arad climbed a broad flight of travertine steps. Fat-bellied columns lined it, rising up to support a vaulted roof paneled with cypress and pine hexagons. Many lanterns blazed along the walls, though the palace was deep in slumber. The lower floors showed all the signs of a lavish feast and lengthy entertainment. The great hall that bisected the building was still being cleared by dozens of slaves. Many of the guests slept on couches against the walls, and some, in the rooms curtained off from the main hall, still celebrated. The watchful eyes of the Pushtigbhan were everywhere. A dozen of the stocky guardsmen loitered about the base of the grand staircase. Arad had shown the parchment and, again, was allowed past.

A hallway lined with sconces and flat wall panels showing scenes of the hunt and battle led him to a foyer. Here the floor was tiled with alternating silver- and gold-washed bricks. Arad looked around, marking the hanging silks and the fine stone and marble. Here, ostentation and raw wealth expressed the power of the Persian state. A memory came to him despite his resolute desire to keep all such things from his thought—a memory of a quiet garden and slim pillars of alabaster. That had been a place no less costly in construction, but it held grace and beauty and refinement. There had been peace there. This place was filled with nervous energy and the desire to impress.

But this stands, whispered the sorcerer, *and that so-peaceful city is now filled with the bones of the dead.*

Arad shook his head, trying to drive out the cloying words and the horror lurking behind them. It was useless. He paused, seeing that the main doorway out of the foyer was closed. No guardsmen stood before it, and there was a low mutter of voices beyond. The priest frowned and moved to the door, raising his staff to knock on the burnished cedarwood panels.

"Hold there, stranger!" The slap of sandals on the stone of the floor drew Arad's attention. He turned, lowering the staff. A short, round man in enveloping white and crimson robes hurried up, his face flushed red with effort. An orange sash over his shoulder and a heavily ornamented staff told Arad that the man was one of the magi, the priests of Ahura-Madza, the Lord of the Eternal Fire. This one's plump face was tight with suspicion, and his beard, trimmed short to make an arc along his chin, jutted forward belligerently. "What business do you have with the Queens of Heaven at this late hour?"

"Your pardon, Holy One. I come bearing a message for the Empresses from a close relative. I come late as I have just arrived from a long journey. Pray, is there someone to announce me?"

The magi drew himself up, puffing out his chest and rapped his staff on the floor with asperity.

"No one, not even another priest, may enter the presence of their Majesties without first passing me. These are dangerous times, and all precautions must be taken. If I say it, you may—perhaps—look upon the radiance of their Imperial presence."

Arad smiled faintly. The presence of the sorcerer had receded in the face of this new development, but the priest could feel mocking laughter at a great distance.

"Of course," Arad said, looking upon the little round man with interest. "What steps need be taken?"

The magi sniffed and frowned in concentration. Arad raised an eyebrow as he felt the patterns of force in the foyer shift and tremble. The little man commanded some power. The other man's breathing slowed, and a gelid sphere of pale white light sprang into being around the two men. For an instant, Arad felt the tendril of thought that tied him to the sorcerer weaken and bend, almost severed by the expansion of the ward. A burst of hope in his heart was stilled and then mercilessly crushed as the sorcerer wrenched the tendril of control out of phase with the ward that the little magi had established.

"I am not without powers . . . ," the round-faced magi gasped for breath, and one hand drew a sign in the air— "I can ken threat and malice and falsehood."

The sign in the air hummed and buzzed, and Arad felt his skin crawl. The sign was the linchpin of an invocation of similarity. It was in the old language that the sorcerer spoke in his mind and called to harm and treachery and slaughter and betrayal. Arad stood silently, leaning on his staff. At last the magi huffed and puffed and let go of a long, shuddering breath. The sign faded away quickly, and the sphere of ward passed away as well. Arad blinked, seeing sweat beading the man's face.

"This is taxing to you," Arad stated. The man was strong, but his skills were poor and ill trained. Such effort as he had expended should have sufficed to lay low every miscreant within the palace and the grounds without. Yet it had found nothing, sliding aside from the sorcerer's skill like water over the surface of a granite boulder. "Are you well?"

The magi drew a rich-colored handkerchief out of his robe and dabbed at his forehead. "In the service of their Majesties, all men must give all that they can. You mean them no harm. I will announce you to their august presence. Do you have a letter or token?"

"Yes, Holy One." Arad gave over the sheet of parchment. "My name is Arad."

The little man nodded and took the sheet without looking at it, then opened the door. He did not think to introduce himself. The sound of flutes and lyres and people talking in overly loud voices spilled out for a moment before the panel closed with a click.

Harm? Dahak settled into Arad's mind, radiating smug satisfaction. For a moment Arad glimpsed dark buildings passing and the swaying motion of a horse between his legs. *I have nothing but the most dear love for my nieces. It pains me, dear Arad, that we missed one of those puling maggots . . . later I will find how his marrow tastes.*

The door opened again, much quicker than Arad would have supposed, and the little magi poked his head out and beckoned. Arad entered, his staff making a soft *tinking* sound on the floor of polished sea green marble. His eyebrows rose again, taking in the unfettered opulence that oozed and spilled from the walls.

Five walls bounded the room, rising up a double height, and they were covered in rich, alternating panels of polished wood—both dark and light. Clear lanterns of colored glass burned, casting a shifting elusive glow over the men and women seated at ease within. Two thrones of gold dominated the room, sitting on a raised pedestal. During the day, tall triangular windows would allow light to flood into the room, silhouetting the high seat. Arad paced forward to the edge of an ermine carpet that lay before the thrones and the two women sitting in them. He bowed, kneeling and touching his forehead to the sea green floor.

You are quite the courtier, dear Arad, the sorcerer thought, snickering, but his attention was elsewhere, on his horse, which was clattering up the rampart road on the palace hill. The gate captain had been easily swayed once the Lord Dahak turned his attention upon him.

"Rise," came a languid voice, and Arad stood, looking upon the two young women who would rule this vast and strange land. To his left sat the Princess Azarmidukht, a glittering creature draped in purple silk and jewels, and with long red fingernails. Like her mother, the Imperial Princess Maria, she possessed a striking, strong face dominated by a fine Greek nose. She was not beautiful in a classic way, but the fervor in her dark brown eyes and the opulent display that her bosom made, glittering with amethyst and ruby and topaz, strove to overcome that lack. Her hair was invisible behind an elaborate crown of white gold and tiny pearls. Likewise, her face and eyes were carefully enhanced by artful paints. Arad bowed low again before her. "Glory to your name, Radiance of the World."

To his right sat Purandokht, her twin sister, though Arad

marked that her eyes were a watery green. They did not match well with the floor, but he forbore mentioning this. Purandokht, too, was encrusted with finery and gold and gems of a thousand colors. Each sat at ease, though Arad could taste fear in the air from the courtiers and nobles who made up their court. To her, he bowed low again and then stood. "Glory to your name, Flame of the East."

A servant kneeling on the step below Azarmidukht held the parchment in his hands. The Princess made a small motion with her hand, barely moving a fingernail. "You bring us news of our uncle, priest?" Her voice was strong, but none would call it melodious. "We are puzzled, thinking him long dead, banished beyond the edge of the world."

"Yes," Purandokht said smoothly, following on her sister's words without a pause. "What favor does he seek of our Royal mercy?" The green-eyed Princess smiled, though it was hard to make out on her henna-etched lips.

"I beg your indulgence, Crowns of the Firmament of Heaven, your noble uncle had heard that some ignorant men disputed your claim to the throne of your father. He comes to lend you his arm in support of your rightful patrimony."

Arad bowed again, his forehead barely grazing the cool tile of the floor. It seemed appropriate. There was a rustling in the court—their neighbors had roused many who had fallen asleep during the revels. Arad had only glanced around for an instant as he had walked from the door up the long aisle among the couches and low tables, but he knew that none of the great *spabahadan* were present. The true powers in the land were waiting to see if the Empresses could gather any strength at all.

Azarmidukht's eyes narrowed, and she leaned forward slightly, a movement that sent a trill of chiming metal and crystal across the room.

"How strong is this arm? Does he command more than a rabble? None have seen him for nearly twenty years, if my memory of ancient times does serve."

Arad, still facing the floor, smiled bitterly at the brash words. How could anyone not know the power of the Lord Dahak, now that he moved in the world?

"Light of the Coming Sun, your uncle comes with a strength of twenty thousand men, all pledged to your cause."

All around the room was a titter of incredulity and some small hiss of fear. The disaster at Kerenos River and the failed campaigns of the dead King Chrosoes had beggared Persia for men and treasure. Once an army of twenty thousand would be the matter of mustering a great Prince's country estates, but now it was a force to be reckoned with and more. Purandokht had opened her mouth to make a scathing remark, but now she closed it with a snap and sought her sister's eye.

Azarmidukht remained composed and raised an eyebrow. "And when, priest, may we expect our uncle to attend us?"

Arad rose, leaving the staff lying on the floor, and met the eyes of the two Queens. "Within moments, Blessed of the Flame That Does Not Die. I hurried ahead to bring you this news, lest there be confusion, fear, or unwary words. Here, your uncle bade me bring you these tokens of the love that he holds for you."

Arad removed a package of cloth-of-gold from his robe and ascended the steps. The Pushtigbhan behind the thrones, a full score of them, tensed. Purandokht caught the eye of their captain and shook her head slightly. Arad knelt on the step at their feet, fighting hard to keep from sneezing. A slowly shifting cloud of myrrh and rose-attar surrounded the Princesses. He unwrapped the package, untying silk twine and showing first an inner covering of silver mesh and then, in his upraised hands, two slim black bracelets.

Purandokht started in utter surprise, her hand flying to her mouth, the rattle of her garments as she made to rise echoing loud in the expectant quiet of the court. Her sister's fingers tightened on the arms of the throne, and a thin hiss of rage escaped her lips.

"Where . . . ?" Azarmidukht could barely speak.

Arad separated the cloths, taking one bracelet in cloth-of-gold and the other in silver mesh. He turned to his left, to Azarmidukht, and held the bracelet up to her.

"In the last days of her life your mother gave this into the keeping of your uncle. She commanded him to bring them to you when her husband, your father, at last lay dead. Rustam protested, knowing that these things should go to you straightaway, but she insisted. Now he sends them to you, a token of his love and hers. Pray, lady, take it as your mother intended."

Arad cursed himself for a coward, raging at himself in his mind. Still, he could not prevent his hands from slipping the thin black bracelet—its fine mesh of scales glinting in the light of the lanterns—around the pale white wrist of the Princess. Azarmidukht stared down at it as it closed on her wrist, sliding snug, and in her eyes the priest could see the reflection of a band of white gold blazing with emeralds. In that brief moment Arad saw into the heart of the Princess and felt the crushing weight of love long thought denied. The sorcerer's will kept him from tears at this betrayal, but he turned and slid the other onto the waiting arm of Purandokht, who was already crying, her tears cutting deep tracks in the arsenic paste makeup that kept her skin so pure and white.

"Your uncle bade me say this." Arad's voice sank to a whisper that did not reach beyond the ears of the two young women. "As she lay dying, your mother said to him that she loved you both very much and was so proud of you. She regretted the long coldness she had showed you, but it was necessary. To come to this day, as you stand Empresses of all Persia, it was vital that she make you strong. These tokens, things that were denied you in life, she passed on that you would know, today, that you were her most beloved."

Arad felt the doors to the hall open, and he stood, turning, and took the hands of the two Princesses. Even Azarmidukht was crying now, though she did not speak. Purandokht was gasping for breath, feeling the long years of bitter hatred she had held for her mother crumble and collapse. The rush of emotion washed over Arad like a shock of icy water, and his hatred for the sorcerer had never been greater. Even so, he helped them rise.

The Lord Dahak entered the chamber. Khadames and a dozen Pushtigbhan were at his back. He strode across the marble; rich brown hair tied back behind his head, ruddy pink in his cheeks, and knelt with impeccable grace before the two princesses. "Beloved nieces, it has been too long. You were so small when I saw you last." His voice filled the room with a rich baritone, and every heart there leapt at the surety of command ringing in those words. Dahak raised his eyes, meeting each Princess in turn. Behind them, Arad stepped away behind the golden thrones, unleashed from his master's will for just a moment. Dahak brought the two young women into a close embrace, bending his head to speak softly to each. Azarmidukht was sobbing now, seeing love and acceptance and guileless welcome in the sorcerer's eyes.

In this light, under these lanterns, the face of the sorcerer was the very image of the dead king.

ROMA MATER

The wagon rattled through hills of debris rising higher than a villa roof. The road here was elevated on an embankment and sealed with close-fitted paving stones. Krista dozed lightly, leaning back on a frayed cushion wedged against the wooden back of the driver's seat. The little black cat was a warm presence on her chest, where it had curled up inside her cloak. This close to the city a haze of wood smoke clouded the sky and lent the air a bitter taste. The road ran straight as a die, coming out of the valley behind and running ahead to the rising wall of the city. A vast tumbled pile of broken pottery, wine jars, and amphorae rose up on the left. To their right, acres of discarded furniture, substandard building tile, cracked brick, and splintered barrels humped toward the horizon. Among the hills, curls of smoke rose up from funerary temples and the camps of rag pickers and vagrants.

Even with most of the debris of the city being carried down to Portus on barges returning to the great port to pick up new shipments of trade goods, the waste heap of the ancient capital was enormous. Clouds of tiny brown birds swept and dove over the hills, sometimes blocking the sun.

Krista had a bag on her lap as well, with her hand inside, riding on the hilt of a cheap iron knife. The wagoneer was a surly man with an evil black beard and a sullen disposition. He had taken her copper coin and let her ride with him, but he kept glancing at her out of the corner of his eye and, despite being exhausted, she did not sleep. Even this catnap seemed to have encouraged him, and she felt the wagon slow. She cracked an eyelid and measured the distance to the Via Appia gate. No more than a mile, she supposed. *I could get out and walk*, she thought.

She yawned, stretching, and sat up. The driver's hand snatched away from over her knee. Krista stared at him, and he looked away. Clouds were edging into the sky from the east, threatening to cut off the pale sunlight. Krista shivered and wished she had thought to bring a heavier cloak. It could be quite cold in Rome, even in summer. The wagon jounced and banged as it crossed a bad section of road. Krista slid the little cat into her bag, ignoring the plaintive *mew* of protest.

Motion on a nearby mound of cracked olive jars and discarded racing chits drew her eye. A man in a dirty brown-and-white cloak was scrambling up the side of the road embankment. His face and hands were wrapped in grimy linen. Krista snapped the iron knife out of its sheath and whirled around. The driver, startled by her motion, looked back toward her. Four more men had appeared out of the rubble on the other side of the road and were running toward the wagon. The driver shouted in fear and cracked his whip over the heads of the oxen.

Krista rolled off of the seat as the cart jerked forward, hitting the ground hard on the balls of her feet and then bouncing back up. The bag with the little cat was clutched tight to her chest. The four men reached the road, ignored the cart, and ran toward her. The lead man was shouting something, but the rags that covered his face muffled the sound. Krista dodged across the road toward the single man who had just managed to make it up the road embankment. He was just standing up, brushing dirt from his tunic, when she spun into him, her right foot flashing around and up to crack against the side of his head.

The man cried out and staggered back. Krista dropped down lightly and then jumped over the side of the embankment. Dirt fountained under her feet as she slid down the side of the road. The man, stunned by her kick, toppled off the road and bounced down the slope, crashing into a great pile of half-burned wicker baskets. Krista hit the bottom of the slope running, and dodged off through the smoldering piles of refuse.

On the road behind her, the leader of the four men cursed and ground his fist into his thigh in disgust. "Krista!" He cupped his hands to make his voice carry farther, but the girl was already gone.

It was well past sunset when Krista finally entered the city. After the close shave on the Via Appia, she had picked her way through the rubbish yards to the Ostia gate—the next closest entrance in the wall—but some suspicious characters had been loitering in the shade of the gate towers. She crouched in the shadow of a mound of broken statuary for almost two hours before one of the ragged men she had seen before appeared and spoke quietly to one of the watchers. It was afternoon, then, and she took her time working through the debris and smoke and funereal tombs to the east. The city of Rome was entered by many gates, but all of them had guards. Some of the watchers would be more alert than others, and she had no idea how many of the ragged men there were.

At nightfall she fed the little cat the last of the smoked fish from Herculaneum and scratched its ears. She sat in deep shadow under a curving section of wall at the eastern end of the city. The wall was odd looking, lined with arches and pillars in three courses. The main wall ran into it at an angle and stopped abruptly. The archways were filled in with mixed brick and concrete. Over the walls, the daytime din and clatter of the Asinara district was fading as people went home and closed up shop. The little cat was nosing about, looking for mice in the high grass that grew along the verge of the rampart. Not more than ten feet away, a doorway was set into the wall in a very shallow embrasure. The door was iron and heavy and locked, but Krista could smell the rank odor of urine on the bricks that filled the archways on either side.

The curved section of wall was known to her, too; it was the outer face of the amphitheater of Castrense—a theater of moderate size that had been incorporated in the outer city wall hundreds of years ago. Once, she supposed, official games and pageants would have been held in it. Now she knew that it hosted a stodgy succession of theater revivals, religious festivals, and—in the evening—it was rented out for private parties. Even with the height of the wall above her, she could hear the tinny clash of cymbals and the racket of young boys singing. The little black cat sidled back up to her, nosing at her hand. Krista smiled and opened her palm. There was no more fish. The little cat gave a quiet sigh and crawled into her lap.

She sat quietly, waiting for an overindulgence of wine to take its inevitable effect.

*   *   *

Krista glided into the alleyway behind the Duchess' villa with trepidation. Rome after midnight was still a dangerous proposition—filled with footpads and murderers—even under the firm rule of the Emperor Galen. The city was just too big and crowded and filled with foreigners to police properly. It had taken almost three hours for Krista to make her way across the city to the Quirinal hill and home, but now she was at the back gate, feeling the strain of the long day in her calves. Luckily, the Duchess had great call for people to come and go quietly from her house so there was always a watchman on duty.

She rapped on the stout wooden panel with the pommel of the iron knife and, after a moment, there was a rattling as the spyhole cover was moved aside. A bleary blue eye peered out and widened at the sight of Krista standing under the gate lamp. Krista made a half snarl and bobbed her head. "Let me in." She was very tired and very grumpy. The door clanked as the locking bar was thrown back, and she pushed in before it was even open. The man on watch made to say something, but Krista raised a hand to silence him. "Later, Macrus, later. After a bath and sleep. Oh, what happened to your eye?"

The servant, a burly man with thick forearms and a trunklike neck, had a bandage wrapped around his head and over one eye. He made to speak, but Krista ignored him and carried on. "Oh, it doesn't matter. I'll find the Duchess by myself. You can tell me tomorrow."

She hurried off, her whole body aching with desire for a hot bath and a bed with fresh, clean sheets. At the gate, Macrus closed his mouth with a snap and shook his head in amusement as he locked the gate again.

Krista clattered down the steps into the gymnasium and the baths, her cloak already bundled under one arm with the bag and the cat. On the lower level, she turned left in the round atrium, intending to enter the series of rooms that held marble tubs set into the floor, but the ring of steel drew her attention. On the right-hand side of the gymnasium was a practice floor of sand surrounded by an arcade of columns. Krista slipped into the room, her sandals off, and came to stand next to one of the fluted green pillars. Oil lamps in bronze holders burned on each acanthus capital, casting a steady, warm glow over the rectangle of sand in the middle of the room.

In the fighting square, Thyatis attacked furiously, her Indian-steel blade flickering in the air. She was clad in only a short kilt and a twisted cloth *strophium* that bound her breasts close to her chest. Her long hair was pinned back in a bun and away from her face. Her skin was slick with sweat and silver droplets flew off her arms as she pressed the attack. Nikos faced her, stripped to a loincloth as well, his own sword a blur in the air as he matched her stroke for stroke. Thyatis bounced back, the tip of her blade trapping his on the withdraw. Nikos lunged in, striking for the inside of her arm. She blocked downward and turned on her heel, trying to lead him past her. He countered and threw an elbow at her face.

Thyatis leaned aside, slipping the blow. Her sword flashed back at his throat, and he parried furiously. They traded a passage of lunge and thrust and parry and then stood back, chests heaving with exertion. The echoes of steel on steel faded in the high arch of the roof. Nikos' bald head and bare chest gleamed with sweat. Krista started breathing again. Both of them seemed possessed.

"That is enough." The deep husky contralto of the Duchess filled the air, and Krista started in surprise. Anastasia appeared between the pillars on the far side of the fighting square, her oval face filled with weariness. Krista frowned, seeing that the Duchess was wearing only a very simple gown. The lady's hair was bound up in a silver net, and her makeup was unusually heavy. Behind the striated green pillar, Krista licked her lips. There was some great trouble in the air.

"If you press yourselves more, you will only gain exhaustion, not skill." The Duchess' voice was already weary, and she stepped down onto the sand with the assistance of a little blond slave. Krista raised an eyebrow, seeing her replacement already in train. The girl was watching Nikos, however, and Krista smiled to see the intent look on her face. The Illyrian was rubbing his face with a towel, having put his blade away in its old, weathered leather sheath. The sweat-soaked loincloth left very little of his tough, muscular physique to the imagination. Thyatis turned to face the Duchess, her face grim and set. "We need a little more time on the sand," the young woman said. "Everyone's timing is off."

Anastasia nodded and handed another towel to Thyatis. The young woman smiled back and took it, drying her face and arms. The little blond slave sidled up to Nikos to take his towel away. The Illyrian grinned at her, and she glowered back before escaping with the towels through the pillars.

"I know." The Duchess sighed and pinched her nose. "My men have yet to find the Prince, so we can only train and wait. His caravan disappeared before it reached Cumae, but I have agents quartering the entire province in search of him."

Krista swallowed and stepped out between the columns. In her arms the little black cat poked its head out of the bag, looking around in interest.

"Mistress?" All four heads turned as one, and Krista saw incredulity and amazement and, best of all, joy in the face of the Duchess as she was recognized. "Which Prince would that be?"

Morning sun shone down on the garden, casting long slats of warm light on the wooden table and the chairs pulled up around it. Some of the servants had pulled an awning out over the terrace to shade the Duchess, and it blocked off part of the clear blue sky. The haze of the previous day had been driven off by a cool breeze, and larks and robins sang in the trees. Small puffy white clouds tracked across the sky, looking like so many wayward sheep. Glass tinkled as Krista put an empty sherbet plate back on the table. She had slept very late, drugged with exhaustion and the lassitude of a long, hot bath. She held the memory of the Duchess' warm embrace and greeting close to her heart. The remains of a huge lunch of fresh bread, scented olive oil, cut fruit, thin slices of lamb, fresh pomegranates, and light sweet wine cluttered the table. Krista leaned back in her chair, feeling the softness of the cushions under her head. She was very tired, the more so for having spent the last three hours pouring out the tale of her long absence.

The Duchess held her right hand fiercely tight, and the older woman's face was a mask of pain. The shadow in her eyes had grown deeper and deeper as Krista had related the events of her journey in the east with the Prince—their excavations in Rome and Constantinople, the flight on the great Engine into Persia, the battles in the crypts under Dastagird, the opening of the tomb of gold and lead. The others had listened quietly, though the tension around their eyes as she related these events had chilled the air. Now, even in the late morning heat, Krista could feel their grim humor. Thyatis, in particular, had drawn her long sword near the beginning of the tale and was now working the edge of it with a whetstone. The metallic scrape of the stone seemed to calm her, but it put everyone else under a pall.

Krista watched the Duchess carefully. She had not told her mistress everything by any means, only the skeleton of the tale. But Krista knew that the Duchess, somehow, held the missing portion—the matter of the Oath—the part that could not be said aloud. Anastasia stirred among the cushions in her chair and slowly released the clawlike grip on Krista's hand. The older woman put her hand on the man sitting next to her for support. Krista suppressed a frown at this—she had never known the Duchess to need the help or support of a man for anything. This barbarian was well made; tall and muscular, with a noble bearing and liquid dark eyes, but Krista did not trust him.

Indeed, many of the man's kinsmen were in attendance,

and Krista wondered what had happened to the merry band of rogues who had served Thyatis before. A great deal seemed to have changed in her absence! These barbarians seemed quite at home, sitting on the tiled floor of the terrace and eating a great deal of the Duchess' food and drink.

"And now the tale is known in full." Anastasia sat upright, drawing strength from some inner reserve. A hint of the vigor she usually showed reappeared. "We know the provenance of the creature you fought in the house in the hills; we know whereat the Prince has been, who he has consorted with, and what he has been about."

"And we know where he now resides." Thyatis leaned forward, chin on her palm. Her gray-green eyes surveyed the little group, passing over Nikos, Anagathios, the Khazar Jusuf, Krista, and finally alighting on the Duchess. "But there are things left unsaid in this tale. There is the question of why the Prince should attempt to move heaven and earth in his search for the body of this Greek. Why be so secretive? What does the Prince intend? How is the Emperor involved in all this?"

Krista met the red-haired woman's gaze without flinching, but she could think of nothing to say that would not put everyone in danger.

"The Prince," Anastasia said, breaking the silence, "I believe, intends the Emperor harm."

"But . . . ," Thyatis stopped, for the Duchess had raised a pale, jeweled hand. "There are matters afoot here that will not be discussed. It is enough for you to know, as we suspected before, that the Prince has fallen under evil influences and must be dealt with."

Thyatis grimaced and steepled her fingers, frowning over them at the Duchess. "Do you wish this Prince dead, or alive? What says the Emperor of this?"

Krista grinned, seeing that the redheaded woman had grown, too, while she was away. Thyatis and the Duchess matched flinty stares. After a tense moment, the Duchess nodded her head and looked to the side. Krista thought she was expecting someone to be standing behind her, but no one was there.

"The Emperor says and knows nothing of this." Anastasia's voice was tired. "My command is that the Prince shall be put to death. Should the fates smile and he is taken alive, then I shall deliver him to the Emperor, but I fear that he has grown too powerful in this dark magic to be an easy captive. Prepare and plan that this young man shall be slain and his body burned in fire until there is nothing but ash. Even those remains we shall cast into the sea."

Krista, hearing the words said aloud that she had chanted to herself for the past three days, felt a chill wash over her like the exhalation of a tomb. A memory of the Prince's face came to her, his dark brown eyes smiling, the white flash of his grin as they lay close together in a tangle of quilts and sheets. The vision of him, haggard and bleeding, in the crypt of the magi, silhouetted in fire and smoke. His dark, intent countenance leaning over the table of parchments and scrolls in the house in Constantinople. His face wreathed in lightning and thunder as he summoned the walking fire. She put a hand over her mouth and closed her eyes, blinking to keep tears from trickling down her cheek.

The Duchess continued to speak, for Nikos had asked some question.

". . . there will be only those whom we can trust, and no thaumaturge has answered my plea. The Prince is still a man, and he must sleep. Krista can provide all pertinent information about this house at Ottaviano. We will strike by night and swiftly, within the next week. It will take time, even with fast horses, to reach the villa, so you must be ready to leave within a day."

Thyatis nodded, and her attention turned inward, measuring time and distance in her mind. The Duchess turned to the tall, lean man at her side, her hand creeping into his. "And you, my Lord Jusuf, shall leave as well—but for the east and beyond, not upon this errand."

The Khazar sat up, his face intent on Anastasia's. "My

lady—are you sure? With me on the team, there will be three strong blades, not just two."

The Duchess shook her head, through Krista could see a great sense of loss hiding behind the older woman's calm appearance. "You must return to your people, as we have discussed. Time seems to press upon me, and if things go wrong here, you must be far away. Kahrmi and Efraim will remain and go in your place."

Jusuf bowed his head, accepting her judgment. Krista hid a puzzled frown; the Duchess was playing some other game, as well—which was not surprising. Nikos and Thyatis, however, were not involved, which was a little odd.

Anastasia sighed and put the little oil lamp down on the table by the head of her bed. It was very late at night, again, and she did not look forward to sleep. The day had been long and arduous, not only for the chilling tale that Krista had brought, but for the tension and outright anger among Thyatis and her men. Thyatis was hurt that Anastasia would not, could not, tell her the full story. The others felt her displeasure and echoed it. It was very tiring.

The Duchess removed the silver pins from her hair one by one, letting the black cloud drift down over her shoulders. Tomorrow would be worse; she would have to go the offices and speak with the Emperor. Galen had settled back into the business of running his Empire with renewed vigor, and a number of massive public projects were in the offing. For each of these things, he wanted to know who would benefit and who would not. The Emperor had a good head for the politics of his state, and he relied on Anastasia for current information about all of the players in his great game. *Such a meeting would be a major effort at another time, but now? With this other matter obsessing her every thought?*

The door creaked a little as it opened, and the Duchess turned, expecting to see the shy face of Betia with her combs and brushes. Anastasia smiled wanly, seeing that it was Krista. The young woman did have Betia's basket in her hand, along with a flask of oil and clean cloths. A little black cat that had recently made itself a member of the household padded along behind her, its curious yellow eyes examining the corners of the room for mice.

"You needn't do this," Anastasia said, sitting on the edge of the bed. "You've promoted yourself from my maidservant. I have Betia to take care of me. . . ."

Krista settled on the bed by Anastasia's side and smiled, running her hand through the older woman's hair. "The little blond shrimp? She is occupied elsewhere, I think. I told her to make herself scarce."

Anastasia turned a little, arching a thin, elegant eyebrow. "Were you mean? She is very sweet, you know . . ."

Krista made a sour face. "She almost squeaked in fear when I sent her off. But she does seem to have a good heart. I know this place is lost to me now." Anastasia touched Krista's cheek, seeing the frightened, wide-eyed little girl she had brought into her service for a moment. That child was gone now, leaving a skilled, tough young woman.

"I am so glad you came back." Anastasia smiled sadly and dabbed at her eye. There was something in it. "I feared you were dead a dozen times over. Then I thought you would choose to stay with the Prince."

Krista shook her head, letting curls of her thick dark hair fall in front of her face. Disappointed at the lack of fat brown mice or other playthings, the little black cat sprang lightly up onto the bed and nosed around among the pillows.

"The Prince was a fine young man," she said softly, "but this is my home. There is a doom over him that poisons everything he touches. He must be stopped."

The Duchess sighed. She felt the same way. This was one of those days that felt like the whole of the world was crushing her into the ground. "Do you think that he is right? The Emperor told me about the curse that only Maxian can see—is it real? Must such steps be taken?"

Krista shrugged and flipped the stray tendrils of hair out

of her face. Behind her, the little black cat found a corner of turned-up quilt and wormed itself under the covers, making itself a cave.

"My lady, I know that *he* believes, and that poor Abdmachus believed. I have not their powers or skills, so I have not seen anything myself, but they are dead set upon it. Those others, Gaius and Alexandros, they want only continued life and power. They are the real danger to the Emperor; how could they stand to live as ordinary men after a taste of the Imperial drug?"

Anastasia rubbed her face with one of the cloths soaked in oil. Her makeup came off at the touch, and she continued until it was all cleaned away. She picked up a silverbacked mirror and squinted at it. In the hazy reflection she seemed to still have her looks. She put the mirror down. "Are they real? These men—are they, in truth, these ancient legends come alive again? They are not mountebanks or some deluded fools . . ."

The young woman nodded, her eyes dark with memory. "They are. It seems impossible, but . . ." Krista shrugged her tunic off one shoulder and showed Anastasia the thin, puckered scar she had gained in the collapse of the Egyptian House. "The Prince has brought me back from the edge of death twice. These others, he plucked them from the halls of Hades itself. The strength of their legend gives them life and power and the lever the Prince desires."

Anastasia sighed, thinking that on another day this would be a wonder past compare.

Krista touched her cheek and turned the Duchess' head away. There was a rustling sound as the girl picked up a comb of ivory and horn from the basket.

"Tell me the good things that have happened while I was away." Krista began combing out the Duchess' long, dark hair. It would take a good hour, for the flood of deep blue-black spilled to Anastasia's lower back. Krista smiled to herself, remembering how nervous she had been the first time she had done this. It seemed an eternity ago, something that had happened to a wholly different person.

"Well," the Duchess said, sighing after a moment, "I made Petro take out all of the gladiolas that used to line the northern edge of the big garden and put in roses and lilies instead. He was furious, and we had a huge argument about it. He swore to leave and never return, to die before committing such a sacrilege—but he is a slave, of course, so eventually he gave in. But now they look beautiful, and he thinks it was his own idea. . . ."

Under the covers, the little black cat settled into her nest, putting her head on her paws, and went to sleep.

Krista found Thyatis in the gymnasium right after breakfast. The redheaded woman was reviewing corselets of mail laid on the big wooden table in the armory. The room smelled of oil and metal and sweat, and here, among the racks of spears and swords and tools, Thyatis seemed most at home. The sounds of the Khazars engaged in a furious training session echoed through the doorway to the fighting sallé. The clatter of metal on metal made quite a din. Krista paused in the doorway, unconsciously fingering the spring-gun strapped to her left forearm. Like Thyatis, she wore a short linen kilt held up by a stout belt, a long knife slapping at her thigh in a wooden sheath, high-laced boots of kid leather, and a loose blouse of fine dark green wool with long sleeves.

"Lady Thyatis? Do you have a moment?" Krista was unsure how to deal with the "peasant girl." When they had last parted, Thyatis had been little more than a sellsword the Duchess used to tidy up the Emperor's dirty laundry. Krista had been, by her own admission, a petulant servant girl with a sharp tongue. The intervening year had put its mark on both of them. Thyatis seemed larger somehow, more complete, more real than she had before. Krista just felt older.

Thyatis turned, gray-green eyes narrowing as she took in Krista's costume. "No," she said simply, and turned back to checking the links of the chain mail.

Krista almost backed up a step, feeling like she had been

slapped in the face. "Your pardon, Lady Thyatis, but—"

"No." Thyatis turned, her face grim and set. She shook her head. "You will not go with us to Ottaviano. You will stay here, with the Duchess."

"Why?" Krista's voice trembled on the edge of open rage. "No one else here knows the land, the buildings, the enemies, the Prince, as well as I do! I brought you the news of his location; I sent the messages that tipped the Duchess to what he plans! I will go, and I will see this thing finished."

The noise of training in the gymnasium stopped, and it was very quiet. Thyatis put down the heavy shirt of mail and turned to face Krista. "You know the Prince too well." Thyatis' voice was steady and calm and utterly final. "I watched you as you told your story yesterday. You love this Prince Maxian, for all that you have betrayed him to the Duchess."

Krista flinched at the words. She was sure that the Prince had let her go unpursued, unmolested, because he loved *her* and would not try to keep her if she wanted to leave. He had been true to her, and she had repaid him now with this: a hunting party armed with steel and iron. Thyatis stepped closer, her voice dropping in volume.

"If we are in the heat of it and the Prince lies under my knife, or yours, could you bring yourself to drive the point into his heart? Could you stand to see me or Nikos spill the red life from him? I do not think you could. He is in your heart, and you are in his. Should you think of him now, a smile would come to your face. You are here"— Thyatis gestured to encompass the house and the city— "because of duty and honor. But when the die is cast and spins upon the table, you may still choose love."

Krista tried to speak, but words did not come to her. Memories of the Prince were still strong in her mind. The thought of him lying dead, or dying, bleeding out his life on the floor of the kitchen at Ottaviano, filled her with horror and dread. She raised a hand and batted at the air, causing Thyatis to step back. Odd, dark motes danced in the air before her eyes, and Krista felt a sharp pain in her gut.

"I will not risk my men on the balance of your heart." Thyatis turned away, the line of her jaw stiff.

Krista gasped silently, feeling some great pressure closing on her. She put out a hand to the edge of the door and struggled to keep upright. This was far worse than it had been on the mountainside. She struggled for breath. "I"— she wheezed, and Thyatis stopped, her slim hand on the haft of a spear—"I will . . . I will kill him." The pressure eased a little, and Krista could draw a ragged breath. Air in her lungs had never seemed so sweet. "I will kill him." Her voice was stronger. "I must kill him, Lady Thyatis. I will drive this knife into his eye if I must, but he will die by my hand."

Krista pushed away from the wall, feeling stronger and able to breathe freely at last. The black haze in the air was gone. She felt giddy and almost euphoric with relief.

Thyatis looked her up and down, a quizzical frown on her face. But she shook her head. "No. I will not take you."

Krista stiffened and turned on her heel. If the pigeon-brained peasant refused her help, she would find another way. She had to end this thing and soon.

"The Duchess already said no." Thyatis' voice echoed down the hallway, but Krista ignored her.

THE WINE DARK SEA, SOUTH OF THE ISLAND OF CRETA

Foam curled away from the knife-edge prow of the Tyrean coaster, sending up a fine, cool spray. Dwyrin sat, his legs hanging over the side of the ship, one arm casually wrapped around a stay. He had stripped down to sweat-stained woolen breeches and had been barefoot for days. A new layer of calluses was growing on his feet, joining those added by marching the length of the Empire. The coaster had found a quartering wind and was doglegging its way south from the rocky cliffs of Creta, now a day behind. The Tyrean crew were truly lax fellows, rarely leaving the shade of a big awning that stretched over the back half of the ship. Nicholas was back there now, testing his luck against theirs at bones.

Dwyrin spent most of his time watching the sea. It cheered him up to see the waves sparkle and dance under the sun. The sea was alive, too, and many a day passed with dolphins or short-backed whales accompanying them on their journey south. Once past the coast of Creta, the Tyrean captain had agreed to sail by night as well as day, since the sea was open and free of reefs or islands until they reached the Egyptian shore. They were making for the way marker of the great Pharos at Alexandria. Then they would hug the coast of the delta and make their way northeast to the ports of Judea.

Dwyrin lay back, resting against a coil of rope that was stowed in the prow. The cool wind of their passage made the hot day quite bearable. He considered taking a nap, but kept his eyes propped open. As they neared the mouth of the delta, they might encounter other ships. With luck they would see one of the massive grain haulers. That would be a sight!

"Pardon, lad, do you mind if I sit with you?"

Dwyrin looked up, canting back his straw hat. It was the beast-man, Vladimir, looking a little peaked. Dwyrin shrugged. It was unusual for the Walach to come out of the cabin during the day. The motion and vastness of the sea seemed to make him uneasy. "Surely. Pick a plank."

Vladimir sat oddly, with his legs crossed over each other. Like Dwyrin, he had shed shirt and boots, leaving just long linen trousers. These were a fine weave, though, and dyed a dark woad blue. Lacings in green-dyed leather ran down the outside of each leg. Vladimir looked out over the water, shading his eyes with a thick hand. "Do you love the sea?"

Dwyrin raised an eyebrow and pushed his hat back, turning to face the Walach. "The sea is in my blood," he said, pressing two fingers to his chest. "All of my people came to Hibernia from the sea in the great migration. Even if we live in the green heart of the land, the ocean is never far away. You can hear the beat of the surf in the ground, it seems. Of course, it's nothing like this tranquil lake." He indicated the horizon, "The true ocean, beyond the Pillars, is mighty and awesome."

Vladimir nodded, scratching the side of his head with a thick fingernail. "My people . . . we came out of the Sea of Grass, but even then, when we came to the waters of the Sea of Darkness and tasted them, we knew that something lay beyond. Our old legends, the ones that the *k'shapâcara* elders learn from the memory chant, speak of the great ocean that circles the world. We must have seen it once, long ago."

Dwyrin nodded companionably. He no longer felt ill in the presence of the beast-man, seeing that he and Nicholas were fast friends. It was good that the Walach had come out of his cabin to sit under the open sky. It did no one good to spend their days mewed up in some dank hole. The clear clean air was better. Dwyrin suddenly realized that the dark feeling that had lain over him since Antioch was gone. He missed Zoë and Odenathus terribly, but he hoped to see them again, one day.

Perhaps they will have put their anger aside. It was a hope, anyway.

"I would like to see the great ocean," Vladimir said, still talking and looking out over the waters. "Some day, before I am called into the close darkness. There are many stories, in the old tales, of the endless sea and the water-that-tastes-like-blood."

Dwyrin clapped the Walach on the shoulder, feeling the fine, soft fur. "You will see it, then, my friend. It is a journey of many days, but between us we can convince

Nicholas to turn the ship and take us there. Then you will see the gray vastness. . . ."

Vladimir laughed, a deep throaty sound that reminded Dwyrin of a forest stream spilling over mossy stones.

THE SIQ, NEAR PETRA, ROMAN NABATEA

Torches flared in the wind, casting red-and-orange light high on the walls of the canyon. The shadows of men trembled across the water-carved stone surfaces, growing enormous and small by turns. Fitted stones making a metaled road covered the floor of the canyon where the native stone had not been planed smooth. Boots clattered on the flagstones, and the jingle of armor and the creak of leather filled the air. Water, carried in round, ceramic pipes fitted into channels in the wall of the canyon, gurgled past. Somewhere high above, catchment dams and cisterns gathered the rain and the seepage of tiny springs. The men were tired and footsore and hungry, and the canyon continued to narrow. Even the night sky above, strewn with a field of stars, was soon closed off, and they marched under striated red walls.

At the head of the column, Odenathus led a weary horse by its bridle. He was tired, too, for the sprint across the flat desert wasteland to the east of these hills had been taxing. Ahead of him, the lead scout suddenly stopped and raised a hand in warning. Odenathus shook his head, trying to clear the fog of fatigue away. He handed off the bridle of his horse to one of the Palmyrenes in the van and splashed forward. The scout, a Bostran shepherd who had joined them a week ago, was standing at a turn in the canyon. It was very narrow here, barely wide enough for a horse to pass through.

"What is it?" Odenathus kept his voice down, though the racket of the army at his back was sure to have alerted anyone who might be about. The scout nodded ahead, his dark eyes glittering in the torchlight. The Bostran was clad in the enveloping desert robes of the southern tribes, leaving only the bridge of his nose and his eyes showing. Odenathus stepped to the turn and looked around the corner.

The passage widened out, and there, carved from the living rock of the canyon wall, was a towering palace with doors and windows and deep embrasures holding statues of men and Amazons. Odenathus hissed, seeing the gorgeous building illuminated by the light of a bonfire on the floor of the canyon. Then he silenced himself, for a gate of worked stone stood at the end of the canyon. It stood wide open, though men in desert robes and armor loitered just beyond it. Indeed, banners fluttered in the breeze that forced its way down the narrow slot canyon, and it seemed that they were expected.

The Palmyrene turned and signaled to the men following. A muttered message was passed down the line. Odenathus waited in the shadow of the canyon, watching the men standing in the light of the bonfires. They seemed to be waiting, too. At last there was a muted rattle of boots on stone, and two figures trotted up to his side. Odenathus smiled in relief, seeing that Zoë did not have the dead Queen strapped to her back. The long march across the Hauran and the rough passage of the Trachontis had convinced her that she did not need to carry the corpse herself. Another wagon had been acquired in a town south of Jerash and outfitted as a catafalque. Now the dead Queen rode in majesty, lying on a bed of rose petals and cedar. Incense and aromatic candles were burned around her at dawn and dusk, shrouding the faint smell of desiccated flesh.

Beyond that, however, Zoë spent much time with her aunt, sometimes sleeping under the funeral wagon. Odenathus and the other men had, slowly, grown used to its presence and now ignored it.

Zoë brushed a trailing lock of raven dark hair out of her face as she came up to Odenathus.

"Our way is blocked?" Here in the dark, with this firelight, she seemed her old self, unmarked by torment and inner demons. Odenathus nodded in the direction of the gate.

"The city is defended—men stand at the door yonder. Lord Prince, is this the usual practice here?"

The man standing at Zoë's side was their new ally, Zamanes, Prince of Bostra and Jerash, the King of Gerasa. He was a stoutly built man of middle height with a thick, curly beard ornamented with small jewels. Despite his young age, he was afflicted with a slight limp and poor vision. The Prince looked around the corner of the cliff as well, then tugged at his beard. "Those are no Petrans," he growled. "That merchant must have been right."

Two days before, as the combined army—such that it was—of the Palmyrenes and Bostrans reached the eastern end of the fertile valley that had led them to this slot canyon, their outriders had captured an Arab merchant on the Roman road. The man was walking alone with his goods in a bag held by a carry-strap that circled his forehead. Zamanes had questioned him while Odenathus watched. The merchant had related an odd tale that "Southerners" had captured the Red City in the mountains and had thrown down all the idols of the gods. This struck Odenathus as being particularly unlucky, but he knew that the southern tribes believed all sorts of superstitions.

"They are enemies of the Empire." Zoë's voice was flat. Odenathus started to dispute the statement, but paused and realized that it might well be true. Anyone who would attack and capture a provincial capital had to be an enemy of the Romans. *But does that make them our friends?*

"Let us speak with their chieftain." Zoë pushed away from the wall and walked out onto the sandy canyon floor, her arms raised high in greeting. Odenathus, without thinking, jumped after her and then found himself in the full view of thirty or forty men waiting in the wide oval space between the exit from the slot canyon and the huge rock temple. He looked from side to side and counted the number of bows trained upon him. It would be very difficult to take this place, emerging one at a time from the canyon mouth into a storm of arrows, spears, and javelins.

"Ho! We come to speak with your master. Call him to us, or let us enter." Zoë's voice, high and strong, rang off of the canyon walls, echoing among the entablature and free-standing statues on the pediment of the tomb. On the ramp of steps leading up into the rock temple, a man with thick, broad shoulders looked down upon them. He wore a cloak of white and green over burnished metal armor. Odenathus squinted into the firelight, seeing that he wore the habitual headdress of the southern tribes and bore a long, recurved bow in a wooden case on his back.

"Our lord awaits you, strangers. Send your embassy forward, and we will take you to him."

Within a circling ring of mountains, Petra nestled in a rich and crowded valley. Hundreds of villas and shops climbed the hills that stood on either side of the main road into the city. Above those hills, cliffs rose on every side, riddled with carved tombs and grand funerary temples. Though the city was well-illuminated at night by lanterns and torches, the surrounding mountains were dark. The tomb doors gaped, showing black yawning pits where the old doors had been cracked open by earthquake or vandal.

Odenathus followed Zoë and Zamanes as they passed down the avenue of the city. Everything was built of blocks of stone and roofs of tile or slate. In the darkness he could make out the murmur of many horses and camels, and the smell of water and growing things. *There must be gardens behind these bare walls*, he thought. The stream of the Siq ran through the middle of the city alongside a raised roadbed lined with beautiful columns of marble. Little arched bridges crossed the streambed, though unless there were heavy rains, he could see no use for them. They passed an open market on their left, raised up on a great platform and built out from the side of a hill. A Roman-style triumphal gate followed, thick with devotive statues and carved wreaths. Beyond the gate was a long, rectangular plaza fronting a Greek-style temple. A great baths crouched at the side of the elegant temple, seeming crude in comparison.

Unexpectedly, for Odenathus had expected them to be taken to the palace of the Kings of Petra, they turned and climbed the steps leading up into the temple. At the top of the steps their escort paused, a constantly moving ring of Arabs in long cloaks, and the wall-captain—that great-shouldered bowman—spoke with the commander of the watch. After a moment they were allowed within, entering first a portico of fat-bellied pillars in shades of red, and then a vaulted hall lined with statues of men in regal garb. At the end of the hall of statues, was a square room with many tables. Behind the tables, a great statue rose up, but it was covered in cloth from head to toe. At the largest table, leaning his chin on his fist, was a man of middle years with startling white streaks running through his beard. His face was dominated by a scar, a strong nose, and brilliant dark eyes. The man looked up as they approached, and gestured for the servants lurking about in the corners of the room to leave.

"I am Mohammed, Lord of the City."

Odenathus started, as he had expected the rough, uncultured voice of a barbarian chieftain, but this man spoke Greek like a philosopher of Alexandria or Antioch. "Welcome to Petra. Please, sit and take some tea."

Odenathus accepted a chair, as did Zamanes and Zoë, though the woman was staring fixedly at the desert chieftain. Servants hurried back, carrying trays of beaten gold that held cups of porcelain and a kettle of steaming water.

"I do not imbibe wine," the desert chieftain continued as he took a small yellow cup from the tray. "Nor do my men. Tea, therefore, is in short supply among us. But, please, drink. Are you hungry?"

In answer, Odenathus' stomach growled. Rations had been short since they had left the fertile valleys around Damascus. Even adding the Bostrans to their number, with the support of the tribes that followed Zamanes, had not eased the logistical problems they faced. This was a barren country, not suited for the movement of armies that did not own the cities and towns. Mohammed grinned and rattled off an order to the nearest servant.

"Soon there will be food, my guests. Now, I know you well, Prince Zamanes, but you—young lady and young man—you are new to me. What are your names?"

Zamanes stiffened, cocking his head toward the chieftain with a perplexed look on his face. "You know me, Lord Mohammed? Where have we met?"

Mohammed laughed, a short, sharp bark. He fingered the white in his beard. "Most like you thought me dead, Prince Zamanes. My men and I held your left on the field at Emesa, before the cowardice of that Palmyrene cur Zabda lost us the day."

Odenathus was standing, a snarl on his lips and his sword half drawn before the words fully registered in his mind. The desert men behind him reacted swiftly, and he found the point of a spear at his throat. Zamanes had also risen, his face wreathed in shock, but now he too froze.

"If you impugn the name of Zabda," snapped Odenathus, "Lord Mohammed, you insult all Palmyra. You insult me and my house, for that noble lord was my father."

Mohammed turned, his eyes hard and the line of his mouth grim. "You seem a likely lad, and if you hail from fair Palmyra I would call you friend. But the Queen herself cursed his name on that black day and bade him never set foot within the city again. We were inches from victory o'er the damnable Persians before his caution threw it all away." The desert chieftain's voice rapped like a chisel on stone.

Odenathus flushed beet red, and his heart hammered.

The news of his father's death, delivered in a leaden voice by his own mother, had been very hard to take. This was harder still—his family disgraced by cowardice on the field of battle. The young man struggled with his temper and then slid the gladius back into its sheath with an audible click. "Your pardon, Lord Mohammed. I am your guest and spoke out of turn." Odenathus sat down.

"I thought you dead when we saw your banner fall. . . ." Zamanes plucked nervously at his beard. "My men and I only fought free at great cost and scattered to the south. We heard that the Queen escaped with some portion of her army, but the Persians filled the countryside."

"It was very close," Mohammed said, a fingertip touching a scar on his neck and face. "But the Queen held us together. I woke in a litter on the road to Palmyra." He put the thought away and turned again to Zoë and Odenathus. "What are your names, children of that city?"

"I am Odenathus, son of Zabda." Odenathus rose, slowly, mindful of the guards close at hand, and bowed, touching his fingers to his forehead. "Now captain of the host of Palymra, such that it be."

Mohammed bowed in turn, returning the salute. His dark eyes turned to Zoë, who had said nothing, sitting like a stone in her chair, hands clasped in her lap.

"And you, lady? What is your name?" His voice gentled as he took in the dark shadows around her eyes and the thin, wasted look in her face.

"I am Zoë," she said at last. "Regent for the Queen, Zenobia Septima. These men command in my name and hers in war."

"Regent?" Mohammed was puzzled, and he looked first to Zamanes and then to Odenathus. They could not meet his eyes, and at last he looked back to Zoë. "What mean you, Lady Zoë? I saw the Queen laid in her tomb myself; with my own hand I carved the blessing on her resting place."

Zoë looked up, her face filled with fear and loss. Her voice, when it came, was hoarse and thick. "The Queen does not lie dead, Lord Mohammed. She but sleeps, waiting to awaken. She rides with us. Even now she is without the city, patient, resting that she may enter in splendor."

Zoë stood, one thin, white hand on her stomach, the other trembling on the tabletop. "Did you see her fall, so wounded that she lay as in death? Were you there, on that last day?"

Mohammed stepped back, seeing madness burning in the young woman's eyes. "Yes," he said slowly, eyes searching the face of this apparition. He could see, now that he looked past the lines of sorrow and pain, the echo of Zenobia's smile and laugh and smooth white cheek. This must be—not a daughter, for he knew from his time with her that Zenobia had borne no living children—but her sister's daughter. "I was there on the last day. I saw the sorcerer come forth and raise his hand against us. . . ."

Odenathus listened, his heart sick and torn, as the desert chieftain related the tale of the fall of the city in his deep, carrying voice. With each word, the Palmyrene felt anew the pain of his city's death. His sorrow and loss were renewed, and with it, his resolve to bring down the powers that had wreaked such betrayal and slaughter.

". . . so it was that I have come into Roman lands again with a host of men."

A litter of plates and cups lay on the table. Servants had come and gone, and Odenathus had eaten his fill. Zamanes had done his appetite proud, as well, and even Zoë had picked at the grouse and hen and sliced fruit that the kitchens had conjured up. During the course of the tale, many of the Arabs had also joined them, coming quietly and sitting on the floor around the table. Looking at their faces, Odenathus realized that many of them had never heard the full story before.

Mohammed took a long drink of water and sighed. The room was quiet, save for the hiss of the little oil lamps.

"What do you intend?" Zoë's voice, still hoarse, broke

the silence. "Will you pit your strength against Rome, or against Persia?"

Mohammed leaned forward, his face partially in shadow as he moved. "The Persians killed my dear friends and put the torch to your city, but they came against us in open battle. The great and merciful God weighs all men in the scales of His justice, and I know that the Persians traffic in dark arts. The God who speaks in the wasteland will see to them. Even now Persia is in disarray, shattered by civil war. Rome. . . . Rome has taken a faithless course, betraying states and peoples that have stood by it for six hundred years. On this day, Rome is my foe . . . more, the Emperor Heraclius himself is my enemy."

Odenathus stirred, thinking of the oaths that he and Zoë had sworn when they entered the Legion. Did they bind him now? He thought not, for they had completed their service and mustered out. It was still strange, hearing the Emperor impugned in such a way.

"My enemy," Mohammed continued, "is not the Roman people. They did not betray us, leading to the slaughter of tens of thousands. It is not the army of Rome—no, it is a man, this fool Heraclius, who saw fit to send the armies of the Decapolis and Palmyra and Nabatea forth as bait and a lure. The blood and bone of those cities served him well, delaying the Persian army until he could strike the head from the Persian monster. This thing I cannot forgive. I will see it done that he pays for this crime."

There was a murmur from the Arabs, and Odenathus joined in. Zamanes, the Prince, also nodded and raised a cup in salute of the desert chieftain. "You speak truly, Lord Mohammed. All throughout the ten cities, the name of the Emperor is reviled. There is no family that did not send a son, or sons, north to fight Persia. Now nearly all are dead. Our lands and cities are numb with grief, but hate burns there, too, a guttering spark . . . but one that could be coaxed to open flame."

Zamanes stopped and looked around, meeting Odena-thus' eyes for a moment, then surveying the assembly in the hall. He stood, turning to address everyone. "The son and daughter of Palmyra came into my lands with a ragged band. I had heard from the *cursus publicus* that bandits and landless men were on the loose, so I took what few bowmen and lancers remained to me and sought them out. I found them by the spring of Goliath, watering their horses. I looked upon them from cover, seeing the gaunt weariness in their faces and the paltry number of their men. Then, I looked again and saw that they bore the standard of the royal house of Palmyra.

"These did not seem to be bandits! I came forth and spoke with them and heard of the destruction of that city. Now, hear me! All the cities and towns of the Decapolis and Judea have heard of the Emperor's great victory in Persia. All have heard of his conquests and his triumphs. Rome bestrides the world, unmatched in power. All the lands beyond the two rivers will come under the sway of Rome. These words made me sick at heart, for I see only the grave markers and funereal processions that bought Heraclius this glory."

Zamanes turned, bowing his head toward Zoë. She stirred, inclining her head as well.

"Even as the Lord Mohammed has done, the Lady Zoë had taken up arms against Rome. Her hurts are deep, and the stain upon the honor of Palmyra is black. Yet she does not flinch from the task. I dwelt in thought a long time, there by the waters of the spring, before I pledged myself as well. Gerasa and the ten cities will rise up against Rome the betrayer."

Zamanes turned back to Mohammed, who was watching him intently.

"Lord Mohammed, you are well skilled in battle, as are your captains. Will you accept my hand in alliance and brotherhood against Rome?"

Mohammed stood, his face grave, though his dark eyes were glittering with delight. "Prince Zamanes, Lord of Bostra and Jerash, King of Gerasa, I will take your hand. The Lord of Battles looks down upon us and smiles, seeing that we have delivered ourselves into his keeping."

The two men clasped wrists and bowed. Odenathus made to rise, but Zoë had already risen, her pale face and long dark hair making a still mask. She placed her thin white hand over the two men's. "The Queen speaks. She says this: Palmyra stands with you." Her voice was cold, like a sound from the tomb. Her fingers curled around Mohammed's wrist, and her fingernails dug into his skin. "Death to Rome."

"Death to Rome," the two men echoed, and then, after a pause, the whole room followed.

Odenathus felt a chill wash over him and he shook his shoulders like a wet dog. "Roma delenda est," he whispered, fingering his Legion-issue belt.

"Lejjun? Yes, I spoke with a merchant who had visited the camp not more than a month ago." Zamanes looked puzzled, but he motioned for Mohammed to continue. The cool light of dawn shone in through round windows on the eastern wall of the palace. Odenathus rubbed his eyes, trying to drive the gritty feel of sleep from them. There had been little time to rest, and the call to prayer had come far too early. It had taken hours after the long conference with Mohammed to bring the army into the city and see the men bedded down.

He cradled a tin cup of tea in his hands, warming them. It was cold in the desert in the early morning, and when he had crossed the inner square of the palace he could see his breath. Soon the sun would blaze down over the jagged ridge that surrounded the city, and it would be blisteringly hot, but for the moment he needed his cloak wrapped around him to stay comfortable.

The Lord Mohammed was taking his breakfast on the eastern terrace; a long colonnade of red stone pillars and spit-shined terracotta. It was cool under the arches, and it gave a stunning view of the city in the valley. Houses and temples filled the bowl of stone and climbed up the rocky palisade around it. Long flights of stairs had been cut from the stone, and some of the houses seemed to be driven into the very rock. Everywhere were flowers and fruit trees, and the singing of birds greeting the morning. Mohammed sat at a low wicker table with a top made of a single sheet of porphyry, cut smooth and polished to a high gloss. There was a battered tea kettle on a wooden plate, and little cups, along with a basket of fresh hot flatbread. Odenathus dug in, finding the heavy meal of the night before only a memory for his stomach.

"Has the camp been reoccupied by the Legion?" Mohammed asked, sipping from his own cup.

Zamanes shook his head, occupied with smearing honey and jam on a round of the bread. "No. The merchant—a cousin of my third wife—reported that two cohorts of Syrian archers had taken up residence, along with some Roman officers. They were preparing to reopen all of the buildings, though. There were hundreds of slaves in residence, busily sweeping out."

Mohammed nodded and seemed relieved. "Lord Prince, if my army passes through your lands to reach Lejjun, can your towns and villages supply us with bread and fodder for our animals? May we water at your wells, use your roads?"

Zamanes grinned, stained brown teeth showing briefly in the thicket of his beard. "I would be a poor ally if I did not offer you some hospitality! You intend to seize Lejjun, then? To what end?"

Mohammed put down the cup and signaled to one of the young men loitering around in the doorways to the palace proper. The lad strode over, carrying a leather packet of scrolls and maps. Odenathus looked the fellow up and down—he seemed very young, barely as old as Odenathus himself—but his green and white robes were crisp and of fine Indian cotton. His narrow face was handsome and marked not by the short beard of Mohammed, but by a closely trimmed mustache and goatee that accented his high cheekbones and sharp nose. The youth unrolled a map from the case, placing cups and oranges at the edges to hold it down.

"Lord Zamanes, Prince Odenathus—this is Khalid Al'Walid, the captain of my infantry and admiral of the fleet."

Khalid laughed at the expressions on Zamanes' and Odenathus' faces. It was a rich sound, and guileless. "Yes, my lords, we have a fleet—not more than a dozen barques and a clutch of *dhows*—but it has served us well. Pray, remember that the wealth of Mekkah comes from the sea, not from the land. We are a nation of horsemen, but the sea and its ways are not unknown to us."

Odenathus grinned back, finding himself liking this young rogue. He nodded to himself—the riches of Palmyra had been in ships and sea trade, too. Suddenly he rubbed his chin in thought. The ports along the Mare Internum were the home to many Palmyran ships, bought over the years and supplied with Palmyran captains and sometimes with crew. A lucrative relationship had grown up between the old Phoenician cities along the coast and the inland power. He wondered what had happened to those warehouses, ships, factors, and trade.

"Here is our intent," Mohammed said briskly, bringing everyone's attention back to the map. "At the moment we do not lack for men. There are slightly more than twenty thousand Arabs, two thousand Petrans, your thousand Palmyrans, and—by your count, Lord Zamanes—some five thousand Gerasans we can muster for this campaign."

"Perhaps more," Zamanes interjected, "if the other cities of the Decapolis will rise with us."

"Even so. Our great lack, however, is heavy equipment—shovels, mattocks, wagons, barrels, all manner of siege works like catapults and ballistae. Then there is the matter of our armor, which is spotty. We have gathered some formations of heavy horse, but most of my army is armed with javelin, bow, and perhaps only a shield for protection. If we are to deal with Rome, we need to supplement that armament."

"You intend to seize the supplies at Lejjun," Odenathus said, "if you can reach the camp before it is properly garrisoned."

Mohammed nodded at the young Palmyrene. "Exactly. With the tools of war held therein, we can strike to the coast."

Zamanes frowned. "Not at Damascus? It is the linchpin of the entire frontier defense, the hub of the Strata Diocletiana, and now the richest city in the region. Should not that be our goal?"

"No," Mohammed said, his face split by a grin. "Our aim is not the conquest of Phoenicia and Syria—in truth, we do not have the men we need to garrison so much land—our aim is to seize the Roman port of Caesarea Maritima, here on the coast of Judea. Look upon the map, my friends—the Roman provinces are a long strip between the sea and the sand. All their forces have been withdrawn to the north to deal with the Persians. If we were to strike north, along the axis of the Strata, we would expose a lengthy flank. Rome still controls the sea, allowing them to land armies behind us at any point.

"Further, with Anatolia and Cilicia still unsettled from the Persian invasions, it will take more time for them to bring an army over land to meet us. The enemy will come by sea, so we must wrest from Rome the one thing that has maintained its power for all these long centuries."

The desert chieftain moved his hand across the blue-tinted map. "Control of the Mare Internum is the key. At Caesarea Maritima are both an Imperial naval base and a fleet. We will seize that fleet, recrewing the ships with our own men, and wrest Rome's monopoly of the sea from them. Then, Lord Prince, then we will see about the cities of the plain."

"A bold plan." Zoë's voice broke in, cold and formal. The men started, for they had not heard her approach. Odenathus rose and offered her his chair, sweeping his cloak behind him as he made a slight bow. Zoë met his eyes and summoned a smile, though her own were cold and bleak. She settled in the chair, her dark gray cloak falling around her like a thundercloud. She had pulled her hair back from her face in a severe manner, and the heavy clink of iron rings came as she arranged herself. Odenathus stood at the back of the chair, worried that she had taken to wearing armor under her linen blouse. "What do you intend after that?"

Mohammed sat again, his face grave, and he waited a moment, watching the face of the young woman opposite him. Odenathus could see that the desert chieftain was troubled by the pain and sorrow etched so clearly on the young woman's face.

"Lady Zoë, I intend to seek out the Emperor Heraclius and put him to death for the murders he had caused and the destruction he has wreaked. I hope he will come against us, as is his wont, with an army. Then I shall face him on the field of battle and the Merciful and Compassionate One will judge. But should he hide in his city of stone, then I will dig him out. For that, I need a fleet."

Zoë smiled, though there was no warmth in it.

"You would storm the walls of Constantinople with this rabble?"

Zamanes flinched at the scorn in her voice, but Odenathus put a gentling hand on the Prince's shoulder.

Zoë ignored the motion. "I served, of late, in the army of the Empire," Zoë said. "You would face not thirty thousand men, or even fifty thousand, but upward of a hundred thousand trained men. Your enemy commands fleets, he commands thaumaturges, he commands an empire. You are a desert bandit with only the men at your back to support you."

Mohammed nodded, then said, "And you, my lady, what are you? You have taken up the same cause, to repay the death of your beloved Queen. How will you take vengeance?"

Zoë stiffened, and her pale face became ashy. She rose from the chair, her hands curling into fists.

"The Queen," she rasped, "is not dead! She sleeps, waiting for her time to return. She will lead us to victory. Can your great and merciful God say the same?"

Mohammed blanched and put his hands on the arms of his chair, willing them to lie still. "The voice that speaks from the clear air has told me what I must do. My men and I will stand against the dark powers that threaten the earth. I have seen them with my own eyes. We submit to the will of the Loving and Compassionate One, and we will be delivered."

"Will you?" Zoë sneered down at the desert chieftain. "Can your God of the Wasteland restore strength to the weak limbs of my Queen? Can He raise her up, that she might walk among us once again, hale and strong? Can He?"

Mohammed matched gazes with the young woman, seeing horror and pain and madness there. He slowly shook his head. "The God passes judgment upon all men. If He wills that she rise again, she will. And if not, it is not our place to question His will."

"I have no use for your God, bandit! May He rot and burn in His own fire." Zoë wrapped her cloak around her with a snap and strode away, leaving her angry words ringing in the air.

Odenathus made to follow her, but then stopped himself and turned back to the table. "My apologies, Lord Mohammed. As you see, my cousin took the loss of the Queen badly."

The Quryash nodded, looking after Zoë as she walked away down the terrace. His face was sad. "She is not alone in that."

A centipede, long and glistening, a deep burnished red highlighted by glossy black chitin, rippled across a floor of fitted stone. A shaft of light, sparkling with slow-falling dust, fell across the vestibule of the grave house. In the midday sun, even attenuated by its fall from the window high above, it burned like fire as it crossed the doorway. Within, past the threshold, cool darkness held sway. The air was a little thick, filled with dust, and it tickled the throat. The centipede slithered down the steps and disappeared between the stone feet of a statue standing at the side of the door.

"Where are the gods and their divine justice?"

The voice was raspy with exhaustion. A young woman, her thin shoulders marked by the sun, and half clad in a grimy black robe, crouched against the wheel of a wagon. Her hair fell in a tangle around her face. The wagon sat in the center of an old tomb, one of many cut from the soft sandstone walls of the canyons that ringed Petra. The doorway, broad and imposing, had been just wide enough to allow it entrance. The Queen's servants had sweated and groaned in the darkness to place it here, but now they were gone, leaving the woman and her burden behind.

"Where are the Furies and their whips? Does not Zeus Ammon look down from on high and see the sins of men? Where is his wrath?"

The sides of the wagon had been etched and carved by the soldiers. An echo of a city filled with prosperous families and gardens and high, arching, colonnades peered out of the wood. The work was not done, only two sides of the wagon were finished. The other surfaces were marked with lines and curves in bits of chalk and cut with the tip of a knife. Slim, fluted wooden posts had been erected at each corner. These held up a canvas awning. The top was rough and unfinished, but hidden beneath, where it could only been seen by the passenger, was a painted sun of many rays.

The woman stood, shakily, and leaned on the side of the wagon, pressing her forehead to the smooth wood. She spoke, but did not know that the words flowed, aloud, from her mouth.

"This man, this Heraclius, should be driven into the field with invisible whips and stings! His flesh should run red with the blood of a thousand cuts. Madness should be his reward."

Within the wagon, laid on a soft bed of cloths and dried

flower petals, the withered corpse of a woman of middle height and age lay, half curled. Robes of silk and linen had been placed upon her with care. Her flesh was dry and brittle, and broke easily, cracking into a slippery dust with mishandling.

"Why do the gods not strike him down? Why does he rule the land in glory and splendor? Why is his name praised to the heavens?"

Zoë ground her fist against the stone of the tomb wall. Blood seeped from her knuckles. There was a heat in her mind, a fury and a rage, and it seeped out of her, smoking from her fingertips. It washed over the stones, cracking and discoloring the old worn surface. The spots of blood slid down the wall, hissing like a snake. Black scoring marked their passage.

Daughter, do not despair.

Zoë turned, her eyes wide, the world wheeling around her. The tomb seemed both infinitely vast and crushingly close. She fell to her knees, mindless of the pain. Something rustled in the wagon, the sound of garments shifting. There was a skittering sound, and the *click-clack* of beetles. The sound filled the space, enormously loud, and Zoë pressed her hands against her ears, crying out.

You are the child of my heart, said a voice from the wagon, echoing in her mind. *I bore no child of my own flesh, yet you came to me and filled those empty places. You are my daughter of spirit. In you, I live. In your memories and thoughts, I am still alive.*

The sound died, leaving a great stillness. Zoë crawled to the edge of the wagon and gripped the planks for support. The rustling came again, and something moved at the lip of the panel. Zoë pressed her forehead against the smooth wood again, her eyes smarting with tears.

"Auntie, what should I do? This chieftain, this Mohammed, he desires to strive against Rome, yet the Persians who murdered you are still alive and loose in the world. How can I let you go unavenged? Fate pushes me west, yet my heart tells me otherwise. . . ."

Dear child, life would remain in my breast and we would be sitting in my garden, laughing and talking, were it not for the perfidy of Rome. All those things that are lost to us would be restored. . . . You must go west, and strike down the Roman. Let that be my vengeance.

Zoë nodded, tears streaming from her face, and made to rise. There was a soft touch on her hair and she froze, trembling. Fingertips stroked her hair, and the side of her head, soft and warm, and the air was filled with the subtle fragrance of orange and myrrh.

OTTAVIANO

〠

Maxian dozed on the short, springy grass that covered the floor of the grotto. He lay in sunshine, warm and comfortable, and above him the bowl of the sky was a fine rich blue. Individual clouds, each fluffy and white, drifted across his vision. Hawks and eagles soared on the updraft off the mountain slopes. Somewhere among the mossy stones, frogs peeped from a hidden spring. The Prince felt almost content, lulled by the sleepy rumble of the mountain. Respite from the crawling insidious attack of the curse drew him here each day, and he spent long hours sleeping or reading, his back against one of the boulders. He missed Krista dreadfully, particularly when he thought of the lunch hamper she could pack.

Often he looked up suddenly, expecting to see her walking out from the shade of the overhanging trees.

It had taken him three days to mark her absence, and he still felt ashamed by that. The hurly-burly of setting up his library and cleaning out the buildings at the villa had occupied him, but she had been such a constant presence for the past year that he should have known immediately when she was gone. Gaius Julius and Alexandros, for their part, had not seemed to care at all. The Walach boys had moped around for a day or two before the Prince had given them leave to hunt for their dinner on the estate grounds. Then they were rarely seen at all, though there was a fine fresh supply of venison, quail, rabbit, and pheasant for the dinner table. *What we lack*, he thought sourly, *is a cook to make good of it*. "No," he said suddenly aloud, and he rolled over and stood up. "That is the least of what I miss about her."

Maxian looked around and brushed his hands clean of the rich black dirt that lay under the grass. "Galen was right," he mused to himself. "With some sleep and rest, my mind is much the clearer."

Despite seeming indolent, he had been thinking hard the past day. He was sure that Krista had left him because she had come to view his quest as a mad obsession. He could not fault her, for twice it had nearly cost her life. To his mind, he reasoned that she had come to the conclusion that the Oath could not be overturned and to remain with him would mean—in short order—her death. To preserve her life, she had gone away. Likewise, he was confident that she would not attempt to interfere with him once she had found safety.

The puzzle that racked him now revolved around what he should do next. He was greatly troubled by what he had done and condoned in the last year. A man he thought of as a good friend—the little old Persian wizard Abdmachus—had been tortured, killed, and then raised as his thrall *by his own command*. Before even that had happened, men and children had been abducted by his servants and subjected to heinous torments and experiments in the cellars under the Egyptian House.

"These are not the acts of a man in his right mind!"

Maxian pressed his palms against one of the big glassy black boulders that surrounded the grotto. He felt a curious sense of detachment from all that had occurred before he came to this place. The fire and darkness and blood all seemed part of another life, one lived by another man, one that had replaced the young healer Maxian when he had entered a boat workshop in Ostia. He rubbed his face, feeling stubble on his chin. *What must my brothers think? Galen seemed so odd when I saw him last—but if he knows what I have been about, then he, too, thinks me mad.*

The Prince thought of his mother, whose dowry had included this villa, and her kind face silhouetted by the light from the kitchen windows in their old house in Narbo. Would she approve of what he had done? *Surely not!* Maxian felt sick, and he sat down, the full import of all that he had done washing over him. *Gods! I am a monster.*

A memory intruded, breaking out of the waves of his guilt. It was his old teacher, Tarsus, speaking in the gallery of the school near Pergamum. The deep basso voice had thundered off the vaulted ceiling, sounding like the pronouncement of Zeus on high Olympus.

Each of you possesses a great power, highly prized and respected, that gift of the loving God that lets you bind and heal, restoring the withered limb and the sightless eye. Men will look upon you as a demigod, serene and without reproach. But you are not gods; you are men and prone to men's failings. This is the first law of our order—bring no harm to others by our actions.

Maxian shook his head, but the memory that came upon him was strong, and he recited aloud what he had first learned that day:

"I swear by Apollo the physician, and Asclepius the teacher, and all the gods and goddesses, that, according to my ability and judgment, I will keep this Oath and this stipulation to reckon he who taught me this Art equally dear to me as my parents, to share my substance with him, and relieve his necessities if required; to look upon his offspring in the same footing as my own brothers, and to teach them this art, if they shall wish to learn it, without fee or stipulation. I swear that by precept, lecture, and every other mode of instruction, I will impart a knowledge of the Art to my own sons, and those of my teachers, and to disciples bound by a stipulation and oath according to the law of medicine, but to none others."

His voice shook, but he continued. "I will follow that system of regimen which, according to my ability and judgment, I consider for the benefit of my patients, and abstain from whatever is deleterious and mischievous. I will give no deadly medicine to anyone if asked, nor suggest any such counsel. With purity and with holiness I will pass my life and practice my Art. Into whatever houses I enter, I will go into them for the benefit of the sick and no other reason. Whatever, in connection with my professional practice or not, in connection with it, I see or hear, in the lives of men, which ought not to be spoken of abroad, I will not divulge, as reckoning that all such should be kept secret. While I continue to keep this Oath unviolated, may it be granted to me to enjoy life and the practice of the Art, respected by all men, in all times! But should I trespass and violate this Oath, may the reverse be my lot!"

The words seemed an anchor, a lifeline across these black days to the man who had stood in front of the boat shed in Ostia. Maxian smoothed back his hair nervously. The words had been cut into a great slab of fine Cosian marble in the foyer of the temple. It was the first task of each initiate to commit them to memory. He knew what he should do, but it would be dangerous, and it might even cost him his life. *But what then of my oath to myself and to the brothers of my craft? What of Krista? What of my brothers?*

He pushed away from the stone and the friendly calming vibration that suffused it. If he was the man he thought himself to be, he would betake himself back to Rome and surrender himself to the mercy of his Imperial brother. Maxian grinned to himself. The Engine, at least, would be a worthy gift to Galen!

"Maxian! Lord Maxian!"

The Prince looked up, shading his eyes with a hand. There was a scrabbling sound, and rocks tumbled down from above. He craned his neck and stepped out into the center of the grotto. One of the Walach boys—Anatol?— was perched on the top of a pinnacle.

"Down here!" Maxian waved his arms, drawing the boy's attention. "What is it?"

"They've found it, my lord! Lord Gaius says that he's found it!" Anatol's voice echoed from the mossy stones and was quickly swallowed up by the wilderness of thorn bush and ivy.

"Found what?" Maxian tried not to let his impatience show.

"The text you sought, my lord. The original notes for the Oath!"

Maxian raised both eyebrows in surprise and then he jogged across the grotto to the hidden trail.

"You've read this, of course." The Prince held up a thin sheet of papyrus, old and yellowed, with crumbling edges, to the light from one of the library windows. Unlike most of the windows in the villa, these were covered with small squares of clear glass set into a metal frame. They allowed light even when the day was cold or blustery, unlike most of the others, which were covered with wooden shutters or lattices. Maxian frowned; the writing on the paper was in a weak, spidery hand, and the ink, over the centuries, had faded. "Did you make a translation?"

Gaius Julius nodded and pushed a sheet of fresh parchment, almost white, across the surface of the plank table they had dragged in from the stables. Alexandros was sitting next to him, perched on the back of a chair, looking for all the world like a blond crow. Maxian picked up the sheet and settled in the chair, comparing the original— which was in Greek—and Gaius' translation, which was in his simple, straightforward Latin. Maxian had once chaffed the old Roman about his writing style in comparison to the noble orators, to which Gaius had replied, in an arch tone, that "Cicero can stuff himself."

Maxian's face turned grave as he read the text of the paper. In the original there had been emendations and notes inked in along the margins. Gaius had listed these as well on a second sheet, with circled numbers indicating where each one had appeared in the original. The Prince put the translation aside once he had read it through and laid the old scroll carefully down on the table. He pinched his nose and closed his eyes for a moment, then drew a box around the papyrus with his fingertip.

Gaius Julius and Alexandros shared a glance, shrugged, then turned to watch the Prince.

Maxian rested his hands on the tabletop, palms down, on either side of the invisible box. His attention turned inward—this much was clear—and a low, faint hum rose up. Motes of dust sparkled in the air, glittering in the falling rays of the sun. On the tabletop, the scroll shifted by itself, making a faint rattle. The Prince's head slumped low on his chest. Dust spun through the air, blown on an invisible wind. Gaius Julius inched back, feeling a draft on his neck. The motes whirled through the sunstreaked air, collecting within the box. The scroll lifted into the air, no more than the width of a man's small fingertip. Dust rushed to it, filling the cracked and broken edges, restoring—suddenly—the yellowed surface to a delicate cream. The ink congealed on the page, becoming dark and clear.

Alexandros whistled in surprise. The dust continued to fill in the page, but it began to form in the air beside the sheet with dizzying speed. A second page of papyrus spun out of gossamer crept through the air. It built mote by mote, atom of dust by atom. Diagrams and signs in unknown tongues filled the sheet, the ink seemingly welling up out of the papyrus. The edge of this new sheet composed itself with a crisp snap. Then another began to build, above the first.

"Hades . . . it's a whole bloody book!" Gaius Julius fell silent, watching the drawn, pale face of the Prince. Pages continued to build out of the thin air, filled with the spidery

crabbed writing and a wild confusion of diagrams, gruesome pictures, and astronomical patterns. The hum rose in
pitch until it shook the table legs, making them dance, and
set Gaius' teeth on edge. Sunlight fled, and evening came.

At last, when nearly a hundred sheets had appeared, the
Prince looked up, his face haggard. "It is done." He raised
his hands from the tabletop, and the hundred sheets,
stacked in the air, collapsed with a soft flutter to the planks.
The room was unnaturally clean, every surface shining and
dust free. Maxian opened his eyes and looked around, lost
for a moment.

Alexandros circled the table and, very gently, touched
the edge of the manuscript. The papyrus rustled. "It's
real . . ." The Macedonian smiled in delight and withdrew
his finger.

"Yes," the Prince said in a weary voice. "Whole and
complete in sentence, word, and verse, as it was on the
first day it was written down at the command of the Emperor Augustus."

Gaius Julius made a clicking sound with his teeth. He
pointed with his chin at the book.

"This is what you call similarity? Like these lattices
within the Oath?"

Maxian nodded and leafed through the sheets of paper.
He found the original page, now gleaming white, and
turned over the book to expose it. The emendations stood
out in slightly different colored ink. "This book was done
as a whole, by one person working at a furious pace, at
one time. That man—his name was Khamûn, a Greek-
speaking Egyptian—was under deadly pressure. He held
the whole of this document in his mind as he wrote each
page. He was a wizard, even as Abdmachus was, and the
strength of his vision impressed itself upon the whole. It
was a simple thing to call it forth from the one surviving
page."

At the mention of the Egyptian's name, Gaius Julius had
made a face and was now lost in thought. Maxian tapped

on the tabletop, drawing his attention. "Is this man known to you? He lived in your time."

"Yes . . ." Gaius Julius seemed hesitant, but then he forged ahead. "During my time in Egypt, there was trouble among the Royal House of Ptolemy. On one side stood the boy-prince, and on the other, his sister. Each desired nothing so much as the other's death—I remember that the boy had taken a sorcerer into his employ. He made some trouble for the Queen, but my soldiers sorted it out."

Gaius clicked his nails against his teeth, lost in an ancient vision. "He was a funny old bird. I may . . . I may have sent him home, for my Triumph . . ."

Maxian raised an eyebrow at that and scowled. Alexandros laughed, draping himself over a chair.

"That was wise," snapped the Prince. "Sending a man of unknown powers home to dawdle among the idlers of the city. Your esteemed nephew, I warrant, did not miss the opportunity to take him into his household. I wondered how this whole business came about. Now it is rather unpleasantly clear."

"You know, then? This treatise tells you?" Alexandros swung up out of his chair, eager for the hunt. "How it came about, I mean, the Oath. How to break it?"

Maxian turned to look at the Macedonian and nodded, his face still and quiet.

"I know."

"Then?" Alexandros was ready to spring up from his chair, spear and sword in hand, and test his strength against anything—visible or invisible. Energy seemed to flow from him, now that he was roused by the thought of an end to their struggle. "What need we do?"

"Nothing," Maxian said coldly and he stood, gathering up the book. "We will do nothing."

"What!" Even Gaius Julius was on his feet, fists on the table. Alexandros was fairly dancing from foot to foot. "After all this, you say we will do nothing?"

"I do," the Prince said, eyeing the two men. He sighed and turned back to them. "Gaius Julius, your intuition was right. Augustus put Khamûn to the task of safeguarding his reign by devising an Oath that would bind the common soldier directly to the Emperor. Upon reflection, he demanded an extension of that guard to include his office and his heirs as well. The defection of the eastern Legions to Antony during their little war must have galled him! Khamûn will have been put to death immediately afterward, I suppose. He was a superlative architect, a true master of the art."

"And so?" Gaius Julius moved around the table to stand by Alexandros. The hairs on the backs of his arms were standing up. The Prince seemed strange, and Gaius felt danger in the air around him. "What does all that mean to us?"

"It means, Gaius, that while the Emperor lives, the State endures. If I am to throw down the lattice of forms at the core of this thing, I shall have to murder my brother and take his mantle as my own."

The words hung in the air of the library. Maxian turned again to leave, but Alexandros suddenly stepped forward and grasped the Prince by his arm. "Then do it! Man, you are to be a king! Flinching from blood will not make it easier. Trust me, I know full well the cost of Empire— have I not born it myself, on the bodies of my brothers and my father? If your brother must die to succor your people, is his single death not worth the freedom of millions?"

Maxian wrenched his arm from the Macedonians grasp, an angry look settling over his face. "No," snapped the Prince, his voice hot. "It is *not* worth it. I am putting this task aside. This I resolved today, on the mountaintop, and this"—he raised the book up—"only makes my will the surer. I have killed, murdered, maimed in the pursuit of this, and it is *not worth it!*"

Gaius felt the full chill of nearing death wash over him. It was worse than the hot shock of the blood-fire in battle, or the whisper of a Gaulish axe flying past his head. He remembered dank, close woods and the howling of his enemies. He gripped a nearby chair and coughed. Alexandros turned, and Gaius caught his eye with a sharp glare.

"Lord Prince, if this is your will, so be it. But what of us? You gave us life again and purpose. Will you put us aside now, like discarded toys after the gifting feast?"

Maxian sighed, weary, and raised a hand in dismissal. "Go. I will not withdraw the power that gives you motion. Find your own way in the world." Then he was gone, his charcoal cloak blending with the dark corridor and the rap of his boots echoing on the square tiles. When it faded, Gaius Julius turned to Alexandros.

"Well, I believe that we have reached a time of parting from these dear friends." The old Roman smiled, and his teeth were very bright in the dim light. Alexandros shook his shaggy curls away from his eyes, then smoothed it back with a trim muscular hand. Gaius touched the disk the Macedonian wore around his neck on a copper chain.

"We shall have to test these," he said, laughter bubbling in his voice. "Should they work—"

"We shall find a new world before us," finished Alexandros, and he, too, was smiling.

"And where will you go, my lad?" Gaius was already considering what to take from the villa. Gold first, of course, as much as he could find. Then fine horses and some of the local wine.

"To Rome, old man, where else?" Alexandros seemed to have settled the nervous energy that had filled him before. Now his mind was waking, rising up from the lulling doze it had assumed for the time when the Prince was his master.

"To Rome, then." The two men clasped forearms and bowed, one to the other. "To Rome."

Terns wheeled and swooped over the water, lazing through the afternoon sky. The air shimmered with thermals rising from the marble docks of the harbor. Nicholas tramped down the gangway of the Tyrean coaster, his kit bag slung over one shoulder and his shirt half-undone. The sky and sun seemed unnaturally bright and the glare of gleaming sandstone quays and dockside buildings hurt his eyes. The harbor of the city was justly renowned throughout the Mare Internum for its smart appointments and the engineering marvel that it represented—having been built on an otherwise barren and useless shore.

For some reason the port was nearly empty of ships, so the coaster had found a tie-up close to the tall white shape of the Pharos at the southern end of the docks. Vladimir groaned behind him; the Walach hated bright sun even worse than Nicholas did. Only Dwyrin seemed happy. Despite moping over some sprig of a girl for the last week, this landfall had made him positively cheery.

"Ah . . . warm at last!" Dwyrin stretched his arms and grinned, viewing the sand dunes and dusty brown hills that rose up behind the port with delight. Nicholas shook his head in dismay—he had thought that Greece was hot, but this? It was still the edge of spring but the air shimmered with heat like the haze over a hot griddle pan. What would it be like in full summer?

"Is it usually like this?" There was an aggrieved tone in Vladimir's voice. He was squinting ferociously.

Dwyrin nodded, breathing deep of the arid desert air. "It is. This is a fine day, in fact. Look at that sky! I'd almost forgotten how blue it can be . . . Don't worry, Vlad, you'll love it here!"

"Of course," snarled the Walach, "just as soon as my eyeballs dry up and I go blind."

Dwyrin clapped Vladimir on the shoulder in a companionable way. "Don't fret so," he said. "Just drink lots of water."

"Water?" Nicholas turned from his survey of the tan-and-white warehouses, offices, and boat sheds. "Is it fit to drink? Wouldn't we be safer with wine?"

The Hibernian shrugged and hitched his carry bag up on his shoulder. Nicholas saw that the boy had produced an evil-looking straw hat from somewhere and had crammed it down over his long red braids. He made a note to get one too. The sun was already burning on the back of his neck.

"Wine makes you thirstier. The water has a funny taste, but better than in Constantinople. Take it from me, Centurion, you don't want to go short of aqua in these parts."

"Fair enough. Let's find some lodgings and our new comrades."

Vladimir led off, making a beeline for a series of buildings stacked in a row along the road that wound out of the port side. Even from here, Nicholas could see the garish sign boards and ornamental wooden statues that advertised strong drink, cheap food, and sympathetic women. He sighed and hurried up. They needed a billet in the Legion camp, not a doss-house by the docks. The thought made him itch already.

Dwyrin started whistling a tune. By his estimation, if they made their way to this Aelia Capitolina, they would be only a week's ride from Damascus. He guessed that Zoë would wind up there if it was true that her city was destroyed. She would need supplies and food and water—what better place to get them?

"You're the First Century, Ninth Cohort, Sixth Ferrata?" Nicholas unfolded the briefing sheet and turned it over so he could read the names. "Gnaeus Parsos commanding?"

He looked up, his eyes running over the crowd of men rising from their bunks when he had rapped on the door to the barracks building. By his count there were nearly the hundred the Magister Militatum's Office had promised, which surprised him. The Ferrata had just been posted back to Judea from the war against Persia and would not have had time to replace any men lost or invalided out of service. He was perplexed by the men he saw—they were all dark-haired and Latin looking, with hardly a blond or redhead among them. Not the usual run of Eastern troops. True, they seemed stout fellows with muscular frames and thick wrists, but in the brief moment he had been in the doorway he had seen a marked lack of scars, missing ears, broken noses, or any of the other impedimenta Legion soldiers tended to acquire. They weren't even particularly tan and he expected veterans of the Ferrata, which had been garrisoning the Judean frontier for almost four hundred years, would have caught a little sun.

One of the soldiers looked around quizzically and then stepped forward. He was a balding fellow with sleepy-looking eyes, week-old sunburn, and a neck like a tree trunk. Nicholas squinted at his rank insignia. It didn't look quite right, being formed of a circular wheel with some kind of a triangle within it. The man coughed and said something that Nicholas did not quite catch.

"Sorry," Nicholas said, speaking slowly, "Latin is not my best tongue."

The man nodded and then, with the air of someone dredging his memory for words, said, "Centurion, we're not from the Sixth Ferrata. And there's just no Gnaeus Parsos here."

Nicholas was taken aback and looked over to Vladimir and Dwyrin, who were lounging against the doorpost sharing a bread roll with cheese and salami they'd gotten from a caupona on the way to the barracks. Vladimir, his mouth filled with flatbread and cheese, shook his head in amusement. He was no help.

"All right!" Nicholas gestured at the men standing around. "You're the First of the Ninth of the Sixth by this mustering order! You're assigned to me for the duration of this mission. Everyone should bunk out their kit for inspection."

The man with the funny-looking insignia shook his head. "But sir, we're not them! This is the Fourth Engineer's cohort of the First Minerva! I'm Sextus Verus, lead surveyor. Are you Nicholas of Roskilde?"

Nicholas frowned, thinking of delightful torments to apply to the clerks at the Office of Barbarians.

"Yes," he allowed grudgingly, "I am."

"Oh good! We've been waiting *weeks* for you to show up." Sextus dug into a wallet he had hung from his shoulder on a stout leather strap. It was filled with folded sheets of paper, unsharpened quills, and a stoppered bottle of blue ink. Dwyrin peered into it with interest—there were all sorts of odd pieces of metal and string in the wallet. Sextus closed it with a snap and a frown and Dwyrin stepped back, grinning in apology. The surveyor handed a sheet of parchment over to Nicholas.

It was an order writ, signed by the tribune in charge of military assignments at Antioch. Nicholas read it with a face that grew longer and longer. His century of canny grizzled veterans was nowhere to be seen. Instead, he had been assigned a gang of mathematicians and hydrologists.

"What do you do?" Nicholas put the writ away and looked around, a perplexed look on his face. "You're all listed by these Latin technical terms, which I, for one, do not know!"

"Oh," said Sextus, brightening. He had lost one of his teeth in the front. "These are the lads—normally, you know, we're attached to the Minerva, building bridges and aqueducts and the like—Batavia is a messy country for water. . . ." He waved a hand at the men standing around.

"Batavia?" Nicholas snapped in irritation. "That's a humid, low-lying, half-inundated, gnat-infested Western Empire province." He looked at his order sheet again. "You're supposed to be veterans of the Judean frontier, and Eastern troops to boot!"

"Oh no," said Sextus sadly, shaking his head. Some of the other men shook their heads in disgust. Most had returned to their bunks to play draughts or cards or sleep. If there was some cock-up with the orders, the centurions could sort it out. "We're Western troops all right. Stuck here on the edge of nowhere . . . You know, there's not a good aqueduct in this whole province? Everything is wells and these underground channels! What good is that? There's hardly any gravity feed on an underground channel . . ."

"Stop." Nicholas frowned his best Centurion-in-a-bad-mood frown. "What happened to the men from the Ferrata?"

"They bunkered off," interjected a thin-looking man with a squint. He had lank dark hair cropped close above his eyes and chipped fingernails. "I heard it from the optio when we were back in Damascus. That lot had been thrown in the lockup for breaking up a taverna." The man punctuated each word with a nod as he spoke. Nicholas glared but the man blithely ignored him.

"From who?" Sextus did not believe it. "From that fat bastard Crassus?"

"No," said the thin man, making a waving motion with his hands. Nicholas saw that they were stained with ink. "From Martus—we had a drink right before we got our orders. We were talking about the public sewer and the pooling problem in the east quarter. You know, the one where the temple foundation had settled and tipped the conduit . . ."

"Enough!" Nicholas moved physically between the two men, his hand over Sextus' mouth before he could reply. "You—squinty—what's your name?"

"Julius Frontius Alba, sir, begging your pardon."

Nicholas leaned close to Frontius and smiled. It was not

a pleasant smile. "You'll get no pardon from me, squinty, if you don't keep on the road with your story. What happened to the men from the Ferrata?"

Frontius squeaked a little and backed up, his hands fluttering in front of him. "They got sent off on some bandit-chasing expedition, sir! Really, it's true!"

"Settling foundations!" Sextus was ready to spit nails. "Why didn't you tell me that then? Now we're three provinces away from our real posting and you . . ." He jabbed a finger at Frontius, "knew why the whole time!"

"I did not," Frontius said, leaning around Nicholas to wag a finger at the surveyor. "No one knew that the Ferrata First and Ninth was supposed to come down here!"

Nicholas clapped a hand over Frontius' mouth and silenced the man with a steely glare.

"You, Sextus, what was your assigned posting before you were sent here?"

"Ah, Centurion!" Sextus grinned wistfully. He put his hand over his heart. "That would have been a bonny job! We'd been left off by Emperor Galen as loaners to the Eastern wigs to take care of infrastructure shortfall and the legate—before he left us for home—said we'd drawn the ticket for Mesopotamia."

"Mesopotamia?" Nicholas made a face. He had heard tales of the land between the two rivers from soldiers returned with the Imperial Army. An endless bog of mud, flies, bad water, rivers too wide to see across, a vast and hostile native population, and truly pitiful wine. "What's so great about Mesopotamia?"

Both Sextus and Frontius sighed, shaking their heads and sharing a long-suffering glance. Who knew where the Empire got these officers?

"Bridges by the hundred," said Sextus brightly.

"Canals by the mile," put in Frontius. "And dams and dikes and water mills bigger than the Saepta Julia!"

"Don't forget the sewers," answered Sextus. "Ctesiphon had nearly five hundred thousand citizens before the big boots knocked it over. That's nearly two hundred miles of conduit! We were right glad for the opportunity to show these effete Persians how to deal with such things, too. But here we are, sitting beside as fine an artificial harbor as ever built, five hundred miles from Babylon and all its ancient wonders. . . ."

Frontius sighed again. "And barely a serviceable aqueduct in the whole province."

Sextus turned to Nicholas, his face grave, and put his hand on the thin man's shoulder. "Aqueducts are what Frontius here does best. He's one of the masters of the craft."

Frontius shook his head severely and raised a finger. "No, I am but an apprentice. No Vetruvius I!"

Nicholas pressed his fingers to his forehead, hoping to forestall an incipient headache.

"I don't suppose," he said slowly and carefully, "that any of you are actual legionnaires? Like the kind who march on roads, with say a *pilum* or spear or perhaps a *scutum* among you?"

Sextus and Frontius stared at him in surprise, taken aback.

"Why surely, Centurion!" Sextus gestured to a stack of tools set beside the barracks door. A collection of hardened leather *lorica*, iron helmets with hinged neck flaps, short swords in wooden cases, and throwing spears lay against the wall in neat bundles. "Every Legion engineer has to train beside his fellows. We're just . . ." He paused, then smiled and said, "We're specialists!"

"I'm a specialist too," sneered Nicholas, "but it's rather more specific to what we're actually supposed to be *doing* than you are."

Frontius frowned, his face quizzical. "Centurion, you *always* need an engineer along. You're just blessed by having a whole century of them! How much luckier could a field commander get? Often I've heard a tribune or general complain about the lack of sappers or engineers."

"Or surveyors," interjected Sextus, looking solemn. "Can't have too many surveyors about! You know, sir, there's many a time I've had to sneak about under the noses of the Germanii—it's not an easy life of draughts and wine cups for a *librator*, no indeed!" He picked up the hem of his tunic, showing a length of hairy thigh marked with a curling puckered scar. "Got that from a Frankish throwing axe I did, when we were putting a pontoon bridge across the Rhenus at Bonna. That was a close thing."

Nicholas looked around and sat on the nearest bunk. The previous inhabitant, seeing that the centurion was coming his way, had decided he really needed to use the privy. The Scandian laid his orders packet on the thin cotton sheet and put the palms of his hands over his eyes. He wondered for a moment if it were too early to get a stiff drink at the caupona they had passed.

"Tell me," he said after a moment of reflection, "what you do . . . what your specialties are."

Sextus narrowed his eyes and surveyed the room, taking a tally in his head. Dwyrin and Vladimir, seeing that things were going to go on for a while, made themselves scarce. Nicholas was sure he could find them later in the caupona, half-sick from strange local food and too many overripe olives in garlic pickle.

"Well, sir, we've nine lead surveyors with me as their chief, a senior, and a junior-level man each as assistants. Then there are the stonemasons, another dozen, with about twenty apprentices for the smoothing, tunneling, and the detail work. Frontius has his pack of carpenters, calculators, and copyists—that's an easy fifteen fellows right there. We've two cooks, that's a bit of luck for you there, sir, you won't have to eat the local food. Oh wait, Frontius has two more draftsmen who work for him—his assistants really. How many does that make?"

Nicholas sneered, saying, "Eighty and two. And the rest of these layabouts?"

"Ah," said Sextus sagely, "those will be the semaphore men—for six—and the runners for the last four. I always forget about them . . . but, sir, you'll miss them if they're not about!"

"Fine," said Nicholas, rubbing his chin. "Have you any experience riding?"

Sextus beamed and rubbed the top of his head. "Sir, we ride everywhere."

"On horses?" Nicholas gritted his teeth. *It had better not be shanks-mare!*

"Not at all, sir. Nasty balky beasts, always biting you when you're not looking! No sir, like any engineer's cohort we've a good twenty military *reda* for the equipment, plus the cook's *carruca*. We can all fit quite handily on board. You needn't worry, Centurion, we've got all our kit, baggage, and mules ready to go."

"Those things you mentioned," said Nicholas, racking his brain for what little Latin he had gathered while in the Empire, "those would be . . . wagons?"

"Yes, Centurion, fine steel-sprung wagons, too. Very comfortable."

Nicholas grimaced, then fought down a surge of bile.

"Sextus," he asked politely. "Have you ever chased bandits over hill and dale in your . . . wagons?"

The engineer thought for a moment and then shook his head sadly, *no*.

The Scandian repressed another sigh and opened one of the sheets of his briefing packet. He spread it out on the bedsheet.

"Our orders are to proceed from the port here . . ." His thumb indicated the symbol for Caesarea. ". . . to here, Aelia Capitolina, to deal with some provincial troubles. I expect that those troubles will involve bandits who will take great delight in flitting about on horses over the local hills while we are stuck on the local roads with these wagons . . ."

Frontius sniffed and turned up his nose. "No aqueducts for Capitolina. No need—whole town's fed by springs right within the walls. A silly place to build it too, right on the highest ground thereabouts . . . can't get water to run uphill, you know." He paused. "Well, that's not exactly true . . . you can get it to run uphill, but you need a big mountain to start from."

Sextus shrugged, saying "well, sir, I suppose we can swan about on horses with the best of them."

"Good," muttered Nicholas, gathering up his papers. "We leave in the morning."

It got worse, as far as Nicholas could see, the farther inland you went. Barren dry hills rose up on either side of the road and the bottomland wasn't much greener. Even the olives and junipers were stunted and the air had a funny brittle quality to it. All the villages seemed to be crouched on hilltops and were mean places with reclusive citizens, stout walls, and an angry feeling in the air. Nicholas' heart sank the higher they went into the hills. The only birds seemed to be crows and buzzards.

"This has all the signs of a badly managed province," he muttered to Vladimir, who was riding at his side, wrapped in a white-and-tan striped cloak and a sun hat. The Walach grunted in agreement, keeping his hands inside his cloak. Vladimir's pale skin had started to burn on the voyage from Constantinople and now he was peeling and in a particularly bad mood. "This may take some doing."

Nicholas wheeled his bay mare around and dropped back to allow the first engineer's wagon to catch up with him. He and Vladimir had been in the lead, a dozen paces ahead of the first wagon, with the surveyors out in front of them as scouts. The rest of Sextus' apprentices and the semaphore men made the rear guard. In his usual good humor, Sextus grinned at the centurion as he came alongside. Despite his fear the engineer's wagons would slow him down, Nicholas was impressed by the conveyance.

The *reda* was a four-wheeled box with high hinged sides and an elevated riding seat for a driver and passenger. A long wooden tongue ran out to harness four fast-stepping mules. The wheel rims were of a standard size and covered with layers of heavy canvas, which seemed to reduce the noise and rattle that wagons usually generated. Nicholas had inspected the wagons before they had left the Legion camp at the port. They were impressive; carefully packed full of all the materials and tools that the engineers would need in their work. Spades, picks, mauls, adzes, axes large and small, chisels, precut support timbers, five big *dioptra* for taking sightings and finding levels, broken-down leveling tables called *chorobates*, metal fittings for ballista and onagers, water screws, and barrels and barrels of nails and precut wooden pegs. Each man had his own kit, too, in addition to the light leather armor cuirass of a Legion *auxillia;* a saw, a heavy hand-hammer, a plane, and a hand-held water level as well as plumb bobs and a *groma* for finding straight lines and right angles. The stonemasons had a whole other set of gear in their wagons, too, all designed for finding, cutting, moving, finishing, and cementing stone. Each wagon had its own packing order, which had really impressed Nicholas—used, as he was, to the lax logistical methods of the Scandian tribes or the Eastern Empire—which was tracked by square-cut leather tags tied to each piece of equipment.

Finally, a high-hooped frame of laminated wood covered the wagon. A leather shade was lashed to this, which left a covered space on top of the equipment for the men to sleep in while they rode along. Sextus' *reda*, as it was the lead surveyor's wagon, was also equipped with a measuring device that dropped stones into a tin bucket, measuring the passage of the miles as the wagon rolled along. If his task had been to build a new road or repair just about anything in the world, Nicholas would have been a happy man.

As it was, he felt obscurely depressed as he rode along beside the wagon.

"While you were waiting at the port, did you hear anything about why these bandits are running wild?"

Sextus leaned back against the padded seat of the wagon

and nodded his head. He looked a little sad.

"Surely, Centurion. This province has been a spot of trouble for centuries. It's always been a hotbed of religious fanatics, madmen, separatists, reckless builders, and outlawed cults. The senior *optio* at the port let me in on a little of it—the entire province of Judea has risen up in full-scale revolt against the Empire twice—on the second time the native population was deported en masse and scattered throughout the Empire. Those were religious troubles, over sacred sites at this place we're going. They didn't ken much to the Capitoline Triad, I guess."

Nicholas nodded—the Empire did not take recurring trouble lightly. Threats to the divinity of the Emperor and the gods of Rome were treated harshly.

"And today?" he asked, twitching the reins to keep his horse moving. "What gripes them now?"

Sextus smiled grimly. He scratched the side of his nose and looked the centurion up and down.

"Well, sir, seeing as how you're an Eastern officer, I should be politic. But you seem a right fellow, so . . . the big trouble here is taxes, like it always is. It's a poor province and really not worth that much. All the riches are across the river in Nabatea or the Decapolis, where the trade runs up from the Sinus Arabicus to Damascus. A few weeks ago the word went out that Emperor Heraclius had called for a fresh census, which means, of course . . ."

"That taxes will go up," finished Nicholas sourly. That was surely the way of the world. He looked around, seeing the barren hills and the scattered scrawny flocks of sheep, the dry watercourses and the pitiful gardens, the poor villages. New taxes would go down hard here, he thought. This was a land with very little margin in it. If there was already resentment from past grievances, a few hotheads could make a lot of trouble.

"Sir!" Dwyrin spurred his horse up. The thaumaturge had been placed in the middle of the caravan with an escort of burly stonecutters to back him up. The boy looked alert and wary. "I feel something in the aether, maybe trouble ahead."

Nicholas nodded sharply—the storm lords of the Dannmark could smell ambuscade in the air, too.

"Pass the word to stand ready," he rapped at Sextus and the stonemasons, then he turned and rode back to the point. Vladimir had perked up too and was sniffing the air.

"Yes," said Nicholas in a low voice as he cantered alongside, "time to earn your pay."

Vladimir's teeth flashed in the shade of his broad-brimmed hat. "Time for lunch, you mean."

Nicholas made a shushing motion and grimaced. It might be true for the Walach, but this was not the time or place to discuss it. Vlad's sense of humor tended to the grisly.

Dwyrin came up behind Vlad and Nicholas, guiding his pony with his knees. He had picked it out because it liked to stand around thinking and not move much. He wrapped the bridle around his wrist and cleared his thoughts, calling forth the words of the meditations that would open his mind to the hidden world. Ahead of him, the two older men drew their swords quietly and continued riding, watching the steep hillsides with a wary eye. The pony ambled along. The road turned, running under a crumbling cliff of cracked pale gray limestone. At some time in the past, a smooth-faced cut had been made in the side of the hill. Most of that had tumbled away, but the way narrowed sharply in the turn. Dwyrin let his senses expand, seeing the invisible currents in the air and the chuckling green flow of water deep under the dry streambed. Threat was waiting in the air. Beyond the curve of the hill he could feel the burning orange flicker of men crouched among the rocks.

The surveyors in the lead turned the corner and Nicholas and Vladimir spurred their horses, galloping around after them. Dwyrin let the pony follow and dug his will into rock and stone, drawing forth a stream of power. Distantly, he heard a sudden shout and then men howling war cries. The red figures gleamed in his sight, charging down the hill. Others rose up, sending arrows and javelins into the air in a cloud.

Dwyrin raised a hand, mouthing the mnemonics of a wind-ward that Zoë had taught him. It seemed to come so slowly! He stumbled among the intricacies of the pattern and a gusty breeze rushed through the canyon. Dust and grit spun up into the eyes of the men rushing downslope toward the wagons. The arrows and javelins he had tried to slap aside fell undeterred among the Romans. One of the surveyor's apprentices in the van cried out in pain as a wooden shaft sank into his leg. His horse bucked, pricked by the metal tip, and he was thrown off, screaming. The bandits rushed onto the road and Nicholas and Vladimir were among them, blades out and flashing in the sun.

Dwyrin cursed, feeling embarrassment and panic war in him. The slope was aboil with men, over two hundred of them, rushing down with spears and small round shields. More had appeared on the road ahead, running forward with a shout. Nicholas was a whirlwind of brilliant white light—the thing that lived in his blade was shrieking with joy in the hidden world—and two men went down. The Hibernian cursed at himself. Since parting from Blanco he had not practiced the forms and patterns and he was very rusty. In a moment, though, the caravan would be overrun. He folded thought into himself, digging down for the pure hot spark of power that he remembered from the siege of Tauris.

Nicholas slammed the pommel of *Brunhilde* down on a bandit's face as the man grabbed at his reins. Bone crunched and blood smeared the side of the man's head as he went down. The mare shied from two spearmen, but Nicholas wrenched her around, dancing between the thrusts, and *Brunhilde* licked out and slid sideways between the bearded one's ribs. Bright red blood welled around the wound and Nicholas ran the falling man over.

He could hear Vladimir screaming a high-pitched war cry like the shriek of a hunting cat. Nicholas parried another spearman and swung the mare around hard. He followed with *Brunhilde* and the steel blade sheared through the next bandit's shield and arm like a carving knife in a hot lamb roast.

A heavy javelin thudded into the ground only inches from the horse's hooves and she skipped aside.

Screams and shouts rose up all around amid the din of iron on iron. The stonemasons had dismounted and were fighting on foot, their rectangular shields close together. The surveyors had fallen back onto their position. Nicholas could hear the rattle of fighting from farther back along the line of the wagons. He had not expected so many bandits! Another man rushed him with sword and a heavy square shield. Nicholas' eyes widened in surprise, seeing that the fellow had a Legion issue *spatha* and *scutum*. One corner of the painted leather facing on the shield had torn off, showing the crossed plywood slats behind it. He knew how to use the long straight blade too, and Nicholas fended off two hard stabs at the mare's legs. The man reversed his stance, blocking with the shield and dodged toward the back of the horse.

Nicholas spun the horse in place, his left leg kicking out and caught the man behind the ear with the tip of his boot. The iron studs in the shoe raked the man's skin, tearing a bloody strip. The fellow cried out and made a wild slash. Nicholas leaned under it and stabbed down, feeling *Brunhilde's* triangular tip punch through the clavicle and then tear out his throat. Blood fountained, spattering in the mare's eyes. The horse reared and Nicholas fought to stay in the saddle.

Arrows whistled past Dwyrin's head and one tangled in his cloak. He did not notice, for the bright shuddering spark in his heart had roared to life. *This*, he rejoiced, *is easy!* The fire calling had always been a quick summoning for him, not like the complicated battle wards and strategies of the thaumaturges. Each working had some kind of gradient associated with it and those patterns that drew from the glyph of fire were smooth and effortless. He unfolded his hands and let the flames that lapped around him in the hidden world find release.

Nicholas fell hard on the ground, cracking his shoulder against the stones of the road. By a miracle he managed to hold onto *Brunhilde* and he tried to get up. The nearest bandit ducked around the mare and stabbed at him as he rolled on the ground. One spear caught his side and pinned the edge of his mail shirt into a crevice between two paving stones. He tugged at it, trying to get some leverage, but he had to keep the steel sword between him and the bandit.

The man, his head wrapped in a blue headdress, laughed aloud to see him stuck like a sheep in the pen. He wrenched his spear from between the stones, sunlight flaring off the triangular iron head and the polished faces of the point. Nicholas blanched at the sight, seeing his own death in it.

Flame filled the sky, roaring like the mouth of a furnace a mile tall. A stabbing bolt of shuddering blue enveloped the bandit's head. The man's shriek of horror ended abruptly as the air in his lungs combusted. Nicholas threw up his hand and cried out himself, seeing the man's burnoose char to white ash and his skin shrivel and crisp away from his skull. Still burning furiously, the man toppled over, the iron of the spear point flashing into the air as red-hot globules that spattered on the dust. Nicholas scrabbled away in the dirt, feeling the heat in the sky beat at him. Men were screaming in an odd high-pitched wail all around him. He looked up, squinting into the actinic glare.

Dwyrin was still astride his pony, but the poor creature was trembling from nose to tail, shaking like a reed bank in a high wind. The boy was surrounded by a corona of fire and his mouth was open, shouting words that Nicholas could not hear over the shriek of flame. Bolts of fire winged from the boy's hands, scattering the bandits, shattering rock and stone where they struck. Dozens of the attackers were down, their bodies wrapped in white-hot flame. A few arrows still sliced the air, but most burned away in flight. The legionnaires, showing quite good sense, had thrown themselves to earth after the first sky-ripping blast. The stonemasons had dragged their shields over their heads. The surveyors were huddled under the wagons.

Dry grass on the hillside ignited, sending up a tall column of black smoke. The tamarisk and stunted olive and dry oak in the stream bottom was burning merrily too, clouding the road with drifts of bitter white fog. The last of the bandits fell, struck down by burning motes that flickered through the air to bury themselves in their victims. The men thrashed and sobbed on the ground, then burst into flame and were consumed in an instant.

Dwyrin dropped his hand and the fires died as one, all across the hillside and along the canyon floor.

Nicholas raised his head and peered around, his eyes streaming with tears from the thick smoke. The boy still sat astride his pony, though he swayed a little from side to side. Nicholas spat, trying to clear his throat. He stood, his legs shaking with the blood-fire from his near death and what had come after. *Brunhilde* trembled in his hand, keening softly in fear. He raised her up, caressing her hilts and smooth worn pommel, then he put her away in the close soft darkness of her sheath. She quieted.

Nicholas looked up the road and saw that it was deserted, though billows of smoke drifted across it like winter fog. Even the sun seemed dim, shining through the gray haze that had risen up over the battlefield. He turned back in time to see Dwyrin slump off of his pony into the waiting arms of Vladimir. The Walach grinned back at Nicholas, and his teeth and face were red with blood.

Nicholas whistled softly to himself and motioned for Vlad to wipe his face clean.

"On, then," he said in a low voice no one could hear. "On to Aelia Capitolina."

*   *   *

Another hot dry dusty day ended with the hills of Hierosolyma rising up before them. Nicholas reined his horse to
the side of the road and let it rest for a moment, head low,
panting in the heat. The city spilled down the sides of the
hill in a maze of winding streets and dirty white-and-tan
buildings. The old town rose on the summit of one hill,
surrounded by ancient-looking walls rising up above newer
houses. There was an outer wall for the suburbs and the
city flowed over a second pair of hills to finally end in a
maze of orchards and gardens. In the fierce sunlight, it
seemed to be quiet and peaceful. There was a constant
breeze from the east, but the air was still hot. Nicholas
sighed in disgust and goosed the horse, urging it back onto
the road.

The engineers' wagons rolled past, raising a pall of
tacky white limestone dust that clung to everything. Nicholas walked the horse, letting the *redii* rumble down the
highway. Ahead of them, a triumphal arch squatted athwart
the road. It was still a hundred yards or more from the
nearest building, standing alone in a field of stones. Three
arches opened in it, allowing the road to pass through the
central one. Nicholas shook his head in disbelief. These
Romans tacked an arch on anything in sight. He had not
seen one freestanding before. In a moment, Dwyrin and
Vladimir rode up, chatting amiably. They fell in beside
Nicholas. He smoothed the sharp points of his mustache.

"Seems a peaceful town," he ventured.

Vlad and Dwryin nodded sagely. "Oh yes," they said,
"very peaceful and quiet."

Nicholas glared at them and fell silent, wondering what
troubles awaited him now. They rode under the arch and
he looked up, shaking his head again at the wind eroded
statues and inscriptions. Whoever had built it was long
gone, swallowed by the gulf of time. Even their monuments were decaying.

The city was sleeping—the doors and windows locked up
for an afternoon rest during the worst of the heat—and

they reached the northern gate of the old city itself before they encountered anyone out and about. Even there, under two crumbling square towers, the gates were standing open and there was no guard posted. A local man hurried past, his head wrapped in a headdress, carrying a lamb with its forelegs tied with hemp twine over his shoulder.

"I'll bet he stole it," whispered Dwyrin to Vladimir as they sat on their horses behind Nicholas.

The centurion turned and gave them both a frigid glare. The engineers had halted their wagons, crowding a half-circle piazza that opened up inside the gate. Sextus stood up on his wagon seat and waved Nicholas forward. The Scandian rode around the line of wagons and past a carved column that rose from the center of the public space. Like the arch outside of town, it was worn down by the elements and many surfaces had been defaced by graffiti.

Marcus was here, read one large carving. Nicholas snorted in amusement. *That's original!*

"What is it?"

Sextus frowned and pointed forward. At the edge of the piazza two streets plunged into the town. Unlike most Roman cities, the *cardo* or secondary street was not a broad avenue, but rather a very narrow street snaking off between shuttered shops toward what seemed to be the citadel, which rose on their left. The buildings stood so close that the road quickly disappeared in a dark tunnel made by overhanging roofs. The whole inner town, within these decaying walls, seemed to be built very small.

"There's no way we can get the wagons through there. We'll have to make a camp outside of town."

Nicholas nodded, turning in his saddle. The rest of his century was backed up on the road and in the piazza. He felt a queer crawling sensation and suddenly knew that the locals were watching them from behind the shuttered windows and laughing.

"All right, Sextus, Vladimir, get everyone turned around and out of town. Scout the other gates, if there are any, and find out if there's a Legion encampment here. If not, find one of these springs that Frontius is always going on about and make camp there—a fortified camp, too. Until we set things right, this is hostile country, understood?"

"*Ave!*" Sextus made a half-salute, grinned, and jumped down off the wagon. He scrambled back along the line of the *redii* shouting orders. Nicholas motioned to Dwyrin.

"Come along, lad, we'll find the governor and introduce ourselves."

The streets of the inner city twisted into a maze of dark shadowy corridors. Little temples and shops crowded every available space and the slope of the hill made for a steep climb. Finally, after thirty minutes of trotting along deserted alleys, Nicholas and Dwyrin came out into a tiny square, which abutted against a substantial bridge. The arch of the bridge rose up to the east, their left, and ran through a long tunnel cut into the side of a massive wall.

Nicholas was impressed. Nearly everything that he had seen was built small, but this edifice rising fifty feet over his head was massive. The stones were the size of wagons and fitted in alternating courses. A pair of square towers cut from the same stone loomed over the roofs of the houses, showing archaic-style battlements. The buildings of the town were built right up to the wall, unfortunately, and the ramp rose up over what had been—at some time in the distant past—a moat. Now it was covered over by shops and houses. This gate, too, stood open.

Here, at last, there were two Roman soldiers standing watch. Nicholas dismounted at the bottom of the ramp and led his horse up. Dwyrin's pony ambled up, with the Hibernian leaning forward over its head.

"*Ave*," said Nicholas, saluting the two guards, who were sitting on triangular wooden stools in the deep shade of the gateway. "I've come to report to the praetor of the city."

One of the guards opened an eye and pointed back down the street, across the tiny square. The other continued to sleep, his stool tilted back and his head resting against the big square blocks of the city wall.

"The praetorium is that way," he said gruffly. "This is the Temple of Jupiter. Go past the tetrapylon and you'll come to the Jaffa gate. It's on the left."

"Thanks," grunted Nicholas as he swung back up on his horse.

Dwyrin nodded to the one man who was awake, but the soldier ignored him. Both of the legionnaires were wearing only stained tunics and broad leather belts. Neither was clean shaven. Their helmets, rectangular shields, and *pila* were piled in a heap behind them against the wall. Even their sandals were kicked under the chairs. The gruff man settled back to sleep, idly brushing a fly away from his nose as they rode away.

Like everything else in the city, the praetorium was a hastily built building, three stories high, packed into a space behind the Jaffa gate. Of a wonder, it had a cleared space around it, though Nicholas could see that during market day the area was crowded with temporary stalls, lines of donkeys, and heaps of rubbish. The rubbish was still there, along with the donkey's contributions to the close, fetid smell of the city. However, less than a block to the south of the praetorium building, which was heralded by an Imperial standard leaning drunkenly from a second-floor window, there was a real wall of dressed stone and a closed military gate.

Above the military gate, another pair of standards hung limply in the hot afternoon air. Underneath them was a wooden placard covered with blocky Latin letters.

Dismounting, Nicholas nodded at the closed gate and gestured for Dwyrin to take his reins.

"There is a Legion encampment of some kind, lad. Make sure the horses are taken care of."

Dwyrin opened his mouth to say he was a sorcerer, not a stable hand, but Nicholas had already stalked off into the shadowy doorway of the praetorium, his back stiff, and the Hibernian sighed and made the best of it.

Besides, he thought, *I can get the latest gossip from the lads in charge of the horses.*

"Come in." Nicholas pushed open a door of light green–painted wood and stepped into the office of the military governor of Aelia Capitolina. The dingy building had indeed proved to be the offices and residence of the praetor. It was just as grim looking inside as out, showing quite a bit of empty corridor, bare wall, and minimally furnished chambers. A sleepy attendant on the ground floor had given Nicholas directions. Despite the close-packed nature of the city buildings, he was beginning to wonder if anyone actually lived here. He had seen barely a dozen people since entering the walls.

"Nicholas of Roskilde, centurion on detached duty, reporting, sir." Nicholas snapped a salute, arm clenched over his heart, then extended, fingers stiff. The man behind the desk raised an eyebrow and motioned to a low wing-backed seat by the side of the marble table that served as a desk. Nicholas handed his travel orders to the man, then sat, his face impassive, and looked the praetor over with a gimlet eye.

"Well met, Nicholas. I am Bardanes Turcus, praetor of Judea and governor of this city. What brings you to Capitolina?" Bardanes took a moment to stack the scrolls in an untidy pile.

Nicholas paused a moment, weighing his words. The lax defense of the city troubled him greatly, particularly since a large and well-armed force of bandits had attacked his century barely a day away. Examining the bodies—or what was left of them after Dwyrin's fire had burned out—had revealed that many of them bore arms and armor of Imperial origin. Nicholas had read over his briefing papers carefully the following night, hunched in his tent with a small candle-lantern for illumination, and there had been no indication that local garrison units had joined the "bandits." Unless there had been a recent defeat for Roman arms, the only other way for such a quantity of weaponry to have gotten into indigenous hands would be for it to have been sold to them. This Bardanes was a stout, almost squat, man with thick black hair on his head and forearms. His face was almost square, with a pug nose and close-set eyes. Today, sitting at ease in his office, he was wearing a fine quality cotton tunic in green with gold edging and lace-up leather boots. The fellow had an open seeming face, but Nicholas was wary. The man reminded him of a badger.

Nicholas had never been fond of badgers.

"Lord Bardanes, I have been sent by the Imperial Offices in Constantinople to see about the ... bandit ... problem the province has been suffering. As my orders relate, I am to base myself and my men here in the city and see that order is restored in the surrounding countryside. A letter was supposed to have been sent to you. Have you received it?"

Bardanes shook his head slowly and opened the orders packet, his thick fingers spreading the documents out on the top of the desk. "I have received no notice of this in the usual dispatches. What bandits were these?"

Nicholas felt the hackles rise on the back of his neck. The man was either utterly ignorant of conditions in the countryside or a brazen liar.

"Reports, sir, had been received in the capital that at least one band of brigands had caused unrest in Judea and that other trouble was expected. A request was made for additional assistance. It was indicated that the local garrison was already occupied."

The praetor smiled genially and put down one of the papers. "There has been a great deal of trouble, Centurion, across the river in the Decapolis. But here? Sheep thieves, petty crime, drunkenness ... those are the kinds of problems that we suffer here. Capitolina is a sleepy town on the edge of nowhere. Now, across the river, I have heard they have some troubles ... wandering bands of Persian soldiers, desert raiders, all that sort of thing. Did you have any problems on the road from Caesarea?"

Nicholas held his temper and willed his fingers to lie still on his knees. He matched his gaze with the praetor's and considered his options. He could accuse the man openly of lying, or let it go. If he confronted Bardanes now, without anyone to back him up, it might become ugly. Nicholas smiled tightly.

"No . . . nothing that my men could not handle. Do you think, if there is trouble across the river, that it might spread here?"

Bardanes smiled again, seemingly a man at peace with the world. He shook his head.

"Things are well in hand here, Centurion. My garrison and the local militia are more than adequate to deal with anything that may arise. But I know that you will need to see things for yourself and make your own judgment. I think, however, that you will soon find that any disturbances have their source on the other side of the river Jordanus."

Nicholas nodded, wanting to seem like a man taking careful note of the praetor's experience.

"My lord, if things are peaceful, then my men will get a good rest. They are weary from the recent war and the march from the coast. I will send a dispatch to the legate in Damascus for further orders."

"Good!" Bardanes smiled, showing a mouth of crooked brown teeth. "I have the garrison officers over to dinner regularly—I'll be sure to invite you. Samuel!"

The praetor pulled a rope that hung from the wall. A moment later there was a distant ringing sound. Bardanes smiled again. "Samuel is the chief of my servants—he will help you barrack your men in the old Legion camp and stable your animals. While you are here, you may draw stores and feed from the Imperial granary. How many men did you bring?"

Nicholas noted that the praetor finally seemed interested in something. He smiled, the edges of his eyes crinkling up.

"A full century, Lord Bardanes. Veterans every one."

There was a patter of feet outside the office and then a tall man entered, ducking under the lintel. Bardanes glowered at the man as he entered. He seemed to have dismissed the matter of Nicholas' troops.

"Samuel, you are as slow a servant as I've ever suffered in my house! This is Centurion Nicholas of Roskilde. He and his men will be occupying the old Legion quarters for a week or two before they head across the river into the territories of the Gerasans. See that they have what they need."

Bardanes nodded to Nicholas and turned back to considering the papers on his desk. Nicholas rose and saluted, then followed the majordomo out into the hallway. Bardanes was already engrossed in his ledgers. Samuel was a tall thin man with a close-cut head of very curly brown hair. He wore a simple robe of cream-colored cotton, belted, with the edge of a blue shirt peeking out at his collar. In youth he had suffered some disease that left his face marked with small half-moon scars. He did not meet Nicholas' eyes, wearing an air of indifference. He preceded the centurion, descending the stairs to the main floor with a loping gait.

"We have wagons and mules," said Nicholas as they reached the cool dim space of the main hall. "Does the old camp have sufficient room for a dozen large wagons? We can camp outside the city, if necessary."

Samuel turned, his dark eyes finally focussing on Nicholas. The Scandian felt a shock, meeting that gaze. This man was hiding deep and abiding anger. In her sheath, *Brunhilde* trembled a little, but so faintly that Nicholas barely perceived it. Here was a slave that did not wear the yoke of Rome gently.

"Master, the Imperial Army has leave to camp where it will. However, when the Tenth Legion was based here, it was at full strength, so I think that the camp on Zion mount will suit you."

The man's voice was soft and submissive, which made Nicholas feel a cold chill creep on his arms. Now that he saw the hatred in the man, the dissonance between his words and hidden thoughts bespoke danger.

"I saw . . ." Nicholas cleared his throat. "I saw no aqueducts upon our arrival. The city is watered by springs? They are all within the walls?"

Samuel paused at the door to the plaza. He turned, his head silhouetted against the brightness of the day outside.

"Master, there are some small springs outside the walls, but they are difficult to reach. The pool of Solomon, for example, or the spring of Sion are high on the cliffs that line the eastern side of the city. The camp of the Tenth is watered by cisterns. They should be full."

Nicholas nodded, his hand on the doorjamb. "I understand. I'm sure we'll find it a suitable camp. I will need a chit for the granary."

The man bowed and then handed Nicholas a tablet bearing the seal of the praetor and the city. Nicholas took it, suppressing an arched eyebrow. There was no name or other directive on the tablet. Any man that held it could, theoretically, request anything they wanted from the Imperial granaries, stables, or armory. *A blank pass,* he thought. Samuel, without speaking, turned away and disappeared into the gloom of the house. Nicholas took one last look around and left, though he still felt on edge as he walked out into the burning heat. A sullen and angry servant coupled with an oblivious master; that was a poor combination.

Dwyrin was waiting in the shade in front of the stables. As Nicholas passed under the wooden porch that lined the front of it, he saw that it was part of some larger building that had been partially torn down. The paint on the walls had flaked away in places, revealing bits and pieces of murals and paintings that had adorned the original walls. The columns, too, were not of Roman manufacture, or even Greek. Nicholas ran his hand over one of them. They were fat-bellied and tapered toward the summit. Round bands formed their bases and capitals. The garish red paint crumbled under his touch, revealing a dark finish and a fine-grained wood underneath.

"Cedar, I think," said the Hibernian, pushing away from the wall he had been holding up. "There are the same kind of columns inside, and tessellated flooring under the straw and dirt. These stables were an audience hall once, I think, and there were upper floors, not just one."

Nicholas scraped away some of the paint on the columns with his belt-knife. The wood underneath was as smooth as silk and had, in some past time, been polished to a high gloss.

"Whoever ruled before Rome, then . . ." Nicholas put the knife away. "No matter. What gossip did you squeeze out of the grooms?"

Dwyrin shrugged and looked about in a nonchalant matter. "Nothing worth talking about."

"Not here, you mean," said Nicholas with a wry grin. "Let's be on our way, then. I shudder to think what kind of trouble those pioneers and Vladimir are up to."

It only took a moment to find the engineers. They had circled the city, starting at the northern gate and going west. The hill of the city was steep on the south, the west, and the east. A barren slope dropped away from the Jaffa gate to the west. Despite this, the engineers had found that the Jaffa gate was wide enough to admit their wagons and it was a simple right turn in the public area fronting the praetorium to reach the Legion encampment.

Nicholas stood in the shade of the gate, watching the wagons roll in, their muffled wheels still loud on the limestone cobbles of the street. The Roman city sprawled away to the north on the flat, shimmering in the heat. Everywhere the land was barren and pale, overgrazed by sheep and goats and sapped by the constant dry wind from the east. Here and there bare hills of white limestone punched through the dry brown soil, assuming the characteristics of old bone under the round white disk of the sun.

"Not much for a farmer . . ." Dwyrin looked around in

mild puzzlement. "Doesn't it seem odd that most of this land should be so grim looking, but people are still here, clinging to it?"

Nicholas rubbed his jaw, feeling the need for a shave. "Many places are like this—the people have always been here, even if it is desolate. They stay because they have always stayed. There must be fertile valleys nearby, though, or it *would* be abandoned. How went things with the groomsmen and servants?"

"Not well," Dwyrin made a face. "I learned quite a bit, though more about the tavernae and cauponae of the city than the lay of the land, so to speak. There is trouble . . . your orders were right about that, but not the kind that you might think."

"Tell me," said Nicholas, turning a little sideways to watch the boy. The last of the engineers' wagons had passed the gate, kicking up a pall of white dust that coated their legs. They began walking back toward the encampment.

"This praetor," the Hibernian began, "he was sent here not too long ago by the Emperor with orders to begin a census—as you heard before—so that there could be a tax. There was a bit of trouble right away, which was bad because all of the Legions in the area had been recalled to Constantinople for the war against Persia. This Bardanes—apparently an Epirote, if you believe the groomsmen—took some initiative to deal with it. He had only brought two or three hundred men with him, but not legionnaires."

"Household troops?" Nicholas interjected. The near collapse of Imperial authority in the east had driven many of the great landowners to raise their own private militias. Many of the traditional authorities—chiefs, princes, and potentates—had armed retainers already. The Emperor frowned upon such things, of course, but with the capital besieged, who could blame a local governor for seeing to the maintenance of order?

"No," Dwyrin mused. "Mercenaries I think, like those guards at the temple gate. In any case he apparently hired the largest local clan, the Persee, to see that order was restored in the countryside and taxes collected. Aelia Capitolina, of course, he garrisoned with his own men."

Nicholas raised an eyebrow at that, though it was a common practice on the borders of the Empire to employ local troops. Still, the Roman landowners in the province would be beside themselves at the thought of some barbarians banging on their gates, demanding the tax.

"The Persee," Dwyrin continued, "faced down the other clans and things settled out. Now, the taxes have not been collected yet, because Bardanes is waiting for the Persee to finish the census. That will be done in a month or two when the official rate comes down from Constantinople."

"You said he hired the Persee," Nicholas said. "With what? Did he bring his own coin or did he use the Emperor's voucher?"

"Better!" grinned Dwyrin as they entered the double-wide gate of the camp within the walls of the city. "He promised them a cut of the taxes that they are to collect."

Nicholas growled in disgust. "Then they get to gouge their neighbors with the Imperial writ, not pay themselves, keep their own percentage, and make this backwoods tax-farmer Bardanes rich." He drummed his fingers on the saddle horn. "This," he pronounced to the nearby buildings and Dwryin, "is the kind of thing that winds up requiring three full Legions, a bushel of tribunes, and an ocean of blood to clean up. Anything else?"

"No," sighed Dwyrin. "Unless you count a fervent argument over which of the local tavern girls is the prettiest."

"Halt!" Nicholas stopped, seeing that a guard had already been posted inside the first row of buildings in the camp. Two of the surveyors stepped out into the sun, their helmets on and spears up. Nicholas nodded to the lead man in greeting. The soldier looked up and down the road and then saluted. "Welcome to the camp, Centurion! Sextus and Frontius are over yonder, near the main building."

Nicholas saluted in return and then walked past, noting

that two more sentries were still in the shade of the nearest barracks, arms in hand. Thankfully the streets of the camp were regular, bisecting the hilltop with a regulation-width road. It seemed that some of the buildings, like the stables, had been converted from some previous edifice, but most of them seemed—in comparison to the rest of the city— to be new. The wagons had stopped, lined up along the main street—the cardo—and the engineers were busily unloading, passing bags and crates from hand to hand. Nicholas came to the lead wagon and stopped, casting a glance down the shorter road, the decumanus, that bisected the camp from east to west.

To the east, there was a slope leading down into some kind of a shallow valley that cut across the city. Beyond the crowded rooftops and towers of the main part of the city, rose the massive bulk of the Temple of Jupiter. From this vantage, raised above the rest of the urb, he could see that the impressive wall was the base of a monumental platform that occupied fully a quarter of the whole city. It rose up, over the nearest houses, like a giant. Atop it was a girdling battlemented wall, and just above the rampart, he could make out the roof line of a classically styled temple.

"That must be the Temple of Jupiter."

"Aye," said Sextus, musing. "A fine piece of work it looks from here. That wall and platform are all artificial, I'd wager. Tens of thousands of tons of dirt and stone to build it up around whatever hill was there originally. Then that facing! They must have dragged those slabs from miles away—there's certainly no good stone around here. Those Greeks . . . they were some builders!"

Nicholas nodded, he had seen the walls of Constantinople, too. This place was on that scale.

With the lead engineer at his side, he stomped into the principa, or headquarters building. Vladimir and Dwyrin had already chosen rooms for themselves, and some of the surveyors were moving his goods and the staff billet into the main room.

"This was the best location?" Nicholas unstrapped the helmet from his head and hung it from the hook on his armor at the right shoulder. The engineer looked around and nodded. His men were using felt-wrapped hammers to tap dowels into the legs of the commander's field table.

"I can't say that I'm happy about the town buildings being so close to the interior wall, but we abut the outer rampart on two sides. There are two main gates, the one at the north you came in through, then one at the south, which goes outside. A steep cliff beneath the walls both to south and west. Not too bad, though we need to dig around in the cisterns to see if there is actually a spring within the precinct." Sextus shrugged. "What can you do?"

Nicholas fingered his chin, looking around at the brisk efficiency that would provide him with a cleaned and garrisoned base within the next three hours. By turns he lamented the veteran infantry that he had been promised and then praised the work of these men. No wonder the Western Empire had ridden out the last three centuries of disaster, plague, invasion, and catastrophe and still stood.

"Good work. Once the camp is secure, call a meeting of the section commanders. Tomorrow we need to start finding the lay of the land hereabouts and making ourselves at home. I want sentries on all four walls right now, and throughout the night. This might be a Roman city, but I fear it is not a friendly one. Dwyrin, here lad, I need you to make a working . . ."

OTTAVIANO

Anatol shuffled his feet on the tile floor. They were bare and covered with a bristly black pelt of fur. Like the other Walach, he had given up wearing a shirt during the day. They spent most of their time sleeping on the patio of the villa or slinking through the flowering bushes along the farm lanes. He didn't need a shirt or tunic for that. Such things just got in the way of the hunt.

"Do you know why I've summoned you here?" Maxian had slept for a long time after the effort of rebuilding the book of Khamûn. Today, after a lengthy spell in the little bathhouse, he felt almost restored. Had the tome been a ruined body, its restoration would have been far easier for the Prince, but he was still exploring the power that let him affect the inanimate world.

"No," Anatol said, staring at the floor. The other Walach stood hunched or squatted behind him. Maxian made a face in disgust. Since Krista had left, the barbarians had become less talkative and more feral. True, he had let them run wild in the woods, but he had no time to watch over them. That had been one of the things that Krista had taken care of, quietly and unobtrusively, while his attention was elsewhere. But she was gone and now they were one of the matters that he had to see to before he returned to the city.

"I am releasing you from the binding," he said and placed a glass vial filled with dark red liquid on the table-top. Maxian had moved his bedding into the library and now used it as office and study and sleeping quarters all in one. He suspected that the Walach slept in the barn in a big pile, all snoring fur, but had never ventured to find out. Gaius and Alexandros had cleared their belongings out of the upstairs rooms and were long gone. Maxian had not even noticed when they slipped away, but he knew that four of the horses and most of the silver was missing. "Do you know what this is?"

Anatol nodded, his eyes now fixed on the vial. A hungry expression slowly filled his face, causing his lips to stretch back from his white canines. The other Walach had become quite still and their eyes were also trained on the glass. "Pain-go-away," hissed the boy.

"It is your freedom," said Maxian, feeling the air tremble with tension. "I am giving you each enough for six months."

Anatol tensed as if to snatch the glass away from the tabletop, but Maxian shook his head minutely. The undercurrent of fear and hunger and hatred and desire in the room was flooding his senses. One eyelid flickered and an invisible ward rose around him, shining blue and pearl in the hidden world. Speech could still flow through it, but the Prince relaxed once the defense was in place. Anatol moved his hand back, obviously struggling with rampant desire.

"Each of you," pronounced Maxian slowly and clearly. Not all the Walach spoke Latin well. "Each of you will have such a vial. Just a drop of the essence on your tongue, once a week, will keep the hunger at bay. Each of you will have an equal amount."

Anatol swayed minutely to the side, his head turning. Maxian watched the Walach measure each other. Fourteen of their number had sworn themselves to his service in Constantinople, brought to him by their pack leader, the Lady Alais. Some had perished in the fighting under Dastagird, while others had been lost in the house in the hills. Now there were seven. *Enough to claw and bite and die, struggling over the serum, until only one lives.* The Prince shook his head at the waste of it all. Still, these not-men were his responsibility. His father had set great store by duty and taking care of those who looked to you as a patron.

"This is the important thing," he continued, taking a wooden case out of his tunic. It was thin and polished to a dark brown sheen. He had found it among the debris in the upper rooms, pushed into a corner. It was plain, without any markings, but it was large enough for a pendant to be enclosed, laid out on a bed of velvet. Now it was large enough to hold four folded sheets of good parchment covered with carefully inked directions and formulae. "This is a message for your mistress, the dark Queen. Take it to her with my apologies for stealing you away."

Maxian paused, thinking of the brilliant eyes and stern countenance of the night visitor. He wondered suddenly if any of these children—for he guessed that among their kind they were children, barely kids, whelped from their mothers—would be allowed to live in the face of her anger. Still, they had served him well and now his use for them was at an end. He would do the best he could for them, though he could not protect them from themselves.

"Take this, too." He removed a chain of copper from his neck. On it hung a silver coin, pierced with a hole for the chain to run through. "It passed between us once as a token. It may do such service again."

He stood and handed the wooden box and the coin to Anatol. The boy clutched them to his thin wiry chest, close to the nap of the fur.

"This is my gift to her, freely given, in hope of peace between our peoples."

Maxian pressed the glass vial into Anatol's hand and curled the long fingers around it.

"Remember," he said, looking down at the boy. "One drop each week, upon the tongue. No more and no less. Now go, lad, and carry my message homeward."

Anatol slid away, his back to the wall, and crept out of the room. Some of the others considered loping off after him, but Maxian made a rattling sound with the remaining vials and they slunk forward to the edge of the table.

"There is enough for all of you . . ." The Prince's voice fell to a whisper. The first Walach stared up at him with shining eyes. Maxian smiled back, closing the furry hand around the vial.

Gaius Julius tipped back the brim of his sun hat, squinting in the hazy air off to the right of the road. He was riding a roan mare he had purchased in the Forum Boarium when they had returned to Italia. She was a pleasant horse with an even gait and she did not shy away from him or Alexandros. Gaius figured that she had no sense of smell or she would have bolted long ago. Mid-day was fast ap-

proaching and the fields of Latium stretched in all directions around him, rich with grain and fruit trees and small
farm buildings of white stone and red terra-cotta roofs. A
packhorse trailed behind the roan, laden with bags of
books and trinkets and amphorae of wine. That one didn't
like Gaius, so he got the heavy lifting.

Alexandros was staring off toward the northeast as well,
his head bare and golden curls spilling down his back like
a wave. Gaius had tried to get him to wear a shirt the first
day they had taken to the road, but the youth refused. In
truth, Gaius could not fault him. The last three days had
been almost perfect—warm and breezy during the day,
cool but not cold at night. The grapes were preparing to
ripen on the vine and all the land was moseying into summer with aplomb. Today the skies were clear, too, and the
sun shone down on a drowsy land.

"What lies yonder?" Alexandros was trying to keep a
tinge of awe from his voice.

Beyond his pointing finger, marching north across the
Latin plain, was a massive stonework of three arched
courses. It loomed a hundred feet high over farmhouses
and woodlots alike, coming out of the east from hazy indistinct hills and curving toward the bluish smoke that rose
above the city of Rome. From the vantage of the road,
which was raised above the surrounding land on an embankment, the miles of arches and pillars were even more
impressive. To Gaius' eye, it was a sight most pleasant to
look upon.

"That is the Aqua Anio Novus," he said with pride.
"One of the arteries of Rome. It is an aqueduct, my friend,
carrying the fresh sweet water of the Tiber down to the
baths and cisterns and stew pots of the city. A stupendous
undertaking worthy of my people."

Alexandros turned and grinned, his blue eyes glinting.
"It must have taken a mighty effort to build that—how
many tens of thousands of slaves perished·in the undertaking? The Egyptians would be proud of you, seeing that
you followed their example."

Gaius Julius sniffed and turned his nose up in the air. "Romans built the Aquae, not Egyptians, and by our own wit and strength, too. I was once custodian of the public waters, my fine Macedonian lad, and it is not a business to be trifled with."

"Indeed," said Alexandros, nodding sagely. "They're almost as big as a pyramid."

"Bigger," snapped Gaius, leaning forward on his saddle horn. "There are more stones in a single one of the eight waterways that feed Rome than in one of those moldering Egyptian monuments. We built them faster, too, the greatest only taking twelve years—far better than a generation for a useless pile of blocks."

Alexandros looked back at the aqueduct and Gaius could see the younger man's thought calculating and considering: *What if I were to attempt such a thing?* Gaius smiled, knowing that the seeming lad at his side had dreamed bigger dreams, done greater things in his time. "Rome builds well," said the Macedonian at last, in a grudging voice.

"It does," said Gaius sympathetically. "As did you."

"No," snarled Alexandros, his face gloomy. "All my dreams were ruins in a generation. Yours—they still stand, seven centuries after you went under the earth. Men I thought my brothers slaughtered my child, murdered my wife, hanged my mother from a limb. All that I hoped to build turned to destruction. Even the memory of me is strange, my tomb looted, my line lost."

"Not lost," said Gaius sharply. "You still live in men's dreams and in the histories. A man may travel from Britannia to Sercia and speak your name—be it Alexander, Alexandros, or Iskander—and all, *all*, will know of it. You are forever young and strong, the brilliant general and able statesman. Your mother tongue, this damnable Greek, is spoken across the world. The works of your poets, artists, sculptors, playwrights are acclaimed everywhere. You traded better than Achilles, my friend, for you gained your fame and now—after a little sleep—you live again."

Alexandros shook himself like a dog wet from the river. Then he smiled and the dark mood passed.

"I do live, do I not? And you as well . . . we are an odd pair. But what will we do when we come again to the city?"

The Macedonian pointed forward to where, now that they had ridden up onto a bit of a hill, he could spy the white walls of Rome rising up from the plain.

"Well, my lad, I have given it some thought. This is no Pella, or Persepolis, where we may strike down the King and take his place by strength of arms. The Empire is too vast and too well-regulated by the rule of law to allow such a thing. Then, too, we are sorely lacking in the funds to buy allies and patrons. We need money and followers and friends. Oh, and we need to establish ourselves in the public eye, but not—of course—as ourselves!"

Alexandros nodded his head sagely. "I see you've been thinking this over."

"I have," gloated Gaius Julius, rubbing a hand over his bald pate. "This will be such a joy! First, we must find a patron—someone we may ably serve while we go about finding the friends that we need, the gold that we require, and the men that will do our bidding. I think I know of such a man—I heard the Prince mention him to Abdmachus as a *friend of convenience*. That is an appealing term."

"And then? What then, O noblest of the Romans? Do you think that this power that creeps among the stones and pervades the water we drink, the air we breathe, will let you topple the state and set yourself up in its place?" Alexandros' tone was light, but Gaius Julius knew that the young man was serious. He understood perfectly—he had no desire to abandon this existence either.

"Remember the words of our dear Prince . . . the Oath is without forethought." Gaius wagged an admonishing finger at the younger man. "It only cares that the Empire should sustain itself—it does not care who the Emperor is. Men live and die. Emperors may perish from disease or accident or old age. The State endures, and with it, the Oath. Any man may make himself Emperor, as long as in doing so he furthers the survival of the Empire."

Alexandros whistled in delight and bowed in the saddle to the old Roman.

"Your training in the forum serves us well, old man."

Gaius Julius accepted the compliment. He had been considering his freedom for some time.

Come, steed of fire. Leap leagues for me, pinions of iron beat the wind, bringing you hither!

Maxian stood in darkness, his booted feet on the highest pinnacle of the mountain. His right hand was raised and blue-green fire shuddered within his fingertips. Wind eddied around his feet, blowing his long cloak to and fro. The night sky was clear and cold, filled with an abyss of stars. Far below his feet, the plain of Campania spread away, the curve of the bay outlined by thin traces of sparkling lights. The moon had not risen, leaving the land in shadow.

Come, cold Pegasus, seek me out, find me in a faraway place, race zephyrs and comets with iron hooves, come!

Among the stars, a red spark moved, rushing through the cold upper air. Maxian saw it and spread his hands, the blue radiance stabbing out in the night sky.

Come, foal of the crucible, speed to me on wings of steel! I summon you, come!

The wind flared up, shaking the trees and then died out. Maxian stood on the crest of the mountain, looking up into the sky. He lowered his hands and let the chant die away. The red spark rushed ever closer, growing into a trail of flame and then, as it swooped down, into the huge bat-winged shape of the Engine. It blotted the stars and smoke and steam boiled off of it, making a trailing cloud. Stooping low, it crunched to earth, iron forelimbs digging deep into the loamy black soil. Once it had alighted, the iron pinions folded in upon themselves with a squealing sound and the great wings ratcheted shut. The ground shook for a moment as the weight settled. A wash of red light illuminated the boulders and trees. Maxian squinted until the glare of the Engine's eyes died down. There was the sharp crack of a tree splitting, brushed by the long tail as it flexed and curled before settling at the rear of the thing.

Maxian stepped close, looking up into the dimming eyes of the Engine with fondness. This was the first thing that he had conceived and built with the labor of his own hands. It had begun in the pages of an old, nearly ruined book—just fragments of drawings by one of the ancients, describing a thing that might possibly exist in dreams. The prince had need of a conveyance and the skills and knowledge of his friend had allowed him to bend his power to its construction.

Maxian leaned against the warm iron scales of the Engine and shuddered, feeling the pain and loss of Abdmachus' death gnaw at him. *I did not mean it to end that way between us!* Tears, despite his fierce attempt to screw his eyes shut and hold them in, leaked down his face. He knew that he had killed a man who had only treated him with kindness. The guilt of using Abdmachus and then discarding him as an empty shell ate at the Prince.

He pushed away from the Engine and walked to the hatchway. It was closed and impossible to see among the interlocking and overlapping scales, but Maxian raised his hand and spoke a word of opening. Then it folded down on sliding metal rods and ruddy red light spilled out onto the ground. The Prince ducked inside and his boots rang hollowly on the honeycombed metal decking.

Behind him, still shrouded in night, a wagon waited on the mountainside and beside it, waiting patiently, stood the homunculus, Khiron.

"Come, Khiron. Unload the wagon and place the books in the hold." The Prince's voice echoed in the belly of the Engine. More words were swallowed by the confines of the machine as the Prince moved away.

Khiron bestirred himself, moving from utter stillness to motion within the space of a heartbeat. He lifted a crate made of pine boards out of the wagon. It was filled with a portion of the books and scrolls and tomes that had been gathered for the library. The wagon was filled with more like it. Khiron's bare feet padded on the decking, his long curved nails making a *tik-tik* sound as he walked.

<hr />

THE BUCOLEON PALACE, CONSTANTINOPLE

Heraclius was biting his palm, feeling springy scar tissue under his teeth, and trying to keep from crying out. He was sitting on a privy with a board on his lap. It was cold in the urinal. Small round windows were set high in the wall above his head and they let a cold draft seep into the small room. Even the simplest business of his life was painful and degrading. He leaned on the board, feeling his arms tremble with the effort of keeping his corrupted body upright. There was restless movement outside in the dark little hallway where his guards and keepers were waiting. He needed help to get anywhere.

"Rufio?" The querulous sound of his voice echoed from the bare walls. "Attend me."

The guard captain entered the room; his face an impassive mask as he slid his arm under Heraclius. Another man of the Faithful Guard entered as well. Heraclius looked away from the Northerner; he could not stand to see the pity in the Scandian's eyes. Rufio grunted a little, but the Emperor rose with some assistance and smoothed his robe down with a trembling hand.

"Take me to the balcony. There is work to be done today."

The dark-haired guard captain nodded and motioned to the other guardsmen to precede them down the hallway.

With the help of one of the Scandians—the blond one with long braids—Rufio helped the Emperor into his chair. It was more a sling that supported Heraclius under his arms and midsection, and left his bloated legs to rest on a fabric of silk straps. Four of the guardsmen lifted it with oaken handles. When the Emperor moved in his palace now, all other men and women were sent away. Only stoic Rufio, the Faithful Guard, and the Emperor's brother were allowed to look upon him. Rooms and chambers would be cleared as he moved. The vast warren of the Bucoleon now seemed a dead and empty place to Heraclius and he often gazed about in confusion as he was carried from room to room. *Where has everyone gone?*

He saw that it was a cloudy day as the guardsmen carried him out onto the balcony. This was the one place that he could look at the sky; a third-floor terrace that looked north upon the towering dome of the Temple of Zeus Pankrator. Small trees rooted in wooden boxes surrounded the terrace and it could not be seen from the ground or the windows of the palace. Most importantly, it did not look upon the sea.

Since the swelling in his legs had begun, the sight of water filled Heraclius with unreasoning fear. He knew it was madness, but could not bring himself to look upon the dark blue waters of the Propontis or even the marble-lined tub of a bath. When he looked upon water, he thought of the clear fluid that bulged under the distended skin of his legs and he shuddered. He thirsted constantly, but could barely bring himself to drink. Only resinated wine, or perhaps the juice of some sweet berries, could pass his lips.

A host of fluffy white clouds thronged the sky, passing in front of the sun in endless procession. When they parted, the sun shone down bright and clear. Heraclius sighed, feeling the warmth on his face. Here in the protected little garden, surrounded only by trusted friends, he felt almost well. The guardsmen put his chair down carefully at an ornamented wooden table set underneath a pair of flowering lemon trees. A number of papers were laid out on the table, along with quills and ink and a sand block.

"What," gasped Heraclius, feeling a twinge in his legs as he settled, "is the business of the day?"

Rufio nodded to the guardsmen, who withdrew to the edges of the terrace, becoming invisible among the planters and trees and ornamental bushes. The scarred guard captain stood at ease beside the table, his hands clasped behind his back.

"Avtokrator, the first item is the setting of the Imperial rate. Each province within your realm has reported that it has completed the initial census. Each governor and legate now awaits your decision about the rate of taxation that they will apply."

Heraclius smiled wanly, feeling pain trickling through his legs. Despite it, he picked up the first of the papers and read the summaries compiled by his clerks.

"Good. We shall surprise them then, good Rufio. I am reducing the rate."

He picked up a quill, wetted it in the inkpot, and then wrote as strongly as he could the edict that would go out to tax the world. He ignored the surprised look that flickered across the guard captain's face. *Let them be astonished at my generosity! We shall make the shortfall back, and more, from the new lands under my demesne.* When he was done, Heraclius looked up and handed the paper to the man.

"Sand this," he said, his voice quavering. Heraclius leaned back in the chair, breathing heavily. "See that copies are made for each governor by the end of the day and check them to see that they are copied dutifully. Then . . ." He paused, catching his breath. Even this little effort was exhausting. "Then, send copies forth by Imperial courier to each town and city. This edict is to be posted in every forum and agora, in a plain and public place. Each and every citizen within my realm is to know, before the month is out, what is expected of him."

Rufio bowed and walked to one of the terrace doors. In the room beyond, Heraclius knew, there were a clutch of sallow-faced clerks, scribes, ministers, and copyists waiting about for him to deal with the matters of state. He had always disliked them—conniving men with small minds and a greedy penchant for bribes. Now, he had every excuse to ban them from his presence. It was a carefully hoarded spot of joy.

When the guard captain returned, the Emperor motioned to him weakly.

"What is the second item?"

Rufio's face became even more impassive and still. Even his dark eyes seemed to shrink into immobility. The guard captain removed two parchment sheets, folded letters, with purple edging on one side. Heraclius stiffened and his mouth twisted into a grimace. Such papers were reserved for petitions from the Imperial family. He tried to raise a hand and wave them away, but Rufio spoke regardless.

"Avtokrator . . . your wife requests an audience with you. She wishes to show you your son."

Heraclius flinched as if struck by a mailed glove. Before this torment he had not thought that Rufio possessed even the faintest hint of a conscience or sympathy or love, but even with his voice as cold and even as a gravestone, the Emperor could hear the entreaty in the man's words. Heraclius thought of his wife, his niece—young and beautiful, filled with a lively wit and an unquenchable desire for knowledge—and the pain was worse than that from his tortured legs and lower body. *If she saw me, she would flinch away and those gorgeous brown eyes would fill with the most dreadful fear . . .*

"Is . . . is my son healthy? Is he strong?"

Rufio remained immobile, staring into the space above the Emperor's head. He said nothing.

"Answer me!" Heraclius hissed in rage, his hand scrabbling on the tabletop, seeking a weapon.

"He lives," said Rufio at last, after a long silence. "There is every hope that he will grow strong and hale and straight."

"Enough . . ." Heraclius looked away. *Even my blood is corrupt. I am cursed by the gods.*

"I will see the Empress on another day," said the Emperor, and put the letter aside, unread. "What is this other?"

Rufio unfolded the letter and placed it before the Emperor. Heraclius frowned, seeing the stiffness in the man's fingers. Where the first petition had inspired love, this one roused disgust or hate in his guard captain. Heraclius caught Rufio's eye and cocked his head in question.

"What is this?"

"The Lord Theodore," said Rufio, his jaw clenched. "requests your permission to send another physician to attend you. This one is a master of the Order of Asklepios."

"How has this transpired?" Heraclius was outraged. "What is he still doing within the city? He should be on his way to take up residence in Ctesiphon by now." The Emperor's hand was shaking and he pressed it firmly on the tabletop, trying to make it stop.

Rufio nodded stiffly, then said, "So you directed him, my lord, but he has refused to go. He claims that he loves you too much to abandon you here, while you are still sick." The guard captain seemed about to say more, but did not.

"Foolishness! If he waits here, the Persian *dihquans* will gather themselves together and reestablish order and control over the land between the two rivers. Bring him to me immediately."

Rufio nodded, then turned and strode to the nearest guardsmen. Heraclius gnawed on his knuckle, his thoughts occupied with incipient fury. Sometimes his reckless brother taxed him too much. Something was going on behind his back, too. He was not so far gone to miss the unspoken meaning in Rufio's words. If the Prince were loitering about the capital while his brother lay sick, Theodore would be prey to all kinds of conniving sycophants and intriguers. It had been far too long since the Emperor had appeared in public. Rumors would be rife in the markets and among the padded seats in the Hippodrome that he was dead, or mad, or worse. An ambitious and healthy brother could easily see an opportunity in such a time.

And, growled Heraclius to himself, *he cannot stand Martina . . . I must do something.*

"You will take yourself immediately to Tyre on the coast of Phoenicia with the greater part of the fleet and four Legions. There is already a Legion at Damascus that can join you."

Heraclius bit out the words, glowering at his brother, who stood before him on the terrace, a little stunned. The Emperor did not fail to note that Theodore was looking very smart today in a crisp red robe with purple edging, golden boots, and a polished breastplate worked with eagles and a laurel crown. He had trimmed his beard close to his jaw and his hair was carefully arranged. A striking image of a modern officer fresh from victory. Very Western, too. *And so strong looking on those fit tan legs . . .*

"With these men at your command, plus those local auxiliaries that prove trustworthy, you will establish direct Imperial control over those lands that had previously been the domain of the rulers of Palmyra and Nabatea. You will place garrisons in each city and provide administrators, governors, and judges in replacement of those that are already there."

Theodore blanched at the cold tone in the Emperor's voice.

"But . . ." He stammered, then paused and gained control of his voice. "I was to go to Persia? What about all our plans to rebuild Ctesiphon as the capital of a Roman Asia?"

Heraclius looked over at Rufio, though it cost him blinding pain to do so.

"Who . . ." He gasped. "Who now stands in command of the army at Antioch?"

"Vahan, my lord. The Armenian."

"I remember him." Heraclius thought for a moment. "Send new orders to him. He is to take the five Legions under his command east to ensure that we retain control of the roads to Ctesiphon and the lands thereabout. My brother, after securing the cities of the Arabian frontier, may join him. Vahan will be proclaimed governor of Persia for the nonce."

Theodore made an abortive half-bleat of outrage. He had just been demoted from the prize he had so greedily accepted, replaced by a mercenary from a barbarian nation. The Prince made to speak again. The Emperor turned, his face bilious with fatigue. He jabbed a gray finger at his brother.

"You. You will see that the Empire directly taxes the cities of the Decapolis. Their armies were shattered at Emesa or ground to meal-paste at Palmyra, so most of your work is already done. Be quick about it, too. You will leave the capital within the week."

"But . . ." Theodore spread his hands in an entreaty. "I've brought another physician . . ."

"Out," snarled Heraclius and he turned away, breathing heavily, and refused to look at his brother. "I've enough of your charlatans." Seven times the mummers had leaned over him, their fat faces sweating, using their *powers* to heal him. Seven times they had failed. Who could stand against the displeasure of the gods?

Rufio took the Prince by the arm, gently, and escorted him to the arched doorway that led into the palace. After a moment, Theodore shook his arm free and glared at the scarred guard captain. Rufio met his gaze with equanimity and after a moment the Prince stormed off, his cloak snapping in the air behind him. When he was gone, Rufio pursed his lips in thought. The Emperor was very tired and would need to be taken to bed soon. It was hurting the State for him to be so weak.

"Sviod, come here."

The strapping young Scandian with long blond braids who had helped carry the Emperor was standing in the hallway, talking in low tones with a middle-aged man with a thick gray beard and the robes of one of the Achaean priesthoods. Sviod bowed to the priest and then stepped to Rufio's side. Unlike many of his fellows, Sviod spoke good Greek. Rufio leaned close, one eye on the Emperor, who was staring at the sky.

"Find the Empress and see if she will grant an audience today. Then find me. Most likely I will be with the Emperor in his quarters."

THE QUIRINAL HILL, ROMA MATER

T hyatis puffed air from her cheeks, watching the frosty cloud dissipate in the air in front of her. The weather had turned cold, startling the citizens who had decided that summer had come for good, and putting a chill on the flowers in the Duchess's garden. Petro the gardener had been beside himself, cursing the fickle gods, and driving his assistants to cover everything with burlap and cheesecloth. In the hour before dawn, as Thyatis stood in the stable yard of the house on the Quirinal, it seemed even colder.

"Why does it always seem colder now, when day approaches?" Despite a thick German-style cloak with a fur lining, Thyatis had her hands in her armpits, hoping that they would warm up. She always had cold hands and this was worse, since she had gotten very little sleep. She felt grainy and irritable. The yard was filled with muffled sounds of men moving about, checking their weapons and preparing to leave. "Night is almost done, it should be warmer."

"It's not that cold," said Nikos as he walked past with a bundle of long boar-spears on his shoulder. He was only

wearing a light shirt and woolen breeches. Thyatis threw
a glare in his direction, but the Illyrian ignored her. She
entertained dark thoughts, watching him swing the heavy
load into the back of their wagon. Centuries of forebears
who had culled their living from the cold Adriaticum in
open skiffs had thickened his blood. *And his skull*, she
thought in disgust. Nikos loved the cold. But then, he liked
it when it was hot, too. Thyatis found this very disturbing.
The world, she thought, should be an even temperature all
year round.

"My lady." Thyatis turned and saw that Jusuf had come
down the steps from the house. Lanterns faced with panes
of cut crystal had been put out to shed some light on the
preparations. The Khazar's long face was half cast in
shadow. Thyatis smiled in greeting; she had not had much
chance to catch up with the Prince since her return.

"You will be leaving today?"

Jusuf nodded. He fingered his tunic. It was a dark indigo
with subtle red edging in stitched silk and a faintly military
cut. A cape of heavy green wool like the shade under forest
trees hung from his shoulders. Thin bracelets of gold were
clasped around his wrists. The Khazar seemed astonished
at the soft nap of the fabric. He kept rubbing it between
his broad fingertips.

"I will, but first I am to speak with this Emperor of
yours. Anas' tells me that he was one of the last men to
speak with Sahul, before he was killed. We will discuss
'friendship' between our peoples and give the embassy of
the Eastern Court apoplexy."

Thyatis felt a strange sense of disassociation at the
Prince's words. Everything seemed turned about and a
giddy sensation of being outside of herself, looking down
and seeing her body from above, overcame her. Thoughts
tumbled like stones in a millrace; the Duchess referred to
as an intimate, the lanky barbarian in exquisite clothes, the
reminder of her old friend's death. She blinked, feeling
choked up, and coughed, covering her mouth. .

"You've come a little way since I met you crawling about in that thicket." Thyatis smiled sadly.

"Yes," he said, allowing his own grief to show in the shadow behind his eyes. "You have led me astray."

"Not as far as some, I see." Thyatis blushed at the tart sound of her words. "I'm sorry!"

"No need," said Jusuf quietly, looking down. Thyatis craned her neck and saw that he was blushing. "I will have a daredevil tale to tell when I return. I feel foolish . . . I was difficult and pig-headed for months while you drove us into the heart of Persia and then brought us out again."

Thyatis laughed softly, frost puffing from her mouth, and laid a gloved hand on his arm. He covered it with his own. "I could not have succeeded without you. I would never have met Shirin. Her children would have been quietly strangled by now and she a jeweled captive in the Eastern Court."

"So true. You've given my family and me a great deal, Thyatis. Even when I have returned to the open grasslands of Scythia and sit once more among the councils of our people, I will not forget you."

"You should not," said Thyatis, raising a haughty eyebrow. "We will be coming to visit you as soon as we can—Shirin and I and the children. When it is safer, we will sail to Tanaïs and come overland. If you have forgotten me when I arrive, I will be forced to thrash you soundly . . ."

Jusuf blushed again, and stood back, making the Roman salute. "Until we meet again, my friend."

"Yes," said Thyatis and she turned away, her thoughts already intent upon the business at hand.

The Duchess had culled her secret enterprises for men who could answer the unexpected with violence. There had been a short and bitter discussion between Thyatis and her patron about the composition of the team that would go to the south. Thyatis had balked at the addition of more fighting men—ones that she did not know and had not worked with before—but Anastasia had been insistent. The stakes were too high in this endeavor to arrive with too few men. There had been discussion of Krista and her place in the enterprise. Again, Thyatis had refused to take the girl. This time, with a wan face, Anastasia had relented and agreed. The dark-haired servant had not been seen since, though Thyatis knew that she was still in the house somewhere.

Seven more men had been added to the core group composed of Thyatis, Nikos, Efraim, Kahrmi, and Anagathios. They were Legion twenty-year men, scarred by fierce service, and patient as hunters. Thyatis had worked long hours to spar with each man in the gymnasium. As she expected, they were superbly skilled with their chosen weapons and quick as vipers. In particular, four of them were experts with the long hunting spear. The other three were archers of repute. There were still rough edges on the team, but she thought that she could make it work. As ever, she relied most on Nikos and the Khazars. The loss of her original team in the ambush at Van still rankled— it would take years to rebuild a maniple like that.

There was a sharp whistle in the courtyard and the mercenaries drew back from the wagon. They had piled the last of the arcuballista and bundles of arrows into the *reda* and laid a thick covering of thatch over the gear. Over that they had put two layers of blankets to make a soft cushion. Nikos and Anagathios came out of one of the half-buried storerooms that lined the courtyard. With the Duchess's villa sitting on the crest of the Quirinal, some of its rooms were cut into the slope of the hill. Each man carried a small oaken barrel, bound with straps of iron. They walked carefully, watching for loose paving stones or slippery places. It would not do for either of these items to be jarred sharply or fall.

Thyatis smiled, showing her teeth in the darkness. If this *homunculus* could not bleed and die like a man, then it would be rendered down into its very constituent atoms. The young Roman woman rocked back and forth on her heels, feeling immense satisfaction. It was good that the Duchess maintained an Empire-wide network of informers, spies, watchers, and messengers. Acquiring these barrels had stretched her power—it was absolutely forbidden by Imperial edict for a private citizen to possess the substance within those close-fitted oaken staves—but what use was power and influence without its exercise?

The Illyrian laid his barrel down carefully in the nest of blankets and wrapped another tightly woven wool quilt around it. Anagathios did likewise and then they piled more blankets on top of that. The jostling of the wagon would barely touch the nervous substance within. Two of the legionnaires climbed up onto the driver's seat. A team of four mules drew the wagon and they were impatient to go.

Thyatis looked around, seeing the rest of her men mounting up. It was time. The nervous tickling in her stomach faded, replaced by the cold certainty that infused her once action was imminent. Half a glass from now, the Via Appia gate would open and they would be on the road south. She counted heads. Everyone was present. A stable boy led her horse up and she took the reins. In defiance of city fashion, she was wearing long warm woolen trousers. She looked up, her eyes scanning the upper floors of the villa.

At one, silhouetted by the warm gold of dozens of candles, the Duchess looked down from a half-open window. The older woman was cowled in a white cape and hood. Thyatis raised a hand in salute and Anastasia answered it.

"Hey-yup! Open the gate." In the still, cold air her voice seemed loud, but the rattle of the gate chains and the rumble of wooden doors quickly drowned the sound as they swung open. Servants darted aside as the wagon rolled out into the black space of the alley. Two lanterns hung on metal posts at the front of the wagon bobbed and flickered, casting a fitful illumination on the road. Thyatis followed, her breath still frosting in the air. Nikos, Anagathios, and the others were close behind, their horses blowing and whickering in complaint. *Sensible creatures*, thought

Thyatis moodily, *they want to be in their nice warm stable, asleep, at such an hour.*

"In a glass or so," Anastasia said, "they will be at the Appia gate and on the road south."

The Duchess turned, her violet eyes gleaming in the candlelight. She had kept Betia very busy at this atrocious hour, carefully anointing her long eyelashes with flecks of gold, accenting her cheekbones, and smoothing her skin with a fine dust of pearl and arsenic. The wearing demands of the Emperor had kept her on edge for months and blemishes had been her reward. Under the supple cloak—a pristine Sabine white—she wore a demure gown of layered charcoal-gray wool edged with silver. Galen's latest innovation of government was a sunrise meeting, accompanied by hot mulled wine and freshly baked bread and butter. The Duchess was all for catching the consuls, tribunes, and ministers at a disadvantage from a night of debauchery, but she preferred to do so while well-rested herself.

"And I?" Krista stood by the door of the little reading room, well away from the window. The young woman had bound her hair back in a tight braid, then wrapped it with a leather thong. Her tunic and cloak and kilt were a deep forest green that verged to black. The weathered brown leather of her girdle was almost invisible against the material. Like the Duchess, her cloak was hooded, though when pulled up, Krista's left her entire face in shadow. Long sleeves covered her arms and two long knives and a short sword were slung at her side from a Legion-style baldric. "Where will I be?"

The Duchess sighed, holding out her hand. Chains of pearls accented her arm, gleaming in the lamplight. Krista stepped up and took her hand. "You will be upon your way to the port at Ostia by a fast horse, my dear. A galley, the *Paris,* is waiting for you there. The captain is one of my couriers. He will take you to Cumae, within hours of the mountain and the villa. You will be ahead of Thyatis and her men by at least two days."

Anastasia pressed a wallet of tooled leather into Krista's hand. It was heavy and clinked as the younger woman hefted it.

"Coin enough," smiled the Duchess. "You can get whatever you need: horses, gladiators, slaves, weapons. Cumae caters to the estates of the rich. It has a sophisticated market." Anastasia paused, her lips pursed. "Are you sure of this?" The Duchess leaned forward a little, closing the space between her and the girl. "You need not put yourself at risk."

Krista laughed, a sharp bitter sound. "While the handsome Prince lives, neither you nor I are safe. If we can kill him, then we can rest easy. My lady, please listen and understand me . . . I *must* kill him." The dark-haired girl clenched her fist hard, turning her knuckles white. "I must."

Anastasia opened her mouth, ready to press her servant for why and how but then relented. Something had transpired between the two, something more than the business of men and women. She could see the closely held determination that sustained Krista. Things were fragile enough already without provoking more trouble. She let it go. It did not matter how the beautiful Prince died.

"Very well," said the Duchess. "Do you need anything else?"

Krista's mouth thinned into a sharp line. She shook her head.

"I have what I need already," Krista said, tucking the wallet away. "Goodbye."

Anastasia inclined her head and let her fingers slip out of Krista's hand. "Good luck."

Without another word, the young woman slipped out the door and took the stairs to the lower floor two and three at a time. When she was gone, the Duchess sat at her desk, her heart heavy, and sighed. The day was only beginning. She flipped open the first briefing booklet and blinked, trying to clear her eyes.

THE RED PALACE, PETRA, NABATEA

Sunlight slanted across a tabletop of mottled travertine. The light brought out the whorls of cream and rust that penetrated the rock, mixing with a flux of darker red material. Mohammed's hands were pressed on the table, flat on the smooth cold surface. A pale green porcelain jug of water stood nearby and an arrangement of fresh-cut flowers held in a copper vase cast a shadow over his fingers. The gardens of the palace, watered by their own spring and culvert, were a wonder to behold. On this day, in the late morning, the scent of thousands of blossoms flooded the air, drifting through the high, arched windows on a light breeze.

Mohammed stood at the side of the table, his eyes staring blankly out the window over the rooftops of the city. His whole body, save for his hands, was trembling. The distant sounds of mules clattering through the streets of the city or the cries of hawkers in the market of Trajan went unheard. Sweat beaded his brow and ran in thin rivulets down the side of his neck. The thin cream-colored cotton shirt that he wore was damp with moisture and clung to the hard muscles of his shoulder and back. Tendrils of pure white striped his thick black beard. An almost inaudible hum trembled in the air.

The power released him and the Quryash gasped softly, suddenly breathing again, seeing again. He staggered a little and groped for a chair.

"Lord Mohammed, I would speak with you." The voice was harsh and brittle, sounding very old for the youthful woman who strode into the room. She stopped, her eyes narrowing at the sight of the Arab chieftain slumping wearily in the wicker chair. "Are you ill?"

Mohammed looked up, his eyebrows bristling. The Palmyrene woman stood, arms akimbo, her legs firmly planted, staring down at him with piercing dark eyes. She was dressed in severe dark colors, a tunic of black cotton over the rippling metal of a scaled iron corselet. Desert robes draped her shoulders, though they bunched at her left shoulder where the hilt of a saber jutted up. She wore Roman-style riding boots and still maintained the thick leather belt of a legionnaire.

"Lady Zoë," Mohammed acknowledged. "Are you ready?"

Zoë's face remained impassive, though one eyebrow hinted at a quirk. "My men and I have been ready for weeks. Yours also—we have sufficient camels and horses for the cavalry. Every wagon within leagues has been confiscated. The water barrels are full, the quartermaster satisfied by the count of wheaten cakes and rashers of bacon. We waste our time in these endless drills and maneuvers so dear to your puppy of a general. Even the weather has refrained from becoming too hot. Yet we wait for your command."

"We have waited," Mohammed said in a soft voice. "We have waited for word to come to me."

"Has it come?" Zoë stepped to the edge of the table, her back stiff with anger. Her impatience was legendary among the Sahaba. Jalal was fond of saying that she would flay the *khamshin* for its sloth in crossing the land.

"Are you ready?" countered Mohammed, rising himself. The strain and weariness of the listening did not take long to pass. He felt certainty and surety of purpose flood his limbs with strength. "I do not speak of your men, or your cousin, I speak of you."

Zoë sneered, her expression filled with bile. Her hair had become lank and spilled from the crown of her head in a tangled mess. Mohammed knew from his spies that she spent long hours closeted in the tomb she shared with the withered corpse of her aunt. The dead Queen had been placed in a catafalque of marble, dredged out of one of the old tombs. When she was not there, she prowled the canyons and ravines that riddled the hills around the city, poking into tombs and crevices. Odd smells and sounds often emanated from the grave-houses of the Petrans. Some of Mohammed's men had reported seeing shapes in the twilight, things like men, but smaller, creeping among the crumbling statues and tombs. Much evil had been done here. Mohammed could feel it like heat radiating off the lava fields of the An'Nafud.

"I am ready," she snapped, her mouth turned down in a grimace. "Are you?"

"Word has come," said Mohammed, bowing his head. "The power that moves the tide and lets sunlight fall has spoken from the clear air. We will leave as soon as the heat of the day begins to fade."

Zoë grinned, showing yellowed teeth. Her eyes lit up. "Praise the gods! I will inform Khalid and Odenathus immediately!" She turned to stride from the room, but Mohammed halted her with a touch on her arm. Under his fingertip, her skin was like ice.

"No," he said. "You and I will go, alone. Camels will be waiting for us under the eaves of the Jebel al'Harun."

Zoë turned, her brow furrowed with confusion. Mohammed almost laughed aloud to see her so vexed. The young woman was filled with enormous impatience. Every sinew of her lithe young body strained to release rage and hate and pain in a frenzy of violence. In the palace, she was the bane of the servants. When she was in a black mood, vases and pots would crack and shatter as she passed. Marble floor tiles had been known to warp and splinter where she walked. Those men and women in the royal enclosure who were sensitive to such things had long ago been sent away. The fury that boiled and curdled in the Palmyrene Queen was dangerous when coupled with the power within her.

"Go where? Alone? Why?"

Mohammed picked up his saber and belt and strapped them around his waist. He took his time, waiting for the young woman to breathe out. At last, with a hiss, she relented and subsided a little.

"There is a city—though it is little more than a town— some days' ride from here. The voice from the clear air bids me take you there and stand upon the summit of a hill. We will ride through the night to reach it. It will not take long."

The Quryash tugged his hood up, letting it cover his head and face. The sun did not spare anyone.

"What town?" Zoë sounded petulant and angry that he did not budge when she tried to bend him to her will. Her forehead creased, and the effort she put forth made a faint haze in the air between them. Mohammed could feel something press against his mind, but it was distant and indistinct like wind on the desert.

"Of old," he said, "men called it Hierosolyma. I name it al'Quds."

Zoë frowned, an expression that only sat well on her face with great practice. "The 'holy'?"

"Yes," said Mohammed as he strode through the door. "It is such a place."

The moon was in the heavens, vast and full, turning a white visage to the earth. Zoë felt it shining on her face, almost like the pressure of the sun, though the light was cold. They had been riding since the day-star had dipped below the rugged tan mountains beyond the Red City. As soon as the last glowing pink light of the sun had faded from the monuments and temples of Petra, Mohammed had set out. They rode two rangy black camels with tasseled tack and bit. The creatures made good speed across the desert, ambling along in their disjointed gait. Swaying atop her mount, Zoë watched the desert go past, sleeping under a wash of silver light. The moon was so bright all but the most brilliant stars were hidden.

Time passed slowly, though the camels did not falter or

complain. The moon had risen first behind them, a huge bloated yellow sphere that seemed to fill half the sky. By the time that it had climbed high, they were trotting along a sandy shore. A long narrow lake of silver water lay on their right and its surface blazed with moonlight like mercury. To their left, a line of jagged cliffs and mountains blocked the horizon. Zoë had seen no lights or dwellings or sign of man for hours. Beyond the end of the lake, they climbed up into hills on an ancient road. At intervals, milestones rose up beside the path—carven oblong monoliths—and then fell away again behind.

In all this time, as they passed under the night sky, Mohammed did not speak.

Even Zoë felt no reason to break the silence. The snuffling of the camels, the rattle of stones under their three-toed paws, the creak and rattle of the saddles—those sounds were enough to fill the night. The thought of human words filled her with weariness. She dozed in the saddle, letting the camel carry her onwards. After a time, a light breeze sprang up, ruffling her robes and stirring her air. Its touch was pleasant on her face and she raised her head.

The road wound up through hills with barren crowns. Bare stones jagged up out of fields bordered by low fences of piled rock. Below the hills, sandy valleys were filled with orchards and garden plots. The camels and their riders padded down lanes between the villages. The moon was still high, but westering. In its silver light, the buildings they passed slept. For a wonder, no dogs barked in the night. Zoë looked into the pens and yards as the camels loped along, seeing the sheep and goats and kine sleeping peacefully.

They passed through an orchard of sweet-smelling orange trees and stood at the top of a ridge looking across a bowl-shaped valley. On the far side, atop a craggy hill, the lights of a city twinkled in the night. Deep shadows lay below the hill, for the moon had consented, at last, to touch the western horizon.

"Hierosolyma," said Mohammed in a hushed voice. "We have arrived."

Zoë stared at him in astonishment. To reach the Judean hill-town from Petra should take no less than two full days and nights of travel, even on barrel-chested camels like these.

"How . . . ?" She could think of nothing to say. Mohammed turned, his eyes shrouded in shadow.

"Those who go about in the land upon the business of the Great and Merciful God go quickly."

The Quryash turned his camel and tapped it sharply on the thigh with a cane. It harrumphed and then jolted into a walk. The road, now broad enough for two carts to pass, wound down the hill into the dark valley. Zoë twitched her own beast into motion and followed.

Beneath the high-sided hill, orchards of olive trees pressed close to the chalky limestone. Mohammed let the camel pick its way through the trees. The moon was hidden now behind the city and it became very dark. Zoë rode with her head close to the neck of the camel and turned inward. Branches and leaves brushed against her and plucked at her cloak. The camels stopped. Boulders nestled among the tree trunks and a slope canted up above them. Mohammed dismounted and tied his mount to a sapling.

"There is a path," he said in a soft voice. "It is steep and it leads to a hidden gate."

Zoë swung down, feeling a twinge in her thighs. It did feel as if they had ridden for days. She hobbled after the chieftain. The Quryash had already gone off through the trees and was climbing up the slope. The Palmyrene girl hurried after, cursing her balky legs under her breath.

From a distance, it did not seem that there was any trail through the tumbled stones and rugged cliffs, but Zoë found that Mohammed's footsteps led unerringly to a sloping path. It wound up through a rocky defile and then switchbacked up the face of the hill. It was very steep and her ankles began to complain fiercely at the effort. The path was littered with stones.

THE SLOPES OF VESUVIUS

)(

Thyatis padded along the line of a brick wall, her hood thrown back, the water-steel blade bare in her hand. A leather sling-bag hung on her back, holding diverse items. Her left hand brushed along the wall, guiding her in the darkness. Ivy studded with sweet-smelling flowers hung down from the top of the wall. The Roman woman had entered the villa grounds from the southeast, coming up through the overgrown vineyards. Two of the legionnaires were a pace behind her, one with a long boar spear, the other with a heavy bow in hand. The archer had a fire-arrow nocked but not lit. The long wooden shaft was topped by a sharpened copper cage in the shape of a diamond. A plug of bitumen had been packed into the cage, ready for the touch of a flame to set it hissing to life. Thyatis stopped. She had reached an arched gateway with a wooden door.

She listened, but heard nothing but the susurration of the night wind through the tall cypresses that lined the edge of the villa. Even the usual sounds of a sleeping residence were absent—no dogs, no restless horses. The place felt empty, but that could be a simple deception. She tested the lock on the gate. It was unlocked and swung open with a creak at her touch. The two legionnaires froze, their weapons raised, but Thyatis let the gate swing wide. The yard beyond was empty, save for two big wagons parked by the wall of what must be a barn.

Thyatis ducked inside, sliding to the left into the shadow of the wall. Then she waited, letting her eyes lose focus, feeling the currents of the air on her face, letting the sense of the place settle on her. It still seemed abandoned. The side of the main house rose up before her, a two-story affair with a canted, tiled roof. Rows of dark windows on the second floor stared down at her. There were no lights. The moon was enough, though, and she made a clicking sound with her mouth. The spearman entered and moved to the right, allowing the archer to take up a position in the gate.

Chopping her hand down to the left, she motioned the spearman to lead off. Her intent was to enter the house from the rear, where the kitchens should be. The spearman darted out across the space between the garden wall and the house. Thyatis remained watchful, but there was still no sign of movement or alarm. Then she followed and the archer after her.

"Nothing, not so much as a mouse." Nikos sounded disgusted. Thyatis ignored him for the moment, stooping to look under the table of planks that stood against one wall of a room near the front of the villa. She held a collapsible metal lantern in one hand. The Illyrian was kitted out in a mail *lorica* with studded leather forearm braces. The shirt of iron rings fell to his midthigh and was covered with a linen tabard. Beneath that he wore a felt undershirt and a cotton tunic close to his flesh. Unlike Thyatis, who was going bare-headed, he was wearing an old-style Legion helmet with a smooth crown and metal flaps and nose guard that tied under his chin, protecting his cheeks. He had considered a cavalry helmet with a full face mask, but that would have cost him too much peripheral vision. After his last encounter with the *homunculus* he was taking as few chances as possible.

Of course, after watching the creature eviscerate a dozen praetorians in their last match, the only sensible option would be to avoid any further test of strength at all. He had given up his gladius, too, for a long iron-bladed spear with a crossbar welded at the base of the head. The image of the homunculus dragging itself up that poor soldier's spear had stayed with Nikos. He did not fancy the same fate.

Thyatis wiped a finger across the table and it came away dusty. It was obvious that the room had been used for storage recently, there were empty shelves made of raw new pine and some empty wooden crates in the corner. Bits of spilled food lay under the table and there was a relatively fresh wine stain on one corner of the table. Anything that might have been stored here, however, or anyone who had been living in the villa was gone.

"Was there anything in the stables?"

Nikos shook his head in negation. "No. Signs of horses and fodder for them, but nothing recent. It seems that we are too late."

Thyatis nodded absently. She reminded herself of the things that the girl, Krista, had told them about the Prince and his habits. By her count, if it could be trusted, there should have been almost a dozen people living in the villa; the Prince, his *homunculus*, the two risen dead, and the Walachs. From what she had seen of the ground floor, and heard of the other buildings, it seemed that they had decamped. All signs pointed to a hurried but thorough evacuation of the premises.

"Search the grounds," she said, turning back to Nikos and the other men clustered in the doorway. "They brought many heavy crates and boxes with them, but the wagons are still here. They cannot have gone far."

Nikos nodded and turned, but halted at the doorway, one hand on the wall. He looked back in question. Thyatis raised an eyebrow and smiled.

"Search in teams of three, like we trained," she said, hitching up her sword-belt. "Check the road for tracks of a single wagon going out and any other lanes or tracks that leave these buildings. The archers are to keep a signal arrow nocked." Nikos nodded and went out.

Thyatis looked around the room again, then bent to pick up her lantern. As she did so, the shadows shifted and she saw a crumpled piece of parchment behind the table. It was at the edge of her reach, but she snagged it with a fingertip. It was not dusty. The parchment crinkled as she unfolded it.

Lord Prince, it said in simple letters, *I have gone and taken the little cat. My desire for life exceeds my love for you. If the gods will, we will meet again in a safe place, Krista.*

Thyatis grunted. She had expected as much. The slave girl had told the truth, then. Thyatis folded the parchment into a tiny square and put it in her girdle before jogging out into the big echoing hallway that ran down the center of the house. Her nerves hissed with the blood-fire. The Prince would be close by.

THE GATE OF SIHON, AELIA CAPITONLINA

The steep narrow trail ended in a gate set into the base of the city wall. The rampart rose up from the top of the cliff like an extension of the hill itself. Zoë was panting in effort by the time they reached the shadowy vestibule. She glared at the desert chieftain's back—he did not seem tired. Given that he was easily twice her age, Zoë did not think it fair at all. The gate was small, shorter than most men, which would force anyone to bend down to pass through it. The face of it was covered with riveted iron plates and a square tower blocked out the night sky above. Anyone attempting to force the iron door would pay grievously for the privilege.

Mohammed moved into the shadows, bending down, and Zoë heard a rattle and click. The moon was well behind the bulk of the city now and it was very dark in the space before the gate. She shivered and pulled her cloak

tight around her. From this vantage, she could look down
upon the valley behind them. It was quite dark, save for a
cluster of fires burning just a little way from where they
had left the camels.

"Follow," came Mohammed's voice and she turned. The
gate was open and led into utter darkness. Air rolled slowly
out, heavy and humid with the smell of rotted cabbage and
urine and offal. Zoë gulped and pulled an edge of her cloak
over her mouth. The Quryash had already vanished inside
and she hurried to catch up with the sound of his boots on
the flagstones. His voice drifted back to her. "Do not
speak. There may be guards."

The passage sloped upwards for a time, then rose
sharply on a flight of broad steps, worn by the passage of
many feet. The curved depressions on the stairs made it
hard to keep one's feet, but Zoë staggered along in darkness for a time. Part of the passage was half-buried in
debris. They rose out of the funk that had collected in the
midden and her mind seemed to wake from a dream.

When it did, she felt the ache in her thighs and buttocks
flare up into serious pain. She gasped aloud in alarm and
stopped, leaning against the wall. The surface was mossy
and slippery.

"Wait," she called. There was no answer. The sound of
footsteps receded in the murk.

Zoë cursed, but with the lifting of the haze in her mind,
she thought to calm her thought and call upon the powers
that coursed in her blood. Two deep breaths settled her
thought and allowed the first entrance. With it came the
flowering of perception and the darkness fell away like a
dropped veil. The walls stood out in sharp relief. Now she
could see that under the patina of moss and age there were
paintings and mosaics inset into the walls. The rounded
steps had once been sharp-cut marble and a series of delicate arches crowned the hallway. She hissed in surprise,
but saw too that the figure of the desert chieftain had almost disappeared up ahead.

Muttering, she jogged up the stairs. Her legs complained

bitterly. They wanted a nice bed and a bath, not more climbing.

At the top of the stairway, there was another door, which now stood open, and a vaulted chamber beyond. She stepped through the archway and found herself standing on a broad open plaza, a thousand yards wide. The moon was low in the sky, but its light glittered back from limestone paving and lines of ornamental trees. Off to her left, to the south, a monumental statue rose up from the plaza, one arm raised to the heavens. Even cast in shadow, she could see that it was the form of an emperor.

She spat on the ground.

At the center of the plaza, where arcs of trees converged, a massive temple rose up on a stepped platform. It was open on three sides, with bulky columns rising like tree trunks. Its ridgeline was crowded with statues and votive sculptures. Within, half obscured by the colonnade, she could make out a sanctuary and something unexpected.

Unlike the usual run of Roman temples, there was a humped shape underneath the shadowed roof, taking the place of the usual walled sanctuary. Too, the back wall was not a solid surface, but it too was columns.

Halfway between the stairway house and the temple, she could see Mohammed, striding swiftly along the line of one of the curving roads. Ignoring the pain in her legs, she hurried after. Within moments, he had vanished up the steps.

Zoë passed between the pillars, her shadow falling on richly layered paint. Her boots clicked on the marble tiling. It had grown cold as the night passed, and here, in this exposed place, a ghost of breath puffed from her lips. She came out into the open space around the strange humped structure at the back of the temple.

A slab of rock, dark and pitted, thrust up from the marble floor. Indeed, the edges of the flooring tile had been worked to fit against it. A low barricade of wooden railing ran around it, keeping onlookers away from the massive plinth. Looking upon it, all unexpected, Zoë realized that it was the crown of the hill below them. This temple, the great plaza, the city, had grown up around it, everything here was focused upon this stone. It was very old and dragged at the will. Some momentous weight gathered around it. Zoë felt the air, letting her mage-sight expand to take in the temple and the buildings that surrounded it.

Everything in the temple complex, even the curve of the walkways and the ranks of planted trees, was oriented toward the stone. Each building, each statue, each arc weighed against it, binding it, trying to restrain the power that throbbed and radiated and spilled from the crevices and pits in that ancient, blackened surface.

Mohammed stood at the northern end of the slab, his hand on a column that still towered above him, reaching into the inky darkness of the roof. Something about the line of his shoulders alarmed Zoë and she vaulted over the barricade. Atop the stone, climbing toward him, she heard a sound. It was a ragged moan and a bubbling gasp in one. She halted, hands on the rough surface of the rock, feeling something fill the air around her. A power was moving in the hidden world.

A knocking sound startled the air. Under her hands, the stone quivered.

Without thinking, she summoned a ward and a shield and then gasped aloud herself.

The Quryash lashed out with a fist, striking at the empty air. The man shouted, his voice ringing with defiance. In her other sight, Zoë could see darkness boiling from the smooth surface of the pillars and curling through the air around her. Heat flushed from the slab and from the marble tiles. The wavering thin blue orb of her ward buckled as the black clouds washed over her. Anger and fear and hatred in the tile and marble yielded up enormous strength to the cloud and Zoë fell to her knees, chanting a calming meditation.

The tendrils curled around Mohammed's arms and limbs like grotesque vines digging into rock. Zoë saw him crushed down against the slab and saw the stone crack and flake under the impact. Darkness curdled at his feet, dragging at his legs. The tendrils thickened and grew a forest of thin black tongues tipped with a red glow. One tongue snapped through the air, lashing Mohammed's cheek. A burning red welt appeared and the Quryash screamed again, this time in horrible pain.

The black cloud eddied around the fringe of Zoë's sphere, flowing past toward the man struggling at the peak of the slab. The power brushed her aside and she fell to the marble floor, sending the wooden barricade clattering down. She gripped the tile with both hands, her back hunched, trying to leach power from the old flooring. It was barren and dry, long ago drained of the vitality of living rock. She wept, feeling the pitiful weakness of her ward.

Mohammed grappled with the darkness, wrestling tentacles away from his body. Now they had grown as thick as tree trunks and they coiled close, crushing his ribcage. Even through the shimmer of her ward, Zoë could hear the grinding of bones breaking under the pressure. Fear boiled up in her, threatening to close her throat. It was hard to breathe. The black tide lapped up around her. In the inky depths, she could see visions and torments. Fires burned in the depths of the earth, where emaciated figures writhed in torment. With an enormous effort, she forced herself to stand. Her ward flexed pearlescent, straining against the lake of ink, and matched her movement. The power that chuckled and hissed inside her demanded release, but it was hot with anger and hate. It yearned to join with the spinning black lake that surrounded her.

With a heave, Mohammed rose to his feet, though he still crouched on the tip of the slab. The initial fear had passed and his eyes cleared. Suddenly, as Zoë watched, he stopped struggling and fell back into the black embrace. The red-tipped tongues slid over his flesh, pressing at his eyelids and slithering into his mouth and nostrils. Zoë tried to cry out to him, but no sound came.

The black tide rushed up, covering her ward and sight of the desert chieftain.

In the ocean of night, Zoë saw visions unfold:

Siege towers loomed over the wall of a city, spitting flame. Men ran in the streets, thin and starved, with mad eyes. The earth shook and a gate tower cracked lengthwise. Hundreds of tons of stone and brick cascaded down into the street. The gate itself toppled, falling to one side. Its exposed limestone face was already burning fiercely. Men in bronze helmets stormed through the breach, scattering the few defenders before them. Eagle-headed standards moved through the smoke at the heads of columns of grim-faced men.

The Palmyrene girl blinked furiously, her hand out in front of her face. The phantasm dissolved, though she could still feel the heat of the burning buildings on her hands and face. Smoke curled in her nostrils.

A glorious temple filled with fat-bellied pillars shuddered, its tiled roof rippling with flame. On broad white steps, hundreds of men were struggling. Most of them wore horse-tail helmets and iron armor. The others were bearded, clad in mismatched armor, fighting with a hopeless ferocity. Clouds of arrows filled the sky, raking the ranks of the defenders. Again, eagle-headed standards advanced and the men of the city fell under hobnailed boots. Lightning snaked through the sky, lighting black clouds of smoke and ash. At the heart of the temple, priests waged a furious defense, their backs to an inner building of stone. Scintillating wards crumpled under the rage that fell from the sky. Amid the iron-armored soldiers, thaumaturges strode forward, spiking fire from their hands.

Zoë felt cold stone under her back and realized that she had fallen. Everything around her was black as pitch, yet filled with a sensation of writhing movement. She closed her eyes, feeling the pain and loss of her aunt's death swell in her chest. It was hard to breathe again.

A man stood on a barren hill, a bloody knife in his hand, his face raised to a storm-tossed sky. Lightning rippled, fierce and azure, between the clouds. Beneath his feet, a dark stone dripped with blood. The body of a boy lay sprawled on the cracked and riven slab. The man screamed at the sky and the sky answered. That sound cracked like a whip, breaking stone and setting trees alight, driving the man to his feet. Tears smoked from his face. He wept, seeing the body of his son.

The man had the face of Mohammed.

Blue-white light stabbed through the murk and the enormous pressure against her battle ward suddenly slackened. A single point of incredibly bright white light blossomed in the darkness and the black tide rushed back. The tendrils and waving forest of tongues shuddered and slowly withdrew, though to Zoë they seemed to resist mightily. Mohammed was revealed, lying at the base of the column. The red-and-black vines that had wormed into every orifice of his body were shaking as if in a high breeze.

The sky, enraged, rippled like a sea in full storm. Rain fell, lashing the man. Rivers of water ran, carrying away the blood and the tears in a slurry of mud. In the rain, in the stuttering flare of the lightning, the hand of the dead boy twitched.

Something was standing over the fallen body of the Quryash. Zoë turned away, blinded, with the streaked afterimage of something with coruscating wings bestride him and rising colossally above the building. Blinded, she pressed her face against the cold tesserae of the floor. The world was silent and still, but she felt the tremble of the darkness in the air around her. The hidden world was in chaos, with mighty powers striving back and forth. Mohammed's left boot beat a sharp tattoo on the rooftop.

Vision returned and Zoë stared down at her hands, seeing them outlined in a soft white glow. She looked up, and for an instant she saw the temple around her as it had stood on the day it had been completed. It was vast with a two-story central hall. Ranks of round-bellied pillars lined the sides of the great open space. The walls gleamed in pale white outline and domes arched toward the heavens. Hundreds of windows pierced the upper walls. She stood, reaching out her hand to the nearest column, which rose up perfect and whole toward the distant, vaulted ceiling.

It faded, slowly growing fainter and fainter. The roof went first, replaced by winking stars, and then the soaring walls dissolved. In only moments the looming shape of the Roman temple returned. Zoë felt tears seep from her eyes and loss churned in her stomach. She looked out upon the city, seeing the white roofs and winding narrow streets for the first time. The white radiance was flowing away from her, touching the windowsills and vine arbors as it passed. Zoë held her breath, seeing the soft white light pass over the land, illuminating everything with the refulgence of day. Olive trees, stockyards, temples, hilltops, tents were all thrown in sharp relief and then shadow came along behind as night closed in.

The light passed and darkness settled around Zoë like a comfortable cloak. The writhing ebon tendrils were gone as well, swallowed up in the blood-stained slab and into the body of the Quryash, who lay still on the rooftop. Zoë ventured to move a foot and found that she could. Even the blindness had passed, leaving only sparkles at the edges of her vision. She felt lighter, as if a great oppressive weight had been taken from her shoulders. Kneeling, she touched the side of Mohammed's throat. There was a pulse, at first thready, but rapidly growing stronger. His skin was hot to her touch and she realized that she was very cold.

In the distance, a dog awoke and began barking furiously. Something had troubled its dreams.

Zoë rolled back Mohammed's eyelid with a thumb and froze in shock. Darkness, live and twisting, had shimmered in his pupil for a moment. Taking a breath to steady herself, she pressed her hands to his temples and settled within herself. Her own power woke and stretched and tested the confines of the world. Mohammed's body glowed between her hands and she felt, for the first time, an enormous strength in him. It was like banked coals burning white hot—not noticeable from a distance, but should you come within their proximity—like the heart of a sun. Echoes of conflict still drifted about him—both the cruel bitter darkness and that brilliant light.

The Palmyrene stood up suddenly, shaking, and shook her hands as if they were wet.

Something has entered him. The thought was plain and appalling. The man at her feet had become the vessel of some power. It slept within him now, but could wake at any moment. Her head rang like a temple bell with the brush of its strength. Pure and unalloyed, it nestled at the heart of the man.

Is this the God of the Wasteland that he worships? Zoë was daunted by the prospect. In all the days of her life she had been told that the powers of the gods—Zeus Ammon, Bel the Guardian, all their ilk—were expressed through men, through their priests. Once she had joined the Legions of Rome, Zoë had learned that she herself—a mortal woman—possessed powers of her will and mind that could mimic or surpass any prelate or high priest. In that light, she had found the gods paltry and weak, perhaps no more than the fantasies of men. Tools that the cunning might use to bend the common people to their will.

But this? This was the hem of a garment far beyond her ken. She pressed the palms of her hands to her eyes, willing the images to pass and the memory to be blotted from her mind.

Lights at the edge of the plaza caught her attention. Men with torches had come out of the buildings, drawn by the disturbance in the night. She crouched down and gathered up the old man's body. It was heavy, but she was young and strong. With a grunt, she managed to slide him onto her shoulders and then stand. His head lolled against her shoulder and he began to snore.

Just like a man, she cursed to herself, *fall asleep after everything's done and leave a woman to clean up!*

Staggering under the weight, she made her way out of the temple and to the top of the stairs. One foot was on the top step before she realized that a flicker of torchlight was gleaming below. The mutter of sleepy voices rose up. Snarling at the ill-luck, she backed away, casting about with her mage-sight for another way off of the plaza.

On the southern side of the vast open space, a light caught her eye. It was a wisp of blue, hanging in the air like a candle flame. Below her the sound of voices strengthened.

"Search the compound," came a gruff voice. It had the ring of a Legion centurion. She moved farther away from the stairwell. The hanging flame beckoned and, without any better ideas, she hurried over to where it flickered in the darkness. As she came closer, it disappeared, falling below the level of the platform. There was an opening between her feet, round and dark, with the smell of water rising out of it.

The flame fluttered away, swirling down the well. There were steps cut into the wall, winding down into the foundation. Somewhere below, water dripped into a pool. Zoë shifted the Quryash on her shoulders to a more comfortable position and put her foot on the first step.

Gingerly, she descended into the encompassing dark.

THE PALATINE HILL, ROMA MATER

Good evening, Augustus, Lord and God Galen, Emperor of the Romans." Anastasia bowed formally, a single curl of her dark hair falling over one eye. It was evening and the lights of the city twinkled through the windows of the Emperor's study, high on the southern face

of the Palatine hill. The Duchess turned, the doubled necklace of black pearls around her pale neck glinting in the
lantern light. She bowed as well to Aurelian, who like his
brother, had risen at her entrance. "Aurelian, Caesar,
Prince of the Empire, greetings unto you."

The two men were sitting at ease over the remains of a
light dinner of roasted black grouse brushed with garlic,
cardoon in vinegar and oil, and hard-boiled goose eggs
dusted with paprika. With the weather tending toward the
heat of summer, everyone was beginning to avoid heavy
foods. Still, the night threatened enough of a chill to warrant woolen tunics, and for Aurelian, a half-cape. Despite
his heavier build, it seemed that he was more sensitive than
his brother to changes in temperature.

One of the servants who had been standing in an alcove
off the study brought out a slim-legged oak chair and
placed it beside the pair of couches.

The Duchess sat delicately, letting the long drape of her
charcoal gray gown fall naturally. Her hair was bound up
in a cloud on the top of her head, shot with silver pins.
Even her sandals were in fine leather dyed a very dark
brown. Anastasia did not come bearing good news and her
garments reflected her mood. Galen coughed, his nervous
eyes darting over her face, hands, and clothes. The Duchess repressed a wry smile; she could ken his thought, di-
vining some unexpected disaster. His brother, the bluff
Aurelian, was just frowning, wondering why she had interrupted their little moment of privacy and quiet.

"What has happened?" Galen's voice was sharp and flat.
His attention focussed on her, fierce and intent, and Anastasia felt the familiar shock of his personality. Usually it
would stir her blood in competition, but tonight it only
made her weary. The Emperor carried his power well, and
part of that effectiveness was his will to use it. "You seem
somber this evening, my lady de'Orelio."

"I am distressed, my lord Galen. I come to you with
poor news."

She withdrew a package of papers from a hidden pocket

in the over-cape of her gown. They were almost pure white—exceptionally fine parchment sanded smooth—and bound in a black ribbon. These she placed on the edge of the dining table, making space between a plate that had held candied mushrooms and a bronze ewer holding sour wine. The Duchess then removed a heavy signet ring from one hand and placed it atop the papers.

"By the law of the State, those who conspire against the person of the Emperor, or his family, forfeit all titles, properties, usages, and rights to the person of the Emperor, who shall—as the Divine Augustus first said—best dispose of them." Anastasia's voice was calm, though her hand trembled a little as she briefly touched the ring and then drew away.

"This is the House de'Orelio and all its lands and chattels. It is yours."

Her pale finger, lightly coated with a matte of white lead powder, drifted to the ribbon around the parchment sheets.

"These are the business concerns; the *fabricae*, the ships, the granary shares, the wine shops, the investments in Gaulish iron and British tin, the vineyards in Terraconensis and Sicilia. With them, my lords, is my signed confession and statement of guilt. I pray you, do not waste the time of the Senate with a public trial. I am guilty, but I throw myself upon your mercy, hoping for a discrete and private end."

Galen was standing, his eyes bright with fear and anger. His voice shook when he spoke. "Guilty of what? Has some madness overcome you? What is this conspiracy against me?"

Anastasia looked up, her face pale in its subtle makeup, her violet eyes huge and accented by a thin outline of kohl. She pressed her slim fingers to her chest. Unlike most of her gowns, this one had a high collar and her hand lay like a dying swan on that velvet surface.

"Not you, my lord. Never you. I have sent my men to take arms against your brother, the Prince Maxian, in his refuge at Ottaviano near Cumae." She paused, and it seemed that her voice might break. "I have sent them there to kill the young Prince and return his lifeless body to Rome in a casket of iron."

Galen staggered, his face blanching white, and he sat down. One hand gripped the edge of the couch. Aurelian's eyes had assumed a dreadful aspect and his fist curled around the hilt of a short stabbing sword at his waist.

"You would kill our little piglet?" Aurelian's deep voice ground like stones in a whirlpool. He stood, his brow furrowing, and he stepped to the Duchess' side, his thick-fingered hand touching her neck. Anastasia steeled herself and turned her face away, letting her hair fall loose in front of her eyes. "Our brother? You would send your footpads and *sicaraii* to seek him out in our mother's house?"

Aurelian's voice was rising, sending echoes ringing from the tall columns and the glazed tiles of the domed roof. The sword rasped from its sheath and settled in his hand, a gleaming extension of his arm.

"Yes," said the Duchess in a faint voice. She clasped her right hand around Aurelian's wrist, pressing his muscular palm against her neck. Her fingers were not long enough to encircle the thick muscles. "Tonight, beyond the speed of messenger on horse or ship to warn him, he will die. I have taken every precaution . . ." her voice strengthened and she looked up at Aurelian ". . . every precaution that he be slain."

Aurelian had raised the blade, preparing to give his rage vent in her body, but the sight of her calm eyes, ready and waiting for death, stilled his hand. His face contorted, filled with confusion and fear.

"Why?" Galen's voice was drained and possessed of a depth of grief. "He could not be brought before me in chains? Unconscious? Even blinded and helpless?"

"No, my lord." Anastasia turned, leaning her head on Aurelian's arm. She too was weary. "All that I have learned tells the tale of a man grown so strong in the dark arts, so practiced, that he can take mortal wounds and live, regrow the eye plucked from his head, slip any bond, suborn any guard. He has drunk deep of ancient Oriental poisons—he trafficks with the dead, he raises up grave-wights and commands them, his fingers are thick with tomb dust and lost secrets. Persians whisper in his ear. This dear boy, your brother, has set himself to replace you, to throw down the Senate and the people, to raise himself up in your stead."

"Impossible!" Aurelian shouted, but he turned to Galen, his face showing him lost in a strange land. "Gales, this is the piglet! Our little brother, a priest of blessed Asclepius! He has taken oaths . . . he cannot be a monster!"

"He is," Anastasia said, taking Aurelian's hand in both of hers and drawing him down to sit beside her at the end of the dining couch. "He has murdered foundling children and pensioned soldiers, he has placed workings upon men so that they might obey his will in all things. He has raised up a thing, a *homunculus*, that has murdered and consumed dozens of citizens, even strong men of the Praetorian Guard. He rides a serpent of fire."

Anastasia stroked the side of Aurelian's head, feeling the thick oily heaviness of his bushy red hair. The man seemed about to weep. The Duchess turned again to Galen, her face pensive with worry.

"My lord and god, all these things I have learned very recently. You knew some of them before, but not their entire scope. I know . . . I know that you wanted to give your brother time to heal and rest. I know that he has gone to your mother's estate at Ottaviano. An agent of mine has been close to him and recently returned to me. Things are far worse than you or I believed."

Galen raised a hand, his face terrible in repressed fury. A thin finger extended, jabbing at the Duchess.

"You took upon yourself to execute the Emperor's justice outside the sanction of the Twelve Tables. You usurp my authority, woman. If this man, my brother, is to die, it should be by my hand and order, not yours." The Emperor ground out each word like copper curling away from an iron die. Anastasia made a half-bow, still sitting and holding Aurelian's hand.

"I know, my lord. I am a traitor to the State. I will accept my punishment and death. But I could not wait, or risk that you would grant this man mercy. For the good of the Senate and the people of Rome, the Prince must be killed. I am sorry."

Galen looked away, his fists clenched. A vein throbbed in his forehead. When he looked back, after a long moment, his eyes seemed dead and clouded. His voice was bitter.

"There will be no punishment. This thing must be done. You have the will to lance this wound upon the body of the State."

The Duchess bowed her head again, disguising tears that pearled at the corners of her eyes. In the Emperor's voice, she heard the judgment and sentence of the Senate and the people of Rome.

VESUVIUS

T he gloom of the bowl-shaped grotto seemed to fold around Maxian like a comfortable old cloak, warm and soft, with a few tears and patches, but so well known that it was a relief just to settle into it. Night had fallen again after a sunny cloudless day. The Prince had tarried on the mountain, meditating and napping in the warmth. The last wagonload of books and sundries had been brought up from the villa and stowed in the Engine. Khiron was somewhere in the crevices and gullies among the boulders, waiting for word to climb into the iron hull of the Engine and depart.

Maxian sat at one edge of the grotto, his back to a sloping boulder, feeling the cool moss and the subtle comforting rumble of the mountain. He could see an arc of stars in the sky. Soon the moon might rise high enough to shine down into the bowl, filling it with a quiet silver light. Faced with the prospect of going out, beyond the point of balance between the Oath and the forces restrained within the mountain, he tarried. It was peaceful here and calm. He could doze in the sun without the worry of maintaining a vigilant shield. Khiron watched over him, keeping shepherds or wayward youths from disturbing his rest. Once he left, he would plunge back into the constant struggle with the corrosive power of the Oath. There would be no rest then.

So, he had stayed overlong, days past when he had intended to return to Rome and his brothers.

Maxian started awake, hearing the rattle of a stone falling somewhere in the grotto. He stood up, feeling stiffness in his arms and legs. He laughed softly to himself and patted the flank of the boulder. With the warm ground and the constant faint rumble of the mountain, it was easy to fall asleep here. The heat of the rocks made the bowl a little warmer than the night should be, raising a faint dewy mist. Maxian cracked his neck and walked toward the southern end of the grassy lawn. It was time to depart.

"Khiron! Come out, dead thing. It is time to go." Maxian heard his voice echo from the rocks.

He reached the far side of the glade and turned, looking up at the rim of the bowl. Where was the creature? It never went far away, even when it nosed about for living things among the rocks.

"Khiron, attend me!" The Prince put a tone of command into his call.

There was movement in the darkness at the side of the bowl and a lithe figure slipped down out of the shadows. Maxian frowned at it—the creature's head was turning this way and that and it moved quickly and low to the ground.

He looked around the great circle of rocks again. It was very quiet. Khiron passed through a bit of starlight, his glistening skin shining, loping along in a crouch.

"Khiron? What . . . ?"

Fire bloomed in the night, a sudden sharp orange wash of light that stabbed at the Prince's eyes and threw the boulders and mossy trees into high relief. Something hissing and spitting flame tumbled out of the sky and bounced toward him on the grass. Gobbets of flame scattered, clinging to the stones. Maxian jumped back in alarm and saw Khiron suddenly straighten up, its mouth yawning in a scream of rage.

"Yaaaaaarrr!"

The Prince staggered, slammed back into the bole of a cypress tree by a cold slapping shock to his diaphragm. He looked down, stunned, and gaped at a length of arrow shaft that jutted from his stomach. Blood welled up from the entry wound, wicking down the length of the arrow and fouling the fletching. In the hissing red light of the flames, each drop of blood turned golden as it fell toward the ground.

Time slowed as the Prince watched his life blood spill out.

Another arrow slammed into his shoulder, punching through bone and cartilage with a broad triangular head, lodging in the tree behind him. Pinned, the Prince struggled against a flood of pain and shock to raise his head. Despite the mortal wounds, his mind still seemed whole and aware, though everything was moving so slowly that he was disoriented. With a great effort, he managed to look up.

Men rushed out of the gloom, their helmets and iron mail glinting in the firelight. Another of the burning pots had fallen from above, breaking on a huge looming boulder, and long streams of burning liquid sputtered and snapped as they flowed down its sides. The mist had blown back, leaving a glowing roof over the grotto. Khiron was in motion at the center of the space, though Maxian saw that a dozen heavy black arrows had pierced the *homunculus*. Shrieking, Khiron leapt toward the nearest man, talons outstretched. The man, a heavy-set fellow with a full helm, skipped aside and Khiron caught the tip of the man's spear with his shoulder. There was a gelid sound of razor-sharp metal punching through sinew and stitches of twisted gut, then a slap as the crossbar at the base of the spearhead arrested the passage of the weapon.

Khiron shrieked again, seeing his prey beyond his reach. The creature slashed at the haft of the spear, catching it and wrenching it away. The spearhead twisted in the wound, then popped free. The armored man scrambled away and Khiron reversed the spear with a flip. Bowstrings, somewhere above, snapped with a musical *twang* and more arrows suddenly stabbed from Khiron's back. The *homunculus* shrieked again, but ignored the pain and hurled the spear with a convulsive heave. The left arm flopped, broken and shattered, at its side.

Maxian blinked, suddenly feeling horrible weakness wash over him. The scream of the armored man as the spear tore through his mailed armor from back to front and pinned him to the face of a slab-sided boulder was lost on him. Chill flooded through the Prince and he patted fruitlessly at the blood welling from his stomach. It was hard, caught against the tree, to move.

I must call my power, he realized dimly. Events had moved so fast . . .

A figure rushed forward out of the shadows, a long red braid gleaming in the firelight. A long stabbing sword was bare in her hand. The Prince looked up, taking an eternity to raise his head. A face swam forward out of the firelight, a strong oval with burning gray eyes, silhouetted by flame and smoke. A woman in armor, her mouth in a grim line, and the sharp point of an Indian-steel blade arrowing for him. Maxian tried to raise a hand in defense, but it was too late.

The sword slipped sideways through his ribs, transfixing his heart. The Prince stared, his eyes wide in surprise and recognition. She was close—he could feel her breath on his face—and she jerked the sword from his chest with a little grunt. It came away black and wet. The woman's hand moved and Maxian felt his throat constrict, crushed by powerful fingers. He could barely feel his body, there was only an encompassing, numbing cold. He saw the blade rise, shedding blood in a fine spray, for a slashing cut.

Khiron spun and leapt in one motion. Its powerful legs flung it into the air, over the head of a startled soldier, missing the spear that stabbed at it. Firelight gleamed on its flesh and it struck the ground running. The thicket of arrows that jutted from back and side and thigh did not slow it. The *homunculus* did not feel pain, only hunger and the driving fear of dissolution. Before it, two men turned to meet it, their blades glittering in the flame-shot air. They were armored, too, with heavy iron plates covering their chests and stout helmets of steel. Khiron did not care; all it knew was that its master was just beyond, on the verge of final death.

Heedless of the sword blades hacking for its joints, Khiron bulled into the two men, crashing into one with its ruined shoulder. The man grunted and was thrown back sprawling on the turf. The other hacked deeply into the other arm, but Khiron spun inside the man's reach and smashed its head into the face of the man's helmet. Bony ancient skull rang on metal and the soldier crumpled to the ground. Khiron rushed through the opening.

Thyatis leapt aside, reversing the stroke that would have cut the Prince's head from his body, and slashed the long sword across the face of the horror that lunged at her out of the night. The fire-pots continued to burn brightly, and the flames licking up from them had caught among the trees and undergrowth at the sides of the grotto. Smoke billowed up from the damp grass and wood. More of her men were rushing forward, though the archers had stopped firing once things had reached close quarters. The tip of the water-steel blade slashed across the creature's nose, tearing through cartilage and bone. The vaguely reptilian head jerked aside, but the ruin and wound did not seem to slow it. Thyatis dropped into a crouch, finding her footing, and circled.

In the ruddy glare, the naked body of the thing seemed a disaster, torn with arrows and covered with ragged wounds. One arm flopped at its side, though the other was still outstretched, diamond-bright talons winking in the air. The thing scuttled to one side like a crab and Thyatis gave ground, though that meant it was now between her and the Prince. Her ears roared with the blood-fire and she felt very light, almost floating on the grass.

Thyatis attacked, feinting at the thing's eyes, then weaved aside as its claw lashed through the air where she had been. She tumbled aside and it barely snatched a leg away as she tried to drive the sword into one of its knee-caps. It spun, slashing with a taloned foot and she had to block, feeling the strength of it slam into her shoulder. Her arm went numb at the blow, but the blood-fire roared up and everything disappeared into a tunnel of swirling gray, focussed on the grinning charnel face of the thing.

Nikos staggered up, levering himself upright with a gloved hand. With a gasp, he tore the helmet from his head. Half of it was caved in by the creature's blow, and blood slicked his face and blinded him in one eye. The world seemed unsteady, but he managed to gain his feet. Men were shouting at him and he looked around just in time.

Thyatis and the creature were a blur of limbs and blades, surging back and forth across the grassy field. As he watched, she sprang into the air, going into a sharp side-kick that clipped the thing's head with the iron-shod toe of her boot. It fell away into a roll and then came up again, lashing out with its remaining good arm. The woman, her braids flying behind her head, slid the blow with a forearm, then countered with an elbow strike to the creature's chest.

The thing shuddered, but was not rocked back. It twisted like a snake and caught Thyatis in the chest with its shattered arm, swinging it like a club. The woman, caught out of balance, was flung back to bounce off of one of the boulders. The sound of her impact rang like a wagonload of kettles dropped in the street.

"Fire!" screamed Nikos in panic, seeing the horror lurch forward toward his commander. He scuttled back, groping for a weapon on the ground. "Fire now!"

The *homunculus* turned, grinning, its shattered face lit by the flames. It hissed, a long dry sound, and rushed at Nikos like a lion. The Illyrian threw himself aside, feeling heavy and slow in the armor. There was a grunting sound behind him, the smacking sound of meat and steel and then a gelid pop. Nikos rolled up, wiping blood from his eye. His scalp cut was bleeding freely.

The creature stood frozen, pierced by a long heavy spear. Karhmi and Efraim had run forward at the same moment that Nikos had jumped aside. Between them they held a long pike, a *sarissa*, and when the *homunculus* leapt for the Illyrian, they caught it on the foot-long tip like a gar-pike on a hook. A bladder had been lashed to the crossbars of the weapon and the fluid inside, black and sticky, splashed over the creature's chest and arms.

"Fire!" shrieked Nikos and he backpedaled. The two soldiers dodged away as well, dropping the pike. The bowmen hiding atop the boulders had been waiting, fire-arrows at the ready. Now the air hissed with bowshot and flaming streaks of light flashed toward the creature. It moved abruptly, tearing the spear from its side, and sprang back, sending droplets of the black liquid flying in all directions. Arrows, burning with pitch, thudded into the ground where it had been. One struck at the edge of the broad arc of splashed liquid and there was a sudden guttural roar and blue-white flame leapt up from the turf.

Nikos ran sideways, one hand up to shade his eyes. The *phlogiston* splashed on the ground was burning furiously, filling the grotto with the sound of its combustion. He had lost sight of the creature, which was death in such a tight space as this. Bitter white smoke boiled up, obscuring everyone's vision.

Thyatis shook off the concussion and rolled up, feeling giddy. A bright lancet of pain crawled across her side, telling her that at least one rib had broken on the boulder's unyielding surface. She had lost the sword somewhere, but she still had at least one long knife. It was already in her hand, snatched from her sheath without conscious thought. Her men were shouting in alarm, but she ignored that for the moment. She darted to the right, toward where the Prince had lain against the tree. The *homunculus* was a deadly threat, but the Prince was the mission.

Maxian's eyes fluttered open, seeing a blinding white light. A sharp acrid smell assaulted his nostrils. He was tremendously cold. Blood bubbled from his lips, spilling down his chin.

What is this? The Prince's mind shuddered with waves of pain. *Is this the ferryman? Where is the black river?*

With an enormous effort, the Prince tried to raise a hand. He could not. He was too weak.

A silhouette suddenly came into focus against the actinic glare. It moved and sharpened into focus. It was the woman, her hair in disarray, soot smudged along one high cheekbone. There was steel in her hand, a long knife with a wicked edge. Her gray eyes bored into his, filled with intense determination. Her free hand grasped his hair, bending his head sharply back.

Maxian tried to speak, but blood clogged his throat and there was only a ghastly bubbling sound. The cold edge of the knife pressed against his throat. Out of the corner of his eye, he saw that the woman was wearing a brooch or pendant that bound her hair back. It had fallen to one side, and it gleamed brightly in the shuddering light. On it, incised in the bronze surface, was the sigil of an eye flanked by curved wings.

The Imperial Office of Barbarians. The thought forced

its way through the roaring pain. *My brother. Galen. Aurelian. The Emperor.*

Maxian's heart seemed to stop. Awareness flooded him. The well-equipped soldiers. The forbidden chemicals. The speed and ferocity of the attack. A vision of his brother's face swam into view, Galen's dark eyes hooded, face drawn and fatigued, that one lock of hair lying across his forehead. Metal sawed into the flesh of his throat.

You would kill me? Maxian felt his heart crush under the weight of that betrayal. The vision turned, staring at him across the leagues. The nervous bright eyes were grim and filled with pain. *You would order my death?*

This thing must be done, said the vision. *The State must endure.*

Then Maxian's heart did break.

Thyatis saw the man's eyes flutter closed and felt his pulse stagger and stop under her hand. She drew back the knife, hesitating for a moment. A shriek from behind her made her spin and drop into a crouch. The creature had suddenly bolted out of the shadows of a boulder and had ripped the throat from one of the soldiers. The men had moved out into the open ground, their spears at the ready, but no one had expected the thing to spring from atop one of the smaller boulders. The other men converged on the thing, and the air filled with burning arrows again. Thyatis ran forward, shying away from the pool of burning *phlogiston*.

Khiron wrenched the man's head from his neck and blood sprayed out, blinding the first man that rushed at it. Heedless of the arrows that filled the air, the *homunculus* leapt past the spear and punched two stiffened fingers tipped with hardened bone into the blinded soldiers' eye sockets. There was a wet spattering sound and red gore slimed its fingers. The man fell without a sound. Another spear jabbed in from the side, but Khiron weaved away from it.

Thyatis, running up to the edge of the fray, ground her teeth. Fighting the thing one on one would do nothing!

She opened her mouth to shout a command, but there was a swinging motion at the edge of her vision and she ducked instinctively.

Nikos overhanded a branch, torn from one of the burning trees, into the creature's back as it was wrenching a long spear from a legionnaire's hands. The oak leaves, wreathed in their own sputtering flame, struck the back of the *homunculus* and the *phlogiston* that had clung like black oil to the rippling muscle and flesh and sinew flashed alight. Khiron leapt straight up, howling in despair, and then burst into flame like a flower opening to the sun with impossible speed. The legionnaires scattered.

Khiron slammed back down to earth, a frenzy of thrashing limbs, rolling frantically and clawing at the earth. The *phlogiston* crackled and hissed, burning furiously. It wailed in a high-pitched voice like a baby frying in its own fat. The ancient flesh, held together only by will and sorcery, burned with an amazingly hot blue flame. The creature staggered up, wreathed in a corona of almost invisible fire. Nikos fell back, holding his hand up to shield his face from the intense heat. The thing took a step, but its flesh and muscle were already dissolving into a burning jelly.

Thyatis fell back, too, turning her head away from the gruesome sight. She had unfinished business. She sprinted back toward the Prince.

Maxian's heart stuttered and stopped and then, as the last flicker of thought curdled down into a black abyss, something bright and burning like the sun rose up. Hate flared in the man's heart, and something enormous was shrieking at him, demanding release. The fragile last tendril of will stabbed out into the cold darkness and found power waiting for it: colossal untapped power that had been restrained for centuries, building and building in strength, deep under the earth.

Gods, raged Maxian, *my brother kills me? My family treats me as a mad dog?*

The crumbling lattice of his thought and will flared to life, stitching itself into a feeble semblance of its full shape. His body was destroyed, ruined, slashed and cut, pierced. Flames lapped at his feet, burning through his boots. But in the earth below him, a brilliant green flood of power surged up, slipping through cracks and crevices in the binding that had lain upon it for so long. The Prince, lying near death at the summit of the mountain, reached out, spending the last of his own rage to touch the heart of the volcano.

Thyatis staggered, nearly losing her footing. The ground rumbled from a massive shock. The green turf had lifted up, sending her toppling and then slammed down again. All around her, the air was filled with a great creaking sound and then the rattle of falling rock and the grinding of boulders sliding into new positions. A despairing scream echoed across the grotto. One of the archers had been thrown from his perch and a seventy-ton boulder had shifted, grinding him into paste against one of its brethren. The woman gingerly got to her feet, keeping her hands low to the ground.

She looked up and saw the Prince and a snarl cut her features.

Life flooded him, rushing through his limbs like a mountain freshet in full spate. Broken bone, torn muscle and sinew, shattered organs rippled with virulent power. His torso convulsed and the arrows spit from his flesh. Ragged edges of the entry wounds turned pink, drinking up clotted blood, and then crawled back together. Internal organs knit themselves anew. Awareness poured into his darkened mind, banishing phantoms of pain. He stood, whole, feeling light and almost giddy with the escape from death. He saw the woman with the knife, running full tilt at him, the blade shining in her fist. The Prince smiled, taking joy from the movement and play of his muscles, now restored to full vigor. He raised a hand and blue fire spun out in a tight ring before him.

Thyatis was smashed to the ground again, crying out as her broken ribs ground against one another. Her armor had stopped the brunt of the flare but now it popped and sizzled with tremendous heat. She rolled over, groaning, seeing the knife sticking from the ground a dozen feet away. The breastplate of her cuirass was glowing like an ember and she could feel her flesh crisping in the heat. Frantically, she tugged at the straps that held it closed, feeling the burning sensation spread across her chest.

At the edge of her vision, the Prince walked forward, his steps light on the ground, almost floating. He raised his hand again and ultraviolet lightning snapped and cracked from his palm. Out of her field of view, a man shrieked briefly and there was the roll of thunder. The Prince was glowing slightly, surrounded by a corona of shuddering indigo fire. Men, heedless of imminent death, rushed forward. Arrows filled the air around the Prince.

Thyatis managed to get the straps on her left side undone and prised the breastplate away with trembling fingers. Underneath it, her felt jacket was smoking and tiny flames were licking along the cloth. Gasping at the pain, she tore it off and threw it aside. Beneath that her linen tunic was soaked with sweat and steaming. Luckily, the perspiration trapped in the layers of her clothing had kept the fire from her skin.

Nikos dodged in low, a *spatha* bare in his hand. The glowing man had swiveled as he advanced and the flare of that black coruscating lightning flooded the air. One of the archers, still hanging onto his perch on a tipped boulder, exploded in a red spray as the bolt licked across him. Behind the dead man, trees bloomed into flame and joined their brothers in the conflagration raging around the circumference of the grotto.

The Illyrian leapt into the Prince, hacking sideways with

all the strength in his broad shoulders and powerful back. The keen edge of the *spatha* bit through the corona of fire and then, with a greasy sliding sensation, into the neck of the Prince. Then it stopped, jarring against the man's spine. Nikos dropped down, wrenching the blade away. The Prince turned, his eyes burning with carnelian flame. The Illyrian gaped, seeing the mortal wound gel and the skin rush closed like water over a stone striking the surface of a lake. The Prince smiled and there was nothing human in his face. Arrows slapped through the air, striking the indigo corona and shattering as if they had struck a wall of tempered steel.

Maxian let the tiniest fragment of the roaring, shrieking power that flooded into him from the heart of the mountain fly forth from his fingertips. The essence ignited in the air, unfolding into a ravening burst of flame that caught the swordsman half-turned to dodge aside. The molten air enveloped the man for a brief instant, then seemed to sink into his flesh and armor. Fractions of a second later, the body incandesced into a blue-white pyre and then ash exploded in all directions, filling the air with a haze of dust.

"No!" Thyatis halted in her headlong rush, seeing Nikos die. Efraim and Kahrmi rushed in on the other side of the Prince, their faces masks of death, their legs pumping as they sprinted across the grass. Thyatis was unable to move, seeing her beloved friend shatter in the wind and drift downward in a rain of gray particles. Her limbs seemed made of lead, impossible to move.

Maxian grinned, feeling the joy of the mountain flood his thought. Two more of the soldiers were attacking, pitiful weapons of iron and wood raised against him. He clenched his right fist, sending thought and will into the earth. The ground underneath the two men erupted in rushing orange-red flame and they shrieked in torment as they fell, burning fiercely at his feet.

The Prince bent, feeling the life of the first man rush through his fingers as the flames consumed him. There was a tingling feeling as the breath of life fluttered past and the Prince stood, staring at his hand. Tongues of fire danced on his fingertips, mirroring the strength that was now his. They made beautiful patterns.

Blinking back tears, Thyatis cast about on the grass for a weapon. A wall of flame roared around the fringe of the grotto now, closing off all avenues of escape. It was as bright as day, though the air was thin and very hot. She gasped for breath. Movement was difficult, for the trembling in the ground had increased, shaking the turf like a bowl of gelatin. Her fingers touched the hilt of a fallen sword and curled around it. With an effort, for the mountain suddenly heaved like a wet dog shaking water from its back, she got up on her knees.

At least Anagathios will live, she thought with black humor. *And the Duchess will get her wagons back . . .*

She could see the Prince; he was smiling beatifically and staring at his hands, which shimmered with patterns of color. Above him, the sky was a boiling murk, filled with surging black clouds and lit by the fires roaring below. Entranced, he turned away, spinning slowly in the air. Thyatis stood warily, waiting for the next shock to shift the earth. The sword felt right in her hand as she crouched and scuttled forward.

Footsteps whispered on the grass behind her.

"No," came a tight voice and Thyatis turned in surprise, feeling a hand on her shoulder.

Krista was there, clad in dark clothing, her face grim as any fury. Her forearms were bare and a knife was in her hand. It shone with a black light of its own. "He is mine. You must flee."

Thyatis gaped as the younger woman bolted past her, murder shining in every smooth motion.

Maxian's thought whipped back and forth; the power in the mountain sang to him of ultimate release, of an orgiastic flood of power that would burst forth from the earth in a single stunning blow. His own mind was wrapped in a shell of rage and the burning vision of his brother hung before him in the air.

You brought this upon me, he howled in his mind, tears sparkling at the edges of his eyes. *You, the Emperor who would place the State before your own brother! You would kill me?*

With an effort, he restrained the surging billow of power in the mountain, feeling it press against his will. It had been held back for so long, balanced delicately by the lattices of the Oath, that it hungered and yearned only to be free, to rush out across the land. Maxian stood at the plug, a new balance point, allowing some tiny fragment of it to come forth to be wielded at his hand. Beyond the mountain, the Prince could feel the Oath shudder in retreat, driven back by waves of raw strength.

With this thing at my command, he exulted, *I could smash those forms and specters into nothing!*

He raised a hand, voice rising in words of power and command.

"Maxian!" A cry came, shouting above the roar of the flames. A familiar voice. He turned.

Krista was there, sprinting toward him, her dear face silhouetted by fire and smoke. She was smiling and there was undying love in her eyes. Maxian's heart leapt and his hands dropped, turning to embrace her outstretched arms. Giddy joy shouted in him. *One, at least, of all the world still loves me!*

Krista felt the heat flare from the Prince's body, but ignored it, throwing herself into his arms. He burned and the indigo corona was hotter than a forge, igniting her clothing. She screamed, her eyes blinded by the leaping fire, but she could still feel his thick hair under her hands. Krista flexed her left forearm and felt the cool bronze ring on her thumb take the tension of the spring.

*   *   *

Maxian cried out in dismay, seeing the flames lapping around Krista. The girl was gritting her teeth in pain. He put forth his power to enclose her in a shield of protection. There was a snapping sound close by his ear and then a shocking pain greater than he had ever experienced burst in the side of his skull. He fell back, letting the wash of flame flare up around Krista, catching in her hair. Trembling fingers touched the side of his head. Cold iron met his fingertips, jutting from his ear. Blackness rushed up around him, cutting off all sight and sound and sensation.

Thyatis crawled across the dying grass, her head low. Smoke billowed only a dozen feet above her and the heat beat at her like a fist. There was very little air left to breathe. The mountain, at least, had suddenly gone still and quiet. One arc of the grotto remained free of flames, flanked on either side by towering boulders. Something crouched there in the darkness, but it was free of the burning woods. When the turf steadied, she risked rising up and scurried across the ground toward the rocks.

There was something between the smoking trees, a great shape of iron curled up like a snake in its winter den. Thyatis skidded to a halt, staring in awe at the enormous round golden eyes that suddenly opened before her. The lids slid back, rasping metal on metal, and orbs of gold stared out. The thing was enormous and now it moved, iron scales sliding with a brittle rasp over iron scales. Thyatis fell down, stunned at this sight upon sights. Black wings unfolded, massive and articulated like those of a bat. Forearms as thick as temple columns moved and flexed, supporting its weight. The Engine rose from its slumber and moved forward into the open space of the grotto.

Thyatis scrambled aside, barely avoiding being crushed by a giant taloned paw. The thing was a hundred *pedes* long if it was an *uncia*, with a reticulated snaky tail and massive rear legs like those of a lion. As it moved, there was the ratcheting of gears and wheels and a door opened in its belly. Wings drifted by overhead, touching the walls of the grotto. Trees, nearly consumed by the wildfire, cracked and shattered at the touch. The hot air rushing up caught under the pinions and the whole Engine shuddered, lifting a little. The Roman woman ran underneath it, seeing a hatch lever down.

With a heave, she leapt up and grabbed the edge and swung herself onto the ramp as it descended.

By all accounts, she thought, rolling up into the cargo hold, *this thing can fly us away from here!*

Maxian staggered, feeling poison flood into his skull like a black river. The Oath had come against him, all disguised in the face of love, and now it clawed at his mind and body. Even the power of the mountain seemed faint and weak beside the concentrated venom that hissed like acid inside his head. The Prince felt memories of joy and love and pain and hate flee, consumed by the damage to his mind.

Enough! There was power enough and more at his command. Was not his the will that could mend the shattered body, restore the dead to life, bring fruit from barren soil? He opened his thought to the full power of the mountain and let all restraint flee. *I will live!*

In darkness, crowned with a haze of smoke, the mountain trembled. Far down the cone, on slopes covered with woodlots, pasture, and vineyards, the earth shifted and trembled. Stone grated on stone, and in every farmyard the animals were bawling with terror. Men woke from troubled sleep and stared out into the night. But there was nothing to see save some dim lights on the height.

Clouds had gathered, thick and dark, around the periphery of the mountain. Yellow lightning flickered and rumbled in them, but they formed a swirling broad ring a dozen miles out. No rain fell from them, but in the streets of Cumae and Herculaneum, late-night revelers marked the oppression in the air and the feeling of tension. Some, suddenly nervous, went home in haste. It did not feel safe to be out.

The iron spike oozed from the side of Maxian's head, making a popping sound as it came free. The Prince was on his knees, thrown down by the incessant shaking in the earth. He stared at the bloody bit of metal with his one working eye. The other shimmered with cerulean waves of power as the optic nerve was rebuilt and the eyelid regrew an atom at a time. His lips contorted in something like a laugh—he knew this thing. Once he had touched it with his own power, making it a puissant weapon. With a jerk, he threw it aside and rose up, floating above the quivering ground.

Krista, her body burned beyond recognition, lay at his feet, twisted into a curl. The Prince gulped, his mouth twisting into a grimace. *Come my love*, he whispered to his thought. The corpse rose up, shedding ash and burned cloth. Conveyed by his will, it floated before him into the maw of the Engine, which had lowered itself to receive its master.

The fury of the mountain was about to find release and Maxian, mindful of his own existence, put forth his strength to form a sphere of ward around himself and the Engine. Flying, his cloak fluttering behind him, he soared up and into the cargo hold of the iron drake. The forest that had ringed the grotto was almost burned out, leaving only smoldering patches. Smoke and fumes still rose up, however, and steam jetted from cracks yawning in the ground.

Above the summit of the mountain, a haze was billowing up, climbing into the clear night sky.

Maxian settled onto the honeycombed decking of the Engine and laid Krista's corpse on a crate of books lashed to the metal floor. Numbly, he lashed the body to the crate with leather straps. His mind whirled with thoughts and it seemed that his hands and the charred skull of the young woman were very far away. Only the trembling in the air and the mounting pressure from the mountain could catch his attention.

"Away," he whispered to the Engine that enclosed him. "Take us away."

Outside, iron wings extended, bolts and cogs whining with the strain, and then the Engine kicked off from the ground and soared up into the night sky. In the hold, Maxian gripped one of the wall struts with a white-knuckled hand. The steed born from the forge climbed steeply, sending unsecured crates and boxes sliding across the metal decking. In a moment, wind rushing under its wings, it burst free of the haze collecting above the summit of the mountain and flashed east into the clear air.

THE PALATINE HILL, ROMA

An ewer of wine rattled sharply, then danced across the edge of the tabletop and tipped clattering to the floor. Galen leapt up at the unexpected sound and then swayed drunkenly. Anastasia, still holding Aurelian's arm, felt the room jump and the rattle and crash of toppling vases and statuary was obscenely loud. Plaster dust cascaded from the ceiling in a white mist. The Emperor fell backward, striking the dining couch, and fell over onto the floor. Distantly, the Duchess could hear shouts of fear and the clanging of alarm bells. The floor steadied, though there was still a queasy feeling in the air.

"An earth tremor?" Galen grasped the edge of the couch and pulled himself up. "I've never heard of such a thing in Rome!" Plaster dust settled on his brown hair.

Aurelian stood as well, his bearded face streaked with tears. "What do we do?"

"A doorway or arch," said Anastasia, striding to the heavy archway that led out onto the balcony overlooking the Forum. "It is safest there."

Galen hurried to her side, dragging his brother behind him.

The earth trembled again, but it was not as sharp. Only an echo of what had gone before. The marble flooring quivered and the walls gave forth an alarming groan, but nothing fell and there were no screams of pain.

Anastasia looked out over the rooftops, her dark eyes seeking out the shape of the Quirinal and her house. Lights still sparkled there and the city seemed the same. She felt herself breathe at last. *Perhaps there will be only one tremor?*

"Look!" Aurelian shouted in fear. The Duchess turned and saw, to the south, over the roofs of the palace and the walls of the circus, a great red glow filling the night sky. It flickered and pulsed and then suddenly died away.

"Fire in the city," whispered the Duchess, voicing the single great fear of the urban Roman. Despite the presence of numerous public and private fire brigades and strict building codes, the tenements of Rome, particularly those on the Aventine and beyond, were deathtraps waiting for a stray spark to set them alight. With the earth shaking, it would be nothing to have an oil lamp skitter off a table and fall into papers or hay or old clothing. A tiny apartment would be an inferno in moments, wicking up the poorly plastered walls and catching the dry exposed roof beams. Thousands could die in such an inferno. She grasped the Emperor for support.

His face grim, Galen stared at the southern horizon.

"That is not a fire in the city," he said. His voice was like iron, inflexible and certain sure. "That is far away and big, bigger than any fire we have ever seen."

Ж

Long-lashed eyelids flickered open, revealing pupils of a rich yellow. Narrow irises of red flickered and a membrane occluded the surface of the eye, then slid away. The eye moved in darkness, seeing that the candles had burned down to stubs on the copper holders. There was movement and a rustling like beetles squirming in a dry well and the figure stood up.

Dahak, scion of the House of Sassan, once brother of the King of Kings, raised a hand. A leprous pale light sprang from the walls, flickering with viridian and indigo. The sorcerer stood in a small bare chamber buried deep under the Palace of Seven Gates. It was round and lined with walls of flat ochre bricks. There was one door, still closed. The floor was covered with hexagonal tiles, each incised with a single spiky glyph.

The sorcerer hissed in wonder, his will and thought turned inward. Far to the west, beyond the curve of the world, enormous power had been uncorked with traumatic results. Even from here, from within a shielded chamber built by the Old Ones, he could taste the death-flower. It was bitter on his tongue, attenuated with such distance. He craved it and his body trembled with need.

Someone drinks deep tonight, the sorcerer's thought was sick with envy. *Another power is waking*. He wondered whom this new one served. Then Dahak shivered, feeling the cold of the abyss between the stars and he put the thought away. Even in memory, the will of his master burned him. Day would come soon and he would need to take a pleasing shape. It was a small effort, but it whetted the edge of his hunger.

Garbing himself in black and gray and crimson, the sorcerer went out, closing the lead door behind him. Despite its vast weight, it moved gently, like a feather. *That fat priest is still about*, he thought, smiling to himself. *Very plump indeed.*

ABOVE VESUVIUS

)I(

The Engine screamed high into the air, shedding a contrail of white behind it, letting the power of the thick crystalline spheres in its heart find full release. It was not enough. Below it, below the layer of cloud and haze, the mountain—at last released from ancient constraint—gaped wide and let fury spew.

The top quarter of the cone ripped away in one all-encompassing titanic blast of superheated compressed gas. A mile of corroded lava and soil vaporized in an instant and the sky lit up with a conflagration like the heart of the sun unfolding on earth. Pumice and ash and boulders bigger than the Flavian were ejected into the air, shrieking upward like comets. A shockwave of sound thundered across the land, shattering windows, knocking down trees. It was the forefront of an incandescent cloud of burning gas that swept down the side of the mountain.

The Engine, feeling the power hurtling toward it, banked sharply and screeched off to the north in a steep dive. Air whipped past, over surfaces poorly designed for such velocities. Iron scales tore loose from the skin and sailed away in the slipstream. The great iron wings groaned in torment and in its heart, the pressure of such speed caused the crystal spheres to ring and crack. Tiny fissures rippled over the surface of the globes, spalling flakes of microthin glass into the air. Still, the Engine hurtled on, speeding away in front of the wall of fire.

Seconds after the roof of the mountain had torn away, the deserted villa at Ottaviano was smashed flat by the near-solid wave of air that pressed before the gas cloud. Then the fire swept across it and the trees and fences were consumed. The incandescent gas cloud boiled downslope, consuming everything in its path.

On the seaward side of the mountain, the rupture tore a vast chasm in the side of the cone and the molten heart surged forth, spilling down cliffs and over pastures in a swiftly flowing river. Within minutes, the first vomit of fire had separated into dozens of streams rolling inexorably down toward the shore.

At the back of the Engine, in the cargo hold, Thyatis clung for dear life to a metal spar. The wooden crates had crashed forward with the steep dive, tearing loose from their moorings. After climbing into the hold, she had crawled into a space along the wall where she would hide. Now she braced one leg, bleeding from a long slashing cut, against the forward support and put her back to another. Air roared around her, but she was close to blacking out as a vacuum formed in the hold.

The front of the incandescent cloud smashed over the Engine and it lost all flight control. It spun like a leaf in a tornado, cartwheeling through the sky. One wing, stressed beyond even the powerful incantations of the Persian magi, tore from its moorings and vanished into the night. Only the wavering, simmering ward that the Prince had summoned allowed the body of the machine to survive.

In the forward control space, his face smeared again with blood from an exploding glass plate, Maxian clung to a metal support, his fingers white on the iron. Everything tumbled around him, flying up into the air, as the

Engine plummeted toward the earth. Outside the oval windows at the front of the Engine, the sky was a blanket of flame. The Prince struggled to maintain the sphere of defense, drawing on the reservoir of power that still spewed from the mountain.

The initial shockwave of superheated air rushed past them, leaving the Engine spinning out of the sky. Maxian dragged himself to the window, his thought stiffening the machine, willing it to restore control. Like a snake, it writhed sideways but suddenly leveled off and hurtled through the air.

Thyatis collapsed back against the spar in stunned relief. With the drop in speed, air circulated in the hold once more and she could breathe. She turned in her little sanctuary, seeing crates slide past her. The rear cargo door, half-twisted by the shock of the wing tearing free, hung open. Scrolls and papers fluttered out of broken crates, snatched by a vicious wind that howled and tore at the chamber. Out there, in the open air, she could see that the world was on fire. But they were low, very low. Burning trees and then a ruined two-story house flashed past.

She swung out of her hiding place, any thought of pain or broken bones banished by the sight of that ragged rectangle and the earth below. Wincing at another tear in her flesh, she pushed the ruined door aside. The wind lashed at her, tearing at her hair. The Engine was still streaking across the flat plain north of the mountain at tremendous speed. Grunting, she put her shoulder against the cargo door and felt it give. There was a giddy sensation of standing at the edge of a vast chasm. She did not look down.

"Stop!" A man's voice, hoarse and ruined by the scalding air, rang out behind her. Thyatis turned and saw the Prince, standing in the doorway from the front of the machine. He was haggard, his dark gray cloak in shreds, his face matted with blood. Curlicues of pale blue-and-gold flame flickered around him in an oblate spheroid. When he moved, reaching toward her, it moved like a shadow with him. "You mustn't! The height!"

Thyatis, her face a grim mask, holding only hate in her eyes, pushed away. She fell. Air whipped past and the last thing that she saw was the agonized face of the boy-prince silhouetted in the shattered door of the Engine.

"Fool of a girl!" Maxian reached the cargo door too late. She was gone, sucked away by the whistling blast of wind that roared outside the Engine. "A certain death. . . ."

He turned away. Such reckless abandon had a certain reward. The Engine trembled, fighting through the air. The missing wing crippled it, but Maxian felt such strength at his command that he could will it to fly regardless. He commanded that it soar and seek the cool heavens beyond this inferno. Maxian halted by the big crate, which had jammed itself into the other passageway door. Krista's body, shrunken in death and scored with fire, was still strapped to it. He leaned close and pressed his lips to the charred forehead. Tears fell, sparkling on the ashy flesh.

Then he returned to the command chamber and slumped into the chair that sat there, bolted to the floor. Krista had found it in a shop on the Porticus Aemilla, a heavy block of mahogany carved with ram's head arms and a curved back and covered with soft leather held down by brass nails. The Walach boys had worked for a week to fit it into the control room and get it secured to the decking.

"Rise," he whispered, and the Engine obeyed, soaring into the cold night sky.

Below, a thick choking fog boiled into the air in the wake of the wall of fire. Poison gases curdled and seeped across the land, choking those few animals and men who had survived the first blows. A rain of ash fell as well, settling out of the sky like an ebon blanket. Great stones, flung from the furnace of the mountain, smashed down, sending gouts of water up from the bay at Neapolis. Inland, they crashed into buildings and shattered temples. The coastal towns of Herculaneum and Baiae were first flattened by the blast of burning air, then buried by a thick fall of hot ash and massive stones. Thousands perished trying to flee the conflagration.

The rivers of molten stone continued to rush down the mountainside, burying everything they crossed in a tide of red-hot magma. On the southern side of the mountain, where a gentle slope swept down to the city of Pompeii, there was nothing to arrest the flow. The burning tide rushed on, consuming buildings, barns, fieldstone walls, temples, even the three-tiered bridge on the road to Herculaneum.

Fifteen and twenty miles away, where the distant rumble of the mountain was all but forgotten in the confusion following the earth-shock, the night was disturbed by the whistling impact of foot-wide chunks of superheated lava. The bombs rained down into courtyards and forums, smashing roofs and setting fires in a wide swath across the land.

High above, where the glowing clouds lit by hellish fires and burning cities seemed distant and serene, the Engine flew. A stupendous cloud had formed above the mountain, rising like a temple pillar into the sky. At a vast height, it stalled on a layer of bitterly cold air and began to flatten. The Engine whispered through these rarified strata, circling the mountain and the plume of dust and ash that now leaned away from it.

In the control room, Maxian lay on the heavy chair, his mouth slack, his hands trembling. The gory light reflecting from the windows lighted his face. One pane had survived intact, but the other had cracked and then flaked away, letting chill air whistle into the chamber. The Prince shuddered from foot to crown, his eyes distant and unseeing.

Below him, under the pretty clouds that pulsed and glowed in so many colors, tens of thousands were dying; poisoned by gas, consumed by fire, crushed by falling stones, buried alive in slithery ash, drowned as they attempted to flee in ships from the burning harbors. Others were trampled in the press of the frenzied crowds fleeing the dying cities of Oplontis and Baiae and Pompeii. Each life perished in fear and terror and the minute spark of life that motivated them and drove them into the world was set free.

The Engine plowed through the upper air, heedless of the death and disaster below. The rain of ash was spreading downwind, to the south, and would bury a hundred miles of Campanian countryside under a black shroud. The hammerhead cloud of dust that had vomited into the sky was already beginning to spread in the upper air. By the following noon, the skies over Rome would be a dreary brown and flakes of pumice would rain down for days.

Maxian shuddered, his legs quivering, as he drank in all the power and souls that had been so violently liberated from their mortal shells. He had opened himself on the mountaintop, standing at the maw of the power that now shook the land. He had tasted the dying life of the swordsman and supped greedily at the strength it offered. Now ten thousand times more rushed into him, charging each atom of his being with incalculable force. His mind dissolved, overwhelmed by the millions of memories that rushed past, fleeting and brilliant.

The Engine flew on, drifting out over the sea, a dark shape in a moonlit sky.

THE SEA, OFF OF NEAPOLIS

A red-hot block of ejecta, trailing a long streamer of smoke, plunged into the sea not more than a dozen yards off the bow of the *Pride of Cos*. The sea heaved at the impact, throwing up a billowing cloud of steam. Spray pattered down on the foredeck of the *Cos*, hissing and steaming. Clinging to one of the guy lines, Shirin stared at the shore in utter horror. The sky was streaked with falling stones, glowing and smoking in flight. The debris from the burning mountain rained down all across the bay, intermittently lighting the thick murky night.

Ash was falling too, and it slithered down out of the sky to coat everything—her hair, the deck, the ropes, the other passengers huddled below. Landward, huge fires were burning. Smoke belched from glowing windows. A long line of villas crowded the beach of Oplontis, the *Cos's* destination of record, and most of them were afire. In the dim flickering light, Shirin could see that the beach itself was crowded with thousands of people fleeing the ruin of their homes. Many were in the water, bundles of belongings held over their heads, wading out as far as they could. The air was foul and filled with noisome vapors. Above the town, rivers of flame crawled down the flanks of the mountain, carrying burning trees, wagons, and all kinds of debris.

Another stone shrieked down out of the heavens and arrowed into the sea within a dozen feet of the ship. Shirin, her face wrapped with a gauze veil to keep the hot ash from her throat, turned and shouted at the ship's captain.

"Get us away from the shore, fool! We'll be holed by one of these meteors! Back us away!"

The captain stared back at her, his face blank with fear. He had been useless since the shockwave from the exploding mountain had torn the sail away and nearly capsized the ship. Shirin had been below, in her tiny cabin, sleeping, when the sky lit up with a sudden new dawn. The *boom* of the eruption had shocked her awake, just in time to be thrown fiercely against the wall. She would sport a fine bruise on the right side of her head for that. By great good luck, the ship had been angled almost directly in line with the mountain, and the hell-wind that had rushed after the sound had only torn the lesser mast away and shredded the main sail.

By rights, the *Cos* should have been moored off one of the headlands by Surrentum for the night. But this same captain had thought that he could make up time lost off the coast of Sicilia by tracking on the lights of Oplontis and Baiae and Herculaneum to bring him into harbor. Now his fat-bellied merchantman wallowed in an uneasy sea just off the burning shore.

"You men, put out the harbor oars!" Shirin strode across the deck, her cloak billowing behind her in the hot fetid air. She had taken to wearing a long severe gown with a veil and a woolen wrap. Since taking passage on a leaky coaster from the island port of Naxos, she had been forced to do bodily harm to five or six different men who thought that a woman traveling alone was fair game. Too, at Brundusium, she had purchased a fine knife, two hands long, with a glittering sharp edge. "Now!"

The sailors stared up at her in fear. They had been praying and sacrificing grain and wine from the moment that the mountain had cracked open. They cowered on the main deck, huddled and miserable. Shirin cursed and jumped down the steps among them.

"The oars!" She shouted, kicking the nearest sailor. The man rolled over, curling up into a ball. "We must move away from the shore!"

The others inched away, avoiding her eyes. The Khazar woman stepped to the railing. It was no more than a mile to the beach. She squinted. The strand was seething with dark figures outlined against the burning buildings behind them. More meteors lashed down out of the sky. It seemed that the ash-fall was becoming heavier. *I could swim that*, thought Shirin, sorting possibilities in her mind like a gambler shuffled ivory tokens. She wrenched the cape loose, ignoring the tugging of a cheap copper brooch that snapped and skittered away across the deck. Quick fingers checked her belt, her money, and the knife. Red burned at her throat, where the Eye lay, reflecting the sullen glow in the sky.

A glowing meteor the size of a chariot screamed down out of the sky and crashed through the rear deck of the *Cos*, shaking the whole ship from stem to stern. The deck jumped like a goosed horse and Shirin went sprawling, banging her head on the planks. Splinters and lengths of wood scythed across the deck, killing three of the sailors instantly. Black water vomited up from the gaping wound and the whole ship groaned in pain. Its hull shattered, the *Cos* tipped as the rear hold filled with rushing water.

Shirin lay, dazed, on the decking, staring at the sky swimming queasily above. It was a constant roil of black and red and deep orange. Clouds billowed and surged, driven by the columns of heat rising from the burning cities. Meteors streaked across the sky. Above everything, the mountain glowed and pulsed as it bled fire onto the surrounding land. She blinked, trying to clear hot ash from her eyes. The deck was tipping fast and she began to slide down toward the gaping hole. Struggling, she tangled a hand in a rope and swung to a halt. Soon the ship would be near vertical as it slid into the depths of the sea.

Fighting off vertigo and a pounding headache, Shirin crawled up the rope and hooked an arm over the railing. She had no time to kick off her boots, so she would have to do that in the water. With a great effort, she managed to get both arms over the railing. The ship was settling faster now, sliding down into the oily black water. Swinging a leg, she managed to get her foot over the side.

Able to see the surface of the water once more, she cast about for the shore, trying to get her bearings. She was facing the wrong way, looking out to sea. There was something odd about the water and she paused for a split second.

The waves were gone. The sea seemed oddly flat, like the surface of a still pool. Then it tilted up and Shirin shook her head in puzzlement. That made no sense, the ship should be tilting, not the water. Something appeared up at the mouth of the bay, a white line in the darkness. Then the ship shuddered again, its keel grounding on the seabed. Water rushed past and Shirin felt the *Cos* topple over. The sea was running out, and strongly too, like a racehorse on the home stretch. She clung grimly to the rail as the ship slewed sideways and ground to a halt in suddenly shallow water.

Only a mile away, a wall of black water sixty feet high rushed toward the shore.

Shirin looked up. There was a sound, a sound like a thousand elephants stampeding on a plaza of stone. The wall loomed over the ship, curling up and up and up, its surface slick and shiny, the rumble of its passage filling the world. The *Cos* spun in the eddy before the tidal wave.

She threw up a hand, heedless of the uselessness of the gesture. There was no blur of life images before her eyes, only a deep and abiding anger at being delayed from seeing her children.

THE VALLEY OF SION

D wyrin started awake, his bare skin flushed and slick with sweat. Fragmentary images of a man flying amid a sea of burning clouds faded. The air in the tent was cold. Once night stole over the hills of this barren land, it grew chill very quickly. Given his dubious rank as the senior thaumaturge of Nicholas' detachment, the Hibernian had quarters in the *principa* all to himself. Normally, four men would bunk down in a room this size. Now he was alone. The night was quiet and the deep rumbling sound that he thought he had heard was nowhere in evidence.

He sighed, wiping sweat from his forehead and tucking his long braids behind his ear. Since returning to the desert, the evil dreams that had haunted him on the road from Antioch had passed. He hoped that they were not beginning to recur. Dwyrin sat up and pushed the blankets aside. He felt better in the cold night air. His skin was flushed and hot. *Perhaps I should forgo these blankets . . .* He froze, suddenly aware that someone was sitting in the room with him.

There was only a dark shape, but against the dim light of the lanterns hung along the *via principa* outside the building, he could see the silhouette of a man. There was one wooden folding chair and a little collapsible desk that one of the engineers had loaned him. The man's presence, once noticed, was unmistakable. It filled the chamber like a stormcloud.

"Who are you?" Dwyrin was absurdly pleased—his voice was level and calm.

There is the fire that man makes, and this can be turned to evil use.

Dwyrin's eyes widened in the dark and he closed them, letting the mediation steal over him, opening his sight. When he had done so, he perceived that an old man with a long white beard, matted and tangled with bits of leaf and twig, was sitting in the chair. There was a subtle light that illuminated him from within, showing strong Persian features and a prominent nose. He was garbed in muddy brown robes and a white scarf that lay down on his chest.

"I say again, who are you and what do you want?" Dwyrin tested the hidden waters, feeling the air around him for threat or menace. All seemed unusually still and quiet. A deep sleep lay on the camp, filling men's dreams with thoughts of home and family.

There is the fire that makes men, and this cannot be touched by corruption.

The old man stood, moving in complete silence, and looked down on Dwyrin. The boy felt a shock of recognition—he had seen the old man before, had insulted him, had reviled him. But now he looked down with kind eyes, ancient and filled with hard-won wisdom. Dwyrin saw, too, that the man bore a ring on one hand, shaped like a leaping flame.

"You are a spirit," said the boy, his voice calm. He had seen too much, now, to be startled by apparitions and visions. "What brings you here?"

The old man turned away, stepping to the door. At the jamb, he looked over his shoulder, his eyes bright as a bird. Dwyrin felt a constriction in his chest, as if the air had become thin.

There is a fire that fills the heart, driving man to overcome. This is the flame that must be sheltered and given fuel, exalted and inspired. This is the spear of fire.

Then he was gone. Dwyrin blinked. The plain wooden door remained closed, apparently untouched. The air was hot, now, and close. The Hibernian stood and shuffled outside, pulling a ratty old tunic with moth-eaten holes in it over his head.

The night sky was bright with stars and the moon. For an instant, as he stepped out of the building, Dwyrin could have sworn that a glowing white light touched the tops of the olive trees and cypresses that surrounded the encampment. But now it was dark and very quiet.

Somewhere, at one of the farmhouses in the valley, a dog was barking furiously.

Dawn was touching the walls of the city when Nicholas returned to the Legion camp. He was bone tired from the effort of wearing half-armor all night and quite irritable. Nestled in the corner of the city, the camp itself was still resting in darkness and it was cold enough for him to see his breath. The centurion stomped up to the gate and waited while the guards on duty opened the wooden barrier.

"*Ave*," he snarled at them as he stalked inside. The alarms and excursions of the night just past had produced nothing and he thought of his bed—even a hard Legion cot in a drafty room—with longing. The two stonemasons on the watch saluted smartly and refrained from comment. Even Nicholas' jaunty mustaches were drooping.

Once in his chamber, he unstrapped his armor and let it fall in an untidy pile by the door. He noted that Vladimir was not in the pile of blankets the Northerner preferred and wondered if the Walach had risen early or if he simply had not come in yet.

Despite the seeming peacefulness of the surrounding countryside, every dog in the city had begun raising a howl an hour or so before dawn. In response, the governor had sent a runner to request Nicholas' presence at his residence. After several hours of rooting about in the dark and questioning guardsmen and wayward youths who had been up far past their bedtimes, Nicholas had determined that some kind of light in the sky had started the whole thing. No one, however, had seen anything beyond that. There were no Persian spies or bandits or apparitions in evidence. He had discovered that the city was incredibly dark by night and had an unexpected number of stairs. The governor's guards had insisted that someone had been up on the temple platform, that they had heard voices shouting, but there was no sign that anyone had been there.

The squad of men that he had taken up into the city was still there, nosing about in the old ruins. Later in the day, when he had driven the headache away with sleep, he would roust out the engineers and set them to checking the walls for secret entrances or fallen-down sections. The guards at the city gates had not reported any entries after dark. He could not say why, but he knew that something was up. Some prickling on the back of his neck made him uneasy.

)l(

A rad sat in deep shade, his hands in his lap, wearing little more than a kilt of black cotton and a leather belt. He sat in a gazebo nestled in a garden behind the old palace. The hoary old granite pile of the palace itself and its halls and chambers lay just to the south. Here, encircled by the walls of the citadel and—on the east and north— by the outer rampart of the city, there was a tiny space filled with flowers and fruit trees and ornamentals of all kinds. In these later days, it had seen little use and many of the plants had gone to seed, or run wild, giving the garden an overgrown look.

The gazebo was old and many of the painted latticework boards were rotting away. Still, within its domed space, ringed about by flowering vines and rosebushes, there was as much privacy and solitude as could be found in the citadel. When the twin Empresses had taken up residence, they had filled half of the old palace with their servants and courtiers and hangers-on. Now that the Lord Dahak had come with his army, every inch of the citadel was filled to bursting with his followers. Every nook and cranny and larder had someone sleeping in it.

Each day, now that the word had gone out that the Birds of Paradise had gained a patron of strength, more of the great lords of the land—the *spabahadan* and the *mobeds*— appeared at the gates. Each came with a strong guard and many servants, richly dressed and filled with surety of their own importance. Those men were forced to wait, for the twin Empresses had a sufficiency of things to do with their time now that Dahak had settled between them like a sheltering eagle. The idlers of the court had found little shrift in the new regime and all that remained were Dahak's men, or those who bowed before him.

In the late afternoon, as the sun settled in the west and the sky began to darken, the Empresses were wont to sit in the gazebo, surrounded by their maidservants, in the company of their newly beloved uncle. In this time, the *spabahadan* were allowed an audience, one nobleman at a time, without any advisors or retainers. The Birds of Paradise would interview, it was understood, and choose those whom they would grace with favor.

This was such a time and Arad sat in the shadows at the rear of the gazebo, silent and still, watching with unwavering eyes.

The Lord Dahak sat at ease on a chair of ivory at one side of the gazebo proper. It was draped with a cloth of black silk but bore no other cushion. As was his wont, the sorcerer was dressed in long robes of black and deep gray, with his hair tied back behind his head by a thin scarlet ribbon. Since he had come among the lowland peoples, his appearance had subtly changed, now the seeming of a nobleman lay upon him and his eyes were a dark brown that matched his hair. He wore little jewelry save a single ring on one hand and sometimes, like today, a brooch of worked gold to clasp his cloak at his shoulder. A glass of wine sat close by the chair on a four-legged table of simple wood. Arad had never seen him drink from it.

The change in the twin Empresses was more remarkable, more so that no one in the palace save Arad—and, one presumed, Dahak—had marked upon it. Today, sitting in the slatted sunlight, with a slight breeze passing through the gazebo, each sat at ease on wide chairs of gold and porphyry. They enjoyed silk cushions and glasses of freshly squeezed lemonade cooled by shaved ice. Each wore a simple high-necked traditional gown, finely cut from sheer pale yellow silk. Polished emeralds glittered at their ears and necks, accenting a simple necklace and earrings of beaten gold. Their hair was swept back, making a swan's wing over their shoulders and bound behind in a net of golden thread anchored by garnets. The thick makeup that had turned their faces into masks when Arad had first seen them was gone. A trace of color accented their dark eyes and almost invisible powders smoothed their cheeks, but no more.

Beyond this, each seemed to glow from within with an alluring beauty. Compared to the staggering wealth that they had displayed before, now they showed simple elegance. The plain appearance that they had fought against with overwrought display was gone, replaced by something that drew the hearts of men like a magnet. The scaled black bracelet that Dahak had brought rode like a scepter on Azarmidukht's wrist. So too did Purandokht wear hers as a beloved token. Not too much time passed when they did not, consciously or unconsciously, touch the slick dark metal. Their servants sat quietly, out of the way but ready for a motion or a word to summon them.

The *diquan* Piruz, who had watched the western gate when Arad first entered the city, knelt before the Birds of Paradise. Many great lords had passed this way before his turn had come, but their names and ranks and provinces were meaningless to Arad. Now, with this half-remembered face before the court, the man in the shadows roused himself to pay attention.

"Lord Piruz, welcome," Azarmidukht began, making a slight incline with her head. "Our regrets that we have not spoken with you before. Things have been so busy of late. Pray, tell us of yourself, your lands, and your dreams."

The nobleman blushed, unable to meet the liquid brown eyes of the Empress, and stared down at the worked tesserae of the gazebo floor. It was a hunting scene in green and brown and gold. Men on fine white horses plunged through hedgerows and brush, bows drawn, long-bodied hounds at their feet. Their prey, snarling and rampant, were lions. Arad could see sweat beading Piruz' neck, just above the collar of his ornately embroidered tunic. He was very nervous.

"Flame of the East," he bowed to Azarmidukht.

"Radiance of the World," he turned and bowed to Purandokht. "I come from the furthest eastern reach of your great Empire, from the frontier city of Balkh. We are far from your glorious court, but we are loyal Persians. We hold the fords of the Oxus against the Huns and other barbarians of the north . . ." Arad turned his attention away. It was an old and sorry business—the young lord desired a wife and set his sights high. The Empresses sought husbands as well, but Arad did not think that this border chieftain held lands enough, men enough, or riches enough to entice them.

It was enough that the Lord Dahak was watching the northerner closely, his mind and will intent on the man. Arad settled within himself, drawing back his attention and thought from the world without. The sun between the slats of the gazebo faded, as did the sound of singing birds and the smell of hyacinth and roses. He took it slowly, letting his connection with the outer world fade, releasing even conscious control over his limbs until his *ka* was distilled into an insignificant mote, deep within his corporeal form.

Here, in this black abyss, he was free of the sorcerer and his binding. There was nothing that he could control or touch or affect, but the chill presence of that reptilian mind was gone. *This was reward enough!* Arad felt sure that he could abandon his body and life entirely by retreating here forever. He considered it now, as he had done each day since he had found this refuge. If he ceased to exist, then a powerful weapon would be denied the malignant being.

Too, dreams and phantasms emerged from the darkness. A woman came to him, her black hair a cloud shot with a golden crown, smiling, bright blue eyes flashing. His heart soared to see her, though he could not touch her hand or cheek. The faces of men wavered in his thought—an Arab, his dark beard framing a smiling face—a boy with long red braids—these had been his friends, when his flesh was

warm and his heart beat. Here, in memory, he could be
with them always, free of pain and hurt.

But if he fled, then there would be no chance, no possibility that Arad could ever break the bonds upon his mind
and avenge himself upon the dark power. If he abandoned
the struggle and gave up the hope of escape, then the thing
in the shape of a man would have won another kind of
victory.

Arad did not choose annihilation. He chose to continue.

A pressure changed in the air and Arad swam back up
out of the inky depths, restoring awareness of sight and
sound and the world of physical forms. The Lord Piruz
was standing, holding a scarf the color of crushed onyx in
his hand. The northerner bent his head over the slim white
hand of the Empress Purandokht, taking his leave. He
seemed stunned, a beatific smile on his face. As he went
out, the lean dark shape of the Lord Dahak leaned close,
whispering in his ear.

Arad paid no mind; it was the sorcerer's usual wicked
business. The triangular shape of a leafy vine on the trellis,
glowing with the last rays of the sun, held far more interest.

Bonfires spotted the plain before the lion-gates of the old
city. Thousands of tents dotted the fields and ringed the
walls. The encampments of the Lords of Persia, even reduced by the slaughter of the war against Rome, were still
great. Clouds had covered the sky near sunset and now the
night was as black as pitch. The gate passage stood open,
flanked by its stone guardians, lit by lines of torches. The
general Khadames, the commander of the army of the Empresses of Persia, paced along the paved corridor, deep in
thought.

No word had come from the north. C'hu-lo was late in
sending a messenger. The Lord Dahak had not confided
the substance of the Hun's task to Khadames, but each day
the sorcerer swept into the crowded rooms where the general was working long hours. Each day the Lord Dahak
leaned on his tall iron staff and raised an elegant eyebrow

to Khadames. All the general could do was shrug and return to the business at hand. Usually that business was settling some ancient dispute between the *diquans*, freshly renewed by proximity in the camps around the city.

A man on a massive black charger was waiting at the gate itself, shrouded in a midnight blue cloak and a disreputable felt hat. A leather bowcase was slung at the back of his saddle beside a hand-and-a-half sword wrapped in ragged cloth. The horse's withers were caked with mud and its coat was spotted and dull. Horse and rider had come a long way. Under the brim of the hat, cold eyes glittered.

Khadames halted at the edge of the light spilling from the gate, his thick arms crossed over his chest. He was tired and footsore from tramping around the barren floors of the palace. He could feel the presence of his bodyguards—a dozen men who had followed him from Damawand—behind him. As was his wont, he was wearing a heavy shirt of iron scale mail. It was like a second nature for him now, after so many years.

"You've news for me?" Khadames squinted at the dark figure. He was getting used to the odd comings and goings that seemed parcel in trade for the business of sorcerers. These days it would be startling if someone showed up not on a secret errand. "From whom?"

There was a muted laugh from the dark shape and white teeth flickered in the shadow under the hat. A hand, gloved in fine metal links over leather, emerged from the weather-stained cloak and tossed something to the general. Khadames plucked it easily from the air and then opened his fist. It was a commemorative, a specially struck coin, octagonal and of heavy gold. On one side it bore the eternal flame of Ahura-Mazda and on the other, along with a line of script, the profile of a man with fierce jutting mustaches. Khadames felt a chill pass over him. He held the coin up to the figure on the horse.

"Where?" His blunt tones were sharper than usual, for a fire seemed to have burst into being in his heart. "Tell me, man, or I'll have you flayed to the bone."

"As hasty as ever," came a rumbling voice, like stones falling in a mountain chasm. "In all this time, you've still not learned a hunter's patience."

Khadames swayed on his feet, faint with astonishment. He grasped the side of the man's saddle, unable to believe his ears.

"How . . . ?"

The figure laughed again, and this time the sound boomed from the arch of the gate and startled the guards on the parapet awake. The man leaned down and clasped Khadames' wrist, nearly crushing the bronze armlet with a fierce grip.

"Take me to wine and a warm fire and hot food, my old friend, and I will tell you!"

Over the centuries, fire and earthquake and siege had afflicted the palaces of Ecbatana. They had been rebuilt a dozen times, each new building rising on the foundations of the old. The basements and cellars ran deep, plunging down into the depths of the hill. Khadames descended steps that had been old and worn in the reign of Darius the Great over a thousand years before. Now they were slick with moisture and he kept a hand on the wall for balance. The stairwell was a round drum, dark and filled with the sound of dripping water. Bas-reliefs had once lined the walls, but time had stolen the faces and figures, leaving only a mottled bumpy wall. The general carried a lantern that hissed and spit and let out a foul odor. The citizens of the city were fond of using the thick black fluid that seeped from the broken shale in the hills for lighting. Khadames far preferred a sweet-smelling olive oil.

The stairs reached a stone landing that jutted out over the pit and the general turned, ducking under a door with a triangular lintel. A short passage followed and then it opened into a round chamber with walls made of thin yellow bricks. A squat doorway stood on the other side, nearly closed by a door of heavy bronze. Two figures draped in shadow stood before it. Iron tripods held braziers of hissing coals on either side of the door. A dull red light filled the space and put the iron masks of the door guardians in soft relief.

Khadames ignored the two of the Sixteen and strode between them. The heavy boots of his companion echoed behind him. The guards neither moved to stop them nor queried their intent. They remained motionless, without even the sound of a breath escaping their iron faceplates. Khadames did not know how they differentiated between friend and foe, but the sorcerer seemed to put great store in them. The general put his shoulder to the door and it squealed open, allowing him to step inside.

In eerie similarity to the room deep beneath Damawand, a stone dais stood at the center of the chamber they entered. The Lord Dahak stood at the foot of the slab, his thin fingers just touching the shining black surface. On the basalt table, a muscular man with dark brown skin was struggling silently while four of the Sixteen gripped his arms and legs. The sorcerer ignored Khadames' appearance, though the general did not think for an instant that he had gone unnoticed. Two burly men, blacksmiths from the evidence of their leather aprons and soot-stained arms, were fitting a mask of smooth polished iron over the brown man's head.

Khadames stopped cold, feeling his gorge rise. He stepped aside, into the shadow by the door, and stared at the floor. His companion entered, ducking his head as well. The dark-cloaked figure seemed to fill the room, driving back even the presence of the sorcerer. Khadames felt the surprise and then the disapproval of the figure, but neither man said anything.

Metal grated on the table as the mask was finally wrenched into place. One of the blacksmiths reached into a cloth bag at his belt and took out an iron pin. With a quick motion, he slid the pin into a flange at the back of the mask and riveted it closed with two sharp strokes of his hammer. The ringing sound hung in the air for a moment, then faded sharply. Two more pins were inserted and struck closed. Then the four Sixteen stood aside, loosening their grip, leaving white welts on the flesh of the man.

There was a clank as the man sagged back on the table. He lay still.

After a moment, the Lord Dahak sighed and moved, his robes rustling like a dry carapace. His long pale fingers flexed and then disappeared into the folds of his cloak.

"Rise, my beloved. Show us your new face."

At the words, the man on the table rose up and swung off the table. His body remained trim and corded with muscle. Bands of gold had been placed on his wrists and a pleated kilt of linen hung from his waist. Sandals of white leather were tied around his feet and laced to just beneath his knee. The mask . . . the mask was that of a long-snouted dog with high squared black ears. White teeth jutted from the likeness of a snarl and red markings surrounded the eyeholes that pierced the mask. It was large and it must be heavy, but the man stood straight and tall.

Khadames shuddered, seeing the firelight dance on the iron. In this light and in this place, the lips of the mask seemed to move and the metal pulse with life. Laughter filled the room and it was cold as ice.

"Oh well done." Dahak was most pleased. He turned to the door, his pale yellow eyes lighting up at the look on Khadames' face. "Dear General, he is much improved! Do not blanch so, now he shows his true face to the world."

The massive figure at Khadames' side stirred, twitching the long worn cloak back from the hilt of a heavy sword. The sorcerer moved a little, his face growing pensive. For an instant, something like fear passed over the long face. A pale hand rose to the sorcerer's chest and he made a half-bow, though it was with reluctance.

"Greetings, my lord," said the sorcerer. "It has been a long time since we walked under the moon. I feared . . . I had heard that you were dead."

Khadames felt surprise stir in him, hearing the sorcerer

address another as an equal. But then he took heart, for the man at his side wagered with Kings and Emperors. Even the cancer of the Lord Dahak must find pause somewhere.

"Fancy that," rumbled that powerful voice, filling the room with its sound. "You are looking well, corpsewalker. I see you have taken the face of a dead man for your own. That seems very bold. Do you think that people have forgotten what you have done?"

Dahak flinched and stepped back, then straightened to his full height. His eyes blazed with anger.

"I am a power now, old friend. I do not serve anyone. I am freed of debt and obedience by sweet death. As are you, should you choose to follow your own path."

"This is so . . ." The man in the doorway paused, lost in thought. "All that we built is in ruins. It seems that not a day has passed since the Wooden Man was put to death in the wreck of his treacherous dreams. The land is divided again, preyed upon by Hun in the north and Roman in the west."

"Not for long," said Dahak, stepping forward again. The sorcerer's face was grim, but filled with purpose. "Over half of the great Princes have come to bow before the twins. Soon they will marry, sealing alliances that will bind Persia to the house of Sassan once again. This is only a momentary diversion, this time of anarchy and chaos. Order will return."

"Your order?" Skepticism rang in the powerful voice.

"The order of the King of Kings, my friend." Dahak stood, arms akimbo, matching his gaze against that of the massive warrior. "Neither Radiance has yet wed. Their husbands, whoever they may be, will rule as their councilors and guardians. By my memory, I believe that the girl with brown eyes was birthed first, which makes the bridal dower of Azarmidukht the Radiant the whole of Persia."

Laughter rumbled, shaking the stones of the room.

"And you the dear father, dead man? This will be a fine

wedding. I wonder if the grooms will be able to stand your blessing kiss when they accept your *daughters* from your hands."

Anger flickered again in Dahak's eyes, but it was quickly suppressed. The sorcerer cocked his head to one side.

"It strikes me, great lord, that your wife lies cold in the ground a goodly number of years. Your sons, too, lie dead by the hand of Rome. No blood of yours remains to take your holdings, to bear your banner in battle. Perhaps you should seek a young wife . . ."

A chill developed in the air between the man and the thing in the shape of a man.

"These children? These little girls that I held upon my knee and tickled with my beard? Your thoughts are foul, Wizard. Our discussion comes to a close."

"Wait!" Dahak stepped closer again, and Khadames could see that there was the seeming of honesty in that face. "I mean no disrespect, my lord. You are bereft of a wife and these young women—our most precious possession—are desperately in need of a husband to defend their patrimony. All that they stand to inherit, you built in the name of Chosroes. Without your strong arm, he was nothing, a penniless refugee in a foreign land. Defend his name, his house, his family. Take his daughters as your wives and honor them. In your household, no harm will come to them."

Dahak paused, searching for words. Khadames made to speak, his voice hot, but the man at his side made a slight motion with his hand and the general subsided. The big man waited.

"At one stroke," said the sorcerer, his words and stance free of guile, "you restore Persia. If you do this thing, then there will be no war among the *spabahadan*. No one will dare resist you. One choice and all that is now lost is regained."

Khadames expected the big man to turn on his heel and leave, but the dark-cloaked figure remained. The moment stretched and the general felt a strange silent tension grow in the air. The man at his side seemed to be bending his will upon the sorcerer and, as grains slipped past, the Lord Dahak seemed to shrink and become less.

"Yours was royal blood," said the big man after a long time. His tone was sour. "You were their uncle, a long time ago. Would you drive them to the market to be auctioned to the highest bidder?"

"Is that not the way things have always been?" The sorcerer's voice was equally bitter. "Each of us pays a steep price for what we desire. You, of all of us, have sacrificed the most for Persia. Now the time of your reward has come—the foundation of a strong new dynasty, a crown of gold, peace at long last."

The big man stirred, raising a scarred hand to smooth down the thick, tusk-like mustaches. Khadames swallowed, sensing that his old friend was now seriously considering the situation.

"There will be no war with Rome," said the big man, at last. "We shall bide our time. Too many have died in the service of Empress Maria's revenge. The people must have a reprieve, harvest must be gathered, earthworks repaired, order restored in our own house, the borders strengthened. I have heard that the Huns grow bold."

Dahak bowed in obedience, his arm sweeping out. "As you command, O King of Kings."

The big man laughed at that, a huge booming sound like a temple bell ringing.

"King of Kings! I had not thought to hear that . . ."

The sorcerer smiled, seemingly genuine. He knelt on the hexagonal slabs that covered the floor, and the Sixteen knelt as well. Even the brown-skinned man in the beast mask knelt.

"Hail the Light of the World, Shahr-Baraz, the Mighty Boar, King of Kings, *shahhanshah* of Persia. Hail!"

The words rolled around the chamber and then died away. Shahr-Baraz tugged at his mustaches, looking down upon the sorcerer and his minions with interest. Khadames scratched the back of his head, unable to speak. The world was turning upside down.

The Boar turned to his old friend and grinned, his big white teeth gleaming in the torchlight.

"Well," he said, his voice bubbling with merriment. "The mule of fate kicks like a very devil, does it not? Come, old friend, I must send a message to my men in the hills lest they think that I have been taken captive."

"You have men in the hills?" Khadames' eyebrows rose in dismay. His patrols had been tasked to quarter every copse, valley, and draw for twenty miles in all directions for possible enemies. The gathering of strength to the twin Empresses would gain the attention of many enemies. "How many?"

Shahr-Baraz squinted and counted on his fingers. At last, he smiled and held up both hands.

"More than ten thousand. All of my Immortals who made it out of Kerenos River and whoever we picked up on the way home."

"Ten thousand? The Immortals?" Khadames sputtered in astonishment. His scout commanders would feel the lash on their backs if this were true. "Where are they?"

"Here and there," shrugged Shahr-Baraz. "Many are in the camps just outside the city." He wagged a finger at Khadames. "Your lookouts and scouts are spending too much time looking for *armies* of men. We trickled in ten and twenty at a time, all hidden in the cavalcade of petitioners, jumped-up provincial governors, and second sons who have been flocking here."

Khadames sighed. At least he wouldn't have to bear the burden of command any longer. Just having his old commander at his side made him feel relieved. The Boar turned back to the sorcerer, who had stood silently, his hands hidden in his cloak.

"Let us leave this noisome pit," said Shahr-Baraz. "Let us go up and speak with these Empresses."

Dahak bowed again, smiling. "As you say, O King of Kings."

)-(

Long shadows fell across the ashy gray surface of the Via. Men in plumed helmets, brassy armor, and dull red cloaks rode slowly, their eyes searching the fields on either side of the road. The sun was dim, shrouded by a thick brown haze in the sky. With each step, the horses' hooves raised little clouds of fine gray-black dust. Tiny flakes of ash drifted down from the sky in a constant slow fall like snow. Charred trees jutted from the fields like black posts. The hedgerows and low fieldstone walls were scorched or burned down to the roots. Nothing moved in the dead land save for the party of soldiers on the road.

Amid the red cloaks, Anastasia rode on a brown mare, her face veiled and a hooded robe pulled over her head. Her violet eyes, dark with exhaustion, stared blankly out at the wasteland. She was covered head to toe in dark russet with black edging. The silk over her mouth and nose was already thick with ash. Her escort trotted along at a steady pace.

A cluster of bodies appeared at the side of the road, scattered like fallen logs at the entrance to an estate. All that remained were lumps on the ground, covered with ash, and a burned and twisted hand reaching for the sky. It seemed that they had sought shelter in the arch of the gateway to the villa, though against the firestorm that had swept over them, it had been no protection at all. The Duchess had seen hundreds of these pitiful scenes. Farther from the mountain, there had been whole villages of the dead, only lightly touched by fire. From what she could see, there had been some poison in the air that followed the burning. It seeped into cellars and basements, killing those who had taken shelter there. Nothing was spared, not the birds in the trees or the snakes in the brush beside the road.

The search party clopped into a crossroads town. The buildings were gutted, ripped by fire and buried in drifts of ash. The roof of one building—a public stable by the look—had been smashed in. Anastasia had seen that before too, though it was becoming more common the farther south they went. Great burning stones had been flung from the mountain and had fallen far afield. Two days before she had read a dispatch from the commander of the Imperial fleet base at Misenum. It had been the first report to reach Rome.

In an unsteady hand, on parchment that still reeked of sulfur, the tribune had written:

. . . the cloud was rising from a mountain—at such a distance and in the darkness we couldn't tell which, but afterward learned that it was Vesuvius. I can best describe its shape by likening it to a pine tree. It rose into the sky on a very long "trunk" from which spread some "branches." I imagine it had been raised by a sudden blast, which then weakened, leaving the cloud unsupported so that its own weight caused it to spread sideways. Some of the cloud was glowing like an ember in a fire, in other parts there was only darkness.

The legate (Tacinus Marcus Liva) ordered a boat made ready to investigate. I heard that a cousin of his lived on the slope of the mountain and he feared for her safety. He launched the quadriremes and embarked himself, a source of aid for more people than just Rectina (the cousin), for that delightful shore was a populous one. He hurried to a place from which others were fleeing, and held his course directly into danger. Was he afraid? It seems not, as he kept up a continuous observation of the various movements and shapes of that evil cloud, dictating what he saw.

Ash was falling onto the ships now, darker and denser the closer they went. Now it was bits of pumice, and rocks that were blackened and burned and shattered by the fire. Now the sea is shoal; debris from the mountain blocks the shore. He paused for a moment wondering whether to turn back as the helmsman urged him. "Fortune helps the brave," he said, "Head for Stabiae. There is a squadron there, under the command of Pomponianus."

At Stabiae, on the other side of the bay formed by the gradually curving shore, Pomponianus had loaded up his ships even before the danger arrived, though the burning cloud was visible and indeed extremely close, once it intensified. He had planned to put out as soon as the contrary wind let up. That very wind carried the legate right in, and he embraced the frightened man and gave him comfort and courage. Meanwhile, broad sheets of flame were lighting up many parts of Vesuvius; their light and brightness were the more vivid for the darkness of the night. To alleviate people's fears the legate claimed that the flames came from the deserted homes of farmers who had left in a panic with the hearth fires still alight.

The streets (of Stabiae) rose so high with the mixture of ash and stones that if they had spent anymore time there escape would have been impossible. The buildings were being rocked by a series of strong tremors, and appeared to have come loose from their foundations and to be sliding this way and that. Outside, however, there was danger from the rocks that were coming down, light and fire consumed as these bits of pumice were. Weighing the relative dangers they chose the outdoors; in the legate's case it was a rational decision; others just chose the alternative that frightened them the least.

They tied pillows on top of their heads as protection against the shower of rock. It was daylight now elsewhere in the world, but there the darkness was darker and thicker than any night. But they had torches and other lights. They decided to go down to the shore, to see from close up if anything was possible by sea. But it remained as rough and uncooperative as before. Resting in the shade of a sail the legate drank once or twice from the cold water he had asked for. Then came a smell of sulfur, announcing the flames, and the flames themselves, sending others into flight but reviving him. Supported by two small slaves he stood up, and immediately collapsed. As I understand it, his breathing was obstructed by the dust-laden air, and his innards, which were never strong and often blocked or upset, simply shut down. When daylight came again two days after he died, his body was found untouched, unharmed, in the clothing that he had had on. He looked more asleep than dead.

So Anastasia had found things on the broad plain north of the mountain as well. The citizens and their slaves had fled the eruption and the earthquakes in droves, but the stifling air had overwhelmed them. The dark sky had settled over Rome as well, plunging the capital into constant night. There had been panic and fire—it had taken an hour or so before the skyline of the city had been lit by burning tenements. Galen had taken serious and immediate steps, however, summoning the Second Augustan Legion into the city to assist the *vigiles* and *aediles* in fighting the fires and maintaining order.

The Duchess had hurried home from the Palatine, her heart sick with dread. When word had come that it was Vesuvius that had erupted and that all the lands around that southern mountain were devastated, she had commandeered a troop of cavalry and set off.

She knew, in her heart, that all of the men and women she had sent south were dead. Her only hope, in all this ruin, was that the Prince had died as well. Her heart became numb at the thought and she pushed bleak visions away.

They rode on, out of the village and into a zone of complete destruction at the base of the mountain itself. Vesuvius rose up, its once-smooth sides ripped by long crevices and chasms. The summit, which had tapered to a smooth cone, was now jagged and canted at an angle. A good third of the mountaintop had simply vanished. Anastasia reined her mare to the side of the road. The way was blocked by a drift of large black boulders. The ground still steamed and smoked and the layer of ash was at least a foot deep on the surface of the highway. In the ditches on either side, it was far deeper. She looked up, her exhausted eyes following the line of the summit.

Foul black smoke still belched from the mountain, pluming into the sky. They were now so close that it seemed like late twilight, though far above the murk, the sun rode high in the sky. The Duchess wondered how long the pall would last—days? Months? Galen had already issued a series of edicts placing all grain production in the Western Empire under direct Imperial control. Thousands of acres of agricultural land in Latium had already been destroyed and the price of bread would skyrocket as soon as the grain factors recovered from the shock of the event.

The centurion in command of the detachment of *equites* rode up, his narrow face pale with ash and dust.

"My lady, it would be dangerous to proceed farther. Do you feel the heat in the ground and the thickness of the air? Dangerous vapors have been released from the underworld—we may well find ourselves in Charon's boat if we continue."

Anastasia would have laughed at the allusion on another day, but here, under the black slope of the volcano, it seemed all too appropriate. She nodded wearily and turned her horse around. They had seen nothing but corpses once they had entered the gray land. It seemed passing unlikely that they would find anyone alive. The toll of riding lay heavy on her as well. She had not been on a horse for a lengthy period in years. The pain would be with her for weeks.

They rode back north, following the highway. A wind rose, coming cold out of the east, driving grit and ash into their faces. Anastasia bundled up tighter, feeling chilled to the bone. The horses hung their heads low, fighting through the gray haze.

It was a long way back to Rome.

THE BUCOLEON PALACE, CONSTANTINOPLE

Rufio had served the Emperor of the East for his entire adult life; first as a soldier in the personal army of the Emperor's father, the Exarch of Africa, then, after Constantinople had been taken and the usurper Phocas hacked to bits at the command of the new Emperor Heraclius, in the revitalized Imperial Army. His service during the disaster of the war against the Avars had led him into the service of the Emperor. During all that time, he had murdered men and women, stolen, lied, deceived, faked a kidnapping, misrepresented the use of public funds, forged letters, insulted holy men and priests, and consumed food left on the altars of the gods as sacrifice. Once Heraclius had turned to him, during the driving rain that accompanied their retreat from the dismal field of Adrianople, and called him the only man the Emperor truly trusted.

It had been a moment of weakness, but Rufio, in his stoic way, had let it pass.

Now the scarred, silent Greek had been the captain of the Faithful Guard for three years and seen all that the Empire had lost, regained. He had seen the golden-haired youth become a man and triumph over impossible odds.

It made the guards captain sick to see his master become a delusional cripple, isolating himself from everything that he held dear, letting the Empire that he loved so well slip away into the hands of the great landowners and magnates and priesthoods. Now, he felt uneasy and unfaithful. By Imperial edict, it was treason punishable by dismemberment to stand as he now did. In his own mind, he had already betrayed a man he considered a worthy commander. Now he considered the aspect of real treason and found it palatable.

"He is a stranger, unrecognizable." The Empress' voice was soft and low, barely audible. Her face was in shadow, barely illuminated by a single candle that stood on a long tapering holder by the door to the sleeping chamber. Martina had come by a hidden way, heavily veiled and shrouded in a thick cloak and long gown. The clothes were none of her own. One of the Faithful had purchased them in the city some days before. Rufio had held himself apart from the murk of intrigue and conspiracy that occupied the idle time of the city fathers, but he had not ignored its lessons.

"My lady," he said, his rough voice lowered as well. "In this poor light, he looks more like the man you remember than under the sun. He is not well. His body has rebelled against him."

Martina turned, her glorious brown eyes shining with tears, just visible between two bands of the veil. Rufio could see that the young woman longed to touch her husband's hand, but dared not. Of late, to keep Heraclius in some kind of effective state, Rufio had been adding one or two drops of poppy juice to the heavy wine that the Emperor would consent to drink before sleeping. Even that was difficult, for the Emperor's fears extended to anything liquid. The African knew that this was a dangerous business, but he could see no alternative. If he did not, then the Emperor's sleep would be wracked by terrible dreams.

If the Emperor did not sleep at night, he was in a hallucinatory daze during the day. Too much needed to be done for that to be allowed. Now, with Heraclius in a drugged stupor, Rufio had brought the Empress to look upon him. It was the first time that she had seen her husband in months.

"Is he dying?" For all her youth and bookish nature, the Empress was of a practical mind.

Rufio nodded, his gnarled hands clenching behind his back.

"How long?"

"Perhaps a year . . . he will not allow a priest of Asklepios to attend him. Sviod—one of the Faithful—has seen this kind of thing before. Those so afflicted will linger and slowly decay into death. Madness already comes and goes."

Martina turned away, her hand rising to her lips. Rufio stood, waiting, until she could speak again. "They say that this thing is my fault." The Empress' voice was very faint, barely a whisper. "My handmaids hear them; in the market, in the baths, at the Hippodrome. They are merciless and cruel. Did you know, there are plays in the low houses of the Racing District that . . . that depict what the common people think transpired in our courtship? It is rude work, no Ion of Chios surely, but I know it is what the fine ladies and gentlemen of the nobility are thinking when they titter behind their fans and handkerchiefs."

Rufio said nothing. He had heard all the same spiteful gossip and outright condemnation of the marriage of a niece and uncle. He knew them both, and had seen for three years that they loved one another deeply. What mattered to him, today, was that he needed an ally.

"My lady, there is a thing I would do, but I need your help."

Martina had heard nothing. She stared off into the darkness, her arms crossed over her chest. "They say that the gods have turned their backs on us, because of our marriage. We are cursed, our blood corrupt. My children have all died, save little Heracleonas. He is so small and weak—will he live? Is it true?"

"Empress!" Rufio turned the woman, his big hands enveloping her thin shoulders. *Why not compound two treacheries by laying hands on the body of the Empress, too?* He almost laughed, but stifled it with a cough. "You must listen to me." He bent down, catching her eye.

"Sviod, the blond youth, he says that among his people this affliction is not unknown. He says that if certain medicinal leaves and berries can be acquired, the Emperor may be cured."

Martina stared at him with such a blank expression that Rufio feared she had retreated into her own madness.

"Empress?"

"Oh. Yes, Rufio . . . what did you say?"

The guard captain, quelling an impatience that pressed him to shake her until she came to her senses, repeated what he had said before. The Empress was openly puzzled.

"How can I help you? My husband will not even admit me into his presence, much less allow physicians or priests to attend him. I am imprisoned in my quarters . . . I have no friends or allies . . . His brother hates me and conspires against my son!"

Rufio sighed. The Empress had a great love for the ancient classics, and histories and all matter of obscure things about the natural world. Her education in the matter of palace intrigue, however, was sorely lacking. He raised a finger and pressed it to her lips, halting the flow of words. Her eyes widened in shock, but she remained silent.

"My lady, the medicines that Sviod desires are also used for the treatment of diverse women's ailments. It would be very odd indeed if one of the Faithful were to be seen purchasing such a thing. Your handmaids, however, could seek out a merchant in the lower city and acquire them with ease. No one would think anything of it. Will you help me?"

"Yes," Martina nodded vigorously. "How will you make him take it? I have heard he refuses all medicines . . ."

Rufio nodded, saying, "this is so. But when he sleeps, I believe that his lips may be moistened with the elixir and he will not even be aware of it. His body craves the things he denies—food, sleep, water. While his mind is in the arms of Morpheus, we may yet save him."

Martina smiled and took Rufio's hand in her own and squeezed. The guard captain barely felt the pressure through the sword calluses and muscle. He did not return her smile. His thoughts were occupied with all the things that might go wrong. The Prince Theodore was gone from the city at last, but his adherents and supporters were many in the palace. Soon, the mere possession of the Emperor's body would be crucial.

PETRA, NABATEA

An old man with a snow white beard lay sleeping. Heavy quilts, stitched with squares of green and cream and gold covered him like a mountain. Thick down pillows lay under his head. Long butter yellow slats of sunlight crept down a wall above the bed. The wall was plastered and painted a deep mottled sandstone, though at the joint of the wall and the roof there was a line of black-painted figures and block script. The man's breathing was even and steady, his mustaches riffling with each breath. His beard had been combed out in a fan across the top of the quilts. At his side, her head cushioned on her arms, a young woman was folded up in a wicker chair. Its cushions were skewed under her, and a cotton blanket had been laid over her during the night.

Full day ruled outside the room, though the vines and flowers that grew in the window almost shut out the light. What sun did enter found a dim green place. Circular pipes along the upper course of the walls allowed a breath of air to enter.

The young woman's long black hair was tangled and matted with burrs and dirt. Grime streaked her high-boned cheeks and collected under her fingernails. Despite this, and the filthy tattered clothing she wore, she slept deeply and without dreams. By habit, a knife was clasped in one hand, its sheathed blade resting under her cheek.

The sun settled along the wall, drooping lower and lower until the light, now almost fading, touched the old man's face. His noble nose twitched and he stirred. The heavy quilts made it difficult to move. An eyelid flickered and then opened. Then the other joined it. For a moment, they stared in interest up at the ceiling, seeing a pattern of cross-hatched slats and plaster. Then they became aware and the old man turned his head, seeing the young woman in her chair and then a low table bearing a pottery jar, dark with water sweat.

"Zoë?" The old man's voice was at odds with his snowy beard and thick bushy eyebrows. It was the voice of a man of middle age, strong and powerful, used to making itself heard over the din of battle or the wail of a sandstorm. "Wake, O Queen."

The girl stirred, scratching at her nose and then she too opened her eyes. A flicker of darkness was in them for a moment, and then it passed. The young woman smiled, seeing the face of the old man. "You're awake."

"Help me up and bring some cups. I am thirsty."

Zoë nodded, stretching and yawning. She was sleepy and relaxed. A heavy earthenware cup was fetched from a cupboard and she poured it full.

The old man drank deep of the water, draining three large cups. Zoë laid back the quilts and the sheets beneath. Despite her motion, she still seemed half-asleep, quiet, and introspective. When he had drank his fill, the man put the cup on the table and caught the young woman's hand.

"Are you well?"

Zoë met his eyes with a puzzled look. "I thought I was

dreaming," she said. "There was darkness and then a light. Do you remember what happened?"

Mohammed nodded. He remembered.

"Send word to my captains. We will go to the High Place tonight, as the sun is setting, and I will speak to the multitude. I have seen what must be seen. We are ready."

A thin cold wind gusted, fluttering the green-and-black banners of the Sahaba. Mohammed stood on the altar of stone that stood at the summit of the Jabal al'Madhbah. Sheer cliffs surrounded him on three sides, plunging down a thousand feet into the valley of Petra. The sun, enormous and gold, hung just on the western horizon. From this vantage, the rumpled hills that surrounded the hidden city were a maze of fading golden light and shadow. In the east, the sky was already dark and shadow crept—purple and blue—across the land toward him. There was a smell of night falling in the air. Below him, where night had already filled the canyon of the Siq, he could hear the squeak of bats hunting.

He turned away from the chasm, looking upon the faces of those gathered in the High Place. The pool had been drained and filled with dirt and stones, the altar stone scrubbed until the dark stains faded. The air here, now that the sun and wind had looked upon it, was clean and clear. Even Mohammed could barely feel the lingering echo of the evil that had been done in this place.

Now it was crowded with the nobles of the city, the captains of the Sahaba, the lords of the Decapolis and the Palmyrenes. Hundreds of men and women stood, silently waiting, their robes and veils rustling in the wind. There was no other sound, only the quiet voice of the Lord of the Empty Places gusting over them. The rest of the army stood below, in the canyons and plazas and amphitheaters of the city. It seemed impossible that they would be able to hear him if he spoke from the mountaintop, but certainty rose in his heart.

Leaning on a staff of wood, he took a breath and then, in a strong carrying voice, began to speak.

"The merciful and compassionate one came to me in darkness, saying:

  " '*You alone of men have opened your heart to Our truth. Go forth and travel by night from the Red City to the Farther Mosque whose surroundings We have blessed, so that We might show you Our sign. The Lord of the Air is the Alert, the Observant! A time of great testing is close at hand, and We have warned you.*

  " '*When the first of these warnings came, we dispatched servants of Ours to inflict severe violence upon you. They rampaged through your home, and it served as a warning that you acted upon. Then We offered you another chance against the enemies of men, and reinforced you with wealth and children, and granted you many followers.*

  " '*Thus We sent Our second warning, and so you entered the Mosque and utterly annihilated anything that opposed you. If you heed your Lord he will show mercy to you. If you should turn back from the task He appoints, you will find Hell a confinement for disbelievers! We have reserved painful torment for those who do not believe in the word of the Lord of the Waste.' "*

Mohammed paused, the sound of his voice hanging in the air like the tolling of a great bell. He saw that the faces of the Sahaba were filled with awe and open, like flowers turning toward the rising sun. He knew the effect the words of the God had upon him, but he could not ken their weight to others. It seemed as he searched their faces, that they felt some small echo of the power that filled his mind when the voice came. He hung his head, feeling a wretched sensation of inadequacy. How could his mortal voice convey what he had felt and experienced in the distant temple?

But the voice had bade him recite, to speak to the many. He cleared his throat.

"This is what was said: 'We have granted night and day as twin signs. We blot out the sign of night, and grant the sign of daylight to see by, so you may seek bounty from your Lord and know how to count the years and other such reckoning. Everything We have set forth in detail.

" 'We have tied each man's fate around his neck; and We shall produce a book for him on Resurrection Day that he will find spread open: "Read your book; today there will be none but yourself to call you to account!"

" 'Anyone who submits to guidance will be guided only so far as he himself is concerned, while anyone who strays away, only strays by himself. No burdened soul shall bear another's burden.

" 'We have never acted as punishers until We have dispatched some messenger to warn those who have strayed from the Straight Path. Yet whenever We find that our guidance has been ignored by the depraved and the evil, We do not shrink from annihilation. How many generations did We destroy since the Drowning? Sufficient is it for your Lord to be Informed, Observant of His servants' sins!

" 'For anyone who desires only the fleeting present, We grant this wish. Then Hell waits for him; he will roast in it, condemned, disgraced. Anyone who accepts the Hereafter and makes a proper effort to achieve it while he is a believer will have their effort gratified. Each We shall supply, these as well as those, with a gift from your Lord: your Lord's gift will never be withheld.

" 'What is the law that guides the Straight Path? How may a man walk it, and escape Hell?' "

There was a great rustling in the darkness, for the sun had set in a blaze of gold and yellow and saffron in the west. All those men and women that stood in the High Place knelt, for each had pondered the same question since they had pledged themselves to follow the chieftain.

They had seen his power. They *knew* that his words were the truth.

Among them, at the back, near the twin stone pillars that marked the end of the nine hundred and ninety-nine steps, a young well-dressed man settled to his knees. On the ground before him, he placed a scabbard of plain beaten copper, painted black. A saber hilt jutted from it, wrapped with wire and then a taut covering of linen. He knew, in his heart of hearts, that the balance of the blade was perfect. The swordsmiths of Mekkah, upon learning the destination of this weapon, had excelled themselves. The young man had watched over their process with an eagle eye, for he knew that such a gift needed to dare perfection.

They had done well, though Khalid Al'Walid had not drawn the sword from its sheath since the eldest of the Mekkan guild masters had placed it there with reverent hands. Only one pair of hands should ever touch this weapon or draw it in anger.

"This is the way: Do not place any other deity alongside God, lest you sit back, condemned, forsaken.

"Your Lord has decreed that you should worship nothing except Him, and show kindness to your parents; whether either of them or both of them should attain old age while they are still with you, never curse or scold them. Speak to them in a generous fashion. Protect them carefully from the cruelty of the world, and say 'My Lord, show them mercy, just as they cared for me when I was a little child!'

"Your Lord is quite aware of anything that is on

your minds; if you behave honorably, then He will be forgiving toward those who are attentive.

"Render your close relative his due, as well as the pauper and the wayfarer. Yet do not squander your money extravagantly; spendthrifts are the devil's brethren, and Shaitan has always been ungrateful toward his Lord. Yet if you have to avoid them, seeking some mercy that you may expect from your Lord, still speak a courteous word to them. Your Lord extends sustenance to anyone He wishes, and measures it out; He is Informed, Observant of His servants and their doings.

"Do not kill your children in dread of poverty; We shall provide for both them and you. Do not commit adultery. This is an evil thing, and abhorrent in the eyes of the God that formed men and women from clots of blood.

"Do not kill any soul whom God has forbidden you to, except through the due process of law. We have given his nearest relatives authority for anyone who is killed unjustly—yet let him not overdo things in killing the culprit, inasmuch as he has been so supported.

"Give full measure whenever you measure out anything, and weigh with honest scales; that is better and the finest way of acting.

"Do not worry over something you have no knowledge about: your hearing, eyesight, and vital organs will all be questioned concerning it.

"Do not prance saucily around the earth; you can neither tunnel through the earth nor rival the mountains in height.

"All that is deemed evil by your Lord is to be hated. Such is some of the wisdom your Lord has revealed to you.

"Do not place any other deity alongside your God lest you be tossed into Hell, blamed, rejected.

"The Seven Heavens and Earth, as well as whoever is in them, glorify Him. Nothing exists unless it hymns

His praise; yet you do not understand their glorification. Still He has been lenient.

"Wrongdoers will say: 'You are following a man who is bewitched.' Watch what sort of stories they make up about you. They have strayed away from the Straight Path and are unable to find a way back. They say: 'When we are bones and mortal remains, will we be raised up in some fresh creation?'

"Become stones or iron or any creation that seems important enough to fill your breasts; so they will say: 'Who will bring us back to life?' Say: 'The One Who originated you in the first place.'

"They will wag their heads at you and say: 'When will this come to pass?' Say: 'Perhaps it is near! Someday He will call on you, and you will respond in praise of Him. You will assume you have lingered for only a little while."

Now Mohammed paused, for the weight of the words in his heart had become quite heavy. His fingers gripped the staff, their knuckles turning white with the effort. His voice rolled like thunder, for now the compassionate and the merciful one demanded recompense for the favors He had done the race of men.

Even below, in the gorge of the Siq, where men stood closely packed, shoulder to shoulder, their helmets removed, they could hear the voice ringing in the clear air. It filled the night and settled in their hearts. Each man knew that the excursion of the Sahaba into the lands of the Empire was no raid. That had been clear for weeks. A task had been set them, something mighty. Now they strained to hear of it, their blood slowly building to the race.

Among them, standing in the doorway of the graven temple at the gate of the canyon, Odenathus of Palmyra knelt, the hilt of his sword pressed to his forehead. He had spent many days in the company of the captains of the desert host; he had heard the Young Eagle, Al'Walid, speak of the power and miracles that sprang from the heart of the Quryash. He had seen the utter devotion and loyalty that the hardened mercenaries of the Tanukh afforded the chieftain.

The young man pledged himself, there in the flame-lit darkness, on the cold desert night, to the purpose of the Quryash. Where Mohammed led, Odenathus would follow. He put aside his fear and hate, even the pain of the death of his city. He would submit himself to the will of this God that spoke from the clear air. In this thing there was freedom and blessed purpose.

> *"The lord of the Seven Heavens tasks us: Shaitan stirs up trouble among those who close their hearts to the voice from the clear air; Shaitan is an open enemy of man! Your Lord is quite aware of whoever is in Heaven and Earth.*
>
> *"When we told the angels: 'Bow down on your knees before Adam,' they all knelt down except Shaitan. He said: 'Am I to bow down on my knees before someone you have created out of* clay?' *He said further: 'Have you considered this person yourself whom you have honored more than me? If you will postpone things until the Resurrection Day, then I shall bring all but a few of his offspring under my mastery.'*
>
> *"He, the Merciful and Compassionate One, said: 'Go then! Any of man that follow you will have your reward; it is so ample. Entice any of them whom you can with your voice. Set upon them with your cavalry and your manpower. Share wealth and children with them, and promise them anything. As for My servants, you will have no authority over them; your Lord suffices as a Trustee.'*
>
> *"Your Lord is the One who propels ships for you at sea, so you may seek some of His bounty. He has been so merciful toward you! Whenever some adversity strikes you at sea, anyone you appeal to*

beside Him leaves you to a dreadful fate; yet whenever We bring you safely to port, you all turn away evasively. Man has been so thankless!

"Do you feel so safe that He will not let the land cave in beneath you, or send a sandstorm down upon you? Then you will find no agent to act on your behalf! Or do you feel so secure that He will send you another chance, withholding a smashing gale that would drown you because you have disbelieved? Then you will not find anyone to help you against Us. We have dignified the Children of Adam and transported them across land and sea. We have provided them with wholesome things and favored them especially over many of those whom We have created.

"The day comes when We will call upon the sons of man, whom We have given such shelter. Shaitan is loose in the world. He speaks untruths and turns the unwary from the Straight Path. Men must stand against him, men who follow the Righteous Way.

"Such has been the practice with any of Our messengers whom We have sent before you. You will never find any chance in Our course!

"Keep up prayer from the decline of the sun, until full night comes; and observe the Recital of Our words at daybreak, since reciting at daybreak will be witnessed!

"When you recite, say, 'My Lord, let me enter through a proper entrance and leave by an honest exit! Grant me supporting authority from Your presence.'

"Appeal to God, or appeal to the Mercy-giving: whichever name you may invoke, He still has the Finest Names. Do not shout in your prayer nor say it under your breath; seek a course in between. Praise be to God Who has adopted no son and has no partner in control. He needs no protector against pettiness. Magnify Him greatly!"

Zoë felt a chill pass over her, an invisible wind that cut through her woolen cloak and even the breastplate of iron scales she wore under her tunic. The last words trembled in the air, repeated in a susurrus of hushed voices. Full night had come, covering the sky. It was dark on the summit of the High Place, for no torch or lantern was lit. The moon threw a pale light, but tonight it seemed faint. She felt utterly alone, though she could feel the heavy warm presence of Jalal and Shadin on either side of her. They smelled of horses and oiled metal and well-worn leather and she took great comfort from them. In her heart, she could feel the Queen smiling and it warmed her like the sun.

There was a rustling sound, and Mohammed descended from the high altar. His face was weary and his step uneven. It had taken a great deal from him to let these words find shape in the air. The Tanukh closed around him, supporting his arms. A warm yellow light sprang up. Shadin had lit a small candle-lantern. In the pale light, Zoë could see Mohammed turn to her.

"O Queen," he said, his eyes sparkling in shadow, "summon the captains of the host: Odenathus your cousin, Khalid of the Al'Walid, the Lord of the Ben-Sarid, the Princes of the Decapolis. When the sun comes again, we will leave this place. Lejjun awaits, and then the coast."

Zoë bowed and made to go, but the thin handsome face of the youth Khalid was already there, pushing his way through the crowd. No one had left the High Place, all were waiting for Mohammed to descend the steps. Among all that throng, only Khalid moved. The young man stepped in front of Mohammed and made a deep bow, settling to one knee. A package wrapped in loose cloth was in one hand.

"Lord Mohammed, pause awhile. I have carried a gift from those left behind, your kinfolk in Mekkah and the stalwarts of the city. They cannot join you—being infirm or possessed of responsibilities, but they would have you remember, always, that you are in their hearts. They send you this."

Khalid unwrapped the cloth and the plain unmarked hilt and sheath of a sword stood revealed. With downcast eyes, the youth presented the blade, hilt-first, to the Quryash. Mohammed paused, looking down, his right hand on his own blade.

"I have a sword," said the Quryash. "It suffices."

"Put it aside," said Khalid, his voice solemn. "This is a blade of the heart, not just steel. Draw it, lord, and see what faith has wrought."

One of Mohammed's eyebrows flickered, but he put forth his hand and gripped the hilt. Zoë, watching from the crowd of men, saw his face change at the touch, lighting from within like the sun parting clouds. There was a slithering rasp and the blade flowed free from the sheath.

Zoë gasped.

It was blacker than the barren sky, ebon and indigo. It swallowed light and compressed space. Every eye fixed upon it, seeing infinity in its depths. Colors she could not name crawled across the surface. It was pure and whole, balanced like the tripod of the sun. Mohammed raised the blade above his head and Zoë felt the world shift and center. For an instant, her thought turned to the hidden world, to perceive that which the men of Mekkah had summoned from their forges.

She could not. Such a thing could not be looked upon in life.

"He sings!" Mohammed said, wonder filling his voice. "It is the maker of night."

CAESAREA MARITIMA, PALESTINE

)H(

Banners and pennants snapped in a brisk offshore breeze. Surf beyond the twin breakwaters boomed vigorously. Beyond the twin sea towers, whitecaps stretched to the horizon. On the stone quays, the wind whistled through a forest of masts and sang in the ropes. Nearly a hundred huge grain freighters were tied up. At each massive ship, four gangways—two to a side—had been let down to the docks. Men disbarked in a constant, steady stream from the upper decks. Below them, where the heavier ramps had grounded, wagons were being unloaded, and wobbly horses and mules were being led out.

On the steps of the port master's office, in the shade, Theodore stood with his staff. The Prince wore a heavy red cloak with a purple silk lining. A gilt breastplate molded with rippling muscles shone at his chest. As befitted the commander of an Imperial army, his barbers had shaved his beard close to the jaw and his thick unruly red hair was coifed back. Exquisitely tooled boots with a red stripe, as befitted the brother of the Emperor, were on his feet.

The Prince fairly gleamed in the midday sun, though his staff were similarly well appointed. Theodore did not look kindly upon subordinates who let their armor and helmets be marred by stains or rust. Too, they were men like him, younger and more vigorous than the doddards who served on Heraclius' staff. The Prince had chosen each one from the ranks of the army that had conquered Persia. He understood them well.

Theodore cast a possessive eye over the lines of men

marching past. The army still numbered far too many infantry for his taste, though they did make a stirring sight as they swung past with their spears and bowcases over their shoulders, belongings tied up in a sack on a pole. The tramp of those thousands of feet on the paving stones sent a shiver up his spine.

These are mine, he gloated. *My army, at last.*

With the restoration of Imperial authority over the highlands of Anatolikon and the departure of the Avars to their lands beyond the Danuvius, a flood of manpower had offered itself up to the Emperor. Theodore, acting in his brother's place, had seized upon the fresh levy with alacrity. Nearly half of his *banda* were green troops, but he knew that they would train up quickly. The Anatolians, in particular, were natural soldiers. More to the point, they would form an army that had never known another commander. They had never served under his brother and gained that grating loyalty that seemed to follow the Emperor wherever he went.

The first of the cavalry regiments paraded past, the *equities* raising their arms in salute to the Prince. Theodore grinned, his heart swelling with pride. Here were the finest fighting men in the world, the *cataphracti* of Rome. Today they rode past with their conical helms slung from a strap on their high, four-cornered saddles. Their long curved bows were safely cased away at their sides and the wicked *spatha* were sheathed. Lamellar mail, bound of hundreds of metal lozenges on a leather and felt backing, shimmered in the sunlight. In battle, their horses would bear heavy felted barding, sewn with metal plates. Wagons carried their armor now, for the disembarkment procedure was difficult enough without the extra weight.

The Prince raised his arm in salute and a cheer went up, ringing off the limestone facing on the warehouses and port offices.

"Come," said the Prince, ebullient. "We must make our way to camp and sort things out. Things will be in a right mess there, I am sure. Within the week, once all ships have unloaded, we march to Damascus to see about the suppression of this rabble in the desert and the extension of the rule of law."

The staff officers smiled back, their faces shining with thoughts of victory and conquest. The armies of the frontier states—Palmyra and Nabatea and the Decapolis—had been scattered and destroyed by Persia. The inland cities, grown fat on the Indian trade and the staggering profits of Chin silk, would be a rich prize. Four new provinces were planned, each under the direct rule of a newly appointed Imperial governor.

Theodore stamped down the steps and swung up onto his horse, a massive coal black stallion he had chosen from the stables of the Imperial palace. He felt joy fill him, seeing this pure blue sky and the dry hills above the port. Here was his Empire, waiting for him. He spurred the horse and it clattered up the street, its mane blowing in the wind of his passage.

Behind him, another cohort of infantry marched past the offices, swords and spears jangling. Out at sea, another hundred of the massive transport ships were waiting, heeled against the wind, protected by the prowling galleys of the Imperial fleet. Nearly twenty thousand men would come ashore over the next week.

On the near dock, a centurion cursed at the green troops under his command. They had fouled a line and their supply wagon had tipped, spilling its cargo of arrows, sharpened stakes, bags of millet, and barrels of *acetum* onto the dock.

"Move it, you offal!" His baton made a meaty sound on their backs. The men rushed to turn the wagon back over.

The centurion wiped his brow. It was dreadfully hot here. Soon it would be worse as full summer came. He squinted at the dry hills, snarling in disgust at the thin grass and scrawny trees.

Colonna hated Judea. It was always bad luck to serve here.

To be continued in THE STORM OF HEAVEN

Look for

The STORM

of HEAVEN

by Thomas Harlan
Available in hardcover from Tor Books
June 2001

●

▣⦾-O-⦾-O-⦾-O-⦾-O-⦾-O-⦾-O-⦾-O-⦾-O-⦾-O-⦾-O-⦾-O-⦾-O-⦾-O⦾▣

THE PORT OF KORINTHOS (31 B.C.)

)◫(

The sea gleamed like spoiled glass, a flat murky green. Smoke from the town hung in the air, drifting slowly along the beach in thin gray wisps. The Queen, her pale shoulders covered by a thin rose-colored drape, stood in the surf. Tiny waves lapped around her feet, making silver bangles lift and fall with the water. The sea was as warm as a tepidarium pool.

"No man has ever set foot on the island." The Matron's tone was harsh.

"This is *my son*," said the Queen, her voice urgent. "I need your help."

Sweat beaded on the Greek woman's face, even in the shade of a wide parasol that her servants had lodged in the sand. The Matron stood on the polished plank deck of a small galley, riding low in the water a dozen yards away. Despite the Queen's entreaties, the gray, stiff-backed woman had refused to leave the ship and come ashore.

"We give shelter to women, grown and child, but never to men."

The Queen winced, for the harsh snap of the older woman's voice carried well over the water. There was no wind to break up the sound, or drown it with the crash of surf on the rocky shore.

"He is your get, you must care for him. This is the rule of the Order, as it has been from the beginning."

The Matron turned, flipping the edge of her woolen cloak, black and marked with white checks, over her shoulder. The Queen flinched, feeling the rebuke in her bones. She turned, staring back up the beach to the awnings and pavilions of her camp. The bright colors of the pennants and the cloth that shaded her son and the waiting servants seemed dull and grimy in this still, hot air.

"Have I not given enough?" Despite her best effort, the Queen's voice cracked and rose, shrill and carrying. "Must I give up my son for your faith? He is all that remains of our dream—his father murdered, his patrimony stolen. Hide him for me . . . just for a few months, perhaps a year!"

The women in the galley's rowing deck, responding to the shrill whistle of a flute, raised their long leaf-bladed oars as one. The Matron's figure descended from the platform and paced, slowly, to the foredeck of the vessel. She did not turn or look back, and the angle of her head was canted towards the horizon. A single bank of oars dipped into the water, and the galley turned, swinging easily in the calm sea.

The flute trilled, and the ship slipped across the water, gaining speed with each flashing plunge of the oars.

The Queen felt great weariness crash down upon her, pressing on her shoulders with thick, gnarled fingers. She swayed a little, feeling the sand beneath her feet slip, but then righted herself. Her right hand clutched at a diadem around her neck, slim white fingers covering a golden disk filled with an eight-rayed star.

It would not do, she thought, *to be carried up from the baleful shore by my servants.*